RING LARDNER

RING LARDNER

STORIES & OTHER WRITINGS

Ian Frazier, *editor*

THE LIBRARY OF AMERICA

How To Write Short Stories (With Samples) copyright © 1924 by Charles
Scribner's Sons, renewed 1951 by Ellis A. Lardner. *The Love Nest and
Other Stories* copyright © 1926 by Charles Scribner's Sons, renewed
1953 by Ellis A. Lardner. *Round Up: The Stories of Ring W. Lardner*
copyright © 1924, 1926, 1929 by Charles Scribner's Sons, renewed 1956
by Ellis A. Lardner. "Second-Act Curtain," "Bob's Birthday," "Poodle,"
"Widow," "Insomnia," "Eckie," "Quadroon," and "The Tridget of Greva"
copyright © 2013 by the Estate of Ring Lardner. "The Dames," "Bed-Time
Stories," "'In Conference,'" "Prohibition," "Tennis by Cable," "Who's
Who," "The Other Side," "I. Gaspiri," "Taxidea Americana," and
"Clemo Uti—'The Water Lilies'" from *What Of It?* copyright © 1925 by
Charles Scribner's Sons, renewed 1952 by Ellis A. Lardner. "A Literary Diary,"
"On Conversation," "Odd's Bodkins," "The Bull Pen," "Cora, or Fun at
a Spa," "Dinner Bridge," "Abend di Anni Nouveau," and "Thompson's
Vacation" from *First and Last* copyright © 1934, renewed 1962 by Ring
Lardner, Jr. *Letters of Ring Lardner* copyright © 1979, 1995 by Orchises
Press. Reprinted by arrangement with the Estate of Ring Lardner.

The paper used in this publication meets the
minimum requirements of the American National Standard for
Information Sciences—Permanence of Paper for Printed
Library Materials, ANSI Z39.48—1984.

Distributed to the trade in the United States
by Penguin Group (USA) Inc.
and in Canada by Penguin Books Canada Ltd.

Library of Congress Control Number: 2012954953
ISBN 978-1-59853-253-1

First Printing
The Library of America—244

Manufactured in the United States of America

Contents

YOU KNOW ME AL

A BUSHER'S LETTERS

CONTENTS

CHAPTER I

A Busher's Letters Home

FRIEND AL: Well, Al old pal I suppose you seen in the paper where I been sold to the White Sox. Believe me Al it comes as a surprise to me and I bet it did to all you good old pals down home. You could of knocked me over with a feather when the old man come up to me and says Jack I've sold you to the Chicago Americans.

I didn't have no idea that anything like that was coming off. For five minutes I was just dum and couldn't say a word.

He says We aren't getting what you are worth but I want you to go up to that big league and show those birds that there is a Central League on the map. He says Go and pitch the ball you been pitching down here and there won't be nothing to it. He says All you need is the nerve and Walsh or no one else won't have nothing on you.

So I says I would do the best I could and I thanked him for the treatment I got in Terre Haute. They always was good to me here and though I did more than my share I always felt that my work was appreciated. We are finishing second and I done most of it. I can't help but be proud of my first year's record in professional baseball and you know I am not boasting when I say that Al.

Well Al it will seem funny to be up there in the big show when I never was really in a big city before. But I guess I seen enough of life not to be scared of the high buildings eh Al?

I will just give them what I got and if they don't like it they can send me back to the old Central and I will be perfectly satisfied.

I didn't know anybody was looking me over, but one of the boys told me that Jack Doyle the White Sox scout was down here looking at me when Grand Rapids was here. I beat them twice in that serious. You know Grand Rapids never had a chance with me when I was right. I shut them out in the first game and they got one run in the second on account of Flynn misjuging that fly ball. Anyway Doyle liked my work and he wired Comiskey to buy me. Comiskey come back with an offer and they excepted it. I don't know how much they got but anyway I am sold to the big league and believe me Al I will make good.

Well Al I will be home in a few days and we will have some of the good old times. Regards to all the boys and tell them I am still their pal and not all swelled up over this big league business.

Your pal,   JACK.

Chicago, Illinois, December 14.

OLD PAL: Well Al I have not got much to tell you. As you know Comiskey wrote me that if I was up in Chi this month to drop in and see him. So I got here Thursday morning and went to his office in the afternoon. His office is out to the ball park and believe me its some park and some office.

I went in and asked for Comiskey and a young fellow says He is not here now but can I do anything for you? I told him who I am and says I had an engagement to see Comiskey. He says The boss is out of town hunting and did I have to see him personally?

I says I wanted to see about signing a contract. He told me I could sign as well with him as Comiskey and he took me into another office. He says What salary did you think you ought to get? and I says I wouldn't think of playing ball in the big league for less than three thousand dollars per annum. He laughed and says You don't want much. You better stick round town till the boss comes back. So here I am and it is costing me a dollar a day to stay at the hotel on Cottage Grove Avenue and that don't include my meals.

I generally eat at some of the cafes round the hotel but I had supper downtown last night and it cost me fifty-five cents. If Comiskey don't come back soon I won't have no more money left.

Speaking of money I won't sign no contract unless I get the salary you and I talked of, three thousand dollars. You know what I was getting in Terre Haute, a hundred and fifty a month, and I know it's going to cost me a lot more to live here. I made inquiries round here and find I can get board and room for eight dollars a week but I will be out of town half the time and will have to pay for my room when I am away or look up a new one when I come back. Then I will have to buy cloths to wear on the road in places like New York. When Comiskey comes back I will name him three thousand dollars as my lowest figure and I guess he will come through when he sees I am in ernest. I heard that Walsh was getting twice as much as that.

The papers says Comiskey will be back here sometime to-morrow. He has been hunting with the president of the league so he ought to feel pretty good. But I don't care how he feels. I am going to get a contract for three thousand and if he don't want to give it to me he can do the other thing.

You know me Al.

Yours truly,   JACK.

Chicago, Illinois, December 16.

DEAR FRIEND AL: Well I will be home in a couple of days now but I wanted to write you and let you know how I come out with Comiskey. I signed my contract yesterday afternoon. He is a great old fellow Al and no wonder everybody likes him. He says Young man will you have a drink? But I was to smart and wouldn't take nothing. He says You was with Terre Haute? I says Yes I was. He says Doyle tells me you were pretty wild. I says Oh no I got good control. He says Well do you want to sign? I says Yes if I get my figure. He asks What is my figure and I says three thousand dollars per annum. He says Don't you want the office furniture too? Then he says I thought you was a young ball-player and I didn't know you wanted to buy my park.

We kidded each other back and forth like that a while and then he says You better go out and get the air and come back when you feel better. I says I feel O. K. now and I want to sign a contract because I have got to get back to Bedford. Then he calls the secretary and tells him to make out my contract. He give it to me and it calls for two hundred and fifty a month. He says You know we always have a city serious here in the fall where a fellow picks up a good bunch of money. I hadn't thought of that so I signed up. My yearly salary will be fifteen hundred dollars besides what the city serious brings me. And that is only for the first year. I will demand three thousand or four thousand dollars next year.

I would of started home on the evening train but I ordered a suit of cloths from a tailor over on Cottage Grove and it won't be done till to-morrow. It's going to cost me twenty bucks but it ought to last a long time. Regards to Frank and the bunch.

                    Your Pal,   JACK.

Paso Robles, California, March 2.

OLD PAL AL: Well Al we been in this little berg now a couple of days and its bright and warm all the time just like June. Seems funny to have it so warm this early in March but I guess this California climate is all they said about it and then some.

It would take me a week to tell you about our trip out here. We came on a Special Train De Lukes and it was some train. Every place we stopped there was crowds down to the station to see us go through and all the people looked me over like I was a actor or something. I guess my hight and shoulders attracted their attention. Well Al we finally got to Oakland which is across part of the ocean from Frisco. We will be back there later on for practice games.

We stayed in Oakland a few hours and then took a train for here. It was another night in a sleeper and believe me I was tired of sleepers before we got here. I have road one night at a time but this was four straight nights. You know Al I am not built right for a sleeping car birth.

The hotel here is a great big place and got good eats. We got in at breakfast time and I made a B line for the dining room. Kid Gleason who is a kind of asst. manager to Callahan come in and sat down with me. He says Leave something for the rest of the boys because they will be just as hungry as you. He says Ain't you afraid you will cut your throat with that knife. He says There ain't no extra charge for using the forks. He says You shouldn't ought to eat so much because you're overweight now. I says You may think I am fat, but it's all solid bone and muscle. He says Yes I suppose it's all solid bone from the neck up. I guess he thought I would get sore but I will let them kid me now because they will take off their hats to me when they see me work.

Manager Callahan called us all to his room after breakfast and give us a lecture. He says there would be no work for us the first day but that we must all take a long walk over the hills. He also says we must not take the training trip as a joke. Then the colored trainer give us our suits and I went to my room and tried mine on. I ain't a bad looking guy in the White Sox uniform Al. I will have my picture taken and send you boys some.

My roommate is Allen a lefthander from the Coast League. He don't look nothing like a pitcher but you can't never tell about them dam left handers. Well I didn't go on the long walk because I was tired out. Walsh stayed at the hotel too and when he seen me he says Why didn't you go with the bunch? I says I was too tired. He says Well when Callahan comes back you better keep out of sight or tell him you are sick. I says I don't care nothing for Callahan. He says No but Callahan is crazy about you. He says You better obey orders and you will git along better. I guess Walsh thinks I am some rube.

When the bunch come back Callahan never said a word to me but Gleason come up and says Where was you? I told him I was too tired to go walking. He says Well I will borrow a wheelbarrow some place and push you round. He says Do you sit down when you pitch? I let him kid me because he has not saw my stuff yet.

Next morning half the bunch mostly vetrans went to the ball park which isn't no better than the one we got at home. Most of them was vetrans as I say but I was in the bunch. That makes things look pretty good for me don't it Al? We tossed the ball round and hit fungos and run round and then Callahan asks Scott and Russell and I to warm up easy and pitch a few to the batters. It was warm and I felt pretty good so I warmed up pretty good. Scott pitched to them first and kept laying them right over with nothing on them. I don't believe a man gets any batting practice that way. So I went in and after I lobbed a few over I cut loose my fast one. Lord was to bat and he ducked out of the way and then throwed his bat to the bench. Callahan says What's the matter Harry? Lord says I forgot to pay up my life insurance. He says I ain't ready for Walter Johnson's July stuff.

Well Al I will make them think I am Walter Johnson before I get through with them. But Callahan come out to me and

says What are you trying to do kill somebody? He says Save
your smoke because you're going to need it later on. He says
Go easy with the boys at first or I won't have no batters. But he
was laughing and I guess he was pleased to see the stuff I had.

There is a dance in the hotel to-night and I am up in my
room writing this in my underwear while I get my suit pressed.
I got it all mussed up coming out here. I don't know what
shoes to wear. I asked Gleason and he says Wear your baseball
shoes and if any of the girls gets fresh with you spike them. I
guess he was kidding me.

Write and tell me all the news about home.

Yours truly,   JACK.

Paso Robles, California, March 7.

FRIEND AL: I showed them something out there to-day Al.
We had a game between two teams. One team was made up of
most of the regulars and the other was made up of recruts. I
pitched three innings for the recruts and shut the old birds
out. I held them to one hit and that was a ground ball that the
recrut shortstop Johnson ought to of ate up. I struck Collins
out and he is one of the best batters in the bunch. I used my
fast ball most of the while but showed them a few spitters and
they missed them a foot. I guess I must of got Walsh's goat
with my spitter because him and I walked back to the hotel
together and he talked like he was kind of jealous. He says You
will have to learn to cover up your spitter. He says I could
stand a mile away and tell when you was going to throw it. He
says Some of these days I will learn you how to cover it up. I
guess Al I know how to cover it up all right without Walsh
learning me.

I always sit at the same table in the dining room along with
Gleason and Collins and Bodie and Fournier and Allen the
young lefthander I told you about. I feel sorry for him because
he never says a word. To-night at supper Bodie says How did I
look to-day Kid? Gleason says Just like you always do in the
spring. You looked like a cow. Gleason seems to have the whole
bunch scared of him and they let him say anything he wants to.
I let him kid me to but I ain't scared of him. Collins then says
to me You got some fast ball there boy. I says I was not as fast
to-day as I am when I am right. He says Well then I don't want

to hit against you when you are right. Then Gleason says to Collins Cut that stuff out. Then he says to me Don't believe what he tells you boy. If the pitchers in this league weren't no faster than you I would still be playing ball and I would be the best hitter in the country.

After supper Gleason went out on the porch with me. He says Boy you have got a little stuff but you have got a lot to learn. He says You field your position like a wash woman and you don't hold the runners up. He says When Chase was on second base to-day he got such a lead on you that the little catcher couldn't of shot him out at third with a rifle. I says They all thought I fielded my position all right in the Central League. He says Well if you think you do it all right you better go back to the Central League where you are appresiated. I says You can't send me back there because you could not get waivers. He says Who would claim you? I says St. Louis and Boston and New York.

You know Al what Smith told me this winter. Gleason says Well if you're not willing to learn St. Louis and Boston and New York can have you and the first time you pitch against us we will steal fifty bases. Then he quit kidding and asked me to go to the field with him early to-morrow morning and he would learn me some things. I don't think he can learn me nothing but I promised I would go with him.

There is a little blonde kid in the hotel here who took a shine to me at the dance the other night but I am going to leave the skirts alone. She is real society and a swell dresser and she wants my picture. Regards to all the boys.

Your friend,   JACK.

P. S. The boys thought they would be smart to-night and put something over on me. A boy brought me a telegram and I opened it and it said You are sold to Jackson in the Cotton States League. For just a minute they had me going but then I happened to think that Jackson is in Michigan and there's no Cotton States League round there.

Paso Robles, California, March 9.

DEAR FRIEND AL: You have no doubt read the good news in the papers before this reaches you. I have been picked to go to Frisco with the first team. We play practice games up there about two weeks while the second club plays in Los Angeles. Poor Allen had to go with the second club. There's two other recrut pitchers with our part of the team but my name was first on the list so it looks like I had made good. I knowed they would like my stuff when they seen it. We leave here to-night. You got the first team's address so you will know where to send my mail. Callahan goes with us and Gleason goes with the second club. Him and I have got to be pretty good pals and I wish he was going with us even if he don't let me eat like I want to. He told me this morning to remember all he had learned me and to keep working hard. He didn't learn me nothing I didn't know before but I let him think so.

The little blonde don't like to see me leave here. She lives in Detroit and I may see her when I go there. She wants me to write but I guess I better not give her no encouragement.

Well Al I will write you a long letter from Frisco.

Yours truly,   JACK.

Oakland, California, March 19.

DEAR OLD PAL: They have gave me plenty of work here all right. I have pitched four times but have not went over five innings yet. I worked against Oakland two times and against Frisco two times and only three runs have been scored off me. They should only ought to of had one but Bodie misjuged a easy fly ball in Frisco and Weaver made a wild peg in Oakland that let in a run. I am not using much but my fast ball but I have got a world of speed and they can't foul me when I am right. I whiffed eight men in five innings in Frisco yesterday and could of did better than that if I had of cut loose.

Manager Callahan is a funny guy and I don't understand him sometimes. I can't figure out if he is kidding or in ernest. We road back to Oakland on the ferry together after yesterday's game and he says Don't you never throw a slow ball? I says I don't need no slow ball with my spitter and my fast one. He says No of course you don't need it but if I was you I would get one of the boys to learn it to me. He says And you better watch the way the boys fields their positions and holds up the runners. He says To see you work a man might think they had a rule in the Central League forbidding a pitcher from leaving the box or looking toward first base.

I told him the Central didn't have no rule like that. He says And I noticed you taking your wind up when What's His Name was on second base there to-day. I says Yes I got more stuff when I wind up. He says Of course you have but if you wind up like that with Cobb on base he will steal your watch and chain. I says Maybe Cobb can't get on base when I work against him. He says That's right and maybe San Francisco Bay is made of grapejuice. Then he walks away from me.

He give one of the youngsters a awful bawling out for something he done in the game at supper last night. If he ever talks to me like he done to him I will take a punch at him. You know me Al.

I come over to Frisco last night with some of the boys and we took in the sights. Frisco is some live town Al. We went all through China Town and the Barbers' Coast. Seen lots of swell dames but they was all painted up. They have beer out here that they call steam beer. I had a few glasses of it and it made me logey. A glass of that Terre Haute beer would go pretty good right now.

We leave here for Los Angeles in a few days and I will write you from there. This is some country Al and I would love to play ball round here.

Your Pal,   JACK.

P. S.—I got a letter from the little blonde and I suppose I got to answer it.

Los Angeles, California, March 26.

FRIEND AL: Only four more days of sunny California and then we start back East. We got exhibition games in Yuma and El Paso, Texas, and Oklahoma City and then we stop over in St. Joe, Missouri, for three days before we go home. You know Al we open the season in Cleveland and we won't be in Chi no more than just passing through. We don't play there till April eighteenth and I guess I will work in that serious all right against Detroit. Then I will be glad to have you and the boys come up and watch me as you suggested in your last letter.

I got another letter from the little blonde. She has went back to Detroit but she give me her address and telephone number and believe me Al I am going to look her up when we get there the twenty-ninth of April.

She is a stenographer and was out here with her uncle and aunt.

I had a run in with Kelly last night and it looked like I would have to take a wallop at him but the other boys seperated us. He is a bush outfielder from the New England League. We was playing poker. You know the boys plays poker a good deal but this was the first time I got in. I was having pretty good luck and was about four bucks to the good and I was thinking of quitting because I was tired and sleepy. Then Kelly opened the pot for fifty cents and I stayed. I had three sevens. No one else stayed. Kelly stood pat and I drawed two cards. And I catched my fourth seven. He bet fifty cents but I felt pretty safe even if he did have a pat hand. So I called him. I took the money and told them I was through.

Lord and some of the boys laughed but Kelly got nasty and begun to pan me for quitting and for the way I played. I says Well I won the pot didn't I? He says Yes and he called me something. I says I got a notion to take a punch at you.

He says Oh you have have you? And I come back at him. I says Yes I have have I? I would of busted his jaw if they hadn't stopped me. You know me Al.

I worked here two times once against Los Angeles and once against Venice. I went the full nine innings both times and Venice beat me four to two. I could of beat them easy with any kind of support. I walked a couple of guys in the forth and Chase drops a throw and Collins lets a fly ball get away from him. At that I would of shut them out if I had wanted to cut loose. After the game Callahan says You didn't look so good in there to-day. I says I didn't cut loose. He says Well you been working pretty near three weeks now and you ought to be in shape to cut loose. I says Oh I am in shape all right. He says Well don't work no harder than you have to or you might get hurt and then the league would blow up. I don't know if he was kidding me or not but I guess he thinks pretty well of me because he works me lots oftener than Walsh or Scott or Benz.

I will try to write you from Yuma, Texas, but we don't stay there only a day and I may not have time for a long letter.

　　　　　　　　　　　Yours truly,　　　　　　JACK.

Yuma, Arizona, April 1.

DEAR OLD AL: Just a line to let you know we are on our

way back East. This place is in Arizona and it sure is sandy. They haven't got no regular ball club here and we play a pick-up team this afternoon. Callahan told me I would have to work. He says I am using you because we want to get through early and I know you can beat them quick. That is the first time he has said anything like that and I guess he is wiseing up that I got the goods.

We was talking about the Athaletics this morning and Callahan says None of you fellows pitch right to Baker. I was talking to Lord and Scott afterward and I say to Scott How do you pitch to Baker? He says I use my fadeaway. I says How do you throw it? He says Just like you throw a fast ball to anybody else. I says Why do you call it a fadeaway then? He says Because when I throw it to Baker it fades away over the fence.

This place is full of Indians and I wish you could see them Al. They don't look nothing like the Indians we seen in that show last summer.

                    Your old pal,   JACK.

Oklahoma City, April 4.

FRIEND AL: Coming out of Amarillo last night I and Lord and Weaver was sitting at a table in the dining car with a old lady. None of us were talking to her but she looked me over pretty careful and seemed to kind of like my looks. Finally she says Are you boys with some football club? Lord nor Weaver didn't say nothing so I thought it was up to me and I says No mam this is the Chicago White Sox Ball Club. She says I knew you were athaletes. I says Yes I guess you could spot us for athaletes. She says Yes indeed and specially you. You certainly look healthy. I says You ought to see me stripped. I didn't see nothing funny about that but I thought Lord and Weaver would die laughing. Lord had to get up and leave the table and he told everybody what I said.

All the boys wanted me to play poker on the way here but I told them I didn't feel good. I know enough to quit when I am ahead Al. Callahan and I sat down to breakfast all alone this morning. He says Boy why don't you get to work? I says What do you mean? Ain't I working? He says You ain't improving none. You have got the stuff to make a good pitcher but you don't go after bunts and you don't cover first base and you don't watch the baserunners. He made me kind of sore talking that way and I says Oh I guess I can get along all right.

He says Well I am going to put it up to you. I am going to start you over in St. Joe day after to-morrow and I want you to show me something. I want you to cut loose with all you've got and I want you to get round the infield a little and show them you aren't tied in that box. I says Oh I can field my position if I want to. He says Well you better want to or I will have to ship you back to the sticks. Then he got up and left. He didn't scare me none Al. They won't ship me to no sticks after the way I showed on this trip and even if they did they couldn't get no waivers on me.

Some of the boys have begun to call me Four Sevens but it don't bother me none.

Yours truly,   JACK.

St. Joe, Missouri, April 7.

FRIEND AL: It rained yesterday so I worked to-day instead and St. Joe done well to get three hits. They couldn't of scored if we had played all week. I give a couple of passes but I catched a guy flatfooted off of first base and I come up with a couple of bunts and throwed guys out. When the game was over Callahan says That's the way I like to see you work. You looked better to-day than you looked on the whole trip. Just once you wound up with a man on but otherwise you was all O. K. So I guess my job is cinched Al and I won't have to go to New York or St. Louis. I would rather be in Chi anyway because it is near home. I wouldn't care though if they traded me to Detroit. I hear from Violet right along and she says she can't hardly wait till I come to Detroit. She says she is strong for the Tigers but she will pull for me when I work against them. She is nuts over me and I guess she has saw lots of guys to.

I sent her a stickpin from Oklahoma City but I can't spend no more dough on her till after our first payday the fifteenth of the month. I had thirty bucks on me when I left home and I only got about ten left including the five spot I won in the poker game. I have to tip the waiters about thirty cents a day and I seen about twenty picture shows on the coast besides getting my cloths pressed a couple of times.

We leave here to-morrow night and arrive in Chi the next morning. The second club joins us there and then that night we go to Cleveland to open up. I asked one of the reporters if he knowed who was going to pitch the opening game and he says it would be Scott or Walsh but I guess he don't know much about it.

These reporters travel all round the country with the team all season and send in telegrams about the game every night. I ain't seen no Chi papers so I don't know what they been saying about me. But I should worry eh Al? Some of them are pretty nice fellows and some of them got the swell head. They hang round with the old fellows and play poker most of the time.

Will write you from Cleveland. You will see in the paper if I pitch the opening game.

Your old pal,   JACK.

Cleveland, Ohio, April 10.

OLD FRIEND AL: Well Al we are all set to open the season this afternoon. I have just ate breakfast and I am sitting in the lobby of the hotel. I eat at a little lunch counter about a block from here and I saved seventy cents on breakfast. You see Al they give us a dollar a meal and if we don't want to spend that much all right. Our rooms at the hotel are paid for.

The Cleveland papers says Walsh or Scott will work for us this afternoon. I asked Callahan if there was any chance of me getting into the first game and he says I hope not. I don't know what he meant but he may surprise these reporters and let me pitch. I will beat them Al. Lajoie and Jackson is supposed to be great batters but the bigger they are the harder they fall.

The second team joined us yesterday in Chi and we practiced a little. Poor Allen was left in Chi last night with four others of the recruit pitchers. Looks pretty good for me eh Al? I only seen Gleason for a few minutes on the train last night. He says, Well you ain't took off much weight. You're hog fat. I says Oh I ain't fat. I didn't need to take off no weight. He says One good thing about it the club don't have to engage no birth for you because you spend all your time in the dining car. We kidded along like that a while and then the trainer rubbed my arm and I went to bed. Well Al I just got time to have my suit pressed before noon.

Yours truly,   JACK.

Cleveland, Ohio, April 11.

FRIEND AL: Well Al I suppose you know by this time that I did not pitch and that we got licked. Scott was in there and he didn't have nothing. When they had us beat four to one in the eight inning Callahan told me to go out and warm up and he put a batter in for Scott in our ninth. But Cleveland didn't have to play their ninth so I got no chance to work. But it looks like he means to start me in one of the games here. We got three more to play. Maybe I will pitch this afternoon. I got a postcard from Violet. She says Beat them Naps. I will give them a battle Al if I get a chance.

Glad to hear you boys have fixed it up to come to Chi during the Detroit serious. I will ask Callahan when he is going to pitch me and let you know. Thanks Al for the papers.

Your friend,   JACK.

St. Louis, Missouri, April 15.

FRIEND AL: Well Al I guess I showed them. I only worked one inning but I guess them Browns is glad I wasn't in there no longer than that. They had us beat seven to one in the sixth and Callahan pulls Benz out. I honestly felt sorry for him but he didn't have nothing, not a thing. They was hitting him so hard I thought they would score a hundred runs. A right-hander name Bumgardner was pitching for them and he didn't look to have nothing either but we ain't got much of a batting team Al. I could hit better than some of them regulars. Anyway Callahan called Benz to the bench and sent for me. I was down in the corner warming up with Kuhn. I wasn't warmed up good but you know I got the nerve Al and I run right out there like I meant business. There was a man on second and nobody out when I come in. I didn't know who was up there but I found out afterward it was Shotten. He's the center-fielder. I was cold and I walked him. Then I got warmed up good and I made Johnston look like a boob. I give him three fast balls and he let two of them go by and missed the other one. I would of handed him a spitter but Schalk kept signing for fast ones and he knows more about them batters than me. Anyway I whiffed Johnston. Then up come Williams and I tried to make him hit at a couple of bad ones. I was in the hole with two balls and nothing and come right across the heart with my fast one. I wish you could of saw the hop on it. Williams hit it right straight up and Lord was camped under it. Then up come Pratt the best hitter on their club. You know what I done to him don't you Al? I give him one spitter and another he didn't strike at that was a ball. Then I come back with two fast ones and Mister Pratt was a dead baby. And you notice they didn't steal no bases neither.

In our half of the seventh inning Weaver and Schalk got on and I was going up there with a stick when Callahan calls me back and sends Easterly up. I don't know what kind of managing you call that. I hit good on the training trip and he must of knew they had no chance to score off me in the innings they had left while they were liable to murder his other pitchers. I come back to the bench pretty hot and I says You're making a mistake. He says If Comiskey had wanted you to manage this team he would of hired you.

Then Easterly pops out and I says Now I guess you're sorry you didn't let me hit. That sent him right up in the air and he bawled me awful. Honest Al I would of cracked him right in the jaw if we hadn't been right out where everybody could of saw us. Well he sent Cicotte in to finish and they didn't score no more and we didn't neither.

I road down in the car with Gleason. He says Boy you shouldn't ought to talk like that to Cal. Some day he will lose his temper and bust you one. I says He won't never bust me. I says He didn't have no right to talk like that to me. Gleason says I suppose you think he's going to laugh and smile when we lost four out of the first five games. He says Wait till tonight and then go up to him and let him know you are sorry you sassed him. I says I didn't sass him and I ain't sorry.

So after supper I seen Callahan sitting in the lobby and I went over and sit down by him. I says When are you going to let me work? He says I wouldn't never let you work only my pitchers are all shot to pieces. Then I told him about you boys coming up from Bedford to watch me during the Detroit serious and he says Well I will start you in the second game against

Detroit. He says But I wouldn't if I had any pitchers. He says A girl could get out there and pitch better than some of them have been doing.

So you see Al I am going to pitch on the nineteenth. I hope you guys can be up there and I will show you something. I know I can beat them Tigers and I will have to do it even if they are Violet's team.

I notice that New York and Boston got trimmed to-day so I suppose they wish Comiskey would ask for waivers on me. No chance Al.

Your old pal,   JACK.

P. S.—We play eleven games in Chi and then go to Detroit. So I will see the little girl on the twenty-ninth.

Oh you Violet.

Chicago, Illinois, April 19.

DEAR OLD PAL: Well Al it's just as well you couldn't come. They beat me and I am writing you this so as you will know the truth about the game and not get a bum steer from what you read in the papers.

I had a sore arm when I was warming up and Callahan should never ought to of sent me in there. And Schalk kept signing for my fast ball and I kept giving it to him because I thought he ought to know something about the batters. Weaver and Lord and all of them kept kicking them round the infield and Collins and Bodie couldn't catch nothing.

Callahan ought never to of left me in there when he seen how sore my arm was. Why, I couldn't of threw hard enough to break a pain of glass my arm was so sore.

They sure did run wild on the bases. Cobb stole four and Bush and Crawford and Veach about two apiece. Schalk didn't even make a peg half the time. I guess he was trying to throw me down.

The score was sixteen to two when Callahan finally took me out in the eighth and I don't know how many more they got. I kept telling him to take me out when I seen how bad I was but he wouldn't do it. They started bunting in the fifth and Lord and Chase just stood there and didn't give me no help at all.

I was all O. K. till I had the first two men out in the first inning. Then Crawford come up. I wanted to give him a spitter but Schalk signs me for the fast one and I give it to him. The ball didn't hop much and Crawford happened to catch it just right. At that Collins ought to of catched the ball. Crawford made three bases and up come Cobb. It was the first time I ever seen him. He hollered at me right off the reel. He says You better walk me you busher. I says I will walk you back to the bench. Schalk signs for a spitter and I gives it to him and Cobb misses it.

Then instead of signing for another one Schalk asks for a fast one and I shook my head no but he signed for it again and yells Put something on it. So I throwed a fast one and Cobb hits it right over second base. I don't know what Weaver was doing but he never made a move for the ball. Crawford scored and Cobb was on first base. First thing I knowed he had stole second while I held the ball. Callahan yells Wake up out there and I says Why don't your catcher tell me when they are going to steal. Schalk says Get in there and pitch and shut your mouth. Then I got mad and walked Veach and Moriarty but before I walked Moriarty Cobb and Veach pulled a double steal on Schalk. Gainor lifts a fly and Lord drops it and two more come in. Then Stanage walks and I whiffs their pitcher.

I come in to the bench and Callahan says Are your friends from Bedford up here? I was pretty sore and I says Why don't you get a catcher? He says We don't need no catcher when you're pitching because you can't get nothing past their bats. Then he says You better leave your uniform in here when you go out next inning or Cobb will steal it off your back. I says My arm is sore. He says Use your other one and you'll do just as good.

Gleason says Who do you want to warm up? Callahan says Nobody. He says Cobb is going to lead the league in batting and basestealing anyway so we might as well give him a good start. I was mad enough to punch his jaw but the boys winked at me not to do nothing.

Well I got some support in the next inning and nobody got on. Between innings I says Well I guess I look better now don't I? Callahan says Yes but you wouldn't look so good if Collins hadn't jumped up on the fence and catched that one off Crawford. That's all the encouragement I got Al.

Cobb come up again to start the third and when Schalk signs me for a fast one I shakes my head. Then Schalk says All right pitch anything you want to. I pitched a spitter and Cobb bunts it right at me. I would of threw him out a block but I stubbed my toe in a rough place and fell down. This is the roughest ground I ever seen Al. Veach bunts and for a wonder Lord throws him out. Cobb goes to second and honest Al I forgot all about him being there and first thing I knowed he had stole third. Then Moriarty hits a fly ball to Bodie and Cobb scores though Bodie ought to of threw him out twenty feet.

They batted all round in the forth inning and scored four or five more. Crawford got the luckiest three-base hit I ever see. He popped one way up in the air and the wind blowed it against the fence. The wind is something fierce here Al. At that Collins ought to of got under it.

I was looking at the bench all the time expecting Callahan to call me in but he kept hollering Go on and pitch. Your friends wants to see you pitch.

Well Al I don't know how they got the rest of their runs but they had more luck than any team I ever seen. And all the time Jennings was on the coaching line yelling like a Indian. Some day Al I'm going to punch his jaw.

After Veach had hit one in the eight Callahan calls me to the bench and says You're through for the day. I says It's about time you found out my arm was sore. He says I ain't worrying about your arm but I'm afraid some of our outfielders will run their legs off and some of them poor infielders will get killed. He says The reporters just sent me a message saying they had run out of paper. Then he says I wish some of the other clubs had pitchers like you so we could hit once in a while. He says Go in the clubhouse and get your arm rubbed off. That's the only way I can get Jennings sore he says.

Well Al that's about all there was to it. It will take two or three stamps to send this but I want you to know the truth about it. The way my arm was I ought never to of went in there.

Yours truly,   JACK.

Chicago, Illinois, April 25.

FRIEND AL: Just a line to let you know I am still on earth. My arm feels pretty good again and I guess maybe I will work at Detroit. Violet writes that she can't hardly wait to see me. Looks like I got a regular girl now Al. We go up there the twenty-ninth and maybe I won't be glad to see her. I hope she will be out to the game the day I pitch. I will pitch the way I want to next time and them Tigers won't have such a picnic.

I suppose you seen what the Chicago reporters said about that game. I will punch a couple of their jaws when I see them.

Your pal, JACK.

Chicago, Illinois, April 29.

DEAR OLD AL: Well Al it's all over. The club went to Detroit last night and I didn't go along. Callahan told me to report to Comiskey this morning and I went up to the office at ten o'clock. He give me my pay to date and broke the news. I am sold to Frisco.

I asked him how they got waivers on me and he says Oh there was no trouble about that because they all heard how you tamed the Tigers. Then he patted me on the back and says Go out there and work hard boy and maybe you'll get another chance some day. I was kind of choked up so I walked out of the office.

I ain't had no fair deal Al and I ain't going to no Frisco. I will quit the game first and take that job Charley offered me at the billiard hall.

I expect to be in Bedford in a couple of days. I have got to pack up first and settle with my landlady about my room here which I engaged for all season thinking I would be treated square. I am going to rest and lay round home a while and try to forget this rotten game. Tell the boys about it Al and tell them I never would of got let out if I hadn't worked with a sore arm.

I feel sorry for that little girl up in Detroit Al. She expected me there today.

Your old pal, JACK.

P. S. I suppose you seen where that lucky lefthander Allen shut out Cleveland with two hits yesterday. The lucky stiff.

CHAPTER II

The Busher Comes Back

San Francisco, California, May 13.

Friend Al: I suppose you and the rest of the boys in Bedford will be supprised to learn that I am out here, because I remember telling you when I was sold to San Francisco by the White Sox that not under no circumstances would I report here. I was pretty mad when Comiskey give me my release, because I didn't think I had been given a fair show by Callahan. I don't think so yet Al and I never will but Bill Sullivan the old White Sox catcher talked to me and told me not to pull no boner by refuseing to go where they sent me. He says You're only hurting yourself. He says You must remember that this was your first time up in the big show and very few men no matter how much stuff they got can expect to make good right off the reel. He says All you need is experience and pitching out in the Coast League will be just the thing for you.

So I went in and asked Comiskey for my transportation and he says That's right Boy go out there and work hard and maybe I will want you back. I told him I hoped so but I don't hope nothing of the kind Al. I am going to see if I can't get Detroit to buy me, because I would rather live in Detroit than anywheres else. The little girl who got stuck on me this spring lives there. I guess I told you about her Al. Her name is Violet and she is some queen. And then if I got with the Tigers I wouldn't never have to pitch against Cobb and Crawford, though I believe I could show both of them up if I was right. They ain't got much of a ball club here and hardly any good pitchers outside of me. But I don't care.

I will win some games if they give me any support and I will get back in the big league and show them birds something. You know me, Al.

Your pal,   JACK.

Los Angeles, California, May 20.

Al: Well old pal I don't suppose you can find much news of

22

this league in the papers at home so you may not know that I have been standing this league on their heads. I pitched against Oakland up home and shut them out with two hits. I made them look like suckers Al. They hadn't never saw no speed like mine and they was scared to death the minute I cut loose. I could of pitched the last six innings with my foot and trimmed them they was so scared.

Well we come down here for a serious and I worked the second game. They got four hits and one run, and I just give them the one run. Their shortstop Johnson was on the training trip with the White Sox and of course I knowed him pretty well. So I eased up in the last inning and let him hit one. If I had of wanted to let myself out he couldn't of hit me with a board. So I am going along good and Howard our manager says he is going to use me regular. He's a pretty nice manager and not a bit sarkastic like some of them big leaguers. I am fielding my position good and watching the baserunners to. Thank goodness Al they ain't no Cobbs in this league and a man ain't scared of haveing his uniform stole off his back.

But listen Al I don't want to be bought by Detroit no more. It is all off between Violet and I. She wasn't the sort of girl I suspected. She is just like them all Al. No heart. I wrote her a letter from Chicago telling her I was sold to San Francisco and she wrote back a postcard saying something about not haveing no time to waste on bushers. What do you know about that Al? Calling me a busher. I will show them. She wasn't no good Al and I figure I am well rid of her. Good riddance is rubbish as they say.

I will let you know how I get along and if I hear anything about being sold or drafted.

Yours truly,   JACK.

San Francisco, California, July 20.

FRIEND AL: You will forgive me for not writeing to you oftener when you hear the news I got for you. Old pal I am engaged to be married. Her name is Hazel Carney and she is some queen, Al—a great big stropping girl that must weigh one hundred and sixty lbs. She is out to every game and she got stuck on me from watching me work.

Then she writes a note to me and makes a date and I meet her down on Market Street one night. We go to a nickel show together and have some time. Since then we been together pretty near every evening except when I was away on the road.

Night before last she asked me if I was married and I tells her No and she says a big handsome man like I ought not to have no trouble finding a wife. I tells her I ain't never looked for one and she says Well you wouldn't have to look very far. I asked her if she was married and she said No but she wouldn't mind it. She likes her beer pretty well and her and I had several and I guess I was feeling pretty good. Anyway I guess I asked her if she wouldn't marry me and she says it was O. K. I ain't a bit sorry Al because she is some doll and will make them all sit up back home. She wanted to get married right away but I said No wait till the season is over and maybe I will have more dough. She asked me what I was getting and I told her two hundred dollars a month. She says she didn't think I was getting enough and I don't neither but I will get the money when I get up in the big show again.

Anyway we are going to get married this fall and then I will bring her home and show her to you. She wants to live in Chi or New York but I guess she will like Bedford O. K. when she gets acquainted.

I have made good here all right Al. Up to a week ago Sunday I had won eleven straight. I have lost a couple since then, but one day I wasn't feeling good and the other time they kicked it away behind me.

I had a run in with Howard after Portland had beat me. He says Keep on running round with that skirt and you won't never win another game.

He says Go to bed nights and keep in shape or I will take your money. I told him to mind his own business and then he walked away from me. I guess he was scared I was going to smash him. No manager ain't going to bluff me Al.

So I went to bed early last night and didn't keep my date with the kid. She was pretty sore about it but business before plesure Al. Don't tell the boys nothing about me being engaged. I want to surprise them.

Your pal,   JACK.

Sacramento, California, August 16.

FRIEND AL: Well Al I got the supprise of my life last night. Howard called me up after I got to my room and tells me I am

going back to the White Sox. Come to find out, when they
sold me out here they kept a option on me and yesterday they
exercised it. He told me I would have to report at once. So I
packed up as quick as I could and then went down to say good-
by to the kid. She was all broke up and wanted to go along with
me but I told her I didn't have enough dough to get married.
She said she would come anyway and we could get married in
Chi but I told her she better wait. She cried all over my sleeve.
She sure is gone on me Al and I couldn't help feeling sorry for
her but I promised to send for her in October and then everything will be all O. K. She asked me how much I was going to
get in the big league and I told her I would get a lot more
money than out here because I wouldn't play if I didn't. You
know me Al.

I come over here to Sacramento with the club this morning
and I am leaveing to-night for Chi. I will get there next Tuesday and I guess Callahan will work me right away because he
must of seen his mistake in letting me go by now. I will show
them Al.

I looked up the skedule and I seen where we play in Detroit
the fifth and sixth of September. I hope they will let me pitch
there Al. Violet goes to the games and I will make her sorry
she give me that kind of treatment. And I will make them Tigers sorry they kidded me last spring. I ain't afraid of Cobb or
none of them now, Al.

Your pal,   JACK.

Chicago, Illinois, August 27.

AL: Well old pal I guess I busted in right. Did you notice
what I done to them Athaletics, the best ball club in the country? I bet Violet wishes she hadn't called me no busher.

I got here last Tuesday and set up in the stand and watched
the game that afternoon. Washington was playing here and
Johnson pitched. I was anxious to watch him because I had
heard so much about him. Honest Al he ain't as fast as me. He
shut them out, but they never was much of a hitting club. I
went to the clubhouse after the game and shook hands with
the bunch. Kid Gleason the assistant manager seemed pretty
glad to see me and he says Well have you learned something? I
says Yes I guess I have. He says Did you see the game this

afternoon? I says I had and he asked me what I thought of Johnson. I says I don't think so much of him. He says Well I guess you ain't learned nothing then. He says What was the matter with Johnson's work? I says He ain't got nothing but a fast ball. Then he says Yes and Rockefeller ain't got nothing but a hundred million bucks.

Well I asked Callahan if he was going to give me a chance to work and he says he was. But I sat on the bench a couple of days and he didn't ask me to do nothing. Finally I asked him why not and he says I am saving you to work against a good club, the Athaletics. Well the Athaletics come and I guess you know by this time what I done to them. And I had to work against Bender at that but I ain't afraid of none of them now Al.

Baker didn't hit one hard all afternoon and I didn't have no trouble with Collins neither. I let them down with five blows all though the papers give them seven. Them reporters here don't no more about scoreing than some old woman. They give Barry a hit on a fly ball that Bodie ought to of eat up, only he stumbled or something and they handed Oldring a two base hit on a ball that Weaver had to duck to get out of the way from. But I don't care nothing about reporters. I beat them Athaletics and beat them good, five to one. Gleason slapped me on the back after the game and says Well you learned something after all. Rub some arnicky on your head to keep the swelling down and you may be a real pitcher yet. I says I ain't got no swell head. He says No. If I hated myself like you do I would be a moveing picture actor.

Well I asked Callahan would he let me pitch up to Detroit and he says Sure. He says Do you want to get revenge on them? I says, Yes I did. He says Well you have certainly got some comeing. He says I never seen no man get worse treatment than them Tigers give you last spring. I says Well they won't do it this time because I will know how to pitch to them. He says How are you going to pitch to Cobb? I says I am going to feed him on my slow one. He says Well Cobb had ought to make a good meal off of that. Then we quit jokeing and he says You have improved a hole lot and I am going to work you right along regular and if you can stand the gaff I may be able to use you in the city serious. You know Al the White Sox plays a city serious every fall with the Cubs and the players makes quite a lot of money. The winners gets about eight hundred dollars a peace and the losers about five hundred. We will be the winners if I have anything to say about it.

I am tickled to death at the chance of working in Detroit and I can't hardly wait till we get there. Watch my smoke Al.

Your pal,   JACK.

P. S. I am going over to Allen's flat to play cards a while tonight. Allen is the left-hander that was on the training trip with us. He ain't got a thing, Al, and I don't see how he gets by. He is married and his wife's sister is visiting them. She wants to meet me but it won't do her much good. I seen her out to the game today and she ain't much for looks.

Detroit, Mich., September 6.

FRIEND AL: I got a hole lot to write but I ain't got much time because we are going over to Cleveland on the boat at ten P. M. I made them Tigers like it Al just like I said I would. And what do you think, Al, Violet called me up after the game and wanted to see me but I will tell you about the game first.

They got one hit off of me and Cobb made it a scratch single that he beat out. If he hadn't of been so dam fast I would of had a no hit game. At that Weaver could of threw him out if he had of started after the ball in time. Crawford didn't get nothing like a hit and I whiffed him once. I give two walks both of them to Bush but he is such a little guy that you can't pitch to him.

When I was warming up before the game Callahan was standing beside me and pretty soon Jennings come over. Jennings says You ain't going to pitch that bird are you? And Callahan said Yes he was. Then Jennings says I wish you wouldn't because my boys is all tired out and can't run the bases. Callahan says They won't get no chance to-day. No, says Jennings I suppose not. I suppose he will walk them all and they won't have to run. Callahan says He won't give no bases on balls, he says. But you better tell your gang that he is liable to bean them and they better stay away from the plate. Jennings says He won't never hurt my boys by beaning them. Then I cut in. Nor you neither, I says. Callahan laughs at that so I guess I must of pulled a pretty good one. Jennings didn't have no comeback so he walks away.

Then Cobb come over and asked if I was going to work.

Callahan told him Yes. Cobb says How many innings? Callahan says All the way. Then Cobb says Be a good fellow Cal and take him out early. I am lame and can't run. I butts in then and said Don't worry, Cobb. You won't have to run because we have got a catcher who can hold them third strikes. Callahan laughed again and says to me You sure did learn something out on that Coast.

Well I walked Bush right off the real and they all begun to holler on the Detroit bench There he goes again. Vitt come up and Jennings yells Leave your bat in the bag Osker. He can't get them over. But I got them over for that bird all O. K. and he pops out trying to bunt. And then I whiffed Crawford. He starts off with a foul that had me scared for a minute because it was pretty close to the foul line and it went clear out of the park. But he missed a spitter a foot and then I supprised them Al. I give him a slow ball and I honestly had to laugh to see him lunge for it. I bet he must of strained himself. He throwed his bat way like he was mad and I guess he was. Cobb came prancing up like he always does and yells Give me that slow one Boy. So I says All right. But I fooled him. Instead of giveing him a slow one like I said I was going I handed him a spitter. He hit it all right but it was a line drive right in Chase's hands. He says Pretty lucky Boy but I will get you next time. I come right back at him. I says Yes you will.

Well Al I had them going like that all through. About the sixth inning Callahan yells from the bench to Jennings What do you think of him now? And Jennings didn't say nothing. What could he of said?

Cobb makes their one hit in the eighth. He never would of made it if Schalk had of let me throw him spitters instead of fast ones. At that Weaver ought to of threw him out. Anyway they didn't score and we made a monkey out of Dubuque, or whatever his name is.

Well Al I got back to the hotel and snuck down the street a ways and had a couple of beers before supper. So I come to the supper table late and Walsh tells me they had been several phone calls for me. I go down to the desk and they tell me to call up a certain number. So I called up and they charged me a nickel for it. A girl's voice answers the phone and I says Was they some one there that wanted to talk to Jack Keefe? She says You bet they is. She says Don't you know me, Jack? This is Violet. Well, you could of knocked me down with a peace of bread. I says What do you want? She says Why I want to see you. I says Well you can't see me. She says Why what's the matter, Jack? What have I did that you should be sore at me? I says I guess you know all right. You called me a busher. She says Why I didn't do nothing of the kind. I says Yes you did on that postcard. She says I didn't write you no postcard.

Then we argued along for a while and she swore up and down that she didn't write me no postcard or call me no busher. I says Well then why didn't you write me a letter when I was in Frisco? She says she had lost my address. Well Al I don't know if she was telling me the truth or not but may be she didn't write that postcard after all. She was crying over the telephone so I says Well it is too late for I and you to get together because I am engaged to be married. Then she screamed and I hang up the receiver. She must of called back two or three times because they was calling my name round the hotel but I wouldn't go near the phone. You know me Al.

Well when I hang up and went back to finish my supper the dining room was locked. So I had to go out and buy myself a sandwich. They soaked me fifteen cents for a sandwich and a cup of coffee so with the nickel for the phone I am out twenty cents altogether for nothing. But then I would of had to tip the waiter in the hotel a dime.

Well Al I must close and catch the boat. I expect a letter from Hazel in Cleveland and maybe Violet will write to me too. She is stuck on me all right Al. I can see that. And I don't believe she could of wrote that postcard after all.

Yours truly,   JACK.

Boston, Massachusetts, September 12.

OLD PAL: Well Al I got a letter from Hazel in Cleveland and she is comeing to Chi in October for the city serious. She asked me to send her a hundred dollars for her fare and to buy some cloths with. I sent her thirty dollars for the fare and told her she could wait till she got to Chi to buy her cloths. She said she would give me the money back as soon as she seen me but she is a little short now because one of her girl friends borrowed fifty off of her. I guess she must be pretty soft-hearted Al. I hope you and Bertha can come up for the wedding because I would like to have you stand up with me.

I all so got a letter from Violet and they was blots all over it like she had been crying. She swore she did not write that post-card and said she would die if I didn't believe her. She wants to know who the lucky girl is who I am engaged to be married to. I believe her Al when she says she did not write that postcard but it is too late now. I will let you know the date of my wedding as soon as I find out.

I guess you seen what I done in Cleveland and here. Allen was going awful bad in Cleveland and I relieved him in the eighth when we had a lead of two runs. I put them out in one-two-three order in the eighth but had hard work in the ninth due to rotten support. I walked Johnston and Chapman and Turner sacrificed them ahead. Jackson come up then and I had two strikes on him. I could of whiffed him but Schalk makes me give him a fast one when I wanted to give him a slow one. He hit it to Berger and Johnston ought to of been threw out at the plate but Berger fumbles and then has to make the play at first base. He got Jackson all O. K. but they was only one run behind then and Chapman was on third base. Lajoie was up next and Callahan sends out word for me to walk him. I thought that was rotten manageing because Lajoie or no one else can hit me when I want to cut loose. So after I give him two bad balls I tried to slip over a strike on him but the lucky stiff hit it on a line to Weaver. Anyway the game was over and I felt pretty good. But Callahan don't appresiate good work Al. He give me a call in the clubhouse and said if I ever disobeyed his orders again he would suspend me without no pay and lick me too. Honest Al it was all I could do to keep from wrapping his jaw but Gleason winks at me not to do nothing.

I worked the second game here and give them three hits two of which was bunts that Lord ought to of eat up. I got better support in Frisco than I been getting here Al. But I don't care. The Boston bunch couldn't of hit me with a shovel and we beat them two to nothing. I worked against Wood at that. They call him Smoky Joe and they say he has got a lot of speed.

Boston is some town, Al, and I wish you and Bertha could

come here sometime. I went down to the wharf this morning and seen them unload the fish. They must of been a million of them but I didn't have time to count them. Every one of them was five or six times as big as a blue gill.

Violet asked me what would be my address in New York City so I am dropping her a postcard to let her know all though I don't know what good it will do her. I certainly won't start no correspondents with her now that I am engaged to be married.

Yours truly,   JACK.

New York, New York, September 16.

FRIEND AL: I opened the serious here and beat them easy but I know you must of saw about it in the Chi papers. At that they don't give me no fair show in the Chi papers. One of the boys bought one here and I seen in it where I was lucky to win that game in Cleveland. If I knowed which one of them reporters wrote that I would punch his jaw.

Al I told you Boston was some town but this is the real one. I never seen nothing like it and I been going some since we got here. I walked down Broadway the Main Street last night and I run into a couple of the ball players and they took me to what they call the Garden but it ain't like the gardens at home because this one is indoors. We sat down to a table and had several drinks. Pretty soon one of the boys asked me if I was broke and I says No, why? He says You better get some lubricateing oil and loosen up. I don't know what he meant but pretty soon when we had had a lot of drinks the waiter brings a check and hands it to me. It was for one dollar. I says Oh I ain't paying for all of them. The waiter says This is just for that last drink.

I thought the other boys would make a holler but they didn't say nothing. So I give him a dollar bill and even then he didn't act satisfied so I asked him what he was waiting for and he said Oh nothing, kind of sassy. I was going to bust him but the boys give me the sign to shut up and not to say nothing. I excused myself pretty soon because I wanted to get some air. I give my check for my hat to a boy and he brought my hat and I started going and he says Haven't you forgot something? I guess he must of thought I was wearing a overcoat.

Then I went down the Main Street again and some man

stopped me and asked me did I want to go to the show. He said he had a ticket. I asked him what show and he said the Follies. I never heard of it but I told him I would go if he had a ticket to spare. He says I will spare you this one for three dollars. I says You must take me for some boob. He says No I wouldn't insult no boob. So I walks on but if he had of insulted me I would of busted him.

I went back to the hotel then and run into Kid Gleason. He asked me to take a walk with him so out I go again. We went to the corner and he bought me a beer. He don't drink nothing but pop himself. The two drinks was only ten cents so I says This is the place for me. He says Where have you been? and I told him about paying one dollar for three drinks. He says I see I will have to take charge of you. Don't go round with them ball players no more. When you want to go out and see the sights come to me and I will stear you. So to-night he is going to stear me. I will write to you from Philadelphia.

Your pal,   JACK.

Philadelphia, Pa., September 19.

FRIEND AL: They won't be no game here to-day because it is raining. We all been loafing round the hotel all day and I am glad of it because I got all tired out over in New York City. I and Kid Gleason went round together the last couple of nights over there and he wouldn't let me spend no money. I seen a lot of girls that I would of liked to of got acquainted with but he wouldn't even let me answer them when they spoke to me. We run in to a couple of peaches last night and they had us spotted too. One of them says I'll bet you're a couple of ball players. But Kid says You lose your bet. I am a bellhop and the big rube with me is nothing but a pitcher.

One of them says What are you trying to do kid somebody? He says Go home and get some soap and remove your disguise from your face. I didn't think he ought to talk like that to them and I called him about it and said maybe they was lonesome and it wouldn't hurt none if we treated them to a soda or something. But he says Lonesome. If I don't get you away from here they will steal everything you got. They won't even leave you your fast ball. So we left them and he took me to a picture show. It was some California pictures and they made me think of Hazel so when I got back to the hotel I sent her three postcards.

Gleason made me go to my room at ten o'clock both nights but I was pretty tired anyway because he had walked me all over town. I guess we must of saw twenty shows. He says I would take you to the grand opera only it would be throwing money away because we can hear Ed Walsh for nothing. Walsh has got some voice Al a loud high tenor.

To-morrow is Sunday and we have a double header Monday on account of the rain to-day. I thought sure I would get another chance to beat the Athaletics and I asked Callahan if he was going to pitch me here but he said he thought he would save me to work against Johnson in Washington. So you see Al he must figure I am about the best he has got. I'll beat him Al if they get a couple of runs behind me.

Yours truly,   JACK.

P. S. They was a letter here from Violet and it pretty near made me feel like crying. I wish they was two of me so both them girls could be happy.

Washington, D. C., September 22.

DEAR OLD AL: Well Al here I am in the capital of the old United States. We got in last night and I been walking round town all morning. But I didn't tire myself out because I am going to pitch against Johnson this afternoon.

This is the prettiest town I ever seen but I believe they is more colored people here than they is in Evansville or Chi. I seen the White House and the Monumunt. They say that Bill Sullivan and Gabby St. once catched a baseball that was threw off of the top of the Monumunt but I bet they couldn't catch it if I throwed it.

I was in to breakfast this morning with Gleason and Bodie and Weaver and Fournier. Gleason says I'm supprised that you ain't sick in bed to-day. I says Why?

He says Most of our pitchers gets sick when Cal tells them they are going to work against Johnson. He says Here's these other fellows all feeling pretty sick this morning and they ain't even pitchers. All they have to do is hit against him but it looks like as if Cal would have to send substitutes in for them. Bodie is complaining of a sore arm which he must of strained drawing to two card flushes. Fournier and Weaver have strained their legs doing the tango dance. Nothing could cure them except to hear that big Walter had got throwed out of his machine and wouldn't be able to pitch against us in this serious.

I says I feel O. K. and I ain't afraid to pitch against Johnson and I ain't afraid to hit against him neither. Then Weaver says Have you ever saw him work? Yes, I says, I seen him in Chi. Then Weaver says Well if you have saw him work and ain't afraid to hit against him I'll bet you would go down to Wall Street and holler Hurrah for Roosevelt. I says No I wouldn't do that but I ain't afraid of no pitcher and what is more if you get me a couple of runs I'll beat him. Then Fournier says Oh we will get you a couple of runs all right. He says That's just as easy as catching whales with a angleworm.

Well Al I must close and go in and get some lunch. My arm feels great and they will have to go some to beat me Johnson or no Johnson.

Your pal,   JACK.

Washington, D. C., September 22.

FRIEND AL: Well I guess you know by this time that they didn't get no two runs for me, only one, but I beat him just the same. I beat him one to nothing and Callahan was so pleased that he give me a ticket to the theater. I just got back from there and it is pretty late and I already have wrote you one letter to-day but I am going to sit up and tell you about it.

It was cloudy before the game started and when I was warming up I made the remark to Callahan that the dark day ought to make my speed good. He says Yes and of course it will handicap Johnson.

While Washington was takeing their practice their two coaches Schaefer and Altrock got out on the infield and cut up and I pretty near busted laughing at them. They certainly is funny Al. Callahan asked me what was I laughing at and I told him and he says That's the first time I ever seen a pitcher laugh when he was going to work against Johnson. He says Griffith is a pretty good fellow to give us something to laugh at before he shoots that guy at us.

I warmed up good and told Schalk not to ask me for my spitter much because my fast one looked faster than I ever seen

it. He says it won't make much difference what you pitch to-
day. I says Oh, yes, it will because Callahan thinks enough of
me to work me against Johnson and I want to show him he
didn't make no mistake. Then Gleason says No he didn't make
no mistake. Wasteing Cicotte or Scotty would of been a mistake in this game.

Well, Johnson whiffs Weaver and Chase and makes Lord
pop out in the first inning. I walked their first guy but I didn't
give Milan nothing to bunt and finally he flied out. And then I
whiffed the next two. On the bench Callahan says That's the
way, boy. Keep that up and we got a chance.

Johnson had fanned four of us when I come up with two
out in the third inning and he whiffed me to. I fouled one
though that if I had ever got a good hold of I would of
knocked out of the park. In the first seven innings we didn't
have a hit off of him. They had got five or six lucky ones off of
me and I had walked two or three, but I cut loose with all I
had when they was men on and they couldn't do nothing with
me. The only reason I walked so many was because my fast one
was jumping so. Honest Al it was so fast that Evans the umpire
couldn't see it half the time and he called a lot of balls that was
right over the heart.

Well I come up in the eighth with two out and the score still
nothing and nothing. I had whiffed the second time as well as
the first but it was account of Evans missing one on me. The
eighth started with Shanks muffing a fly ball off of Bodie. It
was way out by the fence so he got two bases on it and he went
to third while they was throwing Berger out. Then Schalk
whiffed.

Callahan says Go up and try to meet one Jack. It might as
well be you as anybody else. But your old pal didn't whiff this
time Al. He gets two strikes on me with fast ones and then I
passed up two bad ones. I took my healthy at the next one and
slapped it over first base. I guess I could of made two bases on
it but I didn't want to tire myself out. Anyway Bodie scored
and I had them beat. And my hit was the only one we got off
of him so I guess he is a pretty good pitcher after all Al.

They filled up the bases on me with one out in the ninth but
it was pretty dark then and I made McBride and their catcher
look like suckers with my speed.

I felt so good after the game that I drunk one of them pink cocktails. I don't know what their name is. And then I sent a postcard to poor little Violet. I don't care nothing about her but it don't hurt me none to try and cheer her up once in a while. We leave here Thursday night for home and they had ought to be two or three letters there for me from Hazel because I haven't heard from her lately. She must of lost my road addresses.

Your pal,   JACK.

P. S. I forgot to tell you what Callahan said after the game. He said I was a real pitcher now and he is going to use me in the city serious. If he does Al we will beat them Cubs sure.

Chicago, Illinois, September 27.

FRIEND AL: They wasn't no letter here at all from Hazel and I guess she must of been sick. Or maybe she didn't think it was worth while writeing as long as she is comeing next week.

I want to ask you to do me a favor Al and that is to see if you can find me a house down there. I will want to move in with Mrs. Keefe, don't that sound funny Al? sometime in the week of October twelfth. Old man Cutting's house or that yellow house across from you would be O. K. I would rather have the yellow one so as to be near you. Find out how much rent they want Al and if it is not no more than twelve dollars a month get it for me. We will buy our furniture here in Chi when Hazel comes.

We have a couple of days off now Al and then we play St. Louis two games here. Then Detroit comes to finish the season the third and fourth of October.

Your pal,   JACK.

Chicago, Illinois, October 3.

DEAR OLD AL: Thanks Al for getting the house. The one-year lease is O. K. You and Bertha and me and Hazel can have all sorts of good times together. I guess the walk needs repairs but I can fix that up when I come. We can stay at the hotel when we first get there.

I wish you could of came up for the city serious Al but anyway I want you and Bertha to be sure and come up for our wedding. I will let you know the date as soon as Hazel gets here.

The serious starts Tuesday and this town is wild over it. The Cubs finished second in their league and we was fifth in ours but that don't scare me none. We would of finished right on top if I had of been here all season.

Callahan pitched one of the bushers against Detroit this afternoon and they beat him bad. Callahan is saveing up Scott and Allen and Russell and Cicotte and I for the big show. Walsh isn't in no shape and neither is Benz. It looks like I would have a good deal to do because most of them others can't work no more than once in four days and Allen ain't no good at all.

We have a day to rest after to-morrow's game with the Tigers and then we go at them Cubs.

Your pal,   JACK.

P. S. I have got it figured that Hazel is fixing to surprise me by dropping in on me because I haven't heard nothing yet.

Chicago, Illinois, October 7.

FRIEND AL: Well Al you know by this time that they beat me to-day and tied up the serious. But I have still got plenty of time Al and I will get them before it is over. My arm wasn't feeling good Al and my fast ball didn't hop like it had ought to. But it was the rotten support I got that beat me. That lucky stiff Zimmerman was the only guy that got a real hit off of me and he must of shut his eyes and throwed his bat because the ball he hit was a foot over his head. And if they hadn't been makeing all them errors behind me they wouldn't of been nobody on bases when Zimmerman got that lucky scratch. The serious now stands one and one Al and it is a cinch we will beat them even if they are a bunch of lucky stiffs. They has been great big crowds at both games and it looks like as if we should ought to get over eight hundred dollars a peace if we win and we will win sure because I will beat them three straight if necessary.

But Al I have got bigger news than that for you and I am the happyest man in the world. I told you I had not heard from Hazel for a long time. To-night when I got back to my room they was a letter waiting for me from her.

Al she is married. Maybe you don't know why that makes me happy but I will tell you. She is married to Kid Levy the middle weight. I guess my thirty dollars is gone because in her letter she called me a cheap skate and she inclosed one one-cent stamp and two twos and said she was paying me for the glass of beer I once bought her. I bought her more than that Al but I won't make no holler. She all so said not for me to never come near her or her husband would bust my jaw. I ain't afraid of him or no one else Al but they ain't no danger of me ever bothering them. She was no good and I was sorry the minute I agreed to marry her.

But I was going to tell you why I am happy or maybe you can guess. Now I can make Violet my wife and she's got Hazel beat forty ways. She ain't nowheres near as big as Hazel but she's classier Al and she will make me a good wife. She ain't never asked me for no money.

I wrote her a letter the minute I got the good news and told her to come on over here at once at my expense. We will be married right after the serious is over and I want you and Bertha to be sure and stand up with us. I will wire you at my own expence the exact date.

It all seems like a dream now about Violet and I haveing our misunderstanding Al and I don't see how I ever could of accused her of sending me that postcard. You and Bertha will be just as crazy about her as I am when you see her Al. Just think Al I will be married inside of a week and to the only girl I ever could of been happy with instead of the woman I never really cared for except as a passing fancy. My happyness would be complete Al if I had not of let that woman steal thirty dollars off of me.

Your happy pal,   JACK.

P. S. Hazel probibly would of insisted on us takeing a trip to Niagara falls or somewheres but I know Violet will be perfectly satisfied if I take her right down to Bedford. Oh you little yellow house.

Chicago, Illinois, October 9.

FRIEND AL: Well Al we have got them beat three games to one now and will wind up the serious to-morrow sure. Callahan sent me in to save poor Allen yesterday and I stopped them dead. But I don't care now Al. I have lost all interest in the game and I don't care if Callahan pitches me to-morrow or not. My heart is just about broke Al and I wouldn't be able to do myself justice feeling the way I do.

I have lost Violet Al and just when I was figureing on being the happyest man in the world. We will get the big money but it won't do me no good. They can keep my share because I won't have no little girl to spend it on.

Her answer to my letter was waiting for me at home to-night. She is engaged to be married to Joe Hill the big lefthander Jennings got from Providence. Honest Al I don't see how he gets by. He ain't got no more curve ball than a rabbit and his fast one floats up there like a big balloon. He beat us the last game of the regular season here but it was because Callahan had a lot of bushers in the game.

I wish I had knew then that he was stealing my girl and I would of made Callahan pitch me against him. And when he come up to bat I would of beaned him. But I don't suppose you could hurt him by hitting him in the head. The big stiff. Their wedding ain't going to come off till next summer and by that time he will be pitching in the Southwestern Texas League for about fifty dollars a month.

Violet wrote that she wished me all the luck and happyness in the world but it is too late for me to be happy Al and I don't care what kind of luck I have now.

Al you will have to get rid of that lease for me. Fix it up the best way you can. Tell the old man I have changed my plans. I don't know just yet what I will do but maybe I will go to Australia with Mike Donlin's team. If I do I won't care if the boat goes down or not. I don't believe I will even come back to Bedford this winter. It would drive me wild to go past that little house every day and think how happy I might of been.

Maybe I will pitch to-morrow Al and if I do the serious will be over to-morrow night. I can beat them Cubs if I get any kind of decent support. But I don't care now Al.

Yours truly,   JACK.

Chicago, Illinois, October 12.

AL: Your letter received. If the old man won't call it off I guess I will have to try and rent the house to some one else. Do you know of any couple that wants one Al? It looks like I would have to come down there myself and fix things up someway. He is just mean enough to stick me with the house on my hands when I won't have no use for it.

They beat us the day before yesterday as you probibly know and it rained yesterday and to-day. The papers says it will be all O. K. to-morrow and Callahan tells me I am going to work. The Cub pitchers was all shot to peaces and the bad weather is just nuts for them because it will give Cheney a good rest. But I will beat him Al if they don't kick it away behind me.

I must close because I promised Allen the little lefthander that I would come over to his flat and play cards a while to-night and I must wash up and change my collar. Allen's wife's sister is visiting them again and I would give anything not to have to go over there. I am through with girls and don't want nothing to do with them.

I guess it is maybe a good thing it rained to-day because I dreamt about Violet last night and went out and got a couple of high balls before breakfast this morning. I hadn't never drank nothing before breakfast before and it made me kind of sick. But I am all O. K. now.

Your pal,   JACK.

Chicago, Illinois, October 13.

DEAR OLD AL: The serious is all over Al. We are the champions and I done it. I may be home the day after to-morrow or I may not come for a couple of days. I want to see Comiskey before I leave and fix up about my contract for next year. I won't sign for no less than five thousand and if he hands me a contract for less than that I will leave the White Sox flat on their back. I have got over fourteen hundred dollars now Al with the city serious money which was $814.30 and I don't have to worry.

Them reporters will have to give me a square deal this time Al. I had everything and the Cubs done well to score a run. I whiffed Zimmerman three times. Some of the boys say he ain't no hitter but he is a hitter and a good one Al only he could not touch the stuff I got. The umps give them their run because in the fourth inning I had Leach flatfooted off of second base and Weaver tagged him O. K. but the umps wouldn't call it. Then Schulte the lucky stiff happened to get a hold of one and pulled it past first base. I guess Chase must of been asleep. Anyway they scored but I don't care because we piled up six runs on Cheney and I drove in one of them myself with one of the prettiest singles you ever see. It was a spitter and I hit it like a shot. If I had hit it square it would of went out of the park.

Comiskey ought to feel pretty good about me winning and I guess he will give me a contract for anything I want. He will have to or I will go to the Federal League.

We are all invited to a show to-night and I am going with Allen and his wife and her sister Florence. She is O. K. Al and I guess she thinks the same about me. She must because she was out to the game to-day and seen me hand it to them. She maybe ain't as pretty as Violet and Hazel but as they say beauty isn't only so deep.

Well Al tell the boys I will be with them soon. I have gave up the idea of going to Australia because I would have to buy a evening full-dress suit and they tell me they cost pretty near fifty dollars.

Yours truly,   JACK.

Chicago, Illinois, October 14.

FRIEND AL: Never mind about that lease. I want the house after all Al and I have got the suprise of your life for you.

When I come home to Bedford I will bring my wife with me. I and Florence fixed things all up after the show last night and we are going to be married to-morrow morning. I am a busy man to-day Al because I have got to get the license and look round for furniture. And I have also got to buy some new cloths but they are haveing a sale on Cottage Grove Avenue at Clark's store and I know one of the clerks there.

I am the happyest man in the world Al. You and Bertha and I and Florence will have all kinds of good times together this winter because I know Bertha and Florence will like each other. Florence looks something like Bertha at that. I am glad I didn't get tied up with Violet or Hazel even if they was a little bit prettier than Florence.

Florence knows a lot about baseball for a girl and you would be suprised to hear her talk. She says I am the best pitcher in the league and she has saw them all. She all so says I am the best looking ball player she ever seen but you know how girls will kid a guy Al. You will like her O. K. I fell for her the first time I seen her.

Your old pal,   JACK.

P. S. I signed up for next year. Comiskey slapped me on the back when I went in to see him and told me I would be a star next year if I took good care of myself. I guess I am a star without waiting for next year Al. My contract calls for twenty-eight hundred a year which is a thousand more than I was getting. And it is pretty near a cinch that I will be in on the World Serious money next season.

P. S. I certainly am relieved about that lease. It would of been fierce to of had that place on my hands all winter and not getting any use out of it. Everything is all O. K. now. Oh you little yellow house.

CHAPTER III

The Busher's Honeymoon

Chicago, Illinois, October 17.

FRIEND AL: Well Al it looks as if I would not be writeing so much to you now that I am a married man. Yes Al I and Florrie was married the day before yesterday just like I told you we was going to be and Al I am the happyest man in the world though I have spent $30 in the last 3 days incluseive. You was wise Al to get married in Bedford where not nothing is nearly half so dear. My expenses was as follows:

License	$ 2.00
Preist	3.50
Haircut and shave	.35
Shine	.05
Carfair	.45
New suit	14.50
Show tickets	3.00
Flowers	.50
Candy	.30
Hotel	4.50
Tobacco both kinds	.25

You see Al it costs a hole lot of money to get married here. The sum of what I have wrote down is $29.40 but as I told you I have spent $30 and I do not know what I have did with that other $0.60. My new brother-in-law Allen told me I should ought to give the preist $5 and I thought it should be about $2 the same as the license so I split the difference and give him $3.50. I never seen him before and probily won't never see him again so why should I give him anything at all when it is his business to marry couples? But I like to do the right thing. You know me Al.

I thought we would be in Bedford by this time but Florrie wants to stay here a few more days because she says she wants to be with her sister. Allen and his wife is thinking about takeing a flat for the winter instead of going down to Waco Texas where they live. I don't see no sense in that when it costs so much to live here but it is none of my business if they want to throw their money away. But I am glad I got a wife with some sense though she kicked because I did not get no room with a bath which would cost me $2 a day instead of $1.50. I says I guess the clubhouse is still open yet and if I want a bath I can go over there and take the shower. She says Yes and I suppose I can go and jump in the lake. But she would not do that Al because the lake here is cold at this time of the year.

When I told you about my expenses I did not include in it the meals because we would be eating them if I was getting married or not getting married only I have to pay for six meals a day now instead of three and I didn't used to eat no lunch in the playing season except once in a while when I knowed I was not going to work that afternoon. I had a meal ticket which had not quite ran out over to a resturunt on Indiana Ave and we eat there for the first day except at night when I took Allen and his wife to the show with us and then he took us to a chop suye resturunt. I guess you have not never had no chop suye Al and I am here to tell you you have not missed nothing but when Allen was going to buy the supper what could I say? I could not say nothing.

Well yesterday and to-day we been eating at a resturunt on Cottage Grove Ave near the hotel and at the resturunt on Indiana that I had the meal ticket at only I do not like to buy no new meal ticket when I am not going to be round here no more than a few days. Well Al I guess the meals has cost me all together about $1.50 and I have eat very little myself. Florrie always wants desert ice cream or something and that runs up into money faster than regular stuff like stake and ham and eggs.

Well Al Florrie says it is time for me to keep my promise and take her to the moveing pictures which is $0.20 more because the one she likes round here costs a dime apeace. So I must close for this time and will see you soon.

Your pal,   JACK.

Chicago, Illinois, October 22.

AL: Just a note Al to tell you why I have not yet came to Bedford yet where I expected I would be long before this time. Allen and his wife have took a furnished flat for the winter and Allen's wife wants Florrie to stay here untill they get settled. Meentime it is costing me a hole lot of money at the hotel and for meals besides I am paying $10 a month rent for the house you got for me and what good am I getting out of it? But Florrie wants to help her sister and what can I say? Though I did make her promise she would not stay no longer than next Saturday at least. So I guess Al we will be home on the evening train Saturday and then may be I can save some money.

I know Al that you and Bertha will like Florrie when you get acquainted with her spesialy Bertha though Florrie dresses pretty swell and spends a hole lot of time fusing with her face and her hair.

She says to me to-night Who are you writeing to and I told her Al Blanchard who I have told you about a good many times. She says I bet you are writeing to some girl and acted like as though she was kind of jealous. So I thought I would tease her a little and I says I don't know no girls except you and Violet and Hazel. Who is Violet and Hazel? she says. I kind of laughed and says Oh I guess I better not tell you and then she says I guess you will tell me. That made me kind of mad because no girl can't tell me what to do. She says Are you going to tell me? and I says No.

Then she says If you don't tell me I will go over to Marie's that is her sister Allen's wife and stay all night. I says Go on and she went downstairs but I guess she probily went to get a soda because she has some money of her own that I give her. This was about two hours ago and she is probily down in the hotel lobby now trying to scare me by makeing me believe she has went to her sister's. But she can't fool me Al and I am now going out to mail this letter and get a beer. I won't never tell her about Violet and Hazel if she is going to act like that.

                    Yours truly,   JACK.

Chicago, Illinois, October 24.
FRIEND AL: I guess I told you Al that we would be home Saturday evening. I have changed my mind. Allen and his wife has a spair bedroom and wants us to come there and stay a week or two. It won't cost nothing except they will probily

want to go out to the moveing pictures nights and we will probily have to go along with them and I am a man Al that wants to pay his share and not be cheap.

I and Florrie had our first quarrle the other night. I guess I told you the start of it but I don't remember. I made some crack about Violet and Hazel just to tease Florrie and she wanted to know who they was and I would not tell her. So she gets sore and goes over to Marie's to stay all night. I was just kidding Al and was willing to tell her about them two poor girls whatever she wanted to know except that I don't like to brag about girls being stuck on me. So I goes over to Marie's after her and tells her all about them except that I turned them down cold at the last minute to marry her because I did not want her to get all swelled up. She made me sware that I did not never care nothing about them and that was easy because it was the truth. So she come back to the hotel with me just like I knowed she would when I ordered her to.

They must not be no mistake about who is the boss in my house. Some men lets their wife run all over them but I am not that kind. You know me Al.

I must get busy and pack my suitcase if I am going to move over to Allen's. I sent three collars and a shirt to the laundrey this morning so even if we go over there to-night I will have to take another trip back this way in a day or two. I won't mind Al because they sell my kind of beer down to the corner and I never seen it sold nowheres else in Chi. You know the kind it is, eh Al? I wish I was lifting a few with you to-night.

Your pal,　　　　　　　　JACK.

Chicago, Illinois, October 28.

DEAR OLD AL: Florrie and Marie has went downtown shopping because Florrie thinks she has got to have a new dress though she has got two changes of cloths now and I don't know what she can do with another one. I hope she don't find none to suit her though it would not hurt none if she got something for next spring at a reduckshon. I guess she must think I am Charles A. Comiskey or somebody. Allen has went to a colledge football game. One of the reporters give him a pass. I don't see nothing in football except a lot of scrapping between little slobs that I could lick the whole bunch of them so I did not care to go. The reporter is one of the guys that travled round with our club all summer. He called up and said he hadn't only the one pass but he was not hurting my feelings none because I would not go to no rotten football game if they payed me.

The flat across the hall from this here one is for rent furnished. They want $40 a month for it and I guess they think they must be lots of suckers running round loose. Marie was talking about it and says Why don't you and Florrie take it and then we can be right together all winter long and have some big times? Florrie says It would be all right with me. What about it Jack? I says What do you think I am? I don't have to live in no high price flat when I got a home in Bedford where they ain't no people trying to hold everybody up all the time. So they did not say no more about it when they seen I was in ernest. Nobody cannot tell me where I am going to live sister-in-law or no sister-in-law. If I was to rent the rotten old flat I would be paying $50 a month rent includeing the house down in Bedford. Fine chance Al.

Well Al I am lonesome and thirsty so more later.

Your pal,   JACK.

Chicago, Illinois, November 2.

FRIEND AL: Well Al I got some big news for you. I am not comeing to Bedford this winter after all except to make a visit which I guess will be round Xmas. I changed my mind about that flat across the hall from the Allens and decided to take it after all. The people who was in it and owns the furniture says they would let us have it till the 1 of May if we would pay $42.50 a month which is only $2.50 a month more than they would of let us have it for for a short time. So you see we got a bargain because it is all furnished and everything and we won't have to blow no money on furniture besides the club goes to California the middle of Febuery so Florrie would not have no place to stay while I am away.

The Allens only subleased their flat from some other people till the 2 of Febuery and when I and Allen goes West Marie can come over and stay with Florrie so you see it is best all round. If we should of boughten furniture it would cost us in the neighborhood of $100 even without no piano and they is a piano in this here flat which makes it nice because Florrie plays pretty good with one hand and we can have lots of good times at home without it costing us nothing except just the bear live- ing expenses. I consider myself lucky to of found out about this before it was too late and somebody else had of gotten the tip.

Now Al old pal I want to ask a great favor of you Al. I all ready have payed one month rent $10 on the house in Bedford and I want you to see the old man and see if he won't call off that lease. Why should I be paying $10 a month rent down there and $42.50 up here when the house down there is not no good to me because I am liveing up here all winter? See Al? Tell him I will gladly give him another month rent to call off the lease but don't tell him that if you don't have to. I want to be fare with him.

If you will do this favor for me, Al, I won't never forget it. Give my kindest to Bertha and tell her I am sorry I and Florrie won't see her right away but you see how it is Al.

Yours,   JACK.

Chicago, Illinois, November 30.

FRIEND AL: I have not wrote for a long time have I Al but I have been very busy. They was not enough furniture in the flat and we have been buying some more. They was enough for some people maybe but I and Florrie is the kind that won't have nothing but the best. The furniture them people had in the liveing room was oak but they had a bookcase bilt in in the flat that was mohoggeny and Florrie would not stand for no joke combination like that so she moved the oak chairs and table in to the spair bedroom and we went downtown to buy some mohoggeny. But it costs too much Al and we was feeling pretty bad about it when we seen some Sir Cashion walnut that was prettier even than the mohoggeny and not near so expensive. It is not no real Sir Cashion walnut but it is just as good and we got it reasonable. Then we got some mission chairs for the dining room because the old ones was just straw and was no good and we got a big lether couch for $9 that somebody can sleep on if we get to much company.

I hope you and Bertha can come up for the holidays and see how comfertible we are fixed. That is all the new furniture we have boughten but Florrie set her heart on some old Rose drapes and a red table lamp that is the biggest you ever seen Al and I did not have the heart to say no. The hole thing cost me in the neighborhood of $110 which is very little for what we got and then it will always be ourn even when we move away from this flat though we will have to leave the furniture that belongs to the other people but their part of it is not no good anyway.

I guess I told you Al how much money I had when the season ended. It was $1400 all told includeing the city serious money. Well Al I got in the neighborhood of $800 left because I give $200 to Florrie to send down to Texas to her other sister who had a bad egg for a husband that managed a club in the Texas Oklahoma League and this was the money she had to pay to get the divorce. I am glad Al that I was lucky enough to marry happy and get a good girl for my wife that has got some sense and besides if I have got $800 left I should not worry as they say.

Your pal,   JACK.

Chicago, Illinois, December 7.

DEAR OLD AL: No I was in ernest Al when I says that I wanted you and Bertha to come up here for the holidays. I know I told you that I might come to Bedford for the holidays but that is all off. I have gave up the idea of comeing to Bedford for the holidays and I want you to be sure and come up here for the holidays and I will show you a good time. I would love to have Bertha come to and she can come if she wants to only Florrie don't know if she would have a good time or not and thinks maybe she would rather stay in Bedford and you come alone. But be sure and have Bertha come if she wants to come but maybe she would not injoy it. You know best Al.

I don't think the old man give me no square deal on that lease but if he wants to stick me all right. I am grateful to you Al for trying to fix it up but maybe you could of did better if you had of went at it in a different way. I am not finding no fault with my old pal though. Don't think that. When I have a pal I am the man to stick to him threw thick and thin. If the old man is going to hold me to that lease I guess I will have to stand it and I guess I won't starv to death for no $10 a month

because I am going to get $2800 next year besides the city se-
rious money and maybe we will get into the World Serious
too. I know we will if Callahan will pitch me every 3d day like
I wanted him to last season. But if you had of approached the
old man in a different way maybe you could of fixed it up. I
wish you would try it again Al if it is not no trouble.

We had Allen and his wife here for thanksgiveing dinner and
the dinner cost me better than $5. I thought we had enough to
eat to last a week but about six o'clock at night Florrie and
Marie said they was hungry and we went downtown and had
dinner all over again and I payed for it and it cost me $5 more.
Allen was all ready to pay for it when Florrie said No this day's
treat is on us so I had to pay for it but I don't see why she did
not wait and let me do the talking. I was going to pay for it any
way.

Be sure and come and visit us for the holidays Al and of
coarse if Bertha wants to come bring her along. We will be
glad to see you both. I won't never go back on a friend and
pal. You know me Al.

Your old pal,   JACK.

Chicago, Illinois, December 20.

FRIEND AL: I don't see what can be the matter with Bertha
because you know Al we would not care how she dressed and
would not make no kick if she come up here in a night gown.
She did not have no license to say we was to swell for her because we did not never think of nothing like that. I wish you
would talk to her again Al and tell her she need not get sore on
me and that both her and you is welcome at my house any
time I ask you to come. See if you can't make her change her
mind Al because I feel like as if she must of took offense at
something I may of wrote you. I am sorry you and her are not
comeing but I suppose you know best. Only we was getting all
ready for you and Florrie said only the other day that she
wished the holidays was over but that was before she knowed
you was not comeing. I hope you can come Al.

Well Al I guess there is not no use talking to the old man no
more. You have did the best you could but I wish I could of
came down there and talked to him. I will pay him his rotten
old $10 a month and the next time I come to Bedford and

meet him on the street I will bust his jaw. I know he is a old man Al but I don't like to see nobody get the best of me and I am sorry I ever asked him to let me off. Some of them old skinflints has no heart Al but why should I fight with a old man over chicken feed like $10? Florrie says a star pitcher like I should not ought never to scrap about little things and I guess she is right Al so I will pay the old man his $10 a month if I have to.

Florrie says she is jealous of me writeing to you so much and she says she would like to meet this great old pal of mine. I would like to have her meet you to Al and I would like to have you change your mind and come and visit us and I am sorry you can't come Al.

Yours truly,   JACK.

Chicago, Illinois, December 27.

OLD PAL: I guess all these lefthanders is alike though I thought this Allen had some sense. I thought he was different from the most and was not no rummy but they are all alike Al and they are all lucky that somebody don't hit them over the head with a ax and kill them but I guess at that you could not hurt no lefthanders by hitting them over the head. We was all down on State St. the day before Xmas and the girls was all tired out and ready to go home but Allen says No I guess we better stick down a while because now the crowds is out and it will be fun to watch them. So we walked up and down State St. about a hour longer and finally we come in front of a big jewlry store window and in it was a swell dimond ring that was marked $100. It was a ladies' ring so Marie says to Allen Why don't you buy that for me? And Allen says Do you really want it? And she says she did.

So we tells the girls to wait and we goes over to a salloon where Allen has got a friend and gets a check cashed and we come back and he bought the ring. Then Florrie looks like as though she was getting all ready to cry and I asked her what was the matter and she says I had not boughten her no ring not even when we was engaged. So I and Allen goes back to the salloon and I gets a check cashed and we come back and bought another ring but I did not think the ring Allen had boughten was worth no $100 so I gets one for $75. Now Al you know I am not makeing no kick on spending a little money for a present for my own wife but I had allready boughten her a rist watch for $15 and a rist watch was just what she had wanted. I was willing to give her the ring if she had not of wanted the rist watch more than the ring but when I give her the ring I kept the rist watch and did not tell her nothing about it.

Well I come downtown alone the day after Xmas and they would not take the rist watch back in the store where I got it. So I am going to give it to her for a New Year's present and I guess that will make Allen feel like a dirty doose. But I guess you cannot hurt no lefthander's feelings at that. They are all alike. But Allen has not got nothing but a dinky curve ball and a fast ball that looks like my slow one. If Comiskey was not good hearted he would of sold him long ago.

I sent you and Bertha a cut glass dish Al which was the best I could get for the money and it was pretty high pricet at that. We was glad to get the pretty pincushions from you and Bertha and Florrie says to tell you that we are well supplied with pincushions now because the ones you sent makes a even half dozen. Thanks Al for remembering us and thank Bertha too though I guess you paid for them.

Your pal,   JACK.

Chicago, Illinois, Januery 3.

OLD PAL: Al I been pretty sick ever since New Year's eve. We had a table at 1 of the swell resturunts downtown and I never seen so much wine drank in my life. I would rather of had beer but they would not sell us none so I found out that they was a certain kind that you can get for $1 a bottle and it is just as good as the kind that has got all them fancy names but this lefthander starts ordering some other kind about 11 oclock and it was $5 a bottle and the girls both says they liked it better. I could not see a hole lot of difference myself and I would of gave $0.20 for a big stine of my kind of beer. You know me Al. Well Al you know they is not nobody that can drink more than your old pal and I was all O. K. at one oclock but I seen the girls was getting kind of sleepy so I says we better go home.

Then Marie says Oh, shut up and don't be no quiter. I says

You better shut up yourself and not be telling me to shut up, and she says What will you do if I don't shut up? And I says I would bust her in the jaw. But you know Al I would not think of busting no girl. Then Florrie says You better not start nothing because you had to much to drink or you would not be talking about busting girls in the jaw. Then I says I don't care if it is a girl I bust or a lefthander. I did not mean nothing at all Al but Marie says I had insulted Allen and he gets up and slaps my face. Well Al I am not going to stand that from nobody not even if he is my brother-in-law and a lefthander that has not got enough speed to brake a pain of glass.

So I give him a good beating and the waiters butts in and puts us all out for fighting and I and Florrie comes home in a taxi and Allen and his wife don't get in till about 5 oclock so I guess she must of had to of took him to a doctor to get fixed up. I been in bed ever since till just this morning kind of sick to my stumach. I guess I must of eat something that did not agree with me. Allen come over after breakfast this morning and asked me was I all right so I guess he is not sore over the beating I give him or else he wants to make friends because he has saw that I am a bad guy to monkey with.

Florrie tells me a little while ago that she paid the hole bill at the resturunt with my money because Allen was broke so you see what kind of a cheap skate he is Al and some day I am going to bust his jaw. She won't tell me how much the bill was and I won't ask her to no more and we had a good time outside of the fight and what do I care if we spent a little money?

Yours truly,   JACK.

Chicago, Illinois, January 20.

FRIEND AL: Allen and his wife have gave up the flat across the hall from us and come over to live with us because we got a spair bedroom and why should they not have the bennifit of it? But it is pretty hard for the girls to have to cook and do the work when they is four of us so I have a hired girl who does it all for $7 a week. It is great stuff Al because now we can go round as we please and don't have to wait for no dishes to be washed or nothing. We generally almost always has dinner downtown in the evening so it is pretty soft for the girl too.

She don't generally have no more than one meal to get because we generally run round downtown till late and don't get up till about noon.

That sounds funny don't it Al, when I used to get up at 5 every morning down home. Well Al I can tell you something else that may sound funny and that is that I lost my taste for beer. I don't seem to care for it no more and I found I can stand allmost as many drinks of other stuff as I could of beer. I guess Al they is not nobody ever lived can drink more and stand up better under it than me. I make the girls and Allen quit every night.

I only got just time to write you this short note because Florrie and Marie is giving a big party to-night and I and Allen have got to beat it out of the house and stay out of the way till they get things ready. It is Marie's berthday and she says she is 22 but say Al if she is 22 Kid Gleason is 30. Well Al the girls says we must blow so I will run out and mail this letter.

Yours truly,   JACK.

Chicago, Illinois, Januery 31.

AL: Allen is going to take Marie with him on the training trip to California and of course Florrie has been at me to take her along. I told her postivly that she can't go. I can't afford no stunt like that but still I am up against it to know what to do with her while we are on the trip because Marie won't be here to stay with her. I don't like to leave her here all alone but they is nothing to it Al I can't afford to take her along. She says I don't see why you can't take me if Allen takes Marie. And I says That stuff is all O. K. for Allen because him and Marie has been grafting off of us all winter. And then she gets mad and tells me I should not ought to say her sister was no grafter. I did not mean nothing like that Al but you don't never know when a woman is going to take offense.

If our furniture was down in Bedford everything would be all O. K. because I could leave her there and I would feel all O. K. because I would know that you and Bertha would see that she was getting along O. K. But they would not be no sense in sending her down to a house that has not no furniture in it. I wish I knowed somewheres where she could visit Al. I would be willing to pay her bord even.

Well Al enough for this time.

Your old pal,   JACK.

Chicago, Illinois, Febuery 4.

FRIEND AL: You are a real old pal Al and I certainly am greatful to you for the invatation. I have not told Florrie about it yet but I am sure she will be tickled to death and it is certainly kind of you old pal. I did not never dream of nothing like that. I note what you say Al about not excepting no bord but I think it would be better and I would feel better if you would take something say about $2 a week.

I know Bertha will like Florrie and that they will get along O. K. together because Florrie can learn her how to make her cloths look good and fix her hair and fix up her face. I feel like as if you had took a big load off of me Al and I won't never forget it.

If you don't think I should pay no bord for Florrie all right. Suit yourself about that old pal.

We are leaveing here the 20 of Febuery and if you don't mind I will bring Florrie down to you about the 18. I would like to see the old bunch again and spesially you and Bertha.

Yours,   JACK.

P. S. We will only be away till April 14 and that is just a nice visit. I wish we did not have no flat on our hands.

Chicago, Illinois, Febuery 9.

OLD PAL: I want to thank you for asking Florrie to come down there and visit you Al but I find she can't get away. I did not know she had no engagements but she says she may go down to her folks in Texas and she don't want to say that she will come to visit you when it is so indefanate. So thank you just the same Al and thank Bertha too.

Florrie is still at me to take her along to California but honest Al I can't do it. I am right down to my last $50 and I have not payed no rent for this month. I owe the hired girl 2 weeks' salery and both I and Florrie needs some new cloths.

Florrie has just came in since I started writeing this letter and we have been talking some more about California and she says maybe if I would ask Comiskey he would take her along as the club's guest. I had not never thought of that Al and maybe he would because he is a pretty good scout and I guess I will go and see him about it. The league has its skedule meeting here to-morrow and may be I can see him down to the hotel where they meet at. I am so worried Al that I can't write no more but I will tell you how I come out with Comiskey.

Your pal,   JACK.

Chicago, Illinois, Febuery 11.

FRIEND AL: I am up against it right Al and I don't know where I am going to head in at. I went down to the hotel where the league was holding its skedule meeting at and I seen Comiskey and got some money off of the club but I owe all the money I got off of them and I am still wondering what to do about Florrie.

Comiskey was busy in the meeting when I went down there and they was not no chance to see him for a while so I and Allen and some of the boys hung round and had a few drinks and fanned. This here Joe Hill the busher that Detroit has got that Violet is hooked up to was round the hotel. I don't know what for but I felt like busting his jaw only the boys told me I had better not do nothing because I might kill him and any way he probily won't be in the league much longer. Well finally Comiskey got threw the meeting and I seen him and he says Hello young man what can I do for you? And I says I would like to get $100 advance money. He says Have you been takeing care of yourself down in Bedford? And I told him I had been liveing here all winter and it did not seem to make no hit with him though I don't see what business it is of hisn where I live.

So I says I had been takeing good care of myself. And I have Al. You know that. So he says I should come to the ball park the next day which is to-day and he would have the secretary take care of me but I says I could not wait and so he give me $100 out of his pocket and says he would have it charged against my salery. I was just going to brace him about the California trip when he got away and went back to the meeting.

Well Al I hung round with the bunch waiting for him to get threw again and we had some more drinks and finally Comiskey was threw again and I braced him in the lobby and asked him if it was all right to take my wife along to California. He says Sure they would be glad to have her along. And then I says Would the club pay her fair? He says I guess you must of spent that $100 buying some nerve. He says Have you not got no sisters that would like to go along to? He says Does your wife insist on the drawing room or will she take a lower birth? He says Is my special train good enough for her?

Then he turns away from me and I guess some of the boys must of heard the stuff he pulled because they was laughing when he went away but I did not see nothing to laugh at. But I guess he ment that I would have to pay her fair if she goes along and that is out of the question Al. I am up against it and I don't know where I am going to head in at.

Your pal,   JACK.

Chicago, Illinois, Febuery 12.

DEAR OLD AL: I guess everything will be all O. K. now at least I am hopeing it will. When I told Florrie about how I come out with Comiskey she bawled her head off and I thought for a while I was going to have to call a doctor or something but pretty soon she cut it out and we sat there a while without saying nothing. Then she says If you could get your salery razed a couple of hundred dollars a year would you borrow the money ahead somewheres and take me along to California? I says Yes I would if I could get a couple hundred dollars more salery but how could I do that when I had signed a contract for $2800 last fall allready? She says Don't you think you are worth more than $2800? And I says Yes of coarse I was worth more than $2800. She says Well if you will go and talk the right way to Comiskey I believe he will give you $3000 but you must be sure you go at it the right way and don't go and ball it all up.

Well we argude about it a while because I don't want to hold nobody up Al but finally I says I would. It would not be holding nobody up anyway because I am worth $3000 to the club if I am worth a nichol. The papers is all saying that the club has got a good chance to win the pennant this year and talking about the pitching staff and I guess they would not be no pitching staff much if it was not for I and one or two others—about one other I guess.

So it looks like as if everything will be all O. K. now Al. I am going to the office over to the park to see him the first thing in the morning and I am pretty sure that I will get what I am after because if I do not he will see that I am going to quit and then he will see what he is up against and not let me get away.

I will let you know how I come out.

               Your pal,   JACK.

Chicago, Illinois, Febuery 14.

FRIEND AL: Al old pal I have got a big supprise for you. I am going to the Federal League. I had a run in with Comiskey yesterday and I guess I told him a thing or 2. I guess he would of been glad to sign me at my own figure before I got threw but I was so mad I would not give him no chance to offer me another contract.

I got out to the park at 9 oclock yesterday morning and it was a hour before he showed up and then he kept me waiting another hour so I was pretty sore when I finally went in to see him. He says Well young man what can I do for you? I says I come to see about my contract. He says Do you want to sign up for next year all ready? I says No I am talking about this year. He says I thought I and you talked business last fall. And I says Yes but now I think I am worth more money and I want to sign a contract for $3000. He says If you behave yourself and work good this year I will see that you are took care of. But I says That won't do because I have got to be sure I am going to get $3000.

Then he says I am not sure you are going to get anything. I says What do you mean? And he says I have gave you a very fare contract and if you don't want to live up to it that is your own business. So I give him a awful call Al and told him I would jump to the Federal League. He says Oh, I would not do that if I was you. They are haveing a hard enough time as it is. So I says something back to him and he did not say nothing to me and I beat it out of the office.

I have not told Florrie about the Federal League business yet as I am going to give her a big supprise. I bet they will take her along with me on the training trip and pay her fair but even if they don't I should not worry because I will make them give me a contract for $4000 a year and then I can afford to take her with me on all the trips.

I will go down and see Tinker to-morrow morning and I will write you to-morrow night Al how much salery they are going to give me. But I won't sign for no less than $4000. You know me Al.

               Yours,   JACK.

Chicago, Illinois, Febuery 15.

OLD PAL: It is pretty near midnight Al but I been to bed a couple of times and I can't get no sleep. I am worried to death Al and I don't know where I am going to head in at. Maybe I will go out and buy a gun Al and end it all and I guess it would be better for everybody. But I cannot do that Al because I have not got the money to buy a gun with.

I went down to see Tinker about signing up with the Federal League and he was busy in the office when I come in. Pretty soon Buck Perry the pitcher that was with Boston last year come out and seen me and as Tinker was still busy we went out and had a drink together. Buck shows me a contract for $5000 a year and Tinker had allso gave him a $500 bonus. So pretty soon I went up to the office and pretty soon Tinker seen me and called me into his private office and asked what did I want. I says I was ready to jump for $4000 and a bonus. He says I thought you was signed up with the White Sox. I says Yes I was but I was not satisfied. He says That does not make no difference to me if you are satisfied or not. You ought to of came to me before you signed a contract. I says I did not know enough but I know better now. He says Well it is to late now. We cannot have nothing to do with you because you have went and signed a contract with the White Sox. I argude with him a while and asked him to come out and have a drink so we could talk it over but he said he was busy so they was nothing for me to do but blow.

So I am not going to the Federal League Al and I will not go with the White Sox because I have got a raw deal. Comiskey will be sorry for what he done when his team starts the season and is up against it for good pitchers and then he will probily be willing to give me anything I ask for but that don't do me no good now Al. I am way in debt and no chance to get no money from nobody. I wish I had of stayed with Terre Haute Al and never saw this league.

Your pal,   JACK.

Chicago, Illinois, Febuery 17.

FRIEND AL: Al don't never let nobody tell you that these here lefthanders is right. This Allen my own brother-in-law who married sisters has been grafting and spongeing on me all winter Al. Look what he done to me now Al. You know how hard I been up against it for money and I know he has got plenty of it because I seen it on him. Well Al I was scared to tell Florrie I was cleaned out and so I went to Allen yesterday and says I had to have $100 right away because I owed the rent and owed the hired girl's salery and could not even pay no grocery bill. And he says No he could not let me have none because he has got to save all his money to take his wife on the trip to California. And here he has been liveing on me all winter and maybe I could of took my wife to California if I had not of spent all my money takeing care of this no good lefthander and his wife. And Al honest he has not got a thing and ought not to be in the league. He gets by with a dinky curve ball and has not got no more smoke than a rabbit or something.

Well Al I felt like busting him in the jaw but then I thought No I might kill him and then I would have Marie and Florrie both to take care of and God knows one of them is enough besides paying his funeral expenses. So I walked away from him without takeing a crack at him and went into the other room where Florrie and Marie was at. I says to Marie I says Marie I wish you would go in the other room a minute because I want to talk to Florrie. So Marie beats it into the other room and then I tells Florrie all about what Comiskey and the Federal League done to me. She bawled something awful and then she says I was no good and she wished she had not never married me. I says I wisht it too and then she says Do you mean that and starts to cry.

I told her I was sorry I says that because they is not no use fusing with girls Al specially when they is your wife. She says No California trip for me and then she says What are you going to do? And I says I did not know. She says Well if I was a man I would do something. So then I got mad and I says I will do something. So I went down to the corner salloon and started in to get good and drunk but I could not do it Al because I did not have the money.

Well old pal I am going to ask you a big favor and it is this I want you to send me $100 Al for just a few days till I can get on my feet. I do not know when I can pay it back Al but I guess you know the money is good and I know you have got it. Who would not have it when they live in Bedford? And besides I let you take $20 in June 4 years ago Al and you give it back but I would not have said nothing to you if you had of kept it. Let me hear from you right away old pal.

Yours truly,   JACK.

Chicago, Illinois, Febuery 19.

AL: I am certainly greatful to you Al for the $100 which come just a little while ago. I will pay the rent with it and part of the grocery bill and I guess the hired girl will have to wait a while for hern but she is sure to get it because I don't never forget my debts. I have changed my mind about the White Sox and I am going to go on the trip and take Florrie along because I don't think it would not be right to leave her here alone in Chi when her sister and all of us is going.

I am going over to the ball park and up in the office pretty soon to see about it. I will tell Comiskey I changed my mind and he will be glad to get me back because the club has not got no chance to finish nowheres without me. But I won't go on no trip or give the club my services without them giveing me some more advance money so as I can take Florrie along with me because Al I would not go without her.

Maybe Comiskey will make my salery $3000 like I wanted him to when he sees I am willing to be a good fellow and go along with him and when he knows that the Federal League would of gladly gave me $4000 if I had not of signed no contract with the White Sox.

I think I will ask him for $200 advance money Al and if I get it may be I can send part of your $100 back to you but I know you cannot be in no hurry Al though you says you wanted it back as soon as possible. You could not be very hard up Al because it don't cost near so much to live in Bedford as it does up here.

Anyway I will let you know how I come out with Comiskey and I will write you as soon as I get out to Paso Robles if I don't get no time to write you before I leave.

Your pal,   JACK.

P. S. I have took good care of myself all winter Al and I guess I ought to have a great season.

P. S. Florrie is tickled to death about going along and her and I will have some time together out there on the Coast if I can get some money somewheres.

Chicago, Illinois, Febuery 21.

FRIEND AL: I have not got the heart to write this letter to you Al. I am up here in my $42.50 a month flat and the club has went to California and Florrie has went too. I am flat broke Al and all I am asking you is to send me enough money to pay my fair to Bedford and they and all their leagues can go to hell Al.

I was out to the ball park early yesterday morning and some of the boys was there allready fanning and kidding each other. They tried to kid me to when I come in but I guess I give them as good as they give me. I was not in no mind for kidding Al because I was there on business and I wanted to see Comiskey and get it done with.

Well the secretary come in finally and I went up to him and says I wanted to see Comiskey right away. He says The boss was busy and what did I want to see him about and I says I wanted to get some advance money because I was going to take my wife on the trip. He says This would be a fine time to be telling us about it even if you was going on the trip.

And I says What do you mean? And he says You are not going on no trip with us because we have got wavers on you and you are sold to Milwaukee.

Honest Al I thought he was kidding at first and I was waiting for him to laugh but he did not laugh and finally I says What do you mean? And he says Cannot you understand no English? You are sold to Milwaukee. Then I says I want to see the boss. He says It won't do you no good to see the boss and he is to busy to see you. I says I want to get some money. And he says You cannot get no money from this club and all you get is your fair to Milwaukee. I says I am not going to no Milwaukee anyway and he says I should not worry about that. Suit yourself.

Well Al I told some of the boys about it and they was pretty sore and says I ought to bust the secretary in the jaw and I was going to do it when I thought No I better not because he is a little guy and I might kill him.

I looked all over for Kid Gleason but he was not nowheres round and they told me he would not get into town till late in the afternoon. If I could of saw him Al he would of fixed me all up. I asked 3 or 4 of the boys for some money but they says they was all broke.

But I have not told you the worst of it yet Al. When I come back to the flat Allen and Marie and Florrie was busy packing up and they asked me how I come out. I told them and Allen just stood there stareing like a big rummy but Marie and Florrie both begin to cry and I almost felt like as if I would like to cry to only I am not no baby Al.

Well Al I told Florrie she might just is well quit packing and make up her mind that she was not going nowheres till I got money enough to go to Bedford where I belong. She kept right on crying and it got so I could not stand it no more so I went out to get a drink because I still had just about a dollar left yet.

It was about 2 oclock when I left the flat and pretty near 5 when I come back because I had ran in to some fans that knowed who I was and would not let me get away and besides I did not want to see no more of Allen and Marie till they was out of the house and on their way.

But when I come in Al they was nobody there. They was not nothing there except the furniture and a few of my things scattered round. I sit down for a few minutes because I guess I must of had to much to drink but finally I seen a note on the table addressed to me and I seen it was Florrie's writeing.

I do not remember just what was there in the note Al because I tore it up the minute I read it but it was something about I could not support no wife and Allen had gave her enough money to go back to Texas and she was going on the 6 oclock train and it would not do me no good to try and stop her.

Well Al they was not no danger of me trying to stop her. She was not no good Al and I wisht I had not of never saw either she or her sister or my brother-in-law.

For a minute I thought I would follow Allen and his wife down to the deepo where the special train was to pull out of and wait till I see him and punch his jaw but I seen that would not get me nothing.

So here I am all alone Al and I will have to stay here till you send me the money to come home. You better send me $25 because I have got a few little debts I should ought to pay before I leave town. I am not going to Milwaukee Al because I did not get no decent deal and nobody cannot make no sucker out of me.

Please hurry up with the $25 Al old friend because I am sick and tired of Chi and want to get back there with my old pal.

Yours,   JACK.

P. S. Al I wish I had of took poor little Violet when she was so stuck on me.

CHAPTER IV

A New Busher Breaks In

Chicago, Illinois, March 2.

FRIEND AL: Al that peace in the paper was all O. K. and the right dope just like you said. I seen president Johnson the president of the league to-day and he told me the peace in the papers was the right dope and Comiskey did not have no right to sell me to Milwaukee because the Detroit Club had never gave no wavers on me. He says the Detroit Club was late in fileing their claim and Comiskey must of tooken it for granted that they was going to wave but president Johnson was pretty sore about it at that and says Comiskey did not have no right to sell me till he was positive that they was not no team that wanted me.

It will probily cost Comiskey some money for acting like he done and not paying no attention to the rules and I would not be supprised if president Johnson had him throwed out of the league.

Well I asked president Johnson should I report at once to the Detroit Club down south and he says No you better wait till you hear from Comiskey and I says What has Comiskey got to do with it now? And he says Comiskey will own you till he sells you to Detroit or somewheres else. So I will have to go out to the ball park to-morrow and see is they any mail for me there because I probily will get a letter from Comiskey telling me I am sold to Detroit.

If I had of thought at the time I would of knew that Detroit never would give no wavers on me after the way I showed Cobb and Crawford up last fall and I might of knew too that Detroit is in the market for good pitchers because they got a rotten pitching staff but they won't have no rotten staff when I get with them.

If necessary I will pitch every other day for Jennings and if I do we will win the pennant sure because Detroit has got a club that can get 2 or 3 runs every day and all as I need to win most of my games is 1 run. I can't hardly wait till Jennings works me against the White Sox and what I will do to them will be a plenty. It don't take no pitching to beat them anyway and when they get up against a pitcher like I they might as well leave their bats in the bag for all the good their bats will do them.

I guess Cobb and Crawford will be glad to have me on the Detroit Club because then they won't never have to hit against me except in practice and I won't pitch my best in practice because they will be teammates of mine and I don't never like to show none of my teammates up. At that though I don't suppose Jennings will let me do much pitching in practice because when he gets a hold of a good pitcher he won't want me to take no chances of throwing my arm away in practice.

Al just think how funny it will be to have me pitching for the Tigers in the same town where Violet lives and pitching on the same club with her husband. It will not be so funny for Violet and her husband though because when she has a chance to see me work regular she will find out what a mistake she made takeing that left-hander instead of a man that has got some future and soon will be makeing 5 or $6000 a year because I won't sign with Detroit for no less than $5000 at most. Of coarse I could of had her if I had of wanted to but still and all it will make her feel pretty sick to see me winning games for Detroit while her husband is batting fungos and getting splinters in his unie from slideing up and down the bench.

As for her husband the first time he opens his clam to me I will haul off and bust him one in the jaw but I guess he will know more than to start trouble with a man of my size and who is going to be one of their stars while he is just holding down a job because they feel sorry for him. I wish he could of got the girl I married instead of the one he got and I bet she would of drove him crazy. But I guess you can't drive a left-hander crazyer than he is to begin with.

I have not heard nothing from Florrie Al and I don't want to hear nothing. I and her is better apart and I wish she would sew me for a bill of divorce so she could not go round claiming she is my wife and disgraceing my name. If she would consent to sew me for a bill of divorce I would gladly pay all the expenses and settle with her for any sum of money she wants say about $75.00 or $100.00 and they is no reason I should give her a nichol after the way her and her sister Marie and her brother-in-law Allen grafted off of me. Probily I could sew her for a bill of divorce but they tell me it costs money to sew and if you just lay low and let the other side do the sewing it don't cost you a nichol.

It is pretty late Al and I have got to get up early to-morrow and go to the ball park and see is they any mail for me. I will let you know what I hear old pal.

Your old pal,   JACK.

Chicago, Illinois, March 4.

AL: I am up against it again. I went out to the ball park office yesterday and they was nobody there except John somebody who is asst secretary and all the rest of them is out on the Coast with the team. Maybe this here John was trying to kid me but this is what he told me. First I says Is they a letter here for me? And he says No. And I says I was expecting word from Comiskey that I should join the Detroit Club and he says What makes you think you are going to Detroit? I says Comiskey asked wavers on me and Detroit did not give no wavers. He says Well that is not no sign that you are going to Detroit. If Comiskey can't get you out of the league he will probily keep you himself and it is a cinch he is not going to give no pitcher to Detroit no matter how rotten he is.

I says What do you mean? And he says You just stick round town till you hear from Comiskey and I guess you will hear pretty soon because he is comeing back from the Coast next Saturday. I says Well the only thing he can tell me is to report to Detroit because I won't never pitch again for the White Sox. Then John gets fresh and says I suppose you will quit the game and live on your saveings and then I blowed out of the office because I was scared I would loose my temper and break something.

So you see Al what I am up against. I won't never pitch for the White Sox again and I want to get with the Detroit Club but how can I if Comiskey won't let me go? All I can do is stick round till next Saturday and then I will see Comiskey and I guess when I tell him what I think of him he will be glad to let me go to Detroit or anywheres else. I will have something on him this time because I know that he did not pay no attention to the rules when he told me I was sold to Milwaukee and if he tries to slip something over on me I will tell president Johnson of the league all about it and then you will see where Comiskey heads in at.

Al old pal that $25.00 you give me at the station the other day is all shot to peaces and I must ask you to let me have $25.00 more which will make $75.00 all together includeing the $25.00 you sent me before I come home. I hate to ask you this favor old pal but I know you have got the money. If I am sold to Detroit I will get some advance money and pay up all my dedts incluseive.

If he don't let me go to Detroit I will make him come across with part of my salery for this year even if I don't pitch for him because I signed a contract and was ready to do my end of it and would of if he had not been nasty and tried to slip something over on me. If he refuses to come across I will hire a attorney at law and he will get it all. So Al you see you have got a cinch on getting back what you lone me but I guess you know that Al without all this talk because you have been my old pal for a good many years and I have allways treated you square and tried to make you feel that I and you was equals and that my success was not going to make me forget my old friends.

Wherever I pitch this year I will insist on a salery of 5 or $6000 a year. So you see on my first pay day I will have enough to pay you up and settle the rest of my dedts but I am not going to pay no more rent for this rotten flat because they tell me if a man don't pay no rent for a while they will put him out. Let them put me out. I should not worry but will go and rent my old room that I had before I met Florrie and got into all this trouble.

The sooner you can send me that $35.00 the better and then I will owe you $85.00 incluseive and I will write and let you know how I come out with Comiskey.

Your pal,   JACK.

Chicago, Illinois, March 12.

FRIEND AL: I got another big supprise for you and this is it I am going to pitch for the White Sox after all. If Comiskey was not a old man I guess I would of lost my temper and beat him up but I am glad now that I kept my temper and did not loose it because I forced him to make a lot of consessions and now it looks like as though I would have a big year both pitching and money.

He got back to town yesterday morning and showed up to his office in the afternoon and I was there waiting for him. He would not see me for a while but finally I acted like as though I was getting tired of waiting and I guess the secretary got scared that I would beat it out of the office and leave them all in the lerch. Anyway he went in and spoke to Comiskey and then come out and says the boss was ready to see me. When I went into the office where he was at he says Well young man what can I do for you? And I says I want you to give me my release so as I can join the Detroit Club down South and get in shape. Then he says What makes you think you are going to join the Detroit Club? Because we need you here. I says Then why did you try to sell me to Milwaukee? But you could not because you could not get no wavers.

Then he says I thought I was doing you a favor by sending you to Milwaukee because they make a lot of beer up there. I says What do you mean? He says You been keeping in shape all this winter by trying to drink this town dry and besides that you tried to hold me up for more money when you allready had signed a contract allready and so I was going to send you to Milwaukee and learn you something and besides you tried to go with the Federal League but they would not take you because they was scared to.

I don't know where he found out all that stuff at Al and besides he was wrong when he says I was drinking to much because they is not nobody that can drink more than me and not be effected. But I did not say nothing because I was scared I would forget myself and call him some name and he is a old man. Yes I did say something. I says Well I guess you found out that you could not get me out of the league and then he says Don't never think I could not get you out of the league. If you think I can't send you to Milwaukee I will prove it to you that I can. I says You can't because Detroit won't give no wavers on me. He says Detroit will give wavers on you quick enough if I ask them.

Then he says Now you can take your choice you can stay

here and pitch for me at the salery you signed up for and you can cut out the monkey business and drink water when you are thirsty or else you can go up to Milwaukee and drownd yourself in one of them brewrys. Which shall it be? I says How can you keep me or send me to Milwaukee when Detroit has allready claimed my services? He says Detroit has claimed a lot of things and they have even claimed the pennant but that is not no sign they will win it. He says And besides you would not want to pitch for Detroit because then you would not never have no chance to pitch against Cobb and show him up.

Well Al when he says that I knowed he appresiated what a pitcher I am even if he did try to sell me to Milwaukee or he would not of made that remark about the way I can show Cobb and Crawford up. So I says Well if you need me that bad I will pitch for you but I must have a new contract. He says Oh I guess we can fix that up O. K. and he steps out in the next room a while and then he comes back with a new contract. And what do you think it was Al? It was a contract for 3 years so you see I am sure of my job here for 3 years and everything is all O. K.

The contract calls for the same salary a year for 3 years that I was going to get before for only 1 year which is $2800.00 a year and then I will get in on the city serious money too and the Detroit Club don't have no city serious and have no chance to get into the World's Serious with the rotten pitching staff they got. So you see Al he fixed me up good and that shows that he must think a hole lot of me or he would of sent me to Detroit or maybe to Milwaukee but I don't see how he could of did that without no wavers.

Well Al I allmost forgot to tell you that he has gave me a ticket to Los Angeles where the 2d team are practicing at now but where the 1st team will be at in about a week. I am leaveing to-night and I guess before I go I will go down to president Johnson and tell him that I am fixed up all O. K. and have not got no kick comeing so that president Johnson will not fine Comiskey for not paying no attention to the rules or get him fired out of the league because I guess Comiskey must be all O. K. and good hearted after all.

I won't pay no attention to what he says about me drinking

this town dry because he is all wrong in regards to that. He must of been jokeing I guess because nobody but some boob would think he could drink this town dry but at that I guess I can hold more than anybody and not be effected. But I guess I will cut it out for a while at that because I don't want to get them sore at me after the contract they give me.

I will write to you from Los Angeles Al and let you know what the boys says when they see me and I will bet that they will be tickled to death. The rent man was round to-day but I seen him comeing and he did not find me. I am going to leave the furniture that belongs in the flat in the flat and allso the furniture I bought which don't amount to much because it was not no real Sir Cashion walnut and besides I don't want nothing round me to remind me of Florrie because the sooner her and I forget each other the better.

Tell the boys about my good luck Al but it is not no luck neither because it was comeing to me.

Yours truly,   JACK.

Los Angeles, California, March 16.

AL: Here I am back with the White Sox again and it seems to good to be true because just like I told you they are all tickled to death to see me. Kid Gleason is here in charge of the 2d team and when he seen me come into the hotel he jumped up and hit me in the stumach but he acts like that whenever he feels good so I could not get sore at him though he had no right to hit me in the stumach. If he had of did it in ernest I would of walloped him in the jaw.

He says Well if here ain't the old lady killer. He ment Al that I am strong with the girls but I am all threw with them now but he don't know nothing about the troubles I had. He says Are you in shape? And I told him Yes I am. He says Yes you look in shape like a barrel. I says They is not no fat on me and if I am a little bit bigger than last year it is because my mussels is bigger. He says Yes your stumach mussels is emense and you must of gave them plenty of exercise. Wait till Bodie sees you and he will want to stick round you all the time because you make him look like a broom straw or something. I let him kid me along because what is the use of getting mad at him? And besides he is all O. K. even if he is a little rough.

I says to him A little work will fix me up all O. K. and he says You bet you are going to get some work because I am going to see to it myself. I says You will have to hurry because you will be going up to Frisco in a few days and I am going to stay here and join the 1st club. Then he says You are not going to do no such a thing. You are going right along with me. I knowed he was kidding me then because Callahan would not never leave me with the 2d team no more after what I done for him last year and besides most of the stars generally allways goes with the 1st team on the training trip.

Well I seen all the rest of the boys that is here with the 2d team and they all acted like as if they was glad to see me and why should not they be when they know that me being here with the White Sox and not with Detroit means that Callahan won't have to do no worrying about his pitching staff? But they is four or 5 young recrut pitchers with the team here and I bet they is not so glad to see me because what chance have they got?

If I was Comiskey and Callahan I would not spend no money on new pitchers because with me and 1 or 2 of the other boys we got the best pitching staff in the league. And instead of spending the money for new pitching recruts I would put it all in a lump and buy Ty Cobb or Sam Crawford off of Detroit or somebody else who can hit and Cobb and Crawford is both real hitters Al even if I did make them look like suckers. Who wouldn't?

Well Al to-morrow A. M. I am going out and work a little and in the P. M. I will watch the game between we and the Venice Club but I won't pitch none because Gleason would not dare take no chances of me hurting my arm. I will write to you in a few days from here because no matter what Gleason says I am going to stick here with the 1st team because I know Callahan will want me along with him for a attraction.

Your pal,   JACK.

San Francisco, California, March 20.

FRIEND AL: Well Al here I am back in old Frisco with the 2d team but I will tell you how it happened Al. Yesterday Gleason told me to pack up and get ready to leave Los Angeles with him and I says No I am going to stick here and wait for the 1st team and then he says I guess I must of overlooked something in the papers because I did not see nothing about you being appointed manager of the club. I says No I am not manager but Callahan is manager and he will want to keep me with him. He says I got a wire from Callahan telling me to keep you with my club but of coarse if you know what Callahan wants better than he knows it himself why then go ahead and stay here or go jump in the Pacific Ocean.

Then he says I know why you don't want to go with me and I says Why? And he says Because you know I will make you work and won't let you eat everything on the bill of fair includeing the name of the hotel at which we are stopping at. That made me sore and I was just going to call him when he says Did not you marry Mrs. Allen's sister? And I says Yes but that is not none of your business. Then he says Well I don't want to butt into your business but I heard you and your wife had some kind of a argument and she beat it. I says Yes she give me a rotten deal. He says Well then I don't see where it is going to be very pleasant for you traveling round with the 1st club because Allen and his wife is both with that club and what do you want to be mixed up with them for? I says I am not scared of Allen or his wife or no other old hen.

So here I am Al with the 2d team but it is only for a while till Callahan gets sick of some of them pitchers he has got and sends for me so as he can see some real pitching. And besides I am glad to be here in Frisco where I made so many friends when I was pitching here for a short time till Callahan heard about my work and called me back to the big show where I belong at and nowheres else.

Yours truly,   JACK.

San Francisco, California, March 25.

OLD PAL: Al I got a supprise for you. Who do you think I seen last night? Nobody but Hazel. Her name now is Hazel Levy because you know Al she married Kid Levy the middle-weight and I wish he was champion of the world Al because then it would not take me more than about a minute to be champion of the world myself. I have not got nothing against him though because he married her and if he had not of I probily would of married her myself but at that she could not of treated me no worse than Florrie. Well they was setting at a table in the cafe where her and I use to go pretty near every night. She spotted me when I first come in and sends a waiter over to ask me to come and have a drink with them. I went over because they was no use being nasty and let bygones be bygones.

She interduced me to her husband and he asked me what I was drinking. Then she butts in and says Oh you must let Mr. Keefe buy the drinks because it hurts his feelings to have somebody else buy the drinks. Then Levy says Oh he is one of these here spendrifts is he? and she says Yes he don't care no more about a nichol than his right eye does. I says I guess you have got no holler comeing on the way I spend my money. I don't steal no money anyway. She says What do you mean? and I says I guess you know what I mean. How about that $30.00 that you borrowed off of me and never give it back? Then her husband cuts in and says You cut that line of talk out or I will bust you. I says Yes you will. And he says Yes I will.

Well Al what was the use of me starting trouble with him when he has got enough trouble right to home and besides as I say I have got nothing against him. So I got up and blowed away from the table and I bet he was relieved when he seen I was not going to start nothing. I beat it out of there a while afterward because I was not drinking nothing and I don't have no fun setting round a place and lapping up ginger ail or something. And besides the music was rotten.

Al I am certainly glad I threw Hazel over because she has grew to be as big as a horse and is all painted up. I don't care nothing about them big dolls no more or about no other kind neither. I am off of them all. They can all of them die and I should not worry.

Well Al I done my first pitching of the year this P. M. and I guess I showed them that I was in just as good a shape as some of them birds that has been working a month. I worked 4 innings against my old team the San Francisco Club and I give them nothing but fast ones but they sure was fast ones and you could hear them zip. Charlie O'Leary was trying to get out of the way of one of them and it hit his bat and went over first base for a base hit but at that Fournier would of eat it up if it had of been Chase playing first base instead of Fournier.

That was the only hit they got off of me and they ought to
of been ashamed to of tooken that one. But Gleason don't
appresiate my work and him and I allmost come to blows at
supper. I was pretty hungry and I ordered some stake and
some eggs and some pie and some ice cream and some coffee
and a glass of milk but Gleason would not let me have the pie
or the milk and would not let me eat more than ½ the stake.
And it is a wonder I did not bust him and tell him to mind his
own business. I says What right have you got to tell me what
to eat? And he says You don't need nobody to tell you what to
eat you need somebody to keep you from floundering yourself.
I says Why can't I eat what I want to when I have worked
good?

He says Who told you you worked good and I says I did not
need nobody to tell me. I know I worked good because they
could not do nothing with me. He says Well it is a good thing
for you that they did not start bunting because if you had of
went to stoop over and pick up the ball you would of busted
wide open. I says Why? and he says because you are hog fat
and if you don't let up on the stable and fancy groceries we will
have to pay 2 fairs to get you back to Chi. I don't remember
now what I says to him but I says something you can bet on
that. You know me Al.

I wish Al that Callahan would hurry up and order me to join
the 1st team. If he don't Al I believe Gleason will starve me to
death. A little slob like him don't realize that a big man like I
needs good food and plenty of it.

Your pal,   JACK.

Salt Lake City, Utah, April 1.

AL: Well Al we are on our way East and I am still with the 2d
team and I don't understand why Callahan don't order me to
join the 1st team but maybe it is because he knows that I am all
right and have got the stuff and he wants to keep them other
guys round where he can see if they have got anything.

The recrut pitchers that is along with our club have not got
nothing and the scout that reckommended them must of been
full of hops or something. It is not no common thing for a
club to pick up a man that has got the stuff to make him a star
up here and the White Sox was pretty lucky to land me but I

don't understand why they throw their money away on new pitchers when none of them is no good and besides who would want a better pitching staff than we got right now without no raw recruts and bushers.

I worked in Oakland the day before yesterday but he only let me go the 1st 4 innings. I bet them Oakland birds was glad when he took me out. When I was in that league I use to just throw my glove in the box and them Oakland birds was licked and honest Al some of them turned white when they seen I was going to pitch the other day.

I felt kind of sorry for them and I did not give them all I had so they got 5 or 6 hits and scored a couple of runs. I was not feeling very good at that and besides we got some awful excuses for a ball player on this club and the support they give me was the rottenest I ever seen gave anybody. But some of them won't be in this league more than about 10 minutes more so I should not fret as they say.

We play here this afternoon and I don't believe I will work because the team they got here is not worth wasteing nobody on. They must be a lot of boobs in this town Al because they tell me that some of them has got ½ a dozen wives or so. And what a man wants with 1 wife is a misery to me let alone a ½ dozen.

I will probily work against Denver because they got a good club and was champions of the Western League last year. I will make them think they are champions of the Epworth League or something.

Yours truly,   JACK.

Des Moines, Iowa, April 10.

FRIEND AL: We got here this A. M. and this is our last stop and we will be in old Chi to-morrow to open the season. The 1st team gets home to-day and I would be there with them if Callahan was a real manager who knowed something about manageing because if I am going to open the season I should ought to have 1 day of rest at home so I would have all my strenth to open the season. The Cleveland Club will be there to open against us and Callahan must know that I have got them licked any time I start against them.

As soon as my name is announced to pitch the Cleveland

Club is licked or any other club when I am right and they don't kick the game away behind me.

Gleason told me on the train last night that I was going to pitch here to-day but I bet by this time he has got orders from Callahan to let me rest and to not give me no more work because suppose even if I did not start the game to-morrow I probily will have to finish it.

Gleason has been sticking round me like as if I had a million bucks or something. I can't even sit down and smoke a cigar but what he is there to knock the ashes off of it. He is O. K. and good-hearted if he is a little rough and keeps hitting me in the stumach but I wish he would leave me alone sometimes espesially at meals. He was in to breakfast with me this A. M. and after I got threw I snuck off down the street and got something to eat. That is not right because it costs me money when I have to go away from the hotel and eat and what right has he got to try and help me order my meals? Because he don't know what I want and what my stumach wants.

My stumach don't want to have him punching it all the time but he keeps on doing it. So that shows he don't know what is good for me. But he is a old man Al otherwise I would not stand for the stuff he pulls. The 1st thing I am going to do when we get to Chi is I am going to a resturunt somewheres and get a good meal where Gleason or no one else can't get at me. I know allready what I am going to eat and that is a big stake and a apple pie and that is not all.

Well Al watch the papers and you will see what I done to that Cleveland Club and I hope Lajoie and Jackson is both in good shape because I don't want to pick on no cripples.

> Your pal,   JACK.

Chicago, Illinois, April 16.

OLD PAL: Yesterday was the 1st pay day old pal and I know I promised to pay you what I owe you and it is $75.00 because when I asked you for $35.00 before I went West you only sent me $25.00 which makes the hole sum $75.00. Well Al I can't pay you now because the pay we drawed was only for 4 days and did not amount to nothing and I had to buy a meal ticket and fix up about my room rent.

And then they is another thing Al which I will tell you about. I come into the clubhouse the day the season opened and the 1st guy I seen was Allen. I was going up to bust him but he come up and held his hand out and what was they for me to do but shake hands with him if he is going to be yellow like that? He says Well Jack I am glad they did not send you to Milwaukee and I bet you will have a big year. I says Yes I will have a big year O. K. if you don't sick another 1 of your sister-in-laws on to me. He says Oh don't let they be no hard feelings about that. You know it was not no fault of mine and I bet if you was to write to Florrie everything could be fixed up O. K.

I says I don't want to write to no Florrie but I will get a attorney at law to write to her. He says You don't even know where she is at and I says I don't care where she is at. Where is she? He says She is down to her home in Waco, Texas, and if I was you I would write to her myself and not let no attorney at law write to her because that would get her mad and besides what do you want a attorney at law to write to her about? I says I am going to sew her for a bill of divorce.

Then he says On what grounds? and I says Dessertion. He says You better not do no such thing or she will sew you for a bill of divorce for none support and then you will look like a cheap guy. I says I don't care what I look like. So you see Al I had to send Florrie $10.00 or maybe she would be mean enough to sew me for a bill of divorce on the ground of none support and that would make me look bad.

Well Al, Allen told me his wife wanted to talk to me and try and fix things up between I and Florrie but I give him to understand that I would not stand for no meeting with his wife and he says Well suit yourself about that but they is no reason you and I should quarrel.

You see Al he don't want no mix-up with me because he knows he could not get nothing but the worst of it. I will be friends with him but I won't have nothing to do with Marie because if it had not of been for she and Florrie I would have money in the bank besides not being in no danger of getting sewed for none support.

I guess you must of read about Joe Benz getting married and I guess he must of got a good wife and 1 that don't bother him all the time because he pitched the opening game and shut Cleveland out with 2 hits. He was pretty good Al, better than I ever seen him and they was a couple of times when his fast ball was pretty near as fast as mine.

I have not worked yet Al and I asked Callahan to-day what was the matter and he says I was waiting for you to get in shape. I says I am in shape now and I notice that when I was pitching in practice this A. M. they did not hit nothing out of the infield. He says That was because you are so spread out that they could not get nothing past you. He says The way you are now you cover more ground than the grand stand. I says Is that so? And he walked away.

We go out on a trip to Cleveland and Detroit and St. Louis in a few days and maybe I will take my regular turn then because the other pitchers has been getting away lucky because most of the hitters has not got their batting eye as yet but wait till they begin hitting and then it will take a man like I to stop them.

The 1st of May is our next pay day Al and then I will have enough money so as I can send you the $75.00.

Your pal,   JACK.

Detroit, Michigan, April 28.

FRIEND AL: What do you think of a rotten manager that bawls me out and fines me $50.00 for loosing a 1 to 0 game in 10 innings when it was my 1st start this season? And no wonder I was a little wild in the 10th when I had not had no chance to work and get control. I got a good notion to quit this rotten club and jump to the Federals where a man gets some kind of treatment. Callahan says I throwed the game away on purpose but I did not do no such a thing Al because when I throwed that ball at Joe Hill's head I forgot that the bases was full and besides if Gleason had not of starved me to death the ball that hit him in the head would of killed him.

And how could a man go to 1st base and the winning run be forced in if he was dead which he should ought to of been the lucky left handed stiff if I had of had my full strenth to put on my fast one instead of being ½ starved to death and weak. But I guess I better tell you how it come off. The papers will get it all wrong like they generally allways does.

Callahan asked me this A. M. if I thought I was hard enough to work and I was tickled to death, because I seen he was going to give me a chance. I told him Sure I was in good shape and if them Tigers scored a run off me he could keep me setting on the bench the rest of the summer. So he says All right I am going to start you and if you go good maybe Gleason will let you eat some supper.

Well Al when I begin warming up I happened to look up in the grand stand and who do you think I seen? Nobody but Violet. She smiled when she seen me but I bet she felt more like crying. Well I smiled back at her because she probily would of broke down and made a seen or something if I had not of. They was not nobody warming up for Detroit when I begin warming up but pretty soon I looked over to their bench and Joe Hill Violet's husband was warming up. I says to myself Well here is where I show that bird up if they got nerve enough to start him against me but probily Jennings don't want to waste no real pitcher on this game which he knows we got cinched and we would of had it cinched Al if they had of got a couple of runs or even 1 run for me.

Well, Jennings come passed our bench just like he allways does and tried to pull some of his funny stuff. He says Hello are you still in the league? I says Yes but I come pretty near not being. I came pretty near being with Detroit. I wish you could of heard Gleason and Callahan laugh when I pulled that one on him. He says something back but it was not no hot comeback like mine.

Well Al if I had of had any work and my regular control I guess I would of pitched a 0 hit game because the only time they could touch me was when I had to ease up to get them over. Cobb was out of the game and they told me he was sick but I guess the truth is that he knowed I was going to pitch. Crawford got a couple of lucky scratch hits off of me because I got in the hole to him and had to let up. But the way that lucky left handed Hill got by was something awful and if I was as lucky as him I would quit pitching and shoot craps or something.

Our club can't hit nothing anyway. But batting against this bird was just like hitting fungos. His curve ball broke about ½ a inch and you could of wrote your name and address on his fast one while it was comeing up there. He had good control but who would not when they put nothing on the ball?

Well Al we could not get started against the lucky stiff and they could not do nothing with me even if my suport was rotten and I give a couple or 3 or 4 bases on balls but when they was men waiting to score I zipped them threw there so as they could not see them let alone hit them. Every time I come to the bench between innings I looked up to where Violet was setting and give her a smile and she smiled back and once I seen her clapping her hands at me after I had made Moriarty pop up in the pinch.

Well we come along to the 10th inning, 0 and 0, and all of a sudden we got after him. Bodie hits one and Schalk gets 2 strikes and 2 balls and then singles. Callahan tells Alcock to bunt and he does it but Hill sprawls all over himself like the big boob he is and the bases is full with nobody down. Well Gleason and Callahan argude about should they send somebody up for me or let me go up there and I says Let me go up there because I can murder this bird and Callahan says Well they is nobody out so go up and take a wallop.

Honest Al if this guy had of had anything at all I would of hit 1 out of the park, but he did not have even a glove. And how can a man hit pitching which is not no pitching at all but just slopping them up? When I went up there I hollered to him and says Stick 1 over here now you yellow stiff. And he says Yes I can stick them over allright and that is where I got something on you.

Well Al I hit a foul off of him that would of been a fare ball and broke up the game if the wind had not of been against it. Then I swung and missed a curve that I don't see how I missed it. The next 1 was a yard outside and this Evans calls it a strike. He has had it in for me ever since last year when he tried to get funny with me and I says something back to him that stung him. So he calls this 3d strike on me and I felt like murdering him. But what is the use?

I throwed down my bat and come back to the bench and I was glad Callahan and Gleason was out on the coaching line or they probily would of said something to me and I would of cut loose and beat them up. Well Al Weaver and Blackburne looked like a couple of rums up there and we don't score where we ought to of had 3 or 4 runs with any kind of hitting.

I would of been all O. K. in spite of that peace of rotten luck if this big Hill had of walked to the bench and not said nothing like a real pitcher. But what does he do but wait out there till I start for the box and I says Get on to the bench you lucky stiff or do you want me to hand you something? He says I don't want nothing more of yourn. I allready got your girl and your goat.

Well Al what do you think of a man that would say a thing like that? And nobody but a left hander could of. If I had of had a gun I would of killed him deader than a doornail or something. He starts for the bench and I hollered at him Wait till you get up to that plate and then I am going to bean you.

Honest Al I was so mad I could not see the plate or nothing. I don't even know who it was come up to bat 1st but whoever it was I hit him in the arm and he walks to first base. The next guy bunts and Chase tries to pull off 1 of them plays of hisn instead of playing safe and he don't get nobody. Well I kept getting madder and madder and I walks Stanage who if I had of been myself would not foul me.

Callahan has Scotty warming up and Gleason runs out from the bench and tells me I am threw but Callahan says Wait a minute he is going to let Hill hit and this big stiff ought to be able to get him out of the way and that will give Scotty a chance to get warm. Gleason says You better not take a chance because the big busher is hogwild, and they kept argueing till I got sick of listening to them and I went back to the box and got ready to pitch. But when I seen this Hill up there I forgot all about the ball game and I cut loose at his bean.

Well Al my control was all O. K. this time and I catched him square on the fourhead and he dropped like as if he had been shot. But pretty soon he gets up and gives me the laugh and runs to first base. I did not know the game was over till Weaver come up and pulled me off the field. But if I had not of been ½ starved to death and weak so as I could not put all my stuff on the ball you can bet that Hill never would of ran to first base and Violet would of been a widow and probily a lot better off than she is now. At that I never should ought to of tried to kill a lefthander by hitting him in the head.

Well Al they jumped all over me in the clubhouse and I had to hold myself back or I would of gave somebody the beating of their life. Callahan tells me I am fined $50.00 and suspended without no pay. I asked him What for and he says They would not be no use in telling you because you have not got no brains. I says Yes I have to got some brains and he says Yes but they is in your stumach. And then he says I wish we had of sent you to Milwaukee and I come back at him. I says I wish you had of.

Well Al I guess they is no chance of getting square treatment on this club and you won't be supprised if you hear of me jumping to the Federals where a man is treated like a man and not like no white slave.

Yours truly,   JACK.

Chicago, Illinois, May 2.

AL: I have got to disappoint you again Al. When I got up to get my pay yesterday they held out $150.00 on me. $50.00 of it is what I was fined for loosing a 1 to 0 10-inning game in Detroit when I was so weak that I should ought never to of been sent in there and the $100.00 is the advance money that I drawed last winter and which I had forgot all about and the club would of forgot about it to if they was not so tight fisted.

So you see all I get for 2 weeks' pay is about $80.00 and I sent $25.00 to Florrie so she can't come no none support business on me.

I am still suspended Al and not drawing no pay now and I got a notion to hire a attorney at law and force them to pay my salery or else jump to the Federals where a man gets good treatment.

Allen is still after me to come over to his flat some night and see his wife and let her talk to me about Florrie but what do I want to talk about Florrie for or talk about nothing to a nut left hander's wife?

The Detroit Club is here and Cobb is playing because he knows I am suspended but I wish Callahan would call it off and let me work against them and I would certainly love to work against this Joe Hill again and I bet they would be a different story this time because I been getting something to eat since we been home and I got back most of my strenth.

Your old pal,   JACK.

Chicago, Illinois, May 5.

FRIEND AL: Well Al if you been reading the papers you will know before this letter is received what I done. Before the

Detroit Club come here Joe Hill had win 4 strate but he has not win no 5 strate or won't neither Al because I put a crimp in his winning streek just like I knowed I would do if I got a chance when I was feeling good and had all my strenth. Callahan asked me yesterday A. M. if I thought I had enough rest and I says Sure because I did not need no rest in the 1st place. Well, he says, I thought maybe if I layed you off a few days you would do some thinking and if you done some thinking once in a while you would be a better pitcher.

Well anyway I worked and I wish you could of saw them Tigers trying to hit me Cobb and Crawford incluseive. The 1st time Cobb come up Weaver catched a lucky line drive off of him and the next time I eased up a little and Collins run back and took a fly ball off of the fence. But the other times he come up he looked like a sucker except when he come up in the 8th and then he beat out a bunt but allmost anybody is liable to do that once in a while.

Crawford got a scratch hit between Chase and Blackburne in the 2d inning and in the 4th he was gave a three-base hit by this Evans who should ought to be writeing for the papers instead of trying to umpire. The ball was 2 feet foul and I bet Crawford will tell you the same thing if you ask him. But what I done to this Hill was awful. I give him my curve twice when he was up there in the 3d and he missed it a foot. Then I come with my fast ball right past his nose and I bet if he had not of ducked it would of drove that big horn of hisn clear up in the press box where them rotten reporters sits and smokes their hops. Then when he was looking for another fast one I slopped up my slow one and he is still swinging at it yet.

But the best of it was that I practally won my own game. Bodie and Schalk was on when I come up in the 5th and Hill hollers to me and says I guess this is where I shoot one of them bean balls. I says Go ahead and shoot and if you hit me in the head and I ever find it out I will write and tell your wife what happened to you. You see what I was getting at Al. I was insinuateing that if he beaned me with his fast one I would not never know nothing about it if somebody did not tell me because his fast one is not fast enough to hurt nobody even if it should hit them in the head. So I says to him Go ahead and shoot and if you hit me in the head and I ever find it out I will write and tell your wife what happened to you. See, Al?

Of coarse you could not hire me to write to Violet but I did not mean that part of it in ernest. Well sure enough he shot at my bean and I ducked out of the way though if it had of hit me it could not of did no more than tickle. He takes 2 more shots and misses me and then Jennings hollers from the bench What are you doing pitching or trying to win a cigar? So then Hill sees what a monkey he is makeing out of himself and tries to get one over, but I have him 3 balls and nothing and what I done to that groover was a plenty. She went over Bush's head like a bullet and got between Cobb and Veach and goes clear to the fence. Bodie and Schalk scores and I would of scored to if anybody else besides Cobb had of been chaseing the ball. I got 2 bases and Weaver scores me with another wallop.

Say, I wish I could of heard what they said to that baby on the bench. Callahan was tickled to death and he says Maybe I will give you back that $50.00 if you keep that stuff up. I guess I will get that $50.00 back next pay day and if I do Al I will pay you the hole $75.00.

Well Al I beat them 5 to 4 and with good support I would of held them to 1 run but what do I care as long as I beat them? I wish though that Violet could of been there and saw it.

Yours truly,   JACK.

Chicago, Illinois, May 29.

OLD PAL: Well Al I have not wrote to you for a long while but it is not because I have forgot you and to show I have not forgot you I am incloseing the $75.00 which I owe you. It is a money order Al and you can get it cashed by takeing it to Joe Higgins at the P. O.

Since I wrote to you Al I been East with the club and I guess you know what I done in the East. The Athaletics did not have no right to win that 1 game off of me and I will get them when they come here the week after next. I beat Boston and just as good as beat New York twice because I beat them 1 game all alone and then saved the other for Eddie Cicotte in the 9th inning and shut out the Washington Club and would of did the same thing if Johnson had of been working against me instead of this left handed stiff Boehling.

Speaking of left handers Allen has been going rotten and I would not be supprised if they sent him to Milwaukee or Frisco or somewheres.

But I got bigger news than that for you Al. Florrie is back and we are liveing together in the spair room at Allen's flat so I hope they don't send him to Milwaukee or nowheres else because it is not costing us nothing for room rent and this is no more than right after the way the Allens grafted off of us all last winter.

I bet you will be supprised to know that I and Florrie has made it up and they is a secret about it Al which I can't tell you now but maybe next month I will tell you and then you will be more supprised than ever. It is about I and Florrie and somebody else. But that is all I can tell you now.

We got in this A. M. Al and when I got to my room they was a slip of paper there telling me to call up a phone number so I called it up and it was Allen's flat and Marie answered the phone. And when I reckonized her voice I was going to hang up the phone but she says Wait a minute somebody wants to talk with you. And then Florrie come to the phone and I was going to hang up the phone again when she pulled this secret on me that I was telling you about.

So it is all fixed up between us Al and I wish I could tell you the secret but that will come later. I have tooken my baggage over to Allen's and I am there now writeing to you while Florrie is asleep. And after a while I am going out and mail this letter and get a glass of beer because I think I have got 1 comeing now on account of this secret. Florrie says she is sorry for the way she treated me and she cried when she seen me. So what is the use of me being nasty Al? And let bygones be bygones.

Your pal,   JACK.

Chicago, Illinois, June 16.

FRIEND AL: Al I beat the Athaletics 2 to 1 to-day but I am writeing to you to give you the supprise of your life. Old pal I got a baby and he is a boy and we are going to name him Allen which Florrie thinks is after his uncle and aunt Allen but which is after you old pal. And she can call him Allen but I will call him Al because I don't never go back on my old pals. The baby was born over to the hospital and it is going to cost me a bunch of money but I should not worry. This is the secret I was going to tell you Al and I am the happyest man in the world and I bet you are most as tickled to death to hear about it as I am.

The baby was born just about the time I was makeing McInnis look like a sucker in the pinch but they did not tell me nothing about it till after the game and then they give me a phone messige in the clubhouse. I went right over there and everything was all O. K. Little Al is a homely little skate but I guess all babys is homely and don't have no looks till they get older and maybe he will look like Florrie or I then I won't have no kick comeing.

Be sure and tell Bertha the good news and tell her everything has came out all right except that the rent man is still after me about that flat I had last winter. And I am still paying the old man $10.00 a month for that house you got for me and which has not never done me no good. But I should not worry about money when I got a real family. Do you get that Al, a real family?

Well Al I am to happy to do no more writeing to-night but I wanted you to be the 1st to get the news and I would of sent you a telegram only I did not want to scare you.

Your pal,   JACK.

Chicago, Illinois, July 2.

OLD PAL: Well old pal I just come back from St. Louis this A. M. and found things in pretty fare shape. Florrie and the baby is out to Allen's and we will stay there till I can find another place. The Dr. was out to look at the baby this A. M. and the baby was waveing his arm round in the air. And Florrie asked was they something the matter with him that he kept waveing his arm. And the Dr. says No he was just getting his exercise.

Well Al I noticed that he never waved his right arm but kept waveing his left arm and I asked the Dr. why was that. Then the Dr. says I guess he must be left handed. That made me sore and I says I guess you doctors don't know it all. And then I turned round and beat it out of the room.

Well Al it would be just my luck to have him left handed and Florrie should ought to of knew better than to name him after

Allen. I am going to hire another Dr. and see what he has to say because they must be some way of fixing babys so as they won't be left handed. And if nessary I will cut his left arm off of him. Of coarse I would not do that Al. But how would I feel if a boy of mine turned out like Allen and Joe Hill and some of them other nuts?

We have a game with St. Louis to-morrow and a double header on the 4th of July. I guess probily Callahan will work me in one of the 4th of July games on account of the holiday crowd.

Your pal,   JACK.

P. S. Maybe I should ought to leave the kid left handed so as he can have some of their luck. The lucky stiffs.

CHAPTER V

The Busher's Kid

FRIEND AL: Well Al what do you think of little Al now? But I guess I better tell you first what he done. Maybe you won't believe what I am telling you but did you ever catch me telling you a lie? I guess you know you did not Al. Well we got back from the East this A. M. and I don't have to tell you we had a rotten trip and if it had not of been for me beating Boston once and the Athaletics two times we would of been ashamed to come home.

I guess these here other pitchers thought we was haveing a vacation and when they go up in the office to-morrow to get there checks they should ought to be arrested if they take them. I would not go nowheres near Comiskey if I had not of did better than them others but I can go and get my pay and feel all O. K. about it because I done something to ern it.

Me loseing that game in Washington was a crime and Callahan says so himself. This here Weaver throwed it away for me and I would not be surprised if he done it from spitework because him and Scott is pals and probily he did not want to see me winning all them games when Scott was getting knocked out of the box. And no wonder when he has not got no stuff. I wish I knowed for sure that Weaver was throwing me down and if I knowed for sure I would put him in a hospital or somewheres.

But I was going to tell you what the kid done Al. So here goes. We are still liveing at Allen's and his wife. So I and him come home together from the train. Well Florrie and Marie was both up and the baby was up too—that is he was not up but he was woke up. I beat it right into the room where he was at and Florrie come in with me. I says Hello Al and what do you suppose he done. Well Al he did not say Hello pa or nothing like that because he is not only one month old. But he smiled at me just like as if he was glad to see me and I guess maybe he was at that.

I was tickled to death and I says to Florrie Did you see that. And she says See what. I says The baby smiled at me. Then she says They is something the matter with his stumach. I says I suppose because a baby smiles that is a sign they is something the matter with his stumach and if he had the toothacke he would laugh. She says You think your smart but I am telling you that he was not smileing at all but he was makeing a face because they is something the matter with his stumach. I says I guess I know the difference if somebody is smileing or make-ing a face. And she says I guess you don't know nothing about babys because you never had none before. I says How many have you had. And then she got sore and beat it out of the room.

I did not care because I wanted to be in there alone with him and see would he smile at me again. And sure enough Al he did. Then I called Allen in and when the baby seen him he begin to cry. So you see I was right and Florrie was wrong. It don't take a man no time at all to get wise to these babys and it don't take them long to know if a man is there father or there uncle.

When he begin to cry I chased Allen out of the room and called Florrie because she should ought to know by this time how to make him stop crying. But she was still sore and she says Let him cry or if you know so much about babys make him stop yourself. I says Maybe he is sick. And she says I was just telling you that he had a pane in his stumach or he would not of made that face that you said was smileing at you.

I says Do you think we should ought to call the doctor but she says No if you call the doctor every time he has the stu-mach acke you might just as well tell him he should bring his trunk along and stay here. She says All babys have collect and they is not no use fusing about it but come and get your breakfast.

Well Al I did not injoy my breakfast because the baby was crying all the time and I knowed he probily wanted I should come in and visit with him. So I just eat the prunes and drunk a little coffee and did not wait for the rest of it and sure enough when I went back in our room and started talking to him he started smileing again and pretty soon he went to sleep so you see Al he was smileing and not makeing no face and that was a hole lot of bunk about him haveing the collect. But I don't suppose I should ought to find fault with Florrie for not knowing no better because she has not never had no babys before but still and all I should think she should ought to of learned something about them by this time or ask somebody.

Well Al little Al is woke up again and is crying and I just about got time to fix him up and get him asleep again and then I will have to go to the ball park because we got a poseponed game to play with Detroit and Callahan will probily want me to work though I pitched the next to the last game in New York and would of gave them a good beating except for Schalk dropping that ball at the plate but I got it on these Detroit babys and when my name is announced to pitch they feel like forfiting the game. I won't try for no strike out record because I want them to hit the first ball and get the game over with quick so as I can get back here and take care of little Al.

                    Your pal,   JACK.
     P. S. Babys is great stuff Al and if I was you I would not wait no longer but would hurry up and adopt 1 somewheres.

Chicago, Illinois, August 15.

OLD PAL: What do you think Al. Kid Gleason is comeing over to the flat and look at the baby the day after to-morrow when we don't have no game skeduled but we have to practice in the A. M. because we been going so rotten. I had a hard time makeing him promise to come but he is comeing and I bet he will be glad he come when he has came. I says to him in the clubhouse Do you want to see a real baby? And he says You're real enough for me Boy.

I says No I am talking about babys. He says Oh I thought you was talking about ice cream soda or something. I says No I want you to come over to the flat to-morrow and take a look at my kid and tell me what you think of him. He says I can tell you what I think of him without takeing no look at him. I think he is out of luck. I says What do you mean out of luck. But he just laughed and would not say no more.

I asked him again would he come over to the flat and look at the baby and he says he had troubles enough without that and kidded along for a while but finally he seen I was in ernest and then he says he would come if I would keep the missus out of the room while he was there because he says if she seen him she would probily be sorry she married me.

He was just jokeing and I did not take no excepshun to his remarks because Florrie could not never fall for him after seeing me because he is not no big stropping man like I am but a little runt and look at how old he is. But I am glad he is comeing because he will think more of me when he sees what a fine baby I got though he thinks a hole lot of me now because look what I done for the club and where would they be at if I had jumped to the Federal like I once thought I would. I will tell you what he says about little Al and I bet he will say he never seen no prettyer baby but even if he don't say nothing at all I will know he is kidding.

The Boston Club comes here to-morrow and plays 4 days includeing the day after to-morrow when they is not no game. So on account of the off day maybe I will work twice against them and if I do they will wish the grounds had of burned down.

Yours truly,   JACK.

Chicago, Illinois, August 17.

AL: Well old pal what did I tell you about what I would do to that Boston Club? And now Al I have beat every club in the league this year because yesterday was the first time I beat the Boston Club this year but now I have beat all of them and most of them severel times.

This should ought to of gave me a record of 16 wins and 0 defeats because the only games I lost was throwed away behind me but instead of that my record is 10 games win and 6 defeats and that don't include the games I finished up and helped the other boys win which is about 6 more alltogether but what do I care about my record Al? because I am not the kind of man that is allways thinking about there record and playing for there record while I am satisfied if I give the club the best I got and if I win all O. K. And if I lose who's fault is it. Not mine Al.

I asked Callahan would he let me work against the Boston Club again before they go away and he says I guess I will have to because you are going better than anybody else on the club. So you see Al he is beginning to appresiate my work and from now on I will pitch in my regular turn and a hole lot offtener then that and probily Comiskey will see the stuff I am made from and will raise my salery next year even if he has got me signed for 3 years and for the same salery I am getting now.

But all that is not what I was going to tell you Al and what I was going to tell you was about Gleason comeing to see the baby and what he thought about him. I sent Florrie and Marie downtown and says I would take care of little Al and they was glad to go because Florrie says she should ought to buy some new shoes though I don't see what she wants of no new shoes when she is going to be tied up in the flat for a long time yet on account of the baby and nobody cares if she wears shoes in the flat or goes round in her bear feet. But I was glad to get rid of the both of them for a while because little Al acts better when they is not no women round and you can't blame him.

The baby was woke up when Gleason come in and I and him went right in the room where he was laying. Gleason takes a look at him and says Well that is a mighty fine baby and you must of boughten him. I says What do you mean? And he says I don't believe he is your own baby because he looks humaner than most babys. And I says Why should not he look human. And he says Why should he.

Then he goes to work and picks the baby right up and I was a-scared he would drop him because even I have not never picked him up though I am his father and would be a-scared of hurting him. I says Here, don't pick him up and he says Why not? He says Are you going to leave him on that there bed the rest of his life? I says No but you don't know how to handle him. He says I have handled a hole lot bigger babys than him or else Callahan would not keep me.

Then he starts patting the baby's head and I says Here, don't do that because he has got a soft spot in his head and you might hit it. He says I thought he was your baby and I says Well he is my baby and he says Well then they can't be no soft spot in his head. Then he lays little Al down because he seen I was in ernest and as soon as he lays him down the baby begins to cry. Then Gleason says See he don't want me to lay him down and I says Maybe he has got a pane in his stumach and he says I would not be supprised because he just took a good look at his father.

But little Al did not act like as if he had a pane in his stumach

and he kept sticking his finger in his mouth and crying. And
Gleason says He acts like as if he had a toothacke. I says How
could he have a toothacke when he has not got no teeth? He
says That is easy. I have saw a lot of pitchers complane that
there arm was sore when they did not have no arm.

Then he asked me what was the baby's name and I told him
Allen but that he was not named after my brother-in-law Allen.
And Gleason says I should hope not. I should hope you would
have better sense then to name him after a left hander. So you
see Al he don't like them no better then I do even if he does
jolly Allen and Russell along and make them think they can
pitch.

Pretty soon he says What are you going to make out of him,
a ball player? I says Yes I am going to make a hitter out of him
so as he can join the White Sox and then maybe they will get a
couple of runs once in a while. He says If I was you I would let
him pitch and then you won't have to give him no educasion.
Besides, he says, he looks now like he would divellop into a
grate spitter.

Well I happened to look out of the window and seen Florrie
and Marie comeing acrost Indiana Avenue and I told Gleason
about it. And you ought to of seen him run. I asked him what
was his hurry and he says it was in his contract that he was not
to talk to no women but I knowed he was kidding because I
allready seen him talking to severel of the players' wifes when
they was on trips with us and they acted like as if they thought
he was a regular comeedion though they really is not nothing
funny about what he says only it is easy to make women laugh
when they have not got no grouch on about something.

Well Al I am glad Gleason has saw the baby and maybe he
will fix it with Callahan so as I won't have to go to morning
practice every A. M. because I should ought to be home takeing care of little Al when Florrie is washing the dishs or helping
Marie round the house. And besides why should I wear myself
all out in practice because I don't need to practice pitching and
I could hit as well as the rest of the men on our club if I never
seen no practice.

After we get threw with Boston, Washington comes here
and then we go to St. Louis and Cleveland and then come
home and then go East again. And after that we are pretty near

threw except the city serious. Callahan is not going to work
me no more after I beat Boston again till it is this here Johnson's turn to pitch for Washington. And I hope it is not his
turn to work the 1st game of the serious because then I would
not have no rest between the last game against Boston and the
1st game against Washington.

But rest or no rest I will work against this here Johnson and
show him up for giveing me that trimming in Washington, the
lucky stiff. I wish I had a team like the Athaletics behind me
and I would loose about 1 game every 6 years and then they
would have to get all the best of it from these rotten umpires.

Your pal,   JACK.

New York, New York, September 16.

FRIEND AL: Al it is not no fun running round the country
no more and I wish this dam trip was over so as I could go
home and see how little Al is getting along because Florrie has
not wrote since we was in Philly which was the first stop on
this trip. I am a-scared they is something the matter with the
little fellow or else she would of wrote but then if they was
something the matter with him she would of sent me a telegram or something and let me know.

So I guess they can't be nothing the matter with him. Still
and all I don't see why she has not wrote when she knows or
should ought to know that I would be worrying about the
baby. If I don't get no letter to-morrow I am going to send her
a telegram and ask her what is the matter with him because I
am positive she would of wrote if they was not something the
matter with him.

The boys has been trying to get me to go out nights and see
a show or something but I have not got no heart to go to shows.
And besides Callahan has not gave us no pass to no show on this
trip. I guess probily he is sore on account of the rotten way the
club has been going but still he should ought not to be sore on
me because I have win 3 out of my last 4 games and would of
win the other if he had not of started me against them with only
1 day's rest and the Athaletics at that, who a man should ought
not to pitch against if he don't feel good.

I asked Allen if he had heard from Marie and he says Yes he
did but she did not say nothing about little Al except that he

was keeping her awake nights balling. So maybe Al if little Al is balling they is something wrong with him. I am going to send Florrie a telegram to-morrow—that is if I don't get no letter.

If they is something the matter with him I will ask Callahan to send me home and he won't want to do it neither because who else has he got that is a regular winner. But if little Al is sick and Callahan won't let me go home I will go home anyway. You know me Al.

Yours truly,   JACK.

Boston, Massachusetts, September 24.

AL: I bet if Florrie was a man she would be a left hander. What do you think she done now Al? I sent her a telegram from New York when I did not get no letter from her and she did not pay no atension to the telegram. Then when we got up here I sent her another telegram and it was not more then five minutes after I sent the 2d telegram till I got a letter from her. And it said the baby was all O. K. but she had been so busy takeing care of him that she had not had no time to write.

Well when I got the letter I chased out to see if I could catch the boy who had took my telegram but he had went allready so I was spending $.60 for nothing. Then what does Florrie do but send me a telegram after she got my second telegram and tell me that little Al is all O. K., which I knowed all about then because I had just got her letter. And she sent her telegram c. o. d. and I had to pay for it at this end because she had not paid for it and that was $.60 more but I bet if I had of knew what was in the telegram before I read it I would of told the boy to keep it and would not of gave him no $.60 but how did I know if little Al might not of tooken sick after Florrie had wrote the letter?

I am going to write and ask her if she is trying to send us both to the Poor House or somewheres with her telegrams. I don't care nothing about the $.60 but I like to see a woman use a little judgement though I guess that is impossable.

It is my turn to work to-day and to-night we start West but we have got to stop off at Cleveland on the way. I have got a nosion to ask Callahan to let me go right on threw to Chi if I win to-day and not stop off at no Cleveland but I guess they would not be no use because I have got that Cleveland Club licked the minute I put on my glove. So probily Callahan will want me with him though it don't make no difference if we win or lose now because we have not got no chance for the pennant. One man can't win no pennant Al I don't care who he is.

Your pal,   JACK.

Chicago, Illinois, October 2.

FRIEND AL: Well old pal I am all threw till the city serious and it is all fixed up that I am going to open the serious and pitch 3 of the games if nessary. The club has went to Detroit to wind up the season and Callahan did not take me along but left me here with a couple other pitchers and Billy Sullivan and told me all as I would have to do was go over to the park the next 3 days and warm up a little so as to keep in shape. But I don't need to be in no shape to beat them Cubs Al. But it is a good thing Al that Allen was tooken on the trip to Detroit or I guess I would of killed him. He has not been going good and he has been acting and talking nasty to everybody because he can't win no games.

Well the 1st night we was home after the trip little Al was haveing a bad night and was balling pretty hard and they could not nobody in the flat get no sleep. Florrie says he was haveing the collect and I says Why should he have the collect all the time when he did not drink nothing but milk? She says she guessed the milk did not agree with him and upsetted his stumach. I says Well he must take after his mother if his stumach gets upsetted every time he takes a drink because if he took after his father he could drink a hole lot and not never be effected. She says You should ought to remember he has only got a little stumach and not a great big resservoire. I says Well if the milk don't agree with him why don't you give him something else? She says Yes I suppose I should ought to give him weeny worst or something.

Allen must of heard us talking because he hollered something and I did not hear what it was so I told him to say it over and he says Give the little X-eyed brat poison and we would all be better off. I says You better take poison yourself because maybe a rotten pitcher like you could get by in the league where you're going when you die. Then I says Besides I would rather my baby was X-eyed then to have him left handed. He says It is better for him that he is X-eyed or else he might get a good look at you and then he would shoot himself. I says Is that so? and he shut up. Little Al is not no more X-eyed than you or I are Al and that was what made me sore because what right did Allen have to talk like that when he knowed he was lying?

Well the next morning Allen nor I did not speak to each other and I seen he was sorry for the way he had talked and I was willing to fix things up because what is the use of staying sore at a man that don't know no better.

But all of a sudden he says When are you going to pay me what you owe me? I says What do you mean? And he says You been liveing here all summer and I been paying all the bills. I says Did not you and Marie ask us to come here and stay with you and it would not cost us nothing. He says Yes but we did not mean it was a life sentence. You are getting more money than me and you don't never spend a nichol. All I have to do is pay the rent and buy your food and it would take a millionare or something to feed you.

Then he says I would not make no holler about you grafting off of me if that brat would shut up nights and give somebody a chance to sleep. I says You should ought to get all the sleep you need on the bench. Besides, I says, who done the grafting all last winter and without no invatation? If he had of said another word I was going to bust him but just then Marie come in and he shut up.

The more I thought about what he said and him a rotten left hander that should ought to be hussling freiht the more madder I got and if he had of opened his head to me the last day or 2 before he went to Detroit I guess I would of finished him. But Marie stuck pretty close to the both of us when we was together and I guess she knowed they was something in the air and did not want to see her husband get the worst of it though if he was my husband and I was a woman I would push him under a st. car.

But Al I won't even stand for him saying that I am grafting off of him and I and Florrie will get away from here and get a flat of our own as soon as the city serious is over. I would like to bring her and the kid down to Bedford for the winter but she wont listen to that.

I allmost forgot Al to tell you to be sure and thank Bertha
for the little dress she made for little Al. I don't know if it will
fit him or not because Florrie has not yet tried it on him yet
and she says she is going to use it for a dishrag but I guess she
is just kidding.

I suppose you seen where Callahan took me out of that
game down to Cleveland but it was not because I was not
going good Al but it was because Callahan seen he was makeing a mistake wasteing me on that bunch who allmost any
pitcher could beat. They beat us that game at that but only by
one run and it was not no fault of mine because I was tooken
out before they got the run that give them the game.

Your old pal,   JACK.

Chicago, Illinois, October 4.

FRIEND AL: Well Al the club winds up the season at Detroit
to-morrow and the serious starts the day after to-morrow and
I will be in there giveing them a battle. I wish I did not have
nobody but the Cubs to pitch against all season and you bet I
would have a record that would make Johnson and Mathewson and some of them other swell heads look like a dirty doose.

I and Florrie and Marie has been haveing a argument about
how could Florrie go and see the city serious games when they
is not nobody here that can take care of the baby because
Marie wants to go and see the games to even though they is
not no more chance of Callahan starting Allen than a rabbit or
something.

Florrie and Marie says I should ought to hire a nurse to take
care of little Al and Florrie got pretty sore when I told her nothing doing because in the first place I can't afford to pay no nurse
a salery and in the second place I would not trust no nurse to
take care of the baby because how do I know the nurse is not
nothing but a grafter or a dope fiend maybe and should ought
not to be left with the baby?

Of coarse Florrie wants to see me pitch and a man can't blame
her for that but I won't leave my baby with no nurse Al and
Florrie will have to stay home and I will tell her what I done
when I get there. I might of gave my consent to haveing a nurse
at that if it had not of been for the baby getting so sick last night
when I was takeing care of him while Florrie and Marie and

Allen was out to a show and if I had not of been home they is no telling what would of happened. It is a cinch that none of them bonehead nurses would of knew what to do.

Allen must of been out of his head because right after supper he says he would take the 2 girls to a show. I says All right go on and I will take care of the baby. Then Florrie says Do you think you can take care of him all O. K.? And I says Have not I tooken care of him before allready? Well, she says, I will leave him with you only don't run in to him every time he cries. I says Why not? And she says Because it is good for him to cry. I says You have not got no heart or you would not talk that way.

They all give me the laugh but I let them get away with it because I am not picking no fights with girls and why should I bust this Allen when he don't know no better and has not got no baby himself. And I did not want to do nothing that would stop him takeing the girls to a show because it is time he spent a peace of money on somebody.

Well they all went out and I went in on the bed and played with the baby. I wish you could of saw him Al because he is old enough now to do stunts and he smiled up at me and waved his arms and legs round and made a noise like as if he was try-ing to say Pa. I did not think Florrie had gave him enough covers so I rapped him up in some more and took a blanket off of the big bed and stuck it round him so as he could not kick his feet out and catch cold.

I thought once or twice he was going off to sleep but all of a sudden he begin to cry and I seen they was something wrong with him. I gave him some hot water but that made him cry again and I thought maybe he was to cold yet so I took an-other blanket off of Allen's bed and wrapped that round him but he kept on crying and trying to kick inside the blankets. And I seen then that he must have collect or something.

So pretty soon I went to the phone and called up our regular Dr. and it took him pretty near a hour to get there and the baby balling all the time. And when he come he says they was nothing the matter except that the baby was to hot and told me to take all them blankets off of him and then soaked me 2 dollars. I had a nosion to bust his jaw. Well pretty soon he beat it and then little Al begin crying again and kept getting worse and worse so finally I got a-scared and run down to the corner where another Dr. is at and I brung him up to see what was the matter but he said he could not see nothing the matter but he did not charge me a cent so I thought he was not no robber like our regular doctor even if he was just as much of a boob.

The baby did not cry none while he was there but the minute he had went he started crying and balling again and I seen they was not no use of fooling no longer so I looked around the house and found the medicine the doctor left for Allen when he had a stumach acke once and I give the baby a little of it in a spoon but I guess he did not like the taste because he hollered like a Indian and finally I could not stand it no longer so I called that second Dr. back again and this time he seen that the baby was sick and asked me what I had gave it and I told him some stumach medicine and he says I was a fool and should ought not to of gave the baby nothing. But while he was talking the baby stopped crying and went off to sleep so you see what I done for him was the right thing to do and them doctors was both off of there nut.

This second Dr. soaked me 2 dollars the 2d time though he had not did no more than when he was there the 1st time and charged me nothing but they is all a bunch of robbers Al and I would just as leave trust a policeman.

Right after the baby went to sleep Florrie and Marie and Allen come home and I told Florrie what had came off but instead of giveing me credit she says If you want to kill him why don't you take a ax? Then Allen butts in and says Why don't you take a ball and throw it at him? Then I got sore and I says Well if I did hit him with a ball I would kill him while if you was to throw that fast ball of yours at him and hit him in the head he would think the musketoes was biteing him and brush them off. But at that, I says, you could not hit him with a ball except you was aiming at something else.

I guess they was no comeback to that so him and Marie went to there room. Allen should ought to know better than to try and get the best of me by this time and I would shut up anyway if I was him after getting sent home from Detroit with some of the rest of them when he only worked 3 innings up there and they had to take him out or play the rest of the game by electrick lights.

I wish you could be here for the serious Al but you would have to stay at a hotel because we have not got no spair room and it would cost you a hole lot of money. But you can watch the papers and you will see what I done.

Yours truly,   JACK.

Chicago, Illinois, October 6.

DEAR OLD PAL: Probily before you get this letter you will of saw by the paper that we was licked in the first game and that I was tooken out but the papers don't know what really come off so I am going to tell you and you can see for yourself if it was my fault.

I did not never have no more stuff in my life then when I was warming up and I seen the Cubs looking over to our bench and shakeing there heads like they knowed they did not have no chance. O'Day was going to start Cheney who is there best bet and had him warming up but when he seen the smoke I had when I and Schalk was warming up he changed his mind because what was the use of useing his best pitcher when I had all that stuff and it was a cinch that no club in the world could score a run off of me when I had all that stuff?

So he told a couple others to warm up to and when my name was announced to pitch Cheney went and set on the bench and this here lefthander Pierce was announced for them.

Well Al you will see by the paper where I sent there 1st 3 batters back to the bench to get a drink of water and all 3 of them good hitters Leach and Good and this here Saier that hits a hole lot of home runs but would not never hit one off of me if I was O. K. Well we scored a couple in our half and the boys on the bench all says Now you got enough to win easy because they won't never score none off of you.

And they was right to because what chance did they have if this thing that I am going to tell you about had not of happened? We goes along seven innings and only 2 of there men had got to 1st base one of them on a bad peg of Weaver's and the other one I walked because this blind Evans don't know a ball from a strike. We had not did no more scoreing off of Pierce not because he had no stuff but because our club could not take a ball in there hands and hit it out of the infield.

Well Al I did not tell you that before I come out to the park I kissed little Al and Florrie good by and Marie says she was going to stay home to and keep Florrie Co. and they was not no reason for Marie to come to the game anyway because they was not a chance in the world for Allen to do nothing but hit fungos. Well while I was doing all this here swell pitching and makeing them Cubs look like a lot of rummys I was thinking about little Al and Florrie and how glad they would be when I come home and told them what I done though of coarse little Al is not only a little over 3 months of age and how could he appresiate what I done? But Florrie would.

Well Al when I come in to the bench after there ½ of the 7th I happened to look up to the press box to see if the reporters had gave Schulte a hit on that one Weaver throwed away and who do you think I seen in a box right alongside of the press box? It was Florrie and Marie and both of them claping there hands and hollering with the rest of the bugs.

Well old pal I was never so suprised in my life and it just took all the heart out of me. What was they doing there and what had they did with the baby? How did I know that little Al was not sick or maybe dead and balling his head off and no-body round to hear him?

I tried to catch Florrie's eyes but she would not look at me. I hollered her name and the bugs looked at me like as if I was crazy and I was to Al. Well I seen they was not no use of stand-ing out there in front of the stand so I come into the bench and Allen was setting there and I says Did you know your wife and Florrie was up there in the stand? He says No and I says What are they doing here? And he says What would they be doing here—mending there stockings? I felt like busting him and I guess he seen I was mad because he got up off of the bench and beat it down to the corner of the field where some of the others was getting warmed up though why should they have anybody warming up when I was going so good?

Well Al I made up my mind that ball game or no ball game I was not going to have little Al left alone no longer and I seen they was not no use of sending word to Florrie to go home because they was a big crowd and it would take maybe 15 or 20 minutes for somebody to get up to where she was at. So I says to Callahan You have got to take me out. He says What is the matter? Is your arm gone? I says No my arm is not gone but my baby is sick and home all alone. He says Where is your wife? And I says She is setting up there in the stand.

Then he says How do you know your baby is sick? And I says I don't know if he is sick or not but he is left home all alone. He says Why don't you send your wife home? And I says I could not get word to her in time. He says Well you have only got two innings to go and the way your going the game will be over in 10 minutes. I says Yes and before 10 minutes is up my baby might die and are you going to take me out or not? He says Get in there and pitch you yellow dog and if you don't I will take your share of the serious money away from you.

By this time our part of the inning was over and I had to go out there and pitch some more because he would not take me out and he has not got no heart Al. Well Al how could I pitch when I kept thinking maybe the baby was dying right now and maybe if I was home I could do something? And instead of paying attension to what I was doing I was thinking about little Al and looking up there to where Florrie and Marie was setting and before I knowed what come off they had the bases full and Callahan took me out.

Well Al I run to the clubhouse and changed my cloths and beat it for home and I did not even hear what Callahan and Gleason says to me when I went by them but I found out after the game that Scott went in and finished up and they batted him pretty hard and we was licked 3 and 2.

When I got home the baby was crying but he was not all alone after all Al because they was a little girl about 14 years of age there watching him and Florrie had hired her to take care of him so as her and Marie could go and see the game. But just think Al of leaveing little Al with a girl 14 years of age that did not never have no babys of her own! And what did she know about takeing care of him? Nothing Al.

You should ought to of heard me ball Florrie out when she got home and I bet she cried pretty near enough to flood the basemunt. We had it hot and heavy and the Allens butted in but I soon showed them where they was at and made them shut there mouth.

I had a good nosion to go out and get a hole lot of drinks and was just going to put on my hat when the doorbell rung and there was Kid Gleason. I thought he would be sore and probily try to ball me out and I was not going to stand for nothing but instead of balling me out he come and shook hands with me and interduced himself to Florrie and asked how was little Al.

Well we all set down and Gleason says the club was depending on me to win the serious because I was in the best shape of all the pitchers. And besides the Cubs could not never hit me when I was right and he was telling the truth to.

So he asked me if I would stand for the club hireing a train nurse to stay with the baby the rest of the serious so as Florrie could go and see her husband win the serious but I says No I would not stand for that and Florrie's place was with the baby.

So Gleason and Florrie goes out in the other room and talks a while and I guess he was persuadeing her to stay home because pretty soon they come back in the room and says it was all fixed up and I would not have to worry about little Al the rest of the serious but could give the club the best I got. Gleason just left here a little while ago and I won't work to-morrow Al but I will work the day after and you will see what I can do when I don't have nothing to worry me.

Your pal,   JACK.

Chicago, Illinois, October 8.

OLD PAL: Well old pal we got them 2 games to one now and the serious is sure to be over in three more days because I can pitch 2 games in that time if nessary. I shut them out to-day and they should ought not to of had four hits but should ought to of had only 2 but Bodie don't cover no ground and 2 fly balls that he should ought to of eat up fell safe.

But I beat them anyway and Benz beat them yesterday but why should he not beat them when the club made 6 runs for him? All they made for me was three but all I needed was one because they could not hit me with a shuvvel. When I come to the bench after the 5th inning they was a note there for me from the boy that answers the phone at the ball park and it says that somebody just called up from the flat and says the baby was asleep and getting along fine. So I felt good Al and I was better then ever in the 6th.

When I got home Florrie and Marie was both there and asked me how did the game come out because I beat Allen home and I told them all about what I done and I bet Florrie was proud of me but I supose Marie is a little jellus because how could she help it when Callahan is depending on me to win the serious and her husband is wearing out the wood on the bench? But why should she be sore when it is me that is winning the serious for them? And if it was not for me Allen and all the rest of them would get about $500.00 apeace instead of the winners' share which is about $750.00 apeace.

Cicotte is going to work to-morrow and if he is lucky maybe he can get away with the game and that will leave me to finish up the day after to-morrow but if nessary I can go in to-morrow when they get to hitting Cicotte and stop them and then come back the following day and beat them again. Where would this club be at Al if I had of jumped to the Federal?

Yours truly,   JACK.

Chicago, Illinois, October 11.

FRIEND AL: We done it again Al and I guess the Cubs won't never want to play us again not so long as I am with the club. Before you get this letter you will know what we done and who done it but probily you could of guessed that Al without seeing no paper.

I got 2 more of them phone messiges about the baby dureing the game and I guess that was what made me so good because I knowed then that Florrie was takeing care of him but I could not help feeling sorry for Florrie because she is a bug herself and it must of been pretty hard for her to stay away from the game espesially when she knowed I was going to pitch and she has been pretty good to sacrifice her own plesure for little Al.

Cicotte was knocked out of the box the day before yesterday and then they give this here Faber a good beating but I wish you could of saw what they done to Allen when Callahan sent him in after the game was gone allready. Honest Al if he had not of been my brother in law I would of felt like laughing at him because it looked like as if they would have to call the fire department to put the side out. They had Bodie and Collins hollering for help and with there tongue hanging out from running back to the fence.

Anyway the serious is all over and I won't have nothing to do but stay home and play with little Al but I don't know yet where my home is going to be at because it is a cinch I won't stay with Allen no longer. He has not came home since the game and I suppose he is out somewheres lapping up some beer and spending some of the winner's share of the money which he would not of had no chance to get in on if it had not of been for me.

I will write and let you know my plans for the winter and I wish Florrie would agree to come to Bedford but nothing doing Al and after her staying home and takeing care of the baby instead of watching me pitch I can't be too hard on her but must leave her have her own way about something.

Your pal,   JACK.

Chicago, Illinois, October 13.

AL: I am all threw with Florrie Al and I bet when you hear about it you won't say it was not no fault of mine but no man liveing who is any kind of a man would act different from how I am acting if he had of been decieved like I been.

Al Florrie and Marie was out to all them games and was not home takeing care of the baby at all and it is not her fault that little Al is not dead and that he was not killed by the nurse they hired to take care of him while they went to the games when I thought they was home takeing care of the baby. And all them phone messiges was just fakes and maybe the baby was sick all the time I was winning them games and balling his head off instead of being asleep like they said he was.

Allen did not never come home at all the night before last and when he come in yesterday he was a sight and I says to him Where have you been? And he says I have been down to the Y. M. C. A. but that is not none of your business. I says Yes you look like as if you had been to the Y. M. C. A. and I know where you have been and you have been out lushing beer. And he says Suppose I have and what are you going to do about it? And I says Nothing but you should ought to be ashamed of yourself and leaveing Marie here while you was out lapping up beer.

Then he says Did you not leave Florrie home while you was getting away with them games, you lucky stiff? And I says Yes but Florrie had to stay home and take care of the baby but Marie don't never have to stay home because where is your baby? You have not got no baby. He says I would not want no

X-eyed baby like yourn. Then he says So you think Florrie stayed to home and took care of the baby do you? And I says What do you mean? And he says You better ask her.

So when Florrie come in and heard us talking she busted out crying and then I found out what they put over on me. It is a wonder Al that I did not take some of that cheap furniture them Allens got and bust it over there heads, Allen and Florrie. This is what they done Al. The club give Florrie $50.00 to stay home and take care of the baby and she said she would and she was to call up every so often and tell me the baby was all O. K. But this here Marie told her she was a sucker so she hired a nurse for part of the $50.00 and then her and Marie went to the games and beat it out quick after the games was over and come home in a taxicab and chased the nurse out before I got home.

Well Al when I found out what they done I grabbed my hat and goes out and got some drinks and I was so mad I did not know where I was at or what come off and I did not get home till this A. M. And they was all asleep and I been asleep all day and when I woke up Marie and Allen was out but Florrie and I have not spoke to each other and I won't never speak to her again.

But I know now what I am going to do Al and I am going to take little Al and beat it out of here and she can sew me for a bill of divorce and I should not worry because I will have little Al and I will see that he is tooken care of because I guess I can hire a nurse as well as they can and I will pick out a train nurse that knows something. Maybe I and him and the nurse will come to Bedford Al but I don't know yet and I will write and tell you as soon as I make up my mind. Did you ever hear of a man getting a rottener deal Al? And after what I done in the serious too.

Your pal,   JACK.

Chicago, Illinois, October 17.

OLD PAL: I and Florrie has made it up Al but we are threw with Marie and Allen and I and Florrie and the baby is staying at a hotel here on Cottage Grove Avenue the same hotel we was at when we got married only of coarse they was only the 2 of us then.

And now Al I want to ask you a favor and that is for you to

go and see old man Cutting and tell him I want to ree-new the lease on that house for another year because I and Florrie has decided to spend the winter in Bedford and she will want to stay there and take care of little Al while I am away on trips next summer and not stay in no high-price flat up here. And may be you and Bertha can help her round the house when I am not there.

I will tell you how we come to fix things up Al and you will see that I made her apollojize to me and after this she will do what I tell her to and won't never try to put nothing over. We was eating breakfast—I and Florrie and Marie. Allen was still asleep yet because I guess he must of had a bad night and he was snoreing so as you could hear him in the next st. I was not saying nothing to nobody but pretty soon Florrie says to Marie I don't think you and Allen should ought to kick on the baby crying when Allen's snoreing makes more noise than a hole wagonlode of babys. And Marie got sore and says I guess a man has got a right to snore in his own house and you and Jack has been grafting off of us long enough.

Then Florrie says What did Allen do to help win the serious and get that $750.00? Nothing but set on the bench except when they was makeing him look like a sucker the 1 inning he pitched. The trouble with you and Allen is you are jellous of what Jack has did and you know he will be a star up here in the big league when Allen is tending bar which is what he should ought to be doing because then he could get stewed for nothing.

Marie says Take your brat and get out of the house. And Florrie says Don't you worry because we would not stay here no longer if you hired us. So Florrie went in her room and I followed her in and she says Let's pack up and get out.

Then I says Yes but we won't go nowheres together after what you done to me but you can go where you dam please and I and little Al will go to Bedford. Then she says You can't take the baby because he is mine and if you was to take him I would have you arrested for kidnaping. Besides, she says, what would you feed him and who would take care of him?

I says I would find somebody to take care of him and I would get him food from a resturunt. She says He can't eat nothing but milk and I says Well he has the collect all the time when he is eating milk and he would not be no worse off if he was eating watermelon. Well, she says, if you take him I will have you arrested and sew you for a bill of divorce for dessertion.

Then she says Jack you should not ought to find no fault with me for going to them games because when a woman has a husband that can pitch like you can do you think she wants to stay home and not see her husband pitch when a lot of other women is cheering him and makeing her feel proud because she is his wife?

Well Al as I said right along it was pretty hard on Florrie to have to stay home and I could not hardly blame her for wanting to be out there where she could see what I done so what was the use of argueing?

So I told her I would think it over and then I went out and I went and seen a attorney at law and asked him could I take little Al away and he says No I did not have no right to take him away from his mother and besides it would probily kill him to be tooken away from her and then he soaked me $10.00 the robber.

Then I went back and told Florrie I would give her another chance and then her and I packed up and took little Al in a taxicab over to this hotel. We are threw with the Allens Al and let me know right away if I can get that lease for another year because Florrie has gave up and will go to Bedford or anywheres else with me now.

Yours truly,   JACK.

Chicago, Illinois, October 20.

FRIEND AL: Old pal I won't never forget your kindnus and this is to tell you that I and Florrie except your kind invatation to come and stay with you till we can find a house and I guess you won't regret it none because Florrie will livun things up for Bertha and Bertha will be crazy about the baby because you should ought to see how cute he is now Al and not yet four months old. But I bet he will be talking before we know it.

We are comeing on the train that leaves here at noon Saturday Al and the train leaves here about 12 o'clock and I don't know what time it gets to Bedford but it leaves here at noon so we shall be there probily in time for supper.

I wish you would ask Ben Smith will he have a hack down to the deepo to meet us but I won't pay no more than $.25 and I should think he should ought to be glad to take us from the deepo to your house for nothing.

Your pal,   JACK.

P. S. The train we are comeing on leaves here at noon Al and will probily get us there in time for a late supper and I wonder if Bertha would have spair ribs and crout for supper. You know me Al.

CHAPTER VI

The Busher Beats It Hence

Friend Al: I guess may be you will begin to think I dont never do what I am going to do and that I change my mind a hole lot because I wrote and told you that I and Florrie and little Al would be in Bedford to-day and here we are in Chi yet on the day when I told you we would get to Bedford and I bet Bertha and you and the rest of the boys will be dissapointed but Al I dont feel like as if I should ought to leave the White Sox in a hole and that is why I am here yet and I will tell you how it come off but in the 1st place I want to tell you that it wont make a diffrence of more then 5 or 6 or may be 7 days at least and we will be down there and see you and Bertha and the rest of the boys just as soon as the N. Y. giants and the White Sox leaves here and starts a round the world. All so I remember I told you to fix it up so as a hack would be down to the deepo to meet us to-night and you wont get this letter in time to tell them not to send no hack so I supose the hack will be there but may be they will be some body else that gets off of the train that will want the hack and then every thing will be all O. K. but if they is not no-body else that wants the hack I will pay them ½ of what they was going to charge me if I had of came and road in the hack though I dont have to pay them nothing because I am not going to ride in the hack but I want to do the right thing and besides I will want a hack at the deepo when I do come so they will get a peace of money out of me any way so I dont see where they got no kick comeing even if I dont give them a nichol now.

I will tell you why I am still here and you will see where I am trying to do the right thing. You knowed of coarse that the White Sox and the N. Y. giants was going to make a trip a round the world and they been after me for a long time to go a long with them but I says No I would not leave Florrie and the kid because that would not be fare and besides I would be paying rent and grocerys for them some wheres and me not getting nothing out of it and besides I would probily be spending a hole lot of money on the trip because though the clubs pays all of our regular expences they would be a hole lot of times when I felt like blowing my self and buying some thing to send home to the Mrs and to good old friends of mine like you and Bertha so I turned them down and Callahan acted like he was sore at me but I dont care nothing for that because I got other people to think a bout and not Callahan and besides if I was to go a long the fans in the towns where we play at would want to see me work and I would have to do a hole lot of pitching which I would not be getting nothing for it and it would not count in no standing because the games is to be just for fun and what good would it do me and besides Florrie says I was not under no circumstance to go and of coarse I would go if I wanted to go no matter what ever she says but all and all I turned them down and says I would stay here all winter or rather I would not stay here but in Bedford. Then Callahan says All right but you know before we start on the trip the giants and us is going to play a game right here in Chi next Sunday and after what you done in the city serious the fans would be sore if they did not get no more chance to look at you so will you stay and pitch part of the game here and I says I would think it over and I come home to the hotel where we are staying at and asked Florrie did she care if we did not go to Bedford for an other week and she says No she did not care if we dont go for 6 years so I called Callahan up and says I would stay and he says Thats the boy and now the fans will have an other treat so you see Al he appresiates what I done and wants to give the fans fare treatment because this town is nuts over me after what I done to them Cubs but I could do it just the same to the Athaletics or any body else if it would of been them in stead of the Cubs. May be we will leave here the A. M. after the game that is Monday and I will let you know so as you can order an other hack and tell Bertha I hope she did not go to no extra trouble a bout getting ready for us and did not order no spair ribs and crout but you can eat them up if she all ready got them and may be she can order some more for us when we come but tell her it dont make no dif- frence and not to go to no trouble because most anything she has is O. K. for I and Florrie accept of coarse we would not want to make no meal off of sardeens or something.

Well Al I bet them N. Y. giants will wish I would of went home before they come for this here exibishun game because my arm feels grate and I will show them where they would be at if they had to play ball in our league all the time though I supose they is some pitchers in our league that they would hit good against them if they can hit at all but not me. You will see in the papers how I come out and I will write and tell you a bout it.

Your pal,   JACK.

Chicago, Ill., Oct. 25.

OLD PAL: I have not only got a little time but I have got some news for you and I knowed you would want to hear all a bout it so I am writeing this letter and then I am going to catch the train. I would be saying good by to little Al instead of writeing this letter only Florrie wont let me wake him up and he is a sleep but may be by the time I get this letter wrote he will be a wake again and I can say good by to him. I am going with the White Sox and giants as far as San Francisco or may be Van Coover where they take the boat at but I am not going a round the world with them but only just out to the coast to help them out because they is a couple of men going to join them out there and untill them men join them they will be short of men and they got a hole lot of exibishun games to play before they get out there so I am going to help them out. It all come off in the club house after the game to-day and I will tell you how it come off but 1st I want to tell you a bout the game and honest Al them giants is the luckyest team in the world and it is not no wonder they keep wining the penant in that league because a club that has got there luck could win ball games with out sending no team on the field at all but staying down to the hotel.

They was a big crowd out to the park so Callahan says to me I did not know if I was going to pitch you or not but the crowd is out here to see you so I will have to let you work so I warmed up but I knowed the minute I throwed the 1st ball warming up that I was not right and I says to Callahan I did not feel good but he says You wont need to feel good to beat this bunch because they heard a hole lot a bout you and you would have them beat if you just throwed your glove out there

in the box. So I went in and tried to pitch but my arm was so
lame it pretty near killed me every ball I throwed and I bet if I
was some other pitchers they would not never of tried to work
with my arm so sore but I am not like some of them yellow
dogs and quit because I would not dissapoint the crowd or
throw Callahan down when he wanted me to pitch and was
depending on me. You know me Al. So I went in there but I
did not have nothing and if them giants could of hit at all in
stead of like a lot of girls they would of knock down the fence
because I was not my self. At that they should not ought to of
had only the 1 run off of me if Weaver and them had not of
begin kicking the ball a round like it was a foot ball or something. Well Al what with dropping fly balls and booting them a
round and this in that the giants was gave 5 runs in the 1st 3
innings and they should ought to of had just the 1 run or may be
not that and that ball Merkle hit in to the seats I was trying to
waist it and a man that is a good hitter would not never of hit
at it and if I was right this here Merkle could not foul me in 9
years. When I was comeing into the bench after the 3th inning
this here smart alex Mcgraw come passed me from the 3 base
coaching line and he says Are you going on the trip and I says
No I am not going on no trip and he says That is to bad because if you was going we would win a hole lot of games and I
give him a hot come back and he did not say nothing so I went
in to the bench and Callahan says Them giants is not such
rotten hitters is they and I says No they hit pretty good when
a man has got a sore arm against them and he says Why did not
you tell me your arm was sore and I says I did not want to
dissapoint no crowd that come out here to see me and he says
Well I guess you need not pitch no more because if I left you
in there the crowd might begin to get tired of watching you a
bout 10 oclock to-night and I says What do you mean and he
did not say nothing more so I set there a while and then went
to the club house. Well Al after the game Callahan come in to
the club house and I was still in there yet talking to the trainer
and getting my arm rubbed and Callahan says Are you getting
your arm in shape for next year and I says No but it give me so
much pane I could not stand it and he says I bet if you was
feeling good you could make them giants look like a sucker
and I says You know I could make them look like a sucker and

he says Well why dont you come a long with us and you will
get an other chance at them when you feel good and I says I
would like to get an other crack at them but I could not go a
way on no trip and leave the Mrs and the baby and then he
says he would not ask me to make the hole trip a round the
world but he wisht I would go out to the coast with them because they was hard up for pitchers and he says Mathewson of
the giants was not only going as far as the coast so if the giants
had there star pitcher that far the White Sox should ought to
have theren and then some of the other boys coaxed me would
I go so finely I says I would think it over and I went home and
seen Florrie and she says How long would it be for and I says
a bout 3 or 4 weeks and she says If you dont go will we start
for Bedford right a way and I says Yes and then she says All
right go a head and go but if they was any thing should happen to the baby while I was gone what would they do if I was
not a round to tell them what to do and I says Call a Dr. in but
dont call no Dr. if you dont have to and besides you should
ought to know by this time what to do for the baby when he
got sick and she says Of coarse I know a little but not as much
as you do because you know it all. Then I says No I dont know
it all but I will tell you some things before I go and you should
not ought to have no trouble so we fixed it up and her and
little Al is to stay here in the hotel untill I come back which
will be a bout the 20 of Nov. and then we will come down
home and tell Bertha not to get to in patient and we will get
there some time. It is going to cost me $6.00 a week at the
hotel for a room for she and the baby besides there meals but
the babys meals dont cost nothing yet and Florrie should not
ought to be very hungry because we been liveing good and
besides she will get all she can eat when we come to Bedford
and it wont cost me nothing for meals on the trip out to the
coast because Comiskey and Mcgraw pays for that.

I have not even had no time to look up where we play at but
we stop off at a hole lot of places on the way and I will get a
chance to make them giants look like a sucker before I get
threw and Mcgraw wont be so sorry I am not going to make
the hole trip. You will see by the papers what I done to them
before we get threw and I will write as soon as we stop some
wheres long enough so as I can write and now I am going to

say good by to little Al if he is a wake or not a wake and wake him up and say good by to him because even if he is not only 5 months old he is old enough to think a hole lot of me and why not. I all so got to say good by to Florrie and fix it up with the hotel clerk a bout she and the baby staying here a while and catch the train. You will hear from me soon old pal.

Your pal,   JACK.

St. Joe, Miss., Oct. 29.

FRIEND AL: Well Al we are on our way to the coast and they is quite a party of us though it is not no real White Sox and giants at all but some players from off of both clubs and then some others that is from other clubs a round the 2 leagues to fill up. We got Speaker from the Boston club and Crawford from the Detroit club and if we had them with us all the time Al I would not never loose a game because one or the other of them 2 is good for a couple of runs every game and that is all I need to win my games is a couple of runs or only 1 run and I would win all my games and would not never loose a game.

I did not pitch to-day and I guess the giants was glad of it because no matter what Mcgraw says he must of saw from watching me Sunday that I was a real pitcher though my arm was so sore I could not hardly raze it over my sholder so no wonder I did not have no stuff but at that I could of beat his gang with out no stuff if I had of had some kind of decent suport. I will pitch against them may be to-morrow or may be some day soon and my arm is all O. K. again now so I will show them up and make them wish Callahan had of left me to home. Some of the men has brung there wife a long and be-sides that there is some other men and there wife that is not no ball players but are going a long for the trip and some more will join the party out the coast before they get a bord the boat but of coarse I and Mathewson will drop out of the party then because why should I or him go a round the world and throw our arms out pitching games that dont count in no standing and that we dont get no money for pitching them out side of just our bare expences. The people in the towns we played at so far has all wanted to shake hands with Mathewson and I so I guess they know who is the real pitchers on these here 2 clubs no matter what them reporters says and the stars is all

ways the men that the people wants to shake there hands with
and make friends with them but Al this here Mathewson
pitched to-day and honest Al I dont see how he gets by and
either the batters in the National league dont know nothing a
bout hitting or else he is such a old man that they feel sorry for
him and may be when he was a bout 10 years younger then he
is may be then he had some thing and was a pretty fare pitcher
but all as he does now is stick the 1st ball right over with 0 on
it and pray that they dont hit it out of the park. If a pitcher like
he can get by in the National league and fool them batters they
is not nothing I would like better then to pitch in the National
league and I bet I would not get scored on in 2 to 3 years. I
heard a hole lot a bout this here fade a way that he is suposed
to pitch and it is a ball that is throwed out between 2 fingers
and falls in at a right hand batter and they is not no body cant
hit it but if he throwed 1 of them things to-day he done it
while I was a sleep and they was not no time when I was not
wide a wake and looking right at him and after the game was
over I says to him Where is that there fade a way I heard so
much a bout and he says O I did not have to use none of my
regular stuff against your club and I says Well you would have
to use all you got if I was working against you and he says Yes
if you worked like you done Sunday I would have to do some
pitching or they would not never finish the game. Then I says
a bout me haveing a sore arm Sunday and he says I wisht I had a
sore arm like yourn and a little sence with it and was your age
and I would not never loose a game so you see Al he has heard a
bout me and is jellus because he has not got my stuff but they
cant every body expect to have the stuff that I got or ½ as
much stuff. This smart alex Mcgraw was trying to kid me to-
day and says Why did not I make friends with Mathewson and
let him learn me some thing a bout pitching and I says
Mathewson could not learn me nothing and he says I guess
thats right and I guess they is not nobody could learn you
nothing a bout nothing and if you was to stay in the league 20
years probily you would not be no better then you are now so
you see he had to add mit that I am good Al even if he has not
saw me work when my arm was O. K.

Mcgraw says to me to-night he says I wisht you was going
all the way and I says Yes you do. I says Your club would look

like a sucker after I had worked against them a few times and
he says May be thats right to because they would not know how
to hit against a regular pitcher after that. Then he says But I
dont care nothing a bout that but I wisht you was going to
make the hole trip so as we could have a good time. He says We
got Steve Evans and Dutch Schaefer going a long and they is
both of them funny but I like to be a round with boys that is
funny and dont know nothing a bout it. I says Well I would go
a long only for my wife and baby and he says Yes it would be
pretty tough on your wife to have you a way that long but still
and all think how glad she would be to see you when you come
back again and besides them dolls acrost the ocean will be pretty
sore at I and Callahan if we tell them we left you to home. I says
Do you supose the people over there has heard a bout me and
he says Sure because they have wrote a lot of letters asking me to
be sure and bring you and Mathewson a long. Then he says I
guess Mathewson is not going so if you was to go and him left
here to home they would not be nothing to it. You could have
things all your own way and probily could marry the Queen of
europe if you was not all ready married. He was giveing me the
strate dope this time Al because he did not crack a smile and I
wisht I could go a long but it would not be fare to Florrie but
still and all did not she leave me and beat it for Texas last winter
and why should not I do the same thing to her only I am not
that kind of a man. You know me Al.

   We play in Kansas city to-morrow and may be I will work
there because it is a big town and I have got to close now and
write to Florrie.

                    Your old pal,   JACK.

                                   Abilene, Texas, Nov. 4.
   AL: Well Al I guess you know by this time that I have worked
against them 2 times since I wrote to you last time and I beat
them both times and Mcgraw knows now what kind of a
pitcher I am and I will tell you how I know because after the
game yesterday he road down to the place we dressed at a long
with me and all the way in the automobile he was after me to
say I would go all the way a round the world and finely it come
out that he wants I should go a long and pitch for his club and
not pitch for the White Sox. He says his club is up against it for

pitchers because Mathewson is not going and all they got left is a man named Hern that is a young man and not got no experiense and Wiltse that is a left hander. So he says I have talked it over with Callahan and he says if I could get you to go a long it was all O. K. with him and you could pitch for us only I must not work you to hard because he is depending on you to win the penant for him next year. I says Did not none of the other White Sox make no holler because may be they might have to bat against me and he says Yes Crawford and Speaker says they would not make the trip if you was a long and pitching against them but Callahan showed them where it would be good for them next year because if they hit against you all winter the pitchers they hit against next year will look easy to them. He was crazy to have me go a long on the hole trip but of coarse Al they is not no chance of me going on acct. of Florrie and little Al but you see Mcgraw has cut out his trying to kid me and is treating me now like a man should ought to be treated that has did what I done.

They was not no game here to-day on acct. of it raining and the people here was sore because they did not see no game but they all come a round to look at us and says they must have some speechs from the most prommerent men in the party so I and Comiskey and Mcgraw and Callahan and Mathewson and Ted Sullivan that I guess is putting up the money for the trip made speechs and they clapped there hands harder when I was makeing my speech then when any 1 of the others was makeing there speech. You did not know I was a speech maker did you Al and I did not know it neither untill to-day but I guess they is not nothing I can do if I make up my mind and 1 of the boys says that I done just as well as Dummy Taylor could of.

I have not heard nothing from Florrie but I guess may be she is to busy takeing care of little Al to write no letters and I am not worring none because she give me her word she would let me know was they some thing the matter.

Yours truly,   JACK.

San Dago, Cal., Nov. 9.

FRIEND AL: Al some times I wisht I was not married at all and if it was not for Florrie and little Al I would go a round the

world on this here trip and I guess the boys in Bedford would
not be jellus if I was to go a round the world and see every thing
they is to be saw and some of the boys down home has not
never been no futher a way then Terre Haute and I dont mean
you Al but some of the other boys. But of coarse Al when a man
has got a wife and a baby they is not no chance for him to go a
way on 1 of these here trips and leave them a lone so they is not
no use I should even think a bout it but I cant help thinking a
bout it because the boys keeps after me all the time to go. Callahan was talking a bout it to me to-day and he says he knowed
that if I was to pitch for the giants on the trip his club would not
have no chance of wining the most of the games on the trip but
still and all he wisht I would go a long because he was a scared
the people over in Rome and Paris and Africa and them other
countrys would be awful sore if the 2 clubs come over there
with out bringing none of there star pitchers along. He says We
got Speaker and Crawford and Doyle and Thorp and some of
them other real stars in all the positions accept pitcher and it will
make us look bad if you and Mathewson dont neither 1 of you
come a long. I says What is the matter with Scott and Benz and
this here left hander Wiltse and he says They is not nothing the
matter with none of them accept they is not no real stars like
you and Mathewson and if we cant show them forreners 1 of
you 2 we will feel like as if we was cheating them. I says You
would not want me to pitch my best against your club would
you and he says O no I would not want you to pitch your best
or get your self all wore out for next year but I would want you
to let up enough so as we could make a run oncet in a while so
the games would not be to 1 sided. I says Well they is not no use
talking a bout it because I could not leave my wife and baby and
he says Why dont you write and ask your wife and tell her how
it is and can you go. I says No because she would make a big
holler and besides of coarse I would go any way if I wanted to
go with out no yes or no from her only I am not the kind of a
man that runs off and leaves his family and besides they is not
nobody to leave her with because her and her sister Allens wife
has had a quarrle. Then Callahan says Where is Allen at now is
he still in Chi. I says I dont know where is he at and I dont care
where he is at because I am threw with him. Then Callahan says
I asked him would he go on the trip before the season was over

but he says he could not and if I knowed where was he I would
wire a telegram to him and ask him again. I says What would
you want him a long for and he says Because Mcgraw is shy of
pitchers and I says I would try and help him find 1. I says Well
you should ought not to have no trouble finding a man like
Allen to go along because his wife probily would be glad to get
rid of him. Then Callahan says Well I wisht you would get a
hold of where Allen is at and let me know so as I can wire him a
telegram. Well Al I know where Allen is at all O. K. but I am not
going to give his adress to Callahan because Mcgraw has treated
me all O. K. and why should I wish a man like Allen on to him
and besides I am not going to give Allen no chance to go a
round the world or no wheres else after the way he acted a bout
I and Florrie haveing a room in his flat and asking me to pay for
it when he give me a invatation to come there and stay. Well Al
it is to late now to cry in the sour milk but I wisht I had not
never saw Florrie untill next year and then I and her could get
married just like we done last year only I dont know would I do
it again or not but I guess I would on acct. of little Al.

Your pal,   JACK.

San Francisco, Cal., Nov. 14.

OLD PAL: Well old pal what do you know a bout me being
back here in San Francisco where I give the fans such a treat 2
years ago and then I was not nothing but a busher and now I
am with a team that is going a round the world and are crazy
to have me go a long only I cant because of my wife and baby.
Callahan wired a telegram to the reporters here from Los Angeles telling them I would pitch here and I guess they is going
to be 20 or 25000 out to the park and I will give them the best
I got.

But what do you think Florrie has did Al. Her and the Allens
has made it up there quarrle and is friends again and Marie told
Florrie to write and tell me she was sorry we had that there argument and let by gones be by gones. Well Al it is all O. K. with
me because I cant help not feeling sorry for Allen because I
dont beleive he will be in the league next year and I feel sorry
for Marie to because it must be pretty tough on her to see how
well her sister done and what a misstake she made when she
went and fell for a left hander that could not fool a blind man

with his curve ball and if he was to hit a man in the head with his fast ball they would think there nose iched. In Florries letter she says she thinks us and the Allens could find an other flat like the 1 we had last winter and all live in it to gether in stead of going to Bedford but I have wrote to her before I started writeing this letter all ready and told her that her and I is going to Bedford and the Allens can go where they feel like and they can go and stay on a boat on Michigan lake all winter if they want to but I and Florrie is comeing to Bedford. Down to the bottom of her letter she says Allen wants to know if Callahan or Mcgraw is shy of pitchers and may be he would change his mind and go a long on the trip. Well Al I did not ask either Callahan nor Mcgraw nothing a bout it because I knowed they was looking for a star and not for no left hander that could not brake a pane of glass with his fast 1 so I wrote and told Florrie to tell Allen they was all filled up and would not have no room for no more men.

It is pretty near time to go out to the ball park and I wisht you could be here Al and hear them San Francisco fans go crazy when they hear my name anounced to pitch. I bet they wish they had of had me here this last year.

Yours truly,   JACK.

Medford, Organ, Nov. 16.

FRIEND AL: Well Al you know by this time that I did not pitch the hole game in San Francisco but I was not tooken out because they was hitting me Al but because my arm went back on me all of a sudden and it was the change in the clime it that done it to me and they could not hire me to try and pitch another game in San Francisco. They was the biggest crowd there that I ever seen in San Francisco and I guess they must of been 40000 people there and I wisht you could of heard them yell when my name was anounced to pitch. But Al I would not never of went in there but for the crowd. My arm felt like a wet rag or some thing and I knowed I would not have nothing and besides the people was packed in a round the field and they had to have ground rules so when a man hit a pop fly it went in to the crowd some wheres and was a 2 bagger and all them giants could do against me was pop my fast ball up in the air and then the wind took a hold of it and dropped it in to the crowd the lucky stiffs. Doyle hit 3 of them pop ups in to the crowd so when you see them 3 2 base hits oposit his name in the score you will know they was not no real 2 base hits and the infielders would of catched them had it not of been for the wind. This here Doyle takes a awful wallop at a ball but if I was right and he swang at a ball the way he done in San Francisco the catcher would all ready be throwing me back the ball a bout the time this here Doyle was swinging at it. I can make him look like a sucker and I done it both in Kansas city and Bonham and if he will get up there and bat against me when I feel good and when they is not no wind blowing I will bet him a $25.00 suit of cloths that he cant foul 1 off of me. Well when Callahan seen how bad my arm was he says I guess I should ought to take you out and not run no chance of you getting killed in there and so I quit and Faber went in to finnish it up because it dont make no diffrence if he hurts his arm or dont. But I guess Mcgraw knowed my arm was sore to because he did not try and kid me like he done that day in Chi because he has saw enough of me since then to know I can make his club look rotten when I am O.K. and my arm is good. On the train that night he come up and says to me Well Jack we catched you off your strid to-day or you would of gave us a beating and then he says What your arm needs is more work and you should ought to make the hole trip with us and then you would be in fine shape for next year but I says You cant get me to make no trip so you might is well not do no more talking a bout it and then he says Well I am sorry and the girls over to Paris will be sorry to but I guess he was just jokeing a bout the last part of it.

Well Al we go to 1 more town in Organ and then to Washington but of coarse it is not the same Washington we play at in the summer but this is the state Washington and have not got no big league club and the boys gets there boat in 4 more days and I will quit them and then I will come strate back to Chi and from there to Bedford.

Your pal,   JACK.

Portland, Organ, Nov. 17.

FRIEND AL: I have just wrote a long letter to Florrie but I feel like as if I should ought to write to you because I wont have no more chance for a long while that is I wont have no more chance to male a letter because I will be on the pacific

Ocean and un less we should run passed a boat that was comeing the other way they would not be no chance of getting no
letter maled. Old pal I am going to make the hole trip clear a
round the world and back and so I wont see you this winter
after all but when I do see you Al I will have a lot to tell you a
bout my trip and besides I will write you a letter a bout it from
every place we head in at.

I guess you will be surprised a bout me changeing my mind
and makeing the hole trip but they was not no way for me to
get out of it and I will tell you how it all come off. While we
was still in that there Medford yesterday Mcgraw and Callahan
come up to me and says was they not no chance of me changeing my mind a bout makeing the hole trip. I says No they was
not. Then Callahan says Well I dont know what we are going
to do then and I says Why and he says Comiskey just got a
letter from president Wilson the President of the united states
and in the letter president Wilson says he had got an other
letter from the king of Japan who says that they would not
stand for the White Sox and giants comeing to Japan un less
they brought all there stars a long and president Wilson says
they would have to take there stars a long because he was a
scared if they did not take there stars a long Japan would get
mad at the united states and start a war and then where would
we be at. So Comiskey wired a telegram to president Wilson
and says Mathewson could not make the trip because he was
so old but would everything be all O.K. if I was to go a long
and president Wilson wired a telegram back and says Yes he
had been talking to the priest from Japan and he says Yes it
would be all O.K. I asked them would they show me the letter
from president Wilson because I thought may be they might
be kiding me and they says they could not show me no letter
because when Comiskey got the letter he got so mad that he
tore it up. Well Al I finely says I did not want to brake up there
trip but I knowed Florrie would not stand for letting me go so
Callahan says All right I will wire a telegram to a friend of mine
in Chi and have him get a hold of Allen and send him out here
and we will take him a long and I says It is to late for Allen to
get here in time and Mcgraw says No they was a train that only
took 2 days from Chi to where ever it was the boat is going to
sale from because the train come a round threw canada and it

was down hill all the way. Then I says Well if you will wire a telegram to my wife and fix things up with her I will go a long with you but if she is going to make a holler it is all off. So we all 3 went to the telegram office to gether and we wired Florrie a telegram that must of cost $2.00 but Callahan and Mcgraw payed for it out of there own pocket and then we waited a round a long time and the anser come back and the anser was longer than the telegram we wired and it says it would not make no diffrence to her but she did not know if the baby would make a holler but he was hollering most of the time any way so that would not make no diffrence but if she let me go it was on condishon that her and the Allens could get a flat to gether and stay in Chi all winter and not go to no Bedford and hire a nurse to take care of the baby and if I would send her a check for the money I had in the bank so as she could put it in her name and draw it out when she need it. Well I says at 1st I would not stand for nothing like that but Callahan and Mcgraw showed me where I was makeing a mistake not going when I could see all them diffrent countrys and tell Florrie all a bout the trip when I come back and then in a year or 2 when the baby was a little older I could make an other trip and take little Al and Florrie a long so I finely says O.K. I would go and we wires still an other telegram to Florrie and told her O.K. and then I set down and wrote her a check for ½ the money I got in the bank and I got $500.00 all together there so I wrote the check for ½ of that or $250.00 and maled it to her and if she cant get a long on that she would be a awfull spendrift because I am not only going to be a way untill March. You should ought to of heard the boys cheer when Callahan tells them I am going to make the hole trip but when he tells them I am going to pitch for the giants and not for the White Sox I bet Crawford and Speaker and them wisht I was going to stay to home but it is just like Callahan says if they bat against me all winter the pitchers they bat against next season will look easy to them and you wont be supprised Al if Crawford and Speaker hits a bout 500 next year and if they hit good you will know why it is. Steve Evans asked me was I all fixed up with cloths and I says No but I was going out and buy some cloths includeing a full dress suit of evening cloths and he says You dont need no full dress suit of evening cloths because you look funny enough with out them.

This Evans is a great kidder Al and no body never gets sore at the stuff he pulls some thing like Kid Gleason. I wisht Kid Gleason was going on the trip Al but I will tell him all a bout it when I come back.

Well Al old pal I wisht you was going a long to and I bet we could have the time of our life but I will write to you right a long Al and I will send Bertha some post cards from the diffrent places we head in at. I will try and write you a letter on the boat and male it as soon as we get to the 1st station which is either Japan or Yokohama I forgot which. Good by Al and say good by to Bertha for me and tell her how sorry I and Florrie is that we cant come to Bedford this winter but we will spend all the rest of the winters there and her and Florrie will have a plenty of time to get acquainted. Good by old pal.

Your pal,

JACK.

Seattle, Wash., Nov. 18.

AL: Well Al it is all off and I am not going on no trip a round the world and back and I been looking for Callahan or Mcgraw for the last ½ hour to tell them I have changed my mind and am not going to make no trip because it would not be fare to Florrie and besides that I think I should ought to stay home and take care of little Al and not leave him to be tooken care of by no train nurse because how do I know what would she do to him and I am not going to tell Florrie nothing a bout it but I am going to take the train to-morrow night right back to Chi and supprise her when I get there and I bet both her and little Al will be tickled to death to see me. I supose Mcgraw and Callahan will be sore at me for a while but when I tell them I want to do the right thing and not give my famly no raw deal I guess they will see where I am right.

We was to play 2 games here and was to play 1 of them in Tacoma and the other here but it rained and so we did not play neither 1 and the people was pretty mad a bout it because I was announced to pitch and they figured probily this would be there only chance to see me in axion and they made a awful holler but Comiskey says No they would not be no game be- cause the field neither here or in Tacoma was in no shape for a game and he would not take no chance of me pitching and may be slipping in the mud and straneing myself and then where would the White Sox be at next season. So we been laying a round all the P. M. and I and Dutch Schaefer had a long talk to gether while some of the rest of the boys was out buying some cloths to take on the trip and Al I bought a full dress suit of evening cloths at Portland yesterday and now I owe Callahan the money for them and am not going on no trip so probily I wont never get to ware them and it is just $45.00 throwed a way but I would rather throw $45.00 a way then go on a trip a round the world and leave my famly all winter.

Well Al I and Schaefer was talking to gether and he says Well may be this is the last time we will ever see the good old US and I says What do you mean and he says People that gos acrost the pacific Ocean most generally all ways has there ship recked and then they is not no more never heard from them. Then he asked me was I a good swimmer and I says Yes I had swam a good deal in the river and he says Yes you have swam in the river but that is not nothing like swimming in the pacific Ocean because when you swim in the pacific Ocean you cant move your feet because if you move your feet the sharks comes up to the top of the water and bites at them and even if they did not bite your feet clean off there bite is poison and gives you the hiderofobeya and when you get that you start barking like a dog and the water runs in to your mouth and chokes you to death. Then he says Of coarse if you can swim with out useing your feet you are all O.K. but they is very few can do that and especially in the pacific Ocean because they got to keep useing there hands all the time to scare the sord fish a way so when you dont dare use your feet and your hands is busy you got nothing left to swim with but your stumach mussles. Then he says You should ought to get a long all O.K. because your stumach mussles should ought to be strong from the ex- ercise they get so I guess they is not no danger from a man like you but men like Wiltse and Mike Donlin that is not hog fat like you has not got no chance. Then he says Of coarse they have been times when the boats got acrost all O.K. and only a few lives lost but it dont offten happen and the time the old Minneapolis club made the trip the boat went down and the only thing that was saved was the catchers protector that was full of air and could not do nothing else but flote. Then he says

May be you would flote to if you did not say nothing for a few days.

I asked him how far would a man got to swim if some thing went wrong with the boat and he says O not far because they is a hole lot of ilands a long the way that a man could swim to but it would not do a man no good to swim to these here ilands because they dont have nothing to eat on them and a man would probily starve to death un less he happened to swim to the sandwich ilands. Then he says But by the time you been out on the pacific Ocean a few months you wont care if you get any thing to eat or not. I says Why not and he says the pacific Ocean is so ruff that not nothing can set still not even the stuff you eat. I asked him how long did it take to make the trip acrost if they was not no ship reck and he says they should ought to get acrost a long in febuery if the weather was good. I says Well if we dont get there until febuery we wont have no time to train for next season and he says You wont need to do no training because this trip will take all the weight off of you and every thing else you got. Then he says But you should not ought to be scared of getting sea sick because they is 1 way you can get a way from it and that is to not eat nothing at all while you are on the boat and they tell me you dont eat hardly nothing any way so you wont miss it. Then he says Of coarse if we should have good luck and not get in to no ship reck and not get shot by 1 of them war ships we will have a grate time when we get acrost because all the girls in europe and them places is nuts over ball players and especially stars. I asked what did he mean saying we might get shot by 1 of them war ships and he says we would have to pass by Swittserland and the Swittserland war ships was all the time shooting all over the ocean and of coarse they was not trying to hit no body but they was as wild as most of them left handers and how could you tell what was they going to do next.

Well Al after I got threw talking to Schaefer I run in to Jack Sheridan the umpire and I says I did not think I would go on no trip and I told him some of the things Schaefer was telling me and Sheridan says Schaefer was kidding me and they was not no danger at all and of coarse Al I did not believe ½ of what Schaefer was telling me and that has not got nothing to do with me changeing my mind but I don't think it is not hardly fare for me to go a way on a trip like that and leave Florrie and the baby and suppose some of them things really did happen like Schaefer said though of coarse he was kidding me but if I of them was to happen they would not be no body left to take care of Florrie and little Al and I got a $1000.00 insurence policy but how do I know after I am dead if the insurence co. comes acrost and gives my famly the money.

Well Al I will male this letter and then try again and find Mcgraw and Callahan and then I will look up a time table and see what train can I get to Chi. I dont know yet when I will be in Bedford and may be Florrie has hired a flat all ready but the Allens can live in it by them self and if Allen says any thing a bout I paying for ½ of the rent I will bust his jaw.

Your pal,   JACK.

Victoria, Can., Nov. 19.

DEAR OLD AL: Well old pal the boat gos to-night I am going a long and I would not be takeing no time to write this letter only I wrote to you yesterday and says I was not going and you probily would be expecting to see me blow in to Bedford in a few days and besides Al I got a hole lot of things to ask you to do for me if any thing happens and I want to tell you how it come a bout that I changed my mind and am going on the trip. I am glad now that I did not write Florrie no letter yesterday and tell her I was not going because now I would have to write her an other letter and tell her I was going and she would be expecting to see me the day after she got the 1st letter and in stead of seeing me she would get this 2nd. letter and not me at all. I have all ready wrote her a good by letter to-day though and while I was writeing it Al I all most broke down and cried and espesially when I thought a bout leaveing little Al so long and may be when I see him again he wont be no baby no more or may be some thing will of happened to him or that train nurse did some thing to him or may be I wont never see him again no more because it is pretty near a cinch that some thing will either happen to I or him. I would give all most any thing I got Al to be back in Chi with little Al and Florrie and I wisht she had not of never wired that telegram telling me I could make the trip and if some thing happens to me think how she will feel when ever she thinks a bout wireing me that telegram and she will feel all most like as if she was a murder.

Well Al after I had wrote you that letter yesterday I found Callahan and Mcgraw and I tell them I have changed my mind and am not going on no trip. Callahan says Whats the matter and I says I dont think it would be fare to my wife and baby and Callahan says Your wife says it would be all O.K. because I seen the telegram my self. I says Yes but she dont know how dangerus the trip is and he says Whos been kiding you and I says They has not no body been kiding me. I says Dutch Schaefer told me a hole lot of stuff but I did not believe none of it and that has not got nothing to do with it. I says I am not a scared of nothing but supose some thing should happen and then where would my wife and baby be at. Then Callahan says Schaefer has been giveing you a lot of hot air and they is not no more danger on this trip then they is in bed. You been in a hole lot more danger when you was pitching some of them days when you had a sore arm and you would be takeing more chances of getting killed in Chi by 1 of them taxi cabs or the dog catcher then on the Ocean. This here boat we are going on is the Umpires of Japan and it has went acrost the Ocean a million times with out nothing happening and they could not nothing happen to a boat that the N. Y. giants was rideing on because they is to lucky. Then I says Well I have made up my mind to not go on no trip and he says All right then I guess we might is well call the trip off and I says Why and he says You know what president Wilson says a bout Japan and they wont stand for us comeing over there with out you a long and then Mcgraw says Yes it looks like as if the trip was off because we dont want to take no chance of starting no war between Japan and the united states. Then Callahan says You will be in fine with Comiskey if he has to call the trip off because you are a scared of getting hit by a fish. Well Al we talked and argude for a hour or a hour and ½ and some of the rest of the boys come a round and took Callahan and Mcgraw side and finely Callahan says it looked like as if they would have to posepone the trip a few days untill he could get a hold of Allen or some body and get them to take my place so finely I says I would go because I would not want to brake up no trip after they had made all there plans and some of the players wifes was all ready to go and would be dissapointed if they was not no trip. So Mcgraw and Callahan says Thats the way to talk and so I am going Al and we are leaveing to-night and may be this is the last letter you will ever get from me but if they does not nothing happen Al I will write to you a lot of letters and tell you all a bout the trip but you must not be looking for no more letters for a while untill we get to Japan where I can male a letter and may be its likely as not we wont never get to Japan.

Here is the things I want to ask you to try and do Al and I am not asking you to do nothing if we get threw the trip all right but if some thing happens and I should be drowned here is what I am asking you to do for me and that is to see that the insurence co. dont skin Florrie out of that $1000.00 policy and see that she all so gets that other $250.00 out of the bank and find her some place down in Bedford to live if she is willing to live down there because she can live there a hole lot cheaper then she can live in Chi and besides I know Bertha would treat her right and help her out all she could. All so Al I want you and Bertha to help take care of little Al untill he grows up big enough to take care of him self and if he looks like as if he was going to be left handed dont let him Al but make him use his right hand for every thing. Well Al they is 1 good thing and that is if I get drowned Florrie wont have to buy no lot in no cemetary and hire no herse.

Well Al old pal you all ways been a good friend of mine and I all ways tried to be a good friend of yourn and if they was ever any thing I done to you that was not O.K. remember by gones is by gones. I want you to all ways think of me as your best old pal. Good by old pal.

Your old pal,   JACK.

P.S. Al if they should not nothing happen and if we was to get acrost the Ocean all O.K. I am going to ask Mcgraw to let me work the 1st game against the White Sox in Japan because I should certainly ought to be right after giveing my arm a rest and not doing nothing at all on the trip acrost and I bet if Mcgraw lets me work Crawford and Speaker will wisht the boat had of sank. You know me Al.

FROM

GULLIBLE'S TRAVELS, ETC.

Carmen

WE WAS playin' rummy over to Hatch's, and Hatch must of fell in a bed of four-leaf clovers on his way home the night before, because he plays rummy like he does everything else; but this night I refer to you couldn't beat him, and besides him havin' all the luck my Missus played like she'd been bought off, so when we come to settle up we was plain seven and a half out. You know who paid it. So Hatch says:

"They must be some game you can play."

"No," I says, "not and beat you. I can run two blocks w'ile you're stoopin' over to start, but if we was runnin' a foot race between each other, and suppose I was leadin' by eighty yards, a flivver'd prob'ly come up and hit you in the back and bump you over the finishin' line ahead o' me."

So Mrs. Hatch thinks I'm sore on account o' the seven-fifty, so she says:

"It don't seem fair for us to have all the luck."

"Sure it's fair!" I says. "If you didn't have the luck, what would you have?"

"I know," she says; "but I don't never feel right winnin' money at cards."

"I don't blame you," I says.

"I know," she says; "but it seems like we should ought to give it back or else stand treat, either one."

"Jim's too old to change all his habits," I says.

"Oh, well," says Mrs. Hatch, "I guess if I told him to loosen up he'd loosen up. I ain't lived with him all these years for nothin'."

"You'd be a sucker if you did," I says.

So they all laughed, and when they'd quieted down Mrs. Hatch says:

"I don't suppose you'd feel like takin' the money back?"

"Not without a gun," I says. "Jim's pretty husky."

So that give them another good laugh; but finally she says:

"What do you say, Jim, to us takin' the money they lose to us and gettin' four tickets to some show?"

135

Jim managed to stay conscious, but he couldn't answer nothin'; so my Missus says:

"That'd be grand of you to do it, but don't think you got to."

Well, of course, Mrs. Hatch knowed all the w'ile she didn't have to, but from what my Missus says she could tell that if they really give us the invitation we wouldn't start no fight. So they talked it over between themself w'ile I and Hatch went out in the kitchen and split a pint o' beer, and Hatch done the pourin' and his best friend couldn't say he give himself the worst of it. So when we come back my Missus and Mrs. Hatch had it all framed that the Hatches was goin' to take us to a show, and the next thing was what show would it be. So Hatch found the afternoon paper, that somebody'd left on the street-car, and read us off a list o' the shows that was in town. I spoke for the Columbia, but the Missus give me the sign to stay out; so they argued back and forth and finally Mrs. Hatch says:

"Let's see that paper a minute."

"What for?" says Hatch. "I didn't hold nothin' out on you."

But he give her the paper and she run through the list herself, and then she says:

"You did, too, hold out on us. You didn't say nothin' about the Auditorium."

"What could I say about it?" says Hatch. "I never was inside."

"It's time you was then," says Mrs. Hatch.

"What's playin' there?" I says.

"Grand op'ra," says Mrs. Hatch.

"Oh!" says my Missus. "Wouldn't that be wonderful?"

"What do you say?" says Mrs. Hatch to me.

"I think it'd be grand for you girls," I says. "I and Jim could leave you there and go down on Madison and see Charley Chaplin, and then come back after you."

"Nothin' doin'!" says Mrs. Hatch. "We'll pick a show that everybody wants to see."

Well, if I hadn't of looked at my Missus then we'd of been O. K. But my eyes happened to light on where she was settin' and she was chewin' her lips so's she wouldn't cry. That finished me. "I was just kiddin'," I says to Mrs. Hatch. "They ain't nothin' I'd like better than grand op'ra."

"Nothin' except gettin' trimmed in a rummy game," says Hatch, but he didn't get no rise.

Well, the Missus let loose of her lips so's she could smile and her and Mrs. Hatch got all excited, and I and Hatch pretended like we was excited too. So Hatch ast what night could we go, and Mrs. Hatch says that depended on what did we want to hear, because they changed the bill every day. So her and the Missus looked at the paper again and found out where Friday night was goin' to be a big special night and the bill was a musical show called *Carmen*, and all the stars was goin' to sing, includin' Mooratory and Alda and Genevieve Farr'r, that was in the movies a w'ile till they found out she could sing, and some fella they called Daddy, but I don't know his real name. So the girls both says Friday night was the best, but Hatch says he would have to go to lodge that evenin'.

"Lodge!" says Mrs. Hatch. "What do you care about lodge when you got a chance to see Genevieve Farr'r in *Carmen?*"

"Chance!" says Hatch. "If that's what you call a chance, I got a chance to buy a thousand shares o' Bethlehem Steel. Who's goin' to pay for my chance?"

"All right," says Mrs. Hatch, "go to your old lodge and spoil everything!"

So this time it was her that choked up and made like she was goin' to blubber. So Hatch changed his mind all of a sudden and decided to disappoint the brother Owls. So all of us was satisfied except fifty per cent., and I and the Missus beat it home, and on the way she says how nice Mrs. Hatch was to give us this treat.

"Yes," I says, "but if you hadn't of had a regular epidemic o' discardin' deuces and treys Hatch would of treated us to groceries for a week." I says: "I always thought they was only twelve pitcher cards in the deck till I seen them hands you saved up to-night."

"You lose as much as I did," she says.

"Yes," I says, "and I always will as long as you forget to fetch your purse along."

So they wasn't no comeback to that, so we went on home without no more dialogue.

Well, Mrs. Hatch called up the next night and says Jim had the tickets boughten and we was to be sure and be ready at seven o'clock Friday night because the show started at eight. So when I was down-town Friday the Missus sent my evenin' dress suit over to Katzes' and had it pressed up and when I come home it was laid out on the bed like a corpse.

"What's that for?" I says.

"For the op'ra," she says. "Everybody wears them to the op'ra."

"Did you ask the Hatches what was they goin' to wear?" I says.

"No," says she. "They know what to wear without me tellin' them. They ain't goin' to the Auditorium in their nightgown."

So I clumb into the soup and fish, and the Missus spent about a hour puttin' on a dress that she could have left off without nobody knowin' the difference, and she didn't have time for no supper at all, and I just managed to surround a piece o' steak as big as your eye and spill some gravy on my clo'es when the bell rung and there was the Hatches.

Well, Hatch didn't have no more evenin' dress suit on than a kewpie. I could see his pants under his overcoat and they was the same old bay pants he'd wore the day he got mad at his kid and christened him Kenneth. And his shoes was a last year's edition o' the kind that's supposed to give your feet a chance, and if his feet had of been the kind that takes chances they was two or three places where they could of got away without much trouble.

I could tell from the expression on Mrs. Hatch's face when she seen our make-up that we'd crossed her. She looked about as comf'table as a Belgium.

"Oh!" she says. "I didn't think you'd dress up."

"We thought you would," says my Frau.

"We!" I says. "Where do you get that 'we'?"

"If it ain't too late we'll run in and change," says my Missus.

"Not me," I says. "I didn't go to all this trouble and expense for a splash o' gravy. When this here uniform retires it'll be to make room for pyjamas."

"Come on!" says Hatch. "What's the difference? You can pretend like you ain't with us."

"It don't really make no difference," says Mrs. Hatch.

And maybe it didn't. But we all stood within whisperin' distance of each other on the car goin' in, and if you had a dollar for every word that was talked among us you couldn't mail a postcard from Hammond to Gary. When we got off at Congress my Missus tried to thaw out the party.

"The prices is awful high, aren't they?" she says.

"Outrageous," says Mrs. Hatch.

Well, even if the prices was awful high, they didn't have nothin' on our seats. If I was in trainin' to be a steeple jack I'd go to grand op'ra every night and leave Hatch buy my ticket. And where he took us I'd of been more at home in overalls and a sport shirt.

"How do you like Denver?" says I to the Missus, but she'd sank for the third time.

"We're safe here," I says to Hatch. "Them French guns can't never reach us. We'd ought to brought more bumbs."

"What did the seats cost?" I says to Hatch.

"One-fifty," he says.

"Very reasonable," says I. "One o' them aviators wouldn't take you more than half this height for a five-spot."

The Hatches had their overcoats off by this time and I got a look at their full costume. Hatch had went without his vest durin' the hot months and when it was alongside his coat and pants it looked like two different families. He had a pink shirt with prune-colored horizontal bars, and a tie to match his neck, and a collar that would of took care of him and I both, and them shoes I told you about, and burlap hosiery. They wasn't nothin' the matter with Mrs. Hatch except she must of thought that, instead o' dressin' for the op'ra, she was gettin' ready for Kenneth's bath.

And there was my Missus, just within the law, and me all spicked and spanned with my soup and fish and gravy!

Well, we all set there and tried to get the focus till about a half-hour after the show was billed to commence, and finally a Lilliputian with a match in his hand come out and started up the orchestry and they played a few o' the hits and then the lights was turned out and up went the curtain.

Well, sir, you'd be surprised at how good we could hear and see after we got used to it. But the hearin' didn't do us no good—that is, the words part of it. All the actors had been smuggled in from Europe and they wasn't none o' them that could talk English. So all their songs was gave in different languages and I wouldn't of never knew what was goin' on only for Hatch havin' all the nerve in the world.

After the first act a lady that was settin' in front of us dropped somethin' and Hatch stooped over and picked it up, and it was one o' these here books they call a liberetto, and it's got all the words they're singin' on the stage wrote out in English.

So the lady begin lookin' all over for it and Hatch was goin' to give it back because he thought it was a shoe catalogue, but he happened to see at the top of it where it says "Price 25 Cents," so he tossed it in his lap and stuck his hat over it. And the lady kept lookin' and lookin' and finally she turned round and looked Hatch right in the eye, but he dropped down inside his collar and left her wear herself out. So when she'd gave up I says somethin' about I'd like to have a drink.

"Let's go," says Hatch.

"No," I says. "I don't want it bad enough to go back to town after it. I thought maybe we could get it sent up to the room."

"I'm goin' alone then," says Hatch.

"You're liable to miss the second act," I says.

"I'd never miss it," says Hatch.

"All right," says I. "I hope you have good weather."

So he slipped me the book to keep for him and beat it. So I seen the lady had forgot us, and I opened up the book and that's how I come to find out what the show was about. I read her all through, the part that was in English, before the curtain went up again, so when the second act begin I knowed what had came off and what was comin' off, and Hatch and Mrs. Hatch hadn't no idear if the show was comical or dry. My Missus hadn't, neither, till we got home and I told her the plot.

Carmen ain't no regular musical show where a couple o' Yids comes out and pulls a few lines o' dialogue and then a girl and a he-flirt sings a song that ain't got nothin' to do with it. *Carmen*'s a regular play, only instead o' them sayin' the lines, they sing them, and in for'n languages so's the actors can pick up some loose change offen the sale o' the liberettos. The music was wrote by George S. Busy, and it must of kept him that way about two mont's. The words was either throwed together by

the stage carpenter or else took down by a stenographer outdoors durin' a drizzle. Anyway, they ain't nobody claims them.
Every oncet in three or four pages they forget themself and
rhyme. You got to read each verse over two or three times before you learn what they're hintin' at, but the management
gives you plenty o' time to do it between acts and still sneak a
couple o' hours' sleep.

The first act opens up somewheres in Spain, about the corner o' Chicago Avenue and Wells. On one side o' the stage
they's a pill mill where the employees is all girls, or was girls a
few years ago. On the other side they's a soldiers' garage where
they keep the militia in case of a strike. In the back o' the stage
they's a bridge, but it ain't over no water or no railroad tracks
or nothin'. It's prob'ly somethin' the cat dragged in.

Well, the soldiers stands out in front o' the garage hittin' up
some barber shops, and pretty soon a girl blows in from the
hero's home town, Janesville or somewheres. She runs a few
steps every little w'ile and then stops, like the rails was slippery.
The soldiers sings at her and she tells them she's came to look
for Don Joss that run the chop-suey dump up to Janesville,
but when they shet down on him servin' beer he quit and
joined the army. So the soldiers never heard o' the bird, but
they all ask her if they won't do just as good, but she says
nothin' doin' and skids off the stage. She ain't no sooner gone
when the Chinaman from Janesville and some more soldiers
and some alley rats comes in to help out the singin'. The book
says that this new gang o' soldiers was sent on to relieve the
others, but if anything happened to wear out the first ones it
must of took place at rehearsal. Well, one o' the boys tells Joss
about the girl askin' for him and he says: "Oh, yes; that must
be the little Michaels girl from up in Wisconsin."

So pretty soon the whistle blows for noon and the girls
comes out o' the pill mill smokin' up the mornin' receipts and
a crowd o' the unemployed comes in to shoot the snipes. So
the soldiers notices that Genevieve Farr'r ain't on yet, so they
ask where she's at, and that's her cue. She puts on a song number and a Spanish dance, and then she slips her bouquet to the
Chink, though he ain't sang a note since the whistle blowed.
But now it's one o'clock and Genevieve and the rest o' the
girls beats it back to the coffin factory and the vags chases

down to the Loop to get the last home edition and look at the want ads to see if they's any jobs open with fair pay and nothin' to do. And the soldiers mosey into the garage for a well-earned rest and that leaves Don all alone on the stage.

But he ain't no more than started on his next song when back comes the Michaels girl. It oozes out here that she's in love with the Joss party, but she stalls and pretends like his mother'd sent her to get the receipt for makin' eggs *fo yung*. And she says his mother ast her to kiss him and she slips him a dime, so he leaves her kiss him on the scalp and he asks her if she can stay in town that evenin' and see a nickel show, but they's a important meetin' o' the Maccabees at Janesville that night, so away she goes to catch the two-ten and Don starts in on another song number, but the rest o' the company don't like his stuff and he ain't hardly past the vamp when they's a riot.

It seems like Genevieve and one o' the chorus girls has quarreled over a second-hand stick o' gum and the chorus girl got the gum, but Genevieve relieved her of part of a earlobe, so they pinch Genevieve and leave Joss to watch her till the wagon comes, but the wagon's went out to the night desk sergeant's house with a case o' quarts and before it gets round to pick up Genevieve she's bunked the Chink into settin' her free. So she makes a getaway, tellin' Don to meet her later on at Lily and Pat's place acrost the Indiana line. So that winds up the first act.

Well, the next act's out to Lily and Pat's, and it ain't no Y. M. C. A. headquarters, but it's a hang-out for dips and policemans. They's a cabaret and Genevieve's one o' the performers, but she forgets the words to her first song and winds up with tra-la-la, and she could of forgot the whole song as far as I'm concerned, because it wasn't nothin' you'd want to buy and take along home.

Finally Pat comes in and says it's one o'clock and he's got to close up, but they won't none o' them make a move, and pretty soon they's a live one blows into the joint and he's Eskimo Bill, one o' the butchers out to the Yards. He's got paid that day and he ain't never goin' home. He sings a song and it's the hit o' the show. Then he buys a drink and starts flirtin' with Genevieve, but Pat chases everybody but the performers and a couple o' dips that ain't got nowheres else to sleep. The dips or stick-up guys, or whatever they are, tries to get Genevieve to go along with them in the car w'ile they pull off somethin', but she's still expectin' the Chinaman. So they pass her up and blow, and along comes Don and she lets him in, and it seems like he'd been in jail for two mont's, or ever since the end o' the first act. So he asks her how everything has been goin' down to the pill mill and she tells him that she's quit and became a entertainer. So he says, "What can you do?" And she beats time with a pair o' chopsticks and dances the Chinese Blues.

After a w'ile they's a bugle call somewhere outdoors and Don says that means he's got to go back to the garage. So she gets sore and tries to bean him with a Spanish onion. Then he reaches inside his coat and pulls out the bouquet she give him in Atto First to show her he ain't changed his clo'es, and then the sheriff comes in and tries to coax him with a razor to go back to his job. They fight like it was the first time either o' them ever tried it and the sheriff's leadin' on points when Genevieve hollers for the dips, who dashes in with their gats pulled and it's good night, Mister Sheriff! They put him in moth balls and they ask Joss to join their tong. He says all right and they're all pretty well lit by this time and they've reached the singin' stage, and Pat can't get them to go home and he's scared some o' the Hammond people'll put in a complaint, so he has the curtain rang down.

Then they's a relapse of it don't say how long, and Don and Genevieve and the yeggs and their lady friends is all out in the country somewheres attendin' a Bohunk Sokol Verein picnic and Don starts whinin' about his old lady that he'd left up to Janesville.

"I wisht I was back there," he says.

"You got nothin' on me," says Genevieve. "Only Janesville ain't far enough. I wisht you was back in Hongkong."

So w'ile they're flatterin' each other back and forth, a couple o' the girls is monkeyin' with the pasteboards and tellin' their fortunes, and one o' them turns up a two-spot and that's a sign they're goin' to sing a duet. So it comes true and then Genevieve horns into the game and they play three-handed rummy, singin' all the w'ile to bother each other, but finally the fellas that's runnin' the picnic says it's time for the fat man's one-legged race and everybody goes offen the stage. So the Michaels girl comes on and is gettin' by pretty good with a song when she's scared by the noise o' the gun that's fired to start the race for the bay-window championship. So she trips back to her dressin'-room and then Don and Eskimo Bill put on a little slap-stick stuff.

When they first meet they're pals, but as soon as they get wise that the both o' them's bugs over the same girl their relations to'rds each other becomes strange. Here's the talk they spill:

"Where do you tend bar?" says Don.

"You got me guessed wrong," says Bill. "I work out to the Yards."

"Got anything on the hip?" says Don.

"You took the words out o' my mouth," says Bill. "I'm drier than St. Petersgrad."

"Stick round a w'ile and maybe we can scare up somethin'," says Don.

"I'll stick all right," says Bill. "They's a Jane in your party that's knocked me dead."

"What's her name?" says Don.

"Carmen," says Bill, Carmen bein' the girl's name in the show that Genevieve was takin' that part.

"Carmen!" says Joss. "Get offen that stuff! I and Carmen's just like two pavin' bricks."

"I should worry!" says Bill. "I ain't goin' to run away from no rat-eater."

"You're a rat-eater yourself, you rat-eater!" says Don.

"I'll rat-eat you!" says Bill.

And they go to it with a carvin' set, but they couldn't neither one o' them handle their utensils.

Don may of been all right slicin' toad-stools for the suey and Bill prob'ly could of massacreed a flock o' sheep with one stab, but they was all up in the air when it come to stickin' each other. They'd of did it better with dice.

Pretty soon the other actors can't stand it no longer and they come on yellin' "Fake!" So Don and Bill fold up their razors and Bill invites the whole bunch to come out and go through the Yards some mornin' and then he beats it, and the Michaels girl ain't did nothin' for fifteen minutes, so the management shoots her out for another song and she sings to Don about how he should ought to go home on account of his old lady bein' sick, so he asks Genevieve if she cares if he goes back to Janesville.

"Sure, I care," says Genevieve. "Go ahead!"

So the act winds up with everybody satisfied.

The last act's outside the Yards on the Halsted Street end. Bill's ast the entire company to come in and watch him croak a steer. The scene opens up with the crowd buyin' perfume and smellin' salts from the guys that's got the concessions. Pretty soon Eskimo Bill and Carmen drive in, all dressed up like a horse. Don's came in from Wisconsin and is hidin' in the bunch. He's sore at Carmen for not meetin' him on the Elevated platform.

He lays low till everybody's went inside, only Carmen. Then he braces her. He tells her his old lady's died and left him the laundry, and he wants her to go in with him and do the ironin'.

"Not me!" she says.

"What do you mean—'Not me'?" says Don.

"I and Bill's goin' to run a kosher market," she says.

Just about now you can hear noises behind the scenes like the cattle's gettin' theirs, so Carmen don't want to miss none of it, so she makes a break for the gate.

"Where you goin'?" says Joss.

"I want to see the butcherin'," she says.

"Stick round and I'll show you how it's done," says Joss.

So he pulls his knife and makes a pass at her, just foolin'. He misses her as far as from here to Des Moines. But she don't know he's kiddin' and she's scared to death. Yes, sir, she topples over as dead as the Federal League.

It was prob'ly her heart.

So now the whole crowd comes dashin' out because they's been a report that the place is infested with the hoof and mouth disease. They tell Don about it, but he's all excited over Carmen dyin'. He's delirious and gets himself mixed up with a Irish policeman.

"I yield me prisoner," he says.

Then the house doctor says the curtain's got to come down to prevent the epidemic from spreadin' to the audience. So the show's over and the company's quarantined.

Well, Hatch was out all durin' the second act and part o' the third, and when he finally come back he didn't have to tell nobody where he'd been. And he dozed off the minute he hit his seat. I was for lettin' him sleep so's the rest o' the audience'd think we had one o' the op'ra bass singers in our party. But Mrs. Hatch wasn't lookin' for no publicity, on account of her costume, so she reached over and prodded him with a hatpin every time he begin a new aria.

Goin' out, I says to him:

"How'd you like it?"

"Pretty good," he says, "only they was too much gin in the last one."

"I mean the op'ra," I says.

"Don't ask him!" says Mrs. Hatch. "He didn't hear half of it and he didn't understand none of it."

"Oh, I wouldn't say that," says I. "Jim here ain't no boob, and they wasn't nothin' hard about it to understand."

"Not if you know the plot," says Mrs. Hatch.

"And somethin' about music," says my Missus.

"And got a little knowledge o' French," says Mrs. Hatch.

"Was that French they was singin'?" says Hatch. "I thought it was Wop or ostrich."

"That shows you up," says his Frau.

Well, when we got on the car for home they wasn't only one vacant seat and, o' course, Hatch had to have that. So I and my Missus and Mrs. Hatch clubbed together on the straps and I got a earful o' the real dope.

"What do you think o' Farr'r's costumes?" says Mrs. Hatch.

"Heavenly!" says my Missus. "Specially the one in the second act. It was all colors o' the rainbow."

"Hatch is right in style then," I says.

"And her actin' is perfect," says Mrs. Hatch.

"Her voice too," says the Wife.

"I liked her actin' better," says Mrs. H. "I thought her voice yodeled in the up-stairs registers."

"What do you suppose killed her?" I says.

"She was stabbed by her lover," says the Missus.

"You wasn't lookin'," I says. "He never touched her. It was prob'ly tobacco heart."

"He stabs her in the book," says Mrs. Hatch.

"It never went through the bindin'," I says.

"And wasn't Mooratory grand?" says the Wife.

"Splendid!" says Mrs. Hatch. "His actin' and singin' was both grand."

"I preferred his actin'," I says. "I thought his voice hissed in the down-stairs radiators."

This give them a good laugh, but they was soon at it again.

"And how sweet Alda was!" my Missus remarks.

"Which was her?" I ast them.

"The good girl," says Mrs. Hatch. "The girl that sung that beautiful aria in Atto Three."

"Atto girl!" I says. "I liked her too; the little Michaels girl. She came from Janesville."

"She did!" says Mrs. Hatch. "How do you know?"

So I thought I'd kid them along.

"My uncle told me," I says. "He used to be postmaster up there."

"What uncle was that?" says my wife.

"He ain't really my uncle," I says. "We all used to call him our uncle just like all these here singers calls the one o' them Daddy."

"They was a lady in back o' me," says Mrs. Hatch, "that says Daddy didn't appear tonight."

"Prob'ly the Missus' night out," I says.

"How'd you like the Tor'ador?" says Mrs. Hatch.

"I thought she moaned in the chimney," says I.

"It wasn't no 'she'," says the Missus. "We're talkin' about the bull-fighter."

"I didn't see no bull-fight," I says.

"It come off behind the scenes," says the Missus.

"When was you behind the scenes?" I says.

"I wasn't never," says my Missus. "But that's where it's supposed to come off."

"Well," I says, "you can take it from me that it wasn't pulled. Do you think the mayor'd stand for that stuff when he won't even leave them stage a box fight? You two girls has got a fine idear o' this here op'ra!"

"You know all about it, I guess," says the Missus. "You talk French so good!"

"I talk as much French as you do," I says. "But not nowheres near as much English, if you could call it that."

That kept her quiet, but Mrs. Hatch buzzed all the way

home, and she was scared to death that the motorman wouldn't know where she'd been spendin' the evenin'. And if there was anybody in the car besides me that knowed *Carmen* it must of been a joke to them hearin' her chatter. It wasn't no joke to me though. Hatch's berth was way off from us and they didn't nobody suspect him o' bein' in our party. I was standin' right up there with her where people couldn't help seein' that we was together.

I didn't want them to think she was my wife. So I kept smilin' at her. And when it finally come time to get off I hollered out loud at Hatch and says:

"All right, Hatch! Here's our street. Your Missus'll keep you awake the rest o' the way with her liberetto."

"It can't hurt no more than them hatpins," he says.

Well, when the paper come the next mornin' my Missus had to grab it up and turn right away to the place where the op'ras is wrote up. Under the article they was a list o' the ladies and gents in the boxes and what they wore, but it didn't say nothin' about what the gents wore, only the ladies. Prob'ly the ladies happened to have the most comical costumes that night, but I bet if the reporters could of saw Hatch they would of gave him a page to himself.

"Is your name there?" I says to the Missus.

"O' course not," she says. "They wasn't none o' them reporters tall enough to see us. You got to set in a box to be mentioned."

"Well," I says, "you don't care nothin' about bein' mentioned, do you?"

"O' course not," she says; but I could tell from how she said it that she wouldn't run down-town and horsewhip the editor if he made a mistake and printed about she and her costume; her costume wouldn't of et up all the space he had neither.

"How much does box seats cost?" I ast her.

"About six or seven dollars," she says.

"Well," I says, "let's I and you show Hatch up."

"What do you mean?" she says.

"I mean we should ought to return the compliment," says I. "We should ought to give them a party right back."

"We'd be broke for six weeks," she says.

"Oh, we'd do it with their money like they done it with ours," I says.

"Yes," she says; "but if you can ever win enough from the Hatches to buy four box seats to the op'ra I'd rather spend the money on a dress."

"Who said anything about four box seats?" I ast her.

"You did," she says.

"You're delirious!" I says. "Two box seats will be a plenty."

"Who's to set in them?" ast the Missus.

"Who do you think?" I says. "I and you is to set in them."

"But what about the Hatches?" she says.

"They'll set up where they was," says I. "Hatch picked out the seats before, and if he hadn't of wanted that altitude he'd of bought somewheres else."

"Yes," says the Missus, "but Mrs. Hatch won't think we're very polite to plant our guests in the Alps and we set down in a box."

"But they won't know where we're settin'," I says. "We'll tell them we couldn't get four seats together, so for them to set where they was the last time and we're goin' elsewheres."

"It don't seem fair," says my wife.

"I should worry about bein' fair with Hatch," I says. "If he's ever left with more than a dime's worth o' cards you got to look under the table for his hand."

"It don't seem fair," says the Missus.

"You should worry!" I says.

So we ast them over the followin' night and it looked for a minute like we was goin' to clean up. But after that one minute my Missus began collectin' pitcher cards again and every card Hatch drawed seemed like it was made to his measure. Well, sir, when we was through the lucky stiff was eight dollars to the good and Mrs. Hatch had about broke even.

"Do you suppose you can get them same seats?" I says.

"What seats?" says Hatch.

"For the op'ra," I says.

"You won't get me to no more op'ra," says Hatch. "I don't never go to the same show twicet."

"It ain't the same show, you goof!" I says. "They change the bill every day."

"They ain't goin' to change this eight-dollar bill o' mine," he says.

"You're a fine stiff!" I says.

"Call me anything you want to," says Hatch, "as long as you don't go over eight bucks' worth."

"Jim don't enjoy op'ra," says Mrs. Hatch.

"He don't enjoy nothin' that's more than a nickel," I says. "But as long as he's goin' to welsh on us I hope he lavishes the eight-spot where it'll do him some good."

"I'll do what I want to with it," says Hatch.

"Sure you will!" I says. "You'll bury it. But what you should ought to do is buy two suits o' clo'es."

So I went out in the kitchen and split a pint one way.

But don't think for a minute that I and the Missus ain't goin' to hear no more op'ra just because of a cheap stiff like him welshin'. I don't have to win in no rummy game before I spend.

We're goin' next Tuesday night, I and the Missus, and we're goin' to set somewheres near Congress Street. The show's *Armour's Do Re Me*, a new one that's bein' gave for the first time. It's prob'ly named after some soap.

Gullible's Travels

I PROMISED the Wife that if anybody ast me what kind of a time did I have at Palm Beach I'd say I had a swell time. And if they ast me who did we meet I'd tell 'em everybody that was worth meetin'. And if they ast me didn't the trip cost a lot I'd say Yes; but it was worth the money. I promised her I wouldn't spill none o' the real details. But if you can't break a promise you made to your own wife what kind of a promise can you break? Answer me that, Edgar.

I'm not one o' these kind o' people that'd keep a joke to themself just because the joke was on them. But they's plenty of our friends that I wouldn't have 'em hear about it for the world. I wouldn't tell you, only I know you're not the village gossip and won't crack it to anybody. Not even to your own Missus, see? I don't trust no women.

It was along last January when I and the Wife was both hit by the society bacillus. I think it was at the opera. You remember me tellin' you about us and the Hatches goin' to *Carmen* and then me takin' my Missus and her sister, Bess, and four of one suit named Bishop to see *The Three Kings?* Well, I'll own up that I enjoyed wearin' the soup and fish and minglin' amongst the high polloi and pretendin' we really was somebody. And I know my wife enjoyed it, too, though they was nothin' said between us at the time.

The next stage was where our friends wasn't good enough for us no more. We used to be tickled to death to spend an evenin' playin' rummy with the Hatches. But all of a sudden they didn't seem to be no fun in it and when Hatch'd call up we'd stall out of it. From the number o' times I told him that I or the Missus was tired out and goin' right to bed, he must of thought we'd got jobs as telephone linemen.

We quit attendin' pitcher shows because the rest o' the audience wasn't the kind o' people you'd care to mix with. We didn't go over to Ben's and dance because they wasn't no class to the crowd there. About once a week we'd beat it to one o' the good hotels down-town, all dressed up like a horse, and have our dinner with the rest o' the E-light. They wasn't no-body talked to us only the waiters, but we could look as much as we liked and it was sport tryin' to guess the names o' the gang at the next table.

Then we took to readin' the society news at breakfast. It used to be that I didn't waste time on nothin' but the market and sportin' pages, but now I pass 'em up and listen w'ile the Missus rattled off what was doin' on the Lake Shore Drive.

Every little w'ile we'd see where So-and-So was at Palm Beach or just goin' there or just comin' back. We got to kiddin' about it.

"Well," I'd say, "we'd better be startin' pretty soon or we'll miss the best part o' the season."

"Yes," the Wife'd say back, "we'd go right now if it wasn't for all them engagements next week."

We kidded and kidded till finally, one night, she forgot we was just kiddin'.

"You didn't take no vacation last summer," she says.

"No," says I. "They wasn't no chance to get away."

"But you promised me," she says, "that you'd take one this winter to make up for it."

"I know I did," I says; "but it'd be a sucker play to take a vacation in weather like this."

"The weather ain't like this everywheres," she says.

"You must of been goin' to night school," I says.

"Another thing you promised me," says she, "was that when you could afford it you'd take me on a real honeymoon trip to make up for the dinky one we had."

"That still goes," I says, "when I can afford it."

"You can afford it now," says she. "We don't owe nothin' and we got money in the bank."

"Yes," I says. "Pretty close to three hundred bucks."

"You forgot somethin'," she says. "You forgot them war ba-bies."

Did I tell you about that? Last fall I done a little dabblin' in Crucial Steel and at this time I'm tellin' you about I still had a hold of it, but stood to pull down six hundred. Not bad, eh?

"It'd be a mistake to let loose now," I says.

"All right," she says. "Hold on, and I hope you lose every cent. You never did care nothin' for me."

Then we done a little spoonin' and then I ast her what was the big idear.

"We ain't swelled on ourself," she says; "but I know and you know that the friends we been associatin' with ain't in our class. They don't know how to dress and they can't talk about nothin' but their goldfish and their meat bills. They don't try to get nowheres, but all they do is play rummy and take in the Majestic. I and you like nice people and good music and things that's worth w'ile. It's a crime for us to be wastin' our time with riff and raff that'd run round barefooted if it wasn't for the police."

"I wouldn't say we'd wasted much time on 'em lately," I says.

"No," says she, "and I've had a better time these last three weeks than I ever had in my life."

"And you can keep right on havin' it," I says.

"I could have a whole lot better time, and you could, too," she says, "if we could get acquainted with some congenial people to go round with; people that's tastes is the same as ourn."

"If any o' them people calls up on the phone," I says, "I'll be as pleasant to 'em as I can."

"You're always too smart," says the Wife. "You don't never pay attention to no schemes o' mine."

"What's the scheme now?"

"You'll find fault with it because I thought it up," she says. "If it was your scheme you'd think it was grand."

"If it really was good you wouldn't be scared to spring it," I says.

"Will you promise to go through with it?" says she.

"If it ain't too ridic'lous," I told her.

"See! I knowed that'd be the way," she says.

"Don't talk crazy," I says. "Where'd we be if we'd went through with every plan you ever sprang?"

"Will you promise to listen to my side of it without actin' cute?" she says.

So I didn't see no harm in goin' that far.

"I want you to take me to Palm Beach," says she. "I want you to take a vacation, and that's where we'll spend it."

"And that ain't all we'd spend," I says.

"Remember your promise," says she.

So I shut up and listened.

The dope she give me was along these lines: We could get special round-trip rates on any o' the railroads and that part of it wouldn't cost nowheres near as much as a man'd naturally think. The hotel rates was pretty steep, but the meals was throwed in, and just imagine what them meals would be! And we'd be stayin' under the same roof with the Vanderbilts and Goulds, and eatin' at the same table, and probably, before we was there a week, callin' 'em Steve and Gus. They was dancin' every night and all the guests danced with each other, and how would it feel fox-trottin' with the president o' the B. & O., or the Delmonico girls from New York! And all Chicago society was down there, and when we met 'em we'd know 'em for life and have some real friends amongst 'em when we got back home.

That's how she had it figured and she must of been practisin' her speech, because it certainly did sound good to me. To make it short, I fell, and dated her up to meet me down-town the next day and call on the railroad bandits. The first one we seen admitted that his was the best route and that he wouldn't only soak us one hundred and forty-seven dollars and seventy cents to and from Palm Beach and back, includin' an apartment from here to Jacksonville and as many stop-overs as we wanted to make. He told us we wouldn't have to write for no hotel accommodations because the hotels had an agent right over on Madison Street that'd be glad to do everything to us.

So we says we'd be back later and then we beat it over to the Florida East Coast's local studio.

"How much for a double room by the week?" I ast the man.

"They ain't no weekly rates," he says. "By the day it'd be twelve dollars and up for two at the Breakers, and fourteen dollars and up at the Poinciana."

"I like the Breakers better," says I.

"You can't get in there," he says. "They're full for the season."

"That's a long spree," I says.

"Can we get in the other hotel?" ast the Wife.

"I can find out," says the man.

"We want a room with bath," says she.

"That'd be more," says he. "That'd be fifteen dollars or six-teen dollars and up."

"What do we want of a bath," I says, "with the whole Atlantic Ocean in the front yard?"

"I'm afraid you'd have trouble gettin' a bath," says the man. "The hotels is both o' them pretty well filled up on account o' the war in Europe."

"What's that got to do with it?" I ast him.

"A whole lot," he says. "The people that usually goes abroad is all down to Palm Beach this winter."

"I don't see why," I says. "If one o' them U-boats hit 'em they'd at least be gettin' their bath for nothin'."

We left him with the understandin' that he was to wire down there and find out what was the best they could give us. We called him up in a couple o' days and he told us we could have a double room, without no bath, at the Poinciana, beginnin' the fifteenth o' February. He didn't know just what the price would be.

Well, I fixed it up to take my vacation startin' the tenth, and sold out my Crucial Steel, and divided the spoils with the railroad company. We decided we'd stop off in St. Augustine two days, because the Missus found out somewheres that they might be two or three o' the Four Hundred lingerin' there, and we didn't want to miss nobody.

"Now," I says, "all we got to do is set round and wait for the tenth o' the month."

"Is that so!" says the Wife. "I suppose you're perfectly satisfied with your clo'es."

"I've got to be," I says, "unless the Salvation Army has somethin' that'll fit me."

"What's the matter with our charge account?" she says.

"I don't like to charge nothin'," I says, "when I know they ain't no chance of ever payin' for it."

"All right," she says, "then we're not goin' to Palm Beach. I'd rather stay home than go down there lookin' like general housework."

"Do you need clo'es yourself?" I ast her.

"I certainly do," she says. "About two hundred dollars' worth. But I got one hundred and fifty dollars o' my own."

"All right," I says. "I'll stand for the other fifty and then we're all set."

"No, we're not," she says. "That just fixes me. But I want you to look as good as I do."

"Nature'll see to that," I says.

But they was no arguin' with her. Our trip, she says, was an investment; it was goin' to get us in right with people worth w'ile. And we wouldn't have a chance in the world unless we looked the part.

So before the tenth come round, we was long two new evenin' gowns, two female sport suits, four or five pairs o' shoes, all colors, one Tuxedo dinner coat, three dress shirts, half a dozen other kinds o' shirts, two pairs o' transparent white trousers, one new business suit and Lord knows how much underwear and how many hats and stockin's. And I had till the fifteenth o' March to pay off the mortgage on the old homestead.

Just as we was gettin' ready to leave for the train the phone rung. It was Mrs. Hatch and she wanted us to come over for a little rummy. I was shavin' and the Missus done the talkin'.

"What did you tell her?" I ast.

"I told her we was goin' away," says the Wife.

"I bet you forgot to mention where we was goin'," I says.

"Pay me," says she.

II

I thought we was in Venice when we woke up next mornin', but the porter says it was just Cairo, Illinois. The river'd went crazy and I bet they wasn't a room without a bath in that old burg.

As we set down in the diner for breakfast the train was goin' acrost the longest bridge I ever seen, and it looked like we was so near the water that you could reach right out and grab a handful. The Wife was a little wabbly.

"I wonder if it's really safe," she says.

"If the bridge stays up we're all right," says I.

"But the question is, Will it stay up?" she says.

"I wouldn't bet a nickel either way on a bridge," I says. "They're treacherous little devils. They'd cross you as quick as they'd cross this river."

"The trainmen must be nervous," she says. "Just see how we're draggin' along."

"They're givin' the fish a chance to get offen the track," I says. "It's against the law to spear fish with a cowcatcher this time o' year."

Well, the Wife was so nervous she couldn't eat nothin' but toast and coffee, so I figured I was justified in goin' to the prunes and steak and eggs.

After breakfast we went out in what they call the sun parlor. It was a glassed-in room on the tail-end o' the rear coach and it must of been a pleasant place to set and watch the scenery. But they was a gang o' missionaries or somethin' had all the seats and they never budged out o' them all day. Every time they'd come to a crossroads they'd toss a stack o' Bible studies out o' the back window for the southern heathen to pick up and read. I suppose they thought they was doin' a lot o' good for their fellow men, but their fellow passengers meanw'ile was gettin' the worst of it.

Speakin' o' the scenery, it certainly was somethin' grand. First we'd pass a few pine trees with fuzz on 'em and then a couple o' acres o' yellow mud. Then they'd be more pine trees and more fuzz and then more yellow mud. And after a w'ile we'd come to some pine trees with fuzz on 'em and then, if we watched close, we'd see some yellow mud.

Every few minutes the train'd stop and then start up again on low. That meant the engineer suspected he was comin' to a station and was scared that if he run too fast he wouldn't see it, and if he run past it without stoppin' the inhabitants wouldn't never forgive him. You see, they's a regular schedule o' duties that's followed out by the more prominent citizens down those parts. After their wife's attended to the chores and got the breakfast they roll out o' bed and put on their overalls and eat. Then they get on their horse or mule or cow or dog and ride down to the station and wait for the next train. When it comes they have a contest to see which can count the passengers first. The losers has to promise to work one day the followin' month. If one fella loses three times in the same month he generally always kills himself.

All the towns has got five or six private residences and seven or eight two-apartment buildin's and a grocery and a post-office. They told me that somebody in one o' them burgs, I forget which one, got a letter the day before we come through. It was misdirected, I guess.

The two-apartment buildin's is constructed on the ground floor, with a porch to divide one flat from the other. One's the housekeepin' side and the other's just a place for the husband and father to lay round in so's they won't be disturbed by watchin' the women work.

It was a blessin' to them boys when their states went dry. Just think what a strain it must of been to keep liftin' glasses and huntin' in their overalls for a dime!

In the afternoon the Missus went into our apartment and took a nap and I moseyed into the readin'-room and looked over some o' the comical magazines. They was a fat guy come in and set next to me. I'd heard him, in at lunch, tellin' the dinin'-car conductor what Wilson should of done, so I wasn't su'prised when he opened up on me.

"Tiresome trip," he says.

I didn't think it was worth w'ile arguin' with him.

"Must of been a lot o' rain through here," he says.

"Either that," says I, "or else the sprinklin' wagon run shy o' streets."

He laughed as much as it was worth.

"Where do you come from?" he ast me.

"Dear old Chicago," I says.

"I'm from St. Louis," he says.

"You're frank," says I.

"I'm really as much at home one place as another," he says. "The Wife likes to travel and why shouldn't I humor her?"

"I don't know," I says. "I haven't the pleasure."

"Seems like we're goin' all the w'ile," says he. "It's Hot Springs or New Orleans or Florida or Atlantic City or California or somewheres."

"Do you get passes?" I ast him.

"I guess I could if I wanted to," he says. "Some o' my best friends is way up in the railroad business."

"I got one like that," I says. "He generally stands on the fourth or fifth car behind the engine."

"Do you travel much?" he ast me.

"I don't live in St. Louis," says I.

"Is this your first trip south?" he ast.

"Oh, no," I says. "I live on Sixty-fifth Street."

"I meant, have you ever been down this way before?"

"Oh, yes," says I. "I come down every winter."

"Where do you go?" he ast.

That's what I was layin' for.

"Palm Beach," says I.

"I used to go there," he says. "But I've cut it out. It ain't like it used to be. They leave everybody in now."

"Yes," I says; "but a man don't have to mix up with 'em."

"You can't just ignore people that comes up and talks to you," he says.

"Are you bothered that way much?" I ast.

"It's what drove me away from Palm Beach," he says.

"How long since you been there?" I ast him.

"How long you been goin' there?" he says.

"Me?" says I. "Five years."

"We just missed each other," says he. "I quit six years ago this winter."

"Then it couldn't of been there I seen you," says I. "But I know I seen you somewheres before."

"It might of been most anywheres," he says. "They's few places I haven't been at."

"Maybe it was acrost the pond," says I.

"Very likely," he says. "But not since the war started. I been steerin' clear of Europe for two years."

"So have I, for longer'n that," I says.

"It's certainly an awful thing, this war," says he.

"I believe you're right," says I; "but I haven't heard nobody express it just that way before."

"I only hope," he says, "that we succeed in keepin' out of it."

"If we got in, would you go?" I ast him.

"Yes, sir," he says.

"You wouldn't beat me," says I. "I bet I'd reach Brazil as quick as you."

"Oh, I don't think they'd be any action in South America," he says. "We'd fight defensive at first and most of it would be along the Atlantic Coast."

"Then maybe we could get accommodations in Yellowstone Park," says I.

"They's no sense in this country gettin' involved," he says. "Wilson hasn't handled it right. He either ought to of went stronger or not so strong. He's wrote too many notes."

"You certainly get right to the root of a thing," says I. "You must of thought a good deal about it."

"I know the conditions pretty well," he says. "I know how far you can go with them people over there. I been amongst 'em a good part o' the time."

"I suppose," says I, "that a fella just naturally don't like to butt in. But if I was you I'd consider it my duty to romp down to Washington and give 'em all the information I had."

"Wilson picked his own advisers," says he. "Let him learn his lesson."

"That ain't hardly fair," I says. "Maybe you was out o' town, or your phone was busy or somethin'."

"I don't know Wilson nor he don't know me," he says.

"That oughtn't to stop you from helpin' him out," says I. "If you seen a man drownin' would you wait for some friend o' the both o' you to come along and make the introduction?"

"They ain't no comparison in them two cases," he says. "Wilson ain't never called on me for help."

"You don't know if he has or not," I says. "You don't stick in one place long enough for a man to reach you."

"My office in St. Louis always knows where I'm at," says he. "My stenographer can reach me any time within ten to twelve hours."

"I don't think it's right to have this country's whole future dependin' on a St. Louis stenographer," I says.

"That's nonsense!" says he. "I ain't makin' no claim that I could save or not save this country. But if I and Wilson was acquainted I might tell him some facts that'd help him out in his foreign policy."

"Well, then," I says, "it's up to you to get acquainted. I'd introduce you myself only I don't know your name."

"My name's Gould," says he; "but you're not acquainted with Wilson."

"I could be, easy," says I. "I could get on a train he was goin' somewheres on and then go and set beside him and begin to talk. Lots o' people make friends that way."

It was gettin' along to'rd supper-time, so I excused myself and went back to the apartment. The Missus had woke up and wasn't feelin' good.

"What's the matter?" I ast her.

"This old train," she says. "I'll die if it don't stop goin' round them curves."

"As long as the track curves, the best thing the train can do is curve with it," I says. "You may die if it keeps curvin', but you'd die a whole lot sooner if it left the rails and went straight ahead."

"What you been doin'?" she ast me.

"Just talkin' to one o' the Goulds," I says.

"Gould!" she says. "What Gould?"

"Well," I says, "I didn't ask him his first name, but he's from St. Louis, so I suppose it's Ludwig or Heinie."

"Oh," she says, disgusted. "I thought you meant one o' the real ones."

"He's a real one, all right," says I. "He's so classy that he's passed up Palm Beach. He says it's gettin' too common."

"I don't believe it," says the Wife. "And besides, we don't have to mix up with everybody."

"He says they butt right in on you," I told her.

"They'll get a cold reception from me," she says.

But between the curves and the fear o' Palm Beach not bein' so exclusive as it used to be, she couldn't eat no supper, and I had another big meal.

The next mornin' we landed in Jacksonville three hours behind time and narrowly missed connections for St. Augustine by over an hour and a half. They wasn't another train till one-thirty in the afternoon, so we had some time to kill. I went shoppin' and bought a shave and five or six rickeys. The Wife helped herself to a chair in the writin'-room of one o' the hotels and told pretty near everybody in Chicago that she wished they was along with us, accompanied by a pitcher o' the Elks' Home or the Germania Club, or Trout Fishin' at Atlantic Beach.

W'ile I was gettin' my dime's worth in the tonsorial parlors, I happened to look up at a calendar on the wall, and noticed it was the twelfth o' February.

"How does it come that everything's open here to-day?" I says to the barber. "Don't you-all know it's Lincoln's birthday?"

"Is that so?" he says. "How old is he?"

III

We'd wired ahead for rooms at the Alcazar, and when we landed in St. Augustine they was a motor-bus from the hotel to meet us at the station.

"Southern hospitality," I says to the Wife, and we was both pleased till they relieved us o' four bits apiece for the ride.

Well, they hadn't neither one of us slept good the night before, w'ile we was joltin' through Georgia; so when I suggested a nap they wasn't no argument.

"But our clo'es ought to be pressed," says the Missus. "Call up the valet and have it done w'ile we sleep."

So I called up the valet, and sure enough, he come.

"Hello, George!" I says. "You see, we're goin' to lay down and take a nap, and we was wonderin' if you could crease up these two suits and have 'em back here by the time we want 'em."

"Certainly, sir," says he.

"And how much will it cost?" I ast him.

"One dollar a suit," he says.

"Are you on parole or haven't you never been caught?" says I.

"Yes, sir," he says, and smiled like it was a joke.

"Let's talk business, George," I says. "The tailor we go to on Sixty-third walks two blocks to get our clo'es, and two blocks to take 'em to his joint, and two blocks to bring 'em back, and he only soaks us thirty-five cents a suit."

"He gets poor pay and he does poor work," says the burglar. "When I press clo'es I press 'em right."

"Well," I says, "the tailor on Sixty-third satisfies us. Suppose you don't do your best this time, but just give us seventy cents' worth."

But they wasn't no chance for a bargain. He'd been in the business so long he'd become hardened and lost all regard for his fellow men.

The Missus slept, but I didn't. Instead, I done a few problems in arithmetic. Outside o' what she'd gave up for postcards and stamps in Jacksonville, I'd spent two bucks for our lunch, about two more for my shave and my refreshments, one for a rough ride in a bus, one more for gettin' our trunk and grips carried round, two for havin' the clo'es pressed, and about half a buck in tips to people that I wouldn't never see again. Somewheres near nine dollars a day, not countin' no hotel bill, and over two weeks of it yet to come!

Oh, you rummy game at home, at half a cent a point!

When our clo'es come back I woke her up and give her the figures.

"But to-day's an exception," she says. "After this our meals will be included in the hotel bill and we won't need to get our suits pressed only once a week and you'll be shavin' yourself and they won't be no bus fare when we're stayin' in one place. Besides, we can practise economy all spring and all summer."

"I guess we need the practise," I says.

"And if you're goin' to crab all the time about expenses," says she, "I'll wish we had of stayed home."

"That'll make it unanimous," says I.

Then she begin sobbin' about how I'd spoiled the trip and I had to promise I wouldn't think no more o' what we were spendin'. I might just as well of promised to not worry when the White Sox lost or when I'd forgot to come home to supper.

We went in the dinin'-room about six-thirty and was showed to a table where they was another couple settin'. They was husband and wife, I guess, but I don't know which was which. She was wieldin' the pencil and writin' down their order.

"I guess I'll have clams," he says.

"They disagreed with you last night," says she.

"All right," he says. "I won't try 'em. Give me cream-o'-tomato soup."

"You don't like tomatoes," she says.

"Well, I won't have no soup," says he. "A little o' the blue-fish."

"The blue-fish wasn't no good at noon," she says. "You better try the bass."

"All right, make it bass," he says. "And them sweet-breads and a little roast beef and sweet potatoes and peas and vanilla ice-cream and coffee."

"You wouldn't touch sweet-breads at home," says she, "and you can't tell what they'll be in a hotel."

"All right, cut out the sweet-breads," he says.

"I should think you'd have the stewed chicken," she says, "and leave out the roast beef."

"Stewed chicken it is," says he.

"Stewed chicken and mashed potatoes and string beans and buttered toast and coffee. Will that suit you?"

"Sure!" he says, and she give the slip to the waiter.

George looked at it long enough to of read it three times if he could of read it once and then went out in the kitchen and got a trayful o' whatever was handy.

But the poor guy didn't get more'n a taste of anything. She was watchin' him like a hawk, and no sooner would he delve into one victual than she'd yank the dish away from him and tell him to remember that health was more important than temporary happiness. I felt so sorry for him that I couldn't enjoy my own repast and I told the Wife that we'd have our breakfast apart from that stricken soul if I had to carry the case to old Al Cazar himself.

In the evenin' we strolled acrost the street to the Ponce— that's supposed to be even sweller yet than where we were stoppin' at. We walked all over the place without recognizin' nobody from our set. I finally warned the Missus that if we didn't duck back to our room I'd probably have a heart attack from excitement; but she'd read in her Florida guide that the decorations and pitchers was worth goin' miles to see, so we had to stand in front o' them for a couple hours and try to keep awake. Four or five o' them was thrillers, at that. Their names was Adventure, Discovery, Contest, and so on, but what they all should of been called was Lady Who Had Mislaid Her Clo'es.

The hotel's named after the fella that built it. He come from Spain and they say he was huntin' for some water that if he'd drunk it he'd feel young. I don't see myself how you could expect to feel young on water. But, anyway, he'd heard that this here kind o' water could be found in St. Augustine, and when he couldn't find it he went into the hotel business and got even with the United States by chargin' five dollars a day and up for a room.

Sunday mornin' we went in to breakfast early and I ast the head waiter if we could set at another table where they wasn't no convalescent and his mate. At the same time I give the said head waiter somethin' that spoke louder than words. We was showed to a place way acrost the room from where we'd been the night before. It was a table for six, but the other four didn't come into our life till that night at supper.

Meanw'ile we went sight-seein'. We visited Fort Marion, that'd be a great protection against the Germans, provided they fought with paper wads. We seen the city gate and the cathedral and the slave market, and then we took the boat over to Anastasia Island, that the ocean's on the other side of it. This trip made me homesick, because the people that was along with us on the boat looked just like the ones we'd often went with to Michigan City on the Fourth o' July. The boat landed on the bay side o' the island and from there we was drug over to the ocean side on a horse car, the horse walkin' to one side o' the car instead of in front, so's he wouldn't get ran over.

We stuck on the beach till dinner-time and then took the chariot back to the pavilion on the bay side, where a whole family served the meal and their pigs put on a cabaret. It was the best meal I had in dear old Dixie—fresh oysters and chicken and mashed potatoes and gravy and fish and pie. And they charged two bits a plate.

"Goodness gracious!" says the Missus, when I told her the price. "This is certainly reasonable. I wonder how it happens."

"Well," I says, "the family was probably washed up here by the tide and don't know they're in Florida."

When we got back to the hotel they was only just time to clean up and go down to supper. We hadn't no sooner got seated when our table companions breezed in. It was a man about forty-five, that looked like he'd made his money in express and general haulin', and he had his wife along and both their mother-in-laws. The shirt he had on was the one he'd started from home with, if he lived in Yokohama. His women-folks wore mournin' with a touch o' gravy here and there.

"You order for us, Jake," says one o' the ladies.

So Jake grabbed the bill o' fare and his wife took the slip and pencil and waited for the dictation.

"Let's see," he says. "How about oyster cocktail?"

"Yes," says the three Mrs. Black.

"Four oyster cocktails, then," says Jake, "and four orders o' bluepoints."

"The oysters is nice, too," says I.

They all give me a cordial smile and the ice was broke.

"Everything's good here," says Jake.

"I bet you know," I says.

He seemed pleased at the compliment and went on dictatin'.

"Four chicken soups with rice," he says, "and four o' the blue-fish and four veal chops breaded and four roast chicken and four boiled potatoes—"

But it seemed his wife would rather have sweet potatoes.

"All right," says Jake; "four boiled potatoes and four sweets. And chicken salad and some o' that tapioca puddin' and ice-cream and tea. Is that satisfactory?"

"Fine!" says one o' the mother-in-laws.

"Are you goin' to stay long?" says Mrs. Jake to my Missus.

The party addressed didn't look very clubby, but she was too polite to pull the cut direct.

"We leave to-morrow night," she says.

Nobody ast her where we was goin'.

"We leave for Palm Beach," she says.

"That's a nice place, I guess," says one o' the old ones. "More people goes there than comes here. It ain't so expensive there, I guess."

"You're some guesser," says the Missus and freezes up.

I ast Jake if he'd been to Florida before.

"No," he says; "this is our first trip, but we're makin' up for lost time. We're seein' all they is to see and havin' everything the best."

"You're havin' everything, all right," I says, "but I don't know if it's the best or not. How long have you been here?"

"A week to-morrow," says he. "And we stay another week and then go to Ormond."

"Are you standin' the trip O. K.?" I ast him.

"Well," he says, "I don't feel quite as good as when we first come."

"Kind o' logy?" I says.

"Yes; kind o' heavy," says Jake.

"I know what you ought to do," says I. "You ought to go to a European plan hotel."

"Not w'ile this war's on," he says, "and besides, my mother's a poor sailor."

"Yes," says his mother; "I'm a very poor sailor."

"Jake's mother can't stand the water," says Mrs. Jake.

So I begun to believe that Jake's wife's mother-in-law was a total failure as a jolly tar.

Social intercourse was put an end to when the waiter staggered in with their order and our'n. The Missus seemed to of lost her appetite and just set there lookin' grouchy and tappin' her fingers on the table-cloth actin' like she was in a hurry to get away. I didn't eat much, neither. It was more fun watchin'.

"Well," I says, when we was out in the lobby, "we finally got acquainted with some real people."

"Real people!" says the Missus, curlin' her lip. "What did you talk to 'em for?"

"I couldn't resist," I says. "Anybody that'd order four oyster cocktails and four rounds o' blue-points is worth knowin'."

"Well," she says, "if they're there when we go in to-morrow mornin' we'll get our table changed again or you can eat with 'em alone."

But they was absent from the breakfast board.

"They're probably stayin' in bed to-day to get their clo'es washed," says the Missus.

"Or maybe they're sick," I says. "A change of oysters affects some people."

I was for goin' over to the island again and gettin' another o' them quarter banquets, but the program was for us to walk round town all mornin' and take a ride in the afternoon.

First, we went to St. George Street and visited the oldest house in the United States. Then we went to Hospital Street and seen the oldest house in the United States. Then we turned the corner and went down St. Francis Street and inspected the oldest house in the United States. Then we dropped into a soda fountain and I had an egg phosphate, made from the oldest egg in the Western Hemisphere. We passed up lunch and got into a carriage drawn by the oldest horse in Florida, and we rode through the country all afternoon and the driver told us some o' the oldest jokes in the book. He felt it was only fair to give his customers a good time when he was chargin' a dollar an hour, and he had his gags rehearsed so's he could tell the same one a thousand times and never change a word. And the horse knowed where the point come in every one and stopped to laugh.

We done our packin' before supper, and by the time we got to our table Jake and the mourners was through and gone. We didn't have to ask the waiter if they'd been there. He was perspirin' like an evangelist.

After supper we said good-by to the night clerk and twenty-two bucks. Then we bought ourself another ride in the motor-bus and landed at the station ten minutes before train-time; so we only had an hour to wait for the train.

Say, I don't know how many stations they is between New York and San Francisco, but they's twice as many between St. Augustine and Palm Beach. And our train stopped twice and started twice at every one. I give up tryin' to sleep and looked out the window, amusin' myself by readin' the names o' the different stops. The only one that expressed my sentiments was Eau Gallie. We was an hour and a half late pullin' out o' that joint and I figured we'd be two hours to the bad gettin' into our destination. But the guy that made out the time-table must of had the engineer down pat, because when we went acrost the bridge over Lake Worth and landed at the Poinciana depot, we was ten minutes ahead o' time.

They was about two dozen uniformed Ephs on the job to meet us. And when I seen 'em all grab for our baggage with one hand and hold the other out, face up, I knowed why they called it Palm Beach.

IV

The Poinciana station's a couple hundred yards from one end o' the hotel, and that means it's close to five miles from the clerk's desk. By the time we'd registered and been gave our key and marathoned another five miles or so to where our room was located at, I was about ready for the inquest. But the Missus was full o' pep and wild to get down to breakfast and look over our stable mates. She says we would eat without changin' our clo'es; people'd forgive us for not dressin' up on account o' just gettin' there. W'ile she was lookin' out the window at the royal palms and buzzards, I moseyed round the room inspectin' where the different doors led to. Pretty near the first one I opened went into a private bath.

"Here," I says; "they've give us the wrong room."

Then my wife seen it and begin to squeal.

"Goody!" she says. "We've got a bath! We've got a bath!"

"But," says I, "they promised we wouldn't have none. It must be a mistake."

"Never you mind about a mistake," she says. "This is our room and they can't chase us out of it."

"We'll chase ourself out," says I. "Rooms with a bath is fifteen and sixteen dollars and up. Rooms without no bath is bad enough."

"We'll keep this room or I won't stay here," she says.

"All right, you win," I says; but I didn't mean it.

I made her set in the lobby down-stairs w'ile I went to the clerk pretendin' that I had to see about our trunk.

"Say," I says to him, "you've made a bad mistake. You told your man in Chicago that we couldn't have no room with a bath, and now you've give us one."

"You're lucky," he says. "A party who had a bath ordered for these two weeks canceled their reservation and now you've got it."

"Lucky, am I?" I says. "And how much is the luck goin' to cost me?"

"It'll be seventeen dollars per day for that room," he says, and turned away to hide a blush.

I went back to the Wife.

"Do you know what we're payin' for that room?" I says. "We're payin' seventeen dollars."

"Well," she says, "our meals is throwed in."

"Yes," says I, "and the hotel furnishes a key."

"You promised in St. Augustine," she says, "that you wouldn't worry no more about expenses."

Well, rather than make a scene in front o' the bellhops and the few millionaires that was able to be about at that hour o' the mornin', I just says "All right!" and led her into the dinin'-room.

The head waiter met us at the door and turned us over to his assistant. Then some more assistants took hold of us one at a time and we was relayed to a beautiful spot next door to the kitchen and bounded on all sides by posts and pillars. It was all right for me, but a whole lot too private for the Missus; so I had to call the fella that had been our pacemaker on the last lap.

"We don't like this table," I says.

"It's the only one I can give you," he says.

I slipped him half a buck.

"Come to think of it," he says, "I believe they's one I forgot all about."

And he moved us way up near the middle o' the place.

Say, you ought to seen that dinin'-room! From one end of it to the other is a toll call, and if a man that was settin' at the table farthest from the kitchen ordered roast lamb he'd get mutton. At that, they was crowded for fair and it kept the head waiters hustlin' to find trough space for one and all.

It was round nine o'clock when we put in our modest order for orange juice, oatmeal, liver and bacon, and cakes and coffee, and a quarter to ten or so when our waiter returned from the nearest orange grove with Exhibit A. We amused ourself meanw'ile by givin' our neighbors the once over and wonderin' which o' them was goin' to pal with us. As far as I could tell from the glances we received, they wasn't no immediate danger of us bein' annoyed by attentions.

They was only a few womenfolks on deck and they was dressed pretty quiet; so quiet that the Missus was scared she'd shock 'em with the sport skirt she'd bought in Chi. Later on in the day, when the girls come out for their dress parade, the Missus' costume made about as much noise as eatin' marsh-mallows in a foundry.

After breakfast we went to the room for a change o' raiment. I put on my white trousers and wished to heaven that the sun'd go under a cloud till I got used to tellin' people without words just where my linen began and I left off. The rest o' my outfit was white shoes that hurt, and white sox, and a two-dollar silk shirt that showed up a zebra, and a red tie and a soft collar and a blue coat. The Missus wore a sport suit that I won't try and describe—you'll probably see it on her sometime in the next five years.

We went down-stairs again and out on the porch, where some o' the old birds was takin' a sun bath.

"Where now?" I says.

"The beach, o' course," says the Missus.

"Where is it at?" I ast her.

"I suppose," she says, "that we'll find it somewheres near the ocean."

"I don't believe you can stand this climate," says I.

"The ocean," she says, "must be down at the end o' that avenue, where most everybody seems to be headed."

"Havin' went to our room and back twice, I don't feel like another five-mile hike," I says.

"It ain't no five miles," she says; "but let's ride, anyway."

"Come on," says I, pointin' to a street-car that was standin' in the middle o' the avenue.

"Oh, no," she says. "I've watched and found out that the real people takes them funny-lookin' wheel chairs."

I was wonderin' what she meant when one o' them pretty near run over us. It was part bicycle, part go-cart and part African. In the one we dodged they was room for one passenger, but some o' them carried two.

"I wonder what they'd soak us for the trip," I says.

"Not more'n a dime, I don't believe," says the Missus.

But when we'd hired one and been w'isked down under the palms and past the golf field to the bath-house, we was obliged to part with fifty cents legal and tender.

"I feel much refreshed," I says. "I believe when it comes time to go back I'll be able to walk."

The bath-house is acrost the street from the other hotel, the Breakers, that the man had told us was full for the season. Both buildin's fronts on the ocean; and, boy, it's some ocean! I bet they's fish in there that never seen each other!

"Oh, let's go bathin' right away!" says the Missus.

"Our suits is up to the other beanery," says I, and I was glad of it. They wasn't nothin' temptin' to me about them man-eatin' waves.

But the Wife's a persistent cuss.

"We won't go to-day," she says, "but we'll go in the bath-house and get some rooms for to-morrow."

The bath-house porch was a ringer for the *Follies*. Here and down on the beach was where you seen the costumes at this time o' day. I was so busy rubberin' that I passed the entrance door three times without noticin' it. From the top o' their heads to the bottom o' their feet the girls was a mess o' colors. They wasn't no two dressed alike and if any one o' them had of walked down State Street we'd of had an epidemic o' stiff neck to contend with in Chi. Finally the Missus grabbed me and hauled me into the office.

"Two private rooms," she says to the clerk. "One lady and one gent."

"Five dollars a week apiece," he says. "But we're all filled up."

"You ought to be all locked up!" I says.

"Will you have anything open to-morrow?" ast the Missus.

"I think I can fix you then," he says.

"What do we get for the five?" I ast him.

"Private room and we take care o' your bathin' suit," says he.

"How much if you don't take care o' the suit?" I ast him. "My suit's been gettin' along fine with very little care."

"Five dollars a week apiece," he says, "and if you want the rooms you better take 'em, because they're in big demand."

By the time we'd closed this grand bargain, everybody'd moved offen the porch and down to the water, where a couple dozen o' them went in for a swim and the rest set and watched. They was a long row o' chairs on the beach for spectators and we was just goin' to flop into two o' them when another bandit come up and told us it'd cost a dime apiece per hour.

"We're goin' to be here two weeks," I says. "Will you sell us two chairs?"

He wasn't in no comical mood, so we sunk down on the sand and seen the show from there. We had plenty o' company that preferred these kind o' seats free to the chairs at ten cents a whack.

Besides the people that was in the water gettin' knocked down by the waves and pretendin' like they enjoyed it, about half o' the gang on the sand was wearin' bathin' suits just to be clubby. You could tell by lookin' at the suits that they hadn't never been wet and wasn't intended for no such ridic'lous purpose. I wisht I could describe 'em to you, but it'd take a female to do it right.

One little girl, either fourteen or twenty-four, had white silk slippers and sox that come pretty near up to her ankles, and from there to her knees it was just plain Nature. North-bound from her knees was a pair o' bicycle trousers that disappeared when they come to the bottom of her Mother Hubbard. This here garment was a thing without no neck or sleeves that begin bulgin' at the top and spread out gradual all the way down, like a croquette. To top her off, she had a jockey cap; and—believe me—I'd of played her mount acrost the board. They was plenty o' class in the field with her, but nothin' that approached her speed. Later on I seen her several times round the hotel, wearin' somethin' near the same outfit, without the jockey cap and with longer croquettes.

We set there in the sand till people begun to get up and leave. Then we trailed along back o' them to the Breakers' porch, where they was music to dance and stuff to inhale.

"We'll grab a table," I says to the Missus. "I'm dyin' o' thirst."

But I was allowed to keep on dyin'.

"I can serve you somethin' soft," says the waiter.

"I'll bet you can't!" I says.

"You ain't got no locker here?" he says.

"What do you mean—locker?" I ast him.

"It's the locker liquor law," he says. "We can serve you a drink if you own your own bottles."

"I'd just as soon own a bottle," I says. "I'll become the proprietor of a bottle o' beer."

"It'll take three or four hours to get it for you," he says, "and you'd have to order it through the order desk. If you're stoppin' at one o' the hotels and want a drink once in a w'ile, you better get busy and put in an order."

So I had to watch the Missus put away a glass of orange juice that cost forty cents and was just the same size as they give us for breakfast free for nothin'. And, not havin' had nothin' to make me forget that my feet hurt, I was obliged to pay another four bits for an Afromobile to cart us back to our own boardin' house.

"Well," says the Missus when we got there, "it's time to wash up and go to lunch."

"Wash up and go to lunch, then," I says; "but I'm goin' to investigate this here locker liquor or liquor locker law."

So she got her key and beat it, and I limped to the bar.

"I want a highball," I says to the boy.

"What's your number?" says he.

"It varies," I says. "Sometimes I can hold twenty and sometimes four or five makes me sing."

"I mean, have you got a locker here?" he says.

"No; but I want to get one," says I.

"The gent over there to the desk will fix you," says he.

So over to the desk I went and ast for a locker.

"What do you drink?" ast the gent.

"I'm from Chicago," I says. "I drink bourbon."

"What's your name and room number?" he says, and I told him.

Then he ast me how often did I shave and what did I think o' the Kaiser and what my name was before I got married, and if I had any intentions of ever running an elevator. Finally he says I was all right.

"I'll order you some bourbon," he says. "Anything else?"

I was goin' to say no, but I happened to remember that the Wife generally always wants a bronix before dinner. So I had to also put in a bid for a bottle o' gin and bottles o' the Vermouth brothers, Tony and Pierre. It wasn't till later that I appreciated what a grand law this here law was. When I got my drinks I paid ten cents apiece for 'em for service, besides payin' for the bottles o' stuff to drink. And, besides that, about every third highball or bronix I ordered, the waiter'd bring back word that I was just out of ingredients and then they'd be another delay w'ile they sent to the garage for more. If they had that law all over the country they'd soon be an end o' drinkin', because everybody'd get so mad they'd kill each other.

My cross-examination had took quite a long time, but when I got to my room the Wife wasn't back from lunch yet and I had to cover the Marathon route all over again and look her up. We only had the one key to the room, and o' course couldn't expect no more'n that at the price.

The Missus had bought one o' the daily programs they get out and she knowed just what we had to do the rest o' the day.

"For the next couple hours," she says, "we can suit ourself."

"All right," says I. "It suits me to take off my shoes and lay down."

"I'll rest, too," she says; "but at half past four we have to be

in the Cocoanut Grove for tea and dancin'. And then we come
back to the room and dress for dinner. Then we eat and then
we set around till the evenin' dance starts. Then we dance till
we're ready for bed."

"Who do we dance all these dances with?" I ast her.

"With whoever we get acquainted with," she says.

"All right," says I; "but let's be careful."

Well, we took our nap and then we followed schedule and had
our tea in the Cocoanut Grove. You know how I love tea! My
feet was still achin' and the Missus couldn't talk me into no dance.

When we'd set there an hour and was saturated with tea, the
Wife says it was time to go up and change into our Tuxedos. I
was all in when we reached the room and willin' to even pass up
supper and nestle in the hay, but I was informed that the biggest
part o' the day's doin's was yet to come. So from six o'clock till
after seven I wrestled with studs, and hooks and eyes that didn't
act like they'd ever met before and wasn't anxious to get acquainted, and then down we went again to the dinin'-room.

"How about a little bronix before the feed?" I says.

"It would taste good," says the Missus.

So I called Eph and give him the order. In somethin' less
than half an hour he come back empty-handed.

"You ain't got no cocktail stuff," he says.

"I certainly have," says I. "I ordered it early this afternoon."

"Where at?" he ast me.

"Over in the bar," I says.

"Oh, the regular bar!" he says. "That don't count. You got
to have stuff at the service bar to get it served in here."

"I ain't as thirsty as I thought I was," says I.

"Me, neither," says the Missus.

So we went ahead and ordered our meal, and w'ile we was
waitin' for it a young couple come and took the other two
chairs at our table. They didn't have to announce through a
megaphone that they was honeymooners. It was wrote all over
'em. They was reachin' under the table for each other's hand
every other minute, and when they wasn't doin' that they was
smilin' at each other or gigglin' at nothin'. You couldn't feel
that good and be payin' seventeen dollars a day for room and
board unless you was just married or somethin'.

I thought at first their company'd be fun, but after a few

meals it got like the southern cookin' and begun to undermine the health.

The conversation between they and us was what you could call limited. It took place the next day at lunch. The young husband thought he was about to take a bite o' the entry, which happened to be roast mutton with sirup; but he couldn't help from lookin' at her at the same time and his empty fork started for his face prongs up.

"Look out for your eye," I says.

He dropped the fork and they both blushed till you could see it right through the sunburn. Then they give me a Mexican look and our acquaintance was at an end.

This first night, when we was through eatin', we wandered out in the lobby and took seats where we could watch the passin' show. The men was all dressed like me, except I was up to date and had on a mushroom shirt, w'ile they was sportin' the old-fashioned concrete bosom. The women's dresses begun at the top with a belt, and some o' them stopped at the mezzanine floor, w'ile others went clear down to the basement and helped keep the rugs clean. They was one that must of thought it was the Fourth o' July. From the top of her head to where the top of her bathin' suit had left off, she was a red, red rose. From there to the top of her gown was white, and her gown, what they was of it—was blue.

"My!" says the Missus. "What stunnin' gowns!"

"Yes," I says; "and you could have one just like 'em if you'd take the shade offen the piano lamp at home and cut it down to the right size."

Round ten o'clock we wandered in the Palm Garden, where the dancin' had been renewed. The Wife wanted to plunge right in the mazes o' the foxy trot.

"I'll take some courage first," says I. And then was when I found out that it cost you ten cents extra besides the tip to pay for a drink that you already owned in fee simple.

Well, I guess we must of danced about six dances together and had that many quarrels before she was ready to go to bed. And oh, how grand that old hay-pile felt when I finally bounced into it!

The next day we went to the ocean at the legal hour—half past eleven. I never had so much fun in my life. The surf was runnin' high, I heard 'em say; and I don't know which I'd rather do, go bathin' in the ocean at Palm Beach when the surf is runnin' high, or have a dentist get one o' my molars ready for a big inlay at a big outlay. Once in a w'ile I managed to not get throwed on my head when a wave hit me. As for swimmin', you had just as much chance as if you was at State and Madison at the noon hour. And before I'd been in a minute they was enough salt in my different features to keep the Blackstone hotel runnin' all through the onion season.

The Missus enjoyed it just as much as me. She tried to pretend at first, and when she got floored she'd give a squeal that was supposed to mean heavenly bliss. But after she'd been bruised from head to feet and her hair looked and felt like spinach with French dressin', and she'd drank all she could hold o' the Gulf Stream, she didn't resist none when I drug her in to shore and staggered with her up to our private rooms at five a week per each.

Without consultin' her, I went to the desk at the Casino and told 'em they could have them rooms back.

"All right," says the clerk, and turned our keys over to the next in line.

"How about a refund?" I ast him; but he was waitin' on somebody else.

After that we done our bathin' in the tub. But we was down to the beach every morning at eleven-thirty to watch the rest o' them get batted round.

And at half past twelve every day we'd follow the crowd to the Breakers' porch and dance together, the Missus and I. Then it'd be back to the other hostelry, sometimes limpin' and sometimes in an Afromobile, and a drink or two in the Palm Garden before lunch. And after lunch we'd lay down; or we'd pay some Eph two or three dollars to pedal us through the windin' jungle trail, that was every bit as wild as the Art Institute; or we'd ferry acrost Lake Worth to West Palm Beach and take in a movie, or we'd stand in front o' the portable Fifth Avenue stores w'ile the Missus wished she could have this dress or that hat, or somethin' else that she wouldn't of looked at if she'd been home and in her right mind. But always at half past four we had to live up to the rules and be in the Cocoanut Grove for tea and some more foxy trottin'. And then it was dress for dinner, eat dinner, watch the parade and wind up the glorious day with more dancin'.

I bet you any amount you name that the Castles in their whole life haven't danced together as much as I and the Missus did at Palm Beach. I'd of gave five dollars if even one o' the waiters had took her offen my hands for one dance. But I knowed that if I made the offer public they'd of been a really serious quarrel between us instead o' just the minor brawls occasioned by steppin' on each other's feet.

She made a discovery one night. She found out that they was a place called the Beach Club where most o' the real people disappeared to every evenin' after dinner. She says we would have to go there too.

"But I ain't a member," I says.

"Then find out how you get to be one," she says.

So to the Beach Club I went and made inquiries.

"You'll have to be introduced by a guy that already belongs," says the man at the door.

"Who belongs?" I ast him.

"Hundreds o' people," he says. "Who do you know?"

"Two waiters, two barkeepers and one elevator boy," I says.

He laughed, but his laugh didn't get me no membership card and I had to dance three or four extra times the next day to square myself with the Missus.

She made another discovery and it cost me six bucks. She found out that, though the meals in the regular dinin'-room was included in the triflin' rates per day, the real people had at least two o' their meals in the garden grill and paid extra for 'em. We tried it for one meal and I must say I enjoyed it—all but the check.

"We can't keep up that clip," I says to her.

"We could," says she, "if you wasn't spendin' so much on your locker."

"The locker's a matter o' life and death," I says. "They ain't no man in the world that could dance as much with their own wife as I do and live without liquid stimulus."

When we'd been there four days she got to be on speakin' terms with the ladies' maid that hung round the lobby and helped put the costumes back on when they slipped off. From this here maid the Missus learned who was who, and the information was relayed to me as soon as they was a chance. We'd be settin' on the porch when I'd feel an elbow in my ribs all of a sudden. I'd look up at who was passin' and then try and pretend I was excited.

"Who is it?" I'd whisper.

"That's Mrs. Vandeventer," the Wife'd say. "Her husband's the biggest street-car conductor in Philadelphia."

Or somebody'd set beside us at the beach or in the Palm Garden and my ribs would be all battered up before the Missus was calm enough to tip me off.

"The Vincents," she'd say; "the canned prune people."

It was a little bit thrillin' at first to be rubbin' elbows with all them celeb's; but it got so finally that I could walk out o' the dinin'-room right behind Scotti, the opera singer, without forgettin' that my feet hurt.

The Washington's Birthday Ball brought 'em all together at once, and the Missus pointed out eight and nine at a time and got me so mixed up that I didn't know Pat Vanderbilt from Maggie Rockefeller. The only one you couldn't make no mistake about was a Russian count that you couldn't pronounce. He was buyin' bay mules or somethin' for the Russian government, and he was in ambush.

"They say he can't hardly speak a word of English," says the Missus.

"If I knowed the word for barber shop in Russia," says I, "I'd tell him they was one in this hotel."

V

In our mail box the next mornin' they was a notice that our first week was up and all we owed was one hundred and forty-six dollars and fifty cents. The bill for room and meals was one hundred and nineteen dollars. The rest was for gettin' clo'es pressed and keepin' the locker damp.

I didn't have no appetite for breakfast. I told the Wife I'd wait up in the room and for her to come when she got through. When she blew in I had my speech prepared.

"Look here," I says; "this is our eighth day in Palm Beach society. You're on speakin' terms with a maid and I've got acquainted with half a dozen o' the male hired help. It's cost us about a hundred and sixty-five dollars, includin' them private rooms down to the Casino and our Afromobile trips, and this and that. You know a whole lot o' swell people by sight, but you can't talk to 'em. It'd be just as much satisfaction and hundreds o' dollars cheaper to look up their names in the telephone directory at home; then phone to 'em and, when you got 'em, tell 'em it was the wrong number. That way, you'd get 'em to speak to you at least.

"As for sport," I says, "we don't play golf and we don't play tennis and we don't swim. We go through the same program o' doin' nothin' every day. We dance, but we don't never change partners. For twelve dollars I could buy a phonograph up home and I and you could trot round the livin'-room all evenin' without no danger o' havin' some o' them fancy birds cave our shins in. And we could have twice as much liquid refreshments up there at about a twentieth the cost.

"That Gould I met on the train comin' down," I says, "was a even bigger liar than I give him credit for. He says that when he was here people pestered him to death by comin' up and speakin' to him. We ain't had to dodge nobody or hide behind a cocoanut tree to remain exclusive. He says Palm Beach was too common for him. What he should of said was that it was too lonesome. If they was just one white man here that'd listen to my stuff I wouldn't have no kick. But it ain't no pleasure tellin' stories to the Ephs. They laugh whether it's good or not, and then want a dime for laughin'.

"As for our clo'es," I says, "they would be all right for a couple o' days' stay. But the dames round here, and the men, too, has somethin' different to put on for every mornin', afternoon and night. You've wore your two evenin' gowns so much that I just have to snap my fingers at the hooks and they go and grab the right eyes.

"The meals would be grand," I says, "if the cook didn't keep gettin' mixed up and puttin' puddin' sauce on the meat and gravy on the pie.

"I'm glad we've been to Palm Beach," I says. "I wouldn't of missed it for nothin'. But the ocean won't be no different tomorrow than it was yesterday, and the same for the daily program. It don't even rain here, to give us a little variety.

"Now what do you say," I says, "to us just settlin' this bill, and whatever we owe since then, and beatin' it out o' here just as fast as we can go?"

The Missus didn't say nothin' for a w'ile. She was too busy cryin'. She knowed that what I'd said was the truth, but she wouldn't give up without a struggle.

"Just three more days," she says finally. "If we don't meet somebody worth meetin' in the next three days I'll go wherever you want to take me."

"All right," I says; "three more days it is. What's a little matter o' sixty dollars?"

Well, in them next two days and a half she done some desperate flirtin', but as it was all with women I didn't get jealous. She picked out some o' the E-light o' Chicago and tried every trick she could think up. She told 'em their noses was shiny and offered 'em her powder. She stepped on their white shoes just so's to get a chance to beg their pardon. She told 'em their clo'es was unhooked, and then unhooked 'em so's she could hook 'em up again. She tried to loan 'em her finger-nail tools. When she seen one fannin' herself she'd say: "Excuse me, Mrs. So-and-So; but we got the coolest room in the hotel, and I'd be glad to have you go up there and quit perspirin'." But not a rise did she get.

Not till the afternoon o' the third day o' grace. And I don't know if I ought to tell you this or not—only I'm sure you won't spill it nowheres.

We'd went up in our room after lunch. I was tired out and she was discouraged. We'd set round for over an hour, not sayin' or doin' nothin'.

I wanted to talk about the chance of us gettin' away the next mornin', but I didn't dast bring up the subject.

The Missus complained of it bein' hot and opened the door to leave the breeze go through. She was settin' in a chair near the doorway, pretendin' to read the *Palm Beach News*. All of a sudden she jumped up and kind o' hissed at me.

"What's the matter?" I says, springin' from the lounge.

"Come here!" she says, and went out the door into the hall.

I got there as fast as I could, thinkin' it was a rat or a fire. But the Missus just pointed to a lady walkin' away from us, six or seven doors down.

"It's Mrs. Potter," she says; "*the* Mrs. Potter from Chicago!"

"Oh!" I says, puttin' all the excitement I could into my voice.

And I was just startin' back into the room when I seen Mrs. Potter stop and turn round and come to'rd us. She stopped again maybe twenty feet from where the Missus was standin'.

"Are you on this floor?" she says.

The Missus shook like a leaf.

"Yes," says she, so low you couldn't hardly hear her.

"Please see that they's some towels put in 559," says *the* Mrs. Potter from Chicago.

VI

About five o'clock the Wife quieted down and I thought it was safe to talk to her. "I've been readin' in the guide about a pretty river trip," I says. "We can start from here on the boat to-morrow mornin'. They run to Fort Pierce to-morrow and stay there to-morrow night. The next day they go from Fort Pierce to Rockledge, and the day after that from Rockledge to Daytona. The fare's only five dollars apiece. And we can catch a north-bound train at Daytona."

"All right, I don't care," says the Missus.

So I left her and went down-stairs and acrost the street to ask Mr. Foster. Ask Mr. Foster happened to be a girl. She sold me the boat tickets and promised she would reserve a room with bath for us at Fort Pierce, where we was to spend the followin' night. I bet she knowed all the w'ile that rooms with a bath in Fort Pierce is scarcer than toes on a sturgeon.

I went back to the room and helped with the packin' in an advisory capacity. Neither one of us had the heart to dress for dinner. We ordered somethin' sent up and got soaked an extra dollar for service. But we was past carin' for a little thing like that.

At nine o'clock next mornin' the good ship *Constitution* stopped at the Poinciana dock w'ile we piled aboard. One bellhop was down to see us off and it cost me a quarter to get that much attention. Mrs. Potter must of overslept herself.

The boat was loaded to the guards and I ain't braggin' when I say that we was the best-lookin' people aboard. And as for manners, why, say, old Bill Sykes could of passed off for Henry Chesterfield in that gang! Each one o' them occupied three o'

the deck chairs and sprayed orange juice all over their neighbors. We could of talked to plenty o' people here, all right;
they were as clubby a gang as I ever seen. But I was afraid if I
said somethin' they'd have to answer; and, with their mouths
as full o' citrus fruit as they was, the results might of been fatal
to my light suit.

We went up the lake to a canal and then through it to Indian
River. The boat run aground every few minutes and had to be
pried loose. About twelve o'clock a cullud gemman come up
on deck and told us lunch was ready. At half past one he served
it at a long family table in the cabin. As far as I was concerned,
he might as well of left it on the stove. Even if you could of bit
into the food, a glimpse of your fellow diners would of stran-
gled your appetite.

After the repast I called the Missus aside.

"Somethin' tells me we're not goin' to live through three
days o' this," I says. "What about takin' the train from Fort
Pierce and beatin' it for Jacksonville, and then home?"

"But that'd get us to Chicago too quick," says she. "We told
people how long we was goin' to be gone and if we got back
ahead o' time they'd think they was somethin' queer."

"They's too much queer on this boat," I says. "But you're
goin' to have your own way from now on."

We landed in Fort Pierce about six. It was only two or three
blocks to the hotel, but when they laid out that part o' town
they overlooked some o' the modern conveniences, includin'
sidewalks. We staggered through the sand with our grips and
sure had worked up a hunger by the time we reached Ye Inn.

"Got reservations for us here?" I ast the clerk.

"Yes," he says, and led us to 'em in person.

The room he showed us didn't have no bath, or even a chair
that you could set on w'ile you pulled off your socks.

"Where's the bath?" I ast him.

"This way," he says, and I followed him down the hall, outdoors and up an alley.

Finally we come to a bathroom complete in all details, except that it didn't have no door. I went back to the room, got
the Missus and went down to supper. Well, sir, I wish you
could of been present at that supper. The choice o' meats was
calves' liver and onions or calves' liver and onions. And I bet if

them calves had of been still livin' yet they could of gave us some personal reminiscences about Garfield.

The Missus give the banquet one look and then laughed for the first time in several days.

"The guy that named this burg got the capitals mixed," I says. "It should of been Port Fierce."

And she laughed still heartier. Takin' advantage, I says:

"How about the train from here to Jacksonville?"

"You win!" says she. "We can't get home too soon to suit me."

VII

The mornin' we landed in Chicago it was about eight above and a wind was comin' offen the Lake a mile a minute. But it didn't feaze us.

"Lord!" says the Missus. "Ain't it grand to be home!"

"You said somethin'," says I. "But wouldn't it of been grander if we hadn't never left?"

"I don't know about that," she says. "I think we both of us learned a lesson."

"Yes," I says; "and the tuition wasn't only a matter o' close to seven hundred bucks!"

"Oh," says she, "we'll get that back easy!"

"How?" I ast her. "Do you expect some tips on the market from Mrs. Potter and the rest o' your new friends?"

"No," she says. "We'll win it. We'll win it in the rummy game with the Hatches."

THE REAL DOPE

CHAPTER I

And Many a Stormy Wind Shall Blow

On the Ship Board, Jan. 15.

FRIEND AL: Well Al I suppose it is kind of foolish to be writeing you a letter now when they won't be no chance to mail it till we get across the old pond but still and all a man has got to do something to keep themself busy and I know you will be glad to hear all about our trip so I might as well write you a letter when ever I get a chance and I can mail them to you all at once when we get across the old pond and you will think I have wrote a book or something.

Jokeing a side Al you are lucky to have an old pal thats going to see all the fun and write to you about it because its a different thing haveing a person write to you about what they see themself then getting the dope out of a newspaper or something because you will know that what I tell you is the real dope that I seen myself where if you read it in a newspaper you know its guest work because in the 1st. place they don't leave the reporters get nowheres near the front and besides that they wouldn't go there if they had a leave because they would be to scared like the baseball reporters that sets a mile from the game because they haven't got the nerve to get down on the field where a man could take a punch at them and even when they are a mile away with a screen in front of them they duck when somebody hits a pop foul.

Well Al it is against the rules to tell you when we left the old U. S. or where we come away from because the pro German spy might get a hold of a man's letter some way and then it would be good night because he would send a telegram to where the submarines is located at and they wouldn't send no 1 or 2 submarines after us but the whole German navy would get after us because they would figure that if they ever got us it would be a rich hall. When I say that Al I don't mean it to sound like I was swell headed or something and I don't mean it would be a rich hall because I am on board or nothing like that but you would know what I am getting at if you seen the bunch we are takeing across.

In the 1st. place Al this is a different kind of a trip then the time I went around the world with the 2 ball clubs because then it was just the 1 boat load and only for two or 3 of the boys on board it wouldn't of made no difference if the boat had of turned a turtle only to pave the whole bottom of the ocean with ivory. But this time Al we have got not only 1 boat load but we got four boat loads of soldiers alone and that is not all we have got. All together Al there is 10 boats in the parade and 6 of them is what they call the convoys and that means war ships that goes along to see that we get there safe on acct. of the submarines and four of them is what they call destroyers and they are little bits of shafers but they say they can go like he—ll when they get started and when a submarine pops up these little birds chases right after them and drops a death bomb on to them and if it ever hits them the capt. of the submarine can pick up what is left of his boat and stick a 2 cent stamp on it and mail it to the kaiser.

Jokeing a side I guess they's no chance of a submarine getting fat off of us as long as these little birds is on watch so I don't see why a man shouldn't come right out and say when we left and from where we come from but if they didn't have some kind of rules they's a lot of guys that wouldn't know no better then write to Van Hinburg or somebody and tell them all they know but I guess at that they could use a post card.

Well Al we been at sea just two days and a lot of the boys has gave up the ghost all ready and pretty near everything else but I haven't felt the least bit sick that is sea sick but I will own up I felt a little home sick just as we come out of the harbor and seen the godess of liberty standing up there maybe for the last time but don't think for a minute Al that I am sorry I come and I only wish we was over there all ready and could get in to it and the only kick I got comeing so far is that we haven't got no further then we are now on acct. that we didn't do nothing the 1st. day only stall around like we was waiting for Connie Mack to waggle his score card or something.

But we will get there some time and when we do you can bet we will show them something and I am tickled to death I am going and if I lay down my life I will feel like it wasn't throwed away for nothing like you would die of tyford fever or something.

Well I would of liked to of had Florrie and little Al come east and see me off but Florrie felt like she couldn't afford to spend the money to make another long trip after making one long trip down to Texas and besides we wasn't even supposed to tell our family where we was going to sail from but I notice they was a lot of women folks right down to the dock to bid us good by and I suppose they just guessed what was comeing off eh Al? Or maybe they was all strangers that just happened to be there but I'll say I never seen so much kissing between strangers. Any way I and my family had our farewells out west and Florrie was got up like a fancy dress ball and I suppose if I die where she can tend the funeral she will come in pink tights or something.

Well Al I better not keep on talking about Florrie and little Al or I will do the baby act and any way its pretty near time for chow but I suppose you will wonder what am I talking about when I say chow. Well Al that's the name we boys got up down to Camp Grant for stuff to eat and when we talk about food instead of saying food we say chow so that's what I am getting at when I say its pretty near time for chow.

Your pal,   JACK.

On the Ship Board, Jan. 17.

FRIEND AL: Well Al here we are out somewheres in the middle of the old pond and I wished the trip was over not because I have been sea sick or anything but I can't hardly wait to get over there and get in to it and besides they got us jammed in like a sardine or something and four of us in 1 state room and I don't mind doubleing up with some good pal but a man can't get no rest when they's four trying to sleep in a room that wouldn't be big enough for Nemo Liebold but I wouldn't make no holler at that if they had of left us pick our own roomys but out of the four of us they's one that looks like he must of bribed the jury or he wouldn't be here and his name is Smith and another one's name is Sam Hall and he has always got a grouch on and the other boy is O. K. only I would like him a whole lot better if he was about ½ his size but no he is as big as me only not put up like I am. His name is Lee and he pulls a lot of funny stuff like this A. M. he says they must of thought us four was a male quartette and they stuck us all in together so as we could get some close harmony. That's what they call it when they hit them minors.

Well Al I always been use to sleeping with my feet in bed with me but you can't do that in the bunk I have got because your knee would crack you in the jaw and knock you out and even if they was room to strech Hall keeps crabbing till you can't rest and he keeps the room filled up with cigarette smoke and no air and you can't open up the port hole or you would freeze to death so about the only chance I get to sleep is up in the parlor in a chair in the day time and you don't no sooner set down when they got a life boat drill or something and for some reason another they have a role call every day and that means everybody has got to answer to their name to see if we are all on board just as if they was any other place to go.

When they give the signal for a life boat drill everybody has got to stick their life belt on and go to the boat where they have been given the number of it and even when everybody knows its a fake you got to show up just the same and yester-day they was one bird thats supposed to go in our life boat and he was sea sick and he didn't show up so they went after him and one of the officers told him that wasn't no excuse and what would he do if he was sea sick and the ship was realy sinking and he says he thought it was realy sinking ever since we started.

Well Al we got some crowd on the boat and they's two French officers along with us that been giveing drills and etc. in one of the camps in the U. S. and navy officers and gunners and a man would almost wish something would happen be-cause I bet we would put up some battle.

Lee just come in and asked me who was I writeing to and I told him and he says I better be careful to not write nothing against anybody on the trip just as if I would. But any way I asked him why not and he says because all the mail would be opened and read by the censor so I said "Yes but he won't see this because I won't mail it till we get across the old pond and then I will mail all my letters at once."

So he said a man can't do it that way because just before we hit land the censor will take all our mail off of us and read it and cut out whatever he don't like and then mail it himself. So I didn't know we had a censor along with us but Lee says we certainly have got one and he is up in the front ship and they call that the censor ship on acct. of him being on there.

Well Al I don't care what he reads and what he don't read because I am not the kind that spill anything about the trip that would hurt anybody or get them in bad. So he is welcome to read anything I write you might say.

This front ship is the slowest one of the whole four and how is that for fine judgment Al to put the slowest one ahead and this ship we are on is the fastest and they keep us behind instead of leaving us go up ahead and set the pace for them and no wonder we never get nowheres. Of course that ain't the censor's fault but if the old U. S. is in such a hurry to get men across the pond I should think they would use some judgment and its just like as if Hughey Jennings would stick Oscar Stanage or somebody ahead of Cobb in the batting order so as Cobb couldn't make to many bases on a hit.

Well Al I will have to cut it out for now because its pretty near time for chow and that's the name we got up out to Camp Grant for meals and now everybody in the army when they talk about food they call it chow.

Your pal,   JACK.

On the Ship Board, Jan. 19.

FRIEND AL: Well Al they have got a new nickname for me and now they call me Jack Tar and Bob Lee got it up and I will tell you how it come off. Last night was one rough bird and I guess pretty near everybody on the boat were sick and Lee says to me how was it that I stood the rough weather so good and it didn't seem to effect me so I says it was probably on acct. of me going around the world that time with the two ball clubs and I was right at home on the water so he says "I guess we better call you Jack Tar."

So that's how they come to call me Jack Tar and its a name they got for old sailors that's been all their life on the water. So on acct. of my name being Jack it fits in pretty good.

Well a man can't help from feeling sorry for the boys that have not been across the old pond before and can't stand a little rough spell but it makes a man kind of proud to think the rough weather don't effect you when pretty near everybody else feels like a churn or something the minute a drop of water splashes vs. the side of the boat but still a man can't hardly help from laughing when they look at them.

Lee says he would of thought I would of enlisted in the navy on acct. of being such a good sailor. Well I would of Al if I had knew they needed men and I told Lee so and he said he thought the U. S. made a big mistake keeping it a secret that they did need men in the navy till all the good ones enlisted in the draft and then of course the navy had to take what they could get.

Well I guess I all ready told you that one of the boys in our room is named Freddie Smith and he don't never say a word and I thought at 1st. it was because he was a kind of a bum like Hall that didn't know nothing and that's why he didn't say it but it seems the reason he don't talk more is because he can't talk English very good but he is a Frenchman and he was a waiter in the big French resturent in Milwaukee and now what do you think Al he is going to learn Lee and I French lessons and Lee fixed it up with him. We want to learn how to talk a little so when we get there we can make ourself understood and you remember I started studing French out to Camp Grant but the man down there didn't know nothing about what he was talking about so I walked out on him but this bird won't try and learn us grammer or how you spell it or nothing like that but just a few words so as we can order drinks and meals and etc. when we get a leave off some time. Tonight we are going to have our 1st. lesson and with a man like he to learn us we ought to pick it up quick.

Well old pal I will wind up for this time as I don't feel very good on acct. of something I eat this noon and its a wonder a man can keep up at all where they got you in a stateroom jammed in like a sardine or something and Hall smoking all the while like he was a freight engine pulling a freight train up grade or something.

Your pal,   JACK.

On the Ship Board, Jan. 20.
FRIEND AL: Just a line Al because I don't feel like writeing as I was taken sick last night from something I eat and who wouldn't be sick jammed in a room like a sardine.

I had a kind of a run in with Hall because he tried to kid me about being sick with some of his funny stuff but I told him where to head in. He started out by saying to Lee that Jack Tar looked like somebody had knocked the tar out of him and after a while he says "What's the matter with the old salt to-night he don't seem to have no pepper with him." So I told him to shut up.

Well we didn't have no French lesson on acct. of me being taken sick but we are going to have a lesson tonight and pretty soon I am going up and try and eat something and I hope they don't try and hand me no more of that canned beans or what-ever it was that effected me and if Uncle Sam wants his boys to go over there and put up a battle he shouldn't try and poison them first.

Your pal,   JACK.

On the Ship Board, Jan. 21.
FRIEND AL: Well Al I was talking to one of the sailors named Doran to-day and he says in a day or 2 more we would be right in the danger zone where all the subs hangs out and then would come the fun and we would probably all have to keep our clothes on all night and keep our life belts on and I asked him if they was much danger with all them convoys guarding us and he says the subs might fire a periscope right between two of the convoys and hit our ship and maybe the convoys might get them afterwards but then it would be to late.

He said the last time he come over with troops they was two subs got after this ship and they shot two periscopes at this ship and just missed it and they seem to be laying for this ship because its one of the biggest and fastest the U. S. has got.

Well I told Doran it wouldn't bother me to keep my clothes on all night because I all ready been keeping them on all night because when you have got a state room like ours they's only one place where they's room for a man's clothes and that's on you.

Well old pal they's a whole lot of difference between learn-ing something from somebody that knows what they are talk-ing about and visa versa. I and Lee and Smith got together in the room last night and we wasn't at it more than an hour but I learned more then all the time I took lessons from that 4

flusher out to Camp Grant because Smith don't waist no time
with a lot of junk about grammer but I or Lee would ask him
what was the French for so and so and he would tell us and we
would write it down and say it over till we had it down pat and
I bet we could pretty near order a meal now without no help
from some of these smart alex that claims they can talk all the
languages in the world.

In the 1st. place they's a whole lot of words in French that
they's no difference you might say between them from the way
we say it like beef steak and beer because Lee asked him if suppose we went in somewheres and wanted a steak and bread and
butter and beer and the French for and is und so we would say
beef steak und brot mit butter schmieren und bier and that's all
they is to it and I can say that without looking at the paper
where we wrote it down and you can see I have got that much
learned all ready so I wouldn't starve and when you want to
call a waiter you call him kellner so you see I could go in a
place in Paris and call a waiter and get everything I wanted.
Well Al I bet nobody ever learned that much in 1 hour off that
bird out to Camp Grant and I'll say its some speed.

We are going to have another lesson tonight but Lee says we
don't want to try and learn to much at once or we will forget
what we all ready learned and they's a good deal to that Al.

Well Al its time for chow again so lebe wohl and that's the
same like good by in French.

                    Your pal,   JACK.

                                        On the Ship Board, Jan. 22.
FRIEND AL: Well Al we are in what they call the danger zone and
they's some excitement these days and at night to because they
don't many of the boys go to sleep nights and they go to their
rooms and pretend like they are going to sleep but I bet you
wouldn't need no alarm clock to make them jump out of bed.

Most of the boys stays out on deck most of the time and I
been staying out there myself most all day today not because I
am scared of anything because I always figure if its going to
happen its going to happen but I stay out because it ain't near
as cold as it was and besides if something is comeing off I don't
want to miss it. Besides maybe I could help out some way if
something did happen.

Last night we was all out on deck in the dark talking about this and that and one of the boys I was standing along side of him made the remark that we had been out nine days and he didn't see no France yet or no signs of getting there so I said no wonder when we had such a he—ll of a censor ship and some other guy heard me say it so he said I better not talk like that but I didn't mean it like that but only how slow it was.

Well we are getting along O. K. with the French lessons and Bob Lee told me last night that he run across one of the two French officers that's on the ship and he thought he would try some of his French on him so he said something about it being a nice day in French and the Frenchman was tickled to death and smiled and bowed at him and I guess I will try it out on them the next time I see them.

Well Al that shows we been learning something when the Frenchmans themself know what we are talking about and I and Lee will have the laugh on the rest of the boys when we get there that is if we do get there but for some reason another I have got a hunch that we won't never see France and I can't explain why but once in a while a man gets a hunch and a lot of times they are generally always right.

Your pal,   JACK.

On the Ship Board, Jan. 23.
FRIEND AL: Well Al I was just out on deck with Lee and Sargent Bishop and Bishop is a sargent in our Co. and he said he had just came from Capt. Seeley and Capt. Seeley told him to tell all the N. C. O. officers like sargents and corporals that if a sub got us we was to leave the privates get into the boats first before we got in and we wasn't to get into our boats till all the privates was safe in the boats because we would probably be cooler and not get all excited like the privates. So you see Al if something does happen us birds will have to take things in hand you might say and we will have to stick on the job and not think about ourselfs till everybody else is taken care of.

Well Lee said that Doran one of the sailors told him something on the quiet that didn't never get into the newspapers and that was about one of the trips that come off in December and it seems like a whole fleet of subs got on to it that some transports was comeing so they layed for them and they shot a periscope at one of the transports and hit it square in the middle and it begun to sink right away and it looked like they wouldn't nobody get into the boats but the sargents and corporals was as cool as if nothing was comeing off and they quieted the soldiers down and finely got them into the boats and the N. C. O. officers was so cool and done so well that when Gen. Pershing heard about it he made this rule about the N. C. O. officer always waiting till the last so they could kind of handle things. But Doran also told Lee that they was some men sunk with the ship and they was all N. C. O. officers except one sailor and of course the ship sunk so quick that some of the corporals and sargents didn't have no time to get off on acct. of haveing to wait till the last. So you see that when you read the newspapers you don't get all the dope because they don't tell the reporters only what they feel like telling them.

Well Al I guess I told you all ready about me haveing this hunch that I wouldn't never see France and I guess it looks now more then ever like my hunch was right because if we get hit I will have to kind of look out for the boys that's in my boat and not think about myself till everybody else is O. K. and Doran says if this ship ever does get hit it will sink quick because its so big and heavy and of course the heavier a ship is it will sink all the sooner and Doran says he knows they are laying for us because he has made five trips over and back on this ship and he never was on a trip when a sub didn't get after them.

Well I will close for this time because I am not feeling very good Al and it isn't nothing I eat or like that but its just I feel kind of faint like I use to sometimes when I would pitch a tough game in St. Louis when it was hot or something.

Your pal,   JACK.

On the Ship Board, Jan. 23.
FRIEND AL: Well I all ready wrote you one letter today but I kind of feel like I better write to you again because any minute we are libel to hear a bang against the side of the boat and you know what that means and I have got a hunch that I won't never get off of the ship alive but will go down with her because I wouldn't never leave the ship as long as they was anybody left on her rules or no rules but I would stay and help out

till every man was off and then of course it would be to late but any way I would go down feeling like I had done my duty. Well Al when a man has got a hunch like that he would be a sucker to not pay no tension to it and that is why I am writing to you again because I got some things I want to say before the end.

Now old pal I know that Florrie hasn't never warmed up towards you and Bertha and wouldn't never go down to Bedford with me and pay you a visit and every time I ever give her a hint that I would like to have you and Bertha come up and see us she always had some excuse that she was going to be busy or this and that and of course I knew she was trying to alibi herself and the truth was she always felt like Bertha and her wouldn't have nothing in common you might say because Florrie has always been a swell dresser and cared a whole lot about how she looked and some way she felt like Bertha wouldn't feel comfortable around where she was at and maybe she was right but we can forget all that now Al and I can say one thing Al she never said nothing reflecting on you yourself in any way because I wouldn't of stood for it but instead of that when I showed her that picture of you and Bertha in your wedding suit she made the remark that you looked like one of the honest homely kind of people that their friends could always depend on them. Well Al when she said that she hit the nail on the head and I always knew you was the one pal who I could depend on and I am depending on you now and I know that if I am laying down at the bottom of the ocean tonight you will see that my wishs in this letter is carried out to the letter.

What I want to say is about Florrie and little Al. Now don't think Al that I am going to ask you for financial assistants because I would know better then that and besides we don't need it on acct. of me having $10000 dollars soldier insurence in Florrie's name as the benefitter and the way she is coining money in that beauty parlor she won't need to touch my insurence but save it for little Al for a rainy day only I suppose that the minute she gets her hands on it she will blow it for widows weeds and I bet they will be some weeds Al and everybody will think they are flowers instead of weeds.

But what I am getting at is that she won't need no money because with what I leave her and what she can make she has got enough and more then enough but I often say that money isn't the only thing in this world and they's a whole lot of things pretty near as good and one of them is kindness and what I am asking from you and Bertha is to drop in on her once in a while up in Chi and pay her a visit and I have all ready wrote her a letter telling her to ask you but even if she don't ask you go and see her any way and see how she is getting along and if she is takeing good care of the kid or leaving him with the Swede nurse all the while.

Between you and I Al what I am scared of most is that Florrie's mind will be effected if anything happens to me and without knowing what she was doing she would probably take the first man that asked her and believe me she is not the kind that would have to wait around on no st. corner to catch somebody's eye but they would follow her around and nag at her till she married them and I would feel like he—ll over it because Florrie is the kind of a girl that has got to be handled right and not only that but what would become of little Al with some horse Dr. for a father in law and probably this bird would treat him like a dog and beat him up either that or make a sissy out of him.

Well Al old pal I know you will do like I ask and go and see her and maybe you better go alone but if you do take Bertha along I guess it would be better and not let Bertha say nothing to her because Florrie is the kind that flare up easy and specially when they think they are a little better then somebody. But if you could just drop her a hint and say that she should ought to be proud to be a widow to a husband that died for Uncle Sam and she ought to live for my memory and for little Al and try and make him as much like I as possible I believe it would make her think and any way I want you to do it for me old pal.

Well good by old pal and I wished I could leave some thing to you and Bertha and believe me I would if I had ever known this was comeing off this way though of course I figured right along that I wouldn't last long in France because what chance has a corporal got? But I figured I would make some arrangements for a little present for you and Bertha as soon as I got to France but of course it looks now like I wouldn't never get there and all the money I have got is tied up so its to late to think of that and all as I can say is good luck to you and Bertha and everybody in Bedford and I hope they will be proud of me and remember I done my best and I often say what more can a man do then that?

Well Al I will say good by again and good luck and now have got to quit and go to chow.

Your pal to the last,   JACK KEEFE.

On the Ship Board, Jan. 24.

FRIEND AL: Well this has been some day and wait till you hear about it and hear what come off and some of the birds on this ship took me for a sucker and tried to make a rummy out of me but I was wise to their game and I guess the shoe is on the other foot this time.

Well it was early this A. M. and I couldn't sleep and I was up on deck and along come one of them French officers that's been on board all the way over. Well I thought I would try myself out on him like Lee said he done so I give him a salute and I said to him "Schones tag nicht wahr." Like you would say its a beautiful day only I thought I was saying it in French but wait till you hear about it Al.

Well Al they ain't nobody in the world fast enough to of caught what he said back to me and I won't never know what he said but I won't never forget how he looked at me and when I took one look at him I seen we wasn't going to get along very good so I turned around and started up the deck. Well he must of flagged the first man he seen and sent him after me and it was a 2d. lieut. and he come running up to me and stopped me and asked me what was my name and what Co. and etc. and at first I was going to stall and then I thought I better not so I told him who I was and he left me go.

Well I didn't know then what was comeing off so I just layed low and I didn't have to wait around long and all of a sudden a bird from the Colonel's staff found me in the parlor and says I was wanted right away and when I got to this room there was the Col. and the two Frenchmans and my captain Capt. Seeley and a couple others so I saluted and I can't tell you exactly what come off because I can't remember all what the Colonel said but it was something like this.

In the first place he says "Corporal Keefe they's some little matters that you have got to explain and we was going to pass

them up first on the grounds that Capt. Seeley said you probably didn't know no better but this thing that come off this
A. M. can't be explained by ignorants."

So then he says "It was reported that you was standing on
deck the night before last and you made the remark that we
had a he—ll of a censor ship." And he says "What did you
mean by that?"

So you see Al this smart alex of a Lee had told me they
called the first ship the censor ship and I believed him at first
because I was thinking about something else or of course I
never would of believed him because the censor ship isn't no
ship like this kind of a ship but means something else. So I
explained about that and I seen Capt. Seeley kind of crack a
smile so then I knew I was O. K.

So then he pulled it on me about speaking to Capt. Somebody of the French army in the German language and of
course they was only one answer to that and you see the way it
was Al all the time Smith was pretending to learn us French he
was learning us German and Lee put him up to it but when the
Colonel asked me what I meant by doing such a thing as talk
German why of course I knew in a minute that they had been
trying to kid me but at first I told the Colonel I couldn't of
said no German because I don't know no more German than
Silk O'Loughlin. Well the Frenchman was pretty sore and I
don't know what would of came off only for Capt. Seeley and
he spoke up and said to the Colonel that if he could have a few
minutes to investigate he thought he could clear things up
because he figured I hadn't intended to do nothing wrong and
somebody had probably been playing jokes.

So Capt. Seeley went out and it seemed like a couple of yrs.
till he came back and he had Smith and Lee and Doran with
him. So then them 3 birds was up on the carpet and I'll say
they got some panning and when it was all over the Colonel
said something about they being a dam site to much kidding
back and fourth going on and he hoped that before long we
would find out that this war wasn't no practicle joke and he
give Lee and Smith a fierce balling out and he said he would
leave Capt. Seeley to deal with them and he would report
Doran to the proper quarters and then he was back on me
again and he said it looked like I had been the innocent victim

of a practicle joke but he says "You are so dam innocent that I figure you are temperately unfit to hold on to a corporal's warrant so you can consider yourself reduced to the ranks. We can't have no corporals that if some comedian told them the Germans was now one of our allies they would try and get in the German trenches and shake hands with them."

Well Al when it was all over I couldn't hardly keep from laughing because you see I come out of it O. K. and the laugh was on Smith and Lee and Doran because I got just what I wanted because I never did want to be a corporal because it meant I couldn't pal around with the boys and be their pals and I never felt right when I was giveing them orders because I would rather be just one of them and make them feel like we were all equals.

O course they wasn't no time on the whole trip when Lee or Doran or Smith either one of them had me fooled because just to look at them you would know they are the kind of smart alex that's always trying to put something over on somebody only I figured two could play at that game as good as one and I would kid them right back and give them as good as they sent because I always figure that the game ain't over till the ninth inning and the man that does the laughing then has got all the best of it. But at that I don't bear no bad will towards neither one of them and I have got a good notion to ask Capt. Seeley to let them off easy.

Well Al this is a long letter but I wanted you to know I wasn't no corporal no more and if a sub hits us now Al I can hop into a boat as quick as I feel like it but jokeing a side if something like that happened it wouldn't make no difference to me if I was a corporal or not a corporal because I am a man and I would do my best and help the rest of the boys get into the boats before I thought about myself.

Your pal,   JACK.

On the Ship Board, Jan. 25.

FRIEND AL: Well old pal just a line to let you know we are out of the danger zone and pretty near in port and I can't tell you where we land at but everybody is hollering and the band's playing and I guess the boys feels a whole lot better then when we was out there where the subs could get at us but between you and I Al I never thought about the subs all the way over only when I heard somebody else talk about them because I always figure that if they's some danger of that kind the best way to do is just forget it and if its going to happen all right but what's the use of worrying about it? But I suppose lots of people is built different and they have just got to worry all the while and they get scared stiff just thinking about what might happen but I always say nobody ever got fat worrying so why not just forget it and take things as they come.

Well old pal they's to many sights to see so I will quit for this time.

Your pal,   JACK.

Somewheres in France, Jan. 26.
FRIEND AL: Well old pal here we are and its against the rules to tell you where we are at but of course it don't take no Shylock to find out because all you would have to do is look at the post mark that they will put on this letter.

Any way you couldn't pronounce what the town's name is if you seen it spelled out because it isn't nothing like how its spelled out and you won't catch me trying to pronounce none of these names or talk French because I am off of languages for a while and good old American is good enough for me eh Al?

Well Al now that its all over I guess we was pretty lucky to get across the old pond without no trouble because between you and I Al I heard just a little while ago from one of the boys that three nights ago we was attacked and our ship just missed getting hit by a periscope and the destroyers went after the subs and they was a whole flock of them and the reason we didn't hear nothing is that the death bombs don't go off till they are way under water so you can't hear them but between you and I Al the navy men say they was nine subs sank.

Well I didn't say nothing about it to the man who tipped me off but I had a hunch that night that something was going on and I don't remember now if it was something I heard or what it was but I knew they was something in the air and I was expecting every minute that the signal would come for us to take to the boats but they wasn't no necessity of that because the destroyers worked so fast and besides they say they don't never give no alarm till the last minute because they don't want to get everybody up at night for nothing.

Well any way its all over now and here we are and you ought to of heard the people in the town here cheer us when we come in and you ought to see how the girls look at us and believe me Al they are some girls. Its a good thing I am an old married man or I believe I would pretty near be tempted to flirt back with some of the ones that's been trying to get my eye but the way it is I just give them a smile and pass on and they's no harm in that and I figure a man always ought to give other people as much pleasure as you can as long as it don't harm nobody.

Well Al everybody's busier then a chicken with their head off and I haven't got no more time to write. But when we get to where we are going I will have time maybe and tell you how we are getting along and if you want drop me a line and I wish you would send me the Chi papers once in a while especially when the baseball training trips starts but maybe they won't be no Jack Keefe to send them to by that time but if they do get me I will die fighting. You know me Al.

Your pal,

JACK.

CHAPTER II

Private Valentine

FRIEND AL: Well Al here I am only I can't tell you where its at because the censor rubs it out when you put down the name of a town and besides that even if I was to write out where we are at you wouldn't have no idear where its at because how you spell them hasn't nothing to do with their name if you tried to say it.

For inst. they's a town a little ways from us that when you say it its Lucy like a gal or something but when you come to spell it out its Loucey like something else.

Well Al any way this is where they have got us staying till we get called up to the front and I can't hardly wait till that comes off and some say it may be tomorrow and others say we are libel to be here a yr. Well I hope they are wrong because I would rather live in the trenches then one of these billets where they got us and between you and I Al its nothing more then a barn. Just think of a man like I Al thats been use to nothing only the best hotels in the big league and now they got me staying in a barn like I was a horse or something and I use to think I was cold when they had us sleeping with imaginery blankets out to Camp Grant but I would prespire if I was there now after this and when we get through here they can send us up to the north pole in our undershirt and we would half to keep moping the sweat off of our forehead and set under a electric fan to keep from sweltering.

Well they have got us pegged as horses all right not only because they give us a barn to live in but also from the way they sent us here from where we landed at in France and we made the trip in cattle cars and 1 of the boys says they must of got us mixed up with the calvary or something. It certainly was some experience to be riding on one of these French trains for a man that went back and fourth to the different towns in the big league and back in a special Pullman and sometimes 2 of them so as we could all have lower births. Well we didn't have no births on the French R. R. and it wouldn't of done us no good to of had them because you wouldn't no sooner dose off when the engine would let off a screem that sounded like a woman that seen a snake and 1 of the boys says that on acct. of all the men being in the army they had women doing the men's work and judgeing by the noise they even had them whistleing for the crossings.

Well we finely got here any way and they signed us to our different billets and they's 20 of us in this one not counting a couple of pigs and god knows how many rats and a cow that mews all night. We haven't done nothing yet only look around but Monday we go to work out to the training grounds and they say we won't only half to march 12 miles through the mud and snow to get there. Mean time we set and look out the cracks onto Main St. and every little wile they's a Co. of pollutes marchs through or a train of motor Lauras takeing stuff up to the front or bringing guys back that didn't duck quick enough and to see these Frenchmens march you would think it was fun but when they have been at it a wile they will loose some of their pep.

Well its warmer in bed then setting here writing so I will close for this time.

Your pal,   Jack.

Somewheres in France, Feb. 4.

Friend Al: Well Al I am writing this in the Y. M. C. A. hut where they try and keep it warm and all the boys that can crowd in spends most of their spare time here but we don't have much spare time at that because its always one thing another and I guess its just as well they keep us busy because every time they find out you are not doing nothing they begin vaxinating everybody.

They's enough noise in here so as a man can't hear yourself think let alone writeing a letter so if I make mistakes in spelling and etc. in this letter you will know why it is. They are singing the song now about the baby's prayer at twilight where the little girl is supposed to be praying for her daddy that's a soldier to take care of himself but if she was here now she would be praying for him to shut up his noise.

Well we was in the trenchs all day not the regular ones but the ones they got for us to train in them and they was a bunch of French officers trying to learn us how to do this in that and etc. and some of the time you could all most understand what they was trying to tell you and then it was stuff we learnt the first wk. out to Camp Grant and I suppose when they get so as they can speak a few words of English they will tell us we ought to stand up when we hear the Star spangle Banner. Well we was a pretty sight when we got back with the mud and slush and everything and by the time they get ready to call us into action they will half to page us in the morgue.

About every 2 or 3 miles today we would pass through a town where some of the rest of the boys has got their billets only they don't call it miles in France because that's to easy to say but instead of miles they call them kilometts. But any way from the number of jerk water burgs we went through you would think we was on the Monon and the towns all looks so much like the other that when one of the French soldiers gets a few days leave off they half to spend most of it looking for land marks so as they will know if they are where they live. And they couldn't even be sure if it was warm weather and their folks was standing out in front of the house because all the familys is just alike with the old Mr. and the Mrs. and pigs and a cow and a dog.

Well Al they say its pretty quite these days up to the front and the boys that's been around here a wile says you can hear the guns when they's something doing and the wind blows this way but we haven't heard no guns yet only our own out to where we have riffle practice but everybody says as soon as spring comes and the weather warms up the Germans is sure to start something. Well I don't care if they start anything or not just so the weather warms up and besides they won't never finish what they start unless they start going back home and they won't even finish that unless they show a whole lot more speed then they did comeing. They are just trying to throw a scare into somebody with a lot of junk about a big drive they are going to make but I have seen birds come up to hit in baseball Al that was going to drive it out of the park but their drive turned out to be a hump back liner to the pitcher. I remember once when Speaker come up with a couple men on and we was 2 runs ahead in the 9th. inning and he says to me "Well busher here is where I hit one a mile." Well Al he hit one a mile all right but it was ½ a mile up and the other ½ a mile down and that's the way it goes with them gabby guys and its the same way with the Germans and they talk all the time so as they will get thirsty and that's how they like to be.

Speaking about thirsty Al its different over here then at home because when a man in uniform wants a drink over here you don't half to hire no room in a hotel and put on your nightgown but you can get it here in your uniform only what they call beer here we would pore it on our wheat cakes at home and they got 2 kinds of wine red and white that you could climb outside of a bbl. of it without asking the head waiter to have them play the Rosery. But they say the champagne is O. K. and I am going to tackle it when I get a chance and you may think from that that I have got jack to throw away but over here Al is where they make the champagne and you can get a qt. of it for about a buck or ½ what you would pay for it in the U. S. and besides that the money they got here is a frank instead of a dollar and a frank isn't only worth about $.19 cents so a man can have a whole lot better time here and not cost him near as much.

And another place where the people in France has got it on the Americans and that is that when they write a letter here they don't half to pay nothing to mail it but when you write to me you have got to stick a 5 cent stamp on it but judgeing by the way you answer my letters the war will be all over before you half to break a dime. Of course I am just jokeing Al and I know why you don't write much because you haven't got nothing to write staying there in Bedford and you could take a post card and tell me all the news that happened in 10 yrs. and still have room enough yet to say Bertha sends kind regards.

But of course its different with a man like I because I am always where they is something big going on and first it was baseball and now its a bigger game yet you might say but whatever is going on big you can always count on me being in the mist of it and not buried alive in no Indiana X roads where they still think the first bounce is out. But of course I know it is not your fault that you haven't been around and seen more and it ain't every man that can get away from a small town and make a name for themself and I suppose I ought to consider myself lucky.

Well Al enough for this time and I will write soon again and I would like to hear from you even if you haven't nothing to say and don't forget to send me a Chi paper when you get a hold of one and I asked Florrie to send me one every day but asking her for favors is like rolling off a duck's back you might say and its first in one ear and then the other.

Your pal,   JACK.

Somewheres in France, Feb. 7.

FRIEND AL: I suppose you have read articles in the papers about the war that's wrote over here by reporters and the way they do it is they find out something and then write it up and send it by cablegrams to their papers and then they print it and that's what you read in the papers.

Well Al they's a whole flock of these here reporters over here and I guess they's one for every big paper in the U. S. and they all wear bands around their sleeves with a C on them for civilian or something so as you can spot them comeing and keep your mouth shut. Well they have got their head quarters in one of the towns along the line but they ride all over the camp in automobiles and this evening I was outside of our billet and one of them come along and seen me and got out of his car and come up to me and asked if I wasn't Jack Keefe the White Sox pitcher. Well Al he writes for one of the Chi papers and of course he knows all about me and has seen me work. Well he asked me a lot of questions about this in that and I didn't give him no military secrets but he asked me how did I like the army game and etc.

I asked him if he was going to mention about me being here in the paper and he says the censors wouldn't stand for mentioning no names until you get killed because if they mentioned your name the Germans would know who all was here but after you are dead the Germans don't care if you had been here or not.

But he says he would put it in the paper that he was talking to a man that use to be a star pitcher on the White Sox and he says everybody would know who it was he was talking about because they wasn't such a slue of star pitchers in the army that it would take a civil service detective to find out who he meant.

So we talked along and finely he asked me was I going to

write a book about the war and I said no and he says all right he would tell the paper that he had ran across a soldier that not only use to be a ball player but wasn't going to write a book and they would make a big story out of it.

So I said I wouldn't know how to go about it to write a book but when I went around the world with the 2 ball clubs that time I use to write some poultry once in a wile just for different occasions like where the boys was called on for a speech or something and they didn't know what to say so I would make up one of my poems and the people would go nuts over them.

So he said why didn't I tear off a few patriotic poems now and slip them to him and he would send them to his paper and they would print them and maybe if some of them was good enough somebody would set down and write a song to them and probably everybody would want to buy it and sing it like Over There and I would clean up a good peace of jack.

Well Al I told him I would see if I could think up something to write and of course I was just stalling him because a soldier has got something better to do than write songs and I will leave that to the birds that was gun shy and stayed home. But if you see in the Chi papers where one of the reporters was talking to a soldier that use to be a star pitcher in the American League or something you will know who they mean. He said he would drop by in a few days again and see if I had something wrote up for him but I will half to tell him I have been to busy to monkey with it.

As far as I can see they's enough songs all ready wrote up about the war so as everybody in the army and navy could have 1 a peace and still have a few left over for the boshs and that's a name we got up for the Germans Al and instead of calling them Germans we call them boshs on acct. of them being so full of bunk.

Well Al one of the burgs along the line is where Jonah Vark was born when she was alive. It seems like France was mixed up in another war along about a 100 yrs. ago and they was getting licked and Jonah was just a young gal but she dressed up in men's coat and pants and went up to the front and led the charges with a horse and she carried a white flag and the Dutchmens or whoever they was fighting against must of thought it was a flag of truants and any way they didn't fire at them and the French captured New Orleans and win the war. The Germans is trying to pull the same stuff on our boys now and lots of times they run up and holler Conrad like they was going to give up and when your back is turned they whang away at you but they won't pull none of that stuff on me and when one of them trys to Conrad me I will perculate them with a bayonet.

Well Al the boys is starting their choir practice and its good night and some times I wished I was a deef and dumb mute and couldn't hear nothing.

Your pal,   JACK.

Somewheres in France, Feb. 9.
FRIEND AL: Well Al I didn't have nothing to do last night and I happened to think about that reporter and how he would be comeing along in a few days asking for that poultry.

I figured I might as well set down and write him up a couple verses because them fellows is hard up for articles to send their paper because in the first place we don't tell them nothing so they could write it up and when they write it the censors smeers out everything but the question marks and dots but of course they would leave them send poems because the Germans couldn't make head or tale out of them. So any way I set down and tore off 3 verses and he says they ought to be something about a gal in it so here is what I wrote:

> *Near a year ago today*
> *Pres. Wilson of the U. S. A.*
> *had something to say,*
> *"Germany you better keep away*
> *This is no time for play."*
> *When it come time to go*
> *America was not slow*
> *Each one said good by to their girl so dear*
> *And some of them has been over here*
> *since last year.*
>
> *I will come home when the war is over*
> *Back to the U. S. A.*
> *So don't worry little girlie*

And now we are going to Berlin
And when we the Kaiser skin
and the war we will win
And make the Kaiser jump out of his skin.

The ones that stays at home
Can subscribe to the liberty loan
And some day we will come home
to the girles that's left alone
Old Kaiser Bill is up against it
For all are doing their bit.
Pres. Wilson says the stars and stripes
Will always fight for their rights.

That's what I tore off and when he comes around again I will have it for him and if you see it in the Chi papers you will know who wrote it up and maybe somebody will write a song to it but of course they can't sign my name to it unless I get killed or something but I guess at that they ain't so many soldiers over here that can turn out stuff like that but what my friends won't be pretty sure who wrote it.

But if something does happen to me I wished you would kind of keep your eyes pealed and if the song comes out try and see that Florrie gets some jack out of it and I haven't wrote nothing to her about it because she is like all other wifes and when somebodys else husband pulls something its O. K. but if their own husband does it he must of had a snoot full.

Well today was so rotten that they didn't make us go nowheres and I'll say its got to be pretty rotten when they do that and the meal they give us tonight wouldn't of bulged out a grandaddy long legs and I and my buddy Frank Carson was both hungry after we eat and I suppose you will wonder what do I mean by buddy. Well Al that's a name I got up for who ever you pal around with or bunk next to them and now everybody calls their pal their buddy. Well any way he says why didn't we go over to the Red X canteen resturent and buy ourself a feed so we went over and its a little shack where the Red X serves you a pretty good meal for 1 frank and that's about $.19 cents and they don't try and make no profits on it but just run them so as a man don't half to go along all the wile on what the army hands out to you.

Well they was 3 janes on the job over there and 2 of them
would be safe anywheres you put them but the other one is
Class A and her old woman must of been pie eyed when she
left her come over here. Well Carson said she belonged to him
because he had seen her before and besides I was a married
man so I says all right go ahead and get her. Well Al it would
be like Terre Haute going after George Sisler or somebody
and the minute we blowed in she didn't have eyes for only me
but I wasn't going to give her no encouragement because we
were here to kill Germans and not ladys but I wished you
could of seen the smile she give me. Well she's just as much a
American as I or you but of course Carson had to be cute and
try to pull some of his French on her so he says Bon soir
Madam Moselle and that is the same like we would say good
evening but when Carson pulled it I spoke up and said "If
your bones is soir why don't you go and take the baths somewhere?" Pretending like I thought he meant his bones were
sore. Well the little lady got it O. K. and pretty near laughed
outright. You see Al when a person has got rhuematism they
go and take the baths like down to Mudlavia so I meant if his
bones was sore he better go somewheres like that. So the little
lady tried to not laugh on acct. of me being a stranger but she
couldn't hardly help from busting out and then I smiled at her
back and after that Carson might as well of been mowing the
lawn out in Nobody's Land. I felt kind of sorry the way things
broke because here he is a man without no home ties and of
course I have all ready got a wife but Miss Moselle didn't have
no eyes for him and that's the way it goes but what can a man
do and Carson seen how it was going and says to me right in
front of her "Have you heard from your Mrs. since we been
over?" And I didn't dast look up and see how she took it.

Well they set us up a pretty good feed and the little lady kept
asking us questions like how long had we been here and what
part of the U. S. we come from and etc. and finely Carson told
her who I was and she popped her eyes out and says she use to
go to the ball games once in a wile in N. Y. city with her old
man and she didn't never think she would meet a big league
pitcher and talk to them and she says she wondered if she ever
seen me pitch. Well I guess if she had she would remember it
specially in N. Y. because there was one club I always made

them look like a fool and they wasn't the only club at that and
I guess they's about 6 other clubs in the American League that
if they had seen my name in the dead they wouldn't shed off
enough tears to gum up the infield.

Well when we come out she asked us would we come again
and we said yes but I guess its best for both she and I if I stay
away but I said we would come again to be polite so she said
au revoir and that's like you would say so long so I said au
reservoir pretending like I didn't know the right way to say it
but she seen I was just kidding and laughed and she is the kind
of a gal that gets everything you pull and bright as a whip and
her and I would make a good team but of course they's no use
talking about it the way I am tied up so even when I'm sick in
tired of the regular rations I won't dast go over there for a feed
because it couldn't do nothing only harm to the both of us and
the best way to do with those kind of affairs is to cut it out
before somebody gets hurt.

Well its time to hop into the feathers and I only wished it
was feathers but feathers comes off a chicken or something and
I guess these matteresses we got is made out to Gary or Indiana Harbor or somewheres.

Your pal,   JACK.

Somewheres in France, Feb. 11.

FRIEND AL: Well Al they's several of the boys that won't need
no motor Laura to carry their pay for the next couple mos. and
if you was to mention champagne to them they would ask for
a barrage. I was over to the Y. M. C. A. hut last night and
when I come back I wished you could of seen my buddys and
they was 2 of them that was still able to talk yet and they was
haveing a argument because one of them wanted to pore some
champagne in a dish so as the rats would get stewed and the
other bird was trying to not let him because he said it always
made them mean and they would go home and beat up their
Mrs.

It seems like one of the boys had a birthday and his folks is
well off and they had sent him some jack from the states to buy
blankets and etc. with it and he thought it would be a sucker
play to load up with bed close when spring was comeing so he
loaded up with something else and some of the boys with him

and for 50 or 60 franks over here you can get enough champagne to keep the dust layed all summer and of course some of
the boys hadn't never tasted it before and they thought you
could bathe in it like beer. They didn't pay no more tension to
revelry this A. M. then if they was a corps and most of them was
at that and out of the whole bunch of us they was only 7 that
didn't get reported and the others got soaked 2 thirds of their
pay and confined to their quarters and Capt. Seeley says if they
was any more birthdays in his Co. we wouldn't wind the celebration up till sunrise and then it would be in front of a fireing
squad. Well Al if the boys can't handle it no better then that
they better leave it alone and just because its cheap that's no
reason to try and get it all at once because the grapes will still
be growing over here yet when all us birds takes our teeth off
at night with our other close.

Well Al the reporter that asked me to write up the verses
ain't been around since and probably he has went up to the
front or somewheres and I am glad of it and I hope he forgets
all about it because in the first place I am not one of the kind
that is crazy to get in the papers and besides I am to busy to be
monking with stuff like that. Yes they keep us on the jump all
the wile and we are pretty well wore out when night comes
around but a man wouldn't mind it if we was learning something but the way it is now its like as if we had graduated from
college and then they sent us to kindegarden and outside of
maybe a few skulls the whole regt. is ready right now to get up
there in the trenches and show them something and I only
wished we was going tomorrow but I guess some of the boys
would like it to never go up there but would rather stay here in
this burg and think they was haveing a good time kidding with
the French gals and etc. but that's no business for a married
man and even if I didn't have no family the French gals I seen
so far wouldn't half to shew me away and I been hearing all my
life what swell dressers they was but a scout for the Follys
wouldn't waist no time in this burg.

But I'm sick in tired of the same thing day in and day out and
here we been in France 2 wks. and all we done is a little riffle
practice and stuff we had back home and get soping wet every day
and no mail and I wouldn't wonder if Florrie and little Al had

forgot all about me and if Secty. Daniels wired them that Jack Keefe had been killed they would say who and the hell is he.

So all and all they can't send us up to the front to quick and it seems like a shame that men like I should be held back just because they's a few birds in the regt. that can't put on a gas mask yet without triping themself up.

Your pal,   JACK.

Somewheres in France, Feb. 13.

FRIEND AL: Well Al wait till you hear this and I bet you will pop your eyes out. I guess I all ready told you about Miss Moselle the little lady over to the Red X canteen. Well I was over there the day before yesterday and she wasn't around nowheres and I was glad of it because I didn't want to see her and just dropped in there to get something to eat and today I was in there again and this time she was there and she smiled when she seen me and come up and begin talking and she asked me how I liked it and I said I would like it a whole lot better if we was in the fighting and she asked me if I didn't like this town and I said well no I wasn't nuts about it and she said she didn't think I was very complementary so then I seen she wanted to get personal.

Well Al she knows I am a married man because Carson just as good as told her so I didn't see no harm in kidding her along a wile so I give her a smile and said well you know the whole town ain't like you and she blushed up and says "Well I didn't expect nothing like that from a great baseball pitcher" so you see Al she had been makeing inquirys about me. So I said "Well they was only one pitcher I ever heard of that couldn't talk and that was Dummy Taylor but at that they's a whole lot of them that if they couldn't say my arm's sore they might as well be tongue tied." But I told her I wasn't one of those kind and I guest when it came to talking I could give as good as I sent and she asked me was I a college man and I kidded her along and said yes I went to Harvard and she said what year so I told her I was there 2 different yrs. and we talked along about this in that and I happened to have them verses in my pocket that I wrote up and they dropped out when I was after my pocket book and she acted like she wanted to know what the writeing was so I showed them to her.

Well Al I wished you could of seen how supprised she was when she read them and she says "So you are a poet." So I said "Yes I am a poet and don't know it" so that made her laugh and I told her about the reporter asking me to write some poems and then she asked me if she could keep a hold of those ones till she made out a copy of them to keep for herself and I said "You can keep that copy and pretend like I was thinking of you when I wrote them." Well Al I wished you could of seen her then and she couldn't say nothing at first but finely she says tomorrow was valentine day and the verses would do for a valentine so just joking I asked her if she wouldn't rather have a comical valentine and she says those ones would do O. K. so then I told her I would write her a real valentine for herself but I might maybe not get it ready in time to give her tomorrow and she says she realized it took time and any time would do.

Well of course I am not going to write up nothing for her and after this I will keep away from the canteen because it isn't right to leave her see to much of me even if she does know I am married but if I do write her something I will make it comical and no mushy stuff in it. But it does seem like fate or something that the harder I try and not get mixed up in a flirtation I can't turn around you might say but what they's some gal poping up on my trail and if it was anybody else only Miss Moselle I wouldn't mind but she is a darb and I wouldn't do nothing to hurt her for the world but they can't nobody say this is my fault.

Well Al I pretty near forgot to tell you that the boys is putting on a entertainment over to the Y. M. C. A. Saturday night and they will be singing and gags and etc. and they asked me would I give them a little talk on baseball and I said no at first but they begged me and finely I give my consent but you know how I hate makeing speeches and etc. but a man don't hardly feel like refuseing when they want me so bad so I am going to give them a little talk on my experiences and make it comical and I will tell you about the entertainment when its over.

Your pal,   JACK.

Somewheres in France, Feb. 15.

FRIEND AL: Well Al I just been over to the canteen and I give

the little lady the valentine I promised to write up for her and
I wasn't going to write it up only I happened to remember that
I promised so I wrote something up and I was going to make
it comical but I figured that would disappoint her on acct. of
the way she feels towards me so here is what I wrote up.

> *To Miss Moselle*
> *(Private)*
> *A soldier don't have much time*
> *To set down and write up a valentine*
> *but please bear in mind*
> *That I think about you many a time*
> *And I wished I could call you mine*
> *And I hope they will come a time*
> *When I will have more time*
> *And then everything will be fine*
> *And if you will be my valentine*
> *I will try and show you a good time.*

Well after I had wrote it I thought I better have it fixed up
like a valentine and they's one of the boys in our Co. named
Stoops that use to be a artist so I had him draw me a couple of
hearts with a bow and arrow sticking through them and a few
flowers on a peace of card board and I coppied off the valentine
on the card in printing and stuck it in a envelope and took it
over to her and I didn't wait for her to open it up and look at
it and I just says here is that valentine I promised you and its I
day late and she blushed up and couldn't say nothing and I
come away. Well Al she has read it by this time and I hope she
don't take nothing I said serious but of course she knows I am
a married man and she can read between the lines and see
where I am trying to let her down easy and telling her to not
expect no more tensions from me and its just like saying good
by to her in a way only not as rough as comeing right out and
saying it. But I won't see her no more and its all over before it
begun you might say.

Well we passed some German prisoners today and believe
me we give them a ride. Everybody called them Heinie and
Fritz and I seen one of them giveing me a look like he was
wondring if all the U. S. soldiers was big stroppers like I but I
stuck out my tongue at him and said "What do you think you

are looking at you big pretzel" and he didn't dast say nothing back. Well they was a fine looking gang and they's been a lot of storys going the rounds about no soap in Germany. Well Al its all true.

Well I finely got a letter from Florrie that is if you could call it a letter and to read it you wouldn't never guess that she had a husband over here in France and maybe never see him again but you would think I had went across the st. to get a bottle of ketchup and all as she said about little Al was that he needed a new pair of shoes and they's about as much news in that as if she said he woke up in the night. And the rest of the letter was about how good she was doing in the beauty parlor and for me not to worry about her because she was O. K. only for a callous on her heel and I suppose she will go to the hospital with it and here I am with so many of them that if they was worth a frank a peace I could pay the Kaiser's gas bill. And she never asked me did I need anything or how was I getting along. And she enclosed a snapshot of herself in one of these here war bride outfits and she looks so good in it that I bet she goes to church every Sunday and asks god to prolongate the war.

Your pal,   JACK.

Somewheres in France, Feb. 16.

FRIEND AL: Well Al they's a certain bird in this camp that if I ever find out who he is they won't need no tonnages to carry him back when the war's over. Let me tell you what come off tonight and what was pulled off on the little lady and I and if you read about me getting in front of the court marshall for murder you will know how it come off.

I guess I all ready told you about the show that was comeing off tonight and they asked me to make a little talk on baseball. Well they was as many there as could crowd in and the band played and they was singing and gags and storys and etc. and they didn't call on me till pretty near the last. Well Al you ought to of heard the crowd when I got up there and it sounded like old times to have them all cheering and clapping and I stepped to the front of the platform and give them a bow and it was the first time I was ever on the stage but I wasn't scared only at first.

Well I had wrote out what I was going to say and learnt the

most of it by heart and here is what I give them only I won't give you only part of it because it run pretty long.

"Gentlemen and friends. I am no speech maker and I guess if I had to make speeches for a liveing I am afraid I couldn't do it but the boys is anxious I should say a few words about baseball and I didn't want to disappoint them. They may be some of you boys that has not followed the great American game very close and maybe don't know who Jack Keefe is. Well gentlemen I was boughten from Terre Haute in the Central League by that grand old Roman Charley Comiskey owner of the Chicago White Sox in 1913 and I been in the big league ever since except one year I was with Frisco and I stood that league on their head and Mr. Comiskey called me back and I was still starring with the Chicago White Sox when Uncle Sam sent out the call for men and I quit the great American game to enlist in the greatest game of all the game we are playing against the Kaiser and we will win this game like I have win many a game of baseball because I was to fast for them and used my brains and it will be the same with the Kaiser and America will fight to the drop of the hat and make the world safe for democracy."

Well Al I had to stop 2 or 3 minutes while they give me a hand and they clapped and hollered at pretty near everything I said. So I said "This war reminds me a good deal like a incident that happened once when I was pitching against the Detroit club. No doubt you gentlemen and officers has heard of the famous Hughey Jennings and his eeyah and on the Detroit club is also the famous Tyrus Cobb the Georgia Peach as he is called and I want to pay him a tribute right here and say he is one of the best ball players in the American League and a great hitter if you don't pitch just right to him. One time we was in Detroit for a serious of games and we had loose the first two games do to bad pitching and the first game Eddie Cicotte didn't have nothing and the second game Faber was in the same boat so on this morning I refer to Manager Rowland come up to me in the lobby of the Tuller hotel and said how do you feel Jack and I said O. K. Clarence why do you ask? And he said well we have loose 2 games here and we have got to grab this one this P. M. and if you feel O. K. I will work you because I know you have got them licked as soon as you walk out there. So I said all right Clarence you can rely on me. And

that P. M. I give them 3 hits and shut them out and Cobb come
up in the ninth innings with two men on bases and two men
out and Ray Schalk our catcher signed me for a curve ball but
I shook my head and give him my floater and the mighty Cobb
hit that ball on a line to our right fielder Eddie Murphy and
the game was over.

"This war is a good deal like baseball gentlemen because it is
stratejy that wins and no matter how many soldiers a gen. has
got he won't get nowheres without he uses his brains and its the
same in baseball and the boys that stays in the big league is the
boys that can think and when this war is over I hope to go back
and begin where I left off and win a pennant for Charley Comiskey the old Roman in the American League."

Well Al they was a regular storm when I got through and I
bowed and give them a smile and started off of the platform
but a sargent named Avery from our Co. stopped me and set
me down in a chair and says I was to wait a minute and I
thought of course they was going to give me a cup or something though I didn't expect nothing of the kind but I hadn't
no sooner set down when Sargent Avery stepped up to the
front of the platform and says "Gentlemen I want to say to you
that Private Jack Keefe the great stratejest is not only a great
pitcher and a great speech maker but he is also a great poet and
if you don't believe me I will read you this beautiful valentine
that he wrote to a certain lady that we all admire and who was
in the Red X canteen up till today when she went back to Paris
to resume other dutys."

Well before I could make a move he read that crazy valentine
and of course they wasn't a word in it that I was serious when
I wrote it and it was all a joke with me only not exactly a joke
neither because I was really trying to let the little lady down
easy and tell her good by between the lines without being
rough with it. But of course these boobs pretended like they
thought I meant it all and was love sick or something and they
hollered like a bunch of Indians and clapped and razed he—ll.

Well Al I didn't get a chance to see Sargent Avery after it was
over because he blowed right out but I will see him tomorrow
and I will find out from him who stole that poem from Miss
Moselle and I wouldn't be supprised if the reason she blowed
to Paris was on acct. of missing the poem and figureing some

big bum had stole it off her and they would find out her secret and make things misable for her and the chances is that's why she blowed. Well wait till I find out who done it and they will be one less snake in this regt. and the sooner you weed those kind of birds out of the army you will get somewheres and if you don't you won't.

But the poor little lady Al I can't help from feeling sorry for her and I only wished I could go to Paris and find her and tell her to not worry though of course its best if she don't see me again but I'm sorry it had to come off this way.

Your pal,   JACK.

Somewheres in France, Feb. 18.

FRIEND AL: Well Al this may be the last letter you will ever get from me because I am waiting now to find out what they are going to do with me and I will explain what I mean.

Yesterday A. M. I seen Sargent Avery and I asked him if I could talk to him a minute and he says yes and I said I wanted to find out from him who stole that valentine from Miss Moselle. So he says "Who is Miss Moselle?" So I said "Why that little lady in the canteen that's blowed to Paris." So he says "Well that little lady's name isn't Miss Moselle but her name is Ruth Palmer and she is the daughter of one of the richest birds in N. Y. city and they wasn't nobody stole no valentine from her because she give the valentine to me before she left." So I said "What do you mean she give it to you?" So he says "I mean she give it to me and when she give it to me she said us birds was in the same Co. with a poet and didn't know it and she thought it was about time we was finding it out. So she laughed and give me the valentine and that's the whole story."

Well Al I had a 20 frank note on me and I asked Sargent Avery if he wouldn't like some champagne and he said no he wouldn't. But that didn't stop me Al and I got all I could hold onto and then some and I snuck in last night after lights out and I don't know if anybody was wise or not but if they are its libel to go hard with me and Capt. Seeley said something about the fireing squad for the next bird that cut loose.

Well I reported sick this A. M. and they could tell to look at me that it wasn't no stall so I'm here and the rest of the boys is gone and I am waiting for them to summons me before the court marshall. But listen Al if they do like Capt. Seeley said you can bet that before they get me I will get some of these birds that's been calling me Private Valentine ever since Saturday night.

Your pal,   JACK.

CHAPTER III

Stragety and Tragedy

FRIEND AL: Well Al if it rains a couple more days like its been they will half to page the navy and at that its about time they give them something to do and I don't mean the chasers and destroyers and etc. that acts like convoys for our troop ships and throws them death bombs at the U boats but I mean the big battle ships and I bet you haven't heard of a supper dread o doing nothing since we been in the war and they say they can't do nothing till the German navy comes out and that's what they're waiting for. Well Al that's a good deal like waiting for the 30nd. of Feb. or for Jennings to send his self up to hit for Cobb and they can say all they want about the Germans being bullet proof from the neck up but they got some brains and you can bet their navy ain't comeing out no more then my hair. So as far as I can see a man being on a supper dread o is just like you owned a private yatch without haveing to pay for the keep up and when they talk about a man on a big U. S. battle ship in danger they mean he might maybe die because he eat to much and no exercise.

So if I was them I would send the big ships here so as we could use them for motor Lauras and I guess they's no place in our whole camp where you couldn't float them and I don't know how it is all over France but if they was a baseball league between the towns where they have got us billeted the fans would get blear eyed looking at the no game sign and if a mgr. worked their pitchers in turn say it was my turn tomorrow and the next time my turn come around some of little Al's kids would half to help me out of the easy chair and say "Come on granpa you pitch this afternoon."

Jokeing a side Al if I was running the training camps like Camp Grant back home instead of starting the men off with the regular drills and hikes like they give them now I would stand them under a shower bath with their close on about ½ the time and when it come time for a hike I would send them back and fourth across Rock River and back where they wasn't no bridge. And then maybe when they got over here France wouldn't be such a big supprise.

One of the boys has put a sign up on our billet and it says Noahs Ark on it and maybe you have heard that old gag Al about the big flood that everybody was drownded only Noah and his folks and a married couple of every kind of animals in the world and they wasn't drownded because Noah had a Ark for them to get in out of the wet. Well Noahs Ark is a good name for our dump and believe me they haven't none of the animals been overlooked and we are also going Noah one better and sheltering all the bugs and some of them is dressed in cocky.

Well I am in this war to the finish and you couldn't hire me to quit till we have ran them ragged but I wished they had of gave us steel helmets wide enough so as they would make a bumber shoot and I hope the next war they have they will pick out Arizona to have it there.

Your pal,   JACK.

Somewheres in France, March 6.
FRIEND AL: Well Al I suppose you have read in the communicates that comes out in the paper where the Americans that's all ready in the trenchs has pulled off some great stuff and a whole lot of them has been sighted and give meddles and etc. by the Frenchmens for what they have pulled off and the way they work it Al when one of the soldiers wrists his life or something and pulls off something big like takeing a mess of prisoners and bringing them back here where they can get something to eat the French pins a meddle on them and sometimes they do it if you don't do nothing but die only then of course they send it to your family so as they will have something to show their friends besides snapshots of Mich. City.

Well we was kidding back and fourth about it today and one of the smart alex in our Co. a bird named Johnny Alcock that is always trying to kid somebody all the time he said to me "Well I suppose they will half to build more tonnages to carry all the meddles you will win back to the states." So I said "Well I guess I will win as many of them as you will win." That shut him up for a wile but finely he says "You have got enough chest to wear a whole junk shop on it." So I said "Well I am not the baby that can't win them." So he says "If you ever happen to be snooping around the bosh trenchs when Fritz climbs over the top you will come back so fast that the Kaiser will want to know who was that speed merchant that led the charge and decorate you with a iron cross." So I said "I will decorate you right in the eye one of these days." So he had to shut up and all the other boys give him the laugh.

Well Al jokeing to one side if I half to go back home without a meddle it will be because they are playing favorites but I guess I wouldn't be left out at that because I stand ace high with most of the Frenchmens around here because they like a man that's always got a smile or a kind word for them and they would like me still better yet if they could understand more English and get my stuff better but it don't seem like they even try to learn and I suppose its because they figure the war is in their country so everybody should ought to talk their language but when you get down to cases they's a big job on both our hands and if one of us has got to talk the others language why and the he—ll should they pick on the one that's hard to learn it and besides its 2 to 1 you might say because the U. S. and the English uses the same language and they's nobody only the French that talks like they do because they couldn't nobody else talk that way so why wouldn't it be the square thing for them to forget theirs and tackle ours and it would prolongate their lifes to do it because most of their words can't be said without straining yourself and no matter what kind of a physic you got its bound to wear you down in time.

But I suppose the French soldiers figure they have got enough of a job on their hands remembering their different uniforms and who to salute and etc. and they have got a fine system in the French army Al because you wear whatever you was before you got to be what you are that is sometimes. For inst. suppose you use to be in the artillery and now you are a aviator you still wear a artillery uniform part of the time and its like I use to pitch for the White Sox and I guess I would be a pretty looking bird if I waddled around in the mire here a wile with my old baseball unie on me and soon people would begin to think I was drafted from the Toledo Mud Hens.

Seriously Al sometimes you see 4 or 5 French officers comeing along and they haven't one of them got the same color uniform on but they are all dressed up like a Roman candle you might say and if their uniforms run when they got wet a man could let them drip into a pail and drink it up for a pussy cafe.

Well Al the boys in our regt. is going to get out a newspaper and get it out themself and it will be just the news about our regt. and a few gags and comical storys about the different boys and they are going to get it out once per wk.

Corp. Pierson from our Co. that use to work on a newspaper somewheres is going to be the editor and he wants I should write them up something about baseball and how to pitch and etc. but I don't believe in a man waisting their time on a childs play like writeing up articles for a newspaper but just to stall him I said I would try and think up something and give it to him when I had it wrote up. Well him waiting for my article will be like me waiting for mail because I don't want nobody to take me for a newspaper man because I seen enough of them in baseball and one time we was playing in Phila. and I had them shut out up to the 8th inning and all of a sudden Weaver and Collins got a stroke of paralysis and tipped their caps to a couple ground balls that grazed their shoe laces and then Rube Oldring hit one on a line right at Gandil and he tried to catch it on the bounce off his lap and Bill Dinneen's right arm was lame and he begin calling everything a ball and first thing you know they beat us 9 to 2 or something and Robbins one of the Chi paper reporters that traveled with us wired a telegram home to his paper that Phila. was supposed to be a town where a man could get plenty of sleep but I looked like I had set up all the nights we was there and of course Florrie seen it in the paper and got delirious and I would of busted Robbins in the jaw only I wasn't sure if he realy wrote it that way or the telegraph operator might of balled it up.

So they won't be no newspaper articles in mine Al but I will be anxious to see what Pierson's paper looks like when it comes out and I bet it will be a fine paper if our bunch have the writeing of it because the most of them would drop in a swoon if you asked them how to spell their name.

Your pal,   JACK.

Somewheres in France, March 9.
FRIEND AL: Well Al I guess I all ready told you about them

getting up a newspaper in our regt. and Joe Pierson asked me
would I write them up something for it and I told him no I
wouldn't but it seems like he overheard me and thought I said
I would so any way he was expecting something from me so
last night I wrote them up something and I don't know if the
paper will ever get printed or not so I will coppy down a part
of what I wrote to give you a idear of what I wrote. He wanted
I should write them up something about the stragety of baseball and where it was like the stragety in the war because one
night last month I give them a little talk at one of their entertainments about how the man that used their brains in baseball
was the one that win just like in the army but I guess I all ready
told you about me giveing them that little talk and afterwards
I got a skinfull of the old grape and I thought sure they would
have me up in front of the old court marshall but they never
knowed the difference on acct. of the way I can handle it and
you take the most of the boys and if they see a cork they want
to kiss the Colonel. Well any way here is the article I wrote up
and I called it War and Baseball 2 games where brains wins.

"The gen. public that go out to the baseball park and set
through the games probably think they see everything that is
going on on the field but they's a lot of stuff that goes on on
the baseball field that the gen. public don't see and don't know
nothing about and I refer to what we baseball boys calls inside
baseball.

"No one is in a better position to know all about inside
baseball then a man like I who have been a pitcher in the big
league because it is the pitchers that has to do most of the
thinking and pull off the smart plays that is what wins ball
games. For inst. I will write down about a little incidents that
come off one time 2 yrs. ago when the Boston club was playing
against the Chicago White Sox where I was one of the stars
when the U. S. went into the war and then I dropped baseball
and signed up a contract with Uncle Sam to play for my country in the big game against the Kaiser of Germany. This day I
refer to I was in there giveing them the best I had but we was
in a tight game because the boys was not hitting behind me
though Carl Mays that was pitching for the Boston club didn't
have nothing on the ball only the cover and after the ball left
his hand you could have ran in the club house and changed

your undershirt and still be back in time to swing when the ball got up there.

"Well it come along the 9th. inning and we was tied up with the score 2 and 2 and I had Larry Gardner swinging like a hammock all day but this time he hit a fly ball that either Weaver or Jackson ought to of caught in a hollow tooth but they both layed down and died on it and Gardner got on second base. Well they was 2 men out and Hoblitzel was the next man up and the next man after he was Scott their shortstop that couldn't take the ball in his hand and make a base hit off a man like I so instead of me giveing Hobby a ball to hit I walked him as we call it and then of course it was Scott's turn to bat and Barry their mgr. hesitated if he should send Ruth up to hit for Scott or not but finely he left Scott go up there and he was just dragging his bat off his shoulder to swing at the first strike when I whizzed the third one past him.

"That is what we call inside baseball or stragety whether its in baseball or war is walking a man like Hoblitzel that might be lucky enough to hit one somewheres but if you don't give him nothing to hit how can he hit it and then I made Scott look like he had been sent for but couldn't come. Afterwards in the 11th. inning Duffy Lewis hit a ball that he ought to of been traded for even swinging at it because it come near clipping his ear lob but any way he swang at it and hit it for three bases because Jackson layed down and died going after it and Lewis scored on a past ball and they beat us 3 to 2.

"So that is what we call stragety on the baseball field and it wins there the same like in war and this war will be win by the side that has gens. with brains and use them and I figure where a man that has been in big league baseball where you can't never make a success out of it unless you are a quick thinker and they have got a big advantage over men that's been in other walks of life where its most all luck and I figure the army would be a whole lot better off if all the officers and gens. had of played baseball in the big leagues and learned to think quick, but of course they ain't everybody that have got the ability to play baseball and stand the gaff but the man that has got the ability and been through the ropes is just that much ahead of the rest of them and its to bad that most of our gens.

is so old that they couldn't of knew much about baseball since it become a test of brains like it is now.

"I am afraid I have eat up a lot of space with my little Article on War and Baseball so I will end this little article up with a little comical incidents that happened dureing our training trip down in Mineral Wells, Tex. a year ago this spring. The first day we was out for practice they was a young outfielder from a bush league and Mgr. Rowland told him to go out in right field and shag and this was his reply. 'I haven't never been in this park before so you will half to tell me which is right field.' Of course right field is the same field in all parks and that is what made the incidents so comical and some of the boys is certainly green when they first break in and we have manys the laugh at their expense."

That is what I wrote up for them Al and I wound it up with that little story and I was reading over what I wrote and Johnny Alcock seen me reading it and asked me to leave him see it so I showed it to him and he said it was great stuff and he hadn't never dreamt they was that much stragety in baseball and he thought if some of the officers seen it they would pop their eyes out and they would want to talk to me and get my idears and see if maybe they couldn't some of them be plied to war fair and maybe if I showed them where it could I would get promoted and stuck on to the gen. staff that's all made up from gens. that lays out the attacks and etc.

Well Al Alcock is a pretty wise bird and a fine boy to if you know how to take him and he seen right off what I was getting at in my article and its true Al that the 2 games is like the other and quick thinking is what wins in both of them. But I am not looking for no staff job that you don't half to go up in the trenchs and fight but just lay around in some office some-wheres and stick pins in a map while the rest of the boys is sticking bayonets in the Dutchmen's maps so I hope they don't none of the gens. see what I wrote because I come over here to fight and be a soldier and carry a riffle instead of a pin cushion.

But it don't hurt nothing for me to give them a few hints once in a wile about useing their brains if they have got them and if I can do any good with my articles in the papers why

I would just as leaf wear my fingers to the bone writeing them up.

Your pal,   JACK.

Somewheres in France, March 13.

FRIEND AL: Well Al I bet you will pretty near fall over in a swoon when you read what I have got to tell you. Before you get this letter you will probably all ready of got a coppy of the paper I told you about because it come out the day before yesterday and I sent you a coppy with my article in it only they cut a part of it out on acct. of not haveing enough space for all of it but they left the best part of it in.

Well Al somebody must of a sent a coppy to Gen. Pershing and marked up what I wrote up so as he would be sure and see it and probably one of the officers done it. Well that's either here or there but this afternoon when we come in they was a letter for me and who do you think it was from Al. Well you can't never even begin to guess so I will tell you. It was from Gen. Pershing Al and it come from Paris where he is at and I have got it here laying on the table and I would send it to you to look at only I wouldn't take no chances of looseing it and I don't mean you wouldn't be carefull of it Al but of course the mail has got to go across the old pond and if the Dutchmens periscoped the boat the letter was on it it would be good night letter and a letter like this here is something to be proud of and hold onto it and keep it for little Al till he grows up big enough to appreciate it. But they's nothing to prevent me from copping down the letter so as you can read what it says and here it is.

PRIVATE KEEFE,

Dear Sir: My attention was called today to an article written by you in your regimental paper under the title War and Baseball: Two Games Where Brains Wins. In this article you state that our generals would be better able to accomplish their task if they had enjoyed the benefits of strategic training in baseball. I have always been a great admirer of the national game of baseball and I heartily agree with what you say. But unfortunately only a few of us ever possessed the ability to play your game and the few never were proficient enough to play it professionally. Therefore the general staff is obliged to blunder along without that capacity for quick thinking which is acquired only on the baseball field.

But I believe in making use of all the talent in my army, even among the rank and file. Therefore I respectfully ask whether you think some of your baseball secrets would be of strategic value to us in the prosecution of this war and if so whether you would be willing to provide us with the same.

If it is not too much trouble, I would be pleased to hear from you along these lines, and if you have any suggestion to make regarding a campaign against our enemy, either offensive or defensive, I would be pleased to have you outline it in a letter to me.

By the way I note with pleasure that our first names are the same. It makes a sort of bond between us which I trust will be further cemented if you can be of assistance to me in my task.

I shall eagerly await your reply.

Sincerely,
BLACK JACK PERSHING,
Folies Bergere, Paris, France.

That is the letter I got from him Al and I'll say its some letter and I bet if some of these smart alex officers seen it it would reduce some of the swelling in their chest but I consider the letter confidential Al and I haven't showed it to nobody only 3 or 4 of my buddys and I showed it to Johnny Alcock and he popped his eyes out so far you could of snipped them off with a shears. And he said it was a cinch that Pershing realy wrote it on acct. of him signing it Black Jack Pershing and they wouldn't nobody else sign it that way because it was a private nickname between he and some of his friends and they wouldn't nobody else know about it.

So then he asked was I going to answer the letter and I said of course I was and he says well I better take a whole lot of pains with my answer and study up the situation before I wrote it and put some good idears in it and if my letters made a hit with Gen. Pershing the next thing you know he would probably summons me to Paris and maybe stick me on the war board so as all I would half to do would be figure up plans of attacks and etc. and not half to go up in the trenchs and wrist my life and probably get splattered all over France.

So I said "Well I am not looking for no excuse to get out of the trenchs but its just the other way and I am nuts to get in them." So he says "You must be." But he showed me where it would be a great experience to set in at them meetings even if I didn't have much to say and just set there and listen and hear their plans and what's comeing off and besides I would get a chance to see something of Paris and it don't look like none of us only the officers would be give leave to go there but of course I would go if Black Jack wanted me and after all Al I am here to give Uncle Sam the best I have got and if I can serve the stars and strips better by sticking pins in a map then getting in the trenchs why all right and it takes more than common soldiers to win a war and if I am more use to them as a kind of adviser instead of carrying a bayonet why I will sacrifice my own feelings for the good of the cause like I often done in baseball.

But they's another thing Alcock told me Al and that is that the war board they have got has got gens. on it from all the different countrys like the U. S. and England and France and Spain and of course they are more French gens. than anything else on acct. of the war being here in France so probably they do some of their talking in French and Alcock says if he was I he would get busy and try and learn enough French so as I could make myself understood when I had something to say and of course they probably won't nothing come out of it all but still and all I always says its best to be ready for whatever comes off and if the U. S. had of been ready for this war I wouldn't be setting here writeing this letter now but I would be takeing a plunge in one of them Berlin brewry vats.

Any way I have all ready picked enough French so as I can talk it pretty good and I would be O. K. if I could understand it when they are talking it off but to hear them talk it off you would think they seen their dinner at the end of the sentence.

Well Al I will tell you how things comes out and I hope Black Jack will forget all about it and lay off me so as I can get into the real fighting instead of standing in front of a map all the wile like a school teacher or something and I all most wished I hadn't never wrote that article and then of course the idear wouldn't of never came to Black Jack that I could help him but if he does take me on his staff it will be some pair of Jacks eh Al and enough to open the pot and if the Germans is sucker enough to stay in they will get their whiskers cinched.

Your pal,   JACK.

Somewheres in France, March 14.

FRIEND AL: Well this is the second letter I have wrote today and the other one is to Gen. Pershing and I have still got the letter here yet Al and I will coppy it down and tell you what I wrote to him.

GEN. JACK PERSHING,
            Care Folies Bergere, Paris, France.

Dear Gen: You can bet I was supprised to get a letter from you and when I wrote that article I didn't have no idear that they would something come out of it. Well Gen. I come into the army expecting to fight and lay down my life if nessary and I am not one of the kind that are looking for an out and trying to hide behind a desk or something because I am afraid to go into the trenchs but I guess if you know something about baseball you won't accuse me from not having the old nerve because they can't no man hold onto a job in the big leagues unless a man is fearless and does their best work under fire and especially a pitcher. But if you figure that I can serve old glory better some other way then in the rank and files I am willing to sacrifice myself like I often done in baseball. Anything to win Gen. is the way I look at it.

You asked me in your letter did I think some of my idears would help out well gen. a man don't like to sound like they was bragging themself up but this isn't no time for monking and I guess you want the truth. Well gen. I don't know much about running a army and their plans but stragety is the same if its on the battle field or the baseball diamond you might say and it just means how can we beat them and I often say that the men that can use their brains will win any kind of a game except maybe some college Willy boy game like football or bridge whist.

Well gen. without no bragging myself up I learned a whole lot about stragety on the baseball field and I think I could help you in a good many ways but before I tried to tell you how to do something I would half to know what you was trying to do and of course I know you can't tell me in a letter on acct. of the censors and of course they are Americans to but they's a whole lot of the boys that don't mean no harm but they are gabby and can't keep their mouth shut and who knows who would get a hold of it and for the same reason I don't feel like I should give you any of my idears by mail but if I could just see you and we could have a little talk and talk things over but I don't suppose they's any chance of that unless I could get leave off to run down to Paris for a wile and meet you somewheres but they won't give us no leave to go to Paris but of course a letter from you that I could show it to Capt. Seeley would fix it up and no questions asked.

So I guess I better wait till I hear from you along these lines and in the mean wile I will be thinking the situation over and see what I can think up and I all ready got some idears that I feel like they would work out O. K. and I hope I will get a chance in the near future to have a little chat with you.

I note what you say about our name being both Jack and I was thinking to myself that lots of times in a poker game a pair of jacks is enough to win and maybe it will be the same way in the war game and any way I guess the 2 of us could put up a good bluff and bet them just as if we had them. Eh gen?

Respy,
JACK KEEFE.

That's what I wrote to him Al and he will get it some time tomorrow or the next day and I should ought to hear from him back right away and I hope he will take my hint and leave me stay here with my regt. where I can see some real action. But if he summonses me I will go Al and not whine about getting a raw deal.

Well I happened to drop into a estaminet here yesterday and that's kind of a store where a man can buy stuff to take along with him or you can get a cup of coffee or pretty near anything and they was a girl on the job in there and she smiled when I come in and I smiled at her back and she seen I was American so she begin talking to me in English only she has got some brogue and its hard to make it out what she is trying to get at. Well we talked a wile and all of a sudden the idear come to me that I and her could hit it off and both do the other some good by her learning me French and I could learn her English and so I sprung it on her and she was tickled to death and we called it a bargain and tomorrow we are going to have our first lessons and how is that Al for a bargain when I can pick up French without it costing me a nickle and of course they won't be only time for 1 or 2 lessons before I hear from Black Jack but I can learn a whole lot in 2 lessons if she will tend to business but the way she smiled at me when I come out and the

looks she give me I am afraid if she seen much of me it would
be good night so I will half to show her I won't stand for no
foolishness because I had enough flirtations Al and the next
woman that looks X eyed at me will catch her death of cold.

Your pal,   JACK.

Somewheres in France, March 16.

FRIEND AL: Well old pal it looks like they wouldn't be no front
line trenchs for this baby and what I am getting at is that the
word was past around today that Black Jack himself is comeing
and they isn't no faulse alarm about it because Capt. Seeley told
us himself and said Gen. Pershing would be here in a day or 2 to
overlook us and he wanted that everybody should look their best
and keep themself looking neat and clean and clean up all the
billets and etc. because that was what Gen. Pershing was comeing
to see, how we look and how we are getting along and etc.

Well Al that's what Capt. Seeley said but between you and I
they's another reason why he is comeing and I guess he figures
they will be a better chance to talk things over down here then
if I was to go to Paris and I am not the only one that knows why
he is comeing because after supper Alcock called me over to 1
side and congratulated me and said it looked like I was in soft.

Well I will be ready for him when he comes and I will be
ready to pack up and blow out of here at a minute's notice and
I can't help from wondring what some of these smart alex officers will say when they see what's comeing off. So this won't
be only a short letter Al because I have got a lot to do to get
ready and what I am going to do is write down some of my
idears so as I can read them off to him when he comes and if I
didn't have them wrote down I might maybe get nervous
when I seen him and maybe forget what I got to say because
the boys says he's a tough bird for a man to see for the first
time till you get to know him and he acts like he was going to
eat you alive but he's a whole lot like a dog when you get to
know him and his bark is worse then a bite.

Well Al how is that for news and I guess you will be prouder
then ever of your old pal before this business gets over with
and I would feel pretty good with everything breaking so good
only I am getting worried about Ernestine that little French gal
in the estaminet and I wished now I hadn't never seen her or

made no bargain with her and I didn't do it so much for what I could learn off of her but these French gals Al has had a tough time of it and if a man can bring a little sunshine into their life he wouldn't be a man unless he done it. So I was just trying to be a good fellow and here is what I get for it because I caught her today Al with that look in her eye that I seen in so many of them and I know what it means and I guess about the best thing for me to do is run away from Gen. Pershing and go over the top or something and leave the boshs shoot my nose off or mess me up some way and then maybe I won't get pestered to death every time I try and be kind to some little gal.

I guess the French lessons will half to be cut out because it wouldn't be square to leave her see me again and it would be different if I could tell her I am married but I don't know the French terms for it and besides it don't seem to make no difference to some of them and the way they act you would think a wife was just something that come out on you like a sty and the best way to do was just to forget it.

Well Al as I say I caught her looking at me like it was breaking her heart and I wouldn't be supprised if she cried after I come away, but what can a man do about it Al and I have got a good notion to wear my gas mask everywhere I go and then maybe I will have a little peace once in a wile.

I must close now for this time and get busy on some idears so as Black Jack won't catch me flat footed but I guess they's no danger of that eh Al?

Your pal,   JACK.

Somewheres in France, March 18.

FRIEND AL: Well old pal I am all set for Gen. Pershing when he comes and I have got some of my idears wrote down just the bear outlines of them and when he asks me if I have got any I can just read them off from my notes like I was a lecture and here is a few of the notes I have got wrote down so you can get some idear of what I am going to spring on him.

I

In baseball many big league mgrs. before a game they talk it over in the club house with their men and disgust the weakness of the other club and how is the best way to beat them and etc. For inst. when I was pitching for the White Sox and suppose we was going to face a pitcher that maybe he was weak on fielding bunts so before the game Mgr. Rowland would say to us "Remember boys this baby so and so gets the rabbis if you lay down bunts on him." So we would begin laying them down on him and the first thing you know he would be frothing at the mouth and triping all over himself and maybe if he did finely get a hold of the ball he would throw it into the Southren League or somewheres and before the other mgr. could get another bird warmed up they would half to hire a crossing policeman to straiten out the jam at the plate. And the same thing would be in war like in baseball and instead of a army going into it blind you might say, why the gens. ought to get together before the battle and fix it up to work on the other side's weakness. For inst. suppose the Germans is weak on getting out of the way of riffle bullets why that's the weapon to use on them and make a sucker out of them.

2

Getting the jump on your oppts. is more then ½ the battle whether its in the war or on the baseball field and many a game has been win by getting the jump on your oppts. For inst. that reminds me of a little incidents that happened one day when we was playing the Washington club and I was pitching against the notorious Walter Johnson and before they was a man out Geo. McBride booted one and Collins and Jackson got a couple hits and we was 2 runs to the good before they was a man out. Well Johnson come back pretty good and the rest of the game the boys acted like they was scared of him and kept one foot in the water bucket but we would of win the game at that only in the 9th. inning Schalk dropped a third strike on me and Judge and Milan hit a couple of fly balls that would of been easy outs only for the wind but the wind raised havioc with the ball and they both went for hits and they beat us 3 to 2 and that's the kind of luck I genally always had against the Washington club.

3

In baseball of course they's only nine men on a side and that is where a gen. in the war has got the advantage on a mgr. in baseball because they's no rules in war fair to keep a man from useing all the men he feels like so it looks to me like a gen. had all the best of it because suppose the other side only had say 50 thousand men in a certain section they's nothing to prevent a gen. from going after them with a 100 thousand men and if he can't run them ragged when you got to them 2 to 1 its time to enlist in the G. A. R. All though as I say a mgr. can't only use nine men at a time in baseball, but at that I know of incidents where a mgr. has took advantage of the oppts. being shy of men and one time the St. Louis club came to Chi and Jones was all crippled up for pitchers but the game was on our home grounds so it was up to Mgr. Rowland to say if the game should be played or if he should call it off on acct. of cold weather because it was in the spring. But he knowed Jones was shy of pitchers so he made him play the game and Jones used big Laudermilk to pitch against us and they beat us 5 and 2.

4

Another advantage where a gen. got it on a baseball mgr. because in baseball the game begins at 3 o'clock and the other club knows when its going to begin just the same as your club so they can't neither club beat the other one to it and start the game wile the other club is looking out the window.

But a gen. don't half to tell the other side when he is going to attack them but of course they have observers that can see when you are going to get ready to pull something. But it looks to me like the observers wouldn't be worth a hoop and he—ll if the other gen. made his preparations at night when it was dark like bringing up the troops and artilery and supplys and etc. and in that way you could take them by supprise and make them look like a fool, like in baseball I have often crossed the batter up and one day I had Cobb 3 and 2 and he was all set to murder a fast one and I dinked a slow one up there to him and the lucky stiff hit it on the end of his bat just inside third base and 2 men scored on it.

That's about the idears I am going to give him Al only of course I can talk it off better then I can write it because wile I am talking I can think up a lot more incidents to tell him and him being a baseball fan he will set there pop eyed with his mouth open as long as I want to talk. But now I can't hardly wait for him to get here Al and it seems funny to think that here I am a $30 dollar a mo. doughboy and maybe in a few days I will be on the staff and they don't have nobody only officers and even a lieut. gets 5 or 6 times as much as a doughboy and how is that for a fine nickname Al for men that all the dough they are getting is a $1 per day and the pollutes only gets 2 Sues a day and that's about 2 cents so I suppose we ought to call them the Wall St. crowd.

Well Al you should ought to be thankfull you are there at home with your wife where you can watch her and keep your eyes on her and find out what she is doing with her spare time though I guess at that they wouldn't be much danger of old Bertha running a muck and I don't suppose she would half to wear bob wire entanglements to keep Jack the Kisser away but when a man has got a wife like Florrie and here I am over here and there she is over there well Al a man don't get to sleep no quicker nights from thinking about it and I lay there night after night and wonder what and the he—ll can she be doing and she might be doing most anything Al and they's only the one thing that its a cinch she ain't doing and that's writeing a letter to me and a man would pretty near think she had forgot my first name but even at that she could set down and write to me and start it out Dear Husband.

But the way she acts why even if they was any fun over here I wouldn't be haveing it and suppose I do get on Gen. Pershing's staff and get a lieut. or something and write and tell her about it, why she would probably wait till a legal holiday to answer me back and then she would write about 10 words and say she went to the Palace last week and when she come out after the show it was raining.

Well Al you can't blame a man for anything he pulls off when their wife acts like that and if I give that little Ernestine a smack the next time she bulges her lips out at me whose fault is it Al? Not mine.

Your pal,   JACK.

Somewheres in France, March 20.
FRIEND AL: Well Al the sooner the Germans starts their drive

let them come and I only hope we are up there when they start
it and believe me Al if they come at us with the gas I will dive
into it with my mouth wide open and see how much of it I can
get because they's no use Al of a man trying to live with the
kind of luck I have got and I'm sick in tired of it all.

Wait till you hear what come off today Al. In the first place
my feet's been going back on me for a long wile and they
walked us all over France yesterday and this A. M. I couldn't
hardly get my shoes on and they was going out for riffle practice and I don't need no riffle practice Al and besides that I
couldn't of stood it so I got excused and I set around a wile
after the rest of the bunch was gone and finely my feet got
feeling a little better and I walked over to the estaminet where
that little gal's at to see if maybe I couldn't brighten things up
a little for her and sure enough she was all smiles when she
seen me and we talked a wile about this in that and she tried to
get personal and called me cherry which is like we say dearie
and finely I made the remark that I didn't think we would be
here much longer and then I seen she was going to blubber so
I kind of petted her hand and stroked her hair and she poked
her lips out and I give her a smack Al but just like you would
kiss a kid or something after they fell down and hurt themself.
Well Al just as this was comeing off the door to the other part
of the joint opened up and in come her old man and seen it
and I thought all Frenchmens talked fast Al but this old bird
made them sound like a impediment and he come at me and if
he hadn't been so old I would of crowned him but of course I
couldn't do nothing only let him rave and finely I felt kind of
sorry for him and I had a 20 frank note on me so I shoved it at
him and it struck him dumb Al and I got out of there and
come back to the Ark and it seems like I had been away a
whole lot longer then I meant to and any way I hadn't hardly
no more then got my shoes off and layed down when in come
some of the boys.

Well Al what do you think? Gen. Pershing was out there to
the riffle practice to overlook them and I suppose he heard we
was going to be out there and he went out there to be sure
and catch me and he was makeing a visit around the camp and
instead of him stopping here he went out there to see us
and instead of me being out there Al, here I was mixed up in a

riot with an old goof over nothing you might say and Black Jack wondring where and the he—ll could I be at because Alcock told me he noticed him looking around like he mist somebody. And now he's on his way back to Paris and probably sore as a boil and I can't do nothing only wait to hear from him and probably he will just decide to pass me up.

And the worst of it is Al that when they brought us the mail they was 2 letters for me from Florrie and I couldn't of asked for nicer letters if I had wrote them myself only why and the he—ll couldn't she of wrote them a day sooner and I would of no more thought of getting excused today then fly because if I had knew how my Mrs. mist me and how much she cares I wouldn't of been waisting no time on no Ernestine but its to late now and Black Jack's gone and so is my 20 franks and believe me Al 20 frank notes is tray pew over here. I'll say they are.

Your pal,   JACK.

CHAPTER IV

Decorated

FRIEND AL: Well Al yesterday was April Fool and you ought to seen what I pulled on 1 of the boys Johnny Alcock and it was a screen and some of the boys is still laughing over it yet but he is 1 of the kind that he can't see a joke at their own expenses and he swelled up like a poison pup and now he is talking about he will get even with me, but the bird that gets even with me will half to get up a long time before revelry eh Al.

Well Al I will tell you what I pulled on him and I bet you will bust your sides. Well it seems like Johnny has got a girl in his home town Riverside, Ill. near Chi and that is he don't know if he has got her or not because him and another bird was both makeing a play for her, but before he come away she told him to not worry, but the other bird got himself excused out of the draft with a cold sore or something and is still there in the old town yet where he can go and call on her every night and she is libel to figure that maybe she better marry him so as she can have some of her evenings to herself and any way she might as well of told Johnny to not scratch himself over here as to not worry because for some reason another the gal didn't write to him last month at lease he didn't get no letters and maybe they got lost or she had writers cramps or something but any way every time the mail come and nothing for him he looked like he had been caught off second base.

Well the day before yesterday he was reading 1 of the letters he got from this baby 5 or 6 wks. ago on acct. of not haveing nothing better to read and he left the envelope lay on the floor and I was going to hand it back to him but I happened to think that yesterday would be April Fool so I kept a hold of the envelope and I got a piece of paper and wrote April Fool on it and stuck it in the envelope and fixed it up so as it would look like a new letter and I handed it to him yesterday like it was mail that had only just came for him and you ought to see him when he tore it open and didn't find nothing only April

Fool in it. At first he couldn't say nothing but finely he says "That's some comedy Keefe. You ought to be a end man in the stretcher bearers minstrels" and he didn't crack a smile so I said "What's the matter with you can't you take a joke?" So he said "What I would like to take is a crack at your jaw." So I said "Well it's to bad your arms is both paralyzed." Well Al they's nothing the matter with his arms and I was just kidding him because as far as him hitting anybody is conserned I was just as safe as the gen. staff because he ain't much bigger than a cutie and for him to reach my jaw he would half to join the aviation.

Well of course he didn't start nothing but just said he would get back at me if it took him till the duration of the war and I told some of the other boys about putting it over on him and they couldn't hardly help from smileing but he acts like a baby and don't speak to me and I suppose maybe he thinks that makes me feel bad but I got to be 25 yrs. old before I ever seen him and if his head was blowed off tomorrow A. M. I would try and show up for my 3 meals a day if you could call them that.

But speaking about April Fool Al I just stopped writeing to try and light a cigarette with 1 of these here French matchs and every one of them is a April Fool and I guess the parents of the kids over here don't never half to worry about them smokeing to young because even if they had a box of cigarettes hid in their cradle they would be of age before they would run across a match that lit and I wouldn't be scared to give little Al a bunch and turn him loose in a bbl. of gasoline.

Well Al I suppose you been reading in the papers about the Dutchmens starting a drive vs. the English up in the northren part of the section and at first it looked like the English was going to leave them walk into the Gulf Stream and scald them-self to death, but now it seems like we have got them slowed up at lease that's the dope we get here but for all the news we get a hold of we might as well of jumped to the codfish league on the way over and once in a wile some of the boys gets a U. S. paper a mo. old but they hog onto it and don't leave nobody else see it but as far as I am conserned they can keep it because I haven't no time to waist reading about the Frisco fair or the Federal League has blowed up and etc. And of course they's plenty of newspapers from Paris but all printed in la la la so as every time you come to a word you half to rumage through a dictionary and even when you run it down its libel to mean 20 different articles and by the time you figured out whether they are talking about a st. car or a hot bath or a raisin or what and the he—ll they are talking about they wouldn't be no more news to it then the bible and it looks to me Al like it would be a good idear if you was to drop me a post card when the war is over so as I can tell Capt. Seeley or he will still be running us ragged to get in shape a couple of yrs. after the last of the Dutchmens lays molting in the grave.

Jokeing to 1 side Al you probably know what's going on a long wile before we do and the only chance we would have to know how a battle come out would be if we was in it and they's no chance of that unless they send us up to the northern part of the section to help out because Van Hindenburg must have something under his hat besides bristles and he ain't a sucker enough to start driveing vs. the front that we are behind it unless he is so homesick that he can't stand it no longer in France.

Your pal,   JACK.

Somewheres in France, April 6.

FRIEND AL: Well Al 1 of the Chi newspapers is getting out a paper in Paris and printed in English and I just seen a copy of it where the Allys has finely got wise to themself and made 1 man gen. of all the Allys and it was a sucker play to not do that long ago only it looks to me like they pulled another boner by makeing a Frenchman the gen. and I suppose they done it for a complement to the Frenchmens on acct. of the war being here, but even suppose this here Foch is a smart gen. and use his brains and etc. it looks to me like it would of been a whole lot better to of picked out a man that can speak English because suppose we was all in a big battle or something and he wanted we should go over the top and if he said it in French why most of the boys hasn't made no attempts to master the language and as far as they was conserned he might as well be telling them to wash their neck. Or else they would half to be interpeters to translate it out in English what he was getting at and by the time he give the orders to fire and the interpeter looked it up and seen what it meant in English and then tell us about it the Dutchmens would be putting peep holes through us with a bayonet and besides the French word for fire in English is feu in French and you say it like it was few and if Gen. Foch yelled few we might think he was complaining of the heat.

But at that its better to have 1 man running it even a Frenchman then a lot of different gens. telling us to do this in that and the other thing every one of them different and suppose they done that in baseball Al and a club had 3 or 4 mgrs. and suppose for inst. it come up to the 9th. inning and we needed some runs and it was Benz's turn to hit and 1 mgr. would tell him to go up and hit for himself and another mgr. would tell Murphy to go up and hit for him and another mgr. would send Risberg up and another would send Russell and the next thing you know they would be 2 of them swinging from 1 side of the plate and 2 from the other side and probably busting each other in the bean with their bats but you take most bird's beans and what would break would be Mr. Bat. But its the same in war like in baseball and you got to have 1 man running it. With a lot of different gens. in command, 1 of them might tell the men to charge while another was telling them to pay cash.

Jokeing to 1 side Al some of our boys have overtook a section up along the Moose river and I wouldn't dast write about it only its been printed in the papers all ready so I am not giveing away no secrets to the Dutchmens. At lease they don't mind us writeing something that's came out in the papers though as far as I can see how would the Dutchmens know it any more if it was in the papers or not, because they ain't so choked with jack over in Germany that they are going to spend it on U. S. papers a mo. old and even when they got them they would half to find somebody that could read English and hadn't been killed for it and it would be like as if I should spend part of my $15 a mo. subscribeing to the Chop Suey Bladder that you would half to lay on your stomach and hold it with your feet to get it right side up and even then it wouldn't mean nothing. But any way the Dutchmens is going to know sooner or later that we are in the war and what's the differents if they meet us at the Moose or the Elks? Jokeing a side Al I guess you won't be supprised to hear how I have picked up in the riffle practice and I knew right along that I couldn't hardly help from being a A No. 1 marksman because a man that had almost perfect control in pitching you might say would be bound to shoot straight when they got the hang of it and don't be supprised if I write you 1 of these days that I been appointed a snipper that sets up in a tree somewheres and picks off the boshs whenever they stick their head up and they call them snippers so pretty soon my name is libel to be Jake Snipe instead of Jack Keefe, but seriously Al I can pick off them targets like they was cherrys or something and maybe I won't half to go in the trenchs at all.

I guess I all ready told you about that little trick I pulled on Johnny Alcock for a April Fool gag and at first he swelled up like a poison pup and wouldn't talk to me and said he wouldn't never rest till he got even. Well he finely got a real letter from the gal back home and she is still waiting for him yet so he feels O. K. again and I and him are on speaking turns again and I am glad to not be scraping with him because I don't never feel right unless I am pals with everybody but they can't nobody stay sore at me very long and even when some of the boys in baseball use to swell up when I pulled 1 of my gags on them it wouldn't last long because I would just smile at them and they would half to smile back and be pals and I always say that if a man can't take a joke he better take acid or something and make a corps out of himself instead of a monkey.

Your pal,   JACK.

Somewheres in France, April 11.

FRIEND AL: Well Al I don't suppose you knew I was a detective but when it comes to being a dick it looks like I don't half to salute Wm. Burns or Shylock or none of them.

Seriously Al I come onto something today that may turn out to be something big and then again it may not but it looks like it was something big only of course it has got to be kept a secret till I get the goods on a certain bird and I won't pull it till I have got him right and in that way he won't suspect nothing until its to late. But I know you wouldn't breath a word about it and besides it wouldn't hurt nothing if you did because by the time you get this letter the whole thing will be over and this bird to who I refer will probably own a peace of land in France with a 2 ft. frontidge and 6 ft. deep. But you will wonder what am I trying to get at so maybe I better explain myself.

Well Al they's a big bird in our Co. name Geo. Shaffer and that's a German name because look at Schaefer that use to play ball in our league and it was spelt different but they called him Germany and he thought he was funny and use to pull gags on the field but I guess he didn't feel so funny the day Griffith sent him up to hit against me in the pinch 1 day at Washington and if the ball he hit had of went straight out instead of straight up it would of pretty near cleared the infield. But any way this bird Shaffer in our Co. is big enough to have a corporal to himself and they must of spent the first Liberty Loan on his uniform and he hasn't hardly said a word since we been in France and for a wile we figured it was just because he was a crab and to grouchy to talk, but now I wouldn't be supprised Al if the real reason was on acct. of him being a Dutchman and maybe can't talk English very good. Well I would feel pretty mean to be spying on most of the boys that's been good pals with me, but when a man is a pro German spy himself they's no question of friendship and etc. and whatever I can do to show this bird up I won't hesitate a minute.

Well Al this bird was writeing a letter last night and he didn't have no envelope and he asked me did I have 1 and I said no and he wouldn't of never spoke only to say Gimme but when I told him I didn't have no envelope he started off somewheres to get 1 and he dropped the last page out of the letter he had been writeing and it was laying right there along side of me and of course I wouldn't of paid no tension to it only it was face up so as I couldn't help from seeing it and what I seen wasn't no words like a man would write in a letter but it was a bunch of marks like a x down at the bottom and they was a whole line of them like this

x x x x x x x x x x x

Well that roused up my suspicions and I guess you know I am not the kind that reads other people's letters even if I don't get none of my own to read but this here letter I kind of felt like they was something funny about it like he was writeing in ciphers or something so I picked the page up and read it through and sure enough they was parts of it in ciphers and if a man didn't have the key you couldn't tell what and the he—ll he was getting at.

Well Al I was still studing the page yet when he come back in and they wasn't nothing for me to do only set on it so as he wouldn't see I had it and he come over and begin looking for it and I asked him had he lost something to throw him off the track and he said yes but he didn't say what it was and that made it all the more suspicious so he finely give up looking and went out again.

Well I have got it put away where he can't get a hold of it because I showed it to Johnny Alcock this A. M. and asked him if it didn't look like something off color and he said yes it did and if he was me he would turn it over to Capt. Seeley but on 2d thoughts he said I better keep it a wile and at the same time keep a eye on Shaffer and get more evidents vs. him and then when I had him dead to rights I could turn the letter and the rest of the evidents over to Capt. Seeley and then I would be sure to get the credit for showing him up.

Well Al I figure this 1 page of his letter is enough or more then enough only of course its best to play safe and keep my eyes pealed and see what comes off and I haven't got time to copy down the whole page Al and besides they's a few sentences that sounds O. K. and I suppose he put them in for a blind but you can't get away from them x marks Al and I will write down a couple other sentences and I bet you will agree that they's something fishy about them and here is the sentences to which I refer:

"In regards to your question I guess I understand O. K. In reply will say yes I. L. Y. more than Y. L. M. Am I right."

"Have you saw D. Give him a ring and tell the old spinort I am W. C. T. U. outside of a little Vin Blank."

Can you make heads or tales out of that Al? I guess not and neither could anybody else except they had the key to it and the best part of it is his name is signed down at the bottom and if he can explain that line of talk he is a wonder but he can't explain it Al and all as he can do is make a clean brest of the whole business and Alcock thinks the same way and Alcock says he wished he had of been the 1 that got a hold of this evidents because whoever turned it over to Capt. Seeley along with what other facts I can get a hold of will just about get a commission in the intelligents dept. and that's the men that looks after the pro German spys Al and gets the dope on them and shows them up and I would probably have my head quarters in Paris and get good money besides my expenses and I would half to pass up the chance to get in the trenchs and fight but they's more ways of fighting then 1 and in this game Al a man has got to go where they send you and where they figure they would do the most good and if my country needs me to track after spys I will sacrifice my own wishs though I would a whole lot rather stay with my pals and fight along side of them and not snoop round Paris fondleing door nobs like a night watchman. But Alcock says he would bet money that is where I will land and he says "You ought to feel right at home in the intelligents dept. like a camel in Lake Erie" and he says the first chance I get I better try and start up a conversation with Shaffer and try and lead him on and that is the way they trap them is to ask them a whole lot of questions and see what they have got to say and if you keep fireing questions at them they are bound to get balled up and then its good night.

Well I don't suppose it seems possible to you stay at homes that they could be such a thing like a pro German spy in the U. S. army and how did he get there and why did they leave him in and etc. Well Al you would be supprised to know how many of them has slipped in and Alcock says that at first it amounted to about 200% but the intelligents officers has been on their sent all the wile and most of them has been nailed and when they get them they shoot them down like a dog and that's what Shaffer will get Al and he is out of luck to be so big because all as the fireing squad would half to do would be look at their compass and see if he was east or west of them and then face their riffle in that direction and let go.

I will write and let you know how things comes along.

Your pal,   JACK.

Somewheres in France, April 14.
FRIEND AL: Well Al I am closeing the net of evidents around Shaffer and I guess I all ready got enough on him to make out a case that he couldn't never wrinkle out of it but Capt. Seeley is away and I can't do nothing till he gets back.

I had my man on the grill today Al and I thought he would be a fox and not criminate himself but I guess I went at him so smooth he didn't never suspect nothing till along towards the finish and then it was to late. I don't remember all that was said but it run along these lines like as follows: In the first place I asked him where he lived and he said Milwaukee Ave. in Chi and I don't know if you know it or not Al but that's a st. where they have got traffic policemens at the corners to blow their whistles once for the Germans to go north and south and twice for them to go east and west. So then I said was he married and he says no. So then I asked him where he was born and he said "What and the he—ll are you the personal officer?" So I laughed it off and said "No but I thought maybe we come from the same part of the country." So he says something about everybody didn't half to come from the country but he wouldn't come out and say where he did come from so then I kind of led around to the war and I made the remark that the German drive up on the north side of France didn't get very far and he says maybe they wasn't through. How was that for a fine line of talk Al and he might as well have said he hoped the Germans wouldn't never be stopped.

Well for a minute I couldn't hardly help from takeing a crack at him but in these kind of matters Al a man has got to keep a hold of themself or they will loose their quarry so I kind of forced a smile and said "Well I guess they would have kept going if they could of." And then he says "Yes but they half to stop every once in a wile to bring up Van Hindenburg." So I had him traped Al and quick is a flash I said "Who told you their plans?" And he says "Oh he—ll my mother in law" and walked away from me.

Well Al it was just like sometimes when they are trying a man for murder and he says he couldn't of did it because he was over to the Elite jazing when it come off and a little wile later the lawyer asks him where did he say he was at when the party was croked and he forgets what he said the 1st. time and says he was out to Lincoln Pk. kidding the bison or something and the lawyer points out to the jury where his storys don't jib and the next thing you know he is dressed up in a hemp collar a couple sizes to small.

And that's the same way I triped Shaffer getting him to say he wasn't married and finely when I have him cornered he busts out about his mother in law. Well Al I don't know of no way to get a mother in law without marrying into one. So I told Alcock tonight what had came off and he says it looked to him like I had a strong case and if he was me he would spill it to Capt. Seeley the minute he gets back. And he said "You lucky stiff you won't never see the inside of a front line trench." So I asked him what he meant and he repeated over again what he said about them takeing me in the intelligents dept. So it looks like I was about through being a doughboy Al and pretty soon I will probably be writeing to you from Paris but I don't suppose I will be able to tell you what I am doing because that's the kind of a job where mum is the word.

Your pal,   JACK.

Somewheres in France, April 16.
FRIEND AL: Well old pal don't be supprised if I write you the next time from Paris. I have got a date to see Capt. Seeley to-morrow and Lieut. Mather fixed it up for me to see him but I had to convince the lieut. that it wasn't no monkey business because they's always a whole lot of riffs and raffs asking Capt. Seeley can they have a word with him and what they want is to borry his knife to pair their finger nails.

But I guess he won't be sorry he seen me Al not when I show him the stuff I have got on this bird and he will probably shake me by the hand and say "Well Keefe Uncle Sam is proud of you but you are waisting your time here and I will be sorry to loose you but it looks like you belong in other fields." And he will wire a telegram to the gen. staff reccomending me to go to Paris.

I guess I all ready told you some of the stuff I have got on this bird but I have not told you all because the best one didn't only happen last night. Well on acct. of I and Alcock being friends he has kind of been keeping a eye pealed on Shaffer to help me out and he found a letter last night that Shaffer had wrote and this time it was the whole letter with the address and everything and who do you suppose it was to? Well Al it was to Van Hindenburg himself and I have got it right here where I can keep a eye on it and believe me it's worth watching and I wished I could send it to you so you could see for yourself what kind of a bird we are dealing with. But that's impossible Al but they's nothing to keep me from copping it off.

Well the letter is wrote in German and to show you what a foxy bird he is he wrote it out in printing so as if it got found by somebody they couldn't prove he wrote it because when words is wrote out in printing it looks just the same who ever wrote it and you can't tell. But he wasn't foxy enough to not sign G. S. down to the bottom of it and that stands for his name George Shaffer and he is the only G. S. in the Co. so it looks like we had him up in a tree. Here is what the letter says:

"Field Marshall Van Hindenburg, c/o Die Vierten Dachshunds, Deutscher Armee, Flanders. 500,000 U. S. Soldaten schon in Frankreich doch. In Lauterbach habe Ich mein Strumpf verloren und ohne Strumpf gehe Ich nicht heim. xxxxxxx G. S."

Notice them x marks again Al like in the other letter and the other letter was probably to Van Hindenburg to and I only wished I knew what the x marks means but maybe some of the birds that's all ready in the intelligents dept. can figure it out. But they's no mystery about the rest of it Al because Alcock understands German and he translated it out what the German words means and here is what it means:

500,000 United States soldiers in France all ready yet. Will advise you when to attack on this front.

How is that Al for a fine trader and spy to tell the gen. of the German army how many soldiers we got over here and to not attack till Shaffer says the word and he was probably going to say it wile we was all asleep or something. But thanks to me Al he will be the one that is asleep and it will be some sleep Al and it will make old Rip and Winkle look like they had the colic and when the boys finds out what I done for them I guess they won't be nothing to good for me. But it will be to late for them to show their appreciations because I won't be here no more and the boys probably won't see me again till its all over and we are back in the old U. S. because Alcock was talking to a bird that's in the int. dept. and he says 1 of their dutys was to keep away from everybody and not leave them know who you are. Because of course if word got out that you was a spy chaser the spys wouldn't hardly run up and kiss you on the st. but they would duck when they seen you and you would have as much chance to catch them as though you was trolling for wales with a grass hopper.

And from this bird's dope that Alcock was talking to I will half to leave off my uniform and wear plain close and maybe wear false whiskers and etc. so as people who see me the 1st. time I will look different to them the next time they see me and maybe I will half to let my mustache grow and grease it so as they will think maybe I am a Dutchman and if they are working for the Kaiser I could maybe pump them.

But they's 1 thing I don't like about it Al because Alcock says Paris is full of women that isn't exactly spys but they have been made a fool out of and they are some German's duke but the Dutchmens tells them a whole lot of things that Uncle Sam would like to know and I would half to find them things out and the only way to do that would be to get them stuck on me and I guess that wouldn't be no chore but when a gal gets stuck on you they will tell you everything they know and wile with most gals I ever seen they could do that without dropping another nickle still and all it would be different with these gals in Paris that's been the tools of some Dutchmens because you take a German and he don't never stop braging till he inhales a bayonet.

But it don't seem fair to make love to them and pertend like I was nuts over them and then when I had learned all they was to know I would half to get rid of them and cast them to 1 side and god knows how many wounds I will leave behind me but probably as many as though I was a regular soldier or snipper but then I wouldn't feel so bad about it because it would be men and not girlies but everything goes in war fair as they say Al and if Uncle Sam and Gen. Pershing asks me to do it I will do whatever they ask me and they can't nobody really hold it vs. me because of why I am doing it.

But talking about snippers Al I noticed today that I wasn't near as good as usual in the riffle practice and it was like as if I was haveing a slump like some of the boys does in baseball when they go along 5 or 6 days without finding out who is umpireing the bases and I am afraid that is how it would be with me in snipping I would be O. K. part of the time and the rest of the time I couldn't hit Europe and maybe I would fall down when they was depending on me and then I would feel like a rummy so I guess I better not try and show up so good in practice even when I do feel O. K. because they might make a snipper out of me without knowing my weakness and I figure its something the matter with my eyes. Besides Al it don't seem like its a fair game to be pecking away at somebody that they can't see you and aren't looking for no supprise and its a whole lot different then fighting with a bayonet where its man to man and may the best man win.

Well Al I guess I have told you all the news and things is going along about as usual and they don't seem to be no prospects of us overtakeing a section up to the front but its just train and train and train and if the ball clubs had a training trip like we been haveing they would be so tired by the 1 of May that they wouldn't run out a base on balls. Yesterday we past by a flock of motor Lauras that was takeing wounded back to a base hospital somewheres and Alcock was talking to 1 of the drivers and he said that over 100% of the birds that's getting wounded and killed these days is the snippers and the boshs don't never rest till they find out where there nests is at and then they get all their best marksmens and aim at where they think the snipper has got his nest and then its good night snipper and he is either killed right out or looses a couple of legs or something. I certainly feel sorry for the boys that's wounded Al and every time we see a bunch of them all us boys is crazy to get up there to the front and get even for what they done.

Well old pal I will half to get busy now and overlook the dope I have got on Shaffer so as I will have everything in order for Capt. Seeley and I will write and let you know how things comes out.

Your pal,   JACK.

Somewheres in France, April 18.

FRIEND AL: Well Al they's a whole lot of birds that thinks they are wise and always trying to pull off something on somebody but once in a wile they pick out the wrong bird to pull it on and then the laugh is on the smart Alex themself.

Well Alcock and some of them thought they was putting up a game on me and was going to make me look like a monkey but before I get through with them Al they will be the suckers and I will be giveing them the horse laugh but what I ought to do is bust them in the jaw and if I was running this war every bird that tried to pull off some practical joke to put a man in bad, I would give a lead shower in their honor some A. M. before breakfast.

Alcock was trying to make me believe that 1 of the boys in the Co. name Geo. Shaffer was a German spy or something and they framed up a letter like as if he wrote it to Van Hindenburg giveing away secrets in German about our army and etc. but they made the mistake of signing his initials to the letter so when I come to think it over I seen it must be a fake because a bird that was a real spy wouldn't never sign their own name to a letter but they would sign John Smith or something.

But any way I had a hold of this letter and a peace of another letter that Shaffer really did write it and I thought I would show them to Capt. Seeley and play it safe because they might be something in them after all and any way it would give him a good laugh. So yesterday I went and seen him and he says "Well Keefe what can I do for you?" So I said "You can't do nothing for me sir but this time I can do something for you. What would you think if I told you they was a trader and a German spy in your Co." So he says "I would think you were crazy." So I said "I am afraid you will half to think so then but maybe you won't think I am so crazy when I show you the goods."

So then Al I pulled that 1st. peace of a letter on him and showed it to him and he read it and when he got through he says "Well it looks suspicious all right. It looks like the man that wrote it was hacking up a big plot to spring a few dependents on his local board the next time they draft him." So I said "The bird that wrote that letter is a Dutchman name Geo. Shaffer." So Capt. Seeley says "Well I wish him all the luck in the world and a lot of little Shaffers." So I said "Yes but what about them x marks and all them letters without no words to them?" So he said "Didn't you never correspond with a girl and put some of them xs down to the bottom of your letter?" So I says "I have wrote letters to a whole lot of girls but I never had to write nothing in ciphers because I wasn't never ashamed of anything I wrote." So he said "Well your lady friends was all cheated then because this is ciphers all right but its the kind of messages they love to read because it means kisses."

Well Al of course I knew it meant something like that but I didn't think a big truck horse like Shaffer would make such a mushmellow out of himself. But anyway I said to Capt. Seeley I says "All right but what about them other initials without no words to go with them?" And he says "Well that's some more ciphers but they's probably a little gal out in Chi that don't half to look at no key to figure it out."

So then I pulled the other letter on him the I in German and he also smiled when he read this one and finely he says "Some of your pals has been playing a trick on you like when you come over on the ship and the best thing you can do is to tear the letters up and keep it quite and don't leave nobody know you fell for it. And now I have got a whole lot to tend to so good by."

So that's all that was said between us and I come away and come back to quarters and Alcock and 2 or 3 of the other boys was there and Alcock knew where I had been and I suppose he had told the other birds and they was all set to give me the Mary ha ha but I beat them to it.

"Well Alcock" I says when I come in "you are some joke Smith but you wouldn't think you was so funny if I punched your jaw." So he turned kind of pail but he forced a smile and says "Well I guess the Vin Blank is on you this time." So I said "You won't get no Vin Blank off me but what you are libel to get is a wallop in the jaw." So he says "You crabbed at me a wile ago for not takeing a joke but it looks like you was the one that couldn't take them now." So I said "What I would like to take is a poke at your nose." So that shut him up and they didn't none of them get their laugh because I had them scared and if they had of laughed I would of made them swallow it.

So after all Al the laugh is on them because their gag fell dead and I guess the next time they try and pull some gag they will pick out some hick from some X roads to pull it on and not a bird that has traveled all over the big leagues and seen all they is to see.

Well Al I am tickled to death I won't half to give up my uniform and snoop around Paris like a white wings double crossing women and spying and etc. and even if the whole thing hadn't of been just a joke I was going to ask Capt. Seeley to not reccomend me to no int. dept. but jest leave me be where I am at so as when the time comes I can fight fair like man to man and not behind no woman's skirts like a cur.

So you see Al everything is O. K. after all and the laugh is on Alcock and his friends because they was the ones that expected to do all the laughing but instead of that I made a monkey out of them.

Your pal,   JACK.

Somewheres in France, April 23.

FRIEND AL: Well Al if you would see my face you would think I had been attending a barrage or something or else I had been in a bar room fight only of course if it was a fair fight I wouldn't be so kind of marred up like I am. But I had a accident Al and fell over a bunk and lit on the old bean and the result is Al that I have got a black eye and a bad nose and my jaw is swole a little and my ears feels kind of dull like so I guess the ladys wouldn't call me Handsome Jack if they seen me but it will be all O. K. in a few days and I will be the same old Jack.

But I will tell you how it come off. I was setting reading a letter from Florrie that all as she said in it was that she had boughten herself a new suit that everybody says was the cutest she ever had on her back just like I give a dam because by the time I see her in it she will of gave it to little Al's Swede. But any way I was reading this letter when in come Shaffer the bird that was mixed up in that little gag about the fake spy and he come up to me and says "Well you big snake who's male are you reading now?" Well Al him calling me big is like I would say hello Jumbo to a flee. But any way I says "My own male and who and the he—ll male would I be reading?" So he said "Well its hard to tell because you stole some of mine and read it and not only that but you showed it to the whole A. E. F. so now stand up and take what's comeing to you."

Well Al I thought he was just kidding so I says "I come over here to fight Germans and not 1 of my own pals." So he says "Don't call me no pal, but if you come to fight Germans now is your chance because you say I'm 1 of them."

Well he kind of made a funny motion like he wanted to spar or wrestle or something and I thought he meant it in a friendly way like we sometimes pull off a rough house once in a wile so I stood up but before I had a chance to take holds with him he cut loose at me with his fists doubled up and I kind of triped or something and fell over a bench and I must have hit something sharp on the way down and I kind of got scratched up but they are only scratchs and don't amt. to nothing. Only I wished I knew he had of been serious and I would of made a punching bag out of him and you can bet that the next time he wants to start something I won't wait to see if he is jokeing but I will tear into him and he will think he run into a Minnie Weffers.

Well I suppose Alcock was sore at me for getting the best of him and not falling for his gag and he was afraid to tackle me himself and he told big Shaffer a peck of lies about some dam letter or something and said I stole it and it made Shaffer sore and no wonder because who wouldn't be sore if they thought somebody was reading their male. But a man like Shaffer that if he stopped a shell the Dutchmens would half to move back a ways so as they would be room enough in France to bury him hasn't got no right to pick on a smaller man especially when I wasn't feeling good on acct. of something I eat but at that Al size don't make no difference and its the bird that's got the nerve and knows how that can knock them dead and if Shaffer had of gave me any warning he would of been the 1 that is scratched up instead of I though I guess he is to lucky to trip over a kit bag and fall down and cut himself.

But my scratchs don't really amt. to nothing Al and in a few days I will be like new.

                    Your pal,   JACK.

                              Somewheres in France, April 25.
FRIEND AL: Well old pal I have got some big news for you now. We been ordered up to the front and its good by to this Class D burg and now for some real actions and I am tickled to death and I only hope the Dutchmens will loose their minds and try and start something up on the section where we are going to and I can't tell you where its at Al but you keep watching the papers and even if the boshs don't start nothing maybe we will start something on our own acct. and the next thing you know you will read where we have got them on the

Lincoln highway towards Russia and believe me Al we won't half to stop every little wile to bring up no Van Hindenburg but we will run them ragged and they say the Germans is the best singers and when they all bust out with Comrades they will make the Great Lakes band sound like the Russia artillery.

Well Al I am so excited I can't write much and I have got a 100 things to tend to so I will half to cut this letter short.

Well some of the other birds like Alcock and them is pertending like they was tickled to death to but believe me Al if the orders was changed all of a sudden and they told us we was going to stay here till the duration of the war we wouldn't half to call on the Engrs. to dam their tear ducks. But they pertend like they are pleased and keep whistleing so as they won't blubber and today they all laughed their heads off at something that come out in the Co. paper that some of the boys gets out but they laughed like they was nervous instead of enjoying it.

Well what come out in the paper was supposed to be a joke on me and if they think its funny they are welcome and I would send the paper to you that its in only I haven't got only the 1 copy so I will copy it down and you can see for yourself what a screen it is. Well they's 1 peace that's got up to look like it was the casuality list in some regular newspaper and it says:

WOUNDED IN ACTION
Privates
Jack Keefe, Chicago, Ill. (Very)

And then they's another peace that reads like this:

DECORATED

"The Company has won its first war honors and Private Jack Keefe is the lucky dog. Private Keefe has been decorated by Gen. George Shaffer of the 4th. Dachshunds for extreme courage and cleverness in showing up a dangerous nest of spies. Keefe was hit four times by large caliber shells before he could say surrender. He was decorated with the Order of the Schwarz Auge, the Order of the Rot Nase and the Order of the Blumenkohl Ohren, besides which a Right Cross was hung on his jaw. Private Keefe takes his honors very modestly, no one having even heard him mention them except in stifled tones during the night."

Well Al all right if they can find something to amuse themself and they need it I guess. But they better remember that they's plenty of time for the laugh to be on the other foot before this war is over.

Your pal,   JACK.

CHAPTER V

Sammy Boy

In the Trenchs, May 6.

FRIEND AL: Well Al I haven't wrote you no letter for a long wile and I suppose maybe you think something might of happened to me or something. Well old pal they hasn't nothing happened and I only wished they would because anything would be better than laying around here and I would rather stop a shell and get spread all over Europe then lay around here and die a day at a time you might say.

Well I would of wrote you before only we was on the march and by the time night come around my dogs fret me so bad I couldn't think of nothing else and when they told us we was comeing up here I thought of course they would send us up in motor Lauras or something and not wear us all out before we got here but no it was drill every ft. of the way and I said to Johnny Alcock the night we got here that when they was sending us up here to die they might at lease give us a ride and he says no because when they send a man to the electric chair they don't push him up there in a go cart but they make him get there on his own dogs. So I said "Yes but he travels light and he don't half to go far and when he gets there they's a chair waiting for him to set down in it but they load us up like a troop ship and walk us ½ way to Sweden and when we finely get here we can either remain standing or lay down in a mud puddle and tuck ourself in."

And another thing Al I thought they meant we was going right in the front line trenchs where a man has got a chance to see some fun but where we are at is what they call the reserve trenchs and we been here 3 days all ready and have got to stay here 7 days more that is unless they should something happen to the regt. that's up ahead of us in the front line and if they get smashed up or something and half to be sent back to the factory then we will jump right in and take their place and I don't wish them no bad luck but I wished they would get messed up tonight at lease enough so as they would half to come out for repairs but it don't look like they was much chance of that as we are on a quite section where they hasn't been nothing doing since the war begin you might say but of course Jerry is raising he—ll all over the front now and here is where he will probably pick on next and believe me Al we will give him a welcome.

But the way things is mapped out now we will be here another wk. yet and then up in the front row for 10 days and then back to the rest billets for a rest but they say the only thing that gets a rest back there is your stomach but believe me your stomach gets a holiday right here without going to no rest billets.

Well I thought they would be some excitement up here but its like church but everybody says just wait till we get up in front and then we will have plenty of excitement well I hope they are telling the truth because its sure motonus here and about all as we do is have inspections and scratch. As Johnny Alcock says France may of lose a whole lot of men in this war but they don't seem to of been no casualitys amist the cuties.

Well Al they's plenty of other bugs here as well as the kinds that itchs and I mean some of the boys themselfs and here is where it comes out on them is where they haven't nothing to do only lay around and they's 1 bird that his name is Harry Friend but the boys calls him the chicken hawk and its not only on acct. of him loveing the ladys but he is all the wile writeing letters to them and he is 1 of these fancy writers that has to wind up before he comes down on the paper with a word and between every word he sores up and swoops down again like he was over a barn yard and sometimes the boys set around and bets on how many wirls he will take before he will get within writeing distants of the paper.

Well any way he must get a whole lot of letters wrote if he answers all the ones that comes for him because every time you bump into him he pulls one on you that he just got from some gal that's nuts about him somewheres in the U. S. and its always a different 1 and I bet the stores that sells service stars kept open evenings the wk. this bird enlisted in the draft. But today it was a French gal that he had a letter from her some dame in Chalons and he showed me her picture and she's some queen Al and he is pulling for us to be sent there on our leave after we serve our turn up here and I don't blame him for wanting to be where she's at and I wished they was some baby doll that I could pal around with in what ever burg they ship us to. But I don't know nobody Al and besides I'm a married man so no flirting with the parley vous for me and I suppose I will spend most of my time with the 2 Vin sisters and a headache.

Your pal,   JACK.

In the Trenchs, May 9.

FRIEND AL: Well Al I was talking to 1 of the boys Jack Brady today and we was talking about Harry Friend and I told Jack about him getting a letter from this French girlie at Chalons and how he was pulling for us to go there on our leave so as he could see her so Jack said he didn't think we would go there but they would probably send us to 1 of the places where we could get a bath as god knows we will need one and they will probably send us to Aix les Bains or Nice or O. D. Cologne. So I said I didn't care where we was sent as they wouldn't be no gal waiting for me in none of them towns so Jack says it was my own fault if they wasn't as all these places was full of girlies that was there for us to dance with them and etc. and the officers had all their names and addresses and the way to do was write to 1 of them and tell her when you was comeing and would she like to show you around and he said he would see 1 of the lieuts. that he stands pretty good with him and see what he could do for me. Well Al I told him to go ahead as I thought it was just a joke but sure enough he showed up after a wile and he said the lieut. didn't only have 1 name left but she was a queen and he give me her name and address and its Miss Marie Antoinette 14 rue de Nez Rouge, O. D. Cologne.

Well Al I didn't have nothing else to do so I set down and wrote her a note and I will coppy down what I wrote:

"*Dear Miss Antoinette:* I suppose you will be supprised to hear from me and I hope you won't think I am some fresh bird writeing you this letter for a joke or something but I am just 1 of Uncle Sam's soldiers from the U. S. A. and am now in the trenchs fighting for your country. Well Miss Antoinette we expect to be here about 2 wks. more and then we will have a leave off for a few days and some of the boys thinks we may spend it in your city and I thought maybe you might be good enough to show me around when we get there. I was a baseball pitcher back in the U. S. A. tall and athletic build and I don't suppose you know what baseball is but thought maybe you would wonder what I look like. Well if you aren't busy when we get there I will hope to see you and if you are agreeable drop me a line here and I will sure look you up when I get there."

So then I give her my name and where to reach me and of course they won't nothing come out of it Al only a man has got to amuse yourself some way in a dump like this or they would go crazy. But it would sure be a horse on me if she was to answer the letter and say she would be glad to see me and then of course I would half to write and tell her I was a married man or else not write to her at all but of course they won't nothing come out of it and its a good bet we won't never see Cologne as that was just a guess on Brady's part.

Well Al things is going along about like usual with nothing doing only inspections and etc. and telling us how to behave when we get up there in the front row and not to stick our head over the top in the day time and you would think we was the home guards or something and at that I guess the home guards is seeing as much of the war as we are in this old ditch but they say it will be different when we get up in front and believe me I hope so and they can't send us there to soon to suit me.

Your pal,   JACK.

In the Trenchs, May 11.

FRIEND AL: Well Al here we are up in the front line trenchs and we come in here 2 days ahead of time but that's the way they run everything in the army except feed you but they don't never do nothing when they say they are going to and I suppose they want a man to get use to haveing things come by supprise so as it won't interfere with your plans if you get killed a couple days before you was looking for it.

Well Al we are looking for it now most any day and this may be the last letter you will ever get from your old pal and you may think I am kidding when I say that but 1 of the boys told me a wile ago that he heard Capt. Seeley telling 1 of the lieuts. that the reason we come in here ahead of time was on acct. of them expecting the Dutchmans to make their next drive on this section and the birds that we are takeing their place was a bunch of yellow stiffs that was hard of hearing except when they was told to retreat and Gen. Pershing figured that if they was up here when Jerry made a attack they would turn around and open up a drive on Africa and the bosh has been going through the rest of the line like it was held by the ladies aid and Gen. Foch says they have got to be stopped so we are elected Al and you know what that means and it means we can't retreat under no conditions but stay here till we get killed. So you see I wasn't kidding Al and it looks like it was only a question of a few days or maybe not that long but at that I guess most of the boys would just as leave stop a Dutch bayonet as to lay around in this he—ll hole. Believe me Al this is a fine resort to spend 10 days at what with the mud and the perfume and a whole menajery useing you for a parade grounds.

Well Capt. Seeley wants us to get all the rest we can now on acct. of what's comeing off after a wile but believe me I am not going to oversleep myself in this he—ll hole because suppose Jerry would pick out the time wile you was asleep to come over and pay us a visit and they's supposed to be some of the boys on post duty to watch all night and keep their eye pealed and wake us up if they's something stiring but I have been in hotels a lot of times and left a call with some gal that didn't have nothing to do only pair her finger nails and when the time come ring me up but even at that she forgot it so what chance is they for 1 of these sentrys to remember and wake everybody up when maybe they's 5 or 6 Dutchmens divideing him into building lots with their bayonet or something. So as far as I am conserned I will try and keep awake wile I can because it looks like when we do go to sleep we will stay asleep several yrs. and even if we are lucky enough to get back to them rest billets we can sleep till the cows come home a specially if they give us some more of them entertainments like we had in camp.

Well Al before we got here I thought they would be so much fireing back and 4th. up here that a man couldn't hear themself think but I guess Jerry is saveing up for the big show though every little wile they try and locate our batterys and clean them out and once in so often 1 of our big guns replys but as Johnny

Alcock says you couldn't never accuse our artillrys from being to gabby and I guess we are lucky they are pretty near speechless as they might take a notion to fire short but any way a little wile ago 1 of our guns sent a big shell over and Johnny says what and the he—ll can that be and I said its a shell from 1 of our guns and he says he thought they fired 1 yesterday.

Well as I say here we are with 10 days of it stareing us in the eye and the cuties for company and the only way we can get out of here ahead of time is on a stretcher and I wouldn't mind that Al but as I say I want to be awake when my time comes because if I am going to get killed in this war I want to have some idear who done it.

Your pal,   JACK.

In the Trenchs, May 14.

FRIEND AL: Well Al I got the supprise of my life today when Jack Brady handed me a letter that had came for me and that's supprise enough itself but all the more when I opened it up and seen who it was from. Well it was from that baby in Cologne and I will coppy it down as it is short and you can see for yourself what she says. Well here it is:

> "*Dear Mr. Keefe:* Your letter just reached me and you can bet I was glad to get it. I sure will be glad to see you when you come to Cologne and I will be more than glad to show you the sights. This is some town and we sure will have a time when you get here. I am just learning to write English so please excuse mistakes but all I want to say is don't disappoint me but write when you will come so I can be all dressed up comme un cheval. Avec l'amour und kussen.
>
> "MARIE ANTOINETTE."

You see Al they's part of it wrote in French and that last part means with love and kisses. Well I guess that letter I wrote her must have went over strong and any ways it looks like she didn't exactly hate me eh Al? Well it looks like I would half to write to her back and tell her I am a married man and they can't be no flirting between her and I but if she wants to be a good pal and show me around O. K. and no harm done. Well I hope she takes it that way because it sure will seem good to talk to a gal again that can talk a little English and not la la la all the wile but of course its a good bet that I won't never see

her because we are just as libel to go somewheres else as Cologne though Brady seems to think that's where we are headed
for. Well time will tell and in the mean wile we are libel to get
blowed to he—ll and gone and then of course it would be
good by sweet Marie but I was supprised to hear from her as I
only wrote to her in fun and didn't think nothing would come
from it but I guess Harry Friend isn't the only lady killer in the
U. S. army and if I was 1 of the kind that shows off all their
letters I guess I have got 1 now to show.

A side from all that Al we was supposed to have our chow a
hr. ago but no chow and some of the boys says its on acct. of
our back arears being under fire and you see the kitchens is
way back of the front lines and the boys on chow detail is supposed to bring our food up here but when the back arears is
under fire they are scared to bring it up or they might maybe
run into some bad luck on the way. How is that for fine dope
Al when a whole regt. starves to death because a few yellow
stiffs is afraid that maybe a shell might light near them and spill
a few beans. Brady says maybe they are trying to starve us so as
we will get mad and fight harder when the time comes like in
the old days when they use to have fights between men and
lions in Reno and Rome and for days ahead they wouldn't give
the lions nothing to eat so as they would be pretty near wild
when they got in Reno and would make a rush at the gladaters
that was supposed to fight them and try and eat them up on
acct. of being so near starved. Well Al I would half to be good
and hungry before I would want to eat a Dutchman a specially
after they been in the trenchs a wile.

But any way it don't make a whole lot of differents if the
chow gets here or not because when it comes its nothing only
a eye dropper full of soup and coffee and some bread that I
would hate to have some of it fall on my toe and before we left
the U. S. everybody was trying to preserve food so as the boys
in France would have plenty to eat but if they sent any of the
preserves over here the boat they come on must of stopped a
torpedo and I hope the young mackerels won't make themselfs
sick on sweets.

Jokeing to 1 side this is some climate Al and they don't never
a day pass without it raining and I use to think the weather
profits back home had a snap that all they had to do was write

down rain or snow or fair and even if they was wrong they was way up there where you couldn't get at them but they have got a tough job when you look at a French weather profit and as soon as he learns the French for rain he can open up an office and he don't half to hide from nobody because he can't never go wrong though Alcock says they have got a dry season here that begins the 14 of July and ends that night but its a holiday so the weather profit don't half to monkey with it. Any way its so dark here all the wile that you can't hardly tell day and night only at night times the Dutchmens over across the way sends up a flare once in a wile to light things up so as they can see if they's any of us prowling around Nobody's Land and speaking about Nobody's Land Brady says its the ground that lays between the German trenchs and the vermin trenchs but jokeing to 1 side if it wasn't for these here flares we wouldn't know they was anybody over in them other trenchs and when we come in here they was a lot of talk about Jerry sending over a patrol to find out who we was but it looks like he wasn't interested. But all and all Al its nothing like I expected up here and all we have seen of the war is when a shell or 2 busts in back of us or once in a wile 1 of their areoplanes comes over and 1 of ours chases them back and sometimes they have a battle but they always manage to finish it where we can't see it for the fear we might enjoy ourselfs.

Well it looks like we would half to go to bed on a empty stomach if you could call it bed and speaking about stomach Brady says they's a old saying that a army travels on their stomach but a cutie covers a whole lot more ground. But as I say when you don't get your chow you don't miss much only it kills a little time and everybody is sick in tired of doing nothing and 1 of the boys was saying tonight he wished the Dutchmens would attack so as to break the motley and Alcock said that if they did attack he hoped they would do it with gas as his nose needed a change of air.

Your pal,   JACK.

In the Trenchs, May 16.

FRIEND AL: Well old pal I come within a ace you might say of not being here to write you this letter and you may think that's bunk but wait till you hear what come off. Well it seems our scout planes brought back word yesterday that the Dutch regt. over across the way had moved out and another regt. had took their place and it seems when they make a change like that our gens. always trys to find out who the new rivals is so the orders come yesterday that we was to get up a patrol party for last night and go over and take a few prisoners so as we would know what regt. we was up vs. Well as soon as the news come out they was some of the boys volunteered to go in the patrol and they was only a few going so I didn't feel like noseing myself in and maybe crowding somebody out that was set on going and besides what and the he—ll do I care what regt. is there as long as its Germans and its like you lived in a flat and the people across the hall moved out and some people moved in why as long as you knowed they wasn't friends of yours you wouldn't rush over and ring their door bell and say who the he—ll are you but you would wait till they had time to get some cards printed and stick 1 in the mail box. So its like I told Alcock that when the boys come back they would tell the Col. that the people opp. us was Germans and the Col. would be supprised because he probably thought all the wile that they was the Idaho boy scouts or something. But at that I pretty near made up my mind at the last minute to volunteer just to break the motley you might say but it was to late and I lost out.

Well Al the boys that went didn't come back and I hope the Col. is satisfied now because he has lost that many men and he knows just as much as he did before namely that they's some Germans across the way and either they killed our whole bunch or took them a prisoner and instead of us learning who they are they found out who we are because the boys that's gone is all from our regt. and its just like as if we went over and give them the information they wanted to save them the trouble of comeing over here and getting it.

Well it don't make a man feel any happier to think about them poor boys and god only knows what happened to them if they are prisoners or dead and some of them was pals of mine to but the worst part of it is that the word will be sent home that they are missing in actions and their wifes won't know what become of them if they got any and I can't help from thinking I might of been with them only for not wanting to crowd somebody out and if I had of went my name would be in the casuality list as missing in actions but I guess at that if Florrie picked up the paper and seen it she wouldn't know it was her husband its so long since she wrote it on a envelop.

Well Al they's other gals in the world besides Florrie and of course its to late to get serious with them when a man has got a wife and kid but believe me I am going to enjoy myself if they happen to pick out Cologne to send us to and if the little gal down there is 1 of the kind that can be good pals with a man without looseing her head over me I will sure have a good time but I suppose when she sees me she will want to begin flirting or something and then I will half to pass her up before anybody gets hurt. Well any way I wrote her a friendly letter today and just told her to keep me in mind and I stuck a few French words in it for a gag but I will coppy down what I wrote the best I can remember it so you will know what I wrote. Here it is:

Mon cher Marie: Your note recd. and you can bet I was mighty glad to hear from you and learn you would show me around Cologne. That is if they send us there and if we get out of here alive. Well you said you was just learning English well I will maybe be able to help you along and you can maybe help me with the French so you see it will be 50 50. Well I sure hope they send us to Cologne and I will let you know the minute I find out where they are going to send us and maybe even if its somewheres else couldn't you visit there at the same time and maybe I could see you. Well girlie we will be out of here in less then a wk. now if we don't have no bad luck and you can bet I won't waist no time getting to where ever they send us and I hope its Cologne. So in the mean wile don't take no wood nickles and don't get impatient but be a good girlie and save up your loving for me. Tres beaucoup from

Your Sammy Boy,
JACK KEEFE.

That's what I wrote her Al and I bet she can't hardly wait to hear if I'm comeing or not but I don't suppose they's any chance of them sending us there and a specially if they find out that anybody wants to go there but maybe she can fix it to meet me somewheres else and any ways they won't be no lifes lost if I never see her and maybe it would be better that way. But a man has got to write letters or do something to keep your mind off what happened to them poor birds that went in the patrol and a specially when I come so near being 1 of them.

Your pal,   JACK.

In the Trenchs, May 18.

FRIEND AL: Well Al if I am still alive yet its not because I laid back and didn't take no chances and I wished some of the baseball boys that use to call me yellow when I was in there pitching had of seen me last night and I guess they would of sang a different song only in the 1st. place I was where they couldn't nobody see me and secondly they would of been so scared they would of choked to death if they tried to talk let alone sing. But wait till you hear about it.

Well yesterday P. M. Sargent Crane asked me how I liked life in the trenchs and I said O. K. only I got tired on acct. of they not being no excitement or nothing to do and he says oh they's plenty to do and I could go out and help the boys fix up the bob wire in front of the trenchs like we done back in the training camp. So I said I didn't see how they could be any fixing needed as they hadn't nothing happened on this section since the war started you might say and the birds that was here before us had plenty of time to fix it if it needed fixing. So he says "Well any ways they's no excitement to fixing the wire but if you was looking for excitement why didn't you go with that patrol the other night?" So I said "Because I didn't see no sence to trying to find out who was in the other trenchs when we know they are Germans and that's all we need to know. Wait till they's a real job and you won't see me hideing behind nobody." So he says "I've got a real job for you tonight and you can go along with Ted Phillips to the listening post."

Well Al a listening post is what they call a little place they got dug out way over near the German trenchs and its so close you can hear them talk sometimes and you are supposed to hear if they are getting ready to pull something and report back here so as they won't catch us asleep. Well I was wild to go just for something to do but I been haveing trouble with my ears lately probably on acct. of the noise from so much shell fire or something but any ways I have thought a couple times that I was getting a little deef so I thought I better tell him the truth so I said "I would be tickled to death to go only

I don't know if I ought to or not because I don't hear very good even in English and of course Jerry would be telling their plans in German and suppose I didn't catch on to it and I would feel like a murder if they started a big drive and I hadn't gave my pals no warning." So he says "Don't worry about that as Phillips has got good ears and understands German and he has been there before only in a job like that a man wants company and you are going along for company."

Well before we snuck out there Sargent Crane called us to 1 side and says "You boys is takeing a big chance and Phillips knows what to do but you want to remember Keefe to keep quite and not make no noise or talk to each other because if Jerry finds out you are there we probably won't see you again."

Well Al it finely come time for us to go and we went and if anybody asks you how to spend a pleasant evening don't steer them up against a listening post with a crazy man. Well I suppose you think its pretty quite there at home nights and I use to think so to but believe me Al, Bedford at 2 o'clock in the A. M. is a bowling alley along the side of 1 of these here listening posts. It may sound funny but I would of gave a month's pay if somebody would of shot off a fire cracker or anything to make a noise. There was the bosh trench about 20 yds. from us but not a sound out of them and a man couldn't help from thinking what if they had of heard us out there and they was getting ready to snoop up on us and that's why they was keeping so still and it got so as I could feel 1 of their bayonets burrowing into me and I am no quitter Al when it comes to fighting somebody you can see but when you have got a idear that somebody is cralling up on you and you haven't no chance to fight back I would like to see the bird that could enjoy themself and besides suppose my ears had went back on me worse then I thought and the Dutchmens was realy makeing a he—ll of a racket but I couldn't hear them and maybe they was getting ready to come over the top and I wouldn't know the differents and all of a sudden they would lay a garage and dash out behind it and if they didn't kill us we would be up in front of the court's marshal for not warning our pals.

Well as I say I would of gave anything for some one to of fired off a gun or made some noise of some kind but when this here Phillips finely opened up his clam and spoke I would of jumped a mile if they had of been any room to jump anywheres. Well the sargent had told us not to say nothing but all of a sudden right out loud this bird says this is a he—ll of a war. Well I motioned back at him to shut up but of course he couldn't see me and he thought I hadn't heard what he said so he said it over again so then I thought maybe he hadn't heard the sargent's orders so I whispered to him that he wasn't supposed to talk. Well Al they wasn't no way of keeping him quite and he says "That's all bunk because I been out here before and talked my head off and nothing happened." So I says well if you have got to talk you don't half to yell it. So then he tried to whisper Al but his whisper sounded like a jazz record with a crack in it so he says I'm not yelling I am whispering so I said yes I have heard Hughey Jennings whisper like that out on the lines.

So he shut up for a wile but pretty soon he busted out again and this time he was louder then ever and he asked me could I sing and I said no I couldn't so then he says well you can holler can't you so I said I suppose I could so he says "Well I know how we could play a big joke on them square heads. Lets the both of us begin yelling like a Indian and they will hear us and they will think they's a whole crowd of us here and they will begin bombing us or something and think they are goin to kill a whole crowd of Americans but it will only be us 2 and we can give them the laugh for waisting their ammunitions."

Well Al I seen then that I was parked there with a crazy man and for a wile I didn't say nothing because I was scared that I might say something that would encourage him some way so I just shut up and finely he says what is the matter ain't you going to join me? So I said I will join you in the jaw in a minute if you don't shut your mouth and then he quited down a little, but every few minutes he would have another swell idear and once he asked me could I imitate animals and I said no so he says he could mew like a cow and he had heard the boshs was so hard up for food and they would rush out here thinking they was going to find a cow but it wouldn't be no cow but it would be a horse on them.

Well you can imagine what I went through out there with a bird like that and I thought more then once I would catch it from him and go nuts myself but I managed to keep a hold of myself and the happiest minute of my life was when it was time

for us to crall back in our dug outs but at that I can't remember
how we got back here.

This A. M. Sargent Crane asked me what kind of a time did we
have and I told him and I told him this here Phillips was squirrel
meat and he says Phillips is just as sane as anybody usualy only
everybody that went out on the listening post was effected that
way by the quite and its a wonder I didn't go nuts to.

Well its a wonder I didn't Al and its a good thing I kept my
head and kept him from playing 1 of those tricks as god
knows what would of happened and the entire regt. might of
been wipped out. But I hope they don't wish no more listening post on me but if they do you can bet I will pick my own
pardner and it won't be no nut and no matter what Sargent
Crane says if this here Phillips is sane we're stopping at Palm
Beach.

Your pal,   JACK.

In the Trenchs, May 19.
FRIEND AL: Well old pal don't say nothing about this not even
to Bertha what I am going to tell you about as some people
might not understand and a specially a woman and might
maybe think I wasn't acting right towards Florrie or something
though when a man is married to a woman that he has been in
France pretty near 4 mos. and she has wrote him 3 letters I
don't see where she would have a sqawk comeing at whatever
I done but of course I am not going to do nothing that I
wouldn't just as leave tell her about it only I want to tell her
myself and when I get a good ready.

Well I guess I told you we was only supposed to stay here in
the front line 10 days and then they will somebody come and
releive us and take our place and then we go to the rest billets
somewheres and lay around till its our turn to come up here
again. Well Al we been in the front line now eight days and
that means we won't only be here 2 days more so probably we
will get out of here the day after tomorrow night. Well up to
today we didn't have no idear where we was going to get sent
as they's several places where the boys can go on leave like Aix
le Bains and Nice and etc. and we didn't know which 1 it would
be. So today we was talking about it and I said I wished I knew
for sure and Jack Brady stands pretty good with 1 of the lieuts.

so he says he would ask him right out. So he went and asked him and the lieut. told him Cologne.

Well Al I hadn't no sooner found out when 1 of the boys hands me a letter that just come and it was a letter from this baby doll that I told you about that's in Cologne and I will coppy down the letter so you can see for yourself what she says and here it is Al:

> *Dear Sammy Boy:*
>
> I was tres beaucoup to get your letter and will sure be glad to see you and can hardly wait till you get here. Don't let them send you anywhere else as Cologne is the prettiest town in France and the liveliest and we will sure have some time going to shows etc. and I hope you bring along beaucoup francs. Well I haven't time to write you much of a letter as I have got to spend the afternoon at the dressmaker's. You see I am getting all dolled up for my Sammy Boy. But be sure and let me know when you are going to get here and when you reach Cologne jump right in a Noir et Blanc taxi and come up to the house. You know the number so come along Sammy and make it toot sweet.
>
> Yours with tres beaucoup,
MARIE.

So that's her letter Al and it looks like I was going to be in right in old O. D. Cologne and it sure does look like fate was takeing a hand in the game when things breaks this way and when I wrote to this gal the first time I didn't have no idear of ever seeing her but the way things is turning out it almost seems like we was meant to meet each other. Well Al I only hope she has got some sence and won't get to likeing me to well or of course all bets is off but if we can just be good pals and go around to shows etc. together I don't see where I will be doing anything out of the way. Only as I say don't say nothing about it to Bertha or nobody else as people is libel to not understand and I guess most of them women back in the U. S. thinks that when a man has been up at the front as long as we have and then when he gets a few days leave he ought to take a running hop step and jump to the nearest phonograph and put on a Rodeheaver record.

Your pal, JACK.

In the Trenchs, May 20.

FRIEND AL: Well Al just a line and it will probably be the last

time I will write you from the trenchs for a wile as our time is
up tomorrow night and the next time I write you it will probably be from Cologne and I will tell you what kind of a time
they show us there and all about it. I just got through writeing
a note to the little gal there telling her I would get there as
soon as possible but I couldn't tell her when that would be as I
don't know how far it is or how we get there but Brady said he
thought it was about 180 miles so I suppose they will make us
walk.

Well talk about a quite section and they hasn't even been a
gun went off all day or no areoplanes or nothing and here we
thought we was going to see a whole lot of excitement and we
haven't fired a shot or throwed a grenade or even saw a German all the wile we was here and we are just like when we
come only for those poor birds that went on that wild goose
chase and didn't come back and they's been some talk about
sending another patrol over to get revenge for those poor boys
but I guess they won't nothing come of it. It would be like
sending good money after bad is the way I look at it.

Several of the boys has been calling me Sammy Boy today and
I signed my name that way in 1 of the notes I wrote that little gal
and I suppose who ever censored it told some of the boys about
it and now they are trying to kid me. Well Al I don't see where a
censor has got any license to spill stuff like that but they's no
harm done and they can laugh at me all they want to wile we are
here as I will be the 1 that does the laughing when we get to
Cologne. And I guess a whole lot of them will wish they was this
same Sammy Boy when they see me paradeing up and down the
blvd. with the bell of the ball. O you sweet Marie.

> Your pal,   JACK.

In the Trenchs, May 22.

FRIEND AL: Well Al its all off and we are here yet and what is
more we are libel to be here till the duration of the war if we
don't get killed and believe me I would welcome death rather
then stay in this he—ll hole another 10 days and from now on
I am going to take all the chances they is to take and the sooner
they finish me I will be glad of it and it looks like it might
come tonight Al as I have volunteered to go along with the

patrol that's going over and try and get even for what they done to our pals.

Well old pal it was understood when we come up here that we would be here 10 days and yesterday was the 10th. day we was here. Well I happened to say something yesterday to Sargent Crane about what time was we going and he says where to and I said I thought our time was up and we was going to get releived. So he says "Who is going to releive us and what and the he—ll do you want to be releived of?" So I said I understood they didn't only keep a regt. in the front line 10 days and then took them out and sent them to a rest billet somewheres. So he says what do you call this but a rest billet? So then I asked him how long we had to stay here and he said "Well it may be a day or it may be all summer. But if we get ordered out in a hurry it won't be to go to no rest billet but it will be to go up to where they are fighting the war."

So I made the remark that I wished somebody had of tipped me off as I had fixed up a kind of a date thinking we would be through here in 10 days. So he asked me where my date was at and I said Cologne. So then he kind of smiled and said "O and when was you planing to start?" So I said "I was figureing on starting tonight." So he waited a minute and then he said "Well I don't know if I can fix it for you tonight or tomorrow night, but they's some of the boys going to start in that direction one of them times and I guess you can go along."

Well Al I suppose Alcock and Brady and them has been playing another 1 of their gags on me and I hope they enjoyed it and as far as I am conserned they's no harm done. Cologne Al is way back of the German lines and when Sargent Crane said they was some of the boys starting in that direction he meant this here patrol. So I'm in on it Al and they didn't go last night but tonight's the big night. And some of the boys is calling me Sammy Boy and trying to make a monkey out of me but the smart Alex that's doing it isn't none of them going along on this raid and that's just what a man would expect from them. Because they's a few of us Al that come across the old puddle to fight and the rest of them thinks they are at the Young Peoples picnic.

Your pal,   JACK.

CHAPTER VI

Simple Simon

FRIEND AL: Well Al we have been haveing a lot of fun with a bird name Jack Simon only the boys calls him Simple Simon and if you seen him you wouldn't ask why because you would know why as soon as you seen him without asking why as he keeps his mouth open all the wile so as he will be ready to swallow whatever you tell him as you can tell him anything and he eats it up. So the boys has been stuffing him full of storys of all kinds and he eats them all up and you could tell him the reason they had the bob wire out in front was to scratch yourself on it when the cuties was useing you for a race track and he would eat it up.

Well when we come in here and took over this section this bird was sick and I don't know what ailed him only it couldn't of been brain fever but any way he didn't join us in here till the day before yesterday but ever since he joined us the boys has been stuffing him full and enjoying themself at his expenses. Well the 1st. thing he asked me was if we had saw any actions since we been here and I told him about a raid we was on the other night before he come and we layed down a garage and then snuck over to the German trenchs and jumped into them trying to get a hold of some prisoners but we couldn't find head or tale of no Germans where our bunch jumped in as they had ducked and hid somewheres when they found out we was comeing. So he says he wished he could of been along as he might of picked up some souvenirs over in their trenchs.

That's 1 of his bugs Al is getting souvenirs as he is 1 of these here souvenir hounds that it don't make no differents to him who wins the war as long as he can get a ship load of junk to carry it back home and show it off. So I told Johnny Alcock and some of the other boys about Simon wishing he could of got some souvenirs so they framed up on him and begin selling him junk that they told him they had picked it up over in the German trenchs and Alcock blowed some cigarette smoke in a bottle and corked it up and told him it was German tear gas and Simon give him 8 franks for it and Jack Brady showed him a couple of laths tied together with a peace of wire and told him it was a part of the areoplane that belonged to Guy Meyer the French ace that brought down so many Dutchmans before they finely got him and Brady said he hated to part with it as he had took it off a German prisoner that he brought in but if Simon thought it was worth 20 franks he could have it. So Simon bought it off him and wanted to know all about how Brady come to get the prisoner and of course Brady had to make it up as we haven't saw a German let alone take them a prisoner since we was back in the training arears and wouldn't know they was any only for their artillery and throwing up rockets at night and snipping at a man every time you go out on a wire party or something.

But any way Simon eats it up whatever you pull on him and some times I feel sorry for him and feel like tipping him off but the boys fun would be spoiled and believe me they need some kind of sport up here or pretty soon we would all be worse off then Simon and we would be running around fomenting at the mouth.

Well Al I wished you would write once in a wile if its only a line as a man likes to get mail once in a wile and I haven't heard from Florrie for pretty near a month and then all as she said was that the reason she hadn't wrote was because she wasn't feeling the best and I suppose she got something in her eye but anything for an excuse to not write and you would think I had stepped outdoors to wash the windows instead of being away from her since last December.

Your pal,   JACK.

In the Trenchs, June 4.

FRIEND AL: Well Al nothing doing as usual only patching things up once in a wile and it would be as safe here as picking your teeth if our artillery had a few brains as the Germans wouldn't never pay no tension to us if our batterys would lay off them but we don't no sooner get a quite spell when our guns cuts loose and remind Fritz that they's a war and then of course the Dutchmens has got to pay for their board some way and they raise he—ll for a wile and make everybody cross but as far as I can see they don't nobody never get killed on 1 side or the other side but of course the shells mess things up and keeps the boys busy makeing repairs where if our artillery would keep their mouth shut why so would theirs and the boys wouldn't never half to leave their dice game only for chow.

But from all as we hear I guess they's no dice game going on up on some of the other sections but they's another kind of a game going on up there and so far the Dutchmens has got all the best of it but some of the boys says wait till the Allys gets ready to strike back and they will make them look like a sucker and the best way to do is wait till the other side has wore themself out before you go back at them. Well I told them I have had a lot of experience in big league baseball where they's stragety the same like in war but I never heard none of the big league managers tell their boys to not try and score till the other side had all the runs they was going to get and further and more it looked to me like when the Germans did get wore out they could rest up again in the best hotel in Paris. So Johnny Alcock says oh they won't never get inside of Paris because the military police will stop them at the city limits and ask them for their pass and then where would they be? So I says tell that to Simple Simon and he shut up.

Speaking about Simple Simon what do you think they have got him believeing now. Well they told him Capt. Seeley had sent a patrol over the other night to find out what ailed the Germans that they never showed themself or started nothing against us and the patrol found out that Van Hindenburg had took all the men out of the section opp. us and sent them up to the war and left the trenchs opp. us empty so Simon asked him why we didn't go over there and take them then and they told him because our trenchs was warmer on acct. of being farther south. I suppose they will be telling him the next thing that Capt. Seeley and Ludendorf married sisters and the 2 of them has agreed to lay off each other.

Well Al I am glad they have got somebody else to pick on besides me and of course they can have a lot more fun with Simon as they's nothing to raw that he won't eat it up wile in my case I was to smart for them and just pretended like I fell for their gags as they would of been disappointed if I hadn't of and as I say somebody has got to furnish amusement in a he—ll hole like this or we would all be squirrel meat.

Your pal,   JACK.

In the Trenchs, June 7.

FRIEND AL: Well Al here is a hot 1 that they pulled on this Simon bird today and it was all as I could do to help from busting out laughing while they was telling it to him.

Well it seems like he must of been thinking that over what they told him about they not being no Germans in the trenchs over opp. to where we are at and it finely downed on him that if they wasn't nobody over there why who was throwing up them flares and rockets every night. So today he said to Brady he says "Didn't you birds tell me them trenchs over across the way was empty?" So Brady says yes what of it. So Simon says "Well I notice they's somebody over there at night times or else who throws up them flares as they don't throw themselfs up." So Brady says they had probably left a flare thrower over there to do that for them. But Simon says they must of left a lot of flare throwers because the flares come from different places along the line.

So then Alcock cut in and says "Yes but you will notice they don't come from different places at once and the bird that throws them gos from 1 place to another so as we will think the trenchs is full of Germans." So Simon says "They couldn't nobody go from 1 place to another place as fast as them flares shoots up from different places." So Alcock says "No they couldn't nobody do it if they walked but the man that throws them flares don't walk because he hasn't got only 1 leg as his other leg was shot off early in the war. But Van Hindenburg is so hard up for men that even if you get a leg shot off as soon as the Dr. mops up the mess and sticks on the court plaster they send the bird back in the war and put him on a job where you don't half to walk. So they stuck this old guy in the motorcycle dept. and now all as he does is ride up and down some quite section like this here all night and stop every so often and throw up a flare to make us think the place is dirty with Germans."

Well Al Simon thought it over a wile and then asked Alcock how a man could ride a motorcycle with only 1 leg and Alcock says "Why not because you don't half to peddle a motorcycle as they run themself." So Simon says yes but how about it when you want to get off? So Alcock says "What has a man's legs got to do with him getting off of a motorcycle as long as you have got your head to light on?"

That is what they handed him Al and they hadn't hardly no sooner then got through with that dose when Brady begun on the souvenirs. First he asked him if he had got a hold of any new ones lately and Simon says no he hadn't seen nobody that had any for sale and besides his jack was low so Brady asked him how much did he have and he says about 4 franks. So Brady says "Well you can't expect anybody to come across with anything first class for no such chicken's food as that." So Simon says well even if he had a pocket full of jack he couldn't buy nothing with it when they wasn't nothing to buy. Then Brady asked him if he had saw the German speegle Ted Phillips had picked up and Simon says no so Brady went and got Phillips and after a wile he come back with him and Phillips said he had the speegle in his pocket and he would show it to us if we promised to be carefull and not jar it out of his hands wile he was showing it as he wouldn't have it broke for the world. So Simon stood there with his eyes popping out and Phillips pulled the speegle out of his pocket and it wasn't nothing only a dirty little looking glass that you could pretty near crall through the cracks in it and all the boys remarked what a odd little speegle it was and they hadn't never saw 1 like it before and etc. and finely Simon couldn't keep his clam shut no longer so he asked Phillips how much he would take for it. Well Phillips says it wasn't for sale as speegles was scarce in Germany on acct. of the war and that was why the Dutchmens always looked like a bum when you took them a prisoner. So Simon asked him what price he would set on it suppose he would sell it and Phillips says about 8 franks. Well Simon got out all his jack and they wasn't only 4 franks and he showed it to Phillips and said if he would take 10 franks for the speegle he would give him 4 franks down and the other 6 franks when he got hold of some jack so Phillips hummed and hawed a wile and finely said all right Simon could have it but he wouldn't never sell it to him only that it kept worring him so much to carry it in his pocket for the fear he would loose it or break it.

Well Al Phillips has got Simon's last 4 franks and Simon has got Phillips's speegle and I suppose now that the boys sees how soft it is they will be selling him stuff on credit and he will owe them his next months pay before they get through with him and I suppose the next thing you know they will keep their beard when they shave and sell it to him for German tobacco. Well I would half to be pretty hard up before I went in on some skin game like that and I would just as leave go up to 1 of them cripples that use to spraddle all over the walk along 35 st. after the ball game and stick my heel in their eye and romp off with their days receipts.

Your pal,   JACK.

In the Trenchs, June 11.

FRIEND AL: Well Al it seems like Capt. Seeley is up on his ear because they haven't took our regt. out of here yet because it seems Gen. Pershing told Gen. Foch that he was to help himself to any part of the U. S. army and throw them in where ever they was needed and they's been a bunch of the boys throwed in along the other parts of the front to try and stop the Germans and Capt. Seeley is raveing because they keep us here and don't take us where we can get some actions. Any way 1 of the lieuts. told some of the boys that if we didn't get took out of here pretty quick Capt. Seeley would start a war of our own on this section and all the officers was sore because we hadn't done nothing or took no prisoners or nothing you might say only make repairs in the wire and etc. Well Al how in the he—ll can we show them anything when they don't never send us over the top or nowheres else but just leave us here moldering you might say but at that I guess we have showed as much life as the birds that's over there opp. us in them other trenchs that hasn't hardly peeped since we come in here and the boys says they are a Saxon regt. that comes from part of Germany where the Kaiser is thought of the same as a gum boil so the Saxons feels kind of friendly towards us and they will leave us alone as long as we leave them alone and visa and versa. So I don't see where Capt. Seeley and them other officers has got a right to pan us for not showing nothing but I don't blame them for wishing they would take us out of here and show us the war and from all as we hear they's plenty of places where we could do some good or at lease as much good as the birds that has been there.

Well Al they have been stringing poor Simon along and today they give him a song and dance about some bird name

Joe in the regt. that was here ahead of us that got a collection of souvenirs that makes Simon's look rotten and they said the guy's pals called him Souvenir Joe on acct. of him haveing such a fine collection. So Brady says to Simon "All you have got is 5 or 6 articles and the next thing you know they will be takeing us out of here and you might maybe never get another chance to pick up any more rare articles so if I was you I would either get busy and get a real collection or throw away them things you have got and forget it."

So Simon says "How can I get any more souvenirs when I haven't no more jack to buy them and besides you birds haven't no more to sell." So Brady says "Souvenir Joe didn't buy his collection but he went out and got them." So Simon asked him where at and Brady told him this here Joe use to crall out in Nobody's Land every night and pick up something and Simon says it was a wonder he didn't get killed. So Brady says "How would he get killed as the trenchs over across the way was just as empty when he was here as they are now and Old 1 Legged Mike and his motorcycle was on the job then to, so Joe would wait till Mike had throwed a few flares on this section and then he would sneak out and get his souvenirs before Mike come back again on his rounds."

Well then Simon asked him where the souvenirs was out there and Brady says they was in the different shell holes because most of Joe's souvenirs was the insides of German shells that had exploded and they was the best kind of souvenirs as they wasn't no chance of them being a fake.

Well Al I had a notion to take Simon to 1 side and tell him to not pay no tension to these smart alex because the poor crum might go snooping out there some night after the insides of a shell and get the outsides and all and if something like that happened to him I would feel like a murder though I haven't never took no part in makeing a monkey out of him, but I thought well if the poor cheese don't know no more then that he is better off dead so let him go.

Your pal,   JACK.

In the Trenchs, June 13.
FRIEND AL: Just a line Al as I am to excited to write much but I knew you would want to know the big news. Well Al I have

got a daughter born the 18 of May. How is that for a supprise Al but I guess you won't be no more supprised than I was when the news come as Florrie hadn't gave me no hint and a man can't guess a thing like that when you are in France and the lady in question is back in old Chi. But it sure is wonderfull news Al and I only wished I was somewheres where I could celebrate it right but you can't even whistle here or somebody would crown you with a shovle.

Well Al the news come today in a letter from Florrie's sister Marie Allen and she has been down in Texas but I suppose Florrie got her to come up and stay with her though as far as I can see its bad enough to have a baby without haveing that bird in the house to, but they's 1 consolation we haven't got rm. in the apt. for more than 2 kids and 3 grown ups so when I get home if sweet Marie is still there yet we will either half to get rid of the Swede cook or she, and when it comes to a choice between a ski jumper that will work and a sister that won't why Florrie won't be bothered with no family ties.

Any way I haven't no time to worry about no Allen family now as I am feeling to good and all as I wish is that somebody wins this war dam toot sweet so as I can get home and see this little chick Al and I bet she is as pretty as a picture and she couldn't be nothing else you might say and I have wrote to Florrie to not name her or nothing till I have my say as you turn a woman loose on nameing somebody all alone and they go nuts and look through a seed catalog.

Well old pal I know you would congratulate me if you was here and I am only sorry I can't return the complement and if I was you and Bertha I would adopt 1 of these here Belgium orphans that's lost their parents as they's nothing like it Al haveing a kid or 2 in the house and I bet little Al is tickled to death with his little sister.

Well Al I have told all the boys about it and they have been haveing a lot of fun with me but any way they call me Papa now which is a he—ll of a lot better then Sammy Boy.

Your pal,   JACK.

In the Trenchs, June 14.

FRIEND AL: I am all most to nervous to write Al but anything is better then setting around thinking and besides I want you to know what has came off so as you will know what come off in the case something happens.

Well Al Simple Simon's gone. We don't know if he's dead or alive or what the he—ll and all as we know is that he was here last night and he ain't here today and they hasn't nobody seen or heard of him.

Of course Al that isn't all we know neither as we can just about guess what happened. But I have gave my word to not spill nothing about what the boys pulled on him or god knows what Capt. Seeley would do to them.

Well Al I got up this A. M. feeling fine as I had slept better then any time for a wk. and I dreamt about the little gal back home that ain't never seen her daddy or don't know if she's got 1 or not but in my dream she knowed me O. K. as I dreamt I had just got home and Florrie wasn't there to meet me as usual but I rung the bell and the ski jumper let me in and I asked her where Florrie was and she said she had went out somewheres with little Al so I was going out and look for them but the Swede says the baby is here if you want to see her and I asked her what baby and she says why your new little baby girl.

So then I heard a baby crying somewheres in the house and I went in the bed rm. and this little mite jumped right up out of bed and all of a sudden she was 3 yrs. old instead of a mo. and she come running to me and hollered daddy. So then I grabbed her up and we begin danceing around but all of a sudden it was I and Florrie that was danceing together and little Al and the little gal was danceing around us and then I woke up Al and found I was still in this he—ll hole but the dream was so happy that I was still feeling good over it yet and besides it looked like the sun had forgot it was in France and was going to shine for a while.

Well pretty soon along come Corp. Evans and called me to 1 side and asked me what I knew about Simon. So I says what about him. So Corp. Evans says he is missing and they hasn't nobody saw him since last night. So I says I didn't know nothing about him but if anything had happened to him they was a lot of birds in this Co. that ought to pay for it. So Corp. Evans asked me what was I driveing at and I started in to tell him about Alcock and Brady and them kidding this poor bird to death and Corp. Evans says yes he knew all about that and the best thing to do was to shut up about it as it would get every-body in bad. He says "Wait a couple days any way and maybe he will show up O. K. and then they won't be no sence in spilling all this stuff." So I says all right I would wait a couple days but these birds ought to get theirs if something serious has happened and if he don't show up by that time I won't make no promise to spill all I know. So Corp. Evans says I didn't half to make no promise as he would spill the beans himself if Simon isn't O. K.

Well Al of course all the boys had heard the news by the time I got to talk to them and they's 2 or 3 of them that feels pretty sick over it and no wonder and the bird that feels the sickest is Alcock and here is why. Well it seems like yesterday while I was telling all the boys about the news from home Simon was giveing Alcock a ear full of that junk Brady had been slipping him about Souvenir Joe and Simon asked Alcock if he thought they was still any of them souvenirs worth going after out in them shell holes. So Alcock says of course they must be as some of the holes was made new since we been here. But Alcock told him that if he was him he wouldn't waist no time collecting the insides of German shells as the Germans was so hard up for mettle and etc. now days that the shells they was sending over was about ½ full of cheese and stuff that wouldn't keep. So Alcock says to him "What you ought to go after is a Saxon because you can bet that Souvenir Joe didn't get none and if you would get 1 all the boys would begin call-ing you Souvenir Simon instead of Simple Simon and you would make Souvenir Joe look like a dud."

Well Al Simon didn't know a Saxon from a hang nail so he asked Alcock what they looked like and Alcock told him to never mind as he couldn't help from knowing 1 if he ever seen it so then Simon asked him where they was libel to be and Al-cock told him probably over in some of the shell holes near the German trench.

That's what come off yesterday wile I was busy telling every-body about the little gal as you can bet I would of put Simon wise had I of been in on it and now Al he's gone and they don't nobody know what's became of him but they's a lot of us that's got a pretty good idear and as I say they's 2 or 3 feels pretty sick and one a specially. But I guess at that they don't no one feel no worse then me though they can't nobody say I am to blame for what's happened but still in all I might of interfered because I am the only 1 of them that has got a heart Al and the only reason Alcock and Brady is so sick now is that they are scared to death of what will happen to them if they get found out. Because their smartness won't get them nothing up in front of the Court Marshall as he has seen to many birds just like them.

Well Al I am on post duty tonight and maybe you don't know what that means. Well old pal its no Elks carnivle at no time and just think what it will be tonight with your ears straining for a cry from out there. And if the cry comes Al they won't only be the 1 thing to do and I will be the 1 to do it.

So this may be the last time you will hear from me old pal and I wanted you to know in the case anything come off just how it happened as I won't be here to write it to you afterwards.

All as I can think about now Al is 2 things and 1 of them is that little gal back home that won't never see her daddy but maybe when she gets 4 or 5 yrs. old she will ask her mother "Why haven't I got a daddy like other little girls?" But maybe she will have 1 by that time Al. But what I am thinking about the most is that poor ½ wit out there and as Brady says he isn't nothing but a Mormon any way and ought never to of got in the army but still and all he is a man and its our duty to fight and die for him if needs to be.

Your pal,   JACK.

In the Hospital, July 20.

FRIEND AL: You will half to excuse this writeing as I am proped up in a funny position in bed and its all as I can do to keep the paper steady as my left arm ain't no more use then the Russian front.

Well Al yesterday was the 1st. time they left me set up and I wrote a letter to Florrie and told her I was getting along O. K. as I didn't want she should worry and this time I will try and write to you. I suppose you got the note that the little nurse wrote for me about 2 wks. ago and told you I was getting better. Well old pal the gal that wrote you that little note is some baby and if you could see the kid that wrote you that little note you would wished you was laying here in my place. No I guess you wouldn't wished that Al as they's nobody that would want to go through what I have been through and they's very few that could stand it like I have and keep on smileing.

Well old pal they thought for a wile that it was Feeney for yrs. truly as they say over here and believe me I was in such pain that I would of been glad to die to get rid of the pain and the Dr. said it was a good thing I was such a game bird and had such a physic or I couldn't of never stood it. But I am not strong enough yet to set this way very long so if I am going to tell you what happened I had better start in.

Well Al this is the 20 of July and that means I have been in here 5 wks. as it was the 14 of June when all this come off. Well Al I can remember writeing to you the day of the night it come off and I guess I told you about this bird Simon getting lost that was always after the souvenirs and some of the boys told him they wasn't no Germans over in the other trenchs but just a bird name Motorcycle Mike that went up and down the section throwing flares so as we would think they was Germans over there. So they told him if he wanted to go out in No-body's Land and spear souvenirs it was safe if you went just after Mike had made his rounds so as the snippers wouldn't get you.

Well old pal I was standing there looking out over Nobody's Land that night and I couldn't think of nothing only poor Simon and listening to hear if I couldn't maybe hear him call from somewheres out there and I don't know how long I had been standing there when I heard a kind of a noise like some-body scrunching and at the same time they was a flare throwed up from our side and I seen a figure out there cralling on the ground quite a ways beyond our wire. Well Al I didn't wait to look twice but I called Corp. Evans and told him. So he says who did I think it was and I said it must be Simon. So he says "Well Keefe its up to 1 of us to go get him." So I said "Well Corp. I guess its my job." So he says "All right Keefe if you feel that way about it." So I says all right and I'll say Al that he give up his claims without a struggle.

Well I started and I was going without my riffle but the Corp. stopped me and says take it along and I says "What for, do you think I am going to pick Simon up with a bayonet." So he says who told me it was Simon out there. Well Al that's the 1st. time I stopped to think it might maybe be somebody else.

Well Florrie use to say that I couldn't get up in the night for a drink of water without everybody in the bldg. thinking the world serious must of started but I bet I didn't knock over no chairs on this trip. Well Al it took me long enough to get out there as you can bet I wasn't trying for no record and every time they was a noise I had to lay flat and not buge. But I got there Al to where I thought I had saw this bird moveing around but they hadn't no rockets went up since I started and it was like a troop ship and I couldn't make out no figure of a man or nothing else and I was just going to whisper Simon's name when I reached out my hand and touched him. Well Al it wasn't Simon.

Well old pal we had some battle this bird and me and the both of us forgot bayonets and guns and everything else. I would of killed him sure only he got a hold of my left hand between his teeth and I couldn't pry it loose. But believe me Al he took a awful beating with my free hand and I will half to hand it to him for a game bird only what chance did he have? None Al and the battle couldn't only end the 1 way and I was just getting ready to grab his wind pipe and shut off the meter when he left go of my other hand and let out a yell that you could hear all over the great lakes and then all of a sudden it seemed like everybody was takeing a flash light and then the bullets come whizzing from all sides it seemed like and they got me 3 times Al and never pinked this other bird once. Well Al it wasn't till 2 wks. ago that I found out that my opponent was Johnny Alcock.

Just 2 wks. ago yesterday Johnny come in and seen me and told me the whole story and it was the 1st. day they left me see anybody only the Dr. and the little nurse and was the 1st. day Johnny was able to be up and around. How is that Al to put a man in the hospital for 3 wks. without useing no gun or knife or nothing on him only 1 bear fist. Some fist eh Al.

Well it seems like he had been worring so about Simon that he finely went out there snooping around all by himself looking for him and he was the 1 I seen when that flare went up and of course we each thought the other 1 was a German and finely it was him yelling and the rockets going up at the same time that drawed the fire and I got all of it because I was the bird on top.

But listen Al till you hear the funny part of it. Simple Simon the bird that we was both out there looking for him showed up in our trench about a half hr. after we was brought in and he showed up with a Saxon all right but the Saxon was dead. Well Al Simon told them that he had ran into this guy over near their wire and that he was alive when he got him, but Alcock says that Brady said Simon hadn't only been gone 24 hrs. and the Saxon had been gone a he—ll of a lot longer than that.

Well they's no hard feeling between Alcock and I and I guess I more then got even with him for eating out of my hand as they say but Johnny said it was a shame I couldn't of used some of my strength on a German instead of him but any way its all over now and the Dr. says my leg is pretty near O. K. and I can walk on it in a couple wks. but my left arm won't be no use for god knows how long and maybe never and I guess I'm lucky they didn't half to clip it off. So I don't know when I will get out of here or where I will go from here but I guess they's 1 little party that ain't in no hurry to see me go and I wished you could see her look at me Al and you would say its to bad I am a married man with 2 kids.

Your pal,   JACK.

Somewheres in France, Aug. 16.

FRIEND AL: Well Al I don't suppose this will reach you any sooner then if I took it with me and mailed it when I get home but I haven't nothing to do for a few hrs. so I might as well be writeing you the news.

Well old pal I am homewards bound as they say as the war is Feeney as far I am conserned and I am sailing tonight along with a lot of the other boys that's being sent home for good and when I look at some of the rest of them I guess I am lucky to be in as good a shape as I am. I am O. K. only for my arm and wile it won't never be as good as it was I can probably get to use it pretty good in a few months and all as I can say is thank god it is my left arm and not the old souper that use to stand Cobb and them on their head and it will stand them on their head again Al as soon as this war is over and I guess I won't half to go begging to Comiskey to give me another chance after what I have done as even if I couldn't pitch up a alley I would be a money maker for them just setting on the bench and showing myself after this.

Well we are saying good by to old France and I don't know how the rest of the boys feels but I am not haveing no trouble controling myself and when it comes down to cases Al the shoe is on the other ft. and what I am getting at is that France ought to be the 1 that hates to see us leave as I doubt if they will ever get a bunch of spenders like us over here again.

Well Al it certainly seems quite down here in this old sea port town after what we have been through and it seems like I can still hear them big guns roar and them riffles crack and etc. and I feel like I ought to keep my head down all the wile and keep out of the snippers way and I could all most shut my eyes and imagine I was back there again in that he—ll hole but I know I'm not Al as I don't itch.

Well Al my wounds isn't the only reason I am comeing home but they's another reason and that is that they want some of us poplar idles to help rouse up the public on this here next Liberty Loan and I don't mind it as they have promised to send me home to Chi and I can be with Florrie and the kids. I will do what I can Al though I can't figure where the public would need any rouseing up and they certainly wouldn't if they had of been through what I have been through and maybe some of the other boys to. It takes jack to run a war Al even if us boys don't get none of it or what we do get they either send it home to our wife or take it away from us in a crap game.

Well old pal I left the hospital the day before yesterday and that was the only time I felt like crying since they told me I was going home and it wasn't so much for myself Al but that poor little nurse and you would of felt like crying to if you could of seen the look she give me. Her name is Charlotte Warren and she lives in Minneapolis and expects to go right back there after she is through over here but that don't do me no good as a married man with a couple children has got something better to do besides flirting with a pretty little nurse and besides I won't never pitch ball in Minneapolis as I expect to quit the game when I am about 40.

Well Al some of the boys wants to say their farewells to the

Vin Rouge and the la la las and I will half to close and I will write again as soon as I get home and tell you what the baby gal looks like though they's only the 1 way she could look and that's good.

Well here is good by to France and good luck to all the boys that's going to stay over here and Simple Simon with the rest of them and I suppose I ought to of got a few souvenirs off him to bring home with me. But I guess at that I will be carrying a souvenir of this war for a long wile Al and its better than any of them foney ones he has got as the 1 I have got shows I was realy in it and done my bit for old Glory and the U. S. A.

Your pal,   JACK.

Chicago, Aug. 29.

FRIEND AL: Well Al here I am back in old Chi and feeling pretty good only for my arm and my left leg is still stiff yet and I caught a mean cold comeing across the old pond but what is a few little things like that as the main thing is being home.

Well old pal they wasn't nothing happened on the trip across the old pond only it took a whole lot to long and believe me old N. Y. looked good but believe me I wouldn't waist no time in N. Y. only long enough to climb outside a big steak and the waiter had to cut it up for me but even the waiters treated us fine and everywheres we showed up the people was wild about us and cheered and clapped and it sounded like old times when I use to walk out there to warm up.

Well we hit N. Y. in the A. M. and left that night and got here last eve. and I didn't leave Florrie know just when I was comeing as I wanted to supprise her. Well Al I ought to of wired ahead and told her to go easy on my poor old arm because when she opened the door and seen me she give a running hop step and jump and dam near killed me. So then she seen my arm in a sling and cried and cried and she says "Oh my poor boy what have you been through." So I says "Well you have been through something yourself so its 50 50 only I got this from a German."

Well Al little Al was the cutest thing you ever seen and he grabbed me by the good hand and rushed me in to where the little stranger was laying and she was asleep but we broke the rules for once and all and all it was some party and she is some little gal Al and pretty as a picture and when you can say that for a 3 mos. old its going some as the most of them looks like a French breakfast.

Well I finely happened to think of Sister Marie and I asked where she was at and Florrie says she went back to Texas so I says tough luck and Florrie says I needn't get so gay the 1st. evening home and she says "Any way we have still got a Marie in the house as that is what I call the baby." So I says "Well you can think of her that way but her name ain't going to be that as I don't like the name." So she says what name did I like and I pretended like I was thinking a wile and finely I says what is the matter with Charlotte. Well Al you will half to hand it to the women for detectives as I hadn't no sooner said the name when she says "Oh no you can't come home and name my baby after none of your French nurses." And I hadn't told her nothing about a nurse.

Well any way I says I had met a whole lot more Maries then Charlottes in France and she says had I met any Florries and I said no and that was realy the name I had picked out for the kid. So she says well she didn't like the name herself but it was the only name I could pick out that she wouldn't be suspicious of it so the little gal is named after her mother Al and if she only grows up ½ as pretty as her old lady it won't make no differents if she has got a funny name.

Well Al have you noticed what direction the Dutchmens is makeing their drive in now? They started going the other way the 18 of July and it was 2 days ahead of that time that our regt. was moved over to the war and now they are running them ragged. Well Al I wished I was there to help but even if I was worth a dam to fight I couldn't very well leave home just now.

Your pal,   JACK.

THE YOUNG IMMIGRUNTS

By
RING W. LARDNER, JR.

WITH A PREFACE BY
THE FATHER

Portraits by Gaar Williams

The Author — "Bill"

CONTENTS

LIST OF ILLUSTRATIONS

CITY LIMITS
SPEED
NINE (9) MILES

PREFACE

THE person whose name is signed to this novel was born on the nineteenth day of August, 1915, and was therefore four years and three months old when the manuscript was found, late in November, 1919. The narrative is substantially true, with the following exceptions:

1. "My Father," the leading character in the work, is depicted as a man of short temper, whereas the person from whom the character was drawn is in reality as pleasant a fellow as one would care to meet and seldom has a cross word for any one, let alone women and children.

2. The witty speeches accredited to "My Father" have, possibly owing to the limitations of a child's memory, been so garbled and twisted that they do not look half so good in print as they sounded in the open air.

3. More stops for gas were made than are mentioned in the story.

As the original manuscript was written on a typewriter with a rather frayed ribbon, and as certain words were marked out and others handwritten in, I have taken the liberty of copying the entire work with a fresh ribbon and the inclusion of the changes which the author indicated in pencil in the first draft. Otherwise the story is presented to the reader exactly as it was first set down.

THE FATHER.

CHAPTER I

My Parents

MY PARENTS are both married and ½ of them are very good looking. The balance is tall and skiny and has a swarty complexion with moles but you hardly ever notice them on account of your gaze being rapped up in his feet which would be funny if brevvity wasnt the soul of wit. Everybody says I have his eyes and I am glad it didnt half to be something else tho Rollie Zeider the ball player calls him owl eyes for a nick name but if I was Rollie Zeider and his nose I wouldnt pick on somebodys else features.

He wears pretty shirts which he bought off of another old ball player Artie Hofman to attrack tension off of his feet and must of payed a big price for them I heard my ant tell my uncle when they thorght I was a sleep down to the lake tho I guess he pays even more for his shoes if they sell them by the frunt foot.

I was born in a hospittle in Chicago 4 years ago and liked it very much and had no idear we were going to move till 1 day last summer I heard my mother arsk our nurse did she think she could get along O. K. with myself and 3 brothers John Jimmie and David for 10 days wilst she and my old man went east to look for a costly home.

Well yes said our nurse barshfully.

I may as well exclaim to the reader that John is 7 and Jimmie is 5 and I am 4 and David is almost nothing as yet you might say and tho I was named for my father they call me Bill thank God.

The conversation amungst my mother and our nurse took place right after my father came back from Toledo where Jack Dempsey knocked Jessie Willard for a gool tho my father liked the big fellow and bet on him.

David was in his bath at the time and my mother and our nurse and myself and 2 elder brothers was standing around admireing him tho I notice that when the rest of the family takes their bath they dont make open house of the occassion.

The Rest of the family

Well my parents went east and dureing their absents myself and brothers razed hell with David on the night shift but when they come back my mother said to the nurse were they good boys.

Fine replid our nurse lamely and where are you going to live.

Connecticut said my mother.

Our nurse forced a tired smile.

Here we will leave my parents to unpack and end this chapter.

CHAPTER 2

Starting Gaily

WE SPENT the rest of the summer on my granmother in Indiana and my father finley went to the worst series to write it up as he has followed sports of all sorts for years and is a expert so he bet on the wite sox and when he come home he acted rarther cross.

Well said my mother simperingly I suppose we can start east now.

We will start east when we get good and ready said my father with a lordly sneeze.

The next thing was how was we going to make the trip as my father had boughten a new car that the cheepest way to get it there was drive it besides carrying a grate deal of our costly bagage but if all of us went in it they would be no room left for our costly bagage and besides 2 of my brothers always acts like devils incarnite when they get in a car so my mother said to our nurse.

If you think you can manage the 2 older boys and David on the train myself and husband will take Bill in the car said my mother to our nurse.

Fine replid our nurse with a gastly look witch my mother did not see.

Myself and parents left Goshen Indiana on a fine Monday morning leaveing our nurse and brothers to come latter in the weak on the railway. Our plans was to reach Detroit that night and stop with my uncle and ant and the next evening take the boat to Buffalo and thence to Connecticut by motor so the first town we past through was Middlebury.

Elmer Flick the old ball player use to live here said my father modestly.

My mother forced a smile and soon we were acrost the Michigan line and my mother made the remark that she was thirsty.

We will stop at Coldwater for lunch said my father with a strate face as he pulls most of his lines without changeing expressions.

Sure enough we puled up to 1 side of the road just after

Grandmother at Goshen

leaveing Coldwater and had our costly viands of frid chicken and doughnuts and milk fernished by my grate ant and of witch I partook freely.

We will stop at Ypsilanti for supper said my father in calm tones that is where they have the state normal school.

I was glad to hear this and hoped we would get there before dark as I had always wanted to come in contack with normal peaple and see what they are like and just at dusk we entered a large size town and drove past a large size football field.

Heavens said my mother this must be a abnormal school to have such a large football field.

My father wore a qeer look.

This is not Ypsilanti this is Ann Arbor he crid.

But I thorght you said we would go south of Ann Arbor and direct to Ypsilanti said my mother with a smirk.

I did say that but I thorght I would surprise you by comeing into Ann Arbor replid my father with a corse jesture.

Personly I think the suprise was unanimous.

Well now we are here said my mother we might as well look up Bill.

Bill is my uncle Bill so we stoped at the Alfa Delt house and got him and took him down to the hotel for supper and my old man called up Mr. Yost the football coach of the Michigan football team and he come down and visited with us.

What kind of a team have you got coach said my father lamely.

I have got a determined team replid Mr. Yost they are determined to not play football.

At this junction my unlucky mother changed the subjeck to the league of nations and it was 10 o'clock before Mr. Yost come to a semi colon so we could resume our jurney and by the time we past through Ypsilanti the peaple was not only subnormal but unconsius. It was nerly midnight when we puled up in frunt of my ants and uncles house in Detroit that had been seting up since 7 expecting us.

Were sorry to be so late said my mother bruskly.

Were awfully glad you could come at all replid my ant with a ill consealed yawn.

We will now leave my relitives to get some sleep and end this chapter.

Uncle Bill

CHAPTER 3

Erie Lake

THE BOAT leaves Detroit every afternoon at 5 oclock and reachs Buffalo the next morning at 9 tho I would better exclaim to my readers that when it is 9 oclock in Buffalo it is only 8 oclock in Goshen for instants as Buffalo peaple are qeer.

Well said my father the next morning at brekfus I wander what time we half to get the car on the board of the boat.

I will find out down town and call up and let you know replid my uncle who is a engineer and digs soors or something.

Sure enough he called up dureing the fornoon and said the car must be on the board of the boat at 3 oclock so my father left the house at 2 oclock and drove down to the worf tho he had never drove a car in Detroit before but has nerves of steal. Latter my uncle come out to his home and took myself and mother and ant down to the worf where my old man was waiting for us haveing put the car on the board.

What have you been doing ever since 3 oclock arsked my mother as it was now nerly 5.

Haveing a high ball my father replid.

I thorght Detroit was dry said my mother shyly.

Did you said my father with a rye smile and as it was now nerly time for the boat to leave we said good by to my uncle and ant and went on the boat. A messenger took our costly bagage and put it away wilst myself and parents went out on the porch and set looking at the peaple on the worf. Suddenly they was a grate hub bub on the worf and a young man and lady started up the gangs plank wilst a big crowd throwed rice and old shoes at them and made a up roar.

Bride and glum going to Niagara Falls said my father who is well travelled and seams to know everything.

Instantly the boat give a blarst on the wistle and I started with suprise.

Did that scare you Bill said my father and seamed to enjoy it and I suppose he would of laughed out right had I fell overboard and been drowned in the narsty river water.

Uncle and Ant at Detroit

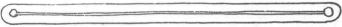

The Bride and Glum

Soon we were steeming up the river on the city of Detroit 3.

That is Canada over there is it not said my mother.

What did you think it was the Austrian Tyrol replid my father explodeing a cough. Dureing our progress up the river I noticed several funny things flotting in the water with lanterns hanging on them and was wandering what they could be when my mother said they seam to have plenty of boys.

They have got nothing on us replid my father quick as a flarsh.

A little latter who should come out on the porch and set themselfs ner us but the bride and glum.

Oh I said to myself I hope they will talk so as I can hear them as I have always wandered what newlyweds talk about on their way to Niagara Falls and soon my wishs was realized.

Some night said the young glum are you warm enough.

I am perfectly comfertible replid the fare bride tho her looks belid her words what time do we arive in Buffalo.

9 oclock said the lordly glum are you warm enough.

I am perfectly comfertible replid the fare bride what time do we arive in Buffalo.

9 oclock said the lordly glum I am afrade it is too cold for you out here.

Well maybe it is replid the fare bride and without farther adieu they went in the spacius parlers.

I wander will he be arsking her 8 years from now is she warm enough said my mother with a faint grimace.

The weather may change before then replid my father.

Are you warm enough said my father after a slite pause.

No was my mothers catchy reply.

Well said my father we arive in Buffalo at 9 oclock and with that we all went inside as it was now pitch dark and had our supper and retired and when we rose the next morning and drest and had brekfus we puled up to the worf in Buffalo and it was 9 oclock so I will leave the city of Detroit 3 tide to the worf and end this chapter.

Buffalo to Rochester 76.4

A s we was leaveing the boat who should I see right along side of us but the fare bride and the lordly glum.

We are right on the dot said the glum looking at his costly watch it is just 9 oclock and so they past out of my life.

We had to wait qite a wile wilst the old man dug up his bill of loading and got the costly moter.

We will half to get some gas he said I wonder where they is a garage.

No sooner had the words fell from his lips when a man with a flagrant Adams apple handed him a card with the name of a garage on it.

Go up Genesee st 5 blks and turn to the left or something said the man with the apple.

Soon we reached the garage and had the gas tank filled with gas it was 27 cents in Buffalo and soon we was on our way to Rochester. Well these are certainly grate roads said my father barshfully.

They have lots better roads in the east than out west replid my mother with a knowing wink.

The roads all through the east are better than out west remarked my father at lenth.

These are wonderfull replid my mother smuggleing me vs her arm.

The time past quickly with my parents in so jocular a mood and all most before I knew it we was on the outer skirts of Batavia.

What town is this quired my mother in a tolerant voice.

Batavia husked my father sloughing down to 15 miles per hour.

Well maybe we would better stop and have lunch here said my mother coyly.

We will have lunch in Rochester replid my father with a loud cough.

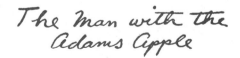

The Man with the
Adams Apple

My mother forced a smile and it was about ½ past 12 when we arived in Rochester and soon we was on Genesee st and finley stoped in front of a elegant hotel and shared a costly lunch.

CHAPTER 5

My Father's Idear

WILST PARTICIPATEING in the lordly viands my father halled out his map and give it the up and down.

Look at here he said at lenth they seams to be a choice of 2 main roads between here and Syracuse but 1 of them gos way up north to Oswego wilst the other gos way south to Geneva where as Syracuse is strate east from here you might say so it looks to me like we would save both millage and time if we was to drive strate east through Lyons the way the railway gos.

Well I dont want to ride on the ties said my mother with a loud cough.

Well you dont half to because they seams to be a little road that gos strate through replid my father removing a flys cadaver from the costly farina.

Well you would better stick to the main roads said my mother tacklessly.

Well you would better stick to your own business replid my father with a pungent glance.

Soon my father had payed the check and gave the waiter a lordly bribe and once more we sprang into the machine and was on our way. The lease said about the results of my fathers grate idear the soonest mended in a word it turned out to be a holycost of the first water as after we had covered miles and miles of ribald roads we suddenly come to a abrupt conclusion vs the side of a stagnant freight train that was stone deef to honks. My father set there for nerly ½ a hour reciteing the 4 Horses of the Apoplex in a under tone but finley my mother mustard up her curage and said affectedly why dont we turn around and go back somewheres. I cant spell what my father replid.

At lenth my old man decided that Lyons wouldnt never come to Mahomet if we set it out on the same lines all winter so we backed up and turned around and retraced 4 miles of shell holes and finley reached our objective by way of Detour.

The Dirty Mechanic

Puling up in front of a garage my father beckoned to a dirty mechanic.

How do we get to Syracuse from here arsked my father blushing furiously.

Go strate south to Geneva and then east to Syracuse replid the dirty mechanic with a loud cough.

Isnt there no short cut arsked my father.

Go strate south to Geneva and then east to Syracuse replid the dirty mechanic.

You see daddy we go to Geneva after all I said brokenly but luckly for my piece of mind my father dont beleive in corporeal punishment a specially in front of Lyons peaple.

Soon we was on a fine road and nothing more hapened till we puled into Syracuse at 7 that evening and as for the conversation that changed hands in the car between Lyons and Syracuse you could stick it in a day message and send it for 30 cents.

CHAPTER 6

Syracuse to Hudson 183.2

Soon we was on Genesee st in Syracuse but soon turned off a blk or 2 and puled up in front of a hotel that I cant ether spell or pronounce besides witch they must of been a convention of cheese sculpters or something stoping there and any way it took the old man a hour to weedle a parler bed room and bath out of the clerk and put up a cot for me.

Wilst we was enjoying a late and futile supper in the hotel dinning room a man named Duffy reckonized my father and came to our table and arsked him to go to some boxing matchs in Syracuse that night.

Thanks very much said my father with a slite sneeze but you see what I have got on my hands besides witch I have been driving all day and half to start out again erly in the morning so I guess not.

Between you and I dear reader my old man has been oposed to pugilisms since the 4 of July holycost.

Who is that man arsked my mother when that man had gone away.

Mr. Duffy replid my father shove the ketchup over this way.

Yes I know he is Mr. Duffy but where did you meet him insisted my mother quaintly.

In Boston my father replid where would a person meet a man named Duffy.

When we got up the next morning it was 6 o'clock and purring rain but we eat a costly brekfus and my father said we would save time if we would all walk down to the garage where he had horded the car witch he stated was only 2 short blks away from the hotel. Well if it was only 2 short blks why peaple that lives next door to each other in Syracuse are by no means neighbors and when we got there the entire party was soping wet and rarther rabid.

We will all catch our death of cold chuckled my mother.

What of it explained my old man with a dirty look at the sky.

Mr. and Mrs. Heywood
and the Closed Car.

Maybe we would better put up the curtains sugested my mother smirking.

Maybe we wouldnt too said my father cordialy.

Well maybe it will clear up said my mother convulsively.

Maybe it wont too replid my father as he capered into the drivers seat.

My father is charming company wilst driveing on strange roads through a purring rain and even when we past through Oneida and he pronounced it like it was a biscuit neither myself or my mother ventured to correct him but finley we reached Utica when we got to witch we puled up along side the kerb and got out and rang ourselfs out to a small extent when suddenly a closed car sored past us on the left.

Why that was Mrs. Heywood in that car explained my mother with a fierce jesture. By this time it was not raining and we got back into the car and presently over took the closed car witch stoped when they reckonized us.

And witch boy is this quired Mrs. Heywood when the usual compliments had been changed.

This is the third he is named for his father replid my mother forceing a smile.

He has his eyes was the comment.

Bill dont you remember Mrs. Heywood said my mother turning on me she use to live in Riverside and Dr. Heywood tended to you that time you had that slite atack of obesity.

Well yes I replid with a slite accent but did not add how rotten the medicine tasted that time and soon we was on Genesee st on our way out of Utica.

I wander why they dont name some of their sts Genesee in these eastren towns said my father for the sun was now shining but no sooner had we reached Herkimer when the clouds bersed with renude vigger and I think my old man was about to say we will stop and have lunch when my mother sugested it herself.

No replid my father with a corse jesture we will go on to Little Falls.

It was raining cats and dogs when we arived at Little Falls and my father droped a quaint remark.

If Falls is a verb he said the man that baptized this town was a practicle joker.

We will half to change our close replid my mother steping into a mud peddle in front of the hotel with a informal look.

When we had done so we partook of a meger lunch and as it was now only drooling resumed our jurney.

They soked me 5 for that room said my father but what is a extra sokeing or 2 on a day like this.

I didnt mean for you to get a room said my mother violently.

Where did you want us to change our close on the register said my old man turning pail.

Wasnt it funny that we should happen to see Mrs. Heywood in Utica said my mother at lenth.

They live there dont they my father replid.

Why yes my mother replid.

Well then my father replid the real joke would of been if we had of happened to see her in Auburn.

A little wile latter we past a grate many signs reading dine at the Big Nose Mountain Inn.

Rollie Zeider never told me they had named a mountain after him crid my father and soon we past through Fonda.

Soon we past through Amsterdam and I guess I must of dosed off at lease I cant remember anything between there and Schenectady and I must apologize to my readers for my laps as I am unable to ether describe the scenery or report anything that may of been said between these 2 points but I recall that as we entered Albany a remark was adrest to me for the first time since lunch.

Bill said my mother with a ½ smirk this is Albany the capital of New York state.

So this is Albany I thorght to myself.

Who is governer of New York now arsked my mother to my father.

Smith replid my father who seams to know everything.

Queer name said my mother sulkily.

Soon we puled up along side a policeman who my father arsked how do we get acrost the river to the New York road and if Albany pays their policemans by the word Ill say we were in the presents of a rich man and by the time he got through it was dark and still drooling and my old man didnt know the road and under those conditions I will not repete the conversation that transpired between Albany and Hudson but will end my chapter at the city limits of the last named settlemunt.

Albany's Rich Policeman

CHAPTER 7

Hudson

WE WERE turing gaily down the main st of Hudson when a man of 12 years capered out from the side walk and hoped on the runing board.

Do you want a good garage he arsked with a dirty look.

Why yes my good man replid my father tenderly but first where is the best hotel.

I will take you there said the man.

I must be a grate favorite in Hudson my father wispered at my mother.

Soon folling the mans directions we puled up in front of a hotel but when my father went at the register the clerk said I am full tonight.

Where do you get it around here arsked my father tenderly.

We have no rooms replid the senile clerk paying no tension to my old mans remark but there is a woman acrost the st that takes loggers.

Not to excess I hope replid my father but soon we went acrost the st and the woman agrede to hord us for the night so myself and mother went to our apartmunts wilst my father and the 12 year old besought the garage. When we finley got reunited and went back to the hotel for supper it was past 8 oclock as a person could of told from the viands. Latter in front of our loggings we again met the young man who had welcomed us to Hudson and called my father to 1 side.

There is a sailer going to spend the night here he said in a horse wisper witch has walked all the way from his home Schenectady and he has got to report on his ship in New York tomorrow afternoon and has got no money so if he dont get a free ride he will be up vs it.

He can ride with us replid my father with a hiccup if tomorrow is anything like today a sailer will not feel out of place in my costly moter.

I will tell him replid the man with a corse jesture.

The Man of Twelve years

Will you call us at ½ past 5 my mother reqested to our lanlady as we entered our Hudson barracks.

I will if I am awake she replid useing her handkerchief to
some extent.

Latter we wandered how anybody could help from being
awake in that hot bed of mones and grones and cat calls and
caterwauls and gulish screaks of all kinds and tho we had rose
erly at Syracuse and had a day of retchedness we was all more
than ready to get up when she wraped on our door long ere
day brake.

Where is that sailer that stoped here last night quired my
father as we was about to make a lordly outburst.

He wouldnt pay his bill and razed hell so I kicked him out
replid the lanlady in her bear feet.

Without farther adieu my father payed his bill and we walked
into the dismul st so I will end this chapter by leaving the fare
lanlady flaping in the door way in her sredded night gown.

ARD
V THE
WEEK,
DAY OR
MEAL

Our lanlady in Hudson

CHAPTER 8

Hudson to Yonkers 106.5

IT WAS raining a little so my father bad my mother and I stand in the st wilst he went to the garage and retained the costly moter. He returned ½ a hour latter with the story that the garage had been locked and he had to go to the props house and roust him out.

How did you know where he lived quired my mother barshfully.

I used the brains god gave me was my fathers posthumous reply.

Soon we rumpled into Rhinebeck and as it was now day light and the rain had siezed we puled up in front of the Beekman arms for brekfus.

It says this is the oldest hotel in America said my mother reading the programme.

The eggs tastes all right replid my father with a corse jesture.

What is the next town quired my mother when we again set sale.

Pokippsie was my fathers reply.

Thats where Vassar is said my mother as my old man stiffled a yawn I wonder if there is a store there that would have a koop for David.

I doubt it they ever heard of him said my father dryly how much do they cost.

Well I dont know.

We entered Pokippsie at lenth and turned to the left up the main st and puled up in front of a big store where myself and mother went in and purchased a koop for my little brother and a kap for me witch only took a ½ hour dureing witch my father lost his temper and when we finley immerged he was barking like a dog and giveing the Vassar yell. 2 men come out of the store with us and tost the koop with the rest of the junk in the back seat and away we went.

Doesnt this look cute on him said my mother in regards to my new kap.

What of it replid my father with a grimace and with that we puled into Garrison.

Isnt this right acrost the river from West Point said my mother with a gastly look.

What of it replid my father tenderly and soon we found ourselfs in Peekskill.

This is where that young girl cousin of mine gos to school said my father from Philadelphia.

What of it said my mother with a loud cough and presently we stoped and bought 15 gals of gas.

I have got a fund of usefull information about every town we come to said my father admireingly for instants this is Harmon where they take off the steem engines and put on the electric bullgines.

My mother looked at him with ill consealed admiration.

And what do you know about this town she arsked as we frisked into Ossining.

Why this is Ossining where they take off the hair and put on the stripes replid my father qick as a flarsh and the next place is Tarrytown where John D. Rockefeller has a estate.

What is the name of the estate quired my mother breathlessly.

Socony I supose was the sires reply.

With that we honked into Yonkers and up the funny looking main st.

What a funny looking st said my mother and I always thorght it was the home of well to do peaple.

Well yes replid my father it is the home of the ruling class at lease Bill Klem the umpire and Bill Langford the referee lives here.

I will end my chapter on that one.

CHAPTER 9

The Bureau of Manhattan

ISN'T IT about time said my mother as we past Spuyten Duyvil and entered the Bureau of Manhattan that we made our plans.

What plans said my father all my plans is all ready made.

Well then you might make me your confident sugested my mother with a quaint smirk.

Well then heres the dope uttered my father in a vage tone I am going to drop you at the 125 st station where you will only half to wait 2 hours and a ½ for the rest of the family as the train from the west is do at 350 at 125 st in the meen wile I will drive out to Grenitch with Bill and see if the house is ready and etc and if the other peaples train is on time you can catch the 44 and I an Bill will meet you at the Grenitch station.

If you have time get a qt of milk for David said my mother with a pail look.

What kind of milk arsked my dad.

Oh sour milk my mother screened.

As she was now in a pretty bad temper we will leave her to cool off for 2 hours and a ½ in the 125 st station and end this chapter.

CHAPTER 10

N. Y. to Grenitch 500.0

THE LEASE said about my and my fathers trip from the Bureau of Manhattan to our new home the soonest mended. In some way ether I or he got balled up on the grand concorpse and next thing you know we was thretning to swoop down on Pittsfield.

Are you lost daddy I arsked tenderly.

Shut up he explained.

At lenth we doubled on our tracks and done much better as we finley hit New Rochelle and puled up along side a policeman with falling archs.

What road do I take for Grenitch Conn quired my father with poping eyes.

Take the Boston post replid the policeman.

I have all ready subscribed to one out of town paper said my father and steped on the gas so we will leave the flat foot gaping after us like a prune fed calf and end this chapter.

The New Rochelle Policeman

CHAPTER II

How It Ended

TRUE TO our promise we were at the station in Grenitch when the costly train puled in from 125 st. Myself and father hoped out of the lordly moter and helped the bulk of the family off of the train and I aloud our nurse and my 3 brothers to kiss me tho Davids left me rarther moist.

Did you have a hard trip my father arsked to our nurse shyly.

Why no she replid with a slite stager.

She did too said my mother they all acted like little devils.

Did you get Davids milk she said turning on my father.

Why no does he like milk my father replid with a gastly smirk.

We got lost mudder I said brokenly.

We did not screened my father and accidently cracked me in the shins with a stray foot.

To change the subjeck I turned my tensions on my brother Jimmie who is nerest my age.

I've seen our house Jimmie I said brokenly I got here first.

Yes but I slept all night on a train and you didnt replid Jimmie with a dirty look.

Nether did you said my brother John to Jimmie you was awake all night.

Were awake said my mother.

Me and David was awake all night and crid said my brother John.

But I only crid once the whole time said my brother Jimmie.

But I didnt cry at all did I I arsked to my mother.

So she replid with a loud cough Bill was a very very good boy.

So now we will say fare well to the characters in this book.

Our Nurse

THE BIG TOWN

*How I and the Mrs. Go To New York
To See Life and Get Katie a Husband*

CONTENTS

CHAPTER I

Quick Returns

THIS IS just a clipping from one of the New York papers; a little kidding piece that they had in about me two years ago. It says:

> HOOSIER CLEANS UP IN WALL STREET.
>
> Employees of the brokerage firm of H. L. Krause & Co. are authority for the statement that a wealthy Indiana speculator made one of the biggest killings of the year in the Street yesterday afternoon. No very definite information was obtainable, as the Westerner's name was known to only one of the firm's employees, Francis Griffin, and he was unable to recall it last night.

You'd think I was a millionaire and that I'd made a sucker out of Morgan or something, but it's only a kid, see? If they'd of printed the true story they wouldn't of had no room left for that day's selections at Pimlico, and God knows that would of been fatal.

But if you want to hear about it, I'll tell you.

Well, the war wound up in the fall of 1918. The only member of my family that was killed in it was my wife's stepfather. He died of grief when it ended with him two hundred thousand dollars ahead. I immediately had a black bandage sewed round my left funny bone, but when they read us the will I felt all right again and tore it off. Our share was seventy-five thousand dollars. This was after we had paid for the inheritance tax and the amusement stamps on a horseless funeral.

My young sister-in-law, Katie, dragged down another seventy-five thousand dollars and the rest went to the old bird that had been foreman in papa's factory. This old geezer had been starving to death for twenty years on the wages my stepfather-in-law give him, and the rest of us didn't make no holler when his name was read off for a small chunk, especially as he didn't have no teeth to enjoy it with.

I could of had this old foreman's share, maybe, if I'd of took advantage of the offer "father" made me just before his daughter and I was married. I was over in Niles, Michigan, where they lived, and he insisted on me seeing his factory, which meant smelling it too. At that time I was knocking out about eighteen hundred dollars per annum selling cigars out of South Bend, and the old man said he would start me in with him at only about a fifty per cent. cut, but we would also have the privilege of living with him and my wife's kid sister.

"They's a lot to be learnt about this business," he says, "but if you would put your mind on it you might work up to manager. Who knows?"

"My nose knows," I said, and that ended it.

The old man had lost some jack and went into debt a good many years ago, and for a long wile before the war begin about all as he was able to do was support himself and the two gals and pay off a part of what he owed. When the war broke loose and leather went up to hell and gone I and my wife thought he would get prosperous, but before this country went in his business went on about the same as usual.

"I don't know how they do it," he would say. "Other leather men is getting rich on contracts with the Allies, but I can't land a one."

I guess he was trying to sell razor strops to Russia.

Even after we got into it and he begin to clean up, with the factory running day and night, all as we knew was that he had contracts with the U. S. Government, but he never confided in us what special stuff he was turning out. For all as we knew, it may of been medals for the ground navy.

Anyway, he must of been hitting a fast clip when the armistice come and ended the war for everybody but Congress! It's a cinch he wasn't amongst those arrested for celebrating too loud on the night of November 11. On the contrary they tell me that when the big news hit Niles the old bird had a stroke that he didn't never recover from, and though my wife and Katie hung round the bedside day after day in the hopes he would tell how much he was going to leave he was keeping his fiscal secrets for Oliver Lodge or somebody, and it wasn't till we seen the will that we knew we wouldn't have to work no more, which is pretty fair consolation even for the loss of a stepfather-in-law that ran a perfume mill.

"Just think," said my wife, "after all his financial troubles, papa died a rich man!"

"Yes," I said to myself, "and a patriot. His only regret was that he just had one year to sell leather to his country."

If the old codger had of only been half as fast a salesman as his two daughters this clipping would of been right when it called me a wealthy Hoosier. It wasn't two weeks after we seen the will when the gals had disposed of the odor factory and the old home in Niles, Michigan. Katie, it seemed, had to come over to South Bend and live with us. That was agreeable to me, as I figured that if two could live on eighteen hundred dollars a year three could struggle along some way on the income off one hundred and fifty thousand dollars.

Only for me, though, Ella and Sister Kate would of shot the whole wad into a checking account so as the bank could enjoy it wile it lasted. I argued and fought and finally persuaded them to keep five thousand apiece for pin money and stick the rest into bonds.

The next thing they done was run over to Chi and buy all the party dresses that was vacant. Then they come back to South Bend and wished somebody would give a party. But between you and I the people we'd always ran round with was birds that was ready for bed as soon as they got home from the first show, and even though it had been printed in the News-Times that we had fell heir to a lot of jack we didn't have to hire no extra clerical help to tend to invitations received from the demi-Monday.

Finally Ella said we would start something ourselves. So she got a lot of invitations printed and sent them to all our friends that could read and hired a cater and a three-piece orchestra and everything, and made me buy a dress suit.

Well, the big night arrived and everybody come that had somebody to leave their baby with. The hosts wore evening clothes and the rest of the merrymakers prepared for the occasion with a shine or a clean collar. At first the cat had everybody's tongue, but when we sat down to eat some of the men folks begun to get comical. For instance, they would say to my wife or Katie, "Ain't you afraid you'll catch cold?" And they'd say to me, "I didn't know you was a waiter at the Oliver." Before the fish course everybody was in a fair way to get the giggles.

After supper the musicians come and hid behind a geranium and played a jazz. The entire party set out the first dance. The second was a solo between Katie and I, and I had the third with my wife. Then Kate and the Mrs. had one together, wile I tried holds with a lady named Mrs. Eckhart, who seemed to think that somebody had ast her to stand for a time exposure. The men folks had all drifted over behind the plant to watch the drummer, but after the stalemate between Mrs. Eckhart and I I grabbed her husband and took him out in the kitchen and showed him a bottle of bourbon that I'd been saving for myself, in the hopes it would loosen him up. I told him it was my last bottle, but he must of thought I said it was the last bottle in the world. Anyway, when he got through they was international prohibition.

We went back in the ballroom and sure enough he ast Katie to dance. But he hadn't no sooner than win one fall when his wife challenged him to take her home and that started the epidemic that emptied the house of everybody but the orchestra and us. The orchestra had been hired to stay till midnight, which was still two hours and a half distance, so I invited both of the gals to dance with me at once, but it seems like they was surfeited with that sport and wanted to cry a little. Well, the musicians had ran out of blues, so I chased them home.

"Some party!" I said, and the two girls give me a dirty look like it was my fault or something. So we all went to bed and the ladies beat me to it on account of being so near ready.

Well, they wasn't no return engagements even hinted at and the only other times all winter when the gals had a chance to dress up was when some second-hand company would come to town with a show and I'd have to buy a box. We couldn't ask nobody to go with us on account of not having no friends that you could depend on to not come in their stocking feet.

Finally it was summer and the Mrs. said she wanted to get out of town.

"We've got to be fair to Kate," she said.

"We don't know no young unmarried people in South Bend and it's no fun for a girl to run round with her sister and brother-in-law. Maybe if we'd go to some resort somewheres we might get acquainted with people that could show her a good time."

So I hired us rooms in a hotel down to Wawasee Lake and we stayed there from the last of June till the middle of September. During that time I caught a couple of bass and Kate caught a couple of carp from Fort Wayne. She was getting pretty friendly with one of them when along come a wife that he hadn't thought was worth mentioning. The other bird was making a fight against the gambling fever, but one night it got the best of him and he dropped forty-five cents in the nickel machine and had to go home and make a new start.

About a week before we was due to leave I made the remark that it would seem good to be back in South Bend and get some home cooking.

"Listen!" says my wife. "I been wanting for a long wile to have a serious talk with you and now's as good a time as any. Here are I and Sis and you with an income of over eight thousand dollars a year and having pretty near as good a time as a bird with habitual boils. What's more, we can't never have a good time in South Bend, but have got to move somewheres where we are unknown."

"South Bend is certainly all of that," I said.

"No, it isn't," said the Mrs. "We're acquainted there with the kind of people that makes it impossible for us to get acquainted with the other kind. Kate could live there twenty years and never meet a decent man. She's a mighty attractive girl, and if she had a chance they's nobody she couldn't marry. But she won't never have a chance in South Bend. And they's no use of you saying 'Let her move,' because I'm going to keep her under my eye till she's married and settled down. So in other words, I want us to pack up and leave South Bend for good and all and move somewheres where we'll get something for our money."

"For instance, where?" I ast her.

"They's only one place," she said; "New York City."

"I've heard of it," said I, "but I never heard that people who couldn't enjoy themselves on eight thousand a year in South Bend could go to New York and tear it wide open."

"I'm not planning to make no big splurge," she says. "I just want to be where they's Life and fun; where we can meet real live people. And as for not living there on eight thousand, think of the families that's already living there on half of that and less!"

"And think of the Life and fun they're having!" I says.

"But when you talk about eight thousand a year," said the Mrs., "why do we have to hold ourselves to that? We can sell some of those bonds and spend a little of our principal. It will just be taking money out of one investment and putting it in another."

"What other?" I ast her.

"Kate," said the wife. "You let me take her to New York and manage her and I'll get her a husband that'll think our eight thousand a year fell out of his vest."

"Do you mean," I said, "that you'd let a sister of yours marry for money?"

"Well," she says, "I know a sister of hers that wouldn't mind if she had."

So I argued and tried to compromise on somewheres in America, but it was New York or nothing with her. You see, she hadn't never been here, and all as she knew about it she'd read in books and magazines, and for some reason another when authors starts in on that subject it ain't very long till they've got a weeping jag. Besides, what chance did I have when she kept reminding me that it was her stepfather, not mine, that had croaked and made us all rich?

When I had give up she called Kate in and told her, and Kate squealed and kissed us both, though God knows I didn't deserve no remuneration or ask for none.

Ella had things all planned out. We was to sell our furniture and take a furnished apartment here, but we would stay in some hotel till we found a furnished apartment that was within reason.

"Our stay in some hotel will be lifelong," I said.

The furniture, when we come to sell it, wasn't worth nothing, and that's what we got. We didn't have nothing to ship, as Ella found room for our books in my collar box. I got two lowers and an upper in spite of the Government, and with two taxi drivers and the baggageman thronging the station platform we pulled out of South Bend and set forth to see Life.

The first four miles of the journey was marked by considerable sniveling on the part of the heiresses.

"If it's so painful to leave the Bend let's go back," I said.

"It isn't leaving the Bend," said the Mrs., "but it makes a person sad to leave any place."

"Then we're going to have a muggy trip," said I. "This train stops pretty near everywheres to either discharge passengers or employees."

They were still sobbing when we left Mishawaka and I had to pull some of my comical stuff to get their minds off. My wife's mighty easy to look at when she hasn't got those watery blues, but I never did see a gal that knocked you for a goal when her nose was in full bloom.

Katie had brought a flock of magazines and started in on one of them at Elkhart, but it's pretty tough trying to read with the Northern Indiana mountains to look out at, to say nothing about the birds of prey that kept prowling up and down the aisle in search of a little encouragement or a game of rhum.

I noticed a couple of them that would of give a lady an answer if she'd approached them in a nice way, but I've done some traveling myself and I know what kind of men it is that allows themselves to be drawed into a flirtation on trains. Most of them has made the mistake of getting married some time, but they don't tell you that. They tell you that you and a gal they use to be stuck on is as much alike as a pair of corsets, and if you ever come to Toledo to give them a ring, and they hand you a telephone number that's even harder to get than the ones there are; and they ask you your name and address and write it down, and the next time they're up at the Elks they show it to a couple of the brothers and tell what they'd of done if they'd only been going all the way through.

"Say, I hate to talk about myself! But say!"

Well, I didn't see no sense in letting Katie waste her time on those kind of guys, so every time one of them looked our way I give him the fish eye and the non-stop signal. But this was my first long trip since the Government started to play train, and I didn't know the new rules in regards to getting fed; otherwise I wouldn't of never cleaned up in Wall Street.

In the old days we use to wait till the boy come through and announced that dinner was now being served in the dining car forward; then we'd saunter into the washroom and wash our hands if necessary, and ramble into the diner and set right down and enjoy as big a meal as we could afford. But the Government wants to be economical, so they've cut down the number of trains, to say nothing about the victuals; and they's two or three times as many people traveling, because they can't throw their money away fast enough at home. So the result is that the wise guys keeps an eye on their watch and when it's about twenty minutes to dinner time they race to the diner and park against the door and get quick action; and after they've eat the first time they go out and stand in the vestibule and wait till it's their turn again, as one Federal meal don't do nothing to your appetite only whet it, you might say.

Well, anyway, I was playing the old rules and by the time I and the two gals started for the diner we run up against the outskirts of a crowd pretty near as big as the ones that waits outside restaurant windows to watch a pancake turn turtle. About eight o'clock we got to where we could see the wealthy dining car conductor in the distance, but it was only about once every quarter of an hour that he raised a hand, and then he seemed to of had all but one of his fingers shot off.

I have often heard it said that the way to a man's heart is through his stomach, but every time I ever seen men and women keep waiting for their eats it was always the frail sex that give the first yelp, and personally I've often wondered what would of happened in the trenches Over There if ladies had of been occupying them when the rations failed to show up. I guess the bombs bursting round would of sounded like Sweet and Low sang by a quextette of deef mutes.

Anyway, my two charges was like wild animals, and when the con finally held up two fingers I didn't have no more chance or desire to stop them than as if they was the Center College Football Club right after opening prayer.

The pair of them was ushered to a table for four where they already was a couple of guys making the best of it, and it wasn't more than ten minutes later when one of these birds dipped his bill in the finger bowl and staggered out, but by the time I took his place the other gent and my two gals was talking like barbers.

The guy was Francis Griffin that's in the clipping. But when Ella introduced us all as she said was, "This is my husband," without mentioning his name, which she didn't know at that time, or mine, which had probably slipped her memory.

Griffin looked at me like I was a side dish that he hadn't

ordered. Well, I don't mind snubs except when I get them, so I ast him if he wasn't from Sioux City—you could tell he was from New York by his blue collar.

"From Sioux City!" he says. "I should hope not!"

"I beg your pardon," I said. "You look just like a photographer I used to know out there."

"I'm a New Yorker," he said, "and I can't get home too soon."

"Not on this train, you can't," I said.

"I missed the Century," he says.

"Well," I says with a polite smile, "the Century's loss is our gain."

"Your wife's been telling me," he says, "that you're moving to the Big Town. Have you ever been there?"

"Only for a few hours," I says.

"Well," he said, "when you've been there a few weeks you'll wonder why you ever lived anywhere else. When I'm away from old Broadway I always feel like I'm only camping out."

Both the gals smiled their appreciation, so I says: "That certainly expresses it. You'd ought to remember that line and give it to Georgie Cohan."

"Old Georgie!" he says. "I'd give him anything I got and welcome. But listen! Your wife mentioned something about a good hotel to stop at wile you're looking for a home. Take my advice and pick out one that's near the center of things; you'll more than make up the difference in taxi bills. I lived up in the Hundreds one winter and it averaged me ten dollars a day in cab fares."

"You must of had a pleasant home life," I says.

"Me!" he said. "I'm an old bachelor."

"Old!" says Kate, and her and the Mrs. both giggled.

"But seriously," he says, "if I was you I would go right to the Baldwin, where you can get a room for twelve dollars a day for the three of you; and you're walking distance from the theaters or shops or cafés or anywheres you want to go."

"That sounds grand!" said Ella.

"As far as I'm concerned," I said, "I'd just as lief be overseas from any of the places you've mentioned. What I'm looking for is a home with a couple of beds and a cookstove in the kitchen, and maybe a bath."

"But we want to see New York first," said Katie, "and we can do that better without no household cares."

"That's the idear!" says Griffin. "Eat, drink and be merry; to-morrow we may die."

"I guess we won't drink ourselves to death," I said, "not if the Big Town's like where we been living."

"Oh, say!" says our new friend. "Do you think little old New York is going to stand for Prohibition? Why, listen! I can take you to thirty places to-morrow night where you can get all you want in any one of them."

"Let's pass up the other twenty-nine," I says.

"But that isn't the idear," he said. "What makes we New Yorkers sore is to think they should try and wish a law like that on Us. Isn't this supposed to be a government of the people, for the people and by the people?"

"People!" I said. "Who and the hell voted for Prohibition if it wasn't the people?"

"The people of where?" he says. "A lot of small-time hicks that couldn't buy a drink if they wanted it."

"Including the hicks," I says, "that's in the New York State legislature."

"But not the people of New York City," he said. "And you can't tell me it's fair to spring a thing like this without warning on men that's got their fortunes tied up in liquor that they can't never get rid of now, only at a sacrifice."

"You're right," I said. "They ought to give them some warning. Instead of that they was never even a hint of what was coming off till Maine went dry seventy years ago."

"Maine?" he said. "What the hell is Maine?"

"I don't know," I said. "Only they was a ship or a boat or something named after it once, and the Spaniards sunk it and we sued them for libel or something."

"You're a smart Aleck," he said. "But speaking about war, where was you?"

"In the shipyards at South Bend painting a duck boat," I says. "And where was you?"

"I'd of been in there in a few more weeks," he says. "They wasn't no slackers in the Big Town."

"No," said I, "and America will never forget New York for coming in on our side."

By this time the gals was both giving me dirty looks, and we'd eat all we could get, so we paid our checks and went back in our car and I felt kind of apologetic, so I dug down in the old grip and got out a bottle of bourbon that a South Bend pal of mine, George Hull, had give me the day before; and Griffin and I went in the washroom with it and before the evening was over we was pretty near ready to forget national boundaries and kiss.

The old bourb' helped me save money the next morning, as I didn't care for no breakfast. Ella and Kate went in with Griffin and you could of knocked me over with a coupling pin when the Mrs. come back and reported that he'd insisted on paying the check. "He told us all about himself," she said. "His name is Francis Griffin and he's in Wall Street. Last year he cleared twenty thousand dollars in commissions and everything."

"He's a piker," I says. "Most of them never even think under six figures."

"There you go!" said the Mrs. "You never believe nothing. Why shouldn't he be telling the truth? Didn't he buy our breakfast?"

"I been buying your breakfast for five years," I said, "but that don't prove that I'm knocking out twenty thousand per annum in Wall Street."

Francis and Katie was setting together four or five seats ahead of us.

"You ought to of seen the way he looked at her in the diner," said the Mrs. "He looked like he wanted to eat her up."

"Everybody gets desperate in a diner these days," I said. "Did you and Kate go fifty-fifty with him? Did you tell him how much money we got?"

"I should say not!" says Ella. "But I guess we did say that you wasn't doing nothing just now and that we was going to New York to see Life, after being cooped up in a small town all these years. And Sis told him you'd made us put pretty near everything in bonds, so all we can spend is eight thousand a year. He said that wouldn't go very far in the Big Town."

"I doubt if it ever gets as far as the Big Town," I said. "It won't if he makes up his mind to take it away from us."

"Oh, shut up!" said the Mrs. "He's all right and I'm for him, and I hope Sis is too. They'd make a stunning couple. I wished I knew what they're talking about."

"Well," I said, "they're both so reserved that I suppose they're telling each other how they're affected by cucumbers."

When they come back and joined us Ella said: "We was just remarking how well you two young things seemed to be getting along. We was wondering what you found to say to one another all this time."

"Well," said Francis, "just now I think we were discussing you. Your sister said you'd been married five years and I pretty near felt like calling her a fibber. I told her you looked like you was just out of high school."

"I've heard about you New Yorkers before," said the Mrs. "You're always trying to flatter somebody."

"Not me," said Francis. "I never say nothing without meaning it."

"But sometimes," says I, "you'd ought to go on and explain the meaning."

Along about Schenectady my appetite begin to come back. I'd made it a point this time to find out when the diner was going to open, and then when it did our party fell in with the door.

"The wife tells me you're on the stock exchange," I says to Francis when we'd give our order.

"Just in a small way," he said. "But they been pretty good to me down there. I knocked out twenty thousand last year."

"That's what he told us this morning," said Ella.

"Well," said I, "they's no reason for a man to forget that kind of money between Rochester and Albany, even if this is a slow train."

"Twenty thousand isn't a whole lot in the Big Town," said Francis, "but still and all, I manage to get along and enjoy myself a little on the side."

"I suppose it's enough to keep one person," I said.

"Well," says Francis, "they say two can live as cheap as one."

Then him and Kate and Ella all giggled, and the waiter brought in a part of what he thought we'd ordered and we eat what we could and ast for the check. Francis said he wanted it and I was going to give in to him after a long hard struggle, but the gals reminded him that he'd paid for breakfast, so he said all right, but we'd all have to take dinner with him some night.

I and Francis set a wile in the washroom and smoked, and then he went to entertain the gals, but I figured the wife would go right to sleep like she always does when they's any scenery to look out at, so I stuck where I was and listened to what a couple of toothpick salesmen from Omsk would of done with the League of Nations if Wilson had of had sense enough to leave it to them.

Pulling into the Grand Central Station, Francis apologized for not being able to steer us over to the Baldwin and see us settled, but said he had to rush right downtown and report on his Chicago trip before the office closed. To see him when he parted with the gals you'd of thought he was going clear to Siberia to compete in the Olympic Games, or whatever it is we're in over there.

Well, I took the heiresses to the Baldwin and got a regular Big Town welcome. Ella and Kate set against a pillar wile I tried different tricks to make an oil-haired clerk look at me. New York hotel clerks always seem to of just dropped something and can't take their eyes off the floor. Finally I started to pick up the register and the guy give me the fish eye and ast what he could do for me.

"Well," I said, "when I come to a hotel I don't usually want to buy a straw hat."

He ast me if I had a reservation and I told him no.

"Can't do nothing for you then," he says. "Not till to-morrow morning anyway."

So I went back to the ladies.

"We'll have to go somewheres else," I said. "This joint's a joint. They won't give us nothing till to-morrow."

"But we can't go nowheres else," said the Mrs. "What would Mr. Griffin think, after recommending us to come here?"

"Well," I said, "if you think I'm going to park myself in a four-post chair all night just because we got a tip on a hotel from Wall Street you're Queen of the Cuckoos."

"Are you sure they haven't anything at all?" she says.

"Go ask them yourself!" I told her.

Well, she did, and in about ten minutes she come back and said everything was fixed.

"They'll give us a single room with bath and a double room with bath for fifteen dollars a day," she said.

"'Give us' is good!" said I.

"I told him we'd wired for reservations and it wasn't our fault if the wire didn't get here," she said. "He was awfully nice."

Our rooms was right close to each other on the twenty-first floor. On the way up we decided by two votes to one that we'd dress for dinner. I was still monkeying with my tie when Katie come in for Ella to look her over. She had on the riskiest dress she'd bought in Chi.

"It's a pretty dress," she said, "but I'm afraid maybe it's too daring for just a hotel dining room."

Say, we hadn't no sooner than set down in the hotel dining room when two other gals come in that made my team look like they was dressed for a sleigh ride with Doc Cook.

"I guess you don't feel so daring now," I said. "Compared to that baby in black you're wearing Jess Willard's ulster."

"Do you know what that black gown cost?" said Ella. "Not a cent under seven hundred dollars."

"That would make the material twenty-one hundred dollars a yard," I says.

"I'd like to know where she got it," said Katie.

"Maybe she cut up an old stocking," said I.

"I wished now," said the Mrs., "that we'd waited till we got here before we bought our clothes."

"You can bet one thing," says Katie. "Before we're ast out anywheres on a real party we'll have something to wear that isn't a year old."

"First thing to-morrow morning," says the Mrs., "we'll go over on Fifth Avenue and see what we can see."

"They'll only be two on that excursion," I says.

"Oh, we don't want you along," said Ella. "But I do wished you'd go to some first-class men's store and get some ties and shirts and things that don't look like an embalmer."

Well, after a wile one of the waiters got it in his head that maybe we hadn't came in to take a bath, so he fetched over a couple of programs.

"Never mind them," I says. "What's ready? We're in a hurry."

"The Long Island Duckling's very nice," he said. "And how about some nice au gratin potatoes and some nice lettuce and tomato salad with Thousand Island dressing, and maybe some nice French pastry?"

"Everything seems to be nice here," I said. "But wait a minute. How about something to drink?"

He give me a mysterious smile.

"Well," he said, "they're watching us pretty close here, but we serve something we call a cup. It comes from the bar and we're not supposed to know what the bartender puts in it."

"We'll try and find out," I said. "And rush this order through, as we're starved."

So he frisked out and was back again in less than an hour with another guy to help carry the stuff, though Lord knows he could of parked the three ducklings on one eyelid and the whole meal on the back of his hand. As for the cup, when you tasted it they wasn't no big mystery about what the bartender had put in it—a bottle of seltzer and a prune and a cherry and an orange peel, and maybe his finger. The check come to eighteen dollars and Ella made me tip him the rest of a twenty.

Before dinner the gals had been all for staying up a wile and looking the crowd over, but when we was through they both owned up that they hadn't slept much on the train and was ready for bed.

Ella and Kate was up early in the morning. They had their breakfast without me and went over to stun Fifth Avenue. About ten o'clock Francis phoned to say he'd call round for us that evening and take us to dinner. The gals didn't get back till late in the afternoon, but from one o'clock on I was too busy signing for packages to get lonesome. Ella finally staggered in with some more and I told her about our invitation.

"Yes, I know," she said.

"How do you know?" I ast her.

"He told us," she said. "We had to call him up to get a check cashed."

"You got plenty nerve!" I said. "How does he know your checks is good?"

"Well, he likes us," she said. "You'll like us too when you see us in some of the gowns we bought."

"Some!" I said.

"Why, yes," said the Mrs. "You don't think a girl can go round in New York with one evening dress!"

"How much money did you spend to-day?" I ast her.

"Well," she said, "things are terribly high—that is, nice things. And then, of course, there's suits and hats and things besides the gowns. But remember, it's our money. And as I told you, it's an investment. When young Mister Wall Street sees Kate to-night it'll be all off."

"I didn't call on you for no speech," I says. "I ast you how much you spent."

"Not quite sixteen hundred dollars."

I was still out on my feet when the phone rung. Ella answered it and then told me it was all right about the tickets.

"What tickets?" I said.

"Why, you see," she says, "after young Griffin fixing us up with that check and inviting us to dinner and everything we thought it would be nice to take him to a show to-night. Kate wanted to see Ups and Downs, but the girl said she couldn't get us seats for it. So I ast that nice clerk that took care of us yesterday and he's fixed it."

"All right," I said, "but when young Griffin starts a party, why and the hell not let him finish it?"

"I suppose he would of took us somewheres after dinner," says the Mrs., "but I couldn't be sure. And between you and I, I'm positive that if he and Kate is throwed together a whole evening, and her looking like she'll look to-night, we'll get mighty quick returns on our investment."

Well, to make a short story out of it, the gals finally got what they called dressed, and I wished Niles, Michigan, or South Bend could of seen them. If boxers wore bathing skirts I'd of thought I was in the ring with a couple of bantams.

"Listen!" I said. "What did them two girdles cost?"

"Mine was three hundred and Kate's three hundred and fifty," said the Mrs.

"Well," I says, "don't you know that you could of went to any cut-rate drug store and wrapped yourself up just as warm in thirty-two cents' worth of adhesive tape? Listen!" I said. "What's the use of me paying a burglar for tickets to a show like Ups and Downs when I could set round here and look at you for nothing?"

Then Griffin rung up to say that he was waiting and we went downstairs. Francis took us in the same dining room we'd been in the night before, but this time the waiters all fought each other to get to us first.

I don't know what we eat, as Francis had something on the hip that kind of dazed me for a wile, but afterwards I know we got a taxi and went to the theater. The tickets was there in my name and only cost me thirteen dollars and twenty cents.

Maybe you seen this show wile it was here. Some show! I didn't read the program to see who wrote it, but I guess the words was by Noah and the music took the highest awards at the St. Louis Fair. They had a good system on the gags. They didn't spring none but what you'd heard all your life and knew what was coming, so instead of just laughing at the point you laughed all the way through it.

I said to Ella, I said, "I bet the birds that run this don't want prohibition. If people paid $3.30 apiece and come in here sober they'd come back the next night with a machine gun."

"I think it's dandy," she says, "and you'll notice every seat is full. But listen! Will you do something for me? When this is over suggest that we go up to the Castle Roof for a wile."

"What for?" I said. "I'm sleepy."

"Just this once," she says. "You know what I told you about quick returns!"

Well, I give in and made the suggestion, and I never seen people so easy coaxed. I managed to get a ringside table for twenty-two bucks. Then I ast the boy how about getting a drink and he ast me if I knew any of the head waiters.

"I do," says Francis. "Tell Hector it's for Frank Griffin's party."

So we ordered four Scotch highballs and some chicken à la King, and then the dinge orchestra tore loose some jazz and I was expecting a dance with Ella, but before she could ask me Francis had ast her, and I had one with Kate.

"Your Wall Street friend's a fox," I says, "asking an old married lady to dance so's to stand in with the family."

"Old married lady!" said Kate. "Sis don't look a day over sixteen to-night."

"How are you and Francis coming?" I ast her.

"I don't know," she says. "He acts kind of shy. He hasn't hardly said a word to me all evening."

Well, they was another jazz and I danced it with Ella; then her and Francis had another one and I danced again with Kate. By this time our food and refreshments was served and the show was getting ready to start.

I could write a book on what I don't remember about that show. The first sip of their idear of a Scotch highball put me down for the count of eight and I was practic'lly unconscious till the waiter woke me up with a check for forty bucks.

Francis seen us home and said he would call up again soon, and when Ella and I was alone I made the remark that I didn't think he'd ever strain his larnix talking to Kate.

"He acts gun-shy when he's round her," I says. "You seem to be the one that draws him out."

"It's a good sign," she says. "A man's always embarrassed when he's with a girl he's stuck on. I'll bet you anything you want to bet that within a week something'll happen."

Well, she win. She'd of win if she'd of said three days instead of a week. It was a Wednesday night when we had that party, and on the Friday Francis called up and said he had tickets for the Palace. I'd been laid up mean wile with the Scotch influenza, so I told the gals to cut me out. I was still awake yet when Ella come in a little after midnight.

"Well," I said, "are we going to have a brother-in-law?"

"Mighty soon," she says.

So I ast her what had came off.

"Nothing—to-night," she says, "except this: He wrote me a note. He wants me to go with him to-morrow afternoon and look at a little furnished apartment. And he ast me if I could come without Sis, as he wants to pull a surprise on her. So I wondered if you couldn't think of some way to fix it so's I can sneak off for a couple of hours."

"Sure!" I said. "Just tell her you didn't sleep all night and you're wore out and you want to take a nap."

So she pulled this gag at lunch Saturday and Katie said she was tired too. She went up to her room and Ella snuck out to keep her date with Francis. In less than an hour she romped into our room again and throwed herself on the bed.

"Well," I says, "it must of been a little apartment if it didn't only take you this long to see it."

"Oh, shut up!" she said. "I didn't see no apartment. And don't say a word to me or I'll scream."

Well, I finally got her calmed down and she give me the details. It seems that she'd met Francis, and he'd got a taxi and they'd got in the taxi and they hadn't no sooner than got in the taxi when Francis give her a kiss.

"Quick returns," I says.

"I'll kill you if you say another word!" she says.

So I managed to keep still.

Well, I didn't know Francis' home address, and Wall Street don't run Sundays, so I spent the Sabbath training on a quart of rye that a bell hop picked up at a bargain sale somewheres for fifteen dollars. Mean wile Katie had been let in on the secret and staid in our room all day, moaning like a prune-fed calf.

"I'm afraid to leave her alone," says Ella. "I'm afraid she'll jump out the window."

"You're easily worried," I said. "What I'm afraid of is that she won't."

Monday morning finally come, as it generally always does, and I told the gals I was going to some first-class men's store and buy myself some ties and shirts that didn't look like a South Bend embalmer.

So the only store I knew about was H. L. Krause & Co. in Wall Street, but it turned out to be an office. I ast for Mr. Griffin and they ast me my name and I made one up, Sam Hall or something, and out he come.

If I told you the rest of it you'd think I was bragging. But I did bust a few records. Charley Brickley and Walter Eckersall both kicked five goals from field in one football game, and they was a bird named Robertson or something out at Purdue that kicked seven. Then they was one of the old-time ball players, Bobby Lowe or Ed Delahanty, that hit four or five home runs in one afternoon. And out to Toledo that time Dempsey made big Jess set down seven times in one round.

Well, listen! In a little less than three minutes I floored this bird nine times and I kicked him for eight goals from the field and I hit him over the fence for ten home runs. Don't talk records to me!

So that's what they meant in the clipping about a Hoosier cleaning up in Wall Street. But it's only a kid, see?

CHAPTER II

Ritchey

WELL, I was just getting used to the Baldwin and making a few friends round there when Ella suddenly happened to remember that it was Griffin who had recommended it. So one day, wile Kate was down to the chiropodist's, Ella says it was time for us to move and she had made up her mind to find an apartment somewheres.

"We could get along with six rooms," she said. "All as I ask is for it to be a new building and on some good street, some street where the real people lives."

"You mean Fifth Avenue," said I.

"Oh, no," she says. "That's way over our head. But we'd ought to be able to find something, say, on Riverside Drive."

"A six room apartment," I says, "in a new building on Riverside Drive? What was you expecting to pay?"

"Well," she said, "you remember that time I and Kate visited the Kitchells in Chi? They had a dandy apartment on Sheridan Road, six rooms and brand new. It cost them seventy-five dollars a month. And Sheridan Road is Chicago's Riverside Drive."

"Oh, no," I says. "Chicago's Riverside Drive is Canal Street. But listen: Didn't the Kitchells have their own furniture?"

"Sure they did," said Ella.

"And are you intending to furnish us all over complete?" I asked her.

"Of course not," she says. "I expect to get a furnished apartment. But that don't only make about twenty-five dollars a month difference."

"Listen," I said: "It was six years ago that you visited the Kitchells; beside which, that was Chi and this is the Big Town. If you find a six room furnished apartment for a hundred dollars in New York City to-day, we'll be on Pell Street in Chinatown, and maybe Katie can marry into a laundry or a joss house."

"Well," said the wife, "even if we have to go to $150 a month for a place on the Drive, remember half of it's my money and half of it's Kate's, and none of it's yours."

"You're certainly letter perfect in that speech," I says.

"And further and more," said Ella, "you remember what I told you the other day. Wile one reason we moved to New York was to see Life, the main idear was to give Kate a chance to meet real men. So every nickel we spend making ourself look good is just an investment."

"I'd rather feel good than look good," I says, "and I hate to see us spending so much money on a place to live that they won't be nothing left to live on. For three or four hundred a month you might get a joint on the Drive with a bed and two chairs, but I can't drink furniture."

"This trip wasn't planned as no spree for you," says Ella. "On the other hand, I believe Sis would stand a whole lot better show of landing the right kind of a man if the rumor was to get out that her brother-in-law stayed sober once in a wile."

"Well," I said, "I don't think my liberal attitude on the drink question affected the results of our deal in Wall Street. That investment would of turned out just as good whether I was a teetotaler or a lush."

"Listen," she says: "The next time you mention ancient history like that, I'll make a little investment in a lawyer. But what's the use of arguing? I and Kate has made up our mind to do things our own way with our own money, and to-day we're going up on the Drive with a real estate man. We won't pay no more than we can afford. All as we want is a place that's good enough and big enough for Sis to entertain her gentleman callers in it, and she certainly can't do that in this hotel."

"Well," I says, "all her gentleman callers that's been around here in the last month, she could entertain them in one bunch in a telephone booth."

"The reason she's been let alone so far," says the Mrs., "is because I won't allow her to meet the kind of men that stays at hotels. You never know who they are."

"Why not?" I said. "They've all got to register their name when they come in, which is more than you can say for people that lives in $100 apartments on Riverside Drive."

Well, my arguments went so good that for the next three days the two gals was on a home-seekers' excursion and I had to spend my time learning the eastern intercollegiate kelly pool rules up to Doyle's. I win about seventy-five dollars.

When the ladies come home the first two nights they was all wore out and singing the landlord blues, but on the third afternoon they busted in all smiles.

"We've found one," says Ella. "Six rooms, too."

"Where at?" I asked her.

"Just where we wanted it," she says. "On the Drive. And it fronts right on the Hudson."

"No!" I said. "I thought they built them all facing the other way."

"It almost seems," said Katie, "like you could reach out and touch New Jersey."

"It's what you might call a near beer apartment," I says.

"And it's almost across the street from Grant's Tomb," says Ella.

"How many rooms has he got?" I says.

"We was pretty lucky," said Ella. "The people that had it was forced to go south for the man's health. He's a kind of a cripple. And they decided to sublet it furnished. So we got a bargain."

"Come on," I says. "What price?"

"Well," she says, "they don't talk prices by the month in New York. They give you the price by the year. So it sounds a lot more than it really is. We got it for $4,000."

"Sweet patootie!" I said. "That's only half your income."

"Well, what of it?" says Ella. "It won't only be for about a year and it's in the nicest kind of a neighborhood and we can't meet nothing only the best kind of people. You know what I told you."

And she give me a sly wink.

Well, it seems like they had signed up a year's lease and paid a month's rent in advance, so what was they left for me to say? All I done was make the remark that I didn't see how we was going to come even close to a trial balance.

"Why not?" said Katie. "With our rent paid we can get along easy on $4,000 a year if we economize."

"Yes," I said. "You'll economize just like the rest of the Riverside Drivers, with a couple of servants and a car and four or five new evening dresses a month. By the end of six months the bank'll be figuring our account in marks."

"What do you mean 'our' account?" says Ella.

"But speaking about a car," said Katie, "do you suppose we could get a good one cheap?"

"Certainly," I said. "They're giving away the good ones for four double coupons."

"But I mean an inexpensive one," says Kate.

"You can't live on the River and ride in a flivver," I said. "Besides, the buses limp right by the door."

"Oh, I love the buses!" said Ella.

"Wait till you see the place," says Katie to me. "You'll go simply wild! They's a colored boy in uniform to open the door and they's two elevators."

"How high do we go?" I said.

"We're on the sixth floor," says Katie.

"I should think we could get that far in one elevator," I says.

"What was it the real estate man told us?" said Ella. "Oh, yes, he said the sixth floor was the floor everybody tried to get on."

"It's a wonder he didn't knock it," I said.

Well, we was to have immediate possession, so the next morning we checked out of this joint and swooped up on the Drive. The colored boy, who I nicknamed George, helped us up with the wardrobe. Ella had the key and inside of fifteen minutes she'd found it.

We hadn't no sooner than made our entree into our new home when I knew what ailed the previous tenant. He'd crippled himself stumbling over the furniture. The living room was big enough to stage the high hurdles, and that's what was in it, only they'd planted them every two feet apart. If a stew with the blind staggers had of walked in there in the dark, the folks on the floor below would of thought he'd knocked the head pin for a goal.

"Come across the room," said Ella, "and look at the view."

"I guess I can get there in four downs," I said, "but you better have a substitute warming up."

"Well," she says, when I'd finally fell acrost the last white chalk mark, "what do you think of it?"

"It's a damn pretty view," I says, "but I've often seen the same view from the top of a bus for a thin dime."

Well, they showed me over the whole joint and it did look
O. K., but not $4,000 worth. The best thing in the place was
a half full bottle of rye in the kitchen that the cripple hadn't
gone south with. I did.

We got there at eleven o'clock in the morning, but at three
P. M. the gals was still hanging up their Follies costumes, so I
beat it out and over to Broadway and got myself a plate of pea
soup. When I come back, Ella and Katie was laying down exhausted. Finally I told Ella that I was going to move back to
the hotel unless they served meals in this dump, so her and
Kate got up and went marketing. Well, when you move from
Indiana to the Big Town, of course you can't be expected to
do your own cooking, so what we had that night was from the
delicatessen, and for the next four days we lived on dill pickles
with dill pickles.

"Listen," I finally says: "The only reason I consented to
leave the hotel was in the hopes I could get a real home cook
meal once in a wile and if I don't get a real home cook meal
once in a wile, I leave this dive."

"Have a little bit of patience," says Ella. "I advertised in the
paper for a cook the day before we come here, the day we
rented this apartment. And I offered eight dollars a week."

"How many replies did you get?" I asked her.

"Well," she said, "I haven't got none so far, but it's probably
too soon to expect any."

"What did you advertise in, the world almanac?" I says.

"No, sir," she says. "I advertised in the two biggest New
York papers, the ones the real estate man recommended."

"Listen," I said: "Where do you think you're at, in Niles,
Michigan? If you get a cook here for eight dollars a week, it'll
be a one-armed leper that hasn't yet reached her teens."

"What would you do, then?" she asked me.

"I'd write to an employment agency," I says, "and I'd tell
them we'll pay good wages."

So she done that and in three days the phone rung and the
agency said they had one prospect on hand and did we want her
to come out and see us. So Ella said we did and out come a colleen for an interview. She asked how much we was willing to pay.

"Well," said Ella, "I'd go as high as twelve dollars. Or I'd
make it fifteen if you done the washing."

Kathleen Mavourneen turned her native color.

"Well," I said, "how much do you want?"

"I'll work for ninety dollars a month," she said, only I can't get the brogue. "That's for the cookin' only. No washin'. And I would have to have a room with a bath and all day Thursdays and Sunday evenin's off."

"Nothing doing," said Ella, and the colleen started for the door.

"Wait a minute," I says. "Listen: Is that what you gals is getting in New York?"

"We're a spalpeen if we ain't," says the colleen bawn.

Well, I was desperate, so I called the wife to one side and says: "For heaven's sakes, take her on a month's trial. I'll pay the most of it with a little piece of money I picked up last week down to Doyle's. I'd rather do that than get dill pickled for a goal."

"Could you come right away?" Ella asked her.

"Not for a couple days," says Kathleen.

"It's off, then," I said. "You cook our supper to-night or go back to Greece."

"Well," she says, "I guess I could make it if I hurried."

So she went away and come back with her suitcase, and she cooked our supper that night. And Oh darlint!

Well, Beautiful Katie still had the automobile bug and it wasn't none of my business to steer her off of it and pretty near every day she would go down to the "row" and look them over. But every night she'd come home whistling a dirge.

"I guess I've seen them all," she'd say, "but they're too expensive or else they look like they wasn't."

But one time we was all coming home in a taxi from a show and come up Broadway and all of a sudden she yelled for the driver to stop.

"That's a new one in that window," she says, "and one I never see before."

Well, the dive was closed at the time and we couldn't get in, but she insisted on going down there the first thing in the morning and I and Ella must go along. The car was a brand new model Bam Eight.

"How much?" I asked him.

"Four thousand," he says.

"When could I get one?" says Katie.

"I don't know," said the salesman.

"What do you mean?" I asked him. "Haven't they made none of them?"

"I don't know," says the salesman. "This is the only one we got."

"Has anybody ever rode in one?" I says.

"I don't know," said the guy.

So I asked him what made it worth four thousand.

"Well," he says, "what made this lady want one?"

"I don't know," I said.

"Could I have this one that's on the floor?" says Katie.

"I don't know," said the salesman.

"Well, when do you think I could get one?" says Katie.

"We can't promise no deliveries," says the salesman.

Well, that kind of fretted me, so I asked him if they wasn't a salesman we could talk to.

"You're talking to one," he said.

"Yes, I know," said I. "But I used to be a kind of a salesman myself, and when I was trying to sell things, I didn't try and not sell them."

"Yes," he says, "but you wasn't selling automobiles in New York in 1920. Listen," he says: "I'll be frank with you. We got the New York agency for this car and was glad to get it because it sells for four thousand and anything that sells that high, why the people will eat up, even if it's a pearl-handle ketchup bottle. If we ever do happen to get a consignment of these cars, they'll sell like oil stock. The last word we got from the factory was that they'd send us three cars next September. So that means we'll get two cars a year from next October and if we can spare either of them, you can have one."

So then he begin to yawn and I said, "Come on, girls," and we got a taxi and beat it home. And I wouldn't of said nothing about it, only if Katie had of been able to buy her Bam, what come off might of never came off.

It wasn't only two nights later when Ella come in from shopping all excited. "Well," she said, "talk about experiences! I just had a ride home and it wasn't in a street car and it wasn't in a taxi and it wasn't on the subway and it wasn't on a bus."

"Let's play charades," said I.

"Tell us, Sis," says Katie.

"Well," said the wife, "I was down on Fifth Avenue, waiting for a bus, and all of a sudden a big limousine drew up to the curb with a livery chauffeur, and a man got out of the back seat and took off his hat and asked if he couldn't see me home. And of course I didn't pay no attention to him."

"Of course not," I said.

"But," says Ella, "he says, 'Don't take no offense. I think we're next door neighbors. Don't you live acrost the hall on the sixth floor of the Lucius?' So of course I had to tell him I did."

"Of course," I said.

"And then he said," says Ella, "'Is that your sister living with you?' 'Yes,' I said, 'she lives with my husband and I.' 'Well,' he says, 'if you'll get in and let me take you home, I'll tell you what a beautiful girl I think she is.' So I seen then that he was all right, so I got in and come home with him. And honestly, Sis, he's just wild about you!"

"What is he like?" says Katie.

"He's stunning," says the wife. "Tall and wears dandy clothes and got a cute mustache that turns up."

"How old?" says Kate, and the Mrs. kind of stalled.

"Well," she said, "he's the kind of a man that you can't tell how old they are, but he's not old. I'd say he was, well, maybe he's not even that old."

"What's his name?" asked Kate.

"Trumbull," said the Mrs. "He said he was keeping bachelor quarters, but I don't know if he's really a bachelor or a widower. Anyway, he's a dandy fella and must have lots of money. Just imagine living alone in one of these apartments!"

"Imagine living in one of them whether you're a bachelor or a Mormon," I says.

"Who said he lived alone?" asked Katie.

"He did," says the Mrs. "He told me that him and his servants had the whole apartment to themselves. And that's what makes it so nice, because he's asked the three of us over there to dinner to-morrow night."

"What makes it so nice?" I asked her.

"Because it does," said Ella, and you can't ever beat an argument like that.

So the next night the two girls donned their undress uniforms and made me put on the oysters and horse radish and
we went acrost the hall to meet our hero. The door was opened
by a rug peddler and he showed us into a twin brother to our
own living room, only you could get around it without being
Houdini.

"Mr. Trumbull will be right out," said Omar.

The ladies was shaking like an aspirin leaf, but in a few minutes, in come mine host. However old Ella had thought he
wasn't, she was wrong. He'd seen baseball when the second
bounce was out. If he'd of started his career as a barber in
Washington, he'd of tried to wish a face massage on Zachary
Taylor. The only thing young about him was his teeth and his
clothes. His dinner suit made me feel like I was walking along
the station platform at Toledo, looking for hot boxes.

"Ah, here you are!" he says. "It's mighty nice of you to be
neighborly. And so this is the young sister. Well," he says to
me, "you had your choice, and as far as I can see, it was heads
you win and tails you win. You're lucky."

So when he'd spread all the salve, he rung the bell and in
come Allah with cocktails. I don't know what was in them, but
when Ella and Katie had had two apiece, they both begin to
trill.

Finally we was called in to dinner and every other course was
hootch. After the solid and liquid diet, he turned on the steam
piano and we all danced. I had one with Beautiful Katie and
the rest of them was with my wife, or, as I have nicknamed
them, quarrels. Well, the steam run out of three of us at the
same time, the piano inclusive, and Ella sat down in a chair
that was made for Eddie Foy's family and said how comfortable it was.

"Yes," says Methuselah, "that's my favorite chair. And I bet
you wouldn't believe me if I told you how much it cost."

"Oh, I'd like to know," says Ella.

"Two hundred dollars," says mine host.

"Do you still feel comfortable?" I asked her.

"Speaking about furniture," said the old bird, "I've got a
few bits that I'm proud of. Would you like to take a look at
them?"

So the gals said they would and we had to go through the

entire apartment, looking at bits. The best bits I seen was tastefully wrapped up in kegs and cases. It seemed like every time he opened a drawer, a cork popped up. He was a hundred per cent. proofer than the governor of New Jersey. But he was giving us a lecture on the furniture itself, not the polish.

"I picked up this dining room suit for eighteen hundred," he says.

"Do you mean the one you've got on?" I asked him, and the gals give me a dirty look.

"And this rug," he says, stomping on an old rag carpet. "How much do you suppose that cost?"

It was my first guess, so I said fifty dollars.

"That's a laugh," he said. "I paid two thousand for that rug."

"The guy that sold it had the laugh," I says.

Finally he steered us into his bedroom.

"Do you see that bed?" he says. "That's Marie Antoinette's bed. Just a cool thousand."

"What time does she usually get in?" I asked him.

"Here's my hobby," he said, opening up a closet, "dressing gowns and bathrobes."

Well, they was at least a dozen of them hanging on hangers. They was all colors of the rainbow including the Scandinavian. He dragged one down that was redder than Ella's and Katie's cheeks.

"This is my favorite bathrobe," he said. "It's Rose D. Barry."

So I asked him if he had all his household goods and garments named after some dame.

"This bathrobe cost me an even two hundred," he says.

"I always take baths bare," I said. "It's a whole lot cheaper."

"Let's go back in the living room," says Katie.

"Come on," said Ella, tugging me by the sleeve.

"Wait a minute," I says to her. "I don't know how much he paid for his toothbrush."

Well, when we got back in the living room, the two gals acted kind of drowsy and snuggled up together on the davenport and I and the old bird was left to ourself.

"Here's another thing I didn't show you," he says, and pulls a pair of African golf balls out of a drawer in his desk. "These dice is real ivory and they cost me twelve and a half berries."

"You mean up to now," I said.

"All right," he said. "We'll make it a twenty-five dollar limit."

Well, I didn't have no business in a game with him, but you know how a guy gets sometimes. So he took them first and rolled a four.

"Listen," I says: "Do you know how many times Willard set down in the first round?"

And sure enough he sevened.

"Now solid ivory dice," I said, "how many days in the week?"

So out come a natural. And as sure as I'm setting here, I made four straight passes with the whole roll riding each time and with all that wad parked on the two thousand dollar rug, I shot a five and a three. "Ivory," I said, "we was invited here to-night, so don't make me pay for the entertainment. Show me eighter from Decatur."

And the lady from Decatur showed.

Just then they was a stir on the davenport, and Ella woke up long enough to make the remark that we ought to go home. It was the first time she ever said it in the right place.

"Oh," I says, "I've got to give Mr. Trumbull a chance to get even."

But I wasn't in earnest.

"Don't bother about that," said Old Noah. "You can accommodate me some other time."

"You're certainly a sport," I says.

"And thanks for a wonderful time," said Ella. "I hope we'll see you again soon."

"Soon is to-morrow night," said mine host. "I'm going to take you all up the river to a place I know."

"Well," I says to Katie, when we was acrost the hall and the door shut, "how do you like him?"

"Oh, shut up!" says Katie.

So the next night he come over and rung our bell and said Ritchey was waiting with the car and would we come down when we was ready. Well, the gals had only had all day to prepare for the trip, so in another half hour they had their wraps on and we went downstairs. They wasn't nothing in front but a Rools-Royce with a livery chauffeur that looked like he'd been put there by a rubber stamp.

"What a stunning driver!" said Katie when we'd parked ourself in the back seat.

"Ritchey?" says mine host. "He is a nice looking boy, but better than that, he's a boy I can trust."

Well, anyway, the boy he could trust took us out to a joint called the Indian Inn where you wouldn't of never knew they was an eighteenth amendment only that the proprietor was asking twenty berries a quart for stuff that used to cost four. But that didn't seem to bother Methuselah and he ordered two of them. Not only that but he got us a table so close to the orchestra that the cornet player thought we was his mute.

"Now, what'll we eat?" he says.

So I looked at the program and the first item I seen was "Guinea Hen, $4.50."

"That's what Katie'll want," I says to myself, and sure enough that's what she got.

Well, we eat and then we danced and we danced and we danced, and finally along about eleven I and Ella was out on the floor pretending like we was enjoying ourself, and we happened to look over to the table and there was Katie and Trumbull setting one out and to look at either you could tell that something was wrong.

"Dance the next one with her," says Ella, "and find out what's the matter."

So I danced the next one with Katie and asked her.

"He squeezed my hand," she says. "I don't like him."

"Well," said I, "if you'd of ordered guinea hen on me I wouldn't of stopped at your hand. I'd of went at your throat."

"I've got a headache," she says. "Take me out to the car."

So they was nothing to it but I had to take her out to the car and come back and tell Ella and Trumbull that she wasn't feeling any too good and wanted to go home.

"She don't like me," says the old guy. "That's the whole trouble."

"Give her time," says Ella. "Remember she's just a kid."

"Yes, but what a kid!" he says.

So then he paid the check without no competition and we went out and clumb in the big limmie. Katie was pretending like she was asleep and neither Ella or Trumbull acted like they wanted to talk, so the conversation on the way home was mostly one-sided, with me in the title rôle. Katie went in the apartment without even thanking mine host for the guinea hen, but he kept Ella and I outside long enough to say that Ritchey and the car was at our service any time we wanted them.

So Ella told her that the next noon at breakfast. "And you'd ought to be ashamed of yourself," says Ella, "for treating a man like that like that."

"He's too fresh," says Katie.

"Well," said Ella, "if he was a little younger, you wouldn't mind him being fresh."

"No," said Katie, "if he was fresh, I wouldn't care if he was fresh. But what's the number of the garage?"

And she didn't lose no time taking advantage of the old bird. That same afternoon it seemed she had to go shopping and the bus wasn't good enough no more. She was out in Trumbull's limmie from two o'clock till pretty near seven. The old guy himself come to our place long about five and wanted to know if we knew where she was at. "I haven't no idear," said Ella. "I expected her home long ago. Did you want to use the car?"

"What's the difference," I said, "if he wanted to use the car or not? He's only the owner."

"Well," says Trumbull, "when I make an offer I mean it, and that little girl is welcome to use my machine whenever she feels like it."

So Ella asked him to stay to dinner and he said he would if we'd allow him to bring in some of his hootch, and of course I kicked on that proposition, but he insisted. And when Katie finally did get home, we was all feeling good and so was she and you'd never of thought they'd been any bad feelings the night before.

Trumbull asked her what she'd been buying.

"Nothing," she says. "I was looking at dresses, but they want too much money."

"You don't need no dresses," he says.

"No, of course not," said Katie. "But lots of girls is wearing them."

"Where did you go?" said Ella.

"I forget," says Katie. "What do you say if we play cards?"

So we played rummy till we was all blear-eyed and the old guy left, saying we'd all go somewheres next day. After he'd gone Ella begin to talk serious.

"Sis," she says, "here's the chance of a lifetime. Mr. Trumbull's head over heels in love with you and all as you have to do is encourage him a little. Can't you try and like him?"

"They's nobody I have more respect for," said Katie, "unless it's George Washington."

And then she give a funny laugh and run off to bed.

"I can't understand Sis no more," said Ella, when we was alone.

"Why not?" I asked her.

"Why, look at this opportunity staring her in the face," says the Mrs.

"Listen," I said: "The first time I stared you in the face, was you thinking about opportunity?"

Well, to make a short story out of it, I was the only one up in the house the next morning when Kathleen said we had a caller. It was the old boy.

"I'm sorry to be so early," he says, "but I just got a telegram and it means I got to run down to Washington for a few days. And I wanted to tell you that wile I'm gone Ritchey and the car is at your service."

So I thanked him and he said good-by and give his regards to the Mrs. and especially Katie, so when they got up I told them about it and I never seen a piece of bad news received so calm as Katie took it.

"But now he's gone," I said at the breakfast table, "why not the three of us run out to Bridgeport and call on the Wilmots?"

They're cousins of mine.

"Oh, fine!" said Ella.

"Wait a minute," says Katie. "I made a kind of an engagement with a dressmaker for to-day."

Well, as I say, to make a short story out of it, it seems like she'd made engagements with the dressmaker every day, but they wasn't no dresses ever come home.

In about a week Trumbull come back from Washington and the first thing he done was look us up and we had him in to dinner and I don't remember how the conversation started, but all of a sudden we was on the subject of his driver, Ritchey.

"A great boy," says Trumbull, "and a boy you can trust. If I didn't like him for nothing else, I'd like him for how he treats his family."

"What family?" says Kate.

"Why," says Trumbull, "his own family: his wife and two kids."

"My heavens!" says Katie, and kind of fell in a swoon.

So it seems like we didn't want to live there no more and we moved back to the Baldwin, having sublet the place on the Drive for three thousand a year.

So from then on, we was paying a thousand per annum for an apartment we didn't live in two weeks. But as I told the gals, we was getting pretty near as much for our money as the people that rented New York apartments and lived in them, too.

CHAPTER III

Lady Perkins

A LONG THE first week in May they was a couple hot days, and Katie can't stand the heat. Or the cold, or the medium. Anyway, when it's hot she always says: "I'm simply stifling." And when it's cold: "I'm simply frozen." And when it ain't neither one: "I wished the weather would do one thing another." I don't s'pose she knows what she's saying when she says any one of them things, but she's one of these here gals that can't bear to see a conversation die out and thinks it's her place to come through with a wise crack whenever they's a vacuum.

So during this hot spell we was having dinner with a bird named Gene Buck that knowed New York like a book, only he hadn't never read a book, and Katie made the remark that she was simply stifling.

"If you think this is hot," says our friend, "just wait till the summer comes. The Old Town certainly steams up in the Old Summer Time."

So Kate asked him how people could stand it.

"They don't," he says. "All the ones that's got a piece of change ducks out somewheres where they can get the air."

"Where do they go?" Katie asked him.

"Well," he says, "the most of my pals goes to Newport or Maine or up in the Adirondacks. But of course them places is out of most people's reach. If I was you folks I'd go over on Long Island somewheres and either take a cottage or live in one of them good hotels."

"Where, for instance?" says my Mrs.

"Well," he said, "some people takes cottages, but the rents is something fierce, and besides, the desirable ones is probably all eat up by this time. But they's plenty good hotels where you get good service and swell meals and meet good people; they won't take in no riffraff. And they give you a pretty fair rate if they know you're going to make a stay."

So Ella asked him if they was any special one he could recommend.

"Let's think a minute," he says.

"Let's not strain ourself," I said.

"Don't get cute!" said the Mrs. "We want to get some real information and Mr. Buck can give it to us."

"How much would you be willing to pay?" said Buck.

It was Ella's turn to make a wise crack.

"Not no more than we have to," she says.

"I and my sister has got about eight thousand dollars per annum between us," said Katie, "though a thousand of it has got to go this year to a man that cheated us up on Riverside Drive.

"It was about a lease. But papa left us pretty well off; over a hundred and fifty thousand dollars."

"Don't be so secret with Mr. Buck," I says. "We've knew him pretty near a week now. Tell him about them four-dollar stockings you bought over on Fifth Avenue and the first time you put them on they got as many runs as George Sisler."

"Well," said Buck, "I don't think you'd have no trouble getting comfortable rooms in a good hotel on seven thousand dollars. If I was you I'd try the Hotel Decker. It's owned by a man named Decker."

"Why don't he call it the Griffith?" I says.

"It's located at Tracy Estates," says Buck. "That's one of the garden spots of Long Island. It's a great big place, right up to the minute, and they give you everything the best. And they's three good golf courses within a mile of the hotel."

The gals told him they didn't play no golf.

"You don't know what you've missed," he says.

"Well," I said, "I played a game once myself and missed a whole lot."

"Do they have dances?" asked Kate.

"Plenty of them," says Buck, "and the guests is the nicest people you'd want to meet. Besides all that, the meals is included in the rates, and they certainly set a nasty table."

"I think it sounds grand," said the Mrs. "How do you get there?"

"Go over to the Pennsylvania Station," says Buck, "and take the Long Island Railroad to Jamaica. Then you change to the Haverton branch. It don't only take a half hour altogether."

"Let's go over to-morrow morning and see can we get rooms," said Katie.

So Ella asked how that suited me.

"Go just as early as you want to," I says. "I got a date to run down to the Aquarium and see the rest of the fish."

"You won't make no mistake stopping at the Decker," says Buck.

So the gals thanked him and I paid the check so as he would have more to spend when he joined his pals up to Newport.

Well, when Ella and Kate come back the next afternoon, I could see without them telling me that it was all settled. They was both grinning like they always do when they've pulled something nutty.

"It's a good thing we met Mr. Buck," said the Mrs., "or we mightn't never of heard of this place. It's simply wonderful. A double room with a bath for you and I and a room with a bath for Katie. The meals is throwed in, and we can have it all summer."

"How much?" I asked her.

"Two hundred a week," she said. "But you must remember that's for all three of us and we get our meals free."

"And I s'pose they also furnish knobs for the bedroom doors," says I.

"We was awful lucky," said the wife. "These was the last two rooms they had, and they wouldn't of had those only the lady that had engaged them canceled her reservation."

"I wished I'd met her when I was single," I says.

"So do I," says Ella.

"But listen," I said. "Do you know what two hundred a week amounts to? It amounts to over ten thousand a year, and our income is seven thousand."

"Yes," says Katie, "but we aren't only going to be there twenty weeks, and that's only four thousand."

"Yes," I said, "and that leaves us three thousand for the other thirty-two weeks, to pay for board and room and clothes and show tickets and a permanent wave every other day."

"You forget," said Kate, "that we still got our principal, which we can spend some of it and not miss it."

"And you also forget," said the Mrs., "that the money belongs to Sis and I, not you."

"I've got a sweet chance of forgetting that," I said. "It's hammered into me three times a day. I hear about it pretty near as often as I hear that one of you's lost their new silk bag."

"Well, anyway," says Ella, "it's all fixed up and we move out there early to-morrow morning, so you'll have to do your packing to-night."

I'm not liable to celebrate the anniversary of the next day's trip. Besides the trunks, the gals had a suitcase and a grip apiece and I had a suitcase. So that give me five pieces of baggage to wrestle, because of course the gals had to carry their parasol in one hand and their wrist watch in the other. A redcap helped load us on over to the station, but oh you change at Jamaica! And when we got to Tracy Estates we seen that the hotel wasn't only a couple of blocks away, so the ladies said we might as well walk and save taxi fare.

I don't know how I covered them two blocks, but I do know that when I reeled into the Decker my hands and arms was paralyzed and Ella had to do the registering.

Was you ever out there? Well, I s'pose it's what you might call a family hotel, and a good many of the guests belongs to the cay-nine family. A few of the couples that can't afford dogs has got children, and you're always tripping over one or the other. They's a dining room for the grown-ups and another for the kids, wile the dogs and their nurses eats in the grillroom à la carte. One part of the joint is bachelor quarters. It's located right next to the dogs' dormitories, and they's a good deal of rivalry between the dogs and the souses to see who can make the most noise nights. They's also a ballroom and a couple card rooms and a kind of a summer parlor where the folks sets round in the evening and listen to a three-piece orchestra that don't know they's been any music wrote since Poets and Peasants. The men get up about eight o'clock and go down to New York to Business. They don't never go to work. About nine the women begins limping downstairs and either goes to call on their dogs or take them for a walk in the front yard. This is a great big yard with a whole lot of benches strewed round it, but you can't set on them in the daytime because the women or the nurses uses them for a place to read to the dogs or kids, and in the evenings you would have to share them with the waitresses, which you have already had enough of them during the day.

When the women has prepared themselves for the long day's grind with a four-course breakfast, they set round on the front porch and discuss the big questions of the hour, like for instance the last trunk murder or whether an Airedale is more loving than a Golden Bantam. Once in a wile one of them cracks that it looks like they was bound to be a panic pretty soon and a big drop in prices, and so forth. This shows they're broad-minded and are giving a good deal of thought to up-to-date topics. Every so often one of them'll say: "The present situation can't keep up." The hell it can't!

By one o'clock their appetites is whetted so keen from brain exercise that they make a bum out of a plate of soup and an order of Long Island duckling, which they figure is caught fresh every day, and they wind up with salad and apple pie à la mode and a stein of coffee. Then they totter up to their rooms to sleep it off before Dear gets home from Business.

Saturday nights everybody puts on their evening clothes like something was going to happen. But it don't. Sunday mornings the husbands and bachelors gets up earlier than usual to go to their real business, which is golf. The womenfolks are in full possession of the hotel till Sunday night supper and wives and husbands don't see one another all day long, but it don't seem as long as if they did. Most of them's approaching their golden-wedding jubilee and haven't nothing more to say to each other that you could call a novelty. The husband may make the remark, Sunday night, that he would of broke one hundred and twenty in the afternoon round if the caddy hadn't of handed him a spoon when he asked for a nut pick, and the wife'll probably reply that she's got to go in Town some day soon and see a chiropodist. The rest of the Sabbath evening is spent in bridge or listening to the latest song hit from The Bohemian Girl.

The hotel's got all the modern conveniences like artificial light and a stopper in the bathtubs. They even got a barber and a valet, but you can't get a shave wile he's pressing your clothes, so it's pretty near impossible for a man to look their best at the same time.

Well, the second day we was there I bought me a deck of cards and got so good at solitary that pretty soon I could play fifty games between breakfast and lunch and a hundred from then till suppertime. During the first week Ella and Kate got on friendly terms with over a half dozen people—the head waiter, our waitress, some of the clerks and the manager and the two telephone gals. It wasn't from lack of trying that they didn't meet even more people. Every day one or the other of them would try and swap a little small talk with one of the other squatters, but it generally always wound up as a short monologue.

Ella said to me one day, she says: "I don't know if we can stick it out here or not. Every hotel I was ever at before, it was easy enough to make a lot of friends, but you could stick a bottle of cream alongside one of these people and it'd stay sweet a week. Unless they looked at it. I'm sick of talking to you and Sis and the hired help, and Kate's so lonesome that she cries herself to sleep nights."

Well, if I'd of only had sense enough to insist on staying we'd of probably packed up and took the next train to Town. But instead of that I said: "What's to prevent us from going back to New York?"

"Don't be silly!" says the Mrs. "We come out here to spend the summer and here is where we're going to spend the summer."

"All right," I says, "and by September I'll be all set to write a book on one-handed card games."

"You'd think," says Ella, "that some of these women was ti-tled royalties the way they snap at you when you try and be friends with them. But they's only one in the bunch that's got any handle to her name; that's Lady Perkins."

I asked her which one was that.

"You know," says Ella. "I pointed her out to you in the din-ing room. She's a nice-looking woman, about thirty-five, that sets near our table and walks with a cane."

"If she eats like some of the rest of them," I says, "she's lucky they don't have to w'eel her."

"She's English," says Ella. "They just come over and her husband's in Texas on some business and left her here. She's the one that's got that dog."

"That dog!" I said. "You might just as well tell me she's the one that don't play the mouth organ. They've all got a dog."

"She's got two," said the wife. "But the one I meant is that big German police dog that I'm scared to death of him. Haven't you saw her out walking with him and the little chow?"

"Yes," I said, "if that's what it is. I always wondered what the boys in the Army was talking about when they said they eat chow."

"They probably meant chowchow," says the Mrs. "They wouldn't of had these kind of chows, because in the first place, who would eat a dog, and besides these kind costs too much."

"Well," I says, "I'm not interested in the price of chows, but if you want to get acquainted with Lady Perkins, why I can probably fix it for you."

"Yes, you'll fix it!" said Ella. "I'm beginning to think that if we'd of put you in storage for the summer the folks round here wouldn't shy away from us like we was leopards that had broke out of a pest-house. I wished you would try and dress up once in a wile and not always look like you was just going to do the chores. Then maybe I and Sis might get some-wheres."

Well, of course when I told her I could probably fix it up with Lady Perkins, I didn't mean nothing. But it wasn't only the next morning when I started making good. I was up and dressed and downstairs about half past eight, and as the gals wasn't ready for their breakfast yet I went out on the porch and set down. They wasn't nobody else there, but pretty soon I seen Lady Perkins come up the path with her two whelps. When she got to the porch steps their nurse popped out of the servants' quarters and took them round to the grillroom for their breakfast. I s'pose the big one ordered sauerkraut and kalter Aufschnitt, wile the chow had tea and eggs fo yung. Anyway, the Perkins dame come up on the porch and flopped into the chair next to mine.

In a few minutes Ed Wurz, the manager of the hotel, showed, with a bag of golf instruments and a trick suit. He spotted me and asked me if I didn't want to go along with him and play.

"No," I said. "I only played once in my life."

"That don't make no difference," he says. "I'm a bum my-self. I just play shinny, you might say."

"Well," I says, "I can't anyway, on account of my dogs. They been giving me a lot of trouble."

Of course I was referring to my feet, but he hadn't no sooner than went on his way when Lady Perkins swung round on me and says: "I didn't know you had dogs. Where do you keep them?"

At first I was going to tell her "In my shoes," but I thought I might as well enjoy myself, so I said: "They're in the dog hospital over to Haverton."

"What ails them?" she asked me.

Well, I didn't know nothing about caynine diseases outside of hydrophobia, which don't come till August, so I had to make one up.

"They got blanny," I told her.

"Blanny!" she says. "I never heard of it before."

"No," I said. "It hasn't only been discovered in this country just this year. It got carried up here from Peru some way another."

"Oh, it's contagious, then!" says Lady Perkins.

"Worse than measles or lockjaw," says I. "You take a dog that's been in the same house with a dog that's got blanny, and it's a miracle if they don't all get it."

She asked me if I'd had my dogs in the hotel.

"Only one day," I says, "the first day we come, about a week ago. As soon as I seen what was the matter with them, I took them over to Haverton in a sanitary truck."

"Was they mingling with the other dogs here?" she says.

"Just that one day," I said.

"Heavens!" said Lady Perkins. "And what's the symptoms?"

"Well," I said, "first you'll notice that they keep their tongue stuck out a lot and they're hungry a good deal of the time, and finally they show up with a rash."

"Then what happens?" she says.

"Well," said I, "unless they get the best of treatment, they kind of dismember."

Then she asked me how long it took for the symptoms to show after a dog had been exposed. I told her any time between a week and four months.

"My dogs has been awful hungry lately," she says, "and they most always keeps their tongue stuck out. But they haven't no rash."

"You're all right, then," I says. "If you give them treatments before the rash shows up, they's no danger."

"What's the treatment?" she asked me.

"You rub the back of their neck with some kind of dope," I told her. "I forget what it is, but if you say the word, I can get you a bottle of it when I go over to the hospital this afternoon."

"I'd be ever so much obliged," she says, "and I hope you'll find your dear ones a whole lot better."

"Dear ones is right," I said. "They cost a pile of jack, and the bird I bought them off of told me I should ought to get them insured, but I didn't. So if anything happens to them now, I'm just that much out."

Next she asked me what kind of dogs they was.

"Well," I said, "you might maybe never of heard of them, as they don't breed them nowheres only way down in Dakota. They call them yaphounds—I don't know why; maybe on account of the noise they make. But they're certainly a grand-looking dog and they bring a big price."

She set there a wile longer and then got up and went inside, probably to the nursery to look for signs of rash.

Of course I didn't tell the Mrs. and Kate nothing about this incidence. They wouldn't of believed it if I had of, and besides, it would be a knock-out if things broke right and Lady Perkins come up and spoke to me wile they was present, which is just what happened.

During the afternoon I strolled over to the drug store and got me an empty pint bottle. I took it up in the room and filled it with water and shaving soap. Then I laid low till evening, so as Perk would think I had went to Haverton.

I and Ella and Kate breezed in the dining room kind of late and we hadn't no more than ordered when I seen the Lady get up and start out. She had to pass right past us, and when I looked at her and smiled she stopped.

"Well," she said, "how's your dogs?"

I got up from the table.

"A whole lot better, thank you," says I, and then I done the honors. "Lady Perkins," I said, "meet the wife and sister-in-law."

The two gals staggered from their chairs, both pop-eyed. Lady Perkins bowed to them and told them to set down. If she hadn't the floor would of bounced up and hit them in the chin.

"I got a bottle for you," I said. "I left it upstairs and I'll fetch it down after supper."

"I'll be in the red card room," says Perk, and away she went.

I wished you could of see the two gals. They couldn't talk for a minute, for the first time in their life. They just set there with their mouth open like a baby blackbird. Then they both broke out with a rash of questions that come so fast I couldn't understand none of them, but the general idear was, What the hell!

"They's no mystery about it," I said. "Lady Perkins was setting out on the porch this morning and you two was late getting down to breakfast, so I took a walk, and when I come back she noticed that I kind of limped and asked me what ailed my feet. I told her they always swoll up in warm weather and she said she was troubled the same way and did I know any medicine that shrank them. So I told her I had a preparation and would bring her a bottle of it."

"But," says Kate, "I can't understand a woman like she speaking to a man she don't know."

"She's been eying me all week," I said. "I guess she didn't have the nerve to break the ice up to this morning; then she got desperate."

"She must of," said Ella.

"I wished," said Kate, "that when you introduce me to people you'd give them my name."

"I'm sorry," I said, "but I couldn't recall it for a minute, though your face is familiar."

"But listen," says the wife. "What ails your dogs is a corn. You haven't got no swelled feet and you haven't got no medicine for them."

"Well," I says, "what I give her won't hurt her. It's just a bottle of soap and water that I mixed up, and pretty near everybody uses that once in a wile without no bad after effects."

Now, the whole three of us had been eating pretty good ever since we'd came to the Decker. After living à la carte at Big Town prices for six months, the American plan was sweet patootie. But this night the gals not only skrimped themselves but they was in such a hurry for me to get through that my molars didn't hardly have time to identify what all was scampering past them. Ella finally got so nervous that I had to take off the feed bag without dipping my bill into the stewed rhubarb.

"Lady Perkins will get tired waiting for you," she says. "And besides, she won't want us horning in there and interrupting them after their game's started."

"Us!" said I. "How many do you think it's going to take to carry this bottle?"

"You don't mean to say we can't go with you!" said Kate.

"You certainly can't," I says. "I and the nobility won't have our little romance knocked for a gool by a couple of country gals that can't get on speaking terms with nobody but the chambermaid."

"But they'll be other people there," says Kate. "She can't play cards alone."

"Who told you she was going to play cards?" I says. "She picked the red card room because we ain't liable to be interrupted there. As for playing cards alone, what else have I done all week? But when I get there she won't have to play solitary. It'll be two-handed hearts; where if you was to crowd in, it couldn't be nothing but rummy."

Well, they finally dragged me from the table, and the gals took a seat in the lobby wile I went upstairs after the medicine. But I hadn't no sooner than got a hold of the bottle when Ella come in the room.

"Listen," she says. "They's a catch in this somewheres. You needn't to try and tell me that a woman like Lady Perkins is trying to start a flirtation with a yahoo. Let's hear what really come off."

"I already told you," I said. "The woman's nuts over me and you should ought to be the last one to find fault with her judgment."

Ella didn't speak for a wile. Then she says: "Well, if you're going to forget your marriage vows and flirt with an old hag like she, I guess two can play at that little game. They's several men round this hotel that I like their looks and all as they need is a little encouragement."

"More than a little, I guess," says I, "or else they'd of already been satisfied with what you and Kate has give them. They can't neither one of you pretend that you been fighting on the defense all week, and the reason you haven't copped nobody is because this place is a hotel, not a home for the blind."

I wrapped a piece of newspaper round the bottle and started for the door. But all of a sudden I heard snuffles and stopped.

"Look here," I said. "I been kidding you. They's no need for you to get sore and turn on the tear ducks. I'll tell you how this thing happened if you think you can see a joke."

So I give her the truth, and afterwards I says: "They'll be plenty of time for you and Kate to get acquainted with the dame, but I don't want you tagging in there with me to-night. She'd think we was too cordial. To-morrow morning, if you can manage to get up, we'll all three of us go out on the porch and lay for her when she brings the whelps back from their hike. She's sure to stop and inquire about my kennel. And don't forget, wile she's talking, that we got a couple of yap-hounds that's suffering from blanny, and if she asks any questions let me do the answering, as I can think a lot quicker. You better tell Kate the secret, too, before she messes everything up, according to custom."

Then I and the Mrs. come downstairs and her and Katie went out to listen to the music wile I beat it to the red card room. I give Perkie the bottle of rash poison and she thanked me and said she would have the dogs' governess slap some of it onto them in the morning. She was playing bridge w'ist with another gal and two dudes. To look at their faces they wasn't playing for just pins. I had sense enough to not talk, but I stood there watching them a few minutes. Between hands Perk introduced me to the rest of the party. She had to ask my name first. The other skirt at the table was a Mrs. Snell and one of the dudes was a Doctor Platt. I didn't get the name of Lady Perkins' partner.

"Mr. Finch," says Perk, "is also a dog fancier. But his dogs is sick with a disease called blanny and he's got them over to the dog hospital at Haverton."

"What kind of dogs?" asked Platt.

"I never heard of the breed before," says Perk. "They're yap-hounds."

"They raise them in South Dakota," I says.

Platt gives me a funny look and said: "I been in South Dakota several times and I never heard of a yaphound neither; or I never heard of a disease named blanny."

"I s'pose not," says I. "You ain't the only old-fashioned doctor that left themself go to seed when they got out of school. I bet you won't admit they's such a thing as appendicitis."

Well, this got a laugh from Lady Perkins and the other dude, but it didn't go very big with Doc or Mrs. Snell. Wile Doc was trying to figure out a come-back I said I must go and look after my womenfolks. So I told the party I was glad to of met them and walked out.

I found Ella and Katie in the summer parlor, and they wasn't alone. A nice-looking young fella named Codd was setting alongside of them, and after we was introduced Ella leaned over and w'ispered to me that he was Bob Codd, the famous aviator. It come out that he had invented some new kind of an aeroplane and had came to demonstrate it to the Williams Company. The company—Palmer Williams and his brother, you know—they've got their flying field a couple miles from the hotel. Well, a guy with nerve enough to go up in one of them things certainly ain't going to hesitate about speaking to a strange gal when he likes their looks. So this Codd baby had give himself an introduction to my Mrs. and Kate, and I guess they hadn't sprained an ankle running away from him.

Of course Ella wanted to know how I'd came out with Lady Perkins. I told her that we hadn't had much chance to talk because she was in a bridge game with three other people, but I'd met them and they'd all seemed to fall for me strong. Ella wanted to know who they was and I told her their names, all but the one I didn't get. She squealed when I mentioned Mrs. Snell.

"Did you hear that, Sis?" she says to Kate. "Tom's met Mrs. Snell. That's the woman, you know, that wears them funny clothes and has the two dogs."

"You're describing every woman in the hotel," I said.

"But this is *the* Mrs. Snell," said the wife. "Her husband's the sugar man and she's the daughter of George Henkel, the banker. They say she's a wonderful bridge player and don't never play only for great big stakes. I'm wild to meet her."

"Yes," I said, "if they's one person you should ought to meet, it's a wonderful bridge player that plays for great big stakes, especially when our expenses is making a bum out of our income and you don't know a grand slam from no dice."

"I don't expect to gamble with her," says Ella. "But she's just the kind of people we want to know."

Well, the four of us set there and talked about this and that, and Codd said he hadn't had time to get his machine put together yet, but when he had her fixed and tested her a few times he would take me up for a ride.

"You got the wrong number," I says. "I don't feel flighty."

"Oh, I'd just love it!" said Kate.

"Well," says Codd, "you ain't barred. But I don't want to have no passengers along till I'm sure she's working O. K."

When I and Ella was upstairs she said that Codd had told them he expected to sell his invention to the Williamses for a cold million. And he had took a big fancy to Kate.

"Well," I said, "they say that the reckless aviators makes the best ones, so if him and Kate gets married he'll be better than ever. He won't give a damn after that."

"You're always saying something nasty about Sis," said the Mrs.; "but I know you just talk to hear yourself talk. If I thought you meant it I'd walk out on you."

"I'd hate to lose you," I says, "but if you took her along I wouldn't write it down as a total loss."

The following morning I and the two gals was down on the porch bright and early and in a few minutes, sure enough, along came Lady Perkins, bringing the menagerie back from the parade. She turned them over to the nurse and joined us. She said that Martha, the nurse, had used the rash poison and it had made a kind of a lather on the dogs' necks and she didn't know whether to wash it off or not, but it had dried up in the sun. She asked me how many times a day the dope should ought to be put on, and I told her before every meal and at bedtime.

"But," I says, "it's best to not take the dogs right out in the sun where the lather'll dry. The blanny germ can't live in that kind of lather, so the longer it stays moist, why, so much the better."

Then she asked me was I going to Haverton to see my pets

that day and I said yes, and she said she hoped I'd find them much improved. Then Ella cut in and said she understood that Lady Perkins was very fond of bridge.

"Yes, I am," says Perk. "Do you people play?"

"No, we don't," says Ella, "but we'd like to learn."

"It takes a long wile to learn to play good," said Perk. "But I do wished they was another real player in the hotel so as we wouldn't have to take Doctor Platt in. He knows the game, but he don't know enough to keep still. I don't mind people talking wile the cards is being dealt, but once the hands is picked up they ought to be absolute silence. Last night I lost about three hundred and seventy dollars just because he talked at the wrong time."

"Three hundred and seventy dollars!" said Kate. "My, you must play for big stakes!"

"Yes, we do," says Lady Perkins; "and when a person is playing for sums like that it ain't no time to trifle, especially when you're playing against an expert like Mrs. Snell."

"The game must be awfully exciting," said Ella. "I wished we could watch it sometime."

"I guess it wouldn't hurt nothing," says Perkie; "not if you kept still. Maybe you'd bring me luck."

"Was you going to play to-night?" asked Kate.

"No," says the Lady. "They's going to be a little dance here to-night and Mr. Snell's dance mad, so he insists on borrowing his wife for the occasion. Doctor Platt likes to dance too."

"We're all wild about it," says Kate. "Is this an invitation affair?"

"Oh, no," says Perk. "It's for the guests of the hotel."

Then she said good-by to us and went in the dining room. The rest of our conversation all day was about the dance and what should we wear, and how nice and democratic Lady Perkins was, and to hear her talk you wouldn't never know she had a title. I s'pose the gals thought she ought to stop every three or four steps and declare herself.

I made the announcement about noon that I wasn't going to partake in the grand ball. My corn was the alibi. But they wasn't no way to escape from dressing up and escorting the two gals into the grand ballroom and then setting there with them.

The dance was a knock-out. Outside of Ella and Kate and the aviator and myself, they was three couple. The Snells was there and so was Doctor Platt. He had a gal with him that looked like she might be his mother with his kid sister's clothes on. Then they was a pair of young shimmy shakers that ought to of been give their bottle and tucked in the hay at six P. M. A corn wouldn't of bothered them the way they danced; their feet wasn't involved in the transaction.

I and the Mrs. and Kate was the only ones there in evening clothes. The others had attended these functions before and knew that they wouldn't be enough suckers on hand to make any difference whether you wore a monkey suit or rompers. Besides, it wasn't Saturday night.

The music was furnished by the three-piece orchestra that usually done their murder in the summer parlor.

Ella was expecting me to introduce her and Kate to the Snell gal, but her and her husband was so keen for dancing that they called it off in the middle of the second innings and beat it upstairs. Then Ella said she wouldn't mind meeting Platt, but when he come past us and I spoke to him he give me a look like you would expect from a flounder that's been wronged.

So poor Codd danced one with Kate and one with Ella, and so on, and so on, till finally it got pretty late, a quarter to ten, and our party was the only merrymakers left in the joint. The orchestra looked over at us to see if we could stand some more punishment. The Mrs. told me to go and ask them to play a couple more dances before they quit. They done what I asked them, but maybe I got my orders mixed up.

The next morning I asked Wurz, the manager, how often the hotel give them dances.

"Oh," he says, "once or twice a month."

I told him I didn't see how they could afford it.

Kate went out after supper this next evening to take an automobile ride with Codd. So when I and Ella had set in the summer parlor a little wile, she proposed that we should go in and watch the bridge game. Well, I wasn't keen for it, but when you tell wife you don't want to do something she always says, "Why not?" and even if you've got a reason she'll make a monkey out of it. So we rapped at the door of the red card room and Lady Perkins said, "Come in," and in we went.

The two dudes and Mrs. Snell was playing with her again, but Perk was the only one that spoke.

"Set down," she said, "and let's see if you can bring me some luck."

So we drawed up a couple of chairs and set a little ways behind her. Her and the anonymous dude was partners against Doc and Mrs. Snell, and they didn't change all evening. I haven't played only a few games of bridge, but I know a little about it, and I never see such hands as Perkie held. It was a misdeal when she didn't have the ace, king and four or five others of one suit and a few picture cards and aces on the side. When she couldn't get the bid herself she doubled the other pair and made a sucker out of them. I don't know what they was playing a point, but when they broke up Lady Perkins and her dude was something like seven hundred berries to the good.

I and Ella went to bed wile they was settling up, but we seen her on the porch in the morning. She smiled at us and says: "You two are certainly grand mascots! I hope you can come in and set behind me again to-night. I ain't even yet, but one more run of luck like last night's and I'll be a winner. Then," she says, "I s'pose I'll have to give my mascots some kind of a treat."

Ella was tickled to death and couldn't hardly wait to slip Sis the good news. Kate had been out late and overslept herself and we was half through breakfast when she showed up. The Mrs. told her about the big game and how it looked like we was in strong with the nobility, and Kate said she had some good news of her own; that Codd had as good as told her he was stuck on her.

"And he's going to sell his invention for a million," says Ella. "So I guess we wasn't as crazy coming out to this place as some people thought we was."

"Wait till the machine's made good," I said.

"It has already," says Kate. "He was up in it yesterday and everything worked perfect and he says the Williamses was wild over it. And what do you think's going to come off to-morrow morning? He's going to take me up with him."

"Oh, no, Sis!" said Ella. "S'pose something should happen!"

"No hope," says I.

"But even if something should happen," said Katie, "what would I care as long as it happened to Bob and I together!"

I told the waitress to bring me another order of fried mush.

"To-night," said Kate, "Bob's going in Town to a theater party with some boys he went to college with. So I can help you bring Lady Perkins good luck."

Something told me to crab this proposition and I tried, but it was passed over my veto. So the best I could do was to re-mind Sis, just before we went in the gambling den, to keep her mouth shut wile the play was going on.

Perk give us a smile of welcome and her partner smiled too.

For an hour the game went along about even. Kate acted like she was bored, and she didn't have nothing to say after she'd told them, wile somebody was dealing, that she was going to have an aeroplane ride in the morning. Finally our side begin to lose, and lose by big scores. They was one time when they was about sixteen hundred points to the bad. Lady Perkins didn't seem to be enjoying herself and when Ella ad-dressed a couple of remarks to her the cat had her tongue.

But the luck switched round again and Lady Perk had all but caught up when the blow-off come.

It was the rubber game, with the score nothing and noth-ing. The Doc dealt the cards. I was setting where I could see his hand and Perk's both. Platt had the king, jack and ten and five other hearts. Lady Perkins held the ace and queen of hearts, the other three aces and everything else in the deck.

The Doc bid two hearts. The other dude and Mrs. Snell passed.

"Two without," says Lady Perkins.

"Three hearts," says Platt.

The other two passed again and Perk says: "Three without."

Katie had came strolling up and was pretty near behind Perk's chair.

"Well," says Platt, "it looks like ——"

But we didn't find out what it looked like, as just then Katie says: "Heavens! Four aces! Don't you wished you was playing penny ante?"

It didn't take Lady Perkins no time at all to forget her title.

"You fool!" she screams, w'eeling round on Kate. "Get out of here, and get out of here quick, and don't never come near me again! I hope your aeroplane falls a million feet. You little fool!"

I don't know how the hand come out. We wasn't there to see it played.

Lady Perkins got part of her hope. The aeroplane fell all right, but only a couple of miles instead of a million feet. They say that they was a defect or something in poor Codd's engine. Anyway, he done an involuntary nose dive. Him and his invention was spilled all over Long Island. But Katie had been awake all night with the hysterics and Ella hadn't managed to get her to sleep till nine A. M. So when Codd had called for her Ella'd told him that Sis would go some other day. Can you beat it?

Wile I and Ella was getting ready for supper I made the remark that I s'posed we'd live in a vale of tears for the next few days.

"No," said Ella. "Sis is taking it pretty calm. She's sensible. She says if that could of happened, why the invention couldn't of been no good after all. And the Williamses probably wouldn't of give him a plugged dime for it."

Lady Perkins didn't only speak to me once afterwards. I seen her setting on the porch one day, reading a book. I went up to her and said: "Hello." They wasn't no answer, so I thought I'd appeal to her sympathies.

"Maybe you're still interested in my dogs," I said. "They was too far gone and the veter'nary had to order them shot."

"That's good," said Perk, and went on reading.

CHAPTER IV

Only One

ABOUT A week after this, the Mrs. made the remark that the Decker wasn't big enough to hold both she and Perkins.

"She treats us like garbage," says the Mrs., "and if I stay here much longer I'll forget myself and do her nose in a braid."

But Perk left first and saved us the trouble. Her husband was down in Texas looking after some oil gag and he wired her a telegram one day to come and join him as it looked like he would have to stay there all summer. If I'd of been him I'd of figured that Texas was a sweet enough summer resort without adding your wife to it.

We was out on the porch when her ladyship and two dogs shoved off.

"Three of a kind," said the Mrs.

And she stuck her tongue out at Perk and felt like that made it all even. A woman won't stop at nothing to revenge insults. I've saw them stagger home in a new pair of 3 double A shoes because some fresh clerk told them the 7 Ds they tried on was too small. So anyway we decided to stay on at the Decker and the two gals prettied themselves up every night for dinner in the hopes that somebody besides the head-waiter would look at them twice, but we attracted about as much attention as a dirty finger nail in the third grade.

That is, up till Herbert Daley come on the scene.

Him and Katie spotted each other at the same time. It was the night he come to the Decker. We was pretty near through dinner when the head-waiter showed him to a table a little ways from us. The majority of the guests out there belongs to the silly sex and a new man is always a riot, even with the married ones. But Daley would of knocked them dead anywheres. He looked like he was born and raised in Shubert's chorus and the minute he danced in all the women folks forgot the feed bag and feasted their eyes on him. As for Daley, after he'd glanced at the bill of fare, he let his peepers roll over towards our table and then they quit rolling. A cold stare from Kate might have scared him off, but if they was ever a gal with "Welcome" embroidered on her pan, she's it.

It was all I could do to tear Ella and Sis from the dining room, though they was usually in a hurry to romp out to the summer parlor and enjoy a few snubs. I'd just as soon of set one place as another, only for the waitress, who couldn't quit till we did and she generally always had a date with the big ski jumper the hotel hires to destroy trunks.

Well, we went out and listened a wile to the orchestra, which had brought a lot of new jazz from the Prince of Pilsen, and we waited for the new dude to show up, but he didn't, and finally I went in to the desk to buy a couple of cigars and there he was, talking to Wurz, the manager. Wurz introduced us and after we'd shook hands Daley excused himself and said he was going upstairs to write a letter. Then Wurz told me he was Daley the horseman.

"He's just came up from the South," says Wurz. "He's going to be with us till the meetings is over at Jamaica and Belmont. He's got a whale of a stable and he expects to clean up round New York with Only One, which he claims can beat any horse in the world outside of Man o' War. They's some other good ones in the bunch, too, and he says he'll tell me when he's going to bet on them. I don't only bet once in a long wile and then never more than $25 at a crack, but I'll take this baby's tips as often as he comes through with them. I guess a man won't make no mistake following a bird that bets five and ten thousand at a clip, though of course it don't mean much to him if he win or lose. He's dirty with it."

I asked Wurz if Daley was married and he said no.

"And listen," he says: "It looks like your little sister-in-law had hit him for a couple of bases. He described where she was setting in the dining room and asked who she was."

"Yes," I said, "I noticed he was admiring somebody at our table, but I thought maybe it was me."

"He didn't mention you," says Wurz, "only to make sure you wasn't Miss Kate's husband."

"If he was smart he'd know that without asking," I said. "If she was my wife I'd be wearing weeds."

I went back to the gals and told them I'd met the guy. They was all steamed up.

"Who is he?" says Kate.

"His name is Herbert Daley," I told her. "He's got a stable over to Jamaica."

"A stable!" says Ella, dropping her jaw. "A man couldn't dress like he and run a livery."

So I had to explain that he didn't run no livery, but owned a string of race horses.

"How thrilling!" says Katie. "I love races! I went to the Grand Circuit once, the time I was in Columbus."

"These is different," I says. "These is thurlbreds."

"So was they thurlbreds!" she says. "You always think a thing can't be no good if you wasn't there."

I let her win that one.

"We must find out when the race is and go," said the Mrs.

"They's six of them every day," I said, "but it costs about five smackers apiece to get in, to say nothing about what you lose betting."

"Betting!" said Katie. "I just love to bet and I never lose. Don't you remember the bet I made with Sammy Pass on the baseball that time? I took him for a five-pound box of candy. I just felt that Cincinnati was going to win."

"So did the White Sox," I says. "But if you bet with the boys over to Jamaica, the only candy they'll take you for is an all-day sucker."

"What did Mr. Daley have to say?" asked Ella.

"He had to say he was pleased to meet me," I told her. "He proved it by chasing upstairs to write a letter."

"Probably to his wife," said Kate.

"No," I said. "Wurz tells me he ain't got no wife. But he's got plenty of jack, so Wurz says."

"Well, Sis," says the Mrs., "that's no objection to him, is it?"

"Don't be silly!" said Katie. "He wouldn't look at me."

"I guess not!" I says. "He was so busy doing it in the dining room, that half his soup never got past his chin. And listen: I don't like to get you excited, but Wurz told me he asked who you was."

"O Sis!" said the Mrs. "It looks like a Romance."

"Wurz didn't say nothing about a Romance," said I. "He may be interested like the rubes who stare with their mouth open at Ringling's 'Strange People.'"

"Oh, you can't tease Sis like that," said Ella. "She's as pretty as a picture to-night and nobody could blame a man from admiring her."

"Especially when we don't know nothing about him," I says. "He may be a snow-eater or his upstairs rooms is unfurnished or something."

"Well," says Ella, "if he shows up again to-night, don't you forget to introduce us."

"Better not be in no hurry," I said.

"Why not?" said Ella. "If him and Sis likes each other's looks, why, the sooner they get acquainted, it won't hurt nothing."

"I don't know," I says. "I've noticed that most of the birds you chose for a brother-in-law only stayed in the family as long as they was strangers."

"Nobody said nothing about Mr. Daley as a brother-in-law," says Ella.

"Oh!" I said. "Then I suppose you want Katie to meet him so as she can land a hostler's job."

Well, in about a half hour, the gals got their wish and Daley showed up. I didn't have to pull no strategy to land him. He headed right to where we was setting like him and I was old pals. I made the introductions and he drawed up a chair and parked. The rest of the guests stared at us goggle-eyed.

"Some hotel!" says Daley.

"We like it," says the Mrs. "They's so many nice people lives here."

"We know by hearsay," I said, but she stepped on my foot.

"It's handy for me," said Daley. "I have a few horses over to the Jamaica race track and it's a whole lot easier to come here than go in Town every night."

"Do you attend the races every day?" says Katie.

"Sure," he says. "It's my business. And they's very few afternoons when one of my nags ain't entered."

"My! You must have a lot of them!" said Kate.

"Not many," says Daley. "About a hundred. And I only shipped thirty."

"Imagine!" said Kate.

"The army's got that many," I said.

"The army ain't got none like mine," says Daley. "I guess

they wished they had of had. I'd of been glad to of helped them out, too, if they'd asked me."

"That's why I didn't enlist," I said. "Pershing never even suggested it."

"Oh, I done my bit all right," says Daley. "Two hundred thousand in Liberty Bonds is all."

"Just like throwing it away!" I says.

"Two hundred thousand!" says Ella. "And you've still got money left?"

She said this in a joking way, but she kept the receiver to her ear.

"I ain't broke yet," says Daley, "and I don't expect to be."

"You don't half know this hotel," I says.

"The Decker does charge good prices," said Daley, "but still and all, a person is willing to pay big for the opportunity of meeting young ladies like the present company."

"O Mr. Daley!" said Kate. "I'm afraid you're a flatter."

"I bet he makes them pretty speeches to every woman he meets," says Ella.

"I haven't met none before who I felt like making them," says Daley.

Wile they was still talking along these lines, the orchestra begin to drool a Perfect Day, so I ducked out on the porch for air. The gals worked fast wile I was gone and when I come back it was arranged that Daley was to take us to the track next afternoon in his small car.

His small car was a toy that only had enough room for the people that finds fault with Wilson. I suppose he had to leave his big car in New York on account of the Fifty-ninth Street bridge being so frail.

Before we started I asked our host if they was a chance to get anything to drink over to the track and he says no, but pretty near everybody brought something along on the hip, so I said for them to wait a minute wile I went up to the room and filled a flask. When we was all in the car, the Mrs. wanted to know if it wasn't risky, me taking the hooch along.

"It's against the prohibition law," she says.

"So am I," I said.

"They's no danger," says Daley. "They ain't began to force

prohibition yet. I only wished they had. It would save me a little worry about my boy."

"Your boy!" said Katie, dropping her jaw a foot.

"Well, I call him my boy," says Daley. "I mean little Sid Mercer, that rides for me. He's the duke of them all when he lays off the liquor. He's gave me his word that he won't touch nothing as long as he's under contract to me, and he's kept straight so far, but I can't help from worr'ing about him. He ought to be good, though, when I pay him $20,000 for first call, and leave him make all he can on the side. But he ain't got much stren'th of character, you might say, and if something upsets him, he's liable to bust things wide open.

"I remember once he was stuck on a gal down in Louisville and he was supposed to ride Great Scott for Bradley in the Derby. He was the only one that could handle Scott right, and with him up Scott would of win as far as from here to Dallas. But him and the gal had a brawl the day before the race and that night the kid got stiff. When it come time for the race he couldn't of kept a seat on a saw horse. Bradley had to hustle round and dig up another boy and Carney was the only one left that could ride at all and him and Great Scott was strangers. So Bradley lose the race and canned Mercer."

"Whisky's a terrible thing," says Ella. A woman'll sometimes pretend for a long wile like she's stupid and all of a sudden pull a wise crack that proves she's a thinker.

"Well," says Daley, "when Bradley give him the air, I took him, and he's been all right. I guess maybe I know how to handle men."

"Men only?" says Katie, smiling.

"Men and horses," said Daley. "I ain't never tried to handle the fair sex and I don't know if I could or not. But I've just met one that I think could handle me." And he give her a look that you could pour on a waffle.

Daley had a table saved for him in the clubhouse and we eat our lunch. The gals had clubhouse sandwiches, probably figuring they was caught fresh there. They was just one of Daley's horses entered that day and he told us he wasn't going to bet on it, as it hadn't never showed nothing and this was just a try-out. He said, though, that they was other horses on the card that looked good and maybe he would play them after he'd been round and talked to the boys.

"Yes," says Kate, "but the men you'll talk to knows all about the different horses and they'll tell you what horses to bet on and how can I win?"

"Why," says Daley, "if I decide to make a little bet on So-and-So I'll tell you about it and you can bet on the same horse."

"But if I'm betting with you," says Kate, "how can we bet on the same horse?"

"You're betting with me, but you ain't betting against me," said Daley. "This ain't a bet like you was betting with your sister on a football game or something. We place our bets with the bookmakers, that makes their living taking bets. Whatever horse we want to bet on, they take the bet."

"They must be crazy!" says Katie. "Your friends tell you what horse is going to win and you bet on them and the book-binders is stung."

"My friends makes mistakes," says Daley, "and besides, I ain't the only guy out here that bets. Pretty near everybody at the track bets and the most of them don't know a race horse from a corn plaster. A bookmaker that don't finish ahead on the season's a cuckoo. Now," he says, "if you'll excuse me for a few minutes, I'll go down to the paddock and see what's new."

So wile he was gone we had a chance to look round and they was plenty to see. It was a Saturday and a big crowd out. Lots of them was gals that you'd have to have a pick to break through to their regular face. Since they had their last divorce, about the only excitement they could enjoy was playing a long shot. Which reminds me that they's an old saying that nobody loves a fat man, but you go out to a race track or down to Atlantic City or any place where the former wifes hangs out and if you'll notice the birds with them, the gents that broke up their home, you'll find out that the most of them is guys with chins that runs into five and six figures and once round their waist is a sleeper jump.

Besides the Janes and the fat rascals with them, you seen a flock of ham actors that looked like they'd spent the night in a Chinese snowstorm, and maybe a half a dozen losers'-end boxers that'd used the bridge of their nose to block with and always got up in the morning just after the clock had struck ten, thinking they'd been counted out.

Pretty near everybody wore a pair of field glasses on a strap and when the race was going on they'd look through them and tell the world that the horse they'd bet on was three len'ths in front and just as good as in, but I never heard of a bookie paying off on that dope, and personally when some one would insist on lending me a pair to look through I couldn't tell if the things out there racing was horses or gnats.

Daley was back with us in a few minutes and says to Kate: "I guess you'll have to bet on yourself in the first race."

So she asked him what did he mean and he said: "I had a tip on a filly named Sweet and Pretty."

"O Mr. Daley!" says Kate.

"They don't expect her to win," says Daley, "but she's six, two and even, and I'm going to play her place and show."

Then he explained what that was and he said he was going to bet a thousand each way and finally the gals decided to go in for $10 apiece to show. It tickled them to death to find out that they didn't have to put up nothing. We found seats down in front wile Daley went to place the bets. Pretty soon the horses come out and Kate and Ella both screamed when they seen how cute the jockeys was dressed. Sweet and Pretty was No. 10 and had a combination of colors that would knock your eye out. Daley come back and explained that every owner had their own colors and of course the gals wanted to know what his was and he told them Navy blue and orange sleeves with black whoops on them and a blue cap.

"How beautiful!" says Ella. "I can't hardly wait to see them!"

"You must have wonderful taste in colors!" says Kate.

"Not only in colors," he says.

"O Mr. Daley!" she says again.

Well, the race was ran and No. 10 was a Sweet and Pretty last.

"Now," I says, "you O Mr. Daley."

The gals had yelped themself hoarse and didn't have nothing to say, but I could tell from their face that it would take something more than a few pretty speeches to make up for that twenty men.

"Never mind that!" says Daley. "She got a rotten ride. We'll get that back on the next one."

His hunch in the next one was Sena Day and he was betting a thousand on her to place at 4 to 1. He made the gals go in for $20 apiece, though they didn't do it with no pep. I went along with him to place the bets and he introduced me to a bookie so as I could bet a few smackers of my own when I felt like it. You know they's a law against betting unless it's a little bet between friends and in order to be a bookie's friend he's got to know your name. A quick friendship sprung up between I and a guy named Joe Meyer, and he not only give me his card but a whole deck of them. You see the law also says that when you make one of these bets with your pals he can't give you no writing to show for it, but he's generally always a man that makes a lot of friends and it seems like they all want to make friendly bets with him, and he can't remember where all his buddies lives, so he makes them write their name and ad- dress on the cards and how much the friendly wager is for and who on, and so forth, and the next day he mails them the bad news and they mail him back a check for same. Once in a wile, of course, you get the bad news and forget to mail him the check and he feels blue over it as they's nothing as sad as breaking up an old friendship.

I laid off Sena Day and she win. Daley smiled at the gals.

"There!" he says. "I'm sorry we didn't play her on the nose, but I was advised to play safe."

"Fine advice!" said Kate. "It's cost Sis and I $60 so far."

"What do you mean?" says Daley.

"We lose $20 on the first race," she says, "and you tell us we'll get it back on the next one and we bet the horse'll come second and it don't."

So we had to explain that if a horse win, why it placed, too, and her and Ella had grabbed $160 on that race and was $140 ahead. He was $2,000 winners himself.

"We'll have a drink on Sena," he says. "I don't believe they was six people out here that bet a nickel on her."

So Katie told him he was wonderful and him and the gals had a sarsaparilla or something and I poured my own. He'd been touting Cleopatra in the third race, but her and every- body else was scratched out of it except Captain Alcock and

On Watch. On Watch was 9 to 10 and Alcock even money and Daley wouldn't let us bet.

"On Watch is best," he says, "but he's giving away twenty pounds and you can't tell. Anyway, it ain't worth it at that price."

"Only two horses in the race?" asked Ella.

"That's all," he says.

"Well, then, listen," she says, all excited: "Why not bet on one of them for place?"

Daley laughed and said it was a grand idear only he didn't think the bookbinders would stand for it.

"But maybe they don't know," she says.

"I guess they do," said Daley. "It's almost impossible to keep a secret like that round a race track."

"Besides," I said, "the bookworms owes you and Kate $70 apiece and if you put something like that over on them and they find it out, they'll probably get even by making you a check on the West Bank of the Hudson River."

So we decided to play fair and lay off the race entirely. On Watch come through and the gals felt pretty bad about it till we showed them that they'd of only grabbed off nine smackers apiece if they'd of plunged on him for $20 straight.

Along toward time for the next race, Daley steered us down by the paddock and we seen some of the nags close up. Daley and the gals raved over this one and that one, and wasn't this one a beauty, and so forth. Personally they was all just a horse to me and I never seen one yet that wasn't homelier than the City Hall. If they left it up to me to name the world's champion eyesore, I'd award the elegant barb' wire wash rag to a horse rode by a woman in a derby hat. People goes to the Horse Show to see the Count de Fault; they don't know a case of withers from an off hind hock. And if the Sport of Kings was patronized by just birds that admires equine charms, you could park the Derby Day crowd in a phone booth.

A filly named Tamarisk was the favorite in the fourth race and Daley played her for eight hundred smackers at 4 to 5. The gals trailed along with $8 apiece and she win from here to Worcester. The fifth was the one that Daley had an entry in— a dog named Fly-by-Night. It was different in the daytime. Mercer had the mount and done the best he could, which was finish before supper. Nobody bet, so nobody was hurt.

"He's just a green colt," Daley told us. "I wanted to see how he'd behave."

"Well," I said, "I thought he behaved like a born caboose."

Daley liked the Waterbury entry in the last and him and the gals played it and win. All told, Daley was $4,000 ahead on the day and Ella and Kate had picked up $160 between them. They wanted to kiss everybody on the way out. Daley sent us to the car to wait for him. He wanted to see Mercer a minute. After a wile he come out and brought Mercer along and introduced him. He's a good-looking kid only for a couple of blotches on his pan and got an under lip and chin that kind of lags behind. He was about Kate's height, and take away his Adams apple and you could mail him to Duluth for six cents. Him and Kate got personal right away and she told him how different he looked now than in his riding make-up. He said he had a new outfit that he'd of wore if he'd knew she was looking on. So I said I hoped he didn't expect to ride Fly-by-Night round the track and keep a suit new, and he laughed, and Daley didn't seem to enjoy the conversation and said we'd have to be going, but when we started off, Kate and Mercer give each other a smile with a future in it. She's one of these gals that can't help from looking open house, even if the guy takes after a pelican.

Daley moved to our table that night and after that we eat breakfast and supper with him pretty near every day. After breakfast the gals would go down to New York to spend what they had win the day before, and I'll admit that Daley give us many a winner. I begin betting a little of my own jack, but I stuck the proceeds in the old sock. I ain't superstitious about living off a woman's money as long as you're legally married, but at the clip the two gals was going, it looked like their old man's war profits was on the way to join their maker, and the more jack I laid by, the less sooner I would have to go to work.

We'd meet every afternoon at the track and after the races Daley'd bring us back to the hotel. After supper we'd set round and chin or play rummy or once in a wile we'd go in Town to a show or visit one of the road houses near the Decker. The mail service on Long Island's kind of rotten and they's a bunch of road houses that hasn't heard of prohibition.

During the time we'd lived in Town Katie had got acquainted

with three or four birds that liked her well enough to take her places where they wasn't no cover charge, but since we'd moved to the Decker we hadn't heard from none of them. That is, till a few days after we'd met Daley, when she told us that one of the New York boys, a guy named Goldberg, had called up and wanted her to come in and see a show with him. He's a golf champion or something. Well, Daley offered to drive her in, but she said no, she'd rather go on the train and Goldberg was going to meet her. So she went, and Daley tried to play cards with Ella and I, but he was too restless and finally snuck up to his room.

They wasn't no question about his feelings toward Kate. He was always trying to fix it to be alone with her, but I guess it was the first time in her life when she didn't have to do most of the leading and she kept him at arm's len'th. Her and Ella had many a battle. Ella told her that the first thing she knowed he'd get discouraged and walk out on her; that she'd ought to quit monking and give him to understand that she was ready to yes him when he spoke up. But Katie said she guessed she could run her own love affairs as she'd had a few more of them than Ella.

So Ella says: "Maybe you have, but which one of us has got the husband?"

"You, thank the Lord!" says Katie.

"Thank him twice," I said.

Kate didn't come home from her New York party till two o'clock and she overslept herself till it was too late to go down again and shop. So we all drove over to the track with Daley and most of the way over he acted like a child. Katie kept talking about what a good show she seen and had a grand time, and so forth, and he pretended he wasn't listening. Finally she cut it out and give him the old oil and by the time we got to the clubhouse he'd tossed in the sponge.

That was the last day at Jamaica and a couple of his horses was in. We was all down on them and they both copped, though Mercer had to give one of them a dude ride to pull us through. Daley got maudlin about what a grand rider the kid was and a grand little fella besides, and he had half a notion to bring him along with us back to the hotel and show him a good time. But Kate said what was the use of an extra man, as it would kind of spoil things and she was satisfied with just

Daley. So of course that tickled him and everybody was feeling good and after supper him and Kate snuck out alone for the first time. Ella made me set up till they come back, so as she could get the news. Well, Daley had asked her all right, but she told him she wanted a little wile to think.

"Think!" says Ella. "What does she want to think for?"

"The novelty, I suppose," said I.

Only One was in the big stake race the next day, when we shifted over to Belmont. They was five or six others in with him, all of them pretty good, and the price on him was 3 to 1. He hadn't started yet since Daley'd brought him here, but they'd been nursing him along and Mercer and the trainer said he was right.

I suppose of course you've been out to Belmont. At that time they run the wrong way of the track, like you deal cards. Daley's table was in a corner of the clubhouse porch and when you looked up the track, the horses was coming right at you. Even the boys with the trick glasses didn't dast pretend they could tell who's ahead.

The Belmont national hymn is Whispering. The joint's so big and scattered round that a German could sing without disturbing the party at the next table. But they seems to be a rule that when they's anything to be said, you got to murmur it with the lips stuck to the opponent's earlobe. They shush you if you ask out loud for a toothpick. Everywheres you'll see two or three guys with their heads together in a whispering scene. One of them has generally always just been down to the horses' dining room and had lunch with Man o' War or somebody and they told him to play Sea Mint in the next race as Cleopatra had walked the stall all night with her foal. A little ways off they'll be another pair of shushers and one of them's had a phone call from Cleopatra's old dam to put a bet on Cleo as Captain Alcock had got a hold of some wild oats and they couldn't make him do nothing but shimmy.

If they's ten horses in a race you can walk from one end of the clubhouse to the other and get a whisper on all ten of them. I remember the second time Man o' War run there. They was only one horse that wanted to watch him from the track and the War horse was 1 to 100. So just before the race, if you want to call it that, I seen a wise cracker that I'd got acquainted with, that had always been out last night with Madden or Waterbury, so just kidding I walked up to him and asked him who he liked. So he motioned me to come over against the wall where they wasn't nobody near us and whispered, "Man o' War's unbeatable." You see if that remark had of been overheard and the news allowed to spread round, it might of forced the price to, say, 1 to a lump of coal, and spoiled the killing.

Well, wile the Jamaica meeting was on, the gals had spent some of their spare time figuring out how much they'd of been ahead if Daley had of let them bet more than ten to twenty smackers a race. So this day at Belmont, they said that if he liked Only One so much, he should ought to leave them raise the ante just once and play fifty apiece.

But he says: "No, not this time. I'm pretty sure he'll win, but he's in against a sweet field and he ain't raced for a month. I'll bet forty on the nose for the two of you, and if he looks good you can gamble some real money the next time he runs."

So Ella and Kate had to be satisfied with $20 apiece. Daley himself bet $2,000 and I piked along with $200 that I didn't tell the gals nothing about. We all got 3 to 1. A horse named Streak of Lightning was favorite at 6 to 5. It was a battle. Only One caught the Streak in the last step and win by a flea's jaw. Everybody was in hysterics and the gals got all messed up clawing each other.

"Nobody but Mercer could of did it!" says Daley, as soon as he could talk.

"He's some jockey!" yelled Kate. "O you Sid!"

Pretty soon the time was give out and Only One had broke the track record for the distance, whatever it was.

"He's a race horse!" said Daley. "But it's too bad he had to extend himself. We won't get no price the next time out."

Well, altogether the race meant $14,000 to Daley, and he said we'd all go to Town that night and celebrate. But when we got back to the Decker, they was a telegram for him and he had to pack up and beat it for Kentucky.

Daley being away didn't stop us from going to the track. He'd left orders with Ernest, his driver, to take us wherever we wanted to go and the gals had it so bad now that they couldn't hardly wait till afternoon. They kept on trimming the books, too. Kate got a phone call every morning that she said was from this Goldberg and he was giving her tips. Her and Ella played them and I wished I had. I would of if I'd knew who they was from. They was from Mercer, Daley's boy. That's who they was from.

I and Ella didn't wise up till about the third night after Daley'd went. That night, Kate took the train to Town right after supper, saying she had a date with Goldberg. It was a swell night and along about eight, I and Ella decided we might as well have a ride. So we got a hold of Ernest and it wound up by us going to New York too. We seen a picture and batted round till midnight and then Ella says why not go down to the Pennsylvania Station and pick Kate up when she come to take the train, and bring her home. So we done it. But when Katie showed up for the train, it was Mercer that was with her, not Goldberg.

Well, Mercer was pretty near out to the car with us when he happened to think that Daley's driver mustn't see him. So he said good night and left us. But he didn't do it quick enough. Daley's driver had saw him and I seen that he'd saw him and I knowed that he wasn't liable to be stuck on another of Daley's employs that was getting ten times as much money as him and all the cheers, and never had to dirty himself up changing a tire. And I bet it was all Ernest could do was wait till Daley come back so as he could explode the boom.

Kate and Ella didn't know Ernest was hep and I didn't tell them for fear of spoiling the show, so the women done their brawling on the way home in a regular race track whisper. The Mrs. told Kate she was a hick to be monking round with a jockey when Daley was ready and willing to give her a modern home with a platinum stopper in the washbowl. Kate told Ella that she wasn't going to marry nobody for their money, and besides, Mercer was making more than enough to support a wife, and how that boy can dance!

"But listen," she says: "I ain't married to neither one of them yet and don't know if I want to be."

"Well," says Ella, "you won't have no chance to marry Daley if he finds out about you and Mercer."

"He won't find out unless you tell him," said Kate.

"Well, I'll tell him," says Ella, "unless you cut this monkey business out."

"I'll cut it out when I get good and ready," says Kate. "You can tell Daley anything you please."

She knew they wasn't no chance of Ella making good.

"Daley'll be back in a couple of days," says the Mrs. "When he comes he'll want his answer and what are you going to say?"

"Yes or no, according to which way I make up my mind," said Kate. "I don't know yet which one I like best."

"That's ridic'lous!" Ella says. "When a girl says she can't make up her mind, it shows they's nothing to make up. Did you ever see me when I couldn't make up my mind?"

"No," said Katie, "but you never had even one whole man to choose between."

The last half of the ride neither of them were talking. That's a world's record in itself. They kind of made up the next morning after I'd told Ella that the surest way to knock Daley's chances for a gool was to paste Mercer.

"Just lay off of it," I told her. "The best man'll win in fair competition, which it won't be if you keep plugging for Daley."

We had two more pretty fair days at the track on Kate's tips that Mercer give her. We also went on a party with him down Town, but we used the train, not Daley's car.

Daley showed up on a Wednesday morning and had Ernest take him right over to the track. I suppose it was on this trip that Ernest squealed. Daley didn't act no different when we joined him on the clubhouse porch, but that night him and Kate took a ride alone and come back engaged.

They'd been pointing Only One for the Merrick Handicap, the fourth race on Saturday. It was worth about $7,000 to the winner. The distance was seven furlongs and Only One had top weight, 126 pounds. But Thursday he done a trial over the distance in 1.22, carrying 130 pounds, so it looked like a set-up.

Thursday morning I and Ella happened to be in Katie's room when the telephone rung. It was Mercer on the other end. He asked her something and she says: "I told you why in my note."

So he said something else and she says: "Not with no jail-bird."

And she hung up.

Well, Ella wanted to know what all the pleasantries was about, but Kate told her to mind her own business.

"You got your wish and I'm engaged to Daley," she says, "and that's all you need to know."

For a gal that was going to marry a dude that was supposed to have all the money in the world, she didn't act just right, but she wouldn't been Kate if she had of, so I didn't think much about it.

Friday morning I got a wire from one of the South Bend boys, Goat Anderson, sent from Buffalo, saying he'd be in New York that night and would I meet him at the Belmont at seven o'clock. So I went in Town from the track and waited round till pretty near nine, but he didn't show up. I started to walk across to the Pennsylvania Station and on the way I dropped in at a place where they was still taking a chance. I had one up at the bar and was throwing it into me when a guy in the back part yelled "Hey! Come here!" It was Mercer yelling and it was me he wanted.

He was setting at a table all alone with a highball. It didn't take no Craig Kennedy to figure out that it wasn't his first one.

"Set down before I bat you down!" he says.

"Listen," I says: "I wished you was champion of the world. You'd hold onto the title just long enough for me to reach over and sock you where most guys has a chin."

"Set down!" he says. "It's your wife I'm going to beat up, not you."

"You ain't going to beat up nobody's wife or nobody's husband," I says, "and if you don't cut out that line of gab you'll soon be asking the nurse how you got there."

"Set down and come clean with me," he says. "Was your wife the one that told Daley about your sister-in-law and I?"

"If she did, what of it?" I says.

"I'm asking you, did she?" he says.

"No, she didn't," I said. "If somebody told him his driver told him. He seen you the other night."

"Ernest!" he says. "Frank and Ernest! I'll Ernest him right in the jaw!"

"You're a fine matchmaker!" I says. "He could knock you for a row of flat tires. Why don't you try and get mad at Dempsey?"

"Set down and have a drink," says Mercer.

"I didn't mean that about your wife. You and her has treated me all right. And your sister-in-law, too, even if she did give me the air. And called me a jail-bird. But that's all right. It's Daley I'm after and it's Daley I'm going to get."

"Sweet chance!" I says. "What could you do to him?"

"Wait and see!" said Mercer, and smiled kind of silly.

"Listen," I says. "Have you forgot that you're supposed to ride Only One to-morrow?"

"Supposed to ride is right," he says, and smiled again.

"Ain't you going to ride him?" I said.

"You bet I am!" he says.

"Well, then," I said, "you better call it a day and go home."

"I'm over twenty-one," he says, "and I'm going to set here and enjoy myself. But remember, I ain't keeping you up."

Well, they wasn't nothing I could do only set there and wait for him to get stiff and then see him to his hotel. We had a drink and we had another and a couple more. Finally he opened up. I wished you could of heard him. It took him two hours to tell his story, and everything he said, he said it over and over and repeated it four and five times. And part of the time he talked so thick that I couldn't hardly get him.

"Listen," he says. "Can you keep a secret? Listen," he says. "I'm going to take a chance with you on account of your sister-in-law. I loved that little gal. She's give me the air, but that don't make no difference; I loved that little gal and I don't want her to lose no money. So I'm going to tell you a secret and if you don't keep your clam shut I'll roll you for a natural. In the first place," he says, "how do you and Daley stack up?"

"That ain't no secret," I said. "I think he's all right. He's been a good friend of mine."

"Oh," says Mercer, "so he's been a good friend of yours, has he? All right, then. I'm going to tell you a secret. Do you remember the day I met you and the gals in the car? Well, a couple of days later, Daley was feeling pretty good about something and he asked me how I liked his gal? So I told him she looked good. So he says, 'I'm going to marry that gal,' he says. He says, 'She likes me and her sister and brother-in-law is encouraging it along,' he says. 'They know I've got a little money and they're making a play for me. They're a couple of rats and I'm the cheese. They're going to make a meal off of me. They think they are,' he says. 'But the brother-in-law's a smart Aleck that thinks he's a wise cracker. He'd be a clown in a circus, only that's work. And his wife's fishing for a sucker with her sister for bait. Well, the gal's a pip and I'm going to marry her,' he says, 'but as soon as we're married, it's good-by, family-in-law! Me and them is going to be perfect strangers. They think they'll have free board and lodging at my house,' he says, 'but they won't get no meal unless they come to the back door for it, and when they feel sleepy they can make up a lower for themself on my cement porch.' That's the kind of a friend of yours this baby is," says Mercer.

I didn't say nothing and he went on.

"He's your friend as long as he can use you," he says. "He's been my friend since I signed to ride for him, that is, up till he found out I was stealing his gal. Then he shot my chances for a bull's-eye by telling her about a little trouble I had, five or six years ago. I and a girl went to a party down in Louisville and I seen another guy wink at her and I asked him what he meant by it and he said he had St. Vitus' dance. So I pulled the iron and knocked off a couple of his toes, to cure him. I was in eleven months and that's what Daley told Kate about. And of course he made her promise to not tell, but she wrote me a good-by note and spilled it. That's the kind of a pal he is.

"After I got out I worked for Bradley, and when Bradley turned me loose, he give me a $10,000 contract."

"He told us twenty," I said.

"Sure he did," says Mercer. "He always talks double. When he gets up after a tough night, both his heads aches. And if he ever has a baby he'll invite you over to see the twins. But anyway, what he pays me ain't enough and after to-morrow I'm through riding. What's ten or fifteen thousand a year when you can't drink nothing and you starve to death for the fear you'll pick up an ounce! Listen," he says. "I got a brother down in Oklahoma that's in the oil lease game. He cleaned up $25,000 last year and he wants me to go in with him. And with what I've saved up and what I'm going to win to-morrow, I should worry if we don't make nothing in the next two years."

"How are you going to win to-morrow?" I said. "The price'll be a joke."

"The price on who?" says Mercer.

"Only One," I said.

He give a silly laugh and didn't say nothing for a minute. Then he asked if Daley done the betting for I and the two gals. I told him he had did it at first, but now I was doing it.

"Well," he says, "you do it to-morrow, see? That little lady called me a jail-bird, but I don't want her to lose her money."

So I asked him what he meant and he asked me for the tenth or eleventh time if I could keep a secret. He made me hold up my hand and swear I wouldn't crack what he was going to tell me.

"Now," he says, "what's the name of the horse I'm riding to-morrow?"

"Only One," I said.

"That ain't all of it," said Mercer. "His name to-morrow is Only One Left. See? Only One Left."

"Do you mean he's going to get left at the post?" I says.

"You're a Ouija board!" says Mercer. "Your name is Ouija and the horse's name is Only One Left. And listen," he says. "Everything but three horses is going to be scratched out of this race and we'll open at about 1 to 3 and back up to 1 to 5. And Daley's going to bet his right eye. But they's a horse in the race named Sap and that's the horse my two thousand smackers is going down on. And you're a sap, too, if you don't string along with me."

"Suppose you can't hold Only One?"

"Get the name right," said Mercer. "Only One Left. And don't worry about me not handling him. He thinks I'm Billy Sunday and everything I say he believes. Do you remember the other day when I beat Streak of Lightning? Well, the way I done that was whispering in One's ear, coming down the stretch. I says to him, 'One,' I says, 'this Lightning hoss has been spilling it round that your father's grandmother was a zebra. Make a bum out of him!' That's what I whispered to him and he got sore and went past Lightning like he was standing still. And to-morrow, just before we're supposed to go, I'll say to him, 'One, we're back at Jamaica. You're facing the wrong way.' And when Sap and the other dog starts, we'll be headed towards Rhode Island and in no hurry to get there."

"Mercer," I said, "I don't suppose they's any use talking to you, but after all, you're under contract to give Daley the best you've got and it don't look to me just like you was treating him square."

"Listen!" he says. "Him and square don't rhyme. And besides, I won't be under contract to nobody by this time tomorrow. So you save your sermon for your own parish."

I don't know if you'll think I done right or not. Or I don't care. But what was the sense of me tipping off a guy that had said them sweet things about I and Ella? And even if I don't want a sister-in-law of mine running round with a guy that's got a jail record, still Daley squealing on him was rotten dope. And besides, I don't never like to break a promise, especially to a guy that shoots a man's toes off just for having St. Vitus' dance.

Well, anyway, the third race was over and the Merrick Handicap was next, and just like Mercer had said, they all quit but our horse and Sap and a ten-ton truck named Honor Bright. He was 20 to 1 and Sap was 6. Only One was 1 to 3 and Daley hopped on him with fifteen thousand men. Before post time the price was 1 to 5 and 1 to 6.

Daley was off his nut all afternoon and didn't object when I said I'd place the gals' money and save him the trouble. Kate and Ella had figured out what they had win up to date. It was about $1,200 and Daley told them to bet it all.

"You'll only make $400 between you," he says, "but it's a cinch."

"And four hundred's pretty good interest on $1,200," says Kate. "About ten per cent., ain't it?"

I left them and went downstairs. I wrote out a card for a hundred smackers on Sap. Then my feet caught cold and I didn't turn it in. I walked down towards the paddock and got there just as the boys was getting ready to parade. I seen Mercer and you wouldn't of never knew he'd fell off the wagon.

Daley was down there, too, and I heard him say: "Well, Sid, how about you?"

"Never better," says Mercer. "If I don't win this one I'll quit riding."

Then he seen me and smiled.

I chased back to the clubhouse, making up my mind on the way. I decided to not bet a nickel for the gals on anything. If Mercer was crossing me, I'd give Ella and Kate their $400 like they had win it, and say nothing. Personally, I was going to turn in the card I'd wrote on Sap. That was my idear when I got to Joe Meyer. But all of a sudden I had the hunch that Mercer was going through; they wasn't a chance in the world for him to weaken. I left Meyer's stand and went to a bookie named Haynes, who I'd bet with before.

Sap had went up to 8 to 1, and instead of a hundred smackers I bet a thousand.

He finished ahead by three len'ths, probably the most surprised horse in history. Honor Bright got the place, but only by a hair. Only One, after being detained for some reason another, come faster at the end than any horse ever run before. And Mercer give him an unmerciful walloping, pretending to himself, probably, that the hoss was its master.

We come back to our table. The gals sunk down in their chairs. Ella was blubbering and Kate was as white as a ghost. Daley finally joined us, looking like he'd had a stroke. He asked for a drink and I give him my flask.

"I can't understand it!" he says. "I don't know what happened!"

"You don't!" hollered Kate. "I'll tell you what happened. You stole our money! Twelve hundred dollars! You cheat!"

"Oh, shut your fool mouth!" says Daley.

And another Romance was knocked for a row of sour apple trees.

Kate brought the mail in the dining room Monday morning. They was a letter for her and one for me. She read hers and they was a couple of tears in her eyes.

"Mercer's quit riding," she says. "This is a farewell note. He's going to Oklahoma."

Ella picked up my envelope.

"Who's this from?" she says.

"Give it here," I said, and took it away from her. "It's just the statement from Haynes, the bookie."

"Well, open it up," she said.

"What for?" said I. "You know how much you lose, don't you?"

"He might of made a mistake, mightn't he?" she says.

So I opened up the envelope and there was the check for $8,000.

"Gosh!" I said. "It looks like it was me that made the mistake!" And I laid the check down where her and Kate could see it. They screamed and I caught Ella just as she was falling off the chair.

"What does this mean?" says Kate.

"Well," I said, "I guess I was kind of rattled Saturday, and when I come to make my bet I got balled up and wrote down Sap. And I must of went crazy and played him for a thousand men."

"But where's our statement, mine and Sis'?" says Ella.

"That's my mistake again," I said. "I wrote out your ticket, but I must of forgot to turn it in."

They jumped up and come at me, and before I could duck I was kissed from both sides at once.

"O Sis!" yelps the Mrs. "Just think! We didn't lose our twelve hundred! We didn't lose nothing at all. We win eight thousand dollars!"

"Try and get it!" I says.

CHAPTER V

Katie Wins a Home

O H YES, we been back here quite a wile. And we're liable to be here quite a wile. This town's good enough for me and it suits the Mrs. too, though they didn't neither one of us appreciate it till we'd give New York a try. If I was running the South Bend Boosters' club, I'd make everybody spend a year on the Gay White Way. They'd be so tickled when they got to South Bend that you'd never hear them razz the old burg again. Just yesterday we had a letter from Katie, asking us would we come and pay her a visit. She's a regular New Yorker now. Well, I didn't have to put up no fight with my Mrs. Before I could open my pan she says, "I'll write and tell her we can't come; that you're looking for a job and don't want to go nowheres just now."

Well, they's some truth in that. I don't want to go nowheres and I'll take a job if it's the right kind. We could get along on the interest from Ella's money, but I'm tired of laying round. I didn't do a tap of work all the time I was east and I'm out of the habit, but the days certainly do drag when a man ain't got nothing to do and if I can find something where I don't have to travel, I'll try it out.

But the Mrs. has still got most of what the old man left her and all and all, I'm glad we made the trip. I more than broke even by winning pretty close to $10,000 on the ponies down there. And we got Katie off our hands, which was one of the objects of us going in the first place—that and because the two gals wanted to see Life. So I don't grudge the time we spent, and we had some funny experiences when you look back at them. Anybody does that goes on a tour like that with a cuckoo like Katie. You hear a lot of songs and gags about mother-in-laws. But I could write a book of them about sister-in-laws that's twenty years old and pretty and full of peace and good will towards Men.

Well, after the blow-off with Daley, Long Island got too slow, besides costing us more than we could afford. So the gals suggested moving back in Town, to a hotel called the Graham on Sixty-seventh Street that somebody had told them was reasonable.

They called it a family hotel, but as far as I could see, Ella and I was the only ones there that had ever forced two dollars on the clergy. Outside of the transients, they was two song writers and a couple of gals that had their hair pruned and wrote for the papers, and the rest of the lodgers was boys that had got penned into a sixteen-foot ring with Benny Leonard by mistake. They looked like they'd spent many an evening hanging onto the ropes during the rush hour.

When we'd staid there two days, Ella and Katie was ready to pack up again.

"This is just a joint," said Ella. "The gals may be all right, but they're never in, only to sleep. And the men's impossible; a bunch of low prize-fighters."

I was for sticking, on account of the place being cheap, so I said:

"Second prize ain't so low. And you're overlooking the two handsome tune thiefs. Besides, what's the difference who else lives here as long as the rooms is clean and they got a good restaurant? What did our dude cellmates out on Long Island get us? Just trouble!"

But I'd of lose the argument as usual only for Kate oversleeping herself. It was our third morning at the Graham and her and Ella had it planned to go and look for a better place. But Katie didn't get up till pretty near noon and Ella went without her. So it broke so's Sis had just came downstairs and turned in her key when the two bellhops reeled in the front door bulging with baggage and escorting Mr. Jimmy Ralston. Yes, Jimmy Ralston the comedian. Or comic, as he calls it.

Well, he ain't F. X. Bushman, as you know. But no one that seen him could make the mistake of thinking he wasn't somebody. And he looked good enough to Kate so as she waited till the clerk had him fixed up, and then ast who he was. The clerk told her and she told us when the Mrs. come back from her hunt. Ella begin to name a few joints where we might move, but it seemed like Sis had changed her mind.

"Oh," she says, "let's stay here a wile longer, a week anyway."

"What's came over you!" ast Ella. "You just said last night that you was bored to death here."

"Maybe we won't be so bored now," said Kate, smiling. "The Graham's looking up. We're entertaining a celebrity— Jimmy Ralston of the Follies."

Well, they hadn't none of us ever seen him on the stage, but of course we'd heard of him. He'd only just started with the Follies, but he'd made a name for himself at the Winter Garden, where he broke in two or three years ago. And Kate said that a chorus gal she'd met—Jane Abbott—had told her about Ralston and what a scream he was on a party.

"He's terribly funny when he gets just the right number of drinks," says Kate.

"Well, let's stay then," says Ella. "It'll be exciting to know a real actor."

"I would like to know him," says Katie, "not just because he's on the stage, but I think it'd be fun to set and listen to him talk. He must say the screamingest things! If we had him round we wouldn't have to play cards or nothing for entertainment. Only they say it makes people fat to laugh."

"If I was you, I'd want to get fat," I said. "Looking like an E string hasn't started no landslide your way."

"Is he attractive?" ast the Mrs.

"Well," said Kate, "he isn't handsome, but he's striking looking. You wouldn't never think he was a comedian. But then, ain't it generally always true that the driest people have sad faces?"

"That's a joke!" I said. "Did you ever see Bryan when he didn't look like somebody was tickling his feet?"

"We'll have to think up some scheme to get introduced to him," says Ella.

"It'll be tough," I says. "I don't suppose they's anybody in the world harder to meet than a member of the Follies, unless it's an Elk in a Pullman washroom."

"But listen," says Kate: "We don't want to meet him till we've saw the show. It'd be awfully embarrassing to have him ask us how we liked the Follies and we'd have to say we hadn't been to it."

"Yes," said the Mrs., "but still if we tell him we haven't been to it, he may give us free passes."

"Easy!" I said. "And it'd take a big load off his mind. They say it worries the Follies people half sick wondering what to do with all their free passes."

"Suppose we go to-night!" says Kate. "We can drop in a hotel somewheres and get seats. The longer we don't go, the longer we won't meet him."

"And the longer we don't meet him," I says, "the longer till he gives you the air."

"I'm not thinking of Mr. Ralston as a possible suitor," says Katie, swelling up. "But I do want to get acquainted with a man that don't bore a person to death."

"Well," I says, "if this baby's anything like the rest of your gentleman friends, he won't hardly be round long enough for that."

I didn't make no kick about going to the show. We hadn't spent no money since we'd moved back to Town and I was as tired as the gals of setting up in the room, playing rummy. They said we'd have to dress, and I kicked just from habit, but I'd got past minding that end of it. They was one advantage in dolling up every time you went anywheres. It meant an hour when they was no chance to do something even sillier.

We couldn't stop to put on the nose bag at the Graham because the women was scared we'd be too late to get tickets. Besides, when you're dressed for dinner, you at least want the waiter to be the same. So we took a taxi down to the Spencer, bought Follies seats in the ninth row, and went in to eat. It's been in all the papers that the price of food has came down, but the hotel man can't read. They fined us eleven smackers for a two-course banquet that if the Woman's Guild, here, would dast soak you four bits a plate for it, somebody'd write a nasty letter to the News-Times.

We got in the theater a half hour before the show begin. I put in the time finding out what the men will wear, and the gals looked up what scenes Ralston'd be in. He was only on once in each act. They don't waste much time on a comedian in the Follies. It don't take long to spring the two gags they can think up for him in a year, and besides, he just interferes with the big gal numbers, where Bunny Granville or somebody dreams of the different flappers he danced with at the prom, and the souvenirs they give him; and one by one the different gals writhes in, dressed like the stage director thinks they dress at the female colleges—a Wesley gal in pink tights, a Vassar dame in hula-hula, and a Smith gal with a sombrero and a sailor suit. He does a couple of steps with them and they each hand him a flower or a vegetable to remember them by. The song winds up:

> *But my most exclusive token*
> *Is a little hangnail broken*
> *Off the gal from Gussie's School for Manicures.*

And his real sweet patootie comes on made up as a scissors.

You've saw Ralston? He's a good comedian; no getting away from that. The way he fixes up his face, you laugh just to look at him. I yelled when I first seen him. He was supposed to be an office boy and he got back late from lunch and the boss ast him what made him late and he said he stopped to buy the extra. So the boss ast him what extra and he says the extra about the New York society couple getting married. So the boss said, "Why, they wouldn't print an extra about that. They's a New York society couple married most every day." So Ralston said, "Yes, but this couple is both doing it for the first time."

I don't remember what other gags he had, and they're old anyway by now. But he was a hit, especially with Ella and Kate. They screamed so loud I thought we'd get the air. If he didn't say a word, he'd be funny with that fool make-up and that voice.

I guess if it wasn't for me the gals would of insisted on going back to the stage door after the show and waiting for him to come out. I've saw Katie bad a lot of times, but never as cuckoo as this. It wasn't no case of love at first or second sight. You couldn't be stuck on this guy from seeing him. But she'd always been kind of stage-struck and was crazy over the idear of getting acquainted with a celebrity, maybe going round to places with him, and having people see her with Jimmy Ralston, the comedian. And then, of course, most anybody wants to meet a person that can make you laugh.

I managed to persuade them that the best dope would be to go back to the Graham and wait for him to come home; maybe we could fix it up with the night clerk to introduce us. I told them that irregardless of what you read in books, they's some members of the theatrical profession that occasionally visits the place where they sleep. So we went to the hotel and set in the lobby for an hour and a half, me trying to keep awake wile the gals played

Ralston's part of the show over again a couple thousand times. They's nothing goes so big with me as listening to people repeat gags out of a show that I just seen.

The clerk had been tipped off and when Ralston finally come in and went to get his key, I strolled up to the desk like I was after mine. The clerk introduced us.

"I want you to meet my wife and sister-in-law," I said.

"Some other time," says Ralston. "They's a matinée to-morrow and I got to run off to bed."

So off he went and I got bawled out for Ziegfeld having matinées. But I squared myself two days afterwards when we went in the restaurant for lunch. He was just having breakfast and the three of us stopped by his table. I don't think he remembered ever seeing me before, but anyway he got up and shook hands with the women. Well, you couldn't never accuse Ella of having a faint heart, and she says:

"Can't we set down with you, Mr. Ralston? We want to tell you how much we enjoyed the Follies."

So he says, sure, set down, but I guess we would of anyway.

"We thought it was a dandy show," says Katie.

"It ain't a bad troupe," says Ralston.

"If you'll pardon me getting personal," said Ella, "we thought you was the best thing in it."

He looked like he'd strain a point and forgive her.

"We all just yelled!" says Katie. "I was afraid they'd put us out, you made us laugh so hard."

"Well," says Ralston, "I guess if they begin putting people out for that, I'd have to leave the troupe."

"It wouldn't be much of a show without you," says Ella.

"Well, all that keeps me in it is friendship for Ziggy," says Ralston. "I said to him last night, I says, 'Ziggy, I'm going to quit the troupe. I'm tired and I want to rest a wile.' So he says, 'Jim, don't quit or I'll have to close the troupe. I'll give you fifteen hundred a week to stay.' I'm getting a thousand now. But I says to him, I said, 'Ziggy, it ain't a question of money. What I want is a troupe of my own, where I get a chance to do serious work. I'm sick of making a monkey of myself in front of a bunch of saps from Nyack that don't appreciate no art but what's wrapped up in a stocking.' So he's promised that if I'll stick it out this year, he'll star me next season in a serious piece."

"Is he giving you the five hundred raise?" I ast him.

"I wouldn't take it," said Ralston. "I don't need money."

"At that, a person can live pretty cheap at this hotel," I says.

"I didn't move here because it was cheap," he said. "I moved here to get away from the pests—women that wants my autograph or my picture. And all they could say how much they enjoyed my work and how did I think up all them gags, and so forth. No real artist likes to talk about himself, especially to people that don't understand. So that's the reason why I left the Ritz, so's I'd be left alone, not to save money. And I don't save no money, neither. I've got the best suite in the house—bedroom, bath and study."

"What do you study?" ast Kate.

"The parts I want to play," he says; "Hamlet and Macbeth and Richard."

"But you're a comedian," says Kate.

"It's just a stepping stone," said Ralston.

He'd finished his breakfast and got up.

"I must go to my study and work," he says. "We'll meet again."

"Yes, indeed," says Ella. "Do you always come right back here nights after the show?"

"When I can get away from the pests," he says.

"Well," says Ella, "suppose you come up to our rooms tonight and we'll have a bite to eat. And I think the husband can give you a little liquid refreshments if you ever indulge."

"Very little," he says. "What is your room number?"

So the Mrs. told him and he said he'd see us after the show that night, and walked out.

"Well," said Ella, "how do you like him?"

"I think he's wonderful!" says Katie. "I didn't have no idear he was so deep, wanting to play Hamlet."

"Pretty near all comedians has got that bug," I says.

"Maybe he's different when you know him better," said Ella.

"I don't want him to be different," says Kate.

"But he was so serious," said the Mrs. "He didn't say nothing funny."

"Sure he did," I says. "Didn't he say artists hate to talk about themselfs?"

Pretty soon the waiter come in with our lunch. He ast us if the other gentleman was coming back.

"No," said Ella. "He's through."

"He forgot his check," says the dish smasher.

"Oh, never mind!" says Ella. "We'll take care of that."

"Well," I says, "I guess the bird was telling the truth when he said he didn't need no money."

I and the gals spent the evening at a picture show and stopped at a delicatessen on the way home to stock up for the banquet. I had a quart and a pint of yearling rye, and a couple of bottles of McAllister that they'd fined me fifteen smackers apiece for and I wanted to save them, so I told Kate that I hoped her friend would get comical enough on the rye.

"He said he drunk very little," she reminded me.

"Remember, don't make him talk about himself," said the Mrs. "What we want is to have him feel at home, like he was with old friends, and then maybe he'll warm up. I hope we don't wake the whole hotel, laughing."

Well, Ralston showed about midnight. He'd remembered his date and apologized for not getting there before.

"I like to walk home from the theater," he says. "I get some of my funniest idears wile I walk."

I come to the conclusion later that he spent practically his whole life riding.

Ella's and my room wasn't no gymnasium for size and after the third drink, Ralston tried to get to the dresser to look at himself in the glass, and knocked a $30 vase for a corpse. This didn't go very big with the Mrs., but she forced a smile and would of accepted his apology if he'd made any. All he done was mumble something about cramped quarters. They was even more cramped when we set the table for the big feed, and it was my tough luck to have our guest park himself in the chair nearest the clothes closet, where my two bottles of Scotch had been put to bed. The fourth snifter finished the pint of rye and I said I'd get the other quart, but before I could stop her, Ella says:

"Let Mr. Ralston get it. It's right there by him."

So the next thing you know, James has found the good stuff and he comes out with both bottles of it.

"McAllister!" he says. "That's my favorite. If I'd knew you had that, I wouldn't of drank up all your rye."

"You haven't drank it all up," I says. "They's another bottle of it in there."

"It can stay there as long as we got this," he says, and helped himself to the corkscrew.

Well, amongst the knickknacks the gals had picked up at the delicatessen was a roast chicken and a bottle of olives, and at the time I thought Ralston was swallowing bones, stones and all. It wasn't till the next day that we found all these keepsakes on the floor, along with a couple dozen assorted cigarette butts.

Katie's chorus gal friend had told her how funny the guy was when he'd had just the right number of shots, but I'd counted eight and begin to get discouraged before he started talking.

"My mother could certainly cook a chicken," he says.

"Is your mother living?" Kate ast him.

"No," he says. "She was killed in a railroad wreck. I'll never forget when I had to go and identify her. You wouldn't believe a person could get that mangled! No," he says, "my family's all gone. I never seen my father. He was in the pesthouse with smallpox when I was born and he died there. And my only sister died of jaundice. I can still ——"

But Kate was scared we'd wake up the hotel, laughing, so she says: "Do you ever give imitations?"

"You mustn't make Mr. Ralston talk about himself," says Ella.

"Imitations of who?" said Ralston.

"Oh, other actors," said Katie.

"No," he says. "I leave it to the other actors to give imitations of me."

"I never seen none of them do it," says Kate.

"They all do it, but they don't advertise it," he says. "Every comic in New York is using my stuff."

"Oh!" said Ella. "You mean they steal your idears."

"Can't you go after them for it?" ast Katie.

"You could charge them with petit larceny," I said.

"I wouldn't be mean," said Ralston. "But they ain't a comic on the stage today that I didn't give him every laugh he's got."

"You ain't only been on the stage three or four years," I says. "How did Hitchcock and Ed Wynn and them fellas get by before they seen you?"

"They wasn't getting by," he says. "I'm the baby that put them on their feet. Take Hitchy. Hitchy come to me last spring and says, 'Jim, I've ran out of stuff. Have you got any notions I could use?' So I says, 'Hitchy, you're welcome to anything I got.' So I give him a couple of idears and they're the only laughs in his troupe. And you take Wynn. He opened up with a troupe that looked like a flop and one day I seen him on Broadway, wearing a long pan, and I says, 'What's the matter, Eddie?' And he brightened up and says, 'Hello, there, Jim! You're just the boy I want to see.' So I says, 'Well, Eddie, I'm only too glad to do anything I can.' So he says, 'I got a flop on my hands unlest I can get a couple of idears, and you're the baby that can give them to me.' So I said, 'All right, Eddie.' And I give him a couple of notions to work on and they made his show. And look at Stone! And Errol! And Jolson and Tinney! Every one of them come to me at one time another, hollering for help. 'Jim, give me a couple of notions!' 'Jim, give me a couple of gags!' And not a one of them went away empty-handed."

"Did they pay you?" ast Ella.

Ralston smiled.

"I wouldn't take no actor's money," he says. "They're all brothers to me. They can have anything I got, and I can have anything they got, only they haven't got nothing."

Well, I can't tell you all he said, as I was asleep part of the time. But I do remember that he was the one that had give Bert Williams the notion of playing coon parts, and learnt Sarah Bernhardt to talk French.

Along about four o'clock, when they was less than a pint left in the second McAllister bottle, he defied all the theater managers in New York.

"I ain't going to monkey with them much longer!" he says. "I'll let you folks in on something that'll cause a sensation on Broadway. I'm going to quit the Follies!"

We was all speechless.

"That's the big secret!" he says. "I'm coming out as a star under my own management and in a troupe wrote and produced by myself!"

"When?" ast Kate.

"Just as soon as I decide who I'm going to let in as part

owner," said Ralston. "I've worked for other guys long enough! Why should I be satisfied with $800 a week when Ziegfeld's getting rich off me!"

"When did he cut you $200?" I says. "You was getting $1,000 last time I seen you."

He didn't pay no attention.

"And why should I let some manager produce my play," he says, "and pay me maybe $1,200 a week when I ought to be making six or seven thousand!"

"Are you working on your play now?" Kate ast him.

"It's done," he says. "I'm just trying to make up my mind who's the right party to let in on it. Whoever it is, I'll make him rich."

"I've got some money to invest," says Katie. "Suppose you tell us about the play."

"I'll give you the notion, if you'll keep it to yourself," says Ralston. "It's a serious play with a novelty idear that'll be a sensation. Suppose I go down to my suite and get the script and read it to you."

"Oh, if you would!" says Kate.

"It'll knock you dead!" he says.

And just the thought of it was fatal to the author. He got up from his chair, done a nose dive acrost the table and laid there with his head in the chili sauce.

I called up the clerk and had him send up the night bellhop with our guest's key. I and the boy acted as pall bearers and got him to his "suite," where we performed the last sad rites. Before I come away I noticed that the "suite" was a ringer for Ella's and mine—a dinky little room with a bath. The "study" was prettily furnished with coat hangers.

When I got back to my room Katie'd ducked and the Mrs. was asleep, so I didn't get a chance to talk to them till we was in the restaurant at noon. Then I ast Kate if she'd figured out just what number drink it was that had started him being comical.

"Now listen," she says: "I don't think that Abbott girl ever met him in her life. Anyway, she had him all wrong. We expected he'd do stunts, like she said, but he ain't that kind that shows off or acts smart. He's too much of a man for that. He's a bigger man than I thought."

"I and the bellhop remarked that same thing," I says.

"And you needn't make fun of him for getting faint," says Katie. "I called him up a wile ago to find out how he was and he apologized and said they must of been something in that second bottle of Scotch."

So I says:

"You tell him they was, but they ain't."

Well, it couldn't of been the Scotch or no other brew that ruined me. Or if it was, it worked mighty slow. I didn't even look at a drink for three days after the party in our room. But the third day I felt rotten, and that night I come down with a fever. Ella got scared and called a doctor and he said it was flu, and if I didn't watch my step it'd be something worse. He advised taking me to a hospital and I didn't have pep enough to say no.

So they took me and I was pretty sick for a couple of weeks—too sick for the Mrs. to give me the news. And it's a wonder I didn't have a relapse when she finally did.

"You'll probably yelp when you hear this," she says. "I ain't crazy about it myself, but it didn't do me no good to argue at first and it's too late for argument now. Well, to begin with, Sis is in love with Ralston."

"What of it!" I said. "She's going through the city directory and she's just got to the R's."

"No, it's the real thing this time," said the Mrs. "Wait till you hear the rest of it. She's going on the stage!"

"I've got nothing against that," I says. "She's pretty enough to get by in the Follies chorus, and if she can earn money that way, I'm for it."

"She ain't going into no chorus," said Ella. "Ralston's quit the Follies and she's going in his show."

"The one he wrote?" I ast.

"Yes," said the Mrs.

"And who's going to put it on?" I ast her.

"That's it," she says. "They're going to put it on themself, Ralston and Sis. With Sis's money. She sold her bonds, fifty thousand dollars' worth."

"But listen," I says. "Fifty thousand dollars! What's the name of the play, Ringling's Circus?"

"It won't cost all that," said Ella. "They figure it'll take less than ten thousand to get started. But she insisted on having the whole thing in a checking account, where she can get at it. If the show's a big success in New York they're going to have a company in Chicago and another on the road. And Ralston says her half of the profits in New York ought to run round $5,000 a week. But anyway, she's sure of $200 a week salary for acting in it."

"Where did she get the idear she can act?" I says.

"She's always had it," said the Mrs., "and I think she made him promise to put her in the show before she agreed to back it. Though she says it's a wonderful investment! She won't be the leading woman, of course. But they's only two woman's parts and she's got one of them."

"Well," I said, "if she's going to play a sap and just acts normal, she'll be a sensation."

"I don't know what she'll be," says Ella. "All I know is that she's mad over Ralston and believes everything he says. And even if you hadn't of been sick we couldn't of stopped her."

So I ast what the play was like, but Ella couldn't tell me. Ralston had read it out loud to she and Kate, but she couldn't judge from just hearing it that way. But Kate was tickled to death with it. And they'd already been rehearsing a week, but Sis hadn't let Ella see the rehearsals. She said it made her nervous.

"Ralson thinks the main trouble will be finding a theater," said the Mrs. "He says they's a shortage of them and the men that owns them won't want to let him have one on account of jealousy."

"Has the Follies flopped?" I ast her.

"No," she says, "but they've left town."

"They always do, this time of year," I said.

"That's what I thought," says the Mrs., "but Ralston says they'd intended to stay here all the year round, but when the news come out that he'd left, they didn't dast. He's certainly got faith in himself. He must have, to give up a $600 a week salary. That's what he says he was really getting."

"You say Katie's in love," I says. "How about him?"

"I don't know and she don't know," says Ella. "He calls her dearie and everything and holds her hands, but when they're alone together, he won't talk nothing but business. Still, as I say, he calls her dearie."

"Actors calls every gal that," I says. "It's because they can't remember names."

Well, to make a short story out of it, they had another couple weeks' rehearsals that we wasn't allowed to see, and they finally got a theater—the Olney. They had to guarantee a $10,000 business to get it. They didn't go to Atlantic City or nowheres for a tryout. They opened cold. And Ralston didn't tell nobody what kind of a show it was.

Of course he done what they generally always do on a first night. He sent out free passes to everybody that's got a dress suit, and they's enough of them in New York to pretty near fill up a theater. These invited guests is supposed to be for the performance wile it's going on. After it's through, they can go out and ride it all over the island.

Well, the rules wasn't exactly lived up to at "Bridget Sees a Ghost." On account of Ralston writing the play and starring in it, the gang thought it would be comical and they come prepared to laugh. It was comical all right, and they laughed. They didn't only laugh; they yelled. But they yelled in the wrong place.

The programme said it was "a Daring Drama in Three Acts." The three acts was what made it daring. It took nerve to even have one. In the first place, this was two years after the armistice and the play was about the war, and I don't know which the public was most interested in by this time—the war or Judge Parker.

Act I was in July, 1917. Ralston played the part of Francis Shaw, a captain in the American army. He's been married a year, and when the curtain goes up, his wife's in their New York home, waiting for him to come in from camp on his weekly leave. She sets reading the war news in the evening paper, and she reads it out loud, like people always do when they're alone, waiting for somebody. Pretty soon in comes Bridget, the Irish maid—our own dear Katie. And I wished you could of heard her brogue. And seen her gestures. What she reminded me most like was a gal in a home talent minstrels giving an imitation of Lew Fields playing the part of the block system on the New York Central. Her first line was, "Ain't der captain home yed?" But I won't try and give you her dialect.

"No," says Mrs. Shaw. "He's late." So Katie says better late than never, and the wife says, yes, but she's got a feeling that some day it'll be never; something tells her that if he ever goes to France, he won't come back. So Bridget says, "You been reading the war news again and it always makes you sad." "I hate wars!" says Mrs. Shaw, and that line got one of the biggest laughs.

After this they was a couple of minutes when neither of them could think of nothing to add, and then the phone rung and Bridget answered it. It was Capt. Shaw, saying he'd be there pretty soon; so Bridget goes right back to the kitchen to finish getting dinner, but she ain't no sooner than left the stage when Capt. Shaw struts in. He must of called up from the public booth on his front porch.

The audience had a tough time recognizing him without his comic make-up, but when they did they give him a good hand. Mrs. Shaw got up to greet him, but he brushed by her and come down to the footlights to bow. Then he turned and went back to his Mrs., saying "Maizie!" like this was the last place he expected to run acrost her. They kissed and then he ast her "Where is Bobbie, our dear little one?"—for fear she wouldn't know whose little one he meant. So she rung a bell and back come Bridget, and he says "Well, Bridget!" and Bridget says, "Well, it's the master!" This line was another riot. "Bring the little one, Bridget," says Mrs. Shaw, and the audience hollered again.

Wile Bridget was after the little one, the captain celebrated the reunion by walking round the room, looking at the pictures. Bridget brings the baby in and the captain uncovers its face and says, "Well, Bobbie!" Then he turns to his wife and says, "Let's see, Maizie. How old is he?" "Two weeks," says Maizie. "Two weeks!" says Captain Shaw, surprised. "Well," he says, "I hope by the time he's old enough to fight for the Stars and Stripes, they won't be no such a thing as war." So Mrs. Shaw says, "And I hope his father won't be called on to make the supreme sacrifice for him and we others that must stay home and wait. I sometimes think that in wartime, it's the women and children that suffers most. Take him back to his cozy cradle, Bridget. We mothers must be careful of our little ones. Who knows when the kiddies will be our only comfort!" So Bridget beat it out with the little one and I bet he hated to leave all the gayety.

"Well," says Shaw to his wife, "and what's the little woman been doing?"

"Just reading," she says, "reading the news of this horrible war. I don't never pick up the paper but what I think that some day I'll see your name amongst the dead."

"Well," says the captain bravely, "they's no danger wile I stay on U. S. soil. But only for you and the little one, I would welcome the call to go Over There and take my place in the battle line. The call will come soon, I believe, for they say France needs men." This rumor pretty near caused a riot in the audience and Ralston turned and give us all a dirty look.

Then Bridget come in again and said dinner was ready, and Shaw says, "It'll seem funny to set down wile I eat." Which was the first time I ever knew that army captains took their meals off the mantelpiece.

Wile the Shaws was out eating, their maid stayed in the living room, where she'd be out of their way. It seems that Ralston had wrote a swell speech for her to make in this spot, about what a tough thing war is, to come along and separate a happy young couple like the Shaws that hadn't only been married a year. But the speech started "This is terrible!" and when Bridget got that much of it out, some egg in the gallery hollered "You said a mouthful, kid!" and stopped the show.

The house finally quieted down, but Katie was dumb for the first time in her life. She couldn't say the line that was the cue for the phone to ring, and she had to go over and answer a silent call. It was for the captain, and him and his wife both come back on the stage.

"Maizie," he says, after he'd hung up, "it's came! That was my general! We sail for France in half an hour!"

"O husband!" says Maizie. "This is the end!"

"Nonsense!" says Shaw with a brave smile. "This war means death for only a small per cent. of our men."

"And almost no captains," yells the guy in the gallery.

Shaw gets ready to go, but she tells him to wait till she puts on her wraps; she'll go down to the dock and see him off.

"No, darling," he says. "Our orders is secret. I can't give you the name of our ship or where we're sailing from."

So he goes and she flops on the couch w'ining because he

wouldn't tell her whether his ship left from Times Square or Grand Central.

They rung the curtain down here to make you think six days has passed. When it goes up again, Maizie's setting on the couch, holding the little one. Pretty soon Bridget comes in with the evening paper.

"They's a big headline, mum," she says. "A troopship has been torpedoed."

Well, when she handed her the paper, I could see the big headline. It said, "Phillies Hit Grimes Hard." But Maizie may of had a bet on Brooklyn. Anyway, she begin trembling and finally fell over stiff. So Bridget picked up the paper and read it out loud:

"Amongst the men lost was Capt. F. Shaw of New York."

Down went the curtain again and the first act was over, and some jokesmith in the audience yelled "Author! Author!"

"He's sunk!" said the egg in the gallery.

Well, Maizie was the only one in the whole theater that thought Shaw was dead. The rest of us just wished it. Still you couldn't blame her much for getting a wrong idear, as it was Nov. 11, 1918—over a year later—when the second act begins, and she hadn't heard from him in all that time. It wasn't never brought out why. Maybe he'd forgot her name or maybe it was Burleson's fault, like everything else.

The scene was the same old living room and Maizie was setting on the same old couch, but she was all dressed up like Elsie Ferguson. It comes out that she's expecting a gentleman friend, a Mr. Thornton, to dinner. She asks Bridget if she thinks it would be wrong of her to accept the guy the next time he proposed. He's ast her every evening for the last six months and she can't stall him much longer. So Bridget says it's all right if she loves him, but Maizie don't know if she loves him or not, but he looks so much like her late relic that she can't hardly tell the difference and besides, she has got to either marry or go to work, or her and the little one will starve. They's a knock at the door and Thornton comes in. Him and the absent captain looks as much alike as two brothers, yours and mine. Bridget ducks and Thornton proposes. Maizie says, "Before I answer, I must tell you a secret. Captain Shaw didn't leave me all alone. I have a little one, a boy." "Oh, I love kiddies," says Thornton. "Can I see him?" So she says it's seven o'clock and the little one's supposed to of been put to bed, but she has Bridget go get him.

The little one's entrance was the sensation of this act. In Act I he was just three or four towels, but now Bridget can't even carry him acrost the stage, and when she put him on his feet, he comes up pretty near to her shoulder. And when Thornton ast him would he like to have a new papa, he says, "Yes, because my other papa's never coming back."

Well, they say a woman can't keep a secret, but if Thornton had been nosing round for six months and didn't know till now that they was a spanker like Bobbie in the family circle, I wouldn't hardly call Maizie the town gossip.

After the baby'd went back to read himself to sleep and Mrs. Shaw had yessed her new admirer, Bridget dashed in yelling that the armistice was signed and held up the evening paper for Maizie and Thornton to see. The great news was announced in code. It said: "Phillies Hit Grimes Hard." And it seemed kind of silly to not come right out and say "Armistice Signed!" Because as I recall, even we saps out here in South Bend had knew it since three o'clock that morning.

The last act was in the same place, on Christmas Eve, 1918.

Maizie and her second husband had just finished doing up presents for the little one. We couldn't see the presents, but I suppose they was giving him a cocktail shaker and a shaving set. Though when he come on the stage you could see he hadn't aged much since Act 2. He hadn't even begin to get bald.

Thornton and the Mrs. went off somewheres and left the kid alone, but all of a sudden the front door opened and in come old Cap Shaw, on crutches. He seen the kid and called to him. "Who are you?" says the little one. "I'm Santa Claus," says the Cap, "and I've broughten you a papa for Christmas." "I don't want no papa," says Bobbie. "I've just got a new one." Then Bridget popped in and seen "the master" and hollered, "A ghost!" So he got her calmed down and she tells him what's came off. "It was in the paper that Capt. F. Shaw of New York was lost," she says. "It must of been another Capt. F. Shaw!" he says.

"It's an odd name," hollered the guy in the gallery.

The Captain thinks it all over and decides it's his move. He makes Bridget promise to never tell that she seen him and he says good-by to she and the kid and goes out into the night.

Maizie comes in, saying she heard a noise and what was it? Was somebody here? "Just the boy with the evening paper," says Bridget. And the cat's got Bobbie's tongue. And Maizie don't even ask for the paper. She probably figured to herself it was the old story; that Grimes was still getting his bumps.

Well, I wished you could of read what the papers wrote up about the show. One of them said that Bridget seen a ghost at the Olney theater last night and if anybody else wanted to see it, they better go quick because it wouldn't be walking after this week. Not even on crutches. The mildest thing they said about Ralston was that he was even funnier than when he was in the Follies and tried to be. And they said the part of Bridget was played by a young actress that they hoped would make a name for herself, because Ralston had probably called her all he could think of.

We waited at the stage door that night and when Kate come out, she was crying. Ralston had canned her from the show.

"That's nothing to cry about," I says. "You're lucky! It's just like as if a conductor had put you off a train a couple of minutes before a big smash-up."

The programme had been to all go somewheres for supper and celebrate the play's success. But all Katie wanted now was to get in a taxi and go home and hide.

On the way, I ast her how much she was in so far.

"Just ten thousand," she says.

"Ten thousand!" I said. "Why, they was only one piece of scenery and that looked like they'd bought it secondhand from the choir boys' minstrels. They couldn't of spent one thousand, let alone ten."

"We had to pay the theater a week's rent in advance," she says. "And Jimmy give five thousand to a man for the idear."

"The idear for what?" I ast.

"The idear for the play," she said.

"That stops me!" I says. "This baby furnishes idears for all the good actors in the world, but when he wants one for himself, he goes out and pays $5,000 for it. And if he got a bargain, you're Mrs. Fiske."

"Who sold him the idear?" ast Ella.

"He wouldn't tell me," says Kate.

"Ponzi," I said.

Ralston called Kate up the next noon and made a date with her at the theater. He said that he was sorry he'd been rough. Before she went I ast her to give me a check for the forty thousand she had left so's I could buy back some of her bonds.

"I haven't got only $25,000," she says. "I advanced Jimmy fifteen thousand for his own account, so's he wouldn't have to bother me every time they was bills to meet."

So I said: "Listen: I'll go see him with you and if he don't come clean with that money, I'll knock him deader'n his play."

"Thank you!" she says. "I'll tend to my own affairs alone."

She come back late in the afternoon, all smiles.

"Everything's all right," she said. "I give him his choice of letting me be in the play or giving me my money."

"And which did he choose?" I ast her.

"Neither one," she says. "We're going to get married."

"Bridget" went into the ashcan Saturday night and the wedding come off Monday. Monday night they left for Boston, where the Follies was playing. Kate told us they'd took Ralston back at the same salary he was getting before.

"How much is that," I ast her.

"Four hundred a week," she says.

Well, two or three days after they'd left, I got up my nerve and says to the Mrs.:

"Do you remember what we moved to the Big Town for? We done it to see Life and get Katie a husband. Well, we got her a kind of a husband and I'll tell the world we seen Life. How about moseying back to South Bend?"

"But we haven't no home there now."

"Nor we ain't had none since we left there," I says. "I'm going down and see what's the first day we can get a couple of lowers."

"Get uppers if it's quicker," says the Mrs.

So here we are, really enjoying ourselfs for the first time in pretty near two years. And Katie's in New York, enjoying herself, too, I suppose. She ought to be, married to a comedian. It must be such fun to just set and listen to him talk.

HOW TO WRITE SHORT
STORIES (WITH SAMPLES)

Preface
How to Write Short Stories

A GLIMPSE at the advertising columns of our leading maga-zines shows that whatever else this country may be shy of, there is certainly no lack of correspondence schools that learns you the art of short-story writing. The most notorious of these schools makes the boast that one of their pupils cleaned up $5000.00 and no hundreds dollars writing short stories ac-cording to the system learnt in their course, though it don't say if that amount was cleaned up in one year or fifty.

However, for some reason another when you skin through the pages of high class periodicals, you don't very often find them cluttered up with stories that was written by boys or gals who had win their phi beta skeleton keys at this or that story-writing college. In fact, the most of the successful authors of the short fiction of to-day never went to no kind of a college, or if they did, they studied piano tuning or the barber trade. They could of got just as far in what I call the literary game if they had of stayed home those four years and helped mother carry out the empty bottles.

The answer is that you can't find no school in operation up to date, whether it be a general institution of learning or a school that specializes in story writing, which can make a great author out of a born druggist.

But a little group of our deeper drinkers has suggested that maybe boys and gals who wants to take up writing as their life work would be benefited if some person like I was to give them a few hints in regards to the technic of the short story, how to go about planning it and writing it, when and where to plant the love interest and climax, and finally how to market the fin-ished product without leaving no bad taste in the mouth.

Well, then, it seems to me like the best method to use in giving out these hints is to try and describe my own personal procedure from the time I get inspired till the time the manu-script is loaded on to the trucks.

The first thing I generally always do is try and get hold of a catchy title, like for instance, "Basil Hargrave's Vermifuge," or

"Fun at the Incinerating Plant." Then I set down to a desk or flat table of any kind and lay out 3 or 4 sheets of paper with as many different colored pencils and look at them cock-eyed a few moments before making a selection.

How to begin—or, as we professionals would say, "how to commence"—is the next question. It must be admitted that the method of approach ("L'approchement") differs even among first class fictionists. For example, Blasco Ibañez usually starts his stories with a Spanish word, Jack Dempsey with an "I" and Charley Peterson with a couple of simple declarative sentences about his leading character, such as "Hazel Gooftree had just gone mah jong. She felt faint."

Personally it has been my observation that the reading public prefers short dialogue to any other kind of writing and I always aim to open my tale with two or three lines of conversation between characters—or, as I call them, my puppets—who are to play important rôles. I have often found that something one of these characters says, words I have perhaps unconsciously put into his or her mouth, directs my plot into channels deeper than I had planned and changes, for the better, the entire sense of my story.

To illustrate this, let us pretend that I have laid out a plot as follows: Two girls, Dorothy Abbott and Edith Quaver, are spending the heated term at a famous resort. The Prince of Wales visits the resort, but leaves on the next train. A day or two later, a Mexican reaches the place and looks for accommodations, but is unable to find a room without a bath. The two girls meet him at the public filling station and ask him for a contribution to their autograph album. To their amazement, he utters a terrible oath, spits in their general direction and hurries out of town. It is not until years later that the two girls learn he is a notorious forger and realize how lucky they were after all.

Let us pretend that the above is the original plot. Then let us begin the writing with haphazard dialogue and see whither it leads:

"Where was you?" asked Edith Quaver.

"To the taxidermist's," replied Dorothy Abbott.

The two girls were spending the heated term at a famous watering trough. They had just been bathing and were now engaged in sorting dental floss.

"I am getting sick in tired of this place," went on Miss Quaver.

"It is mutual," said Miss Abbott, shying a cucumber at a passing paper-hanger.

There was a rap at their door and the maid's voice announced that company was awaiting them downstairs. The two girls went down and entered the music room. Garnett Whaledriver was at the piano and the girls tiptoed to the lounge.

The big Nordic, oblivious of their presence, allowed his fingers to form weird, fantastic minors before they strayed unconsciously into the first tones of Chopin's 121st Fugue for the Bass Drum.

From this beginning, a skilled writer could go most anywheres, but it would be my tendency to drop these three characters and take up the life of a mule in the Grand Canyon. The mule watches the trains come in from the east, he watches the trains come in from the west, and keeps wondering who is going to ride him. But she never finds out.

The love interest and climax would come when a man and a lady, both strangers, got to talking together on the train going back east.

"Well," said Mrs. Croot, for it was she, "what did you think of the Canyon?"

"Some cave," replied her escort.

"What a funny way to put it!" replied Mrs. Croot. "And now play me something."

Without a word, Warren took his place on the piano bench and at first allowed his fingers to form weird, fantastic chords on the black keys. Suddenly and with no seeming intention, he was in the midst of the second movement of Chopin's Twelfth Sonata for Flute and Cuspidor. Mrs. Croot felt faint.

That will give young writers an idea of how an apparently trivial thing such as a line of dialogue will upset an entire plot and lead an author far from the path he had pointed for himself. It will also serve as a model for beginners to follow in regards to style and technic. I will not insult my readers by going on with the story to its obvious conclusion. That simple task they can do for themselves, and it will be good practice.

So much for the planning and writing. Now for the marketing of the completed work. A good many young writers make the mistake of enclosing a stamped, self-addressed envelope, big enough for the manuscript to come back in. This is too much of a temptation to the editor.

Personally I have found it a good scheme to not even sign my name to the story, and when I have got it sealed up in its envelope and stamped and addressed, I take it to some town where I don't live and mail it from there. The editor has no idea who wrote the story, so how can he send it back? He is in a quandary.

In conclusion let me warn my pupils never to write their stories—or, as we professionals call them, "yarns"—on used paper. And never to write them on a post-card. And never to send them by telegraph (Morse code).

Stories ("yarns") of mine which have appeared in various publications—one of them having been accepted and published by the first editor that got it—are reprinted in the following pages and will illustrate in a half-hearted way what I am trying to get at.

RING LARDNER.

"THE MANGE,"
Great Neck, Long Island, 1924.

My Roomy

NO—I ain't signed for next year; but there won't be no trouble about that. The dough part of it is all fixed up. John and me talked it over and I'll sign as soon as they send me a contract. All I told him was that he'd have to let me pick my own roommate after this and not sic no wild man on to me.

You know I didn't hit much the last two months o' the season. Some o' the boys, I notice, wrote some stuff about me gettin' old and losin' my battin' eye. That's all bunk! The reason I didn't hit was because I wasn't gettin' enough sleep. And the reason for that was Mr. Elliott.

He wasn't with us after the last part o' May, but I roomed with him long enough to get the insomny. I was the only guy in the club game enough to stand for him; but I was sorry afterward that I done it, because it sure did put a crimp in my little old average.

And do you know where he is now? I got a letter today and I'll read it to you. No—I guess I better tell you somethin' about him first. You fellers never got acquainted with him and you ought to hear the dope to understand the letter. I'll make it as short as I can.

He didn't play in no league last year. He was with some semi-pros over in Michigan and somebody writes John about him. So John sends Needham over to look at him. Tom stayed there Saturday and Sunday, and seen him work twice. He was playin' the outfield, but as luck would have it they wasn't a fly ball hit in his direction in both games. A base hit was made out his way and he booted it, and that's the only report Tom could get on his fieldin'. But he wallops two over the wall in one day and they catch two line drives off him. The next day he gets four blows and two o' them is triples.

So Tom comes back and tells John the guy is a whale of a hitter and fast as Cobb, but he don't know nothin' about his fieldin'. Then John signs him to a contract—twelve hundred or somethin' like that. We'd been in Tampa a week before he showed up. Then he comes to the hotel and just sits round all day, without tellin' nobody who he was. Finally the bellhops was going to chase him out and he says he's one o' the ball-players. Then the clerk gets John to go over and talk to him. He tells John his name and says he hasn't had nothin' to eat for three days, because he was broke. John told me afterward that he'd drew about three hundred in advance—last winter some-time. Well, they took him in the dinin' room and they tell me he inhaled about four meals at once. That night they roomed him with Heine.

Next mornin' Heine and me walks out to the grounds to-gether and Heine tells me about him. He says:

"Don't never call me a bug again. They got me roomin' with the champion o' the world."

"Who is he?" I says.

"I don't know and I don't want to know," says Heine; "but if they stick him in there with me again I'll jump to the Feder-als. To start with, he ain't got no baggage. I ast him where his trunk was and he says he didn't have none. Then I ast him if he didn't have no suitcase, and he says: 'No. What do you care?' I was goin' to lend him some pajamas, but he put on the shirt o' the uniform John give him last night and slept in that. He was asleep when I got up this mornin'. I seen his collar layin' on the dresser and it looked like he had wore it in Pittsburgh every day for a year. So I throwed it out the window and he comes down to breakfast with no collar. I ast him what size collar he wore and he says he didn't want none, because he wasn't goin' out nowheres. After breakfast he beat it up to the room again and put on his uniform. When I got up there he was lookin' in the glass at himself, and he done it all the time I was dressin'."

When we got out to the park I got my first look at him. Pretty good-lookin' guy, too, in his unie—big shoulders and well put together; built somethin' like Heine himself. He was talkin' to John when I come up.

"What position do you play?" John was askin' him.

"I play anywheres," says Elliott.

"You're the kind I'm lookin' for," says John. Then he says: "You was an outfielder up there in Michigan, wasn't you?"

"I don't care where I play," says Elliott.

John sends him to the outfield and forgets all about him for a while. Pretty soon Miller comes in and says:

"I ain't goin' to shag for no bush outfielder!"

John ast him what was the matter, and Miller tells him that Elliott ain't doin' nothin' but just standin' out there; that he ain't makin' no attemp' to catch the fungoes, and that he won't even chase 'em. Then John starts watchin' him, and it was just like Miller said. Larry hit one pretty near in his lap and he stepped out o' the way. John calls him in and ast him:

"Why don't you go after them fly balls?"

"Because I don't want 'em," says Elliott.

John gets sarcastic and says:

"What do you want? Of course we'll see that you get anythin' you want!"

"Give me a ticket back home," says Elliott.

"Don't you want to stick with the club?" says John, and the busher tells him, no, he certainly did not. Then John tells him he'll have to pay his own fare home and Elliott don't get sore at all. He just says:

"Well, I'll have to stick, then—because I'm broke."

We was havin' battin' practice and John tells him to go up and hit a few. And you ought to of seen him bust 'em!

Lavender was in there workin' and he'd been pitchin' a little all winter, so he was in pretty good shape. He lobbed one up to Elliott, and he hit it 'way up in some trees outside the fence—about a mile, I guess. Then John tells Jimmy to put somethin' on the ball. Jim comes through with one of his fast ones and the kid slams it agin the right-field wall on a line.

"Give him your spitter!" yells John, and Jim handed him one. He pulled it over first base so fast that Bert, who was standin' down there, couldn't hardly duck in time. If it'd hit him it'd killed him.

Well, he kep' on hittin' everythin' Jim give him—and Jim had somethin' too. Finally John gets Pierce warmed up and sends him out to pitch, tellin' him to hand Elliott a flock o' curve balls. He wanted to see if lefthanders was goin' to bother him. But he slammed 'em right along, and I don't b'lieve he hit more'n two the whole mornin' that wouldn't of been base hits in a game.

They sent him out to the outfield again in the afternoon, and after a lot o' coaxin' Leach got him to go after fly balls; but that's all he did do—just go after 'em. One hit him on the bean and another on the shoulder. He run back after the short ones and 'way in after the ones that went over his head. He catched just one—a line drive that he couldn't get out o' the way of; and then he acted like it hurt his hands.

I come back to the hotel with John. He ast me what I thought of Elliott.

"Well," I says, "he'd be the greatest ballplayer in the world if he could just play ball. He sure can bust 'em."

John says he was afraid he couldn't never make an outfielder out o' him. He says:

"I'll try him on the infield to-morrow. They must be some place he can play. I never seen a lefthand hitter that looked so good agin lefthand pitchin'—and he's got a great arm; but he acts like he'd never saw a fly ball."

Well, he was just as bad on the infield. They put him at short and he was like a sieve. You could of drove a hearse between him and second base without him gettin' near it. He'd stoop over for a ground ball about the time it was bouncin' up agin the fence; and when he'd try to cover the bag on a peg he'd trip over it.

They tried him at first base and sometimes he'd run 'way over in the coachers' box and sometimes out in right field lookin' for the bag. Once Heine shot one acrost at him on a line and he never touched it with his hands. It went bam! right in the pit of his stomach—and the lunch he'd ate didn't do him no good.

Finally John just give up and says he'd have to keep him on the bench and let him earn his pay by bustin' 'em a couple o' times a week or so. We all agreed with John that this bird would be a whale of a pinch hitter—and we was right too. He was hittin' 'way over five hundred when the blowoff come, along about the last o' May.

II

Before the trainin' trip was over, Elliott had roomed with pretty near everybody in the club. Heine raised an awful holler after the second night down there and John put the bug in with Needham. Tom stood him for three nights. Then he doubled up with Archer, and Schulte, and Miller, and Leach, and Saier—and the whole bunch in turn, averagin' about two nights with each one before they put up a kick. Then John tried him with some o' the youngsters, but they wouldn't stand for him no more'n the others. They all said he was crazy and they was afraid he'd get violent some night and stick a knife in 'em.

He always insisted on havin' the water run in the bathtub all night, because he said it reminded him of the sound of the dam near his home. The fellers might get up four or five times a night and shut off the faucet, but he'd get right up after 'em and turn it on again. Carter, a big bush pitcher from Georgia, started a fight with him about it one night, and Elliott pretty near killed him. So the rest o' the bunch, when they'd saw Carter's map next mornin', didn't have the nerve to do nothin' when it come their turn.

Another o' his habits was the thing that scared 'em, though. He'd brought a razor with him—in his pocket, I guess—and he used to do his shavin' in the middle o' the night. Instead o' doin' it in the bathroom he'd lather his face and then come out and stand in front o' the lookin'-glass on the dresser. Of course he'd have all the lights turned on, and that was bad enough when a feller wanted to sleep; but the worst of it was that he'd stop shavin' every little while and turn round and stare at the guy who was makin' a failure o' tryin' to sleep. Then he'd wave his razor round in the air and laugh, and begin shavin' agin. You can imagine how comf'table his roomies felt!

John had bought him a suitcase and some clothes and things, and charged 'em up to him. He'd drew so much dough in advance that he didn't have nothin' comin' till about June. He never thanked John and he'd wear one shirt and one collar till some one throwed 'em away.

Well, we finally gets to Indianapolis, and we was goin' from there to Cincy to open. The last day in Indianapolis John come and ast me how I'd like to change roomies. I says I was perfectly satisfied with Larry. Then John says:

"I wisht you'd try Elliott. The other boys all kicks on him, but he seems to hang round you a lot and I b'lieve you could get along all right."

"Why don't you room him alone?" I ast.

"The boss or the hotels won't stand for us roomin' alone," says John. "You go ahead and try it, and see how you make out. If he's too much for you let me know; but he likes you and I think he'll be diff'rent with a guy who can talk to him like you can."

So I says I'd tackle it, because I didn't want to throw John down. When we got to Cincy they stuck Elliott and me in one room, and we was together till he quit us.

III

I went to the room early that night, because we was goin' to open next day and I wanted to feel like somethin'. First thing I done when I got undressed was turn on both faucets in the bathtub. They was makin' an awful racket when Elliott finally come in about midnight. I was layin' awake and I opened right up on him. I says:

"Don't shut off that water, because I like to hear it run."

Then I turned over and pretended to be asleep. The bug got his clothes off, and then what did he do but go in the bathroom and shut off the water! Then he come back in the room and says:

"I guess no one's goin' to tell me what to do in here."

But I kep' right on pretendin' to sleep and didn't pay no attention. When he'd got into his bed I jumped out o' mine and turned on all the lights and begun stroppin' my razor. He says:

"What's comin' off?"

"Some o' my whiskers," I says. "I always shave along about this time."

"No, you don't!" he says. "I was in your room one mornin' down in Louisville and I seen you shavin' then."

"Well," I says, "the boys tell me you shave in the middle o' the night; and I thought if I done all the things you do mebbe I'd get so's I could hit like you."

"You must be superstitious!" he says. And I told him I was. "I'm a good hitter," he says, "and I'd be a good hitter if I never shaved at all. That don't make no diff'rence."

"Yes, it does," I says. "You prob'ly hit good because you shave at night; but you'd be a better fielder if you shaved in the mornin'."

You see, I was tryin' to be just as crazy as him—though that wasn't hardly possible.

"If that's right," says he, "I'll do my shavin' in the mornin'—because I seen in the papers where the boys says that if I could play the outfield like I can hit I'd be as good as Cobb. They tell me Cobb gets twenty thousand a year."

"No," I says; "he don't get that much—but he gets about ten times as much as you do."

"Well," he says, "I'm goin' to be as good as him, because I need the money."

"What do you want with money?" I says.

He just laughed and didn't say nothin'; but from that time on the water didn't run in the bathtub nights and he done his shavin' after breakfast. I didn't notice, though, that he looked any better in fieldin' practice.

IV

It rained one day in Cincy and they trimmed us two out o' the other three; but it wasn't Elliott's fault.

They had Larry beat four to one in the ninth innin' o' the first game. Archer gets on with two out, and John sends my roomy up to hit—though Benton, a lefthander, is workin' for them. The first thing Benton serves up there Elliott cracks it a mile over Hobby's head. It would of been good for three easy—only Archer—playin' safe, o' course—pulls up at third base. Tommy couldn't do nothin' and we was licked.

The next day he hits one out o' the park off the Indian; but we was 'way behind and they was nobody on at the time. We copped the last one without usin' no pinch hitters.

I didn't have no trouble with him nights durin' the whole series. He come to bed pretty late while we was there and I told him he'd better not let John catch him at it.

"What would he do?" he says.

"Fine you fifty," I says.

"He can't fine me a dime," he says, "because I ain't got it."

Then I told him he'd be fined all he had comin' if he didn't get in the hotel before midnight; but he just laughed and says he didn't think John had a kick comin' so long as he kep' bustin' the ball.

"Some day you'll go up there and you won't bust it," I says.

"That'll be an accident," he says.

That stopped me and I didn't say nothin'. What could you say to a guy who hated himself like that?

The "accident" happened in St. Louis the first day. We needed two runs in the eighth and Saier and Brid was on, with two out. John tells Elliott to go up in Pierce's place. The bug goes up and Griner gives him two bad balls—'way outside. I thought they was goin' to walk him—and it looked like good judgment, because they'd heard what he done in Cincy. But no! Griner comes back with a fast one right over and Elliott pulls it down the right foul line, about two foot foul. He hit it so hard you'd of thought they'd sure walk him then; but Griner gives him another fast one. He slammed it again just as hard, but foul. Then Griner gives him one 'way outside and it's two and three. John says, on the bench:

"If they don't walk him now he'll bust that fence down."

I thought the same and I was sure Griner wouldn't give him nothin' to hit; but he come with a curve and Rigler calls Elliott out. From where we sat the last one looked low, and I thought Elliott'd make a kick. He come back to the bench smilin'.

John starts for his position, but stopped and ast the bug what was the matter with that one. Any busher I ever knowed would of said, "It was too low," or "It was outside," or "It was inside." Elliott says:

"Nothin' at all. It was right over the middle."

"Why didn't you bust it, then?" says John.

"I was afraid I'd kill somebody," says Elliott, and laughed like a big boob.

John was pretty near chokin'.

"What are you laughin' at?" he says.

"I was thinkin' of a nickel show I seen in Cincinnati," says the bug.

"Well," says John, so mad he couldn't hardly see, "that show and that laugh'll cost you fifty."

We got beat, and I wouldn't of blamed John if he'd fined him his whole season's pay.

Up 'n the room that night I told him he'd better cut out that laughin' stuff when we was gettin' trimmed or he never would have no pay day. Then he got confidential.

"Pay day wouldn't do me no good," he says. "When I'm all squared up with the club and begin to have a pay day I'll only get a hundred bucks at a time, and I'll owe that to some o' you fellers. I wisht we could win the pennant and get in on that World's Series dough. Then I'd get a bunch at once."

"What would you do with a bunch o' dough?" I ast him.

"Don't tell nobody, sport," he says; "but if I ever get five hundred at once I'm goin' to get married."

"Oh!" I says. "And who's the lucky girl?"

"She's a girl up in Muskegon," says Elliott; "and you're right when you call her lucky."

"You don't like yourself much, do you?" I says.

"I got reason to like myself," says he. "You'd like yourself, too, if you could hit 'em like me."

"Well," I says, "you didn't show me no hittin' to-day."

"I couldn't hit because I was laughin' too hard," says Elliott.

"What was it you was laughin' at?" I says.

"I was laughin' at that pitcher," he says. "He thought he had somethin' and he didn't have nothin'."

"He had enough to whiff you with," I says.

"He didn't have nothin'!" says he again. "I was afraid if I busted one off him they'd can him, and then I couldn't never hit agin him no more."

Naturally I didn't have no comeback to that. I just sort o' gasped and got ready to go to sleep; but he wasn't through.

"I wisht you could see this bird!" he says.

"What bird?" I says.

"This dame that's nuts about me," he says.

"Good-looker?" I ast.

"No," he says; "she ain't no bear for looks. They ain't nothin' about her for a guy to rave over till you hear her sing. She sure can holler some."

"What kind o' voice has she got?" I ast.

"A bear," says he.

"No," I says; "I mean is she a barytone or an air?"

"I don't know," he says; "but she's got the loudest voice I ever hear on a woman. She's pretty near got me beat."

"Can you sing?" I says; and I was sorry right afterward that I ast him that question.

I guess it must of been bad enough to have the water run-nin' night after night and to have him wavin' that razor round; but that couldn't of been nothin' to his singin'. Just as soon as I'd pulled that boner he says, "Listen to me!" and starts in on 'Silver Threads Among the Gold.' Mind you, it was after mid-night and they was guests all round us tryin' to sleep!

They used to be noise enough in our club when we had Hofman and Sheckard and Richie harmonizin'; but this bug's voice was louder'n all o' theirn combined. We once had a pitcher named Martin Walsh—brother o' Big Ed's—and I thought he could drownd out the Subway; but this guy made a boiler fac-tory sound like Dummy Taylor. If the whole hotel wasn't awake when he'd howled the first line it's a pipe they was when he cut loose, which he done when he come to "Always young and fair to me." Them words could of been heard easy in East St. Louis.

He didn't get no encore from me, but he goes right through it again—or starts to. I knowed somethin' was goin' to happen before he finished—and somethin' did. The night clerk and the house detective come bangin' at the door. I let 'em in and they had plenty to say. If we made another sound the whole club'd be canned out o' the hotel. I tried to salve 'em, and I says:

"He won't sing no more."

But Elliott swelled up like a poisoned pup.

"Won't I?" he says. "I'll sing all I want to."

"You won't sing in here," says the clerk.

"They ain't room for my voice in here anyways," he says. "I'll go outdoors and sing."

And he puts his clothes on and ducks out. I didn't make no attemp' to stop him. I heard him bellowin' 'Silver Threads' down the corridor and down the stairs, with the clerk and the dick chasin' him all the way and tellin' him to shut up.

Well, the guests make a holler the next mornin'; and the hotel people tells Charlie Williams that he'll either have to let Elliott stay somewheres else or the whole club'll have to move. Charlie tells John, and John was thinkin' o' settlin' the ques-tion by releasin' Elliott.

I guess he'd about made up his mind to do it; but that after-noon they had us three to one in the ninth, and we got the bases full, with two down and Larry's turn to hit. Elliott had been sittin' on the bench sayin' nothin'.

"Do you think you can hit one today?" says John.

"I can hit one any day," says Elliott.

"Go up and hit that lefthander, then," says John, "and remember there's nothin' to laugh at."

Sallee was workin'—and workin' good; but that didn't bother the bug. He cut into one, and it went between Oakes and Whitted like a shot. He come into third standin' up and we was a run to the good. Sallee was so sore he kind o' forgot himself and took pretty near his full wind-up pitchin' to Tommy. And what did Elliott do but steal home and get away with it clean!

Well, you couldn't can him after that, could you? Charlie gets him a room somewheres and I was relieved of his company that night. The next evenin' we beat it for Chi to play about two weeks at home. He didn't tell nobody where he roomed there and I didn't see nothin' of him, 'cep' out to the park. I ast him what he did with himself nights and he says:

"Same as I do on the road—borrow some dough some place and go to the nickel shows."

"You must be stuck on 'em," I says.

"Yes," he says; "I like the ones where they kill people—because I want to learn how to do it. I may have that job some day."

"Don't pick on me," I says.

"Oh," says the bug, "you never can tell who I'll pick on."

It seemed as if he just couldn't learn nothin' about fieldin', and finally John told him to keep out o' the practice.

"A ball might hit him in the temple and croak him," says John.

But he busted up a couple o' games for us at home, beatin' Pittsburgh once and Cincy once.

V

They give me a great big room at the hotel in Pittsburgh; so the fellers picked it out for the poker game. We was playin' along about ten o'clock one night when in come Elliott—the earliest he'd showed up since we'd been roomin' together. They was only five of us playin' and Tom ast him to sit in.

"I'm busted," he says.

"Can you play poker?" I ast him.

"They's nothin' I can't do!" he says. "Slip me a couple o' bucks and I'll show you."

So I slipped him a couple o' bucks and honestly hoped he'd win, because I knowed he never had no dough. Well, Tom dealt him a hand and he picks it up and says:

"I only got five cards."

"How many do you want?" I says.

"Oh," he says, "if that's all I get I'll try to make 'em do."

The pot was cracked and raised, and he stood the raise. I says to myself: "There goes my two bucks!" But no—he comes out with three queens and won the dough. It was only about seven bucks; but you'd of thought it was a million to see him grab it. He laughed like a kid.

"Guess I can't play this game!" he says; and he had me fooled for a minute—I thought he must of been kiddin' when he complained of only havin' five cards.

He copped another pot right afterward and was sittin' there with about eleven bucks in front of him when Jim opens a roodle pot for a buck. I stays and so does Elliott. Him and Jim both drawed one card and I took three. I had kings or queens—I forget which. I didn't help 'em none; so when Jim bets a buck I throws my hand away.

"How much can I bet?" says the bug.

"You can raise Jim a buck if you want to," I says.

So he bets two dollars. Jim comes back at him. He comes right back at Jim. Jim raises him again and he tilts Jim right back. Well, when he'd boosted Jim with the last buck he had, Jim says:

"I'm ready to call. I guess you got me beat. What have you got?"

"I know what I've got, all right," says Elliott. "I've got a straight." And he throws his hand down. Sure enough, it was a straight, eight high. Jim pretty near fainted and so did I.

The bug had started pullin' in the dough when Jim stops him.

"Here! Wait a minute!" says Jim. "I thought you had somethin'. I filled up." Then Jim lays down his nine full.

"You beat me, I guess," says Elliott, and he looked like he'd lost his last friend.

"Beat you?" says Jim. "Of course I beat you! What did you think I had?"

"Well," says the bug, "I thought you might have a small flush or somethin'."

When I regained consciousness he was beggin' for two more bucks.

"What for?" I says. "To play poker with? You're barred from the game for life!"

"Well," he says, "if I can't play no more I want to go to sleep, and you fellers will have to get out o' this room."

Did you ever hear o' nerve like that? This was the first night he'd came in before twelve and he orders the bunch out so's he can sleep! We politely suggested to him to go to Brooklyn.

Without sayin' a word he starts in on his 'Silver Threads'; and it wasn't two minutes till the game was busted up and the bunch—all but me—was out o' there. I'd of beat it too, only he stopped yellin' as soon as they'd went.

"You're some buster!" I says. "You bust up ball games in the afternoon and poker games at night."

"Yes," he says; "that's my business—bustin' things."

And before I knowed what he was about he picked up the pitcher of ice-water that was on the floor and throwed it out the window—through the glass and all.

Right then I give him a plain talkin' to. I tells him how near he come to gettin' canned down in St. Louis because he raised so much Cain singin' in the hotel.

"But I had to keep my voice in shape," he says. "If I ever get dough enough to get married the girl and me'll go out singin' together."

"Out where?" I ast.

"Out on the vaudeville circuit," says Elliott.

"Well," I says, "if her voice is like yours you'll be wastin' money if you travel round. Just stay up in Muskegon and we'll hear you, all right!"

I told him he wouldn't never get no dough if he didn't be-have himself. That, even if we got in the World's Series, he wouldn't be with us—unless he cut out the foolishness.

"We ain't goin' to get in no World's Series," he says, "and I won't never get a bunch o' money at once; so it looks like I couldn't get married this fall."

Then I told him we played a city series every fall. He'd never thought o' that and it tickled him to death. I told him the losers always got about five hundred apiece and that we were about due to win it and get about eight hundred. "But," I says, "we still got a good chance for the old pennant; and if I was you I wouldn't give up hope o' that yet—not where John can hear you, anyway."

"No," he says, "we won't win no pennant, because he won't let me play reg'lar; but I don't care so long as we're sure o' that city-series dough."

"You ain't sure of it if you don't behave," I says.

"Well," says he, very serious, "I guess I'll behave." And he did—till we made our first Eastern trip.

VI

We went to Boston first, and that crazy bunch goes out and piles up a three-run lead on us in seven innin's the first day. It was the pitcher's turn to lead off in the eighth, so up goes Elliott to bat for him. He kisses the first thing they hands him for three bases; and we says, on the bench: "Now we'll get 'em!"— because, you know, a three-run lead wasn't nothin' in Boston.

"Stay right on that bag!" John hollers to Elliott.

Mebbe if John hadn't said nothin' to him everythin' would of been all right; but when Perdue starts to pitch the first ball to Tommy, Elliott starts to steal home. He's out as far as from here to Seattle.

If I'd been carryin' a gun I'd of shot him right through the heart. As it was, I thought John'd kill him with a bat, because he was standin' there with a couple of 'em, waitin' for his turn; but I guess John was too stunned to move. He didn't even seem to see Elliott when he went to the bench. After I'd cooled off a little I says:

"Beat it and get into your clothes before John comes in. Then go to the hotel and keep out o' sight."

When I got up in the room afterward, there was Elliott, lookin' as innocent and happy as though he'd won fifty bucks with a pair o' treys.

"I thought you might of killed yourself," I says.

"What for?" he says.

"For that swell play you made," says I.

"What was the matter with the play?" ast Elliott, surprised. "It was all right when I done it in St. Louis."

"Yes," I says; "but they was two out in St. Louis and we wasn't no three runs behind."

"Well," he says, "if it was all right in St. Louis I don't see why it was wrong here."

"It's a diff'rent climate here," I says, too disgusted to argue with him.

"I wonder if they'd let me sing in this climate?" says Elliott.

"No," I says. "Don't sing in this hotel, because we don't want to get fired out o' here—the eats is too good."

"All right," he says. "I won't sing." But when I starts down to supper he says: "I'm li'ble to do somethin' worse'n sing."

He didn't show up in the dinin' room and John went to the boxin' show after supper; so it looked like him and Elliott wouldn't run into each other till the murder had left John's heart. I was glad o' that—because a Mass'chusetts jury might not consider it justifiable hommercide if one guy croaked another for givin' the Boston club a game.

I went down to the corner and had a couple o' beers; and then I come straight back, intendin' to hit the hay. The elevator boy had went for a drink or somethin', and they was two old ladies already waitin' in the car when I stepped in. Right along after me comes Elliott.

"Where's the boy that's supposed to run this car?" he says. I told him the boy'd be right back; but he says: "I can't wait. I'm much too sleepy."

And before I could stop him he'd slammed the door and him and I and the poor old ladies was shootin' up.

"Let us off at the third floor, please!" says one o' the ladies, her voice kind o' shakin'.

"Sorry, madam," says the bug; "but this is a express and we don't stop at no third floor."

I grabbed his arm and tried to get him away from the machinery; but he was as strong as a ox and he threwed me agin the side o' the car like I was a baby. We went to the top faster'n I ever rode in an elevator before. And then we shot down to the bottom, hittin' the bumper down there so hard I thought we'd be smashed to splinters.

The ladies was too scared to make a sound durin' the first trip; but while we was goin' up and down the second time— even faster'n the first—they begun to scream. I was hollerin' my head off at him to quit and he was makin' more noise than the three of us—pretendin' he was the locomotive and the whole crew o' the train.

Don't never ask me how many times we went up and down! The women fainted on the third trip and I guess I was about as near it as I'll ever get. The elevator boy and the bellhops and the waiters and the night clerk and everybody was jumpin' round the lobby screamin'; but no one seemed to know how to stop us.

Finally—on about the tenth trip, I guess—he slowed down and stopped at the fifth floor, where we was roomin'. He opened the door and beat it for the room, while I, though I was tremblin' like a leaf, run the car down to the bottom.

The night clerk knowed me pretty well and knowed I wouldn't do nothin' like that; so him and I didn't argue, but just got to work together to bring the old women to. While we was doin' that Elliott must of run down the stairs and slipped out o' the hotel, because when they sent the officers up to the room after him he'd blowed.

They was goin' to fire the club out; but Charlie had a good stand-in with Amos, the proprietor, and he fixed it up to let us stay—providin' Elliott kep' away. The bug didn't show up at the ball park next day and we didn't see no more of him till we got on the rattler for New York. Charlie and John both bawled him, but they give him a berth—an upper—and we pulled into the Grand Central Station without him havin' made no effort to wreck the train.

VII

I'd studied the thing pretty careful, but hadn't come to no conclusion. I was sure he wasn't no stew, because none o' the boys had ever saw him even take a glass o' beer, and I couldn't never detect the odor o' booze on him. And if he'd been a dope I'd of knew about it—roomin' with him.

There wouldn't of been no mystery about it if he'd been a lefthand pitcher—but he wasn't. He wasn't nothin' but a whale of a hitter and he throwed with his right arm. He hit lefthanded, o' course; but so did Saier and Brid and Schulte and me, and John himself; and none of us was violent. I guessed he must of been just a plain nut and li'ble to break out any time.

They was a letter waitin' for him at New York, and I took it, intendin' to give it to him at the park, because I didn't think they'd let him room at the hotel; but after breakfast he come up to the room, with his suitcase. It seems he'd promised John and Charlie to be good, and made it so strong they b'lieved him.

I give him his letter, which was addressed in a girl's writin' and come from Muskegon.

"From the girl?" I says.

"Yes," he says; and, without openin' it, he tore it up and throwed it out the window.

"Had a quarrel?" I ast.

"No, no," he says; "but she can't tell me nothin' I don't know already. Girls always writes the same junk. I got one from her in Pittsburgh, but I didn't read it."

"I guess you ain't so stuck on her," I says.

He swells up and says:

"Of course I'm stuck on her! If I wasn't, do you think I'd be goin' round with this bunch and gettin' insulted all the time? I'm stickin' here because o' that series dough, so's I can get hooked."

"Do you think you'd settle down if you was married?" I ast him.

"Settle down?" he says. "Sure, I'd settle down. I'd be so happy that I wouldn't have to look for no excitement."

Nothin' special happened that night 'cep' that he come in the room about one o'clock and woke me up by pickin' up the foot o' the bed and droppin' it on the floor, sudden-like.

"Give me a key to the room," he says.

"You must of had a key," I says, "or you couldn't of got in."

"That's right!" he says, and beat it to bed.

One o' the reporters must of told Elliott that John had ast for waivers on him and New York had refused to waive, because next mornin' he come to me with that dope.

"New York's goin' to win this pennant!" he says.

"Well," I says, "they will if some one else don't. But what of it?"

"I'm goin' to play with New York," he says, "so's I can get the World's Series dough."

"How you goin' to get away from this club?" I ast.

"Just watch me!" he says. "I'll be with New York before this series is over."

Well, the way he goes after the job was original, anyway. Rube'd had one of his good days the day before and we'd got a trimmin'; but this second day the score was tied up at two runs apiece in the tenth, and Big Jeff'd been wabblin' for two or three innin's.

Well, he walks Saier and me, with one out, and Mac sends for Matty, who was warmed up and ready. John sticks Elliott in in Brid's place and the bug pulls one into the right-field stand.

It's a cinch McGraw thinks well of him then, and might of went after him if he hadn't went crazy the next afternoon. We're tied up in the ninth and Matty's workin'. John sends Elliott up with the bases choked; but he doesn't go right up to the plate. He walks over to their bench and calls McGraw out. Mac tells us about it afterward.

"I can bust up this game right here!" says Elliott.

"Go ahead," says Mac; "but be careful he don't whiff you."

Then the bug pulls it.

"If I whiff," he says, "will you get me on your club?"

"Sure!" says Mac, just as anybody would.

By this time Bill Koem was hollerin' about the delay; so up goes Elliott and gives the worst burlesque on tryin' to hit that you ever see. Matty throws one a mile outside and high, and the bug swings like it was right over the heart. Then Matty throws one at him and he ducks out o' the way—but swings just the same. Matty must of been wise by this time, for he pitches one so far outside that the Chief almost has to go to the coachers' box after it. Elliott takes his third healthy and runs through the field down to the clubhouse.

We got beat in the eleventh; and when we went in to dress he has his street clothes on. Soon as he seen John comin' he says: "I got to see McGraw!" And he beat it.

John was goin' to the fights that night; but before he leaves the hotel he had waivers on Elliott from everybody and had sold him to Atlanta.

"And," says John, "I don't care if they pay for him or not."

My roomy blows in about nine and got the letter from John out of his box. He was goin' to tear it up, but I told him they was news in it. He opens it and reads where he's sold. I was still sore at him; so I says:

"Thought you was goin' to get on the New York club?"

"No," he says. "I got turned down cold. McGraw says he wouldn't have me in his club. He says he'd had Charlie Faust—and that was enough for him."

He had a kind o' crazy look in his eyes; so when he starts up to the room I follows him.

"What are you goin' to do now?" I says.

"I'm goin' to sell this ticket to Atlanta," he says, "and go back to Muskegon, where I belong."

"I'll help you pack," I says.

"No," says the bug. "I come into this league with this suit o'clothes and a collar. They can have the rest of it." Then he sits down on the bed and begins to cry like a baby. "No series dough for me," he blubbers, "and no weddin' bells! My girl'll die when she hears about it!"

Of course that made me feel kind o' rotten, and I says:

"Brace up, boy! The best thing you can do is go to Atlanta and try hard. You'll be up here again next year."

"You can't tell me where to go!" he says, and he wasn't cryin' no more. "I'll go where I please—and I'm li'ble to take you with me."

I didn't want no argument, so I kep' still. Pretty soon he goes up to the lookin'-glass and stares at himself for five minutes. Then, all of a sudden, he hauls off and takes a wallop at his reflection in the glass. Naturally he smashed the glass all to pieces and he cut his hand somethin' awful.

Without lookin' at it he come over to me and says: "Well, good-by, sport!"—and holds out his other hand to shake. When I starts to shake with him he smears his bloody hand all over my map. Then he laughed like a wild man and run out o' the room and out o' the hotel.

VIII

Well, boys, my sleep was broke up for the rest o' the season. It might of been because I was used to sleepin' in all kinds o' racket and excitement, and couldn't stand for the quiet after he'd went—or it might of been because I kep' thinkin' about him and feelin' sorry for him.

I of'en wondered if he'd settle down and be somethin' if he could get married; and finally I got to b'lievin' he would. So when we was dividin' the city series dough I was thinkin' of him and the girl. Our share o' the money—the losers', as usual—was twelve thousand seven hundred sixty bucks or somethin' like that. They was twenty-one of us and that meant six hundred seven bucks apiece. We was just goin' to cut it up that way when I says:

"Why not give a divvy to poor old Elliott?"

About fifteen of 'em at once told me that I was crazy. You see, when he got canned he owed everybody in the club. I guess he'd stuck me for the most—about seventy bucks—but I didn't care nothin' about that. I knowed he hadn't never reported to Atlanta, and I thought he was prob'ly busted and a bunch o' money might make things all right for him and the other songbird.

I made quite a speech to the fellers, tellin' 'em how he'd cried when he left us and how his heart'd been set on gettin' married on the series dough. I made it so strong that they finally fell for it. Our shares was cut to five hundred eighty apiece, and John sent him a check for a full share.

For a while I was kind o' worried about what I'd did. I didn't know if I was doin' right by the girl to give him the chance to marry her.

He'd told me she was stuck on him, and that's the only excuse I had for tryin' to fix it up between 'em; but, b'lieve me, if she was my sister or a friend o' mine I'd just as soon of had her manage the Cincinnati Club as marry that bird. I thought to myself:

"If she's all right she'll take acid in a month—and it'll be my fault; but if she's really stuck on him they must be somethin' wrong with her too, so what's the diff'rence?"

Then along comes this letter that I told you about. It's from some friend of hisn up there—and they's a note from him. I'll read 'em to you and then I got to beat it for the station:

DEAR SIR: They have got poor Elliott locked up and they are goin' to take him to the asylum at Kalamazoo. He thanks you for the check, and we will use the money to see that he is made comf'table.

When the poor boy come back here he found that his girl was married to Joe Bishop, who runs a soda fountain. She had wrote to him about it, but he did not read her letters. The news drove him crazy—poor boy—and he went to the place where they was livin' with a baseball bat and very near killed 'em both. Then he marched down the street singin' 'Silver Threads Among the Gold' at the top of his voice. They was goin' to send him to prison for assault with intent to kill, but the jury decided he was crazy.

He wants to thank you again for the money.

Yours truly,
JIM——

I can't make out his last name—but it don't make no diff'rence. Now I'll read you his note:

OLD ROOMY: I was at bat twice and made two hits; but I guess I did not meet 'em square. They tell me they are both alive yet, which I did not mean 'em to be. I hope they got good curve-ball pitchers where I am goin'. I sure can bust them curves—can't I, sport?

Yours,
B. ELLIOTT.

P. S.—The B stands for Buster.

That's all of it, fellers; and you can see I had some excuse for not hittin'. You can also see why I ain't never goin' to room with no bug again—not for John or nobody else!

Alibi Ike

I

HIS RIGHT name was Frank X. Farrell, and I guess the X stood for "Excuse me." Because he never pulled a play, good or bad, on or off the field, without apologizin' for it.

"Alibi Ike" was the name Carey wished on him the first day he reported down South. O' course we all cut out the "Alibi" part of it right away for the fear he would overhear it and bust somebody. But we called him "Ike" right to his face and the rest of it was understood by everybody on the club except Ike himself.

He ast me one time, he says:

"What do you all call me Ike for? I ain't no Yid."

"Carey give you the name," I says. "It's his nickname for everybody he takes a likin' to."

"He mustn't have only a few friends then," says Ike. "I never heard him say 'Ike' to nobody else."

But I was goin' to tell you about Carey namin' him. We'd been workin' out two weeks and the pitchers was showin' somethin' when this bird joined us. His first day out he stood up there so good and took such a reef at the old pill that he had everyone lookin'. Then him and Carey was together in left field, catchin' fungoes, and it was after we was through for the day that Carey told me about him.

"What do you think of Alibi Ike?" ast Carey.

"Who's that?" I says.

"This here Farrell in the outfield," says Carey.

"He looks like he could hit," I says.

"Yes," says Carey, "but he can't hit near as good as he can apologize."

Then Carey went on to tell me what Ike had been pullin' out there. He'd dropped the first fly ball that was hit to him and told Carey his glove wasn't broke in good yet, and Carey says the glove could easy of been Kid Gleason's gran'father. He made a whale of a catch out o' the next one and Carey says "Nice work!" or somethin' like that, but Ike says he could of caught the ball with his back turned only he slipped when he started after it and, besides that, the air currents fooled him.

"I thought you done well to get to the ball," says Carey.

"I ought to been settin' under it," says Ike.

"What did you hit last year?" Carey ast him.

"I had malaria most o' the season," says Ike. "I wound up with .356."

"Where would I have to go to get malaria?" says Carey, but Ike didn't wise up.

I and Carey and him set at the same table together for supper. It took him half an hour longer'n us to eat because he had to excuse himself every time he lifted his fork.

"Doctor told me I needed starch," he'd say, and then toss a shovelful o' potatoes into him. Or, "They ain't much meat on one o' these chops," he'd tell us, and grab another one. Or he'd say: "Nothin' like onions for a cold," and then he'd dip into the perfumery.

"Better try that apple sauce," says Carey. "It'll help your malaria."

"Whose malaria?" says Ike. He'd forgot already why he didn't only hit .356 last year.

I and Carey begin to lead him on.

"Whereabouts did you say your home was?" I ast him.

"I live with my folks," he says. "We live in Kansas City—not right down in the business part—outside a ways."

"How's that come?" says Carey. "I should think you'd get rooms in the post office."

But Ike was too busy curin' his cold to get that one.

"Are you married?" I ast him.

"No," he says. "I never run round much with girls, except to shows onct in a wile and parties and dances and roller skatin'."

"Never take 'em to the prize fights, eh?" says Carey.

"We don't have no real good bouts," says Ike. "Just bush stuff. And I never figured a boxin' match was a place for the ladies."

Well, after supper he pulled a cigar out and lit it. I was just goin' to ask him what he done it for, but he beat me to it.

"Kind o' rests a man to smoke after a good work-out," he says. "Kind o' settles a man's supper, too."

"Looks like a pretty good cigar," says Carey.

"Yes," says Ike. "A friend o' mine give it to me—a fella in Kansas City that runs a billiard room."

"Do you play billiards?" I ast him.

"I used to play a fair game," he says. "I'm all out o' practice now—can't hardly make a shot."

We coaxed him into a four-handed battle, him and Carey against Jack Mack and I. Say, he couldn't play billiards as good as Willie Hoppe; not quite. But to hear him tell it, he didn't make a good shot all evenin'. I'd leave him an awful-lookin' layout, and he'd gather 'em up in one try and then run a couple o' hundred, and between every carom he'd say he'd put too much stuff on the ball, or the English didn't take, or the table wasn't true, or his stick was crooked, or somethin'. And all the time he had the balls actin' like they was Dutch soldiers and him Kaiser William. We started out to play fifty points, but we had to make it a thousand so as I and Jack and Carey could try the table.

The four of us set round the lobby a wile after we was through playin', and when it got along toward bedtime Carey whispered to me and says:

"Ike'd like to go to bed, but he can't think up no excuse."

Carey hadn't hardly finished whisperin' when Ike got up and pulled it:

"Well, good night, boys," he says. "I ain't sleepy, but I got some gravel in my shoes and it's killin' my feet."

We knowed he hadn't never left the hotel since we'd came in from the grounds and changed our clo'es. So Carey says:

"I should think they'd take them gravel pits out o' the billiard room."

But Ike was already on his way to the elevator, limpin'.

"He's got the world beat," says Carey to Jack and I. "I've knew lots o' guys that had an alibi for every mistake they made; I've heard pitchers say that the ball slipped when somebody cracked one off'n 'em; I've heard infielders complain of a sore arm after heavin' one into the stand, and I've saw outfielders tooken sick with a dizzy spell when they've misjudged a fly ball. But this baby can't even go to bed without apologizin', and I bet he excuses himself to the razor when he gets ready to shave."

"And at that," says Jack, "he's goin' make us a good man."

"Yes," says Carey, "unless rheumatism keeps his battin' average down to .400."

Well, sir, Ike kept whalin' away at the ball all through the trip till everybody knowed he'd won a job. Cap had him in there regular the last few exhibition games and told the newspaper boys a week before the season opened that he was goin' to start him in Kane's place.

"You're there, kid," says Carey to Ike, the night Cap made the 'nnouncement. "They ain't many boys that wins a big league berth their third year out."

"I'd of been up here a year ago," says Ike, "only I was bent over all season with lumbago."

II

It rained down in Cincinnati one day and somebody organized a little game o' cards. They was shy two men to make six and ast I and Carey to play.

"I'm with you if you get Ike and make it seven-handed," says Carey.

So they got a hold of Ike and we went up to Smitty's room.

"I pretty near forgot how many you deal," says Ike. "It's been a long wile since I played."

I and Carey give each other the wink, and sure enough, he was just as ig'orant about poker as billiards. About the second hand, the pot was opened two or three ahead of him, and they was three in when it come his turn. It cost a buck, and he throwed in two.

"It's raised, boys," somebody says.

"Gosh, that's right, I did raise it," says Ike.

"Take out a buck if you didn't mean to tilt her," says Carey.

"No," says Ike, "I'll leave it go."

Well, it was raised back at him and then he made another mistake and raised again. They was only three left in when the draw come. Smitty'd opened with a pair o' kings and he didn't help 'em. Ike stood pat. The guy that'd raised him back was flushin' and he didn't fill. So Smitty checked and Ike bet and didn't get no call. He tossed his hand away, but I grabbed it and give it a look. He had king, queen, jack and two tens. Alibi Ike he must have seen me peekin', for he leaned over and whispered to me.

"I overlooked my hand," he says. "I thought all the wile it was a straight."

"Yes," I says, "that's why you raised twice by mistake."

They was another pot that he come into with tens and fours. It was tilted a couple o' times and two o' the strong fellas drawed ahead of Ike. They each drawed one. So Ike throwed away his little pair and come out with four tens. And they was four treys against him. Carey'd looked at Ike's discards and then he says:

"This lucky bum busted two pair."

"No, no, I didn't," says Ike.

"Yes, yes, you did," says Carey, and showed us the two fours.

"What do you know about that?" says Ike. "I'd of swore one was a five spot."

Well, we hadn't had no pay day yet, and after a wile everybody except Ike was goin' shy. I could see him gettin' restless and I was wonderin' how he'd make the get-away. He tried two or three times. "I got to buy some collars before supper," he says.

"No hurry," says Smitty. "The stores here keeps open all night in April."

After a minute he opened up again.

"My uncle out in Nebraska ain't expected to live," he says. "I ought to send a telegram."

"Would that save him?" says Carey.

"No, it sure wouldn't," says Ike, "but I ought to leave my old man know where I'm at."

"When did you hear about your uncle?" says Carey.

"Just this mornin'," says Ike.

"Who told you?" ast Carey.

"I got a wire from my old man," says Ike.

"Well," says Carey, "your old man knows you're still here yet this afternoon if you was here this mornin'. Trains leavin' Cincinnati in the middle o' the day don't carry no ball clubs."

"Yes," says Ike, "that's true. But he don't know where I'm goin' to be next week."

"Ain't he got no schedule?" ast Carey.

"I sent him one openin' day," says Ike, "but it takes mail a long time to get to Idaho."

"I thought your old man lived in Kansas City," says Carey.

"He does when he's home," says Ike.

"But now," says Carey, "I s'pose he's went to Idaho so as he can be near your sick uncle in Nebraska."

"He's visitin' my other uncle in Idaho."

"Then how does he keep posted about your sick uncle?" ast Carey.

"He don't," says Ike. "He don't even know my other uncle's sick. That's why I ought to wire and tell him."

"Good night!" says Carey.

"What town in Idaho is your old man at?" I says.

Ike thought it over.

"No town at all," he says. "But he's near a town."

"Near what town?" I says.

"Yuma," says Ike.

Well, by this time he'd lost two or three pots and he was desperate. We was playin' just as fast as we could, because we seen we couldn't hold him much longer. But he was tryin' so hard to frame an escape that he couldn't pay no attention to the cards, and it looked like we'd get his whole pile away from him if we could make him stick.

The telephone saved him. The minute it begun to ring, five of us jumped for it. But Ike was there first.

"Yes," he says, answerin' it. "This is him. I'll come right down."

And he slammed up the receiver and beat it out o' the door without even sayin' good-by.

"Smitty'd ought to locked the door," says Carey.

"What did he win?" ast Carey.

We figured it up—sixty-odd bucks.

"And the next time we ask him to play," says Carey, "his fingers will be so stiff he can't hold the cards."

Well, we set round a wile talkin' it over, and pretty soon the telephone rung again. Smitty answered it. It was a friend of his'n from Hamilton and he wanted to know why Smitty didn't hurry down. He was the one that had called before and Ike had told him he was Smitty.

"Ike'd ought to split with Smitty's friend," says Carey.

"No," I says, "he'll need all he won. It costs money to buy collars and to send telegrams from Cincinnati to your old man in Texas and keep him posted on the health o' your uncle in Cedar Rapids, D. C."

III

And you ought to heard him out there on that field! They

wasn't a day when he didn't pull six or seven, and it didn't make no difference whether he was goin' good or bad. If he popped up in the pinch he should of made a base hit and the reason he didn't was so-and-so. And if he cracked one for three bases he ought to had a home run, only the ball wasn't lively, or the wind brought it back, or he tripped on a lump o' dirt, roundin' first base.

They was one afternoon in New York when he beat all records. Big Marquard was workin' against us and he was good.

In the first innin' Ike hit one clear over that right field stand, but it was a few feet foul. Then he got another foul and then the count come to two and two. Then Rube slipped one acrost on him and he was called out.

"What do you know about that!" he says afterward on the bench. "I lost count. I thought it was three and one, and I took a strike."

"You took a strike all right," says Carey. "Even the umps knowed it was a strike."

"Yes," says Ike, "but you can bet I wouldn't of took it if I'd knew it was the third one. The score board had it wrong."

"That score board ain't for you to look at," says Cap. "It's for you to hit that old pill against."

"Well," says Ike, "I could of hit that one over the score board if I'd knew it was the third."

"Was it a good ball?" I says.

"Well, no, it wasn't," says Ike. "It was inside."

"How far inside?" says Carey.

"Oh, two or three inches or half a foot," says Ike.

"I guess you wouldn't of threatened the score board with it then," says Cap.

"I'd of pulled it down the right foul line if I hadn't thought he'd call it a ball," says Ike.

Well, in New York's part o' the innin' Doyle cracked one and Ike run back a mile and a half and caught it with one hand. We was all sayin' what a whale of a play it was, but he had to apologize just the same as for gettin' struck out.

"That stand's so high," he says, "that a man don't never see a ball till it's right on top o' you."

"Didn't you see that one?" ast Cap.

"Not at first," says Ike; "not till it raised up above the roof o' the stand."

"Then why did you start back as soon as the ball was hit?" says Cap.

"I knowed by the sound that he'd got a good hold of it," says Ike.

"Yes," says Cap, "but how'd you know what direction to run in?"

"Doyle usually hits 'em that way, the way I run," says Ike.

"Why don't you play blindfolded?" says Carey.

"Might as well, with that big high stand to bother a man," says Ike. "If I could of saw the ball all the time I'd of got it in my hip pocket."

Along in the fifth we was one run to the bad and Ike got on with one out. On the first ball throwed to Smitty, Ike went down. The ball was outside and Meyers throwed Ike out by ten feet.

You could see Ike's lips movin' all the way to the bench and when he got there he had his piece learned.

"Why didn't he swing?" he says.

"Why didn't you wait for his sign?" says Cap.

"He give me his sign," says Ike.

"What is his sign with you?" says Cap.

"Pickin' up some dirt with his right hand," says Ike.

"Well, I didn't see him do it," Cap says.

"He done it all right," says Ike.

Well, Smitty went out and they wasn't no more argument till they come in for the next innin'. Then Cap opened it up.

"You fellas better get your signs straight," he says.

"Do you mean me?" says Smitty.

"Yes," Cap says. "What's your sign with Ike?"

"Slidin my left hand up to the end o' the bat and back," says Smitty.

"Do you hear that, Ike?" ast Cap.

"What of it?" says Ike.

"You says his sign was pickin' up dirt and he says it's slidin his hand. Which is right?"

"I'm right," says Smitty. "But if you're arguin' about him goin' last innin', I didn't give him no sign."

"You pulled your cap down with your right hand, didn't you?" ast Ike.

"Well, s'pose I did," says Smitty. "That don't mean nothin'. I never told you to take that for a sign, did I?"

"I thought maybe you meant to tell me and forgot," says Ike.

They couldn't none of us answer that and they wouldn't of been no more said if Ike had of shut up. But wile we was settin' there Carey got on with two out and stole second clean.

"There!" says Ike. "That's what I was tryin' to do and I'd of got away with it if Smitty'd swang and bothered the Indian."

"Oh!" says Smitty. "You was tryin' to steal then, was you? I thought you claimed I give you the hit and run."

"I didn't claim no such a thing," says Ike. "I thought maybe you might of gave me a sign, but I was goin' anyway because I thought I had a good start."

Cap prob'ly would of hit him with a bat, only just about that time Doyle booted one on Hayes and Carey come acrost with the run that tied.

Well, we go into the ninth finally, one and one, and Marquard walks McDonald with nobody out.

"Lay it down," says Cap to Ike.

And Ike goes up there with orders to bunt and cracks the first ball into that right-field stand! It was fair this time, and we're two ahead, but I didn't think about that at the time. I was too busy watchin' Cap's face. First he turned pale and then he got red as fire and then he got blue and purple, and finally he just laid back and busted out laughin'. So we wasn't afraid to laugh ourselfs when we seen him doin' it, and when Ike come in everybody on the bench was in hysterics.

But instead o' takin' advantage, Ike had to try and excuse himself. His play was to shut up and he didn't know how to make it.

"Well," he says, "if I hadn't hit quite so quick at that one I bet it'd of cleared the center-field fence."

Cap stopped laughin'.

"It'll cost you plain fifty," he says.

"What for?" says Ike.

"When I say 'bunt' I mean 'bunt,'" says Cap.

"You didn't say 'bunt,'" says Ike.

"I says 'Lay it down,'" says Cap. "If that don't mean 'bunt,' what does it mean?"

"'Lay it down' means 'bunt' all right," says Ike, "but I understood you to say 'Lay on it.'"

"All right," says Cap, "and the little misunderstandin' will cost you fifty."

Ike didn't say nothin' for a few minutes. Then he had another bright idear.

"I was just kiddin' about misunderstandin' you," he says. "I knowed you wanted me to bunt."

"Well, then, why didn't you bunt?" ast Cap.

"I was goin' to on the next ball," says Ike. "But I thought if I took a good wallop I'd have 'em all fooled. So I walloped at the first one to fool 'em, and I didn't have no intention o' hittin' it."

"You tried to miss it, did you?" says Cap.

"Yes," says Ike.

"How'd you happen to hit it?" ast Cap.

"Well," Ike says, "I was lookin' for him to throw me a fast one and I was goin' to swing under it. But he come with a hook and I met it right square where I was swingin' to go under the fast one."

"Great!" says Cap. "Boys," he says, "Ike's learned how to hit Marquard's curve. Pretend a fast one's comin' and then try to miss it. It's a good thing to know and Ike'd ought to be willin' to pay for the lesson. So I'm goin' to make it a hundred instead o' fifty."

The game wound up 3 to 1. The fine didn't go, because Ike hit like a wild man all through that trip and we made pretty near a clean-up. The night we went to Philly I got him cornered in the car and I says to him:

"Forget them alibis for a wile and tell me somethin'. What'd you do that for, swing that time against Marquard when you was told to bunt?"

"I'll tell you," he says. "That ball he throwed me looked just like the one I struck out on in the first innin' and I wanted to show Cap what I could of done to that other one if I'd knew it was the third strike."

"But," I says, "the one you struck out on in the first innin' was a fast ball."

"So was the one I cracked in the ninth," says Ike.

IV

You've saw Cap's wife, o' course. Well, her sister's about twict as good-lookin' as her, and that's goin' some.

Cap took his missus down to St. Louis the second trip and the other one come down from St. Joe to visit her. Her name is Dolly, and some doll is right.

Well, Cap was goin' to take the two sisters to a show and he wanted a beau for Dolly. He left it to her and she picked Ike. He'd hit three on the nose that afternoon—off'n Sallee, too.

They fell for each other that first evenin'. Cap told us how it come off. She begin flatterin' Ike for the star game he'd played and o' course he begin excusin' himself for not doin' better. So she thought he was modest and it went strong with her. And she believed everything he said and that made her solid with him—that and her make-up. They was together every mornin' and evenin' for the five days we was there. In the afternoons Ike played the grandest ball you ever see, hittin' and runnin' the bases like a fool and catchin' everything that stayed in the park.

I told Cap, I says: "You'd ought to keep the doll with us and he'd make Cobb's figures look sick."

But Dolly had to go back to St. Joe and we come home for a long serious.

Well, for the next three weeks Ike had a letter to read every day and he'd set in the clubhouse readin' it till mornin' practice was half over. Cap didn't say nothin' to him, because he was goin' so good. But I and Carey wasted a lot of our time tryin' to get him to own up who the letters was from. Fine chanct!

"What are you readin'?" Carey'd say. "A bill?"

"No," Ike'd say, "not exactly a bill. It's a letter from a fella I used to go to school with."

"High school or college?" I'd ask him.

"College," he'd say.

"What college?" I'd say.

Then he'd stall a wile and then he'd say:

"I didn't go to the college myself, but my friend went there."

"How did it happen you didn't go?" Carey'd ask him.

"Well," he'd say, "they wasn't no colleges near where I lived."

"Didn't you live in Kansas City?" I'd say to him.

One time he'd say he did and another time he didn't. One time he says he lived in Michigan.

"Where at?" says Carey.

"Near Detroit," he says.

"Well," I says, "Detroit's near Ann Arbor and that's where they got the university."

"Yes," says Ike, "they got it there now, but they didn't have it there then."

"I come pretty near goin' to Syracuse," I says, "only they wasn't no railroads runnin' through there in them days."

"Where'd this friend o' yours go to college?" says Carey.

"I forget now," says Ike.

"Was it Carlisle?" ast Carey.

"No," says Ike, "his folks wasn't very well off."

"That's what barred me from Smith," I says.

"I was goin' to tackle Cornell's," says Carey, "but the doctor told me I'd have hay fever if I didn't stay up North."

"Your friend writes long letters," I says.

"Yes," says Ike; "he's tellin' me about a ball player."

"Where does he play?" ast Carey.

"Down in the Texas League—Fort Wayne," says Ike.

"It looks like a girl's writin'," Carey says.

"A girl wrote it," says Ike. "That's my friend's sister, writin' for him."

"Didn't they teach writin' at this here college where he went?" says Carey.

"Sure," Ike says, "they taught writin', but he got his hand cut off in a railroad wreck."

"How long ago?" I says.

"Right after he got out o' college," says Ike.

"Well," I says, "I should think he'd of learned to write with his left hand by this time."

"It's his left hand that was cut off," says Ike; "and he was left-handed."

"You get a letter every day," says Carey. "They're all the same writin'. Is he tellin' you about a different ball player every time he writes?"

"No," Ike says. "It's the same ball player. He just tells me what he does every day."

"From the size o' the letters, they don't play nothin' but double-headers down there," says Carey.

We figured that Ike spent most of his evenin's answerin' the letters from his "friend's sister," so we kept tryin' to date him up for shows and parties to see how he'd duck out of 'em. He was bugs over spaghetti, so we told him one day that they was goin' to be a big feed of it over to Joe's that night and he was invited.

"How long'll it last?" he says.

"Well," we says, "we're goin' right over there after the game and stay till they close up."

"I can't go," he says, "unless they leave me come home at eight bells."

"Nothin' doin'," says Carey. "Joe'd get sore."

"I can't go then," says Ike.

"Why not?" I ast him.

"Well," he says, "my landlady locks up the house at eight and I left my key home."

"You can come and stay with me," says Carey.

"No," he says, "I can't sleep in a strange bed."

"How do you get along when we're on the road?" says I.

"I don't never sleep the first night anywheres," he says. "After that I'm all right."

"You'll have time to chase home and get your key right after the game," I told him.

"The key ain't home," says Ike. "I lent it to one o' the other fellas and he's went out o' town and took it with him."

"Couldn't you borry another key off'n the landlady?" Carey ast him.

"No," he says, "that's the only one they is."

Well, the day before we started East again, Ike come into the clubhouse all smiles.

"Your birthday?" I ast him.

"No," he says.

"What do you feel so good about?" I says.

"Got a letter from my old man," he says. "My uncle's goin' to get well."

"Is that the one in Nebraska?" says I.

"Not right in Nebraska," says Ike. "Near there."

But afterwards we got the right dope from Cap. Dolly'd blew in from Missouri and was goin' to make the trip with her sister.

V

Well, I want to alibi Carey and I for what come off in Boston. If we'd of had any idear what we was doin', we'd never did it. They wasn't nobody outside o' maybe Ike and the dame that felt worse over it than I and Carey.

The first two days we didn't see nothin' of Ike and her except out to the park. The rest o' the time they was sight-seein' over to Cambridge and down to Revere and out to Brook-a-line and all the other places where the rubes go.

But when we come into the beanery after the third game Cap's wife called us over.

"If you want to see somethin' pretty," she says, "look at the third finger on Sis's left hand."

Well, o' course we knowed before we looked that it wasn't goin' to be no hangnail. Nobody was su'prised when Dolly blew into the dinin' room with it—a rock that Ike'd bought off'n Diamond Joe the first trip to New York. Only o' course it'd been set into a lady's-size ring instead o' the automobile tire he'd been wearin'.

Cap and his missus and Ike and Dolly ett supper together, only Ike didn't eat nothin', but just set there blushin' and spillin' things on the tablecloth. I heard him excusin' himself for not havin' no appetite. He says he couldn't never eat when he was clost to the ocean. He'd forgot about them sixty-five oysters he destroyed the first night o' the trip before.

He was goin' to take her to a show, so after supper he went upstairs to change his collar. She had to doll up, too, and o' course Ike was through long before her.

If you remember the hotel in Boston, they's a little parlor where the piano's at and then they's another little parlor openin' off o' that. Well, when Ike come down Smitty was playin' a few chords and I and Carey was harmonizin'. We seen Ike go up to the desk to leave his key and we called him in. He tried to duck away, but we wouldn't stand for it.

We ast him what he was all duded up for and he says he was goin' to the theayter.

"Goin' alone?" says Carey.

"No," he says, "a friend o' mine's goin' with me."

"What do you say if we go along?" says Carey.

"I ain't only got two tickets," he says.

"Well," says Carey, "we can go down there with you and buy our own seats; maybe we can all get together."

"No," says Ike. "They ain't no more seats. They're all sold out."

"We can buy some off'n the scalpers," says Carey.

"I wouldn't if I was you," says Ike. "They say the show's rotten."

"What are you goin' for, then?" I ast.

"I didn't hear about it bein' rotten till I got the tickets," he says.

"Well," I says, "if you don't want to go I'll buy the tickets from you."

"No," says Ike, "I wouldn't want to cheat you. I'm stung and I'll just have to stand for it."

"What are you goin' to do with the girl, leave her here at the hotel?" I says.

"What girl?" says Ike.

"The girl you ett supper with," I says.

"Oh," he says, "we just happened to go into the dinin' room together, that's all. Cap wanted I should set down with 'em."

"I noticed," says Carey, "that she happened to be wearin' that rock you bought off'n Diamond Joe."

"Yes," says Ike. "I lent it to her for a wile."

"Did you lend her the new ring that goes with it?" I says.

"She had that already," says Ike. "She lost the set out of it."

"I wouldn't trust no strange girl with a rock o' mine," says Carey.

"Oh, I guess she's all right," Ike says. "Besides, I was tired o' the stone. When a girl asks you for somethin', what are you goin' to do?"

He started out toward the desk, but we flagged him.

"Wait a minute!" Carey says. "I got a bet with Sam here, and it's up to you to settle it."

"Well," says Ike, "make it snappy. My friend'll be here any minute."

"I bet," says Carey, "that you and that girl was engaged to be married."

"Nothin' to it," says Ike.

"Now look here," says Carey, "this is goin' to cost me real

money if I lose. Cut out the alibi stuff and give it to us straight. Cap's wife just as good as told us you was roped."

Ike blushed like a kid.

"Well, boys," he says, "I may as well own up. You win, Carey."

"Yatta boy!" says Carey. "Congratulations!"

"You got a swell girl, Ike," I says.

"She's a peach," says Smitty.

"Well, I guess she's O. K.," says Ike. "I don't know much about girls."

"Didn't you never run round with 'em?" I says.

"Oh, yes, plenty of 'em," says Ike. "But I never seen none I'd fall for."

"That is, till you seen this one," says Carey.

"Well," says Ike, "this one's O. K., but I wasn't thinkin' about gettin' married yet a wile."

"Who done the askin'—her?" says Carey.

"Oh, no," says Ike, "but sometimes a man don't know what he's gettin' into. Take a good-lookin' girl, and a man gen'ally almost always does about what she wants him to."

"They couldn't no girl lasso me unless I wanted to be lassoed," says Smitty.

"Oh, I don't know," says Ike. "When a fella gets to feelin' sorry for one of 'em it's all off."

Well, we left him go after shakin' hands all round. But he didn't take Dolly to no show that night. Some time wile we was talkin' she'd came into that other parlor and she'd stood there and heard us. I don't know how much she heard. But it was enough. Dolly and Cap's missus took the midnight train for New York. And from there Cap's wife sent her on her way back to Missouri.

She'd left the ring and a note for Ike with the clerk. But we didn't ask Ike if the note was from his friend in Fort Wayne, Texas.

VI

When we'd came to Boston Ike was hittin' plain .397. When we got back home he'd fell off to pretty near nothin'. He hadn't drove one out o' the infield in any o' them other Eastern parks, and he didn't even give no excuse for it.

To show you how bad he was, he struck out three times in Brooklyn one day and never opened his trap when Cap ast him what was the matter. Before, if he'd whiffed oncet in a game he'd of wrote a book tellin' why.

Well, we dropped from first place to fifth in four weeks and we was still goin' down. I and Carey was about the only ones in the club that spoke to each other, and all as we did was remind ourself o' what a boner we'd pulled.

"It's goin' to beat us out o' the big money," says Carey.

"Yes," I says. "I don't want to knock my own ball club, but it looks like a one-man team, and when that one man's dauber's down we couldn't trim our whiskers."

"We ought to knew better," says Carey.

"Yes," I says, "but why should a man pull an alibi for bein' engaged to such a bearcat as she was?"

"He shouldn't," says Carey. "But I and you knowed he would or we'd never started talkin' to him about it. He wasn't no more ashamed o' the girl than I am of a regular base hit. But he just can't come clean on no subjec'."

Cap had the whole story, and I and Carey was as pop'lar with him as an umpire.

"What do you want me to do, Cap?" Carey'd say to him before goin' up to hit.

"Use your own judgment," Cap'd tell him. "We want to lose another game."

But finally, one night in Pittsburgh, Cap had a letter from his missus and he come to us with it.

"You fellas," he says, "is the ones that put us on the bum, and if you're sorry I think they's a chancet for you to make good. The old lady's out to St. Joe and she's been tryin' her hardest to fix things up. She's explained that Ike don't mean nothin' with his talk; I've wrote and explained that to Dolly, too. But the old lady says that Dolly says that she can't believe it. But Dolly's still stuck on this baby, and she's pinin' away just the same as Ike. And the old lady says she thinks if you two fellas would write to the girl and explain how you was always kiddin' with Ike and leadin' him on, and how the ball club was all shot to pieces since Ike quit hittin', and how he acted like he was goin' to kill himself, and this and that, she'd fall for it and maybe soften down. Dolly, the old lady says, would believe you before she'd believe I and the old lady, because she thinks it's her we're sorry for, and not him."

Well, I and Carey was only too glad to try and see what we could do. But it wasn't no snap. We wrote about eight letters before we got one that looked good. Then we give it to the stenographer and had it wrote out on a typewriter and both of us signed it.

It was Carey's idear that made the letter good. He stuck in somethin' about the world's serious money that our wives wasn't goin' to spend unless she took pity on a "boy who was so shy and modest that he was afraid to come right out and say that he had asked such a beautiful and handsome girl to become his bride."

That's prob'ly what got her, or maybe she couldn't of held out much longer anyway. It was four days after we sent the letter that Cap heard from his missus again. We was in Cincinnati.

"We've won," he says to us. "The old lady says that Dolly says she'll give him another chancet. But the old lady says it won't do no good for Ike to write a letter. He'll have to go out there."

"Send him to-night," says Carey.

"I'll pay half his fare," I says.

"I'll pay the other half," says Carey.

"No," says Cap, "the club'll pay his expenses. I'll send him scoutin'."

"Are you goin' to send him to-night?"

"Sure," says Cap. "But I'm goin' to break the news to him right now. It's time we win a ball game."

So in the clubhouse, just before the game, Cap told him. And I certainly felt sorry for Rube Benton and Red Ames that afternoon! I and Carey was standin' in front o' the hotel that night when Ike come out with his suitcase.

"Sent home?" I says to him.

"No," he says, "I'm goin' scoutin'."

"Where to?" I says. "Fort Wayne?"

"No, not exactly," he says.

"Well," says Carey, "have a good time."

"I ain't lookin' for no good time," says Ike. "I says I was goin' scoutin'."

"Well, then," says Carey, "I hope you see somebody you like."

"And you better have a drink before you go," I says.

"Well," says Ike, "they claim it helps a cold."

Champion

MIDGE KELLY scored his first knockout when he was seventeen. The knockee was his brother Connie, three years his junior and a cripple. The purse was a half dollar given to the younger Kelly by a lady whose electric had just missed bumping his soul from his frail little body.

Connie did not know Midge was in the house, else he never would have risked laying the prize on the arm of the least comfortable chair in the room, the better to observe its shining beauty. As Midge entered from the kitchen, the crippled boy covered the coin with his hand, but the movement lacked the speed requisite to escape his brother's quick eye.

"Watcha got there?" demanded Midge.

"Nothin'," said Connie.

"You're a one legged liar!" said Midge.

He strode over to his brother's chair and grasped the hand that concealed the coin.

"Let loose!" he ordered.

Connie began to cry.

"Let loose and shut up your noise," said the elder, and jerked his brother's hand from the chair arm.

The coin fell onto the bare floor. Midge pounced on it. His weak mouth widened in a triumphant smile.

"Nothin', huh?" he said. "All right, if it's nothin' you don't want it."

"Give that back," sobbed the younger.

"I'll give you a red nose, you little sneak! Where'd you steal it?"

"I didn't steal it. It's mine. A lady give it to me after she pretty near hit me with a car."

"It's a crime she missed you," said Midge.

Midge started for the front door. The cripple picked up his crutch, rose from his chair with difficulty, and, still sobbing, came toward Midge. The latter heard him and stopped.

"You better stay where you're at," he said.

"I want my money," cried the boy.

"I know what you want," said Midge.

Doubling up the fist that held the half dollar, he landed with

480

all his strength on his brother's mouth. Connie fell to the floor with a thud, the crutch tumbling on top of him. Midge stood beside the prostrate form.

"Is that enough?" he said. "Or do you want this, too?"

And he kicked him in the crippled leg.

"I guess that'll hold you," he said.

There was no response from the boy on the floor. Midge looked at him a moment, then at the coin in his hand, and then went out into the street, whistling.

An hour later, when Mrs. Kelly came home from her day's work at Faulkner's Steam Laundry, she found Connie on the floor, moaning. Dropping on her knees beside him, she called him by name a score of times. Then she got up and, pale as a ghost, dashed from the house. Dr. Ryan left the Kelly abode about dusk and walked toward Halsted Street. Mrs. Dorgan spied him as he passed her gate.

"Who's sick, Doctor?" she called.

"Poor little Connie," he replied. "He had a bad fall."

"How did it happen?"

"I can't say for sure, Margaret, but I'd almost bet he was knocked down."

"Knocked down!" exclaimed Mrs. Dorgan.

"Why, who—?"

"Have you seen the other one lately?"

"Michael? No, not since mornin'. You can't be thinkin'——"

"I wouldn't put it past him, Margaret," said the doctor gravely. "The lad's mouth is swollen and cut, and his poor, skinny little leg is bruised. He surely didn't do it to himself and I think Helen suspects the other one."

"Lord save us!" said Mrs. Dorgan. "I'll run over and see if I can help."

"That's a good woman," said Doctor Ryan, and went on down the street.

Near midnight, when Midge came home, his mother was sitting at Connie's bedside. She did not look up.

"Well," said Midge, "what's the matter?"

She remained silent. Midge repeated his question.

"Michael, you know what's the matter," she said at length.

"I don't know nothin'," said Midge.

"Don't lie to me, Michael. What did you do to your brother?"

"Nothin'."

"You hit him."

"Well, then, I hit him. What of it? It ain't the first time."

Her lips pressed tightly together, her face like chalk, Ellen Kelly rose from her chair and made straight for him. Midge backed against the door.

"Lay off'n me, Ma. I don't want to fight no woman."

Still she came on breathing heavily.

"Stop where you're at, Ma," he warned.

There was a brief struggle and Midge's mother lay on the floor before him.

"You ain't hurt, Ma. You're lucky I didn't land good. And I told you to lay off'n me."

"God forgive you, Michael!"

Midge found Hap Collins in the showdown game at the Royal.

"Come on out a minute," he said.

Hap followed him out on the walk.

"I'm leavin' town for a w'ile," said Midge.

"What for?"

"Well, we had a little run-in up to the house. The kid stole a half buck off'n me, and when I went after it he cracked me with his crutch. So I nailed him. And the old lady came at me with a chair and I took it off'n her and she fell down."

"How is Connie hurt?"

"Not bad."

"What are you runnin' away for?"

"Who the hell said I was runnin' away? I'm sick and tired o' gettin' picked on; that's all. So I'm leavin' for a w'ile and I want a piece o' money."

"I ain't only got six bits," said Happy.

"You're in bad shape, ain't you? Well, come through with it."

Happy came through.

"You oughtn't to hit the kid," he said.

"I ain't astin' you who can I hit," snarled Midge. "You try to put somethin' over on me and you'll get the same dose. I'm goin' now."

"Go as far as you like," said Happy, but not until he was sure that Kelly was out of hearing.

Early the following morning, Midge boarded a train for Milwaukee. He had no ticket, but no one knew the difference. The conductor remained in the caboose.

On a night six months later, Midge hurried out of the "stage door" of the Star Boxing Club and made for Duane's saloon, two blocks away. In his pocket were twelve dollars, his reward for having battered up one Demon Dempsey through the six rounds of the first preliminary.

It was Midge's first professional engagement in the manly art. Also it was the first time in weeks that he had earned twelve dollars.

On the way to Duane's he had to pass Niemann's. He pulled his cap over his eyes and increased his pace until he had gone by. Inside Niemann's stood a trusting bartender, who for ten days had staked Midge to drinks and allowed him to ravage the lunch on a promise to come in and settle the moment he was paid for the "prelim."

Midge strode into Duane's and aroused the napping bartender by slapping a silver dollar on the festive board.

"Gimme a shot," said Midge.

The shooting continued until the wind-up at the Star was over and part of the fight crowd joined Midge in front of Duane's bar. A youth in the early twenties, standing next to young Kelly, finally summoned sufficient courage to address him.

"Wasn't you in the first bout?" he ventured.

"Yeh," Midge replied.

"My name's Hersch," said the other.

Midge received the startling information in silence.

"I don't want to butt in," continued Mr. Hersch, "but I'd like to buy you a drink."

"All right," said Midge, "but don't overstrain yourself."

Mr. Hersch laughed uproariously and beckoned to the bartender.

"You certainly gave that wop a trimmin' to-night," said the buyer of the drink, when they had been served. "I thought you'd kill him."

"I would if I hadn't let up," Midge replied. "I'll kill 'em all."

"You got the wallop all right," the other said admiringly.

"Have I got the wallop?" said Midge. "Say, I can kick like a mule. Did you notice them muscles in my shoulders?"

"Notice 'em? I couldn't help from noticin' 'em," said Hersch. "I says to the fella settin' alongside o' me, I says: 'Look at them shoulders! No wonder he can hit,' I says to him."

"Just let me land and it's good-by, baby," said Midge. "I'll kill 'em all."

The oral manslaughter continued until Duane's closed for the night. At parting, Midge and his new friend shook hands and arranged for a meeting the following evening.

For nearly a week the two were together almost constantly. It was Hersch's pleasant rôle to listen to Midge's modest revelations concerning himself, and to buy every time Midge's glass was empty. But there came an evening when Hersch regretfully announced that he must go home to supper.

"I got a date for eight bells," he confided. "I could stick till then, only I must clean up and put on the Sunday clo'es, 'cause she's the prettiest little thing in Milwaukee."

"Can't you fix it for two?" asked Midge.

"I don't know who to get," Hersch replied. "Wait, though. I got a sister and if she ain't busy, it'll be O. K. She's no bum for looks herself."

So it came about that Midge and Emma Hersch and Emma's brother and the prettiest little thing in Milwaukee foregathered at Wall's and danced half the night away. And Midge and Emma danced every dance together, for though every little onestep seemed to induce a new thirst of its own, Lou Hersch stayed too sober to dance with his own sister.

The next day, penniless at last in spite of his phenomenal ability to make someone else settle, Midge Kelly sought out Doc Hammond, matchmaker for the Star, and asked to be booked for the next show.

"I could put you on with Tracy for the next bout," said Doc.

"What's they in it?" asked Midge.

"Twenty if you cop," Doc told him.

"Have a heart," protested Midge. "Didn't I look good the other night?"

"You looked all right. But you aren't Freddie Welsh yet by a consid'able margin."

"I ain't scared of Freddie Welsh or none of 'em," said Midge.

"Well, we don't pay our boxers by the size of their chests," Doc said. "I'm offerin' you this Tracy bout. Take it or leave it."

"All right; I'm on," said Midge, and he passed a pleasant afternoon at Duane's on the strength of his booking.

Young Tracy's manager came to Midge the night before the show.

"How do you feel about this go?" he asked.

"Me?" said Midge. "I feel all right. What do you mean, how do I feel?"

"I mean," said Tracy's manager, "that we're mighty anxious to win, 'cause the boy's got a chanct in Philly if he cops this one."

"What's your proposition?" asked Midge.

"Fifty bucks," said Tracy's manager.

"What do you think I am, a crook? Me lay down for fifty bucks. Not me!"

"Seventy-five, then," said Tracy's manager.

The market closed on eighty and the details were agreed on in short order. And the next night Midge was stopped in the second round by a terrific slap on the forearm.

This time Midge passed up both Niemann's and Duane's, having a sizable account at each place, and sought his refreshment at Stein's farther down the street.

When the profits of his deal with Tracy were gone, he learned, by first-hand information from Doc Hammond and the matchmakers at the other "clubs," that he was no longer desired for even the cheapest of preliminaries. There was no danger of his starving or dying of thirst while Emma and Lou Hersch lived. But he made up his mind, four months after his defeat by Young Tracy, that Milwaukee was not the ideal place for him to live.

"I can lick the best of 'em," he reasoned, "but there ain't no more chanct for me here. I can maybe go east and get on somewheres. And besides——"

But just after Midge had purchased a ticket to Chicago with the money he had "borrowed" from Emma Hersch "to buy shoes," a heavy hand was laid on his shoulders and he turned to face two strangers.

"Where are you goin', Kelly?" inquired the owner of the heavy hand.

"Nowheres," said Midge. "What the hell do you care?"

The other stranger spoke:

"Kelly, I'm employed by Emma Hersch's mother to see that you do right by her. And we want you to stay here till you've done it."

"You won't get nothin' but the worst of it, monkeying with me," said Midge.

Nevertheless, he did not depart for Chicago that night. Two days later, Emma Hersch became Mrs. Kelly, and the gift of the groom, when once they were alone, was a crushing blow on the bride's pale cheek.

Next morning, Midge left Milwaukee as he had entered it—by fast freight.

"They's no use kiddin' ourself any more," said Tommy Haley. "He might get down to thirty-seven in a pinch, but if he done below that a mouse could stop him. He's a welter; that's what he is and he knows it as well as I do. He's growed like a weed in the last six mont's. I told him, I says, 'If you don't quit growin' they won't be nobody for you to box, only Willard and them.' He says, 'Well, I wouldn't run away from Willard if I weighed twenty pounds more.'"

"He must hate himself," said Tommy's brother.

"I never seen a good one that didn't," said Tommy. "And Midge is a good one; don't make no mistake about that. I wisht we could of got Welsh before the kid growed so big. But it's too late now. I won't make no holler, though, if we can match him up with the Dutchman."

"Who do you mean?"

"Young Goetz, the welter champ. We mightn't not get so much dough for the bout itself, but it'd roll in afterward. What a drawin' card we'd be, 'cause the people pays their money to see the fella with the wallop, and that's Midge. And we'd keep the title just as long as Midge could make the weight."

"Can't you land no match with Goetz?"

"Sure, 'cause he needs the money. But I've went careful with the kid so far and look at the results I got! So what's the use of takin' a chanct? The kid's comin' every minute and Goetz is goin' back faster'n big Johnson did. I think we could lick him now; I'd bet my life on it. But six mont's from now they won't be no risk. He'll of licked hisself before that time. Then all as we'll have to do is sign up with him and wait for the referee to stop it. But Midge is so crazy to get at him now that I can't hardly hold him back."

The brothers Haley were lunching in a Boston hotel. Dan had come down from Holyoke to visit with Tommy and to watch the latter's protégé go twelve rounds, or less, with Bud Cross. The bout promised little in the way of a contest, for Midge had twice stopped the Baltimore youth and Bud's reputation for gameness was all that had earned him the date. The fans were willing to pay the price to see Midge's hay-making left, but they wanted to see it used on an opponent who would not jump out of the ring the first time he felt its crushing force. But Cross was such an opponent, and his willingness to stop boxing-gloves with his eyes, ears, nose and throat had long enabled him to escape the horrors of honest labor. A game boy was Bud, and he showed it in his battered, swollen, discolored face.

"I should think," said Dan Haley, "that the kid'd do whatever you tell him after all you done for him."

"Well," said Tommy, "he's took my dope pretty straight so far, but he's so sure of hisself that he can't see no reason for waitin'. He'll do what I say, though; he'd be a sucker not to."

"You got a contrac' with him?"

"No, I don't need no contrac'. He knows it was me that drug him out o' the gutter and he ain't goin' to turn me down now, when he's got the dough and bound to get more. Where'd he of been at if I hadn't listened to him when he first come to me? That's pretty near two years ago now, but it seems like last week. I was settin' in the s'loon acrost from the Pleasant Club in Philly, waitin' for McCann to count the dough and come over, when this little bum blowed in and tried to stand the house off for a drink. They told him nothin' doin' and to beat it out o' there, and then he seen me and come over to where I was settin' and ast me wasn't I a boxin' man and I told him who I was. Then he ast me for money to buy a shot and I told him to set down and I'd buy it for him.

"Then we got talkin' things over and he told me his name and told me about fightn' a couple o' prelims out to Milwaukee. So I says, 'Well, boy, I don't know how good or how rotten you are, but you won't never get nowheres trainin' on that stuff.' So he says he'd cut it out if he could get on in a bout and

I says I would give him a chanct if he played square with me and didn't touch no more to drink. So we shook hands and I took him up to the hotel with me and give him a bath and the next day I bought him some clo'es. And I staked him to eats and sleeps for over six weeks. He had a hard time breakin' away from the polish, but finally I thought he was fit and I give him his chanct. He went on with Smiley Sayer and stopped him so quick that Smiley thought sure he was poisoned.

"Well, you know what he's did since. The only beatin' in his record was by Tracy in Milwaukee before I got hold of him, and he's licked Tracy three times in the last year.

"I've gave him all the best of it in a money way and he's got seven thousand bucks in cold storage. How's that for a kid that was in the gutter two years ago? And he'd have still more yet if he wasn't so nuts over clo'es and got to stop at the good hotels and so forth."

"Where's his home at?"

"Well, he ain't really got no home. He came from Chicago and his mother canned him out o' the house for bein' no good. She give him a raw deal, I guess, and he says he won't have nothin' to do with her unlest she comes to him first. She's got a pile o' money, he says, so he ain't worryin' about her."

The gentleman under discussion entered the café and swaggered to Tommy's table, while the whole room turned to look.

Midge was the picture of health despite a slightly colored eye and an ear that seemed to have no opening. But perhaps it was not his healthiness that drew all eyes. His diamond horseshoe tie pin, his purple cross-striped shirt, his orange shoes and his light blue suit fairly screamed for attention.

"Where you been?" he asked Tommy. "I been lookin' all over for you."

"Set down," said his manager.

"No time," said Midge. "I'm goin' down to the w'arf and see 'em unload the fish."

"Shake hands with my brother Dan," said Tommy.

Midge shook with the Holyoke Haley.

"If you're Tommy's brother, you're O. K. with me," said Midge, and the brothers beamed with pleasure.

Dan moistened his lips and murmured an embarrassed reply, but it was lost on the young gladiator.

"Leave me take twenty," Midge was saying. "I prob'ly won't need it, but I don't like to be caught short."

Tommy parted with a twenty dollar bill and recorded the transaction in a small black book the insurance company had given him for Christmas.

"But," he said, "it won't cost you no twenty to look at them fish. Want me to go along?"

"No," said Midge hastily. "You and your brother here prob'ly got a lot to say to each other."

"Well," said Tommy, "don't take no bad money and don't get lost. And you better be back at four o'clock and lay down a w'ile."

"I don't need no rest to beat this guy," said Midge. "He'll do enough layin' down for the both of us."

And laughing even more than the jest called for, he strode out through the fire of admiring and startled glances.

The corner of Boylston and Tremont was the nearest Midge got to the wharf, but the lady awaiting him was doubtless a more dazzling sight than the catch of the luckiest Massachusetts fisherman. She could talk, too—probably better than the fish.

"O you Kid!" she said, flashing a few silver teeth among the gold. "O you fighting man!"

Midge smiled up at her.

"We'll go somewheres and get a drink," he said. "One won't hurt."

In New Orleans, five months after he had rearranged the map of Bud Cross for the third time, Midge finished training for his championship bout with the Dutchman.

Back in his hotel after the final workout, Midge stopped to chat with some of the boys from up north, who had made the long trip to see a champion dethroned, for the result of this bout was so nearly a foregone conclusion that even the experts had guessed it.

Tommy Haley secured the key and the mail and ascended to the Kelly suite. He was bathing when Midge came in, half hour later.

"Any mail?" asked Midge.

"There on the bed," replied Tommy from the tub.

Midge picked up the stack of letters and postcards and glanced them over. From the pile he sorted out three letters and laid them on the table. The rest he tossed into the wastebasket. Then he picked up the three and sat for a few moments holding them, while his eyes gazed off into space. At length he looked again at the three unopened letters in his hand; then he put one in his pocket and tossed the other two at the basket. They missed their target and fell on the floor.

"Hell!" said Midge, and stooping over picked them up.

He opened one postmarked Milwaukee and read:

DEAR HUSBAND:

I have wrote to you so manny times and got no anser and I dont know if you ever got them, so I am writeing again in the hopes you will get this letter and anser. I dont like to bother you with my trubles and I would not only for the baby and I am not asking you should write to me but only send a little money and I am not asking for myself but the baby has not been well a day sence last Aug. and the dr. told me she cant live much longer unless I give her better food and thats impossible the way things are. Lou has not been working for a year and what I make dont hardley pay for the rent. I am not asking for you to give me any money, but only you should send what I loaned when convenient and I think it amts. to about $36.00. Please try and send that amt. and it will help me, but if you cant send the whole amt. try and send me something.

Your wife,

EMMA.

Midge tore the letter into a hundred pieces and scattered them over the floor.

"Money, money, money!" he said. "They must think I'm made o' money. I s'pose the old woman's after it too."

He opened his mother's letter:

dear Michael Connie wonted me to rite and say you must beet the dutchman and he is sur you will and wonted me to say we wont you to rite and tell us about it, but I gess you havent no time to rite or we herd from you long beffore this but I wish you would rite jest a line or 2 boy becaus it wuld be better for Connie then a barl of medisin. It wuld help me to keep things going if you send me money now and then when you can spair it but if you cant send no money try and fine time to rite a letter onley a few lines and it will please Connie. jest think boy he hasent got out of bed in over 3 yrs. Connie says good luck.

Your Mother,

ELLEN F. KELLY.

"I thought so," said Midge. "They're all alike." ˙
The third letter was from New York. It read:

HON:—This is the last letter you will get from me before your champ, but I will send you a telegram Saturday, but I can't say as much in a telegram as in a letter and I am writeing this to let you know I am thinking of you and praying for good luck.

Lick him good hon and don't wait no longer than you have to and don't forget to wire me as soon as its over. Give him that little old left of yours on the nose hon and don't be afraid of spoiling his good looks because he couldn't be no homlier than he is. But don't let him spoil my baby's pretty face. You won't will you hon.

Well hon I would give anything to be there and see it, but I guess you love Haley better than me or you wouldn't let him keep me away. But when your champ hon we can do as we please and tell Haley to go to the devil.

Well hon I will send you a telegram Saturday and I almost forgot to tell you I will need some more money, a couple hundred say and you have to wire it to me as soon as you get this. You will won't you hon.

I will send you a telegram Saturday and remember hon I am pulling for you.

Well good-by sweetheart and good luck.

GRACE.

"They're all alike," said Midge. "Money, money, money."

Tommy Haley, shining from his ablutions, came in from the adjoining room.

"Thought you'd be layin' down," he said.

"I'm goin' to," said Midge, unbuttoning his orange shoes.

"I'll call you at six and you can eat up here without no bugs to pester you. I got to go down and give them birds their tickets."

"Did you hear from Goldberg?" asked Midge.

"Didn't I tell you? Sure; fifteen weeks at five hundred, if we win. And we can get a guarantee o' twelve thousand, with privileges either in New York or Milwaukee."

"Who with?"

"Anybody that'll stand up in front of you. You don't care who it is, do you?"

"Not me. I'll make 'em all look like a monkey."

"Well you better lay down aw'ile."

"Oh, say, wire two hundred to Grace for me, will you? Right away; the New York address."

"Two hundred! You just sent her three hundred last Sunday."

"Well, what the hell do you care?"

"All right, all right. Don't get sore about it. Anything else?"

"That's all," said Midge, and dropped onto the bed.

"And I want the deed done before I come back," said Grace as she rose from the table. "You won't fall down on me, will you, hon?"

"Leave it to me," said Midge. "And don't spend no more than you have to."

Grace smiled a farewell and left the café. Midge continued to sip his coffee and read his paper.

They were in Chicago and they were in the middle of Midge's first week in vaudeville. He had come straight north to reap the rewards of his glorious victory over the broken down Dutchman. A fortnight had been spent in learning his act, which consisted of a gymnastic exhibition and a ten minutes' monologue on the various excellences of Midge Kelly. And now he was twice daily turning 'em away from the Madison Theater.

His breakfast over and his paper read, Midge sauntered into the lobby and asked for his key. He then beckoned to a bellboy, who had been hoping for that very honor.

"Find Haley, Tommy Haley," said Midge. "Tell him to come up to my room."

"Yes, sir, Mr. Kelly," said the boy, and proceeded to break all his former records for diligence.

Midge was looking out of his seventh-story window when Tommy answered the summons.

"What'll it be?" inquired his manager.

There was a pause before Midge replied.

"Haley," he said, "twenty-five per cent's a whole lot o' money."

"I guess I got it comin', ain't I?" said Tommy.

"I don't see how you figger it. I don't see where you're worth it to me."

"Well," said Tommy, "I didn't expect nothin' like this. I thought you was satisfied with the bargain. I don't want to beat nobody out o' nothin', but I don't see where you could have got anybody else that would of did all I done for you."

"Sure, that's all right," said the champion. "You done a lot for me in Philly. And you got good money for it, didn't you?"

"I ain't makin' no holler. Still and all, the big money's still ahead of us yet. And if it hadn't of been for me, you wouldn't of never got within grabbin' distance."

"Oh, I guess I could of went along all right," said Midge. "Who was it that hung that left on the Dutchman's jaw, me or you?"

"Yes, but you wouldn't been in the ring with the Dutchman if it wasn't for how I handled you."

"Well, this won't get us nowheres. The idear is that you ain't worth no twenty-five per cent now and it don't make no diff'rence what come off a year or two ago."

"Don't it?" said Tommy. "I'd say it made a whole lot of difference."

"Well, I say it don't and I guess that settles it."

"Look here, Midge," Tommy said, "I thought I was fair with you, but if you don't think so, I'm willin' to hear what you think is fair. I don't want nobody callin' me a Sherlock. Let's go down to business and sign up a contrac'. What's your figger?"

"I ain't namin' no figger," Midge replied. "I'm sayin' that twenty-five's too much. Now what are you willin' to take?"

"How about twenty?"

"Twenty's too much," said Kelly.

"What ain't too much?" asked Tommy.

"Well, Haley, I might as well give it to you straight. They ain't nothin' that ain't too much."

"You mean you don't want me at no figger?"

"That's the idear."

There was a minute's silence. Then Tommy Haley walked toward the door.

"Midge," he said, in a choking voice, "you're makin' a big

mistake, boy. You can't throw down your best friends and get away with it. That damn woman will ruin you."

Midge sprang from his seat.

"You shut your mouth!" he stormed. "Get out o' here before they have to carry you out. You been spongin' off o' me long enough. Say one more word about the girl or about anything else and you'll get what the Dutchman got. Now get out!"

And Tommy Haley, having a very vivid memory of the Dutchman's face as he fell, got out.

Grace came in later, dropped her numerous bundles on the lounge and perched herself on the arm of Midge's chair.

"Well?" she said.

"Well," said Midge, "I got rid of him."

"Good boy!" said Grace. "And now I think you might give me that twenty-five per cent."

"Besides the seventy-five you're already gettin'?" said Midge.

"Don't be no grouch, hon. You don't look pretty when you're grouchy."

"It ain't my business to look pretty," Midge replied.

"Wait till you see how I look with the stuff I bought this mornin'!"

Midge glanced at the bundles on the lounge.

"There's Haley's twenty-five per cent," he said, "and then some."

The champion did not remain long without a manager. Haley's successor was none other than Jerome Harris, who saw in Midge a better meal ticket than his popular-priced musical show had been.

The contract, giving Mr. Harris twenty-five per cent of Midge's earnings, was signed in Detroit the week after Tommy Haley had heard his dismissal read. It had taken Midge just six days to learn that a popular actor cannot get on without the ministrations of a man who thinks, talks and means business. At first Grace objected to the new member of the firm, but when Mr. Harris had demanded and secured from the vaudeville people a one-hundred dollar increase in Midge's weekly stipend, she was convinced that the champion had acted for the best.

"You and my missus will have some great old times," Harris

told Grace. "I'd of wired her to join us here, only I seen the Kid's bookin' takes us to Milwaukee next week, and that's where she is."

But when they were introduced in the Milwaukee hotel, Grace admitted to herself that her feeling for Mrs. Harris could hardly be called love at first sight. Midge, on the contrary, gave his new manager's wife the many times over and seemed loath to end the feast of his eyes.

"Some doll," he said to Grace when they were alone.

"Doll is right," the lady replied, "and sawdust where her brains ought to be."

"I'm li'ble to steal that baby," said Midge, and he smiled as he noted the effect of his words on his audience's face.

On Tuesday of the Milwaukee week the champion successfully defended his title in a bout that the newspapers never reported. Midge was alone in his room that morning when a visitor entered without knocking. The visitor was Lou Hersch.

Midge turned white at sight of him.

"What do you want?" he demanded.

"I guess you know," said Lou Hersch. "Your wife's starvin' to death and your baby's starvin' to death and I'm starvin' to death. And you're dirty with money."

"Listen," said Midge, "if it wasn't for you, I wouldn't never saw your sister. And, if you ain't man enough to hold a job, what's that to me? The best thing you can do is keep away from me."

"You give me a piece o' money and I'll go."

Midge's reply to the ultimatum was a straight right to his brother-in-law's narrow chest.

"Take that home to your sister."

And after Lou Hersch had picked himself up and slunk away, Midge thought: "It's lucky I didn't give him my left or I'd of croaked him. And if I'd hit him in the stomach, I'd of broke his spine."

There was a party after each evening performance during the Milwaukee engagement. The wine flowed freely and Midge had more of it than Tommy Haley ever would have permitted him. Mr. Harris offered no objection, which was possibly just as well for his own physical comfort.

In the dancing between drinks, Midge had his new manager's wife for a partner as often as Grace. The latter's face as she floundered round in the arms of the portly Harris, belied her frequent protestations that she was having the time of her life.

Several times that week, Midge thought Grace was on the point of starting the quarrel he hoped to have. But it was not until Friday night that she accommodated. He and Mrs. Harris had disappeared after the matinee and when Grace saw him again at the close of the night show, she came to the point at once.

"What are you tryin' to pull off?" she demanded.

"It's none o' your business, is it?" said Midge.

"You bet it's my business; mine and Harris's. You cut it short or you'll find out."

"Listen," said Midge, "have you got a mortgage on me or somethin'? You talk like we was married."

"We're goin' to be, too. And to-morrow's as good a time as any."

"Just about," Midge said. "You got as much chanct o' marryin' me to-morrow as the next day or next year and that ain't no chanct at all."

"We'll find out," said Grace.

"You're the one that's got somethin' to find out."

"What do you mean?"

"I mean I'm married already."

"You lie!"

"You think so, do you? Well, s'pose you go to this here address and get acquainted with my missus."

Midge scrawled a number on a piece of paper and handed it to her. She stared at it unseeingly.

"Well," said Midge, "I ain't kiddin' you. You go there and ask for Mrs. Michael Kelly, and if you don't find her, I'll marry you to-morrow before breakfast."

Still Grace stared at the scrap of paper. To Midge it seemed an age before she spoke again.

"You lied to me all this w'ile."

"You never ast me was I married. What's more, what the hell diff'rence did it make to you? You got a split, didn't you? Better'n fifty-fifty."

He started away.

"Where you goin'?"

"I'm goin' to meet Harris and his wife."

"I'm goin' with you. You're not goin' to shake me now."

"Yes, I am, too," said Midge quietly. "When I leave town to-morrow night, you're going to stay here. And if I see where you're goin' to make a fuss, I'll put you in a hospital where they'll keep you quiet. You can get your stuff to-morrow mornin' and I'll slip you a hundred bucks. And then I don't want to see no more o' you. And don't try and tag along now or I'll have to add another K. O. to the old record."

When Grace returned to the hotel that night, she discovered that Midge and the Harrises had moved to another. And when Midge left town the following night, he was again without a manager, and Mr. Harris was without a wife.

Three days prior to Midge Kelly's ten-round bout with Young Milton in New York City, the sporting editor of *The News* assigned Joe Morgan to write two or three thousand words about the champion to run with a picture lay-out for Sunday.

Joe Morgan dropped in at Midge's training quarters Friday afternoon. Midge, he learned, was doing road work, but Midge's manager, Wallie Adams, stood ready and willing to supply reams of dope about the greatest fighter of the age.

"Let's hear what you've got," said Joe, "and then I'll try to fix up something."

So Wallie stepped on the accelerator of his imagination and shot away.

"Just a kid; that's all he is; a regular boy. Get what I mean? Don't know the meanin' o' bad habits. Never tasted liquor in his life and would prob'bly get sick if he smelled it. Clean livin' put him up where he's at. Get what I mean? And modest and unassumin' as a school girl. He's so quiet you wouldn't never know he was round. And he'd go to jail before he'd talk about himself.

"No job at all to get him in shape, 'cause he's always that way. The only trouble we have with him is gettin' him to light into these poor bums they match him up with. He's scared he'll hurt somebody. Get what I mean? He's tickled to death over this match with Milton, 'cause everybody says Milton can stand the gaff. Midge'll maybe be able to cut loose a little this

time. But the last two bouts he had, the guys hadn't no business in the ring with him, and he was holdin' back all the w'ile
for the fear he'd kill somebody. Get what I mean?"

"Is he married?" inquired Joe.

"Say, you'd think he was married to hear him rave about
them kiddies he's got. His fam'ly's up in Canada to their summer home and Midge is wild to get up there with 'em. He
thinks more o' that wife and them kiddies than all the money
in the world. Get what I mean?"

"How many children has he?"

"I don't know, four or five, I guess. All boys and every one
of 'em a dead ringer for their dad."

"Is his father living?"

"No, the old man died when he was a kid. But he's got a
grand old mother and a kid brother out in Chi. They're the
first ones he thinks about after a match, them and his wife and
kiddies. And he don't forget to send the old woman a thousand
bucks after every bout. He's goin' to buy her a new home as
soon as they pay him off for this match."

"How about his brother? Is he going to tackle the game?"

"Sure, and Midge says he'll be a champion before he's
twenty years old. They're a fightin' fam'ly and all of 'em honest
and straight as a die. Get what I mean? A fella that I can't tell
you his name come to Midge in Milwaukee onct and wanted
him to throw a fight and Midge give him such a trimmin' in
the street that he couldn't go on that night. That's the kind he
is. Get what I mean?"

Joe Morgan hung around the camp until Midge and his
trainers returned.

"One o' the boys from *The News*," said Wallie by way of introduction. "I been givin' him your fam'ly hist'ry."

"Did he give you good dope?" he inquired.

"He's some historian," said Joe.

"Don't call me no names," said Wallie smiling. "Call us up if
they's anything more you want. And keep your eyes on us
Monday night. Get what I mean?"

The story in Sunday's *News* was read by thousands of lovers
of the manly art. It was well written and full of human interest.
Its slight inaccuracies went unchallenged, though three readers, besides Wallie Adams and Midge Kelly, saw and recognized

them. The three were Grace, Tommy Haley and Jerome Harris and the comments they made were not for publication.

Neither the Mrs. Kelly in Chicago nor the Mrs. Kelly in Milwaukee knew that there was such a paper as the New York *News*. And even if they had known of it and that it contained two columns of reading matter about Midge, neither mother nor wife could have bought it. For *The News* on Sunday is a nickel a copy.

Joe Morgan could have written more accurately, no doubt, if instead of Wallie Adams, he had interviewed Ellen Kelly and Connie Kelly and Emma Kelly and Lou Hersch and Grace and Jerome Harris and Tommy Haley and Hap Collins and two or three Milwaukee bartenders.

But a story built on their evidence would never have passed the sporting editor.

"Suppose you can prove it," that gentleman would have said. "It wouldn't get us anything but abuse to print it. The people don't want to see him knocked. He's champion."

Some Like Them Cold

N. Y., Aug. 3.

DEAR MISS GILLESPIE: How about our bet now as you bet me I would forget all about you the minute I hit the big town and would never write you a letter. Well girlie it looks like you lose so pay me. Seriously we will call all bets off as I am not the kind that bet on a sure thing and it sure was a sure thing that I would not forget a girlie like you and all that is worrying me is whether it may not be the other way round and you are wondering who this fresh guy is that is writeing you this letter. I bet you are so will try and refreshen your memory.

Well girlie I am the handsome young man that was wondering round the Lasalle st. station Monday and "happened" to sit down beside of a mighty pretty girlie who was waiting to meet her sister from Toledo and the train was late and I am glad of it because if it had not of been that little girlie and I would never of met. So for once I was a lucky guy but still I guess it was time I had some luck as it was certainly tough luck for you and I to both be liveing in Chi all that time and never get together till a half hour before I was leaveing town for good.

Still "better late than never" you know and maybe we can make up for lost time though it looks like we would have to do our makeing up at long distants unless you make good on your threat and come to N. Y. I wish you would do that little thing girlie as it looks like that was the only way we would get a chance to play round together as it looks like they was little or no chance of me comeing back to Chi as my whole future is in the big town. N. Y. is the only spot and specially for a man that expects to make my liveing in the song writeing game as here is the Mecca for that line of work and no matter how good a man may be they don't get no recognition unless they live in N. Y.

Well girlie you asked me to tell you all about my trip. Well I remember you saying that you would give anything to be makeing it yourself but as far as the trip itself was conserned you ought to be thankfull you did not have to make it as you would of sweat your head off. I know I did specially wile going through Ind. Monday P. M. but Monday night was the worst of all trying to sleep and finely I give it up and just layed there with the prespiration rolling off of me though I was laying on top of the covers and nothing on but my underwear.

Yesterday was not so bad as it rained most of the A. M. comeing through N. Y. state and in the P. M. we road along side of the Hudson all P. M. Some river girlie and just looking at it makes a man forget all about the heat and everything else except a certain girlie who I seen for the first time Monday and then only for a half hour but she is the kind of a girlie that a man don't need to see her only once and they would be no danger of forgetting her. There I guess I better lay off that subject or you will think I am a "fresh guy."

Well that is about all to tell you about the trip only they was one amuseing incidence that come off yesterday which I will tell you. Well they was a dame got on the train at Toledo Monday and had the birth opp. mine but I did not see nothing of her that night as I was out smoking till late and she hit the hay early but yesterday A. M. she come in the dinner and sit at the same table with me and tried to make me and it was so raw that the dinge waiter seen it and give me the wink and of course I paid no tension and I waited till she got through so as they would be no danger of her folling me out but she stopped on the way out to get a tooth pick and when I come out she was out on the platform with it so I tried to brush right by but she spoke up and asked me what time it was and I told her and she said she geussed her watch was slow so I said maybe it just seemed slow on acct. of the company it was in.

I don't know if she got what I was driveing at or not but any way she give up trying to make me and got off at Albany. She was a good looker but I have no time for gals that tries to make strangers on a train.

Well if I don't quit you will think I am writeing a book but will expect a long letter in answer to this letter and we will see if you can keep your promise like I have kept mine. Don't dissapoint me girlie as I am all alone in a large city and hearing from you will keep me from getting home sick for old Chi though I never thought so much of the old town till I found out you lived there. Don't think that is kidding girlie as I mean it.

You can address me at this hotel as it looks like I will be here right along as it is on 47th st. right off of old Broadway and handy to everything and am only paying $21 per wk. for my rm. and could of got one for $16 but without bath but am glad to pay the differents as am lost without my bath in the A. M. and sometimes at night too.

Tomorrow I expect to commence fighting the "battle of Broadway" and will let you know how I come out that is if you answer this letter. In the mean wile girlie au reservoir and don't do nothing I would not do.

Your new friend (?)

CHAS. F. LEWIS.

Chicago, Ill., Aug. 6.

MY DEAR MR. LEWIS: Well, that certainly was a "surprise party" getting your letter and you are certainly a "wonder man" to keep your word as I am afraid most men of your sex are gay deceivers but maybe you are "different." Any way it sure was a surprise and will gladly pay the bet if you will just tell me what it was we bet. Hope it was not money as I am a "working girl" but if it was not more than a dollar or two will try to dig it up even if I have to "beg, borrow or steal."

Suppose you will think me a "case" to make a bet and then forget what it was, but you must remember, Mr. Man, that I had just met you and was "dazzled." Joking aside I was rather "fussed" and will tell you why. Well, Mr. Lewis, I suppose you see lots of girls like the one you told me about that you saw on the train who tried to "get acquainted" but I want to assure you that I am not one of those kind and sincerely hope you will believe me when I tell you that you was the first man I ever spoke to meeting them like that and my friends and the people who know me would simply faint if they knew I ever spoke to a man without a "proper introduction."

Believe me, Mr. Lewis, I am not that kind and I don't know now why I did it only that you was so "different" looking if you know what I mean and not at all like the kind of men that usually try to force their attentions on every pretty girl they see. Lots of times I act on impulse and let my feelings run away from me and sometimes I do things on the impulse of the moment which I regret them later on, and that is what I did this time, but hope you won't give me cause to regret it and I know you won't as I know you are not that kind of a man a specially after what you told me about the girl on the train. But any way as I say, I was in a "daze" so can't remember what it was we bet, but will try and pay it if it does not "break" me.

Sis's train got in about ten minutes after yours had gone and when she saw me what do you think was the first thing she said? Well, Mr. Lewis, she said: "Why Mibs (That is a pet name some of my friends have given me) what has happened to you? I never seen you have as much color." So I passed it off with some remark about the heat and changed the subject as I certainly was not going to tell her that I had just been talking to a man who I had never met or she would of dropped dead from the shock. Either that or she would not of believed me as it would be hard for a person who knows me well to imagine me doing a thing like that as I have quite a reputation for "squelching" men who try to act fresh. I don't mean anything personal by that, Mr. Lewis, as am a good judge of character and could tell without you telling me that you are not that kind.

Well, Sis and I have been on the "go" ever since she arrived as I took yesterday and today off so I could show her the "sights" though she says she would be perfectly satisfied to just sit in the apartment and listen to me "rattle on." Am afraid I am a great talker, Mr. Lewis, but Sis says it is as good as a show to hear me talk as I tell things in such a different way as I cannot help from seeing the humorous side of everything and she says she never gets tired of listening to me, but of course she is my sister and thinks the world of me, but she really does laugh like she enjoyed my craziness.

Maybe I told you that I have a tiny little apartment which a girl friend of mine and I have together and it is hardly big enough to turn round in, but still it is "home" and I am a great home girl and hardly ever care to go out evenings except occasionally to the theatre or dance. But even if our "nest" is small we are proud of it and Sis complimented us on how cozy it is and how "homey" it looks and she said she did not see how we could afford to have everything so nice and Edith (my girl friend) said: "Mibs deserves all the credit for that. I never knew a girl who could make a little money go a long ways like

she can." Well, of course she is my best friend and always saying nice things about me, but I do try and I hope I get results.
Have always said that good taste and being careful is a whole
lot more important than lots of money though it is nice to
have it.

You must write and tell me how you are getting along in the
"battle of Broadway" (I laughed when I read that) and whether
the publishers like your songs though I know they will. Am
crazy to hear them and hear you play the piano as I love good
jazz music even better than classical, though I suppose it is
terrible to say such a thing. But I usually say just what I think
though sometimes I wish afterwards I had not of. But still I
believe it is better for a girl to be her own self and natural instead of always acting. But am afraid I will never have a chance
to hear you play unless you come back to Chi and pay us a visit
as my "threat" to come to New York was just a "threat" and I
don't see any hope of ever getting there unless some rich New
Yorker should fall in love with me and take me there to live.
Fine chance for poor little me, eh Mr. Lewis?

Well, I guess I have "rattled on" long enough and you will
think I am writing a book unless I quit and besides, Sis has
asked me as a special favor to make her a pie for dinner. Maybe
you don't know it, Mr. Man, but I am quite famous for my pie
and pastry, but I don't suppose a "genius" is interested in common things like that.

Well, be sure and write soon and tell me what N.Y. is like
and all about it and don't forget the little girlie who was "bad"
and spoke to a strange man in the station and have been blushing over it ever since.

Your friend (?)

MABELLE GILLESPIE.

N. Y., Aug. 10.

DEAR GIRLIE: I bet you will think I am a fresh guy com-
menceing that way but Miss Gillespie is too cold and a man
can not do nothing cold in this kind of weather specially in this
man's town which is the hottest place I ever been in and I
guess maybe the reason why New Yorkers is so bad is because
they think they are all ready in H—— and can not go no worse
place no matter how they behave themselves. Honest girlie I

certainly envy you being where there is a breeze off the old Lake and Chi may be dirty but I never heard of nobody dying because they was dirty but four people died here yesterday on acct. of the heat and I seen two different women flop right on Broadway and had to be taken away in the ambulance and it could not of been because they was dressed too warm because it would be impossible for the women here to leave off any more cloths.

Well have not had much luck yet in the battle of Broadway as all the heads of the big music publishers is out of town on their vacation and the big boys is the only ones I will do business with as it would be silly for a man with the stuff I have got to waste my time on somebody that is just on the staff and have not got the final say. But I did play a couple of my numbers for the people up to Levy's and Goebel's and they went crazy over them in both places. So it looks like all I have to do is wait for the big boys to get back and then play my numbers for them and I will be all set. What I want is to get taken on the staff of one of the big firms as that gives a man the inside and they will plug your numbers more if you are on the staff. In the mean wile have not got nothing to worry me but am just seeing the sights of the big town as have saved up enough money to play round for a wile and any way a man that can play piano like I can don't never have to worry about starveing. Can certainly make the old music box talk girlie and am always good for a $75 or $100 job.

Well have been here a week now and on the go every minute and I thought I would be lonesome down here but no chance of that as I have been treated fine by the people I have met and have sure met a bunch of them. One of the boys liveing in the hotel is a vaudeville actor and he is a member of the Friars club and took me over there to dinner the other night and some way another the bunch got wise that I could play piano so of course I had to sit down and give them some of my numbers and everybody went crazy over them. One of the boys I met there was Paul Sears the song writer but he just writes the lyrics and has wrote a bunch of hits and when he heard some of my melodies he called me over to one side and said he would like to work with me on some numbers. How is that girlie as he is one of the biggest hit writers in N. Y.

N. Y. has got some mighty pretty girlies and I guess it would not be hard to get acquainted with them and in fact several of them has tried to make me since I been here but I always figure that a girl must be something wrong with her if she tries to make a man that she don't know nothing about so I pass them all up. But I did meet a couple of pips that a man here in the hotel went up on Riverside Drive to see them and insisted on me going along and they got on some way that I could make a piano talk so they was nothing but I must play for them so I sit down and played some of my own stuff and they went crazy over it.

One of the girls wanted I should come up and see her again, and I said I might but I think I better keep away as she acted like she wanted to vamp me and I am not the kind that likes to play round with a gal just for their company and dance with them etc. but when I see the right gal that will be a different thing and she won't have to beg me to come and see her as I will camp right on her trail till she says yes. And it won't be none of these N. Y. fly by nights neither. They are all right to look at but a man would be a sucker to get serious with them as they might take you up and next thing you know you would have a wife on your hands that don't know a dish rag from a waffle iron.

Well girlie will quit and call it a day as it is too hot to write any more and I guess I will turn on the cold water and lay in the tub a wile and then turn in. Don't forget to write to

Your friend,

CHAS. F. LEWIS.

DEAR MR. MAN: Hope you won't think me a "silly Billy" for starting my letter that way but "Mr. Lewis" is so formal and "Charles" is too much the other way and any way I would not dare call a man by their first name after only knowing them only two weeks. Though I may as well confess that Charles is my favorite name for a man and have always been crazy about it as it was my father's name. Poor old dad, he died of cancer three years ago, but left enough insurance so that mother and we girls were well provided for and do not have to do anything to support ourselves though I have been earning my own living for two years to make things easier for mother and also because I simply can't bear to be doing nothing as I feel like a "drone." So I flew away from the "home nest" though mother felt bad about it as I was her favorite and she always said I was such a comfort to her as when I was in the house she never had to worry about how things would go.

But there I go gossiping about my domestic affairs just like you would be interested in them though I don't see how you could be though personly I always like to know all about my friends, but I know men are different so will try and not bore you any longer. Poor Man, I certainly feel sorry for you if New York is as hot as all that. I guess it has been very hot in Chi, too, at least everybody has been complaining about how terrible it is. Suppose you will wonder why I say "I guess" and you will think I ought to know if it is hot. Well, sir, the reason I say "I guess" is because I don't feel the heat like others do or at least I don't let myself feel it. That sounds crazy I know, but don't you think there is a good deal in mental suggestion and not letting yourself feel things? I believe that if a person simply won't allow themselves to be affected by disagreeable things, why such things won't bother them near as much. I know it works with me and that is the reason why I am never cross when things go wrong and "keep smiling" no matter what happens and as far as the heat is concerned, why I just don't let myself feel it and my friends say I don't even look hot no matter if the weather is boiling and Edith, my girl friend, often says that I am like a breeze and it cools her off just to have me come in the room. Poor Edie suffers terribly during the hot weather and says it almost makes her mad at me to see how cool and unruffled I look when everybody else is perspiring and have red faces etc.

I laughed when I read what you said about New York being so hot that people thought it was the "other place." I can appreciate a joke, Mr. Man, and that one did not go "over my head." Am still laughing at some of the things you said in the station though they probably struck me funnier than they would most girls as I always see the funny side and sometimes something is said and I laugh and the others wonder what I am laughing at as they cannot see anything in it themselves, but it is just the way I look at things so of course I cannot explain to them why I laughed and they think I am crazy. But I had rather part with almost anything rather than my sense of humour as it helps me over a great many rough spots.

Sis has gone back home though I would of liked to of kept her here much longer, but she had to go though she said she would of liked nothing better than to stay with me and just listen to me "rattle on." She always says it is just like a show to hear me talk as I always put things in such a funny way and for weeks after she has been visiting me she thinks of some of the things I said and laughs over them. Since she left Edith and I have been pretty quiet though poor Edie wants to be on the "go" all the time and tries to make me go out with her every evening to the pictures and scolds me when I say I had rather stay home and read and calls me a "book worm." Well, it is true that I had rather stay home with a good book than go to some crazy old picture and the last two nights I have been reading myself to sleep with Robert W. Service's poems. Don't you love Service or don't you care for "highbrow" writings?

Personly there is nothing I love more than to just sit and read a good book or sit and listen to somebody play the piano, I mean if they can really play and I really believe I like popular music better than the classical though I suppose that is a terrible thing to confess, but I love all kinds of music but a specially the piano when it is played by somebody who can really play.

Am glad you have not "fallen" for the "ladies" who have tried to make your acquaintance in New York. You are right in thinking there must be something wrong with girls who try to "pick up" strange men as no girl with self respect would do such a thing and when I say that, Mr. Man, I know you will think it is a funny thing for me to say on account of the way our friendship started, but I mean it and I assure you that was the first time I ever done such a thing in my life and would never of thought of doing it had I not known you were the right kind of a man as I flatter myself that I am a good judge of character and can tell pretty well what a person is like by just looking at them and I assure you I had made up my mind what kind of a man you were before I allowed myself to answer your opening remark. Otherwise I am the last girl in the world that would allow myself to speak to a person without being introduced to them.

When you write again you must tell me all about the girl on Riverside Drive and what she looks like and if you went to see her again and all about her. Suppose you will think I am a little old "curiosity shop" for asking all those questions and will wonder why I want to know. Well, sir, I won't tell you why, so there, but I insist on you answering all questions and will scold you if you don't. Maybe you will think that the reason why I am so curious is because I am "jealous" of the lady in question. Well, sir, I won't tell you whether I am or not, but will keep you "guessing." Now, don't you wish you knew?

Must close or you will think I am going to "rattle on" forever or maybe you have all ready become disgusted and torn my letter up. If so all I can say is poor little me—she was a nice little girl and meant well, but the man did not appreciate her.

There! Will stop or you will think I am crazy if you do not all ready.

Yours (?)

MABELLE.

N. Y., Aug. 20.

DEAR GIRLIE: Well girlie I suppose you thought I was never going to answer your letter but have been busier than a one armed paper hanger the last week as have been working on a number with Paul Sears who is one of the best lyric writers in N. Y. and has turned out as many hits as Berlin or Davis or any of them. And believe me girlie he has turned out another hit this time that is he and I have done it together. It is all done now and we are just waiting for the best chance to place it but will not place it nowheres unless we get the right kind of a deal but maybe will publish it ourselves.

The song is bound to go over big as Sears has wrote a great lyric and I have give it a great tune or at least every body that has heard it goes crazy over it and it looks like it would go over bigger than any song since Mammy and would not be surprised to see it come out the hit of the year. If it is handled right we will make a bbl. of money and Sears says it is a cinch we will clean up as much as $25000 apiece which is pretty fair for one song but this one is not like the most of them but has got a great lyric and I have wrote a melody that will knock them out of their seats. I only wish you could hear it girlie and hear it the way I play it. I had to play it over and over about 50 times at the Friars last night.

I will copy down the lyric of the chorus so you can see what it is like and get the idea of the song though of course you can't tell much about it unless you hear it played and sang. The title of the song is When They're Like You and here is the chorus:

> "Some like them hot, some like them cold.
> Some like them when they're not too darn old.
> Some like them fat, some like them lean.
> Some like them only at sweet sixteen.
> Some like them dark, some like them light.
> Some like them in the park, late at night.
> Some like them fickle, some like them true,
> But the time I like them is when they're like you."

How is that for a lyric and I only wish I could play my melody for you as you would go nuts over it but will send you a copy as soon as the song is published and you can get some of your friends to play it over for you and I know you will like it though it is a different melody when I play it or when somebody else plays it.

Well girlie you will see how busy I have been and am libel to keep right on being busy as we are not going to let the grass grow under our feet but as soon as we have got this number placed we will get busy on another one as a couple like that will put me on Easy st. even if they don't go as big as we expect but even 25 grand is a big bunch of money and if a man could only turn out one hit a year and make that much out of it I would be on Easy st. and no more hammering on the old music box in some cabaret.

Who ever we take the song to we will make them come across with one grand for advance royaltys and that will keep me going till I can turn out another one. So the future looks bright and rosey to yours truly and I am certainly glad I come to the big town though sorry I did not do it a whole lot quicker.

This is a great old town girlie and when you have lived here a wile you wonder how you ever stood for a burg like Chi which is just a hick town along side of this besides being dirty etc. and a man is a sucker to stay there all their life specially a man in my line of work as N. Y. is the Mecca for a man that has got the musical gift. I figure that all the time I spent in Chi I was just wasteing my time and never really started to live till I come down here and I have to laugh when I think of the boys out there that is trying to make a liveing in the song writeing game and most of them starve to death all their life and the first week I am down here I meet a man like Sears and the next thing you know we have turned out a song that will make us a fortune.

Well girlie you asked me to tell you about the girlie up on the Drive that tried to make me and asked me to come and see her again. Well I can assure you you have no reasons to be jealous in that quarter as I have not been back to see her as I figure it is wasteing my time to play round with a dame like she that wants to go out somewheres every night and if you married her she would want a house on 5th ave. with a dozen servants so I have passed her up as that is not my idea of home.

What I want when I get married is a real home where a man can stay home and work and maybe have a few of his friends in once in a wile and entertain them or go to a good musical show once in a wile and have a wife that is in sympathy with you and not nag at you all the wile but be a real help mate. The girlie up on the Drive would run me ragged and have me in the poor house inside of a year even if I was makeing 25 grand out of one song. Besides she wears a make up that you would have to blast to find out what her face looks like. So I have not been back there and don't intend to see her again so what is the use of me telling you about her. And the only other girlie I have met is a sister of Paul Sears who I met up to his house wile we was working on the song but she don't hardly count as she has not got no use for the boys but treats them like dirt and Paul says she is the coldest proposition he ever seen.

Well I don't know no more to write and besides have got a date to go out to Paul's place for dinner and play some of my stuff for him so as he can see if he wants to set words to some more of my melodies. Well don't do nothing I would not do and have as good a time as you can in old Chi and will let you know how we come along with the song.

CHAS. F. LEWIS.

Chicago, Ill., Aug. 23.

DEAR MR. MAN: I am thrilled to death over the song and think the words awfully pretty and am crazy to hear the music which I know must be great. It must be wonderful to have the gift of writing songs and then hear people play and sing them and just think of making $25,000 in such a short time. My, how rich you will be and I certainly congratulate you though am afraid when you are rich and famous you will have no time for insignificant little me or will you be an exception and re- member your "old" friends even when you are up in the world? I sincerely hope so.

Will look forward to receiving a copy of the song and will you be sure and put your name on it? I am all ready very con- ceited just to think that I know a man that writes songs and makes all that money.

Seriously I wish you success with your next song and I laughed when I read your remark about being busier than a one armed paper hanger. I don't see how you think up all those comparisons and crazy things to say. The next time one of the girls asks me to go out with them I am going to tell them I can't go because I am busier than a one armed paper hanger and then they will think I made it up and say: "The girl is clever."

Seriously I am glad you did not go back to see the girl on the Drive and am also glad you don't like girls who makes themselves up so much as I think it is disgusting and would rather go round looking like a ghost than put artificial color on my face. Fortunately I have a complexion that does not need "fixing" but even if my coloring was not what it is I would never think of lowering myself to "fix" it. But I must tell you a joke that happened just the other day when Edith and I were out at lunch and there was another girl in the restaurant whom Edie knew and she introduced her to me and I noticed how this girl kept staring at me and finally she begged my pardon and asked if she could ask me a personal question and I said yes and she asked me if my complexion was really "mine." I as- sured her it was and she said: "Well, I thought so because I did not think anybody could put it on so artistically. I certainly envy you." Edie and I both laughed.

Well, if that girl envies me my complexion, why I envy you living in New York. Chicago is rather dirty though I don't let that part of it bother me as I bathe and change my clothing so often that the dirt does not have time to "settle." Edie often says she cannot see how I always keep so clean looking and says I always look like I had just stepped out of a band box. She also calls me a fish (jokingly) because I spend so much time in the water. But seriously I do love to bathe and never feel so happy as when I have just "cleaned up" and put on fresh clothing.

Edie has just gone out to see a picture and was cross at me because I would not go with her. I told her I was going to write a letter and she wanted to know to whom and I told her and she said: "You write to him so often that a person would almost think you was in love with him." I just laughed and turned it off, but she does say the most embarrassing things and I would be angry if it was anybody but she that said them.

Seriously I had much rather sit here and write letters or read or just sit and dream than go out to some crazy old picture show except once in awhile I do like to go to the theater and see a good play and a specially a musical play if the music is catchy. But as a rule I am contented to just stay home and feel cozy and lots of evenings Edie and I sit here without saying hardly a word to each other though she would love to talk but she knows I had rather be quiet and she often says it is just like living with a deaf and dumb mute to live with me because I make so little noise round the apartment. I guess I was born to be a home body as I so seldom care to go "gadding."

Though I do love to have company once in awhile, just a few congenial friends whom I can talk to and feel at home with and play cards or have some music. My friends love to drop in here, too, as they say Edie and I always give them such nice things to eat. Though poor Edie has not much to do with it, I am afraid, as she hates anything connected with cooking which is one of the things I love best of anything and I often say that when I begin keeping house in my own home I will insist on doing most of my own work as I would take so much more interest in it than a servant, though I would want somebody to help me a little if I could afford it as I often think a woman that does all her own work is liable to get so tired that she loses interest in the bigger things of life like books and music. Though after all what bigger thing is there than home making a specially for a woman?

I am sitting in the dearest old chair that I bought yesterday at a little store on the North Side. That is my one extravagance, buying furniture and things for the house, but I always say it is economy in the long run as I will always have them and have use for them and when I can pick them up at a bargain I would be silly not to. Though heaven knows I will never be "poor" in regards to furniture and rugs and things like that as mother's house in Toledo is full of lovely things which she says she is going to give to Sis and myself as soon as we have real homes of our own. She is going to give me the first choice as I am her favorite. She has the loveliest old things that you could not buy now for love or money including lovely old rugs and a piano which Sis wanted to have a player attachment put on it but I said it would be an insult to the piano so we did not get one. I am funny about things like that, a specially old furniture and feel towards them like people whom I love.

Poor mother, I am afraid she won't live much longer to enjoy her lovely old things as she has been suffering for years from stomach trouble and the doctor says it has been worse lately instead of better and her heart is weak besides. I am going home to see her a few days this fall as it may be the last time. She is very cheerful and always says she is ready to go now as she has had enough joy out of life and all she would like would be to see her girls settled down in their own homes before she goes.

There I go, talking about my domestic affairs again and I will bet you are bored to death though personly I am never bored when my friends tell me about themselves. But I won't "rattle on" any longer, but will say good night and don't forget to write and tell me how you come out with the song and thanks for sending me the words to it. Will you write a song about me some time? I would be thrilled to death! But I am afraid I am not the kind of girl that inspires men to write songs about them, but am just a quiet "mouse" that loves home and am not giddy enough to be the heroine of a song.

Well, Mr. Man, good night and don't wait so long before writing again to

Yours (?)

MABELLE.

N. Y., Sept. 8.

DEAR GIRLIE: Well girlie have not got your last letter with

me so cannot answer what was in it as I have forgotten if there was anything I was supposed to answer and besides have only a little time to write as I have a date to go out on a party with the Sears. We are going to the Georgie White show and afterwards somewheres for supper. Sears is the boy who wrote the lyric to my song and it is him and his sister I am going on the party with. The sister is a cold fish that has no use for men but she is show crazy and insists on Paul takeing her to 3 or 4 of them a week.

Paul wants me to give up my room here and come and live with them as they have plenty of room and I am running a little low on money but don't know if I will do it or not as am afraid I would freeze to death in the same house with a girl like the sister as she is ice cold but she don't hang round the house much as she is always takeing trips or going to shows or somewheres.

So far we have not had no luck with the song. All the publishers we have showed it to has went crazy over it but they won't make the right kind of a deal with us and if they don't loosen up and give us a decent royalty rate we are libel to put the song out ourselves and show them up. The man up to Goebel's told us the song was O. K. and he liked it but it was more of a production number than anything else and ought to go in a show like the Follies but they won't be in N. Y. much longer and what we ought to do is hold it till next spring.

Mean wile I am working on some new numbers and also have taken a position with the orchestra at the Wilton and am going to work there starting next week. They pay good money $60 and it will keep me going.

Well girlie that is about all the news. I believe you said your father was sick and hope he is better and also hope you are getting along O. K. and take care of yourself. When you have nothing else to do write to your friend,

CHAS. F. LEWIS.

Chicago, Ill., Sept. 11.

DEAR MR. LEWIS: Your short note reached me yesterday and must say I was puzzled when I read it. It sounded like you was mad at me though I cannot think of any reason why you should be. If there was something I said in my last letter that offended you I wish you would tell me what it was and I will ask your pardon though I cannot remember anything I could of said that you could take offense at. But if there was something, why I assure you, Mr. Lewis, that I did not mean anything by it. I certainly did not intend to offend you in any way.

Perhaps it is nothing I wrote you, but you are worried on account of the publishers not treating you fair in regards to your song and that is why your letter sounded so distant. If that is the case I hope that by this time matters have rectified themselves and the future looks brighter. But any way, Mr. Lewis, don't allow yourself to worry over business cares as they will all come right in the end and I always think it is silly for people to worry themselves sick over temporary troubles, but the best way is to "keep smiling" and look for the "silver lining" in the cloud. That is the way I always do and no matter what happens, I manage to smile and my girl friend, Edie, calls me Sunny because I always look on the bright side.

Remember also, Mr. Lewis, that $60 is a salary that a great many men would like to be getting and are living on less than that and supporting a wife and family on it. I always say that a person can get along on whatever amount they make if they manage things in the right way.

So if it is business troubles, Mr. Lewis, I say don't worry, but look on the bright side. But if it is something I wrote in my last letter that offended you I wish you would tell me what it was so I can apologize as I assure you I meant nothing and would not say anything to hurt you for the world.

Please let me hear from you soon as I will not feel comfortable until I know I am not to blame for the sudden change.

                              Sincerely,

                                   MABELLE GILLESPIE.

                                        N. Y., Sept. 24.

DEAR MISS GILLESPIE: Just a few lines to tell you the big news or at least it is big news to me. I am engaged to be married to Paul Sears' sister and we are going to be married early next month and live in Atlantic City where the orchestra I have been playing with has got an engagement in one of the big cabarets.

I know this will be a surprise to you as it was even a surprise to me as I did not think I would ever have the nerve to ask the girlie the big question as she was always so cold and acted like I was just in the way. But she said she supposed she would have to marry somebody some time and she did not dislike me as much as most of the other men her brother brought round and she would marry me with the understanding that she would not have to be a slave and work round the house and also I would have to take her to a show or somewheres every night and if I could not take her myself she would "run wild" alone. Atlantic City will be O. K. for that as a lot of new shows opens down there and she will be able to see them before they get to the big town. As for her being a slave, I would hate to think of marrying a girl and then have them spend their lives in druggery round the house. We are going to live in a hotel till we find something better but will be in no hurry to start house keeping as we will have to buy all new furniture.

Betsy is some doll when she is all fixed up and believe me she knows how to fix herself up. I don't know what she uses but it is weather proof as I have been out in a rain storm with her and we both got drowned but her face stayed on. I would almost think it was real only she tells me different.

Well girlie I may write to you again once in a wile as Betsy says she don't give a dam if I write to all the girls in the world just so I don't make her read the answers but that is all I can think of to say now except good bye and good luck and may the right man come along soon and he will be a lucky man getting a girl that is such a good cook and got all that furniture etc.

But just let me give you a word of advice before I close and that is don't never speak to strange men who you don't know nothing about as they may get you wrong and think you are trying to make them. It just happened that I knew better so you was lucky in my case but the luck might not last.

Your friend,

CHAS. F. LEWIS.

Chicago, Ill., Sept. 27.

MY DEAR MR. LEWIS: Thanks for your advice and also thank your fiance for her generosity in allowing you to continue your correspondence with her "rivals," but personly I have no desire to take advantage of that generosity as I have something better to do than read letters from a man like you, a specially as I have a man friend who is not so generous as Miss Sears and would strongly object to my continuing a correspondence with another man. It is at his request that I am writing this note to tell you not to expect to hear from me again.

Allow me to congratulate you on your engagement to Miss Sears and I am sure she is to be congratulated too, though if I met the lady I would be tempted to ask her to tell me her secret, namely how she is going to "run wild" on $60.

Sincerely,

MABELLE GILLESPIE.

A Caddy's Diary

I AM 16 of age and am a caddy at the Pleasant View Golf Club but only temporary as I expect to soon land a job some wheres as asst pro as my game is good enough now to be a pro but to young looking. My pal Joe Bean also says I have not got enough swell head to make a good pro but suppose that will come in time, Joe is a wise cracker.

But first will put down how I come to be writeing this diary, we have got a member name Mr Colby who writes articles in the newspapers and I hope for his sakes that he is a better writer then he plays golf but any way I cadded for him a good many times last yr and today he was out for the first time this yr and I cadded for him and we got talking about this in that and something was mentioned in regards to the golf articles by Alex Laird that comes out every Sun in the paper Mr Colby writes his articles for so I asked Mr Colby did he know how much Laird got paid for the articles and he said he did not know but supposed that Laird had to split 50-50 with who ever wrote the articles for him. So I said don't he write the articles himself and Mr Colby said why no he guessed not. Laird may be a master mind in regards to golf he said, but that is no sign he can write about it as very few men can write decent let alone a pro. Writeing is a nag.

How do you learn it I asked him.

Well he said read what other people writes and study them and write things yourself, and maybe you will get on to the nag and maybe you wont.

Well Mr Colby I said do you think I could get on to it?

Why he said smileing I did not know that was your ambition to be a writer.

Not exactly was my reply, but I am going to be a golf pro myself and maybe some day I will get good enough so as the papers will want I should write them articles and if I can learn to write them myself why I will not have to hire another writer and split with them.

Well said Mr Colby smileing you have certainly got the right temperament for a pro, they are all big hearted fellows.

But listen Mr Colby I said if I want to learn it would not do me no good to copy down what other writers have wrote, what I would have to do would be write things out of my own head.

That is true said Mr Colby.

Well I said what could I write about?

Well said Mr Colby why don't you keep a diary and every night after your supper set down and write what happened that day and write who you cadded for and what they done only leave me out of it. And you can write down what people say and what you think and etc., it will be the best kind of practice for you, and once in a wile you can bring me your writeings and I will tell you the truth if they are good or rotten.

So that is how I come to be writeing this diary is so as I can get some practice writeing and maybe if I keep at it long enough I can get on to the nag.

Friday, Apr. 14.

We been haveing Apr. showers for a couple days and nobody out on the course so they has been nothing happen that I could write down in my diary but dont want to leave it go to long or will never learn the trick so will try and write a few lines about a caddys life and some of our members and etc.

Well I and Joe Bean is the 2 oldest caddys in the club and I been cadding now for 5 yrs and quit school 3 yrs ago tho my mother did not like it for me to quit but my father said he can read and write and figure so what is the use in keeping him there any longer as greek and latin dont get you no credit at the grocer, so they lied about my age to the trunce officer and I been cadding every yr from March till Nov and the rest of the winter I work around Heismans store in the village.

Dureing the time I am cadding I genally always manage to play at lease 9 holes a day myself on wk days and some times 18 and am never more then 2 or 3 over par figures on our course but it is a cinch.

I played the engineers course 1 day last summer in 75 which is some golf and some of our members who has been playing 20 yrs would give their right eye to play as good as myself.

I use to play around with our pro Jack Andrews till I got so as I could beat him pretty near every time we played and now he wont play with me no more, he is not a very good player for a pro but they claim he is a good teacher. Personly I think golf teachers is a joke tho I am glad people is suckers enough to fall for it as I expect to make my liveing that way. We have got a member Mr Dunham who must of took 500 lessons in the past 3 yrs and when he starts to shoot he trys to remember all the junk Andrews has learned him and he gets dizzy and they is no telling where the ball will go and about the safest place to stand when he is shooting is between he and the hole.

I dont beleive the club pays Andrews much salery but of course he makes pretty fair money giveing lessons but his best graft is a 3 some which he plays 2 and 3 times a wk with Mr Perdue and Mr Lewis and he gives Mr Lewis a stroke a hole and they genally break some wheres near even but Mr Perdue made a 83 one time so he thinks that is his game so he insists on playing Jack even, well they always play for $5.00 a hole and Andrews makes $20.00 to $30.00 per round and if he wanted to cut loose and play his best he could make $50.00 to $60.00 per round but a couple of wallops like that and Mr Perdue might get cured so Jack figures a small stedy income is safer.

I have got a pal name Joe Bean and we pal around together as he is about my age and he says some comical things and some times will wisper some thing comical to me wile we are cadding and it is all I can do to help from laughing out loud, that is one of the first things a caddy has got to learn is never laugh out loud only when a member makes a joke. How ever on the days when theys ladies on the course I dont get a chance to caddy with Joe because for some reason another the woman folks dont like Joe to caddy for them wile on the other hand they are always after me tho I am no Othello for looks or do I seek their flavors, in fact it is just the opp and I try to keep in the back ground when the fair sex appears on the seen as cadding for ladies means you will get just so much money and no more as theys no chance of them loosning up. As Joe says the rule against tipping is the only rule the woman folks keeps.

Theys one lady how ever who I like to caddy for as she looks like Lillian Gish and it is a pleasure to just look at her and I would caddy for her for nothing tho it is hard to keep your eye on the ball when you are cadding for this lady, her name is Mrs Doane.

Sat. Apr. 15.

This was a long day and am pretty well wore out but must not get behind in my writing practice. I and Joe carried all day for Mr Thomas and Mr Blake. Mr Thomas is the vice president of one of the big banks down town and he always slips you a $1.00 extra per round but beleive me you earn it cadding for Mr Thomas, there is just 16 clubs in his bag includeing 5 wood clubs tho he has not used the wood in 3 yrs but says he has got to have them along in case his irons goes wrong on him. I dont know how bad his irons will have to get before he will think they have went wrong on him but persationly if I made some of the tee shots he made today I would certainly considder some kind of a change of weppons.

Mr Thomas is one of the kind of players that when it has took him more than 6 shots to get on the green he will turn to you and say how many have I had caddy and then you are suppose to pretend like you was thinking a minute and then say 4, then he will say to the man he is playing with well I did not know if I had shot 4 or 5 but the caddy says it is 4. You see in this way it is not him that is cheating but the caddy but he makes it up to the caddy afterwards with a $1.00 tip.

Mr Blake gives Mr Thomas a stroke a hole and they play a $10.00 nassua and niether one of them wins much money from the other one but even if they did why $10.00 is chickens food to men like they. But the way they crab and squak about different things you would think their last $1.00 was at stake. Mr Thomas started out this A. M. with a 8 and a 7 and of course that spoilt the day for him and me to. Theys lots of men that if they dont make a good score on the first 2 holes they will founder all the rest of the way around and raze H with their caddy and if I was laying out a golf course I would make the first 2 holes so darn easy that you could not help from getting a 4 or better on them and in that way everybody would start off good natured and it would be a few holes at lease before they begun to turn sour.

Mr Thomas was beat both in the A. M. and P. M. in spite of my help as Mr Blake is a pretty fair counter himself and I heard him say he got a 88 in the P. M. which is about a 94 but any way it was good enough to win. Mr Blakes regular game is about a 90 takeing his own figures and he is one of these cocky guys that takes his own game serious and snears at men that cant break 100 and if you was to ask him if he had ever been over 100 himself he would say not since the first yr he begun to play. Well I have watched a lot of those guys like he and I will tell you how they keep from going over 100 namely by doing just what he done this A. M. when he come to the 13th hole. Well he missed his tee shot and dubbed along and finely he got in a trap on his 4th shot and I seen him take 6 wallops in the trap and when he had took the 6th one his ball was worse off then when he started so he picked it up and marked a X down on his score card. Well if he had of played out the hole why the best he could of got was a 11 by holeing his next niblick shot but he would of probly got about a 20 which would of made him around 108 as he admitted takeing a 88 for the other 17 holes. But I bet if you was to ask him what score he had made he would say O I was terrible and I picked up on one hole but if I had of played them all out I guess I would of had about a 92.

These is the kind of men that laughs themselfs horse when they hear of some dub takeing 10 strokes for a hole but if they was made to play out every hole and mark down their real score their card would be decorated with many a big casino.

Well as I say I had a hard day and was pretty sore along towards the finish but still I had to laugh at Joe Bean on the 15th hole which is a par 3 and you can get there with a fair drive and personly I am genally hole high with a midiron, but Mr Thomas topped his tee shot and dubbed a couple with his mashie and was still quiet a ways off the green and he stood studing the situation a minute and said to Mr Blake well I wonder what I better take here. So Joe Bean was standing by me and he said under his breath take my advice and quit you old rascal.

Mon. Apr. 17.

Yesterday was Sun and I was to wore out last night to write as I cadded 45 holes. I cadded for Mr Colby in the A. M. and Mr Langley in the P. M. Mr Thomas thinks golf is wrong on the sabath tho as Joe Bean says it is wrong any day the way he plays it.

This A. M. they was nobody on the course and I played 18 holes by myself and had a 5 for a 76 on the 18th hole but the wind got a hold of my drive and it went out of bounds. This P. M. they was 3 of us had a game of rummy started but Miss Rennie and Mrs Thomas come out to play and asked for me to caddy for them, they are both terrible.

Mrs Thomas is Mr Thomas wife and she is big and fat and shakes like jell and she always says she plays golf just to make her skinny and she dont care how rotten she plays as long as she is getting the exercise, well maybe so but when we find her ball in a bad lie she aint never sure it is hers till she picks it up and smells it and when she puts it back beleive me she don't cram it down no gopher hole.

Miss Rennie is a good looker and young and they say she is engaged to Chas Crane, he is one of our members and is the best player in the club and dont cheat hardly at all and he has got a job in the bank where Mr Thomas is the vice president. Well I have cadded for Miss Rennie when she was playing with Mr Crane and I have cadded for her when she was playing alone or with another lady and I often think if Mr Crane could hear her talk when he was not around he would not be so stuck on her. You would be surprised at some of the words that falls from those fare lips.

Well the 2 ladies played for 2 bits a hole and Miss Rennie was haveing a terrible time wile Mrs Thomas was shot with luck on the greens and sunk 3 or 4 putts that was murder. Well Miss Rennie used some expressions which was best not repeated but towards the last the luck changed around and it was Miss Rennie that was sinking the long ones and when they got to the 18th tee Mrs Thomas was only 1 up.

Well we had started pretty late and when we left the 17th green Miss Rennie made the remark that we would have to hurry to get the last hole played, well it was her honor and she got the best drive she made all day about 120 yds down the fair way. Well Mrs Thomas got nervous and looked up and missed her ball a ft and then done the same thing right over and when she finely hit it she only knocked it about 20 yds and this made her lay 3. Well her 4th went wild and lit over in the rough in the apple trees. It was a cinch Miss Rennie would win the hole unless she dropped dead.

Well we all went over to hunt for Mrs Thomas ball but we would of been lucky to find it even in day light but now you could not hardly see under the trees, so Miss Rennie said drop another ball and we will not count no penalty. Well it is some job any time to make a woman give up hunting for a lost ball and all the more so when it is going to cost her 2 bits to play the hole out so there we stayed for at lease 10 minutes till it was so dark we could not see each other let alone a lost ball and finely Mrs Thomas said well it looks like we could not finish, how do we stand? Just like she did not know how they stood.

You had me one down up to this hole said Miss Rennie.

Well that is finishing pretty close said Mrs Thomas.

I will have to give Miss Rennie credit that what ever word she thought of for this occassion she did not say it out loud but when she was paying me she said I might of give you a quarter tip only I have to give Mrs Thomas a quarter she dont deserve so you dont get it.

Fat chance I would of had any way.

Thurs. Apr. 20.

Well we been haveing some more bad weather but today the weather was all right but that was the only thing that was all right. This P. M. I cadded double for Mr Thomas and Chas Crane the club champion who is stuck on Miss Rennie. It was a 4 some with he and Mr Thomas against Mr Blake and Jack Andrews the pro, they was only playing best ball so it was really just a match between Mr Crane and Jack Andrews and Mr Crane win by 1 up. Joe Bean cadded for Jack and Mr Blake. Mr Thomas was terrible and I put in a swell P. M. lugging that heavy bag of his besides Mr Cranes bag.

Mr Thomas did not go off of the course as much as usual but he kept hitting behind the ball and he run me ragged replacing his divots but still I had to laugh when we was playing the 4th hole which you have to drive over a ravine and every time Mr Thomas misses his tee shot on this hole why he makes a squak about the ravine and says it ought not to be there and etc.

Today he had a terrible time getting over it and afterwards

he said to Jack Andrews this is a joke hole and ought to be changed. So Joe Bean wispered to me that if Mr Thomas kept on playing like he was the whole course would be changed.

Then a little wile later when we come to the long 9th hole Mr Thomas got a fair tee shot but then he whiffed twice missing the ball by a ft and the 3d time he hit it but it only went a little ways and Joe Bean said that is 3 trys and no gain, he will have to punt.

But I must write down about my tough luck, well we finely got through the 18 holes and Mr Thomas reached down in his pocket for the money to pay me and he genally pays for Mr Crane to when they play together as Mr Crane is just a employ in the bank and dont have much money but this time all Mr Thomas had was a $20.00 bill so he said to Mr Crane I guess you will have to pay the boy Charley so Charley dug down and got the money to pay me and he paid just what it was and not a dime over, where if Mr Thomas had of had the change I would of got a $1.00 extra at lease and maybe I was not sore and Joe Bean to because of course Andrews never gives you nothing and Mr Blake dont tip his caddy unless he wins.

They are a fine bunch of tight wads said Joe and I said well Crane is all right only he just has not got no money.

He aint all right no more than the rest of them said Joe.

Well at lease he dont cheat on his score I said.

And you know why that is said Joe, neither does Jack Andrews cheat on his score but that is because they play to good. Players like Crane and Andrews that goes around in 80 or better cant cheat on their score because they make the most of the holes in around 4 strokes and the 4 strokes includes their tee shot and a couple of putts which everybody is right there to watch them when they make them and count them right along with them. So if they make a 4 and claim a 3 why people would just laugh in their face and say how did the ball get from the fair way on to the green, did it fly? But the boys that takes 7 and 8 strokes to a hole can shave their score and you know they are shaveing it but you have to let them get away with it because you cant prove nothing. But that is one of the penaltys for being a good player, you cant cheat.

To hear Joe tell it pretty near everybody are born crooks, well maybe he is right.

Wed. Apr. 26.

Today Mrs Doane was out for the first time this yr and asked for me to caddy for her and you bet I was on the job. Well how are you Dick she said, she always calls me by name. She asked me what had I been doing all winter and was I glad to see her and etc.

She said she had been down south all winter and played golf pretty near every day and would I watch her and notice how much she had improved.

Well to tell the truth she was no better then last yr and wont never be no better and I guess she is just to pretty to be a golf player but of course when she asked me did I think her game was improved I had to reply yes indeed as I would not hurt her feelings and she laughed like my reply pleased her. She played with Mr and Mrs Carter and I carried the 2 ladies bags wile Joe Bean cadded for Mr Carter. Mrs Carter is a ugly dame with things on her face and it must make Mr Carter feel sore when he looks at Mrs Doane to think he married Mrs Carter but I suppose they could not all marry the same one and besides Mrs Doane would not be a sucker enough to marry a man like he who drinks all the time and is pretty near always stood, tho Mr Doane who she did marry aint such a H of a man himself tho dirty with money.

They all gave me the laugh on the 3d hole when Mrs Doane was makeing her 2d shot and the ball was in the fair way but laid kind of bad and she just ticked it and then she asked me if winter rules was in force and I said yes so we teed her ball up so as she could get a good shot at it and they gave me the laugh for saying winter rules was in force.

You have got the caddys bribed Mr Carter said to her.

But she just smiled and put her hand on my sholder and said Dick is my pal. That is enough of a bribe to just have her touch you and I would caddy all day for her and never ask for a cent only to have her smile at me and call me her pal.

Sat. Apr. 29.

Today they had the first club tournament of the yr and they have a monthly tournament every month and today was the first one, it is a handicap tournament and everybody plays in it and they have prizes for low net score and low gross score and etc. I cadded for Mr Thomas today and will tell what happened.

They played a 4 some and besides Mr Thomas we had Mr Blake and Mr Carter and Mr Dunham. Mr Dunham is the worst man player in the club and the other men would not play with him a specialy on a Saturday only him and Mr Blake is partners together in business. Mr Dunham has got the highest handicap in the club which is 50 but it would have to be 150 for him to win a prize. Mr Blake and Mr Carter has got a handicap of about 15 a piece I think and Mr Thomas is 30, the first prize for the low net score for the day was a dozen golf balls and the second low score a ½ dozen golf balls and etc.

Well we had a great battle and Mr Colby ought to been along to write it up or some good writer. Mr Carter and Mr Dunham played partners against Mr Thomas and Mr Blake which ment that Mr Carter was playing Thomas and Blakes best ball, well Mr Dunham took the honor and the first ball he hit went strate off to the right and over the fence outside of the grounds, well he done the same thing 3 times. Well when he finely did hit one in the course why Mr Carter said why not let us not count them 3 first shots of Mr Dunham as they was just practice. Like H we wont count them said Mr Thomas we must count every shot and keep our scores correct for the tournament.

All right said Mr Carter.

Well we got down to the green and Mr Dunham had about 11 and Mr Carter sunk a long putt for a par 5, Mr Blake all ready had 5 strokes and so did Mr Thomas and when Mr Carter sunk his putt why Mr Thomas picked his ball up and said Carter wins the hole and I and Blake will take 6s. Like H you will said Mr Carter, this is a tournament and we must play every hole out and keep our scores correct. So Mr Dunham putted and went down in 13 and Mr Blake got a 6 and Mr Thomas missed 2 easy putts and took a 8 and maybe he was not boiling.

Well it was still their honor and Mr Dunham had one of his dizzy spells on the 2d tee and he missed the ball twice before he hit it and then Mr Carter drove the green which is only a midiron shot and then Mr Thomas stepped up and missed the ball just like Mr Dunham. He was wild and yelled at Mr

Dunham no man could play golf playing with a man like you, you would spoil anybodys game.

Your game was all ready spoiled said Mr Dunham, it turned sour on the 1st green.

You would turn anybody sour said Mr Thomas.

Well Mr Thomas finely took a 8 for the hole which is a par 3 and it certainly looked bad for him winning a prize when he started out with 2 8s, and he and Mr Dunham had another terrible time on No 3 and wile they was messing things up a 2 some come up behind us and hollered fore and we left them go through tho it was Mr Clayton and Mr Joyce and as Joe Bean said they was probly dissapointed when we left them go through as they are the kind that feels like the day is lost if they cant write to some committee and preffer charges.

Well Mr Thomas got a 7 on the 3d and he said well it is no wonder I am off of my game today as I was up ½ the night with my teeth.

Well said Mr Carter if I had your money why on the night before a big tournament like this I would hire somebody else to set up with my teeth.

Well I wished I could remember all that was said and done but any way Mr Thomas kept getting sore and sore and we got to the 7th tee and he had not made a decent tee shot all day so Mr Blake said to him why dont you try the wood as you cant do no worse?

By Geo I beleive I will said Mr Thomas and took his driver out of the bag which he had not used it for 3 yrs.

Well he swang and zowie away went the ball pretty near 8 inchs distants wile the head of the club broke off clean and saled 50 yds down the course. Well I have got a hold on myself so as I dont never laugh out loud and I beleive the other men was scarred to laugh or he would of killed them so we all stood there in silents waiting for what would happen.

Well without saying a word he come to where I was standing and took his other 4 wood clubs out of the bag and took them to a tree which stands a little ways from the tee box and one by one he swang them with all his strength against the trunk of the tree and smashed them to H and gone, all right gentlemen that is over he said.

Well to cut it short Mr Thomas score for the first 9 was a even

60 and then we started out on the 2d 9 and you would not think it was the same man playing, on the first 3 holes he made 2 4s and a 5 and beat Mr Carter even and followed up with a 6 and a 5 and that is how he kept going up to the 17th hole.

What has got in to you Thomas said Mr Carter.

Nothing said Mr Thomas only I broke my hoodoo when I broke them 5 wood clubs.

Yes I said to myself and if you had broke them 5 wood clubs 3 yrs ago I would not of broke my back lugging them around.

Well we come to the 18th tee and Mr Thomas had a 39 which give him a 99 for 17 holes, well everybody drove off and as we was following along why Mr Klabor come walking down the course from the club house on his way to the 17th green to join some friends and Mr Thomas asked him what had he made and he said he had turned in a 93 but his handicap is only 12 so that give him a 81.

That wont get me no wheres he said as Charley Crane made a 75.

Well said Mr Thomas I can tie Crane for low net if I get a 6 on this hole.

Well it come his turn to make his 2d and zowie he hit the ball pretty good but they was a hook on it and away she went in to the woods on the left, the ball laid in behind a tree so as they was only one thing to do and that was waste a shot getting it back on the fair so that is what Mr Thomas done and it took him 2 more to reach the green.

How many have you had Thomas said Mr Carter when we was all on the green.

Let me see said Mr Thomas and then turned to me, how many have I had caddy?

I dont know I said.

Well it is either 4 or 5 said Mr Thomas.

I think it is 5 said Mr Carter.

I think it is 4 said Mr Thomas and turned to me again and said how many have I had caddy?

So I said 4.

Well said Mr Thomas personly I was not sure myself but my caddy says 4 and I guess he is right.

Well the other men looked at each other and I and Joe Bean

looked at each other but Mr Thomas went ahead and putted and was down in 2 putts.

Well he said I certainly come to life on them last 9 holes.

So he turned in his score as 105 and with his handicap of 30 why that give him a net of 75 which was the same as Mr Crane so instead of Mr Crane getting 1 dozen golf balls and Mr Thomas getting ½ a dozen golf balls why they will split the 1st and 2d prize makeing 9 golf balls a piece.

Tues. May 2.

This was the first ladies day of the season and even Joe Bean had to carry for the fair sex. We cadded for a 4 some which was Miss Rennie and Mrs Thomas against Mrs Doane and Mrs Carter. I guess if they had of kept their score right the total for the 4 of them would of ran well over a 1000.

Our course has a great many trees and they seemed to have a traction for our 4 ladies today and we was in amongst the trees more then we was on the fair way.

Well said Joe Bean theys one thing about cadding for these dames, it keeps you out of the hot sun.

And another time he said he felt like a boy scout studing wood craft.

These dames is always up against a stump he said.

And another time he said that it was not fair to charge these dames regular ladies dues in the club as they hardly ever used the course.

Well it seems like they was a party in the village last night and of course the ladies was talking about it and Mrs Doane said what a lovely dress Miss Rennie wore to the party and Miss Rennie said she did not care for the dress herself.

Well said Mrs Doane if you want to get rid of it just hand it over to me.

I wont give it to you said Miss Rennie but I will sell it to you at ½ what it cost me and it was a bargain at that as it only cost me a $100.00 and I will sell it to you for $50.00.

I have not got $50.00 just now to spend said Mrs Doane and besides I dont know would it fit me.

Sure it would fit you said Miss Rennie, you and I are exactly the same size and figure, I tell you what I will do with you I will play you golf for it and if you beat me you can have the gown for nothing and if I beat you why you will give me $50.00 for it.

All right but if I loose you may have to wait for your money said Mrs Doane.

So this was on the 4th hole and they started from there to play for the dress and they was both terrible and worse then usual on acct of being nervous as this was the biggest stakes they had either of them ever played for tho the Doanes has got a bbl of money and $50.00 is chickens food.

Well we was on the 16th hole and Mrs Doane was 1 up and Miss Rennie sliced her tee shot off in the rough and Mrs Doane landed in some rough over on the left so they was clear across the course from each other. Well I and Mrs Doane went over to her ball and as luck would have it it had come to rest in a kind of a groove where a good player could not hardly make a good shot of it let alone Mrs Doane. Well Mrs. Thomas was out in the middle of the course for once in her life and the other 2 ladies was over on the right side and Joe Bean with them so they was nobody near Mrs Doane and I.

Do I have to play it from there she said. I guess you do was my reply.

Why Dick have you went back on me she said and give me one of her looks.

Well I looked to see if the others was looking and then I kind of give the ball a shove with my toe and it come out of the groove and laid where she could get a swipe at it.

This was the 16th hole and Mrs Doane win it by 11 strokes to 10 and that made her 2 up and 2 to go. Miss Rennie win the 17th but they both took a 10 for the 18th and that give Mrs Doane the match.

Well I wont never have a chance to see her in Miss Rennies dress but if I did I aint sure that I would like it on her.

Fri. May 5.

Well I never thought we would have so much excitement in the club and so much to write down in my diary but I guess I better get busy writeing it down as here it is Friday and it was Wed. A. M. when the excitement broke loose and I was getting ready to play around when Harry Lear the caddy master come running out with the paper in his hand and showed it to me on the first page.

It told how Chas Crane our club champion had went south with $8000 which he had stole out of Mr Thomas bank and a swell looking dame that was a stenographer in the bank had elloped with him and they had her picture in the paper and I will say she is a pip but who would of thought a nice quiet young man like Mr Crane was going to prove himself a gay Romeo and a specialy as he was engaged to Miss Rennie tho she now says she broke their engagement a month ago but any way the whole affair has certainly give everybody something to talk about and one of the caddys Lou Crowell busted Fat Brunner in the nose because Fat claimed to of been the last one that cadded for Crane. Lou was really the last one and cadded for him last Sunday which was the last time Crane was at the club.

Well everybody was thinking how sore Mr Thomas would be and they would better not mention the affair around him and etc. but who should show up to play yesterday but Mr Thomas himself and he played with Mr Blake and all they talked about the whole P. M. was Crane and what he had pulled.

Well Thomas said Mr Blake I am curious to know if the thing come as a suprise to you or if you ever had a hunch that he was libel to do a thing like this.

Well Blake said Mr Thomas I will admit that the whole thing come as a complete suprise to me as Crane was all most like my son you might say and I was going to see that he got along all right and that is what makes me sore is not only that he has proved himself dishonest but that he could be such a sucker as to give up a bright future for a sum of money like $8000 and a doll face girl that cant be no good or she would not of let him do it. When you think how young he was and the carreer he might of had why it certainly seems like he sold his soul pretty cheap.

That is what Mr Thomas had to say or at lease part of it as I cant remember a ½ of all he said but any way this P. M. I cadded for Mrs Thomas and Mrs Doane and that is all they talked about to, and Mrs Thomas talked along the same lines like her husband and said she had always thought Crane was to smart a young man to pull a thing like that and ruin his whole future.

He was getting $4000 a yr said Mrs Thomas and everybody liked him and said he was bound to get ahead so that is what makes it such a silly thing for him to of done, sell his soul for $8000 and a pretty face.

Yes indeed said Mrs Doane.

Well all the time I was listening to Mr Thomas and Mr Blake and Mrs Thomas and Mrs Doane why I was thinking about something which I wanted to say to them but it would of ment me looseing my job so I kept it to myself but I sprung it on my pal Joe Bean on the way home tonight.

Joe I said what do these people mean when they talk about Crane selling his soul?

Why you know what they mean said Joe, they mean that a person that does something dishonest for a bunch of money or a gal or any kind of a reward why the person that does it is selling his soul.

All right I said and it dont make no differents does it if the reward is big or little?

Why no said Joe only the bigger it is the less of a sucker the person is that goes after it.

Well I said here is Mr Thomas who is vice president of a big bank and worth a bbl of money and it is just a few days ago when he lied about his golf score in order so as he would win 9 golf balls instead of a ½ a dozen.

Sure said Joe.

And how about his wife Mrs Thomas I said, who plays for 2 bits a hole and when her ball dont lie good why she picks it up and pretends to look at it to see if it is hers and then puts it back in a good lie where she can sock it.

And how about my friend Mrs Doane that made me move her ball out of a rut to help her beat Miss Rennie out of a party dress.

Well said Joe what of it?

Well I said it seems to me like these people have got a lot of nerve to pan Mr Crane and call him a sucker for doing what he done, it seems to me like $8000 and a swell dame is a pretty fair reward compared with what some of these other people sells their soul for, and I would like to tell them about it.

Well said Joe go ahead and tell them but maybe they will tell you something right back.

What will they tell me?

Well said Joe they might tell you this, that when Mr Thomas asks you how many shots he has had and you say 4 when you know he has had 5, why you are selling your soul for a $1.00 tip. And when you move Mrs Doanes ball out of a rut and give it a good lie, what are you selling your soul for? Just a smile.

O keep your mouth shut I said to him.

I am going to said Joe and would advice you to do the same.

The Golden Honeymoon

MOTHER SAYS that when I start talking I never know when to stop. But I tell her the only time I get a chance is when she ain't around, so I have to make the most of it. I guess the fact is neither one of us would be welcome in a Quaker meeting, but as I tell Mother, what did God give us tongues for if He didn't want we should use them? Only she says He didn't give them to us to say the same thing over and over again, like I do, and repeat myself. But I say:

"Well, Mother," I say, "when people is like you and I and been married fifty years, do you expect everything I say will be something you ain't heard me say before? But it may be new to others, as they ain't nobody else lived with me as long as you have."

So she says:

"You can bet they ain't, as they couldn't nobody else stand you that long."

"Well," I tell her, "you look pretty healthy."

"Maybe I do," she will say, "but I looked even healthier before I married you."

You can't get ahead of Mother.

Yes, sir, we was married just fifty years ago the seventeenth day of last December and my daughter and son-in-law was over from Trenton to help us celebrate the Golden Wedding. My son-in-law is John H. Kramer, the real estate man. He made $12,000 one year and is pretty well thought of around Trenton; a good, steady, hard worker. The Rotarians was after him a long time to join, but he kept telling them his home was his club. But Edie finally made him join. That's my daughter.

Well, anyway, they come over to help us celebrate the Golden Wedding and it was pretty crimpy weather and the furnace don't seem to heat up no more like it used to and Mother made the remark that she hoped this winter wouldn't be as cold as the last, referring to the winter previous. So Edie said if she was us, and nothing to keep us home, she certainly wouldn't spend no more winters up here and why didn't we just shut off the water and close up the house and go down to

Tampa, Florida? You know we was there four winters ago and staid five weeks, but it cost us over three hundred and fifty dollars for hotel bill alone. So Mother said we wasn't going no place to be robbed. So my son-in-law spoke up and said that Tampa wasn't the only place in the South, and besides we didn't have to stop at no high price hotel but could rent us a couple rooms and board out somewheres, and he had heard that St. Petersburg, Florida, was *the* spot and if we said the word he would write down there and make inquiries.

Well, to make a long story short, we decided to do it and Edie said it would be our Golden Honeymoon and for a present my son-in-law paid the difference between a section and a compartment so as we could have a compartment and have more privatecy. In a compartment you have an upper and lower berth just like the regular sleeper, but it is a shut in room by itself and got a wash bowl. The car we went in was all compartments and no regular berths at all. It was all compartments.

We went to Trenton the night before and staid at my daughter and son-in-law and we left Trenton the next afternoon at 3.23 P. M.

This was the twelfth day of January. Mother set facing the front of the train, as it makes her giddy to ride backwards. I set facing her, which does not affect me. We reached North Philadelphia at 4.03 P. M. and we reached West Philadelphia at 4.14, but did not go into Broad Street. We reached Baltimore at 6.30 and Washington, D.C., at 7.25. Our train laid over in Washington two hours till another train come along to pick us up and I got out and strolled up the platform and into the Union Station. When I come back, our car had been switched on to another track, but I remembered the name of it, the La Belle, as I had once visited my aunt out in Oconomowoc, Wisconsin, where there was a lake of that name, so I had no difficulty in getting located. But Mother had nearly fretted herself sick for fear I would be left.

"Well," I said, "I would of followed you on the next train."

"You could of," said Mother, and she pointed out that she had the money.

"Well," I said, "we are in Washington and I could of borrowed from the United States Treasury. I would of pretended I was an Englishman."

Mother caught the point and laughed heartily.

Our train pulled out of Washington at 9.40 P. M. and Mother and I turned in early, I taking the upper. During the night we passed through the green fields of old Virginia, though it was too dark to tell if they was green or what color. When we got up in the morning, we was at Fayetteville, North Carolina. We had breakfast in the dining car and after breakfast I got in conversation with the man in the next compartment to ours. He was from Lebanon, New Hampshire, and a man about eighty years of age. His wife was with him, and two unmarried daughters and I made the remark that I should think the four of them would be crowded in one compartment, but he said they had made the trip every winter for fifteen years and knowed how to keep out of each other's way. He said they was bound for Tarpon Springs.

We reached Charleston, South Carolina, at 12.50 P. M. and arrived at Savannah, Georgia, at 4.20. We reached Jacksonville, Florida, at 8.45 P. M. and had an hour and a quarter to lay over there, but Mother made a fuss about me getting off the train, so we had the darky make up our berths and retired before we left Jacksonville. I didn't sleep good as the train done a lot of hemming and hawing, and Mother never sleeps good on a train as she says she is always worrying that I will fall out. She says she would rather have the upper herself, as then she would not have to worry about me, but I tell her I can't take the risk of having it get out that I allowed my wife to sleep in an upper berth. It would make talk.

We was up in the morning in time to see our friends from New Hampshire get off at Tarpon Springs, which we reached at 6.53 A. M.

Several of our fellow passengers got off at Clearwater and some at Belleair, where the train backs right up to the door of the mammoth hotel. Belleair is the winter headquarters for the golf dudes and everybody that got off there had their bag of sticks, as many as ten and twelve in a bag. Women and all. When I was a young man we called it shinny and only needed one club to play with and about one game of it would of been a-plenty for some of these dudes, the way we played it.

The train pulled into St. Petersburg at 8.20 and when we got off the train you would think they was a riot, what with all the darkies barking for the different hotels.

I said to Mother, I said:

"It is a good thing we have got a place picked out to go to and don't have to choose a hotel, as it would be hard to choose amongst them if every one of them is the best."

She laughed.

We found a jitney and I give him the address of the room my son-in-law had got for us and soon we was there and introduced ourselves to the lady that owns the house, a young widow about forty-eight years of age. She showed us our room, which was light and airy with a comfortable bed and bureau and washstand. It was twelve dollars a week, but the location was good, only three blocks from Williams Park.

St. Pete is what folks calls the town, though they also call it the Sunshine City, as they claim they's no other place in the country where they's fewer days when Old Sol don't smile down on Mother Earth, and one of the newspapers gives away all their copies free every day when the sun don't shine. They claim to of only give them away some sixty-odd times in the last eleven years. Another nickname they have got for the town is "the Poor Man's Palm Beach," but I guess they's men that comes there that could borrow as much from the bank as some of the Willie boys over to the other Palm Beach.

During our stay we paid a visit to the Lewis Tent City, which is the headquarters for the Tin Can Tourists. But maybe you ain't heard about them. Well, they are an organization that takes their vacation trips by auto and carries everything with them. That is, they bring along their tents to sleep in and cook in and they don't patronize no hotels or cafeterias, but they have got to be bona fide auto campers or they can't belong to the organization.

They tell me they's over 200,000 members to it and they call themselves the Tin Canners on account of most of their food being put up in tin cans. One couple we seen in the Tent City was a couple from Brady, Texas, named Mr. and Mrs. Pence, which the old man is over eighty years of age and they had came in their auto all the way from home, a distance of 1,641 miles. They took five weeks for the trip, Mr. Pence driving the entire distance.

The Tin Canners hails from every State in the Union and in the summer time they visit places like New England and the

Great Lakes region, but in the winter the most of them comes to Florida and scatters all over the State. While we was down there, they was a national convention of them at Gainesville, Florida, and they elected a Fredonia, New York, man as their president. His title is Royal Tin Can Opener of the World. They have got a song wrote up which everybody has got to learn it before they are a member:

"The tin can forever! Hurrah, boys! Hurrah!
    Up with the tin can! Down with the foe!
  We will rally round the campfire, we'll rally once again,
    Shouting, 'We auto camp forever!'"

That is something like it. And the members has also got to have a tin can fastened on to the front of their machine.

I asked Mother how she would like to travel around that way and she said:

"Fine, but not with an old rattle brain like you driving."

"Well," I said, "I am eight years younger than this Mr. Pence who drove here from Texas."

"Yes," she said, "but he is old enough to not be skittish."

You can't get ahead of Mother.

Well, one of the first things we done in St. Petersburg was to go to the Chamber of Commerce and register our names and where we was from as they's great rivalry amongst the different States in regards to the number of their citizens visiting in town and of course our little State don't stand much of a show, but still every little bit helps, as the fella says. All and all, the man told us, they was eleven thousand names registered, Ohio leading with some fifteen hundred–odd and New York State next with twelve hundred. Then come Michigan, Pennsylvania and so on down, with one man each from Cuba and Nevada.

The first night we was there, they was a meeting of the New York–New Jersey Society at the Congregational Church and a man from Ogdensburg, New York State, made the talk. His subject was Rainbow Chasing. He is a Rotarian and a very convicting speaker, though I forget his name.

Our first business, of course, was to find a place to eat and after trying several places we run on to a cafeteria on Central Avenue that suited us up and down. We eat pretty near all our meals there and it averaged about two dollars per day for the two of us, but the food was well cooked and everything nice and clean. A man don't mind paying the price if things is clean and well cooked.

On the third day of February, which is Mother's birthday, we spread ourselves and eat supper at the Poinsettia Hotel and they charged us seventy-five cents for a sirloin steak that wasn't hardly big enough for one.

I said to Mother: "Well," I said, "I guess it's a good thing every day ain't your birthday or we would be in the poorhouse."

"No," says Mother, "because if every day was my birthday, I would be old enough by this time to of been in my grave long ago."

You can't get ahead of Mother.

In the hotel they had a card-room where they was several men and ladies playing five hundred and this new fangled whist bridge. We also seen a place where they was dancing, so I asked Mother would she like to trip the light fantastic toe and she said no, she was too old to squirm like you have got to do now days. We watched some of the young folks at it awhile till Mother got disgusted and said we would have to see a good movie to take the taste out of our mouth. Mother is a great movie heroyne and we go twice a week here at home.

But I want to tell you about the Park. The second day we was there we visited the Park, which is a good deal like the one in Tampa, only bigger, and they's more fun goes on here every day than you could shake a stick at. In the middle they's a big bandstand and chairs for the folks to set and listen to the concerts, which they give you music for all tastes, from Dixie up to classical pieces like Hearts and Flowers.

Then all around they's places marked off for different sports and games—chess and checkers and dominoes for folks that enjoys those kind of games, and roque and horse-shoes for the nimbler ones. I used to pitch a pretty fair shoe myself, but ain't done much of it in the last twenty years.

Well, anyway, we bought a membership ticket in the club which costs one dollar for the season, and they tell me that up to a couple years ago it was fifty cents, but they had to raise it to keep out the riffraff.

Well, Mother and I put in a great day watching the pitchers and she wanted I should get in the game, but I told her I was all out of practice and would make a fool of myself, though I seen several men pitching who I guess I could take their measure without no practice. However, they was some good pitchers, too, and one boy from Akron, Ohio, who could certainly throw a pretty shoe. They told me it looked like he would win the championship of the United States in the February tournament. We come away a few days before they held that and I never did hear if he win. I forget his name, but he was a clean cut young fella and he has got a brother in Cleveland that's a Rotarian.

Well, we just stood around and watched the different games for two or three days and finally I set down in a checker game with a man named Weaver from Danville, Illinois. He was a pretty fair checker player, but he wasn't no match for me, and I hope that don't sound like bragging. But I always could hold my own on a checker-board and the folks around here will tell you the same thing. I played with this Weaver pretty near all morning for two or three mornings and he beat me one game and the only other time it looked like he had a chance, the noon whistle blowed and we had to quit and go to dinner.

While I was playing checkers, Mother would set and listen to the band, as she loves music, classical or no matter what kind, but anyway she was setting there one day and between selections the woman next to her opened up a conversation. She was a woman about Mother's own age, seventy or seventy-one, and finally she asked Mother's name and Mother told her her name and where she was from and Mother asked her the same question, and who do you think the woman was?

Well, sir, it was the wife of Frank M. Hartsell, the man who was engaged to Mother till I stepped in and cut him out, fifty-two years ago!

Yes, sir!

You can imagine Mother's surprise! And Mrs. Hartsell was surprised, too, when Mother told her she had once been friends with her husband, though Mother didn't say how close friends they had been, or that Mother and I was the cause of Hartsell going out West. But that's what we was. Hartsell left his town a month after the engagement was broke off and ain't never been back since. He had went out to Michigan and become a veterinary, and that is where he had settled down, in Hillsdale, Michigan, and finally married his wife.

Well, Mother screwed up her courage to ask if Frank was still living and Mrs. Hartsell took her over to where they was pitching horse-shoes and there was old Frank, waiting his turn. And he knowed Mother as soon as he seen her, though it was over fifty years. He said he knowed her by her eyes.

"Why, it's Lucy Frost!" he says, and he throwed down his shoes and quit the game.

Then they come over and hunted me up and I will confess I wouldn't of knowed him. Him and I is the same age to the month, but he seems to show it more, some way. He is balder for one thing. And his beard is all white, where mine has still got a streak of brown in it. The very first thing I said to him, I said:

"Well, Frank, that beard of yours makes me feel like I was back north. It looks like a regular blizzard."

"Well," he said, "I guess yourn would be just as white if you had it dry cleaned."

But Mother wouldn't stand that.

"Is that so!" she said to Frank. "Well, Charley ain't had no tobacco in his mouth for over ten years!"

And I ain't!

Well, I excused myself from the checker game and it was pretty close to noon, so we decided to all have dinner together and they was nothing for it only we must try their cafeteria on Third Avenue. It was a little more expensive than ours and not near as good, I thought. I and Mother had about the same dinner we had been having every day and our bill was $1.10. Frank's check was $1.20 for he and his wife. The same meal wouldn't of cost them more than a dollar at our place.

After dinner we made them come up to our house and we all set in the parlor, which the young woman had give us the use of to entertain company. We begun talking over old times and Mother said she was a-scared Mrs. Hartsell would find it tiresome listening to we three talk over old times, but as it turned out they wasn't much chance for nobody else to talk with Mrs. Hartsell in the company. I have heard lots of women that could go it, but Hartsell's wife takes the cake of all the women I ever seen. She told us the family history of everybody in the State of Michigan and bragged for a half hour about her son, who she said is in the drug business in Grand Rapids, and a Rotarian.

When I and Hartsell could get a word in edgeways we joked one another back and forth and I chafed him about being a horse doctor.

"Well, Frank," I said, "you look pretty prosperous, so I suppose they's been plenty of glanders around Hillsdale."

"Well," he said, "I've managed to make more than a fair living. But I've worked pretty hard."

"Yes," I said, "and I suppose you get called out all hours of the night to attend births and so on."

Mother made me shut up.

Well, I thought they wouldn't never go home and I and Mother was in misery trying to keep awake, as the both of us generally always takes a nap after dinner. Finally they went, after we had made an engagement to meet them in the Park the next morning, and Mrs. Hartsell also invited us to come to their place the next night and play five hundred. But she had forgot that they was a meeting of the Michigan Society that evening, so it was not till two evenings later that we had our first card game.

Hartsell and his wife lived in a house on Third Avenue North and had a private setting room besides their bedroom. Mrs. Hartsell couldn't quit talking about their private setting room like it was something wonderful. We played cards with them, with Mother and Hartsell partners against his wife and I. Mrs. Hartsell is a miserable card player and we certainly got the worst of it.

After the game she brought out a dish of oranges and we had to pretend it was just what we wanted, though oranges down there is like a young man's whiskers; you enjoy them at first, but they get to be a pesky nuisance.

We played cards again the next night at our place with the same partners and I and Mrs. Hartsell was beat again. Mother and Hartsell was full of compliments for each other on what a good team they made, but the both of them knowed well enough where the secret of their success laid. I guess all and all we must of played ten different evenings and they was only one night when Mrs. Hartsell and I come out ahead. And that one night wasn't no fault of hern.

When we had been down there about two weeks, we spent one evening as their guest in the Congregational Church, at a social give by the Michigan Society. A talk was made by a man named Bitting of Detroit, Michigan, on How I was Cured of Story Telling. He is a big man in the Rotarians and give a witty talk.

A woman named Mrs. Oxford rendered some selections which Mrs. Hartsell said was grand opera music, but whatever they was my daughter Edie could of give her cards and spades and not made such a hullaballoo about it neither.

Then they was a ventriloquist from Grand Rapids and a young woman about forty-five years of age that mimicked different kinds of birds. I whispered to Mother that they all sounded like a chicken, but she nudged me to shut up.

After the show we stopped in a drug store and I set up the refreshments and it was pretty close to ten o'clock before we finally turned in. Mother and I would of preferred tending the movies, but Mother said we mustn't offend Mrs. Hartsell, though I asked her had we came to Florida to enjoy ourselves or to just not offend an old chatterbox from Michigan.

I felt sorry for Hartsell one morning. The women folks both had an engagement down to the chiropodist's and I run across Hartsell in the Park and he foolishly offered to play me checkers.

It was him that suggested it, not me, and I guess he repented himself before we had played one game. But he was too stubborn to give up and set there while I beat him game after game and the worst part of it was that a crowd of folks had got in the habit of watching me play and there they all was, looking on, and finally they seen what a fool Frank was making of himself, and they began to chafe him and pass remarks. Like one of them said:

"Who ever told you you was a checker player!"

And:

"You might maybe be good for tiddle-de-winks, but not checkers!"

I almost felt like letting him beat me a couple games. But the crowd would of knowed it was a put up job.

Well, the women folks joined us in the Park and I wasn't going to mention our little game, but Hartsell told about it himself and admitted he wasn't no match for me.

"Well," said Mrs. Hartsell, "checkers ain't much of a game anyway, is it?" She said: "It's more of a children's game, ain't it? At least, I know my boy's children used to play it a good deal."

"Yes, ma'am," I said. "It's a children's game the way your husband plays it, too."

Mother wanted to smooth things over, so she said:

"Maybe they's other games where Frank can beat you."

"Yes," said Mrs. Hartsell, "and I bet he could beat you pitching horse-shoes."

"Well," I said, "I would give him a chance to try, only I ain't pitched a shoe in over sixteen years."

"Well," said Hartsell, "I ain't played checkers in twenty years."

"You ain't never played it," I said.

"Anyway," says Frank, "Lucy and I is your master at five hundred."

Well, I could of told him why that was, but had decency enough to hold my tongue.

It had got so now that he wanted to play cards every night and when I or Mother wanted to go to a movie, any one of us would have to pretend we had a headache and then trust to goodness that they wouldn't see us sneak into the theater. I don't mind playing cards when my partner keeps their mind on the game, but you take a woman like Hartsell's wife and how can they play cards when they have got to stop every couple seconds and brag about their son in Grand Rapids?

Well, the New York–New Jersey Society announced that they was goin to give a social evening too and I said to Mother, I said:

"Well, that is one evening when we will have an excuse not to play five hundred."

"Yes," she said, "but we will have to ask Frank and his wife to go to the social with us as they asked us to go to the Michigan social."

"Well," I said, "I had rather stay home than drag that chatterbox everywheres we go."

So Mother said:

"You are getting too cranky. Maybe she does talk a little too much but she is good hearted. And Frank is always good company."

So I said:

"I suppose if he is such good company you wished you had of married him."

Mother laughed and said I sounded like I was jealous. Jealous of a cow doctor!

Anyway we had to drag them along to the social and I will say that we give them a much better entertainment than they had given us.

Judge Lane of Paterson made a fine talk on business conditions and a Mrs. Newell of Westfield imitated birds, only you could really tell what they was the way she done it. Two young women from Red Bank sung a choral selection and we clapped them back and they gave us Home to Our Mountains and Mother and Mrs. Hartsell both had tears in their eyes. And Hartsell, too.

Well, some way or another the chairman got wind that I was there and asked me to make a talk and I wasn't even going to get up, but Mother made me, so I got up and said:

"Ladies and gentlemen," I said. "I didn't expect to be called on for a speech on an occasion like this or no other occasion as I do not set myself up as a speech maker, so will have to do the best I can, which I often say is the best anybody can do."

Then I told them the story about Pat and the motorcycle, using the brogue, and it seemed to tickle them and I told them one or two other stories, but altogether I wasn't on my feet more than twenty or twenty-five minutes and you ought to of heard the clapping and hollering when I set down. Even Mrs. Hartsell admitted that I am quite a speechifier and said if I ever went to Grand Rapids, Michigan, her son would make me talk to the Rotarians.

When it was over, Hartsell wanted we should go to their house and play cards, but his wife reminded him that it was after 9.30 P. M., rather a late hour to start a card game, but he had went crazy on the subject of cards, probably because he didn't have to play partners with his wife. Anyway, we got rid of them and went home to bed.

It was the next morning, when we met over to the Park, that Mrs. Hartsell made the remark that she wasn't getting no exercise so I suggested that why didn't she take part in the roque game.

She said she had not played a game of roque in twenty years, but if Mother would play she would play. Well, at first Mother wouldn't hear of it, but finally consented, more to please Mrs. Hartsell than anything else.

Well, they had a game with a Mrs. Ryan from Eagle, Nebraska, and a young Mrs. Morse from Rutland, Vermont, who Mother had met down to the chiropodist's. Well, Mother couldn't hit a flea and they all laughed at her and I couldn't help from laughing at her myself and finally she quit and said her back was too lame to stoop over. So they got another lady and kept on playing and soon Mrs. Hartsell was the one everybody was laughing at, as she had a long shot to hit the black ball, and as she made the effort her teeth fell out on to the court. I never seen a woman so flustered in my life. And I never heard so much laughing, only Mrs. Hartsell didn't join in and she was madder than a hornet and wouldn't play no more, so the game broke up.

Mrs. Hartsell went home without speaking to nobody, but Hartsell stayed around and finally he said to me, he said:

"Well, I played you checkers the other day and you beat me bad and now what do you say if you and me play a game of horse-shoes?"

I told him I hadn't pitched a shoe in sixteen years, but Mother said:

"Go ahead and play. You used to be good at it and maybe it will come back to you."

Well, to make a long story short, I give in. I oughtn't to of never tried it, as I hadn't pitched a shoe in sixteen years, and I only done it to humor Hartsell.

Before we started, Mother patted me on the back and told me to do my best, so we started in and I seen right off that I was in for it, as I hadn't pitched a shoe in sixteen years and didn't have my distance. And besides, the plating had wore off the shoes so that they was points right where they stuck into my thumb and I hadn't throwed more than two or three times when my thumb was raw and it pretty near killed me to hang on to the shoe, let alone pitch it.

Well, Hartsell throws the awkwardest shoe I ever seen pitched and to see him pitch you wouldn't think he would ever come nowheres near, but he is also the luckiest pitcher I ever seen and he made some pitches where the shoe lit five and six feet short and then schoonered up and was a ringer. They's no use trying to beat that kind of luck.

They was a pretty fair size crowd watching us and four or

five other ladies besides Mother, and it seems like, when Hartsell pitches, he has got to chew and it kept the ladies on the anxious seat as he don't seem to care which way he is facing when he leaves go.

You would think a man as old as him would of learnt more manners.

Well, to make a long story short, I was just beginning to get my distance when I had to give up on account of my thumb, which I showed it to Hartsell and he seen I couldn't go on, as it was raw and bleeding. Even if I could of stood it to go on myself, Mother wouldn't of allowed it after she seen my thumb. So anyway I quit and Hartsell said the score was nineteen to six, but I don't know what it was. Or don't care, neither.

Well, Mother and I went home and I said I hoped we was through with the Hartsells as I was sick and tired of them, but it seemed like she had promised we would go over to their house that evening for another game of their everlasting cards.

Well, my thumb was giving me considerable pain and I felt kind of out of sorts and I guess maybe I forgot myself, but anyway, when we was about through playing Hartsell made the remark that he wouldn't never lose a game of cards if he could always have Mother for a partner.

So I said:

"Well, you had a chance fifty years ago to always have her for a partner, but you wasn't man enough to keep her."

I was sorry the minute I had said it and Hartsell didn't know what to say and for once his wife couldn't say nothing. Mother tried to smooth things over by making the remark that I must of had something stronger than tea or I wouldn't talk so silly. But Mrs. Hartsell had froze up like an iceberg and hardly said good night to us and I bet her and Frank put in a pleasant hour after we was gone.

As we was leaving, Mother said to him: "Never mind Charley's nonsense, Frank. He is just mad because you beat him all hollow pitching horse-shoes and playing cards."

She said that to make up for my slip, but at the same time she certainly riled me. I tried to keep ahold of myself, but as soon as we was out of the house she had to open up the subject and begun to scold me for the break I had made.

Well, I wasn't in no mood to be scolded. So I said:

"I guess he is such a wonderful pitcher and card player that you wished you had married him."

"Well," she said, "at least he ain't a baby to give up pitching because his thumb has got a few scratches."

"And how about you," I said, "making a fool of yourself on the roque court and then pretending your back is lame and you can't play no more!"

"Yes," she said, "but when you hurt your thumb I didn't laugh at you, and why did you laugh at me when I sprained my back?"

"Who could help from laughing!" I said.

"Well," she said, "Frank Hartsell didn't laugh."

"Well," I said, "why didn't you marry him?"

"Well," said Mother, "I almost wished I had!"

"And I wished so, too!" I said.

"I'll remember that!" said Mother, and that's the last word she said to me for two days.

We seen the Hartsells the next day in the Park and I was willing to apologize, but they just nodded to us. And a couple days later we heard they had left for Orlando, where they have got relatives.

I wished they had went there in the first place.

Mother and I made it up setting on a bench.

"Listen, Charley," she said. "This is our Golden Honeymoon and we don't want the whole thing spoilt with a silly old quarrel."

"Well," I said, "did you mean that about wishing you had married Hartsell?"

"Of course not," she said, "that is, if you didn't mean that you wished I had, too."

So I said:

"I was just tired and all wrought up. I thank God you chose me instead of him as they's no other woman in the world who I could of lived with all these years."

"How about Mrs. Hartsell?" says Mother.

"Good gracious!" I said. "Imagine being married to a woman that plays five hundred like she does and drops her teeth on the roque court!"

"Well," said Mother, "it wouldn't be no worse than being

married to a man that expectorates towards ladies and is such a fool in a checker game."

So I put my arm around her shoulder and she stroked my hand and I guess we got kind of spoony.

They was two days left of our stay in St. Petersburg and the next to the last day Mother introduced me to a Mrs. Kendall from Kingston, Rhode Island, who she had met at the chiropodist's.

Mrs. Kendall made us acquainted with her husband, who is in the grocery business. They have got two sons and five grandchildren and one great-grandchild. One of their sons lives in Providence and is way up in the Elks as well as a Rotarian.

We found them very congenial people and we played cards with them the last two nights we was there. They was both experts and I only wished we had met them sooner instead of running into the Hartsells. But the Kendalls will be there again next winter and we will see more of them, that is, if we decide to make the trip again.

We left the Sunshine City on the eleventh day of February, at 11 A. M. This give us a day trip through Florida and we seen all the country we had passed through at night on the way down.

We reached Jacksonville at 7 P. M. and pulled out of there at 8.10 P. M. We reached Fayetteville, North Carolina, at nine o'clock the following morning, and reached Washington, D. C., at 6.30 P. M., laying over there half an hour.

We reached Trenton at 11.01 P. M. and had wired ahead to my daughter and son-in-law and they met us at the train and we went to their house and they put us up for the night. John would of made us stay up all night, telling about our trip, but Edie said we must be tired and made us go to bed. That's my daughter.

The next day we took our train for home and arrived safe and sound, having been gone just one month and a day.

Here comes Mother, so I guess I better shut up.

FROM

THE LOVE NEST AND OTHER STORIES

Haircut

I GOT another barber that comes over from Carterville and helps me out Saturdays, but the rest of the time I can get along all right alone. You can see for yourself that this ain't no New York City and besides that, the most of the boys works all day and don't have no leisure to drop in here and get themselves prettied up.

You're a newcomer, ain't you? I thought I hadn't seen you round before. I hope you like it good enough to stay. As I say, we ain't no New York City or Chicago, but we have pretty good times. Not as good, though, since Jim Kendall got killed. When he was alive, him and Hod Meyers used to keep this town in an uproar. I bet they was more laughin' done here than any town its size in America.

Jim was comical, and Hod was pretty near a match for him. Since Jim's gone, Hod tries to hold his end up just the same as ever, but it's tough goin' when you ain't got nobody to kind of work with.

They used to be plenty fun in here Saturdays. This place is jam-packed Saturdays, from four o'clock on. Jim and Hod would show up right after their supper, round six o'clock. Jim would set himself down in that big chair, nearest the blue spittoon. Whoever had been settin' in that chair, why they'd get up when Jim come in and give it to him.

You'd of thought it was a reserved seat like they have sometimes in a theayter. Hod would generally always stand or walk up and down, or some Saturdays, of course, he'd be settin' in this chair part of the time, gettin' a haircut.

Well, Jim would set there a w'ile without openin' his mouth only to spit, and then finally he'd say to me, "Whitey,"—my right name, that is, my right first name, is Dick, but everybody round here calls me Whitey—Jim would say, "Whitey, your nose looks like a rosebud tonight. You must of been drinkin' some of your aw de cologne."

So I'd say, "No, Jim, but you look like you'd been drinkin' somethin' of that kind or somethin' worse."

Jim would have to laugh at that, but then he'd speak up and

say, "No, I ain't had nothin' to drink, but that ain't sayin' I wouldn't like somethin'. I wouldn't even mind if it was wood alcohol."

Then Hod Meyers would say, "Neither would your wife." That would set everybody to laughin' because Jim and his wife wasn't on very good terms. She'd of divorced him only they wasn't no chance to get alimony and she didn't have no way to take care of herself and the kids. She couldn't never understand Jim. He *was* kind of rough, but a good fella at heart.

Him and Hod had all kinds of sport with Milt Sheppard. I don't suppose you've seen Milt. Well, he's got an Adam's apple that looks more like a mushmelon. So I'd be shavin' Milt and when I'd start to shave down here on his neck, Hod would holler, "Hey, Whitey, wait a minute! Before you cut into it, let's make up a pool and see who can guess closest to the number of seeds."

And Jim would say, "If Milt hadn't of been so hoggish, he'd of ordered a half a cantaloupe instead of a whole one and it might not of stuck in his throat."

All the boys would roar at this and Milt himself would force a smile, though the joke was on him. Jim certainly was a card!

There's his shavin' mug, settin' on the shelf, right next to Charley Vail's. "Charles M. Vail." That's the druggist. He comes in regular for his shave, three times a week. And Jim's is the cup next to Charley's. "James H. Kendall." Jim won't need no shavin' mug no more, but I'll leave it there just the same for old time's sake. Jim certainly was a character!

Years ago, Jim used to travel for a canned goods concern over in Carterville. They sold canned goods. Jim had the whole northern half of the State and was on the road five days out of every week. He'd drop in here Saturdays and tell his experiences for that week. It was rich.

I guess he paid more attention to playin' jokes than makin' sales. Finally the concern let him out and he come right home here and told everybody he'd been fired instead of sayin' he'd resigned like most fellas would of.

It was a Saturday and the shop was full and Jim got up out of that chair and says, "Gentlemen, I got an important announcement to make. I been fired from my job."

Well, they asked him if he was in earnest and he said he was and nobody could think of nothin' to say till Jim finally broke the ice himself. He says, "I been sellin' canned goods and now I'm canned goods myself."

You see, the concern he'd been workin' for was a factory that made canned goods. Over in Carterville. And now Jim said he was canned himself. He was certainly a card!

Jim had a great trick that he used to play w'ile he was travelin'. For instance, he'd be ridin' on a train and they'd come to some little town like, well, like, we'll say, like Benton. Jim would look out the train window and read the signs on the stores.

For instance, they'd be a sign, "Henry Smith, Dry Goods." Well, Jim would write down the name and the name of the town and when he got to wherever he was goin' he'd mail back a postal card to Henry Smith at Benton and not sign no name to it, but he'd write on the card, well, somethin' like "Ask your wife about that book agent that spent the afternoon last week," or "Ask your Missus who kept her from gettin' lonesome the last time you was in Carterville." And he'd sign the card, "A Friend."

Of course, he never knew what really come of none of these jokes, but he could picture what *probably* happened and that was enough.

Jim didn't work very steady after he lost his position with the Carterville people. What he did earn, doin' odd jobs round town, why he spent pretty near all of it on gin and his family might of starved if the stores hadn't of carried them along. Jim's wife tried her hand at dressmakin', but they ain't nobody goin' to get rich makin' dresses in this town.

As I say, she'd of divorced Jim, only she seen that she couldn't support herself and the kids and she was always hopin' that some day Jim would cut out his habits and give her more than two or three dollars a week.

They was a time when she would go to whoever he was workin' for and ask them to give her his wages, but after she done this once or twice, he beat her to it by borrowin' most of his pay in advance. He told it all round town, how he had outfoxed his Missus. He certainly was a caution!

But he wasn't satisfied with just outwittin' her. He was sore the way she had acted, tryin' to grab off his pay. And he made up his mind he'd get even. Well, he waited till Evans's Circus was advertised to come to town. Then he told his wife and two kiddies that he was goin' to take them to the circus. The day of the circus, he told them he would get the tickets and meet them outside the entrance to the tent.

Well, he didn't have no intentions of bein' there or buyin' tickets or nothin'. He got full of gin and laid round Wright's poolroom all day. His wife and the kids waited and waited and of course he didn't show up. His wife didn't have a dime with her, or nowhere else, I guess. So she finally had to tell the kids it was all off and they cried like they wasn't never goin' to stop.

Well, it seems, w'ile they was cryin', Doc Stair came along and he asked what was the matter, but Mrs. Kendall was stubborn and wouldn't tell him, but the kids told him and he insisted on takin' them and their mother in the show. Jim found this out afterwards and it was one reason why he had it in for Doc Stair.

Doc Stair come here about a year and a half ago. He's a mighty handsome young fella and his clothes always look like he has them made to order. He goes to Detroit two or three times a year and w'ile he's there he must have a tailor take his measure and then make him a suit to order. They cost pretty near twice as much, but they fit a whole lot better than if you just bought them in a store.

For a w'ile everybody was wonderin' why a young doctor like Doc Stair should come to a town like this where we already got old Doc Gamble and Doc Foote that's both been here for years and all the practice in town was always divided between the two of them.

Then they was a story got round that Doc Stair's gal had throwed him over, a gal up in the Northern Peninsula somewheres, and the reason he come here was to hide himself away and forget it. He said himself that he thought they wasn't nothin' like general practice in a place like ours to fit a man to be a good all round doctor. And that's why he'd came.

Anyways, it wasn't long before he was makin' enough to live on, though they tell me that he never dunned nobody for what they owed him, and the folks here certainly has got the owin' habit, even in my business. If I had all that was comin' to me for just shaves alone, I could go to Carterville and put up at the Mercer for a week and see a different picture every night. For instance, they's old George Purdy—but I guess I shouldn't ought to be gossipin'.

Well, last year, our coroner died, died of the flu. Ken Beatty, that was his name. He was the coroner. So they had to choose another man to be coroner in his place and they picked Doc Stair. He laughed at first and said he didn't want it, but they made him take it. It ain't no job that anybody would fight for and what a man makes out of it in a year would just about buy seeds for their garden. Doc's the kind, though, that can't say no to nothin' if you keep at him long enough.

But I was goin' to tell you about a poor boy we got here in town—Paul Dickson. He fell out of a tree when he was about ten years old. Lit on his head and it done somethin' to him and he ain't never been right. No harm in him, but just silly. Jim Kendall used to call him cuckoo; that's a name Jim had for anybody that was off their head, only he called people's head their bean. That was another of his gags, callin' head bean and callin' crazy people cuckoo. Only poor Paul ain't crazy, but just silly.

You can imagine that Jim used to have all kinds of fun with Paul. He'd send him to the White Front Garage for a left-handed monkey wrench. Of course they ain't no such a thing as a left-handed monkey wrench.

And once we had a kind of a fair here and they was a baseball game between the fats and the leans and before the game started Jim called Paul over and sent him way down to Schrader's hardware store to get a key for the pitcher's box.

They wasn't nothin' in the way of gags that Jim couldn't think up, when he put his mind to it.

Poor Paul was always kind of suspicious of people, maybe on account of how Jim had kept foolin' him. Paul wouldn't have much to do with anybody only his own mother and Doc Stair and a girl here in town named Julie Gregg. That is, she ain't a girl no more, but pretty near thirty or over.

When Doc first come to town, Paul seemed to feel like here was a real friend and he hung round Doc's office most of the w'ile; the only time he wasn't there was when he'd go home to eat or sleep or when he seen Julie Gregg doin' her shoppin'.

When he looked out Doc's window and seen her, he'd run

downstairs and join her and tag along with her to the different stores. The poor boy was crazy about Julie and she always treated him mighty nice and made him feel like he was welcome, though of course it wasn't nothin' but pity on her side.

Doc done all he could to improve Paul's mind and he told me once that he really thought the boy was gettin' better, that they was times when he was as bright and sensible as anybody else.

But I was goin' to tell you about Julie Gregg. Old Man Gregg was in the lumber business, but got to drinkin' and lost the most of his money and when he died, he didn't leave nothin' but the house and just enough insurance for the girl to skimp along on.

Her mother was a kind of a half invalid and didn't hardly ever leave the house. Julie wanted to sell the place and move somewheres else after the old man died, but the mother said she was born here and would die here. It was tough on Julie, as the young people round this town—well, she's too good for them.

She's been away to school and Chicago and New York and different places and they ain't no subject she can't talk on, where you take the rest of the young folks here and you mention anything to them outside of Gloria Swanson or Tommy Meighan and they think you're delirious. Did you see Gloria in Wages of Virtue? You missed somethin'!

Well, Doc Stair hadn't been here more than a week when he come in one day to get shaved and I recognized who he was as he had been pointed out to me, so I told him about my old lady. She's been ailin' for a couple years and either Doc Gamble or Doc Foote, neither one, seemed to be helpin' her. So he said he would come out and see her, but if she was able to get out herself, it would be better to bring her to his office where he could make a completer examination.

So I took her to his office and w'ile I was waitin' for her in the reception room, in come Julie Gregg. When somebody comes in Doc Stair's office, they's a bell that rings in his inside office so as he can tell they's somebody to see him.

So he left my old lady inside and come out to the front office and that's the first time him and Julie met and I guess it was what they call love at first sight. But it wasn't fifty-fifty. This young fella was the slickest lookin' fella she'd ever seen in this town and she went wild over him. To him she was just a young lady that wanted to see the doctor.

She'd came on about the same business I had. Her mother had been doctorin' for years with Doc Gamble and Doc Foote and without no results. So she'd heard they was a new doc in town and decided to give him a try. He promised to call and see her mother that same day.

I said a minute ago that it was love at first sight on her part. I'm not only judgin' by how she acted afterwards but how she looked at him that first day in his office. I ain't no mind reader, but it was wrote all over her face that she was gone.

Now Jim Kendall, besides bein' a jokesmith and a pretty good drinker, well, Jim was quite a lady-killer. I guess he run pretty wild durin' the time he was on the road for them Carterville people, and besides that, he'd had a couple little affairs of the heart right here in town. As I say, his wife could of divorced him, only she couldn't.

But Jim was like the majority of men, and women, too, I guess. He wanted what he couldn't get. He wanted Julie Gregg and worked his head off tryin' to land her. Only he'd of said bean instead of head.

Well, Jim's habits and his jokes didn't appeal to Julie and of course he was a married man, so he didn't have no more chance than, well, than a rabbit. That's an expression of Jim's himself. When somebody didn't have no chance to get elected or somethin', Jim would always say they didn't have no more chance than a rabbit.

He didn't make no bones about how he felt. Right in here, more than once, in front of the whole crowd, he said he was stuck on Julie and anybody that could get her for him was welcome to his house and his wife and kids included. But she wouldn't have nothin' to do with him; wouldn't even speak to him on the street. He finally seen he wasn't gettin' nowheres with his usual line so he decided to try the rough stuff. He went right up to her house one evenin' and when she opened the door he forced his way in and grabbed her. But she broke loose and before he could stop her, she run in the next room and locked the door and phoned to Joe Barnes. Joe's the marshal. Jim could hear who she was phonin' to and he beat it before Joe got there.

Joe was an old friend of Julie's pa. Joe went to Jim the next day and told him what would happen if he ever done it again.

I don't know how the news of this little affair leaked out. Chances is that Joe Barnes told his wife and she told somebody else's wife and they told their husband. Anyways, it did leak out and Hod Meyers had the nerve to kid Jim about it, right here in this shop. Jim didn't deny nothin' and kind of laughed it off and said for us all to wait; that lots of people had tried to make a monkey out of him, but he always got even.

Meanw'ile everybody in town was wise to Julie's bein' wild mad over the Doc. I don't suppose she had any idear how her face changed when him and her was together; of course she couldn't of, or she'd of kept away from him. And she didn't know that we was all noticin' how many times she made excuses to go up to his office or pass it on the other side of the street and look up in his window to see if he was there. I felt sorry for her and so did most other people.

Hod Meyers kept rubbin' it into Jim about how the Doc had cut him out. Jim didn't pay no attention to the kiddin' and you could see he was plannin' one of his jokes.

One trick Jim had was the knack of changin' his voice. He could make you think he was a girl talkin' and he could mimic any man's voice. To show you how good he was along this line, I'll tell you the joke he played on me once.

You know, in most towns of any size, when a man is dead and needs a shave, why the barber that shaves him soaks him five dollars for the job; that is, he don't soak *him*, but whoever ordered the shave. I just charge three dollars because personally I don't mind much shavin' a dead person. They lay a whole lot stiller than live customers. The only thing is that you don't feel like talkin' to them and you get kind of lonesome.

Well, about the coldest day we ever had here, two years ago last winter, the phone rung at the house w'ile I was home to dinner and I answered the phone and it was a woman's voice and she said she was Mrs. John Scott and her husband was dead and would I come out and shave him.

Old John had always been a good customer of mine. But they live seven miles out in the country, on the Streeter road. Still I didn't see how I could say no.

So I said I would be there, but would have to come in a

jitney and it might cost three or four dollars besides the price of the shave. So she, or the voice, it said that was all right, so I got Frank Abbott to drive me out to the place and when I got there, who should open the door but old John himself! He wasn't no more dead than, well, than a rabbit.

It didn't take no private detective to figure out who had played me this little joke. Nobody could of thought it up but Jim Kendall. He certainly was a card!

I tell you this incident just to show you how he could disguise his voice and make you believe it was somebody else talkin'. I'd of swore it was Mrs. Scott had called me. Anyways, some woman.

Well, Jim waited till he had Doc Stair's voice down pat; then he went after revenge.

He called Julie up on a night when he knew Doc was over in Carterville. She never questioned but what it was Doc's voice. Jim said he must see her that night; he couldn't wait no longer to tell her somethin'. She was all excited and told him to come to the house. But he said he was expectin' an important long distance call and wouldn't she please forget her manners for once and come to his office. He said they couldn't nothin' hurt her and nobody would see her and he just *must* talk to her a little w'ile. Well, poor Julie fell for it.

Doc always keeps a night light in his office, so it looked to Julie like they was somebody there.

Meanw'ile Jim Kendall had went to Wright's poolroom, where they was a whole gang amusin' themselves. The most of them had drank plenty of gin, and they was a rough bunch even when sober. They was always strong for Jim's jokes and when he told them to come with him and see some fun they give up their card games and pool games and followed along.

Doc's office is on the second floor. Right outside his door they's a flight of stairs leadin' to the floor above. Jim and his gang hid in the dark behind these stairs.

Well, Julie come up to Doc's door and rung the bell and they was nothin' doin'. She rung it again and she rung it seven or eight times. Then she tried the door and found it locked. Then Jim made some kind of a noise and she heard it and waited a minute, and then she says, "Is that you, Ralph?" Ralph is Doc's first name.

They was no answer and it must of came to her all of a sudden that she'd been bunked. She pretty near fell downstairs and the whole gang after her. They chased her all the way home, hollerin', "Is that you, Ralph?" and "Oh, Ralphie, dear, is that you?" Jim says he couldn't holler it himself, as he was laughin' too hard.

Poor Julie! She didn't show up here on Main Street for a long, long time afterward.

And of course Jim and his gang told everybody in town, everybody but Doc Stair. They was scared to tell him, and he might of never knowed only for Paul Dickson. The poor cuckoo, as Jim called him, he was here in the shop one night when Jim was still gloatin' yet over what he'd done to Julie. And Paul took in as much of it as he could understand and he run to Doc with the story.

It's a cinch Doc went up in the air and swore he'd make Jim suffer. But it was a kind of a delicate thing, because if it got out that he had beat Jim up, Julie was bound to hear of it and then she'd know that Doc knew and of course knowin' that he knew would make it worse for her than ever. He was goin' to do somethin', but it took a lot of figurin'.

Well, it was a couple days later when Jim was here in the shop again, and so was the cuckoo. Jim was goin' duck-shootin' the next day and had came in lookin' for Hod Meyers to go with him. I happened to know that Hod had went over to Carterville and wouldn't be home till the end of the week. So Jim said he hated to go alone and he guessed he would call it off. Then poor Paul spoke up and said if Jim would take him he would go along. Jim thought a w'ile and then he said, well, he guessed a half-wit was better than nothin'.

I suppose he was plottin' to get Paul out in the boat and play some joke on him, like pushin' him in the water. Anyways, he said Paul could go. He asked him had he ever shot a duck and Paul said no, he'd never even had a gun in his hands. So Jim said he could set in the boat and watch him and if he behaved himself, he might lend him his gun for a couple of shots. They made a date to meet in the mornin' and that's the last I seen of Jim alive.

Next mornin', I hadn't been open more than ten minutes when Doc Stair come in. He looked kind of nervous. He asked me had I seen Paul Dickson. I said no, but I knew where he was, out duck-shootin' with Jim Kendall. So Doc says that's what he had heard, and he couldn't understand it because Paul had told him he wouldn't never have no more to do with Jim as long as he lived.

He said Paul had told him about the joke Jim had played on Julie. He said Paul had asked him what he thought of the joke and the Doc had told him that anybody that would do a thing like that ought not to be let live.

I said it had been a kind of a raw thing, but Jim just couldn't resist no kind of a joke, no matter how raw. I said I thought he was all right at heart, but just bubblin' over with mischief. Doc turned and walked out.

At noon he got a phone call from old John Scott. The lake where Jim and Paul had went shootin' is on John's place. Paul had came runnin' up to the house a few minutes before and said they'd been an accident. Jim had shot a few ducks and then give the gun to Paul and told him to try his luck. Paul hadn't never handled a gun and he was nervous. He was shakin' so hard that he couldn't control the gun. He let fire and Jim sunk back in the boat, dead.

Doc Stair, bein' the coroner, jumped in Frank Abbott's fliv-ver and rushed out to Scott's farm. Paul and old John was down on the shore of the lake. Paul had rowed the boat to shore, but they'd left the body in it, waitin' for Doc to come.

Doc examined the body and said they might as well fetch it back to town. They was no use leavin' it there or callin' a jury, as it was a plain case of accidental shootin'.

Personally I wouldn't never leave a person shoot a gun in the same boat I was in unless I was sure they knew somethin' about guns. Jim was a sucker to leave a new beginner have his gun, let alone a half-wit. It probably served Jim right, what he got. But still we miss him round here. He certainly was a card!

Comb it wet or dry?

Mr. and Mrs. Fix-It

THEY'RE CERTAINLY a live bunch in this town. We ain't only been here three days and had calls already from people representin' four different organizations—the Chamber of Commerce, Kiwanis, and I forget who else. They wanted to know if we was comfortable and did we like the town and is they anything they can do for us and what to be sure and see.

And they all asked how we happened to come here instead of goin' somewheres else. I guess they keep a record of everybody's reasons for comin' so as they can get a line on what features tourists is most attracted by. Then they play up them features in next year's booster advertisin'.

Well, I told them we was perfectly comfortable and we like the town fine and they's nothin' nobody can do for us right now and we'll be sure and see all the things we ought to see. But when they asked me how did we happen to come here, I said it was just a kind of a accident, because the real reason makes too long a story.

My wife has been kiddin' me about my friends ever since we was married. She says that judgin' by the ones I've introduced her to, they ain't nobody in the world got a rummier bunch of friends than me. I'll admit that the most of them ain't, well, what you might call hot; they're different somehow than when I first hung around with them. They seem to be lost without a brass rail to rest their dogs on. But of course they're old friends and I can't give 'em the air.

We have 'em to the house for dinner every little w'ile, they and their wives, and what my missus objects to is because they don't none of them play bridge or mah jong or do cross-word puzzles or sing or dance or even talk, but just set there and wait for somebody to pour 'em a fresh drink.

As I say, my wife kids me about 'em and they ain't really nothin' I can offer in their defense. That don't mean, though, that the shoe is all on one foot. Because w'ile the majority of her friends may not be quite as dumb as mine, just the same they's a few she's picked out who I'd of had to be under the ether to allow anybody to introduce 'em to me in the first place.

Like the Crandalls, for instance. Mrs. Crandall come from my wife's home town and they didn't hardly know each other there, but they met again in a store in Chi and it went from bad to worse till finally Ada asked the dame and her husband to the house.

Well, the husband turns out to be the fella that win the war, w'ile it seems that Mrs. Crandall was in Atlantic City once and some movin' picture company was makin' a picture there and they took a scene of what was supposed to be society people walkin' up and down the Boardwalk and Mrs. Crandall was in the picture and people that seen it when it come out, they all said that from the way she screened, why if she wanted to go into the business, she could make Gloria Swanson look like Mrs. Gump.

Now it ain't only took me a few words to tell you these things, but when the Crandalls tells their story themselves, they don't hardly get started by midnight and no chance of them goin' home till they're through even when you drop 'em a hint that they're springin' it on you for the hundred and twelfth time.

That's the Crandalls, and another of the wife's friends is the Thayers. Thayer is what you might call a all-around handy man. He can mimic pretty near all the birds and beasts and fishes, he can yodel, he can play a ocarena, or he can recite Kipling or Robert H. Service, or he can do card tricks, and strike a light without no matches, and tie all the different knots.

And besides that, he can make a complete radio outfit and set it up, and take pictures as good as the best professional photographers and a whole lot better. He collects autographs. And he never had a sick day in his life.

Mrs. Thayer gets a headache playin' bridge, so it's mah jong or rhum when she's around. She used to be a teacher of elocution and she still gives readin's if you coax her, or if you don't, and her hair is such a awful nuisance that she would get it cut in a minute only all her friends tells her it would be criminal to spoil that head of hair. And when she talks to her husband, she always talks baby talk, maybe because somebody has told her that she'd be single if he wasn't childish.

And then Ada has got still another pal, a dame named Peggy Flood who is hospital mad and ain't happy unless she is just goin' under the knife or just been there. She's had everything removed that the doctors knew the name of and now they're probin' her for new giblets.

Well, I wouldn't mind if they cut her up into alphabet soup if they'd only do such a good job of it that they couldn't put her together again, but she always comes through O. K. and she spends the intermissions at our place, describin' what all they done or what they're plannin' to do next.

But the cat's nightgown is Tom Stevens and his wife. There's the team that wins the Olympics! And they're Ada's team, not mine.

Ada met Belle Stevens on the elevated. Ada was invited to a party out on the North Side and didn't know exactly where to get off and Mrs. Stevens seen her talkin' to the guard and horned in and asked her what was it she wanted to know and Ada told her, and Mrs. Stevens said she was goin' to get off the same station Ada wanted to get off, so they got off together.

Mrs. Stevens insisted on goin' right along to the address where Ada was goin' because she said Ada was bound to get lost if she wasn't familiar with the neighborhood.

Well, Ada thought it was mighty nice of her to do so much for a stranger. Mrs. Stevens said she was glad to because she didn't know what would of happened to her lots of times if strangers hadn't been nice and helped her out.

She asked Ada where she lived and Ada told her on the South Side and Mrs. Stevens said she was sure we'd like it better on the North Side if we'd leave her pick out a place for us, so Ada told her we had a year's lease that we had just signed and couldn't break it, so then Mrs. Stevens said her husband had studied law and he claimed they wasn't no lease that you couldn't break and some evening she would bring him out to call on us and he'd tell us how to break our lease.

Well, Ada had to say sure, come on out, though we was perfectly satisfied with our apartment and didn't no more want to break the lease than each other's jaw. Maybe not as much. Anyway, the very next night, they showed up, Belle and Tom, and when they'd gone, I give 'em the nickname—Mr. and Mrs. Fix-It.

After the introductions, Stevens made some remark about what a cozy little place we had and then he asked if I would mind tellin' what rent we paid. So I told him a hundred and a quarter a month. So he said, of course, that was too much and no wonder we wanted to break the lease. Then I said we was satisfied and didn't want to break it and he said I must be kiddin' and if I would show him the lease he would see what loopholes they was in it.

Well, the lease was right there in a drawer in the table, but I told him it was in my safety deposit box at the bank. I ain't got no safety deposit box and no more use for one than Judge Landis has for the deef and dumb alphabet.

Stevens said the lease was probably just a regular lease and if it was, they wouldn't be no trouble gettin' out of it, and meanw'ile him and his wife would see if they couldn't find us a place in the same buildin' with them.

And he was pretty sure they could even if the owner had to give some other tenant the air, because he, the owner, would do anything in the world for Stevens.

So I said yes, but suppose we want to stay where we are. So he said I looked like a man with better judgment than that and if I would just leave everything to him he would fix it so's we could move within a month. I kind of laughed and thought that would be the end of it.

He wanted to see the whole apartment so I showed him around and when we come to the bathroom he noticed my safety razor on the shelf. He said, "So you use one of them things," and I said, "Yes," and he asked me how I liked it, and I said I liked it fine and he said that must be because I hadn't never used a regular razor.

He said a regular razor was the only thing to use if a man wanted to look good. So I asked him if he used a regular razor and he said he did, so I said, "Well, if you look good, I don't want to."

But that didn't stop him and he said if I would meet him downtown the next day he would take me to the place where he bought all his razors and help me pick some out for myself. I told him I was goin' to be tied up, so just to give me the name and address of the place and I would drop in there when I had time.

But, no, that wouldn't do; he'd have to go along with me and introduce me to the proprietor because the proprietor was a great pal of his and would do anything in the world for him, and if the proprietor vouched for the razors, I could be sure I was gettin' the best razors money could buy. I told him again that I was goin' to be tied up and I managed to get him on some other subject.

Meanw'ile, Mrs. Stevens wanted to know where Ada had bought the dress she was wearin' and how much had it cost and Ada told her and Mrs. Stevens said it was a crime. She would meet Ada downtown tomorrow morning and take her to the shop where she bought her clothes and help her choose some dresses that really was dresses.

So Ada told her she didn't have no money to spend on dresses right then, and besides, the shop Mrs. Stevens mentioned was too high priced. But it seems the dame that run the shop was just like a sister to Mrs. Stevens and give her and her friends a big reduction and not only that, but they wasn't no hurry about payin'.

Well, Ada thanked her just the same, but didn't need nothin' new just at present; maybe later on she would take advantage of Mrs. Stevens's kind offer. Yes, but right now they was some models in stock that would be just beautiful on Ada and they might be gone later on. They was nothin' for it but Ada had to make a date with her; she wasn't obliged to buy nothin', but it would be silly not to go and look at the stuff that was in the joint and get acquainted with the dame that run it.

Well, Ada kept the date and bought three dresses she didn't want and they's only one of them she's had the nerve to wear. They cost her a hundred dollars a smash and I'd hate to think what the price would of been if Mrs. Stevens and the owner of the shop wasn't so much like sisters.

I was sure I hadn't made no date with Stevens, but just the same he called me up the next night to ask why I hadn't met him. And a couple of days later I got three new razors in the mail along with a bill and a note from the store sayin' that these was three specially fine razors that had been picked out for me by Thomas J. Stevens.

I don't know yet why I paid for the razors and kept 'em. I ain't used 'em and never intended to. Though I've been tempted a few times to test their edge on Stevens's neck.

That same week, Mrs. Stevens called up and asked us to

spend Sunday with them and when we got out there, the owner of the buildin' is there, too. And Stevens has told him that I was goin' to give up my apartment on the South Side and wanted him to show me what he had.

I thought this was a little too strong and I said Stevens must of misunderstood me, that I hadn't no fault to find with the place I was in and wasn't plannin' to move, not for a year anyway. You can bet this didn't make no hit with the guy, who was just there on Stevens's say-so that I was a prospective tenant.

Well, it was only about two months ago that this cute little couple come into our life, but I'll bet we seen 'em twenty times at least. They was always invitin' us to their place or invitin' themselves to our place and Ada is one of these here kind of people that just can't say no. Which may be why I and her is married.

Anyway, it begin to seem like us and the Stevenses was livin' together and all one family, with them at the head of it. I never in my life seen anybody as crazy to run other people's business. Honest to heavens, it's a wonder they let us brush our own teeth!

Ada made the remark one night that she wished the ski jumper who was doin' our cookin' would get married and quit so's she wouldn't have to can her. Mrs. Stevens was there and asked Ada if she should try and get her a new cook, but Ada says no, the poor gal might have trouble findin' another job and she felt sorry for her.

Just the same, the next afternoon a Jap come to the apartment and said he was ready to go to work and Mrs. Stevens had sent him. Ada had to tell him the place was already filled.

Another night, Ada complained that her feet was tired. Belle said her feet used to get tired, too, till a friend of hers recommended a chiropodist and she went to him and he done her so much good that she made a regular appointment with him for once every month and paid him a flat sum and no matter how much runnin' around she done, her dogs hadn't fretted her once since this cornhusker started tendin' to 'em.

She wanted to call up the guy at his home right then and there and make a date for Ada and the only way Ada could stop her was by promisin' to go and see him the next time her feet hurt. After that, whenever the two gals met, Belle's first question was "How is your feet?" and the answer was always "Fine, thanks."

Well, I'm quite a football fan and Ada likes to go, too, when it's a big game and lots of excitement. So we decided we'd see the Illinois-Chicago game and have a look at this "Red" Grange. I warned Ada to not say nothin' about it to Tom and Belle as I felt like we was entitled to a day off.

But it happened that they was goin' to be a game up at Evanston that day and the Stevenses invited us to see that one with them. So we used the other game as a alibi. And when Tom asked me later on if I'd boughten my tickets yet, instead of sayin' yes, I told him the truth and said no.

So then he said:

"I'm glad you ain't, because I and Belle has made up our mind that the Chicago game is the one we ought to see. And we'll all go together. And don't you bother about tickets because I can get better ones than you can as Stagg and I is just like that."

So I left it to him to get the tickets and we might as well of set on the Adams Street bridge. I said to Stevens, I said:

"If these is the seats Mr. Stagg digs up for his old pals, I suppose he leads strangers twenty or thirty miles out in the country and blindfolds 'em and ties 'em to a tree."

Now of course it was the bunk about he and Stagg bein' so close. He may of been introduced to him once, but he ain't the kind of a guy that Stagg would go around holdin' hands with. Just the same, most of the people he bragged about knowin', why it turned out that he really did know 'em; yes, and stood ace high with 'em, too.

Like, for instance, I got pinched for speedin' one night and they give me a ticket to show up in the Speeders' court and I told Stevens about it and he says, "Just forget it! I'll call up the judge and have it wiped off the book. He's a mighty good fella and a personal friend of mine."

Well, I didn't want to take no chances so I phoned Stevens the day before I was supposed to appear in court, and I asked him if he'd talked to the judge. He said he had and I asked him if he was sure. So he said, "If you don't believe me, call up the judge yourself." And he give me the judge's number. Sure enough, Stevens had fixed it and when I thanked the judge for his trouble, he said it was a pleasure to do somethin' for a friend of Tom Stevens's.

Now, I know it's silly to not appreciate favors like that and not warm up to people that's always tryin' to help you along, but still a person don't relish bein' treated like they was half-witted and couldn't button their shirt alone. Tom and Belle meant all right, but I and Ada got kind of tired of havin' fault found with everything that belonged to us and everything we done or tried to do.

Besides our apartment bein' no good and our clothes terrible, we learned that my dentist didn't know a bridge from a mustache cup, and the cigarettes I smoked didn't have no taste to them, and the man that bobbed Ada's hair must of been mad at her, and neither of us would ever know what it was to live till we owned a wire-haired fox terrier.

And we found out that the liquor I'd been drinkin' and enjoyin' was a mixture of bath salts and assorted paints, and the car we'd paid seventeen hundred smackers for wasn't nowheres near as much of a car as one that Tom could of got for us for eight hundred on account of knowin' a brother-in-law of a fella that used to go to school with the president of the company's nephew, and that if Ada would take up aesthetic dancin' under a dame Belle knew about, why she'd never have no more trouble with her tonsils.

Nothin' we had or nothin' we talked about gettin' or doin' was worth a damn unless it was recommended or suggested by the Stevenses.

Well, I done a pretty good business this fall and I and Ada had always planned to spend a winter in the South, so one night we figured it out that this was the year we could spare the money and the time and if we didn't go this year we never would. So the next thing was where should we go, and we finally decided on Miami. And we said we wouldn't mention nothin' about it to Tom and Belle till the day we was goin'. We'd pretend we was doin' it out of a clear sky.

But a secret is just as safe with Ada as a police dog tethered with dental floss. It wasn't more than a day or two after we'd had our talk when Tom and Belle sprang the news that they was leavin' for California right after New Year's. And why didn't we go with them.

Well, I didn't say nothin' and Ada said it sounded grand, but it was impossible. Then Stevens said if it was a question of money, to not let that bother us as he would loan it to me and I could pay it back whenever I felt like it. That was more than Ada could stand, so she says we wasn't as poor as people seemed to think and the reason we couldn't go to California was because we was goin' to Miami.

This was such a surprise that it almost struck 'em dumb at first and all Tom could think of to say was that he'd been to Miami himself and it was too crowded and he'd lay off of it if he was us. But the next time we seen 'em they had our trip all arranged.

First, Tom asked me what road we was goin' on and I told him the Big Four. So he asked if we had our reservations and I told him yes.

"Well," he said, "we'll get rid of 'em and I'll fix you up on the C. & E. I. The general passenger agent is a friend of mine and they ain't nothin' he won't do for my friends. He'll see that you're treated right and that you get there in good shape."

So I said:

"I don't want to put you to all that trouble, and besides I don't know nobody connected with the Big Four well enough for them to resent me travelin' on their lines, and as for gettin' there in good shape, even if I have a secret enemy or two on the Big Four, I don't believe they'd endanger the lives of the other passengers just to see that I didn't get there in good shape."

But Stevens insisted on takin' my tickets and sellin' 'em back to the Big Four and gettin' me fixed on the C. & E. I. The berths we'd had on the Big Four was Lower 9 and Lower 10. The berths Tom got us on the C. & E. I. was Lower 7 and Lower 8, which he said was better. I suppose he figured that the nearer you are to the middle of the car, the less chance there is of bein' woke up if your car gets in another train's way.

He wanted to know, too, if I'd made any reservations at a hotel. I showed him a wire I had from the Royal Palm in reply to a wire I'd sent 'em.

"Yes," he says, "but you don't want to stop at the Royal Palm. You wire and tell 'em to cancel that and I'll make arrangements for you at the Flamingo, over at the Beach. Charley Krom, the manager there, was born and raised in the same town I was. He'll take great care of you if he knows you're a friend of mine."

So I asked him if all the guests at the Flamingo was friends of his, and he said of course not; what did I mean?

"Well," I said, "I was just thinkin' that if they ain't, Mr. Krom probably makes life pretty miserable for 'em. What does he do, have the phone girl ring 'em up at all hours of the night, and hide their mail, and shut off their hot water, and put cracker crumbs in their beds?"

That didn't mean nothin' to Stevens and he went right ahead and switched me from one hotel to the other.

While Tom was reorganizin' my program and tellin' me what to eat in Florida, and what bait to use for barracuda and carp, and what time to go bathin' and which foot to stick in the water first, why Belle was makin' Ada return all the stuff she had boughten to wear down there and buy other stuff that Belle picked out for her at joints where Belle was so well known that they only soaked her twice as much as a stranger. She had Ada almost crazy, but I told her to never mind; in just a few more days we'd be where they couldn't get at us.

I suppose you're wonderin' why didn't we quarrel with 'em and break loose from 'em and tell 'em to leave us alone. You'd know why if you knew them. Nothin' we could do would convince 'em that we didn't want their advice and help. And nothin' we could say was a insult.

Well, the night before we was due to leave Chi, the phone rung and I answered it. It was Tom.

"I've got a surprise for you," he says. "I and Belle has give up the California idear. We're goin' to Miami instead, and on account of me knowin' the boys down at the C. & E. I., I've landed a drawin' room on the same train you're takin'. How is that for news?"

"Great!" I said, and I went back and broke it to Ada. For a minute I thought she was goin' to faint. And all night long she moaned and groaned and had hysterics.

So that's how we happened to come to Biloxi.

Zone of Quiet

"WELL," SAID the Doctor briskly, "how do you feel?"

"Oh, I guess I'm all right," replied the man in bed. "I'm still kind of drowsy, that's all."

"You were under the anesthetic an hour and a half. It's no wonder you aren't wide awake yet. But you'll be better after a good night's rest, and I've left something with Miss Lyons that'll make you sleep. I'm going along now. Miss Lyons will take good care of you."

"I'm off at seven o'clock," said Miss Lyons. "I'm going to a show with my G. F. But Miss Halsey's all right. She's the night floor nurse. Anything you want, she'll get it for you. What can I give him to eat, Doctor?"

"Nothing at all; not till after I've been here tomorrow. He'll be better off without anything. Just see that he's kept quiet. Don't let him talk, and don't talk to him; that is, if you can help it."

"Help it!" said Miss Lyons. "Say, I can be old lady Sphinx herself when I want to! Sometimes I sit for hours—not alone, neither—and never say a word. Just think and think. And dream.

"I had a G. F. in Baltimore, where I took my training; she used to call me Dummy. Not because I'm dumb like some people—you know—but because I'd sit there and not say nothing. She'd say, 'A penny for your thoughts, Eleanor.' That's my first name—Eleanor."

"Well, I must run along. I'll see you in the morning."

"Good-by, Doctor," said the man in bed, as he went out.

"Good-by, Doctor Cox," said Miss Lyons as the door closed.

"He seems like an awful nice fella," said Miss Lyons. "And a good doctor, too. This is the first time I've been on a case with him. He gives a girl credit for having some sense. Most of these doctors treat us like they thought we were Mormons or something. Like Doctor Holland. I was on a case with him last week. He treated me like I was a Mormon or something. Finally, I told him, I said, 'I'm not as dumb as I look.' She died Friday night."

576

"Who?" asked the man in bed.

"The woman; the case I was on," said Miss Lyons.

"And what did the doctor say when you told him you weren't as dumb as you look?"

"I don't remember," said Miss Lyons. "He said, 'I hope not,' or something. What *could* he say? Gee! It's quarter to seven. I hadn't no idear it was so late. I must get busy and fix you up for the night. And I'll tell Miss Halsey to take good care of you. We're going to see 'What Price Glory?' I'm going with my G. F. Her B. F. gave her the tickets and he's going to meet us after the show and take us to supper.

"Marian—that's my G. F.—she's crazy wild about him. And he's crazy about her, to hear her tell it. But I said to her this noon—she called me up on the phone—I said to her, 'If he's so crazy about you, why don't he propose? He's got plenty of money and no strings tied to him, and as far as I can see there's no reason why he shouldn't marry you if he wants you as bad as you say he does.' So she said maybe he was going to ask her tonight. I told her, 'Don't be silly! Would he drag me along if he was going to ask you?'

"That about him having plenty of money, though, that's a joke. He told her he had and she believes him. I haven't met him yet, but he looks in his picture like he's lucky if he's getting twenty-five dollars a week. She thinks he must be rich because he's in Wall Street. I told her, I said, 'That being in Wall Street don't mean nothing. What does he do there? is the question. You know they have to have janitors in those buildings just the same like anywhere else.' But she thinks he's God or somebody.

"She keeps asking me if I don't think he's the best looking thing I ever saw. I tell her yes, sure, but between you and I, I don't believe anybody'd ever mistake him for Richard Barthelmess.

"Oh, say! I saw him the other day, coming out of the Algonquin! He's the best looking thing! Even better looking than on the screen. Roy Stewart."

"What about Roy Stewart?" asked the man in bed.

"Oh, he's the fella I was telling you about," said Miss Lyons. "He's my G. F.'s B. F."

"Maybe I'm a D. F. not to know, but would you tell me what a B. F. and G. F. are?"

"Well, you *are* dumb, aren't you!" said Miss Lyons. "A G. F., that's a girl friend, and a B. F. is a boy friend. I thought everybody knew that.

"I'm going out now and find Miss Halsey and tell her to be nice to you. But maybe I better not."

"Why not?" asked the man in bed.

"Oh, nothing. I was just thinking of something funny that happened last time I was on a case in this hospital. It was the day the man had been operated on and he was the best looking somebody you ever saw. So when I went off duty I told Miss Halsey to be nice to him, like I was going to tell her about you. And when I came back in the morning he was dead. Isn't that funny?"

"Very!"

"Well," said Miss Lyons, "did you have a good night? You look a lot better, anyway. How'd you like Miss Halsey? Did you notice her ankles? She's got pretty near the smallest ankles I ever saw. Cute. I remember one day Tyler—that's one of the internes—he said if he could just see our ankles, mine and Miss Halsey's, he wouldn't know which was which. Of course we don't look anything alike other ways. She's pretty close to thirty and—well, nobody'd ever take her for Julia Hoyt. Helen."

"Who's Helen?" asked the man in bed.

"Helen Halsey. Helen; that's her first name. She was engaged to a man in Boston. He was going to Tufts College. He was going to be a doctor. But he died. She still carries his picture with her. I tell her she's silly to mope about a man that's been dead four years. And besides a girl's a fool to marry a doctor. They've got too many alibis.

"When I marry somebody, he's got to be a somebody that has regular office hours like he's in Wall Street or somewhere. Then when he don't come home, he'll have to think up something better than being 'on a case.' I used to use that on my sister when we were living together. When I happened to be out late, I'd tell her I was on a case. She never knew the difference. Poor sis! She married a terrible oil can! But she didn't have the looks to get a real somebody. I'm making this for her. It's a bridge table cover for her birthday. She'll be twenty-nine. Don't that seem old?"

"Maybe to you; not to me," said the man in bed.

"You're about forty, aren't you?" said Miss Lyons.

"Just about."

"And how old would you say I am?"

"Twenty-three."

"I'm twenty-five," said Miss Lyons. "Twenty-five and forty. That's fifteen years' difference. But I know a married couple that the husband is forty-five and she's only twenty-four, and they get along fine."

"I'm married myself," said the man in bed.

"You would be!" said Miss Lyons. "The last four cases I've been on was all married men. But at that, I'd rather have any kind of a man than a woman. I hate women! I mean sick ones. They treat a nurse like a dog, especially a pretty nurse. What's that you're reading?"

"'Vanity Fair,'" replied the man in bed.

"'Vanity Fair.' I thought that was a magazine."

"Well, there's a magazine *and* a book. This is the book."

"Is it about a girl?"

"Yes."

"I haven't read it yet. I've been busy making this thing for my sister's birthday. She'll be twenty-nine. It's a bridge table cover. When you get that old, about all there is left is bridge or cross-word puzzles. Are you a puzzle fan? I did them religiously for a while, but I got sick of them. They put in such crazy words. Like one day they had a word with only three letters and it said 'A e-longated fish' and the first letter had to be an *e*. And only three letters. That *couldn't* be right! So I said if they put things wrong like that, what's the use? Life's too short. And we only live once. When you're dead, you stay a long time dead.

"That's what a B. F. of mine used to say. He was a caution! But he was crazy about me. I might of married him only for a G. F. telling him lies about me. And called herself my friend! Charley Pierce."

"Who's Charley Pierce?"

"That was my B. F. that the other girl lied to him about me. I told him, I said, 'Well, if you believe all them stories about me, maybe we better part once and for all. I don't want to be tied up to a somebody that believes all the dirt they hear about me.' So he said he didn't really believe it and if I would take him back he wouldn't quarrel with me no more. But I said I thought it was best for us to part. I got their announcement two years ago, while I was still in training in Baltimore."

"Did he marry the girl that lied to him about you?"

"Yes, the poor fish! And I bet he's satisfied! They're a match for each other! He was all right, though, at that, till he fell for her. He used to be so thoughtful of me, like I was his sister or something.

"I like a man to *respect* me. Most fellas wants to kiss you before they know your name.

"Golly! I'm sleepy this morning! And got a right to be, too. Do you know what time I got home last night, or this morning, rather? Well, it was half past three. What would mama say if she could see her little girl now! But we did have a good time. First we went to the show—'What Price Glory?'—I and my G. F.—and afterwards her B. F. met us and took us in a taxi down to Barney Gallant's. Peewee Byers has got the orchestra there now. Used to be with Whiteman's. Gee! How he can dance! I mean Roy."

"Your G. F.'s B. F.?"

"Yes, but I don't believe he's as crazy about her as she thinks he is. Anyway—but this is a secret—he took down the phone number of the hospital while Marian was out powdering her nose, and he said he'd give me a ring about noon. Gee! I'm sleepy! Roy Stewart!"

"Well," said Miss Lyons, "how's my patient? I'm twenty minutes late, but honest, it's a wonder I got up at all! Two nights in succession is too much for this child!"

"Barney Gallant's again?" asked the man in bed.

"No, but it was dancing, and pretty near as late. It'll be different tonight. I'm going to bed just the minute I get home. But I did have a dandy time. And I'm just crazy about a certain somebody."

"Roy Stewart?"

"How'd you guess it? But honest, he's wonderful! And so different than most of the fellas I've met. He says the craziest things, just keeps you in hysterics. We were talking about books and reading, and he asked me if I liked poetry—only he called it 'poultry'—and I said I was wild about it and Edgar M. Guest was just about my favorite, and then I asked him if he liked Kipling and what do you think he said? He said he didn't know; he'd never kipled.

"He's a scream! We just sat there in the house till half past eleven and didn't do nothing but just talk and the time went like we was at a show. He's better than a show. But finally I noticed how late it was and I asked him didn't he think he better be going and he said he'd go if I'd go with him, so I asked him where could we go at that hour of night, and he said he knew a road-house just a little ways away, and I didn't want to go, but he said we wouldn't stay for only just one dance, so I went with him. To the Jericho Inn.

"I don't know what the woman thought of me where I stay, going out that time of night. But he *is* such a wonderful dancer and such a perfect gentleman! Of course we had more than one dance and it was after two o'clock before I knew it. We had some gin, too, but he just kissed me once and that was when we said good night."

"What about your G. F., Marian? Does she know?"

"About Roy and I? No. I always say that what a person don't know don't hurt them. Besides, there's nothing *for* her to know—yet. But listen: If there was a chance in the world for her, if I thought he cared anything about her, I'd be the last one in the world to accept his intentions. I hope I'm not that kind! But as far as anything serious between them is concerned, well, it's cold. I happen to *know* that! She's not the girl for him.

"In the first place, while she's pretty in a way, her complexion's bad and her hair's scraggy and her figure, well, it's like some woman in the funny pictures. And she's not peppy enough for Roy. She'd rather stay home than do anything. Stay home! It'll be time enough for that when you can't get anybody to take you out.

"She'd never make a wife for him. He'll be a rich man in another year; that is, if things go right for him in Wall Street like he expects. And a man as rich as he'll be wants a wife that can live up to it and entertain and step out once in a while. He don't want a wife that's a drag on him. And he's too good-looking for Marian. A fella as good-looking as him needs a pretty wife or the first thing you know some girl that is pretty will steal him off of you. But it's silly to talk about them marrying each other. He'd have to ask her first, and he's not going to. I know! So I don't feel at all like I'm trespassing.

"Anyway, you know the old saying, everything goes in love. And I—— But I'm keeping you from reading your book. Oh, yes; I almost forgot a T. L. that Miss Halsey said about you. Do you know what a T. L. is?"

"Yes."

"Well, then, you give me one and I'll give you this one."

"But I haven't talked to anybody but the Doctor. I can give you one from myself. He asked me how I liked you and I said all right."

"Well, that's better than nothing. Here's what Miss Halsey said: She said if you were shaved and fixed up, you wouldn't be bad. And now I'm going out and see if there's any mail for me. Most of my mail goes to where I live, but some of it comes here sometimes. What I'm looking for is a letter from the state board telling me if I passed my state examination. They ask you the craziest questions. Like 'Is ice a disinfectant?' Who cares! Nobody's going to waste ice to kill germs when there's so much of it needed in high-balls. Do you like high-balls? Roy says it spoils whisky to mix it with water. He takes it straight. He's a terror! But maybe you want to read."

"Good morning," said Miss Lyons. "Did you sleep good?"

"Not so good," said the man in bed. "I——"

"I bet you got more sleep than I did," said Miss Lyons. "He's the most persistent somebody I ever knew! I asked him last night, I said, 'Don't you never get tired of dancing?' So he said, well, he did get tired of dancing with some people, but there was others who he never got tired of dancing with them. So I said, 'Yes, Mr. Jollier, but I wasn't born yesterday and I know apple sauce when I hear it and I bet you've told that to fifty girls.' I guess he really did mean it, though.

"Of course most anybody'd rather dance with slender girls than stout girls. I remember a B. F. I had one time in Washington. He said dancing with me was just like dancing with nothing. That sounds like he was insulting me, but it was really a compliment. He meant it wasn't any effort to dance with me like with some girls. You take Marian, for instance, and while

I'm crazy about her, still that don't make her a good dancer and dancing with her must be a good deal like moving the piano or something.

"I'd die if I was fat! People are always making jokes about fat people. And there's the old saying, 'Nobody loves a fat man.' And it's even worse with a girl. Besides people making jokes about them and don't want to dance with them and so forth, besides that they're always trying to reduce and can't eat what they want to. I bet, though, if I was fat, I'd eat everything in sight. Though I guess not, either. Because I hardly eat anything as it is. But they do make jokes about them.

"I'll never forget one day last winter, I was on a case in Great Neck and the man's wife was the fattest thing! So they had a radio in the house and one day she saw in the paper where Bugs Baer was going to talk on the radio and it would probably be awfully funny because he writes so crazy. Do you ever read his articles? But this woman, she was awfully sensitive about being fat and I nearly died sitting there with her listening to Bugs Baer, because his whole talk was all about some fat woman and he said the craziest things, but I couldn't laugh on account of she being there in the room with me. One thing he said was that the woman, this woman he was talking about, he said she was so fat that she wore a wrist watch on her thumb. Henry J. Belden."

"Who is Henry J. Belden? Is that the name of Bugs Baer's fat lady?"

"No, you crazy!" said Miss Lyons. "Mr. Belden was the case I was on in Great Neck. He died."

"It seems to me a good many of your cases die."

"Isn't it a scream!" said Miss Lyons. "But it's true; that is, it's been true lately. The last five cases I've been on has all died. Of course it's just luck, but the girls have been kidding me about it and calling me a jinx, and when Miss Halsey saw me here the evening of the day you was operated, she said, 'God help him!' That's the night floor nurse's name. But you're going to be mean and live through it and spoil my record, aren't you? I'm just kidding. Of course I want you to get all right.

"But it *is* queer, the way things have happened, and it's made me feel kind of creepy. And besides, I'm not like some of the girls and don't care. I get awfully fond of some of my cases and I hate to see them die, especially if they're men and not very sick and treat you half-way decent and don't yell for you the minute you go out of the room. There's only one case I was ever on where I didn't mind her dying and that was a woman. She had nephritis. Mrs. Judson.

"Do you want some gum? I chew it just when I'm nervous. And I always get nervous when I don't have enough sleep. You can bet I'll stay home tonight, B. F. or no B. F. But anyway he's got an engagement tonight, some directors' meeting or something. He's the busiest somebody in the world. And I told him last night, I said, 'I should think you'd need sleep, too, even more than I do because you have to have all your wits about you in your business or those big bankers would take advantage and rob you. You can't afford to be sleepy,' I told him.

"So he said, 'No, but of course it's all right for you, because if you go to sleep on your job, there's no danger of you doing any damage except maybe give one of your patients a bichloride of mercury tablet instead of an alcohol rub.' He's terrible! But you can't help from laughing.

"There was four of us in the party last night. He brought along his B. F. and another girl. She was just blah, but the B. F. wasn't so bad, only he insisted on me helping him drink a half a bottle of Scotch, and on top of gin, too. I guess I was the life of the party; that is, at first. Afterwards I got sick and it wasn't so good.

"But at first I was certainly going strong. And I guess I made quite a hit with Roy's B. F. He knows Marian, too, but he won't say anything, and if he does, I don't care. If she don't want to lose her beaus, she ought to know better than to introduce them to all the pretty girls in the world. I don't mean that I'm any Norma Talmadge, but at least—well—but I sure was sick when I *was* sick!

"I must give Marian a ring this noon. I haven't talked to her since the night she introduced me to him. I've been kind of scared. But I've got to find out what she knows. Or if she's sore at me. Though I don't see how she can be, do you? But maybe you want to read."

"I called Marian up, but I didn't get her. She's out of town but she'll be back tonight. She's been out on a case. Hudson, New

York. That's where she went. The message was waiting for her when she got home the other night, the night she introduced me to Roy."

"Good morning," said Miss Lyons.

"Good morning," said the man in bed. "Did you sleep enough?"

"Yes," said Miss Lyons. "I mean no, not enough."

"Your eyes look bad. They almost look as if you'd been crying."

"Who? Me? It'd take more than—I mean, I'm not a baby! But go on and read your book."

"Well, good morning," said Miss Lyons. "And how's my patient? And this is the last morning I can call you that, isn't it? I think you're mean to get well so quick and leave me out of a job. I'm just kidding. I'm glad you're all right again, and I can use a little rest myself."

"Another big night?" asked the man in bed.

"Pretty big," said Miss Lyons. "And another one coming. But tomorrow I won't ever get up. Honest, I danced so much last night that I thought my feet would drop off. But he certainly is a dancing fool! And the nicest somebody to talk to that I've met since I came to this town. Not a smart Alex and not always trying to be funny like some people, but just nice. He understands. He seems to know what you're thinking. George Morse."

"George Morse!" exclaimed the man in bed.

"Why yes," said Miss Lyons. "Do you know him?"

"No. But I thought you were talking about this Stewart, this Roy."

"Oh, him!" said Miss Lyons. "I should say not! He's private property; other people's property, not mine. He's engaged to my G. F. Marian. It happened day before yesterday, after she got home from Hudson. She was on a case up there. She told me about it night before last. I told her congratulations. Because I wouldn't hurt her feelings for the world! But heavens! what a mess she's going to be in, married to that dumb-bell. But of course some people can't be choosey. And I doubt if they ever get married unless some friend loans him the price of a license.

"He's got her believing he's in Wall Street, but I bet if he ever goes there at all, it's to sweep it. He's one of these kind of fellas that's got a great line for a little while, but you don't want to live with a clown. And I'd hate to marry a man that all he thinks about is to step out every night and dance and drink.

"I had a notion to tell her what I really thought. But that'd only of made her sore, or she'd of thought I was jealous or something. As if I couldn't of had him myself! Though even if he wasn't so awful, if I'd liked him instead of loathed him, I wouldn't of taken him from her on account of she being my G. F. And especially while she was out of town.

"He's the kind of a fella that'd marry a nurse in the hopes that some day he'd be an invalid. You know, that kind.

"But say—did you ever hear of J. P. Morgan and Company? That's where my B. F. works, and he don't claim to own it neither. George Morse.

"Haven't you finished that book yet?"

Women

YOUNG JAKE uttered a few words which it would pain me to repeat.

"And what are *you* crabbin' about?" asked Mike Healy from his corner of the bench.

"Oh, nothin'!" said Jake. "Nothin' except that I'm sick of it!"

"Sick of what?" demanded Healy.

"Of settin' here!" Jake replied.

"You!" said Mike Healy, with a short laugh. "You've got a fine license to squawk! Why, let's see: what is it? The third of June, and your first June in the league. You ain't even *begin* to sit! Look at me! Been on this bench since catchers started wearin' a mast, or anyway it seems that long. And you never hear me crab, do you, Lefty?"

"Only when you talk," answered the athlete addressed. "And that's only at table or between meals."

"But if this kid's hollerin' already," said Mike, "what'll he be doin' along in August or September, to say nothin' about next August and the August after that?"

"Don't worry!" said Young Jake. "I'll either be a regular by the end of this season or I won't be on this ball club at all!"

"That-a-boy!" said Healy. "Threaten 'em!"

"I mean what I say!" retorted Jake. "I ain't goin' to spend my life on no bench! I come here to play baseball!"

"Oh, you did!" said Healy. "And what do you think I come here for, to fish?"

"I ain't talkin' about you," said Young Jake. "I'm talkin' about myself."

"That's a novelty in a ball player," remarked Lefty.

"And what I'm sayin'," Jake went on, "is that I'm sick of settin' on this bench."

"This ain't a bad bench," said Healy. "They's a hell of a lot worse places you might sit."

"And a hell of a lot better places!" said Jake. "I can think of one right now. I'm lookin' right at it."

"Where at?"

"Right up in the old stand; the third—no, the fourth row, next to the aisle, the first aisle beyond where the screen leaves off."

"I noticed her myself!" put in Lefty. "Damn cute! Too damn cute for a busher like you to get smoked up over."

"Oh, I don't know!" said Young Jake. "I didn't get along so bad with them dames down South."

"Down South ain't here!" replied Lefty. "Those dames in some of those swamps, they lose their head when they see a man with shoes on. But up here you've got to have something. If you pulled that Calhoun County stuff of yours on a gal like that gal in the stand she'd yell for the dog catcher. She'd——"

"They're all alike!" interrupted Mike Healy. "South, or here, or anywheres, they're all the same, and all poison!"

"What's poison?" asked Jake.

"Women!" said Healy. "And the more you have to do with 'em the better chance you've got of spending' your life on this bench. Why—— That's pitchin', Joe!" he shouted when the third of the enemy batters had popped out and left a runner stranded at second base. "You look good in there today," he added to Joe as the big pitcher approached the dugout.

"I'm all right, I guess," said Joe, pulling on his sweater and moving toward the water bottle. "I wished that wind'd die down."

The manager had come in.

"All right! Let's get at 'em!" he said. "Nice work, Joe. Was that a fast one Meusel hit?"

"No," said Joe. "A hook, but it didn't break."

"A couple of runs will beat 'em the way you're going," said the manager, stooping over to select his bat. "Make this fella pitch, boys," he added. "He was hog wild in Philly the other day."

The half inning wore on to its close, and the noncombatants were again left in possession of the bench. Young Jake addressed Healy.

"What's women done to you, Mike?"

"Only broke me. That's all!" said Healy.

"What do you mean, broke you! The boys tells me you ain't spent nothin' but the summer since you been in the league."

"Oh, I've got a little money," said Healy. "I don't throw it away. I don't go around payin' ten smackers a quart for liquid catnip. But they's more kinds of broke than money broke, a damn sight worse kinds, too. And when I say women has broke me, I mean they've made a bum out of my life; they've wrecked my—what-do-you-call-it?"

"Your career," supplied Lefty.

"Yes, sir," said Healy. "And I ain't kiddin', neither. Why say, listen: Do you know where I'd be if it wasn't for a woman? Right out there in that infield, playin' that old third sack."

"What about Smitty?" asked Young Jake.

"He'd be where I am—on this bench."

"Aw, come on, Mike! Be yourself! You don't claim you're as good as him!" Jake remonstrated.

"I do claim it, but it don't make no difference if I am or I ain't. He shouldn't never ought to of had a chance, not on this club, anyway. You'd say the same if you knowed the facts."

"Well, let's hear 'em."

"It's a long story, and these boys has heard it before."

"That's all right, Mike," said Gephart, a spare catcher. "We ain't listened the last twelve times."

"Well, it was the year I come in this league, four years ago this spring. I'd been with the Toledo club a couple of years. I was the best hitter on the Toledo club. I hit .332 the first year and .354 the next year. And I led the third basemen in fieldin'."

"It would be hard not to," interposed Lefty. "Anything a third baseman don't get they call it a base hit. A third baseman ought to pay to get in the park."

Healy glanced coldly at the speaker, and resumed:

"This club had Johnnie Lambert. He was still about the best third baseman in this league, but he was thirty-five years old and had a bad knee. It had slipped out on him and cost this club the pennant. They didn't have no other third baseman. They lose sixteen out of twenty games. So that learned 'em a lesson, and they bought me. Their idear was to start Johnnie in the spring, but they didn't expect his knee to hold up. And then it was goin' to be my turn.

"But durin' the winter Johnnie got a hold of some specialist somewhere that fixed his knee, and he come South with a new least of life. He hit good and was as fast as ever on the bases. Meanw'ile I had been on a huntin' trip up in Michigan that winter and froze my dogs, and they ailed me so that I couldn't do myself justice all spring."

"I suppose it was some woman made you go huntin'," said Gephart, but Healy continued without replying:

"They was a gal from a town named Ligonier, Indiana, that had visited in Toledo the second year I played ball there. The people where she was visitin' was great baseball fans, and they brought her out to the game with them, and she got stuck on me."

"Ligonier can't be a town! It must be an asylum!" said Lefty.

"She got stuck on me," Healy repeated, "and the people where she was stayin' asked me to their house to supper. After supper the man and his wife said how about goin' to the picture show, and the gal said she was tired and rather stay home. So the man and woman excused themselves. They said it was a picture they wanted to see and would I excuse them runnin' off and leavin' we two together. They were clubbin' on me, see?

"Well, I thought to myself, I'll give this dame an unpleasant surprise, so I didn't even hold her hand all evenin'. When I got up to go she says she supposed it would be the last time she seen me as she expected to go back to Ligonier the next day. She didn't have no more intentions of goin' back the next day than crossin' Lake Erie in a hollow tooth. But she knowed if I thought it was good-by I'd kiss her. Well, I knowed it wasn't good-by, but what the hell! So that's how it started, and I went to Ligonier that fall to see her, and we got engaged to be married. At least she seemed to think so."

"Look at that!" interrupted Young Jake, his eyes on the field of action. "What could Sam of been thinkin'!"

"Thinkin'!" said Gephart. "Him!"

"What would Sam do," wondered Lefty, "if they played baseball with only one base? He wouldn't enjoy the game if he couldn't throw to the wrong one."

"That play's liable to cost us somethin'," said Gephart.

"I went up in Michigan on a huntin' trip with some friends of mine," Healy continued. "I froze my feet and was laid up all through January and February and shouldn't of never went South. It was all as I could do to wear shoes, let alone play baseball. I wasn't really myself till along the first of May. But, as

I say, Johnnie Lambert had a new least of life and was lookin' better than he'd looked for years. His knee wasn't troublin' him at all.

"Well, that's how things went till around the last part of June. I didn't get no action except five or six times goin' up to hit for somebody. And I was like a young colt, crazy to be let loose. I knowed that if I once got in there and showed what I could do Judge Landis himself couldn't keep me on the bench. I used to kneel down every night and pray to God to get to work on Lambert's knee.

"The gal kept writin' me letters and I answered 'em once in a w'ile, but we hadn't saw each other since before Christmas. She hinted once or twice about when was we goin' to get married, but I told her I didn't want to even disgust the subject till I was somethin' besides a bench warmer.

"We had a serious in Chi the tail-end of June, and the first night we was there I got a long-distance call from Ligonier. It was the gal's sister, sayin' the gal was sick. She was delirious part of the time and hollerin' for me, and the doctor said if she could see me, it'd probably do her more good than medicine.

"So I said that's all right, but they ain't no off days in the schedule right now and I can't get away. But they had looked up the time table and seen where I could leave Chi after the ball game, spend the night in Ligonier and get back for the game the next day.

"So I took a train from Englewood in the evenin' and when I got off at Ligonier, there was my gal to meet me. She was the picture of health and no more delirious than usual. They said she had been just about ready to pass out when she learned I was comin' and it cured her. They didn't tell me what disease she'd had, but I suppose it was a grasshopper bite or somethin'.

"When I left next mornin', the weddin' date was set for that fall.

"Somewheres between South Bend and Laporte, the train stopped and liked it so well that we stayed there over three hours. We hit Englewood after four o'clock and I got to the park just in time to see them loadin' Lambert into a machine to take him away. His knee had broke down on him in the first innin's. He ain't never played ball since. And Smitty, who's always been a natural second baseman, he had my job."

"He's filled it pretty good," said Lefty.

"That's either here or there," retorted Healy. "If I'd been around, nobody'd ever knowed if he could play third base or not. And the worst of him is," he added, "that he never gets hurt."

"Maybe you ain't prayed for him like you done for Lambert," said Young Jake. "What happened to the gal? Did you give her the air?"

"No, I didn't," said Healy. "When I give my word, I keep it. I simply wrote and told her that I'd agreed to marry her and I wouldn't go back on it. But that my feelin's towards her was the same as if she was an advanced case of spinal meningitis. She never answered the letter, so I don't know if we're still engaged or not."

The inning was over and the boys were coming in.

"Joe was lucky to get out of that with only two runs," remarked Lefty. "But of course it was Sam that put him in bad."

"I'm goin' to see if he'll leave me get up on the lines," said Young Jake, "so I can get a better look at that dame."

The manager waited for Sam to catch up.

"What the hell was the matter with you, Sam?" he demanded.

Sam looked silly.

"I thought——"

"That's where you make your mistake!" the manager broke in. "Tough luck, Joe! But two runs are nothing. We'll get 'em back."

"Shall I go up on the lines?" asked Young Jake, hopefully.

"You? No!" said the manager. "You, Mike," turning to Healy, "go over and coach at third base. You brought us luck yesterday."

So it was Mike who was held partly responsible a few moments later when Smitty, who had tripled, was caught napping off the bag.

"Nice coachin', Mike!" said Lefty, as Healy came back to the bench.

"Why don't he watch hisself!" growled Mike. "And besides, I did yell at him!"

"You're a liar!" said Lefty. "Your back was to the ball game. You were lookin' up in the stand."

"Why would I be lookin' at the stand!" demanded Healy.

But nobody answered him. There was silence for a time.

The boys were depressed; in their own language, their dauber was down. Finally Young Jake spoke.

"She's starin' right over this way!" he said.

"Who?" asked Gephart.

"That dame I pointed out. In the tan suit. 'Way over behind third base, the other side of the screen, in the fourth row."

"I see her. Not bad!"

"I'll say she's not bad!" said Jake.

"Women!" said Healy. "You better get your mind on base-ball or you'll be back in that silo league, jumpin' from town to town in a w'eelbarrow."

"I don't see why you should be off all women just because one of them brought you a little hard luck."

"She wasn't the only one! Why, say, if it wasn't for women I'd be playin' regular third base for McGraw right now and cuttin' in on the big money every fall."

"I didn't know you was ever with McGraw."

"I wasn't," said Healy, "but I ought to been, and would of been only for a woman. It was when I was playin' with the Dayton club; my first year in baseball. Boy, I was fast as a streak! I was peggin' bunts to first base before the guy could drop his bat. I covered so much ground to my left that I was always knockin' the shortstop down and bumpin' heads with the right fielder. Everybody was marvelin' at me. Some of the old timers said I reminded them of Bill Bradley at his best, only that I made Bradley look like he was out of the game for a few days.

"Baldy Pierce was umpirin' in our league that year. He wasn't a bad umps, but he never left business interfere with pleasure. Many's the time he called the last fella out in the last innin's when the fella was safer than a hot chocolate at the Elks' convention—just because Baldy was hungry for supper.

"He was so homely that dogs wouldn't live in the same town, and his friends used to try and make him wear his mask off the field as well as on. And yet he grabbed some of the prettiest gals you ever see. He said to me once, he said, 'Mike,' he said, 'you tell me I'm homelier than Railroad Street, but I can cop more pips than you can with all your good looks!'"

At this point there were unprintable comments by Lefty, Gephart, and other occupants of the bench.

"One of these gals of his," Healy went on, "was a gal named Helen Buck from Hamilton, Ohio. She was visitin' in Dayton and come out to the ball game. The first day she was there a lot of the boys was hit in the face by thrown balls, and every time a foul went to the stand the whole infield run in to shag it. But she wouldn't look at nobody but Pierce.

"Well, McGraw had heard about me, and he sent a fella named McDonald, that was scoutin' for him, to look me over. It was in September and we was just about through. How the games come out didn't make no difference, but I knowed this McDonald was there and what he was there for, so I wanted to make a showin'. He had came intendin' to stay two days, but he'd overlooked a skip in the schedule that left us without no game the second day, so he said one game would have to be enough, as he had to go somewheres else.

"We was playin' the Springfield club. I had a good day in the field, but Bill Hutton, who started pitchin' for them, he was hog wild and walked me the first two times up. The third time they was a man on third and I had to follow orders and squeeze him home. So I hadn't had no chance to really show what I could do up there at the plate.

"Well, we come into the ninth innin's with the score tied and it was gettin' pretty dark. We got two of them out, and then their first baseman, Jansen, he got a base on balls. Bill Boone caught a hold of one just right and cracked it to the fence and it looked like Jansen would score, but he was a slow runner. Davy Shaw, our shortstop, thought he must of scored and when the ball was thrown to him he throwed it to me to get Boone, who was tryin' for three bases.

"Well, I had took in the situation at a glance; I seen that Jansen hadn't scored and if I put the ball on Boone quick enough, why the run wouldn't count. So I lunged at Boone and tagged him before Jansen had crossed the plate. But Pierce said the score counted and that Boone wasn't out because I'd missed him. Missed him! Say, I bet that where I tagged him they had to take stitches!

"Anyway, that give 'em a one run lead, and when the first two fellas got out in our half everybody thought it was over. But Davy Shaw hit one to right center that a man like I could of ran around twice on it, but they held Davy at third base. And it was up to me to bring him in.

"By this time Jim Preston was pitchin' for Springfield, and Jim was always a mark for me. I left the first one go by, as it was outside, but Pierce called it a strike. Then they was a couple of balls that he couldn't call strikes. I cracked the next one over the left-field fence, but it was a few inches foul. That made it two and two, and the next ball he throwed, well, if I hadn't ducked my head just when I did they'd of been brains scattered all over Montgomery County. And what does Pierce do but yell 'Batter out!' and run for the clubhouse!

"Well, I run after him and asked him what the hell, and here is what he said. He said, 'Mike,' he said, 'these games don't mean nothin', but if this here game had of wound up a tie it would of meant a game tomorrow, when we got a off day. And I made a date for tomorrow to go on a picnic with my little gal in Hamilton. You wouldn't want me to miss that, would you?'"

"Why," inquired Young Jake, "didn't you break his nose or bust him in the chin?"

"His nose was already broke," said Healy, "and he didn't have no chin. I tried to get a hold of McDonald, the fella that was there scoutin' me. I was goin' to explain the thing to him. But he'd left town before I could catch him. It seems, though, that he'd set over to the side where he couldn't see what a lousy strike it was and he told a friend of mine that he couldn't recommend a man that would take a third strike when a base hit would of tied up the game; that on top of me 'missin'' Boone at third——"

Another half inning was over and Healy started for the third-base coaching line without waiting for the manager to reach the bench. His teammates were not in a position to see the glance he threw at a certain spot in the stand as he walked to his "work." When the side was retired scoreless and he had returned to his corner of the dugout he looked more desolate than ever.

"Women!" he said. "Why, if it wasn't for women I'd be playin' third base for Huggins; I'd have Joe Dugan's job; I'd be livin' right here in the capital of the world."

"How do you make that out?" asked Young Jake.

"It's a long story," said Healy, "but I can tell you in a few words. We was playin' the New York Club out home. Frank Baker had began to slip and Huggins was lookin' for a good young fella to take his place. He was crazy to get me, but he had heard that I didn't want to play in New York. This had came from me kiddin' with some of the boys on the New York Club, tellin' 'em I wouldn't play here if they give me the town. So Huggins wanted to make sure before he started a trade. And he didn't want no one to see him talkin' to me. So he came around one night to the hotel where I was livin' at the time. I was up in my room waitin' for the phone gal to be off duty. She was stuck on me and I had a date to take her for a drive. So when Huggins come to see me she said I was out. She was afraid her date was goin' to be interfered with. So Huggins went away and his club left town that night."

"What did you do to her?" asked Jake.

"Oh, I couldn't do nothin' to her," said Healy. "She claimed she didn't know who it was."

"Didn't he give his name?"

"No."

"Then how do you know it was Huggins?"

"She said it was a little fella."

"He ain't the only little fella."

"He's the littlest fella I know," said Healy.

"But you ain't sure what he wanted to see you for."

"What *would* Huggins want to see me for—to scratch my back? But as I say, she didn't know who it was, so I couldn't do nothin' to her except ignore her from then on, and they couldn't of been no worse punishment as far as she was concerned."

"All and all," summed up Lefty, "if it wasn't for women, you'd of been playin' third base for McGraw and Huggins and this club, all at the same time."

"Yes," said Healy, "and with Washin'ton, too. Why——"

"Mike Healy!" interrupted the voice of Dick Trude, veteran usher. "Here's a mash note and it wants an answer."

Healy read the note and crumpled it in his hand.

"Who is she?" he asked.

"Look where I point," said Trude. "It's that good-lookin' dame in the tan suit, in the fourth row, back of third base. There! She asked me who you was when you was out there coachin'. So I told her, and she give me that note. She said you could answer yes or no."

"Make it 'yes,'" said Healy, and Trude went away.

Healy threw the crumpled note under the water bottle and addressed Young Jake.

"What I want you to get through your head, boy——"

"Oh, for God's sakes, shut up!" said Young Jake.

The Love Nest

"I'LL TELL you what I'm going to do with you, Mr. Bartlett," said the great man. "I'm going to take you right out to my home and have you meet the wife and family; stay to dinner and all night. We've got plenty of room and extra pajamas, if you don't mind them silk. I mean that'll give you a chance to see us just as we are. I mean you can get more that way than if you sat here a whole week, asking me questions."

"But I don't want to put you to a lot of trouble," said Bartlett.

"Trouble!" The great man laughed. "There's no trouble about it. I've got a house that's like a hotel. I mean a big house with lots of servants. But anyway I'm always glad to do anything I can for a writing man, especially a man that works for Ralph Doane. I'm very fond of Ralph. I mean I like him personally besides being a great editor. I mean I've known him for years and when there's anything I can do for him, I'm glad to do it. I mean it'll be a pleasure to have you. So if you want to notify your family——"

"I haven't any family," said Bartlett.

"Well, I'm sorry for you! And I bet when you see mine, you'll wish you had one of your own. But I'm glad you can come and we'll start now so as to get there before the kiddies are put away for the night. I mean I want you to be sure and see the kiddies. I've got three."

"I've seen their pictures," said Bartlett. "You must be very proud of them. They're all girls, aren't they?"

"Yes, sir; three girls. I wouldn't have a boy. I mean I always wanted girls. I mean girls have got a lot more zip to them. I mean they're a lot zippier. But let's go! The Rolls is downstairs and if we start now we'll get there before dark. I mean I want you to see the place while it's still daylight."

The great man—Lou Gregg, president of Modern Pictures, Inc.—escorted his visitor from the magnificent office by a private door and down a private stairway to the avenue, where the glittering car with its glittering chauffeur waited.

"My wife was in town today," said Gregg as they glided

northward, "and I hoped we could ride out together, but she called up about two and asked would I mind if she went on home in the Pierce. She was through with her shopping and she hates to be away from the house and the kiddies any longer than she can help. Celia's a great home girl. You'd never know she was the same girl now as the girl I married seven years ago. I mean she's different. I mean she's not the same. I mean her marriage and being a mother has developed her. Did you ever see her? I mean in pictures?"

"I think I did once," replied Bartlett. "Didn't she play the young sister in 'The Cad'?"

"Yes, with Harold Hodgson and Marie Blythe."

"I thought I'd seen her. I remember her as very pretty and vivacious."

"She certainly was! And she is yet! I mean she's even prettier, but of course she ain't a kid, though she looks it. I mean she was only seventeen in that picture and that was ten years ago. I mean she's twenty-seven years old now. But I never met a girl with as much zip as she had in those days. It's remarkable how marriage changes them. I mean nobody would ever thought Celia Sayles would turn out to be a sit-by-the-fire. I mean she still likes a good time, but her home and kiddies come first. I mean her home and kiddies come first."

"I see what you mean," said Bartlett.

An hour's drive brought them to Ardsley-on-Hudson and the great man's home.

"A wonderful place!" Bartlett exclaimed with a heroic semblance of enthusiasm as the car turned in at an *arc de triomphe* of a gateway and approached a white house that might have been mistaken for the Yale Bowl.

"It ought to be!" said Gregg. "I mean I've spent enough on it. I mean these things cost money."

He indicated with a gesture the huge house and Urbanesque landscaping.

"But no amount of money is too much to spend on home. I mean it's a good investment if it tends to make your family proud and satisfied with their home. I mean every nickel I've spent here is like so much insurance; it insures me of a happy wife and family. And what more can a man ask!"

Bartlett didn't know, but the topic was forgotten in the

business of leaving the resplendent Rolls and entering the even more resplendent reception hall.

"Forbes will take your things," said Gregg. "And, Forbes, you may tell Dennis that Mr. Bartlett will spend the night." He faced the wide stairway and raised his voice. "Sweetheart!" he called.

From above came the reply in contralto: "Hello, sweetheart!"

"Come down, sweetheart. I've brought you a visitor."

"All right, sweetheart, in just a minute."

Gregg led Bartlett into a living-room that was five laps to the mile and suggestive of an Atlantic City auction sale.

"Sit there," said the host, pointing to a balloon-stuffed easy chair, "and I'll see if we can get a drink. I've got some real old Bourbon that I'd like you to try. You know I come from Chicago and I always liked Bourbon better than Scotch. I mean I always preferred it to Scotch. Forbes," he addressed the servant, "we want a drink. You'll find a full bottle of that Bourbon in the cupboard."

"It's only half full, sir," said Forbes.

"Half full! That's funny! I mean I opened it last night and just took one drink. I mean it ought to be full."

"It's only half full," repeated Forbes, and went to fetch it.

"I'll have to investigate," Gregg told his guest. "I mean this ain't the first time lately that some of my good stuff has disappeared. When you keep so many servants, it's hard to get all honest ones. But here's Celia!"

Bartlett rose to greet the striking brunette who at this moment made an entrance so Delsarte as to be almost painful. With never a glance at him, she minced across the room to her husband and took a half interest in a convincing kiss.

"Well, sweetheart," she said when it was at last over.

"This is Mr. Bartlett, sweetheart," said her husband. "Mr. Bartlett, meet Mrs. Gregg."

Bartlett shook his hostess's proffered two fingers.

"I'm so pleased!" said Celia in a voice reminiscent of Miss Claire's imitation of Miss Barrymore.

"Mr. Bartlett," Gregg went on, "is with Mankind, Ralph Doane's magazine. He is going to write me up; I mean us."

"No, you mean you," said Celia. "I'm sure the public is not interested in great men's wives."

"I am sure you are mistaken, Mrs. Gregg," said Bartlett

politely. "In this case at least. You are worth writing up aside from being a great man's wife."

"I'm afraid you're a flatterer, Mr. Bartlett," she returned. "I have been out of the limelight so long that I doubt if anybody remembers me. I'm no longer an artist; merely a happy wife and mother."

"And I claim, sweetheart," said Gregg, "that it takes an artist to be that."

"Oh, no, sweetheart!" said Celia. "Not when they have you for a husband!"

The exchange of hosannahs was interrupted by the arrival of Forbes with the tray.

"Will you take yours straight or in a high-ball?" Gregg inquired of his guest. "Personally I like good whisky straight. I mean mixing it with water spoils the flavor. I mean whisky like this, it seems like a crime to mix it with water."

"I'll have mine straight," said Bartlett, who would have preferred a high-ball.

While the drinks were being prepared, he observed his hostess more closely and thought how much more charming she would be if she had used finesse in improving on nature. Her cheeks, her mouth, her eyes, and lashes had been, he guessed, far above the average in beauty before she had begun experimenting with them. And her experiments had been clumsy. She was handsome in spite of her efforts to be handsomer.

"Listen, sweetheart," said her husband. "One of the servants has been helping himself to this Bourbon. I mean it was a full bottle last night and I only had one little drink out of it. And now it's less than half full. Who do you suppose has been at it?"

"How do I know, sweetheart? Maybe the groceryman or the iceman or somebody."

"But you and I and Forbes are the only ones that have a key. I mean it was locked up."

"Maybe you forgot to lock it."

"I never do. Well, anyway, Bartlett, here's a go!"

"Doesn't Mrs. Gregg indulge?" asked Bartlett.

"Only a cocktail before dinner," said Celia. "Lou objects to me drinking whisky, and I don't like it much anyway."

"I don't object to you drinking whisky, sweetheart. I just

object to you drinking to excess. I mean I think it coarsens a woman to drink. I mean it makes them coarse."

"Well, there's no argument, sweetheart. As I say, I don't care whether I have it or not."

"It certainly is great Bourbon!" said Bartlett, smacking his lips and putting his glass back on the tray.

"You bet it is!" Gregg agreed. "I mean you can't buy that kind of stuff any more. I mean it's real stuff. You help yourself when you want another. Mr. Bartlett is going to stay all night, sweetheart. I told him he could get a whole lot more of a line on us that way than just interviewing me in the office. I mean I'm tongue-tied when it comes to talking about my work and my success. I mean it's better to see me out here as I am, in my home, with my family. I mean my home life speaks for itself without me saying a word."

"But, sweetheart," said his wife, "what about Mr. Latham?"

"Gosh! I forgot all about him! I must phone and see if I can call it off. That's terrible! You see," he explained to Bartlett, "I made a date to go up to Tarrytown tonight, to K. L. Latham's, the sugar people. We're going to talk over the new club. We're going to have a golf club that will make the rest of them look like a toy. I mean a real golf club! They want me to kind of run it. And I was to go up there tonight and talk it over. I'll phone and see if I can postpone it."

"Oh, don't postpone it on my account!" urged Bartlett. "I can come out again some other time, or I can see you in town."

"I don't see how you *can* postpone it, sweetheart," said Celia. "Didn't he say old Mr. King was coming over from White Plains? They'll be mad at you if you don't go."

"I'm afraid they would resent it, sweetheart. Well, I'll tell you. You can entertain Mr. Bartlett and I'll go up there right after dinner and come back as soon as I can. And Bartlett and I can talk when I get back. I mean we can talk when I get back. How is that?"

"That suits me," said Bartlett.

"I'll be as entertaining as I can," said Celia, "but I'm afraid that isn't very entertaining. However, if I'm too much of a bore, there's plenty to read."

"No danger of my being bored," said Bartlett.

"Well, that's all fixed then," said the relieved host. "I hope you'll excuse me running away. But I don't see how I can get out of it. I mean with old King coming over from White Plains. I mean he's an old man. But listen, sweetheart—where are the kiddies? Mr. Bartlett wants to see them."

"Yes, indeed!" agreed the visitor.

"Of course you'd say so!" Celia said. "But we *are* proud of them! I suppose all parents are the same. They all think their own children are the only children in the world. Isn't that so, Mr. Bartlett? Or haven't you any children?"

"I'm sorry to say I'm not married."

"Oh, you poor thing! We pity him, don't we, sweetheart? But why aren't you, Mr. Bartlett? Don't tell me you're a woman hater!"

"Not now, anyway," said the gallant Bartlett.

"Do you get that, sweetheart? He's paying you a pretty compliment."

"I heard it, sweetheart. And now I'm sure he's a flatterer. But I must hurry and get the children before Hortense puts them to bed."

"Well," said Gregg when his wife had left the room, "would you say she's changed?"

"A little, and for the better. She's more than fulfilled her early promise."

"I think so," said Gregg. "I mean I think she was a beautiful girl and now she's an even more beautiful woman. I mean wifehood and maternity have given her a kind of a—well, you know—I mean a kind of a pose. I mean a pose. How about another drink?"

They were emptying their glasses when Celia returned with two of her little girls.

"The baby's in bed and I was afraid to ask Hortense to get her up again. But you'll see her in the morning. This is Norma and this is Grace. Girls, this is Mr. Bartlett."

The girls received this news calmly.

"Well, girls," said Bartlett.

"What do you think of them, Bartlett?" demanded their father. "I mean what do you think of them?"

"They're great!" replied the guest with creditable warmth.

"I mean aren't they pretty?"

"I should say they are!"

"There, girls! Why don't you thank Mr. Bartlett?"

"Thanks," murmured Norma.

"How old are you, Norma?" asked Bartlett.

"Six," said Norma.

"Well," said Bartlett. "And how old is Grace?"

"Four," replied Norma.

"Well," said Bartlett. "And how old is baby sister?"

"One and a half," answered Norma.

"Well," said Bartlett.

As this seemed to be final, "Come, girls," said their mother. "Kiss daddy good night and I'll take you back to Hortense."

"I'll take them," said Gregg. "I'm going up-stairs anyway. And you can show Bartlett around. I mean before it gets any darker."

"Good night, girls," said Bartlett, and the children murmured a good night.

"I'll come and see you before you're asleep," Celia told them. And after Gregg had led them out, "Do you really think they're pretty?" she asked Bartlett.

"I certainly do. Especially Norma. She's the image of you," said Bartlett.

"She looks a little like I used to," Celia admitted. "But I hope she doesn't look like me now. I'm too old looking."

"You look remarkably young!" said Bartlett. "No one would believe you were the mother of three children."

"Oh, Mr. Bartlett! But I mustn't forget I'm to 'show you around.' Lou is so proud of our home!"

"And with reason," said Bartlett.

"It *is* wonderful! I call it our love nest. Quite a big nest, don't you think? Mother says it's too big to be cosy; she says she can't think of it as a home. But I always say a place is whatever one makes of it. A woman can be happy in a tent if they love each other. And miserable in a royal palace without love. Don't you think so, Mr. Bartlett?"

"Yes, indeed."

"Is this really such wonderful Bourbon? I think I'll just take a sip of it and see what it's like. It can't hurt me if it's so good. Do you think so, Mr. Bartlett?"

"I don't believe so."

"Well then, I'm going to taste it and if it hurts me it's your fault."

Celia poured a whisky glass two-thirds full and drained it at a gulp.

"It *is* good, isn't it?" she said. "Of course I'm not much of a judge as I don't care for whisky and Lou won't let me drink it. But he's raved so about this Bourbon that I did want to see what it was like. You won't tell on me, will you, Mr. Bartlett?"

"Not I!"

"I wonder how it would be in a high-ball. Let's you and I have just one. But I'm forgetting I'm supposed to show you the place. We won't have time to drink a high-ball and see the place too before Lou comes down. Are you so crazy to see the place?"

"Not very."

"Well, then, what do you say if we have a high-ball? And it'll be a secret between you and I."

They drank in silence and Celia pressed a button by the door.

"You may take the bottle and tray," she told Forbes. "And now," she said to Bartlett, "we'll go out on the porch and see as much as we can see. You'll have to guess the rest."

Gregg, having changed his shirt and collar, joined them.

"Well," he said to Bartlett, "have you seen everything?"

"I guess I have, Mr. Gregg," lied the guest readily. "It's a wonderful place!"

"We like it. I mean it suits us. I mean it's my idear of a real home. And Celia calls it her love nest."

"So she told me," said Bartlett.

"She'll always be sentimental," said her husband.

He put his hand on her shoulder, but she drew away.

"I must run up and dress," she said.

"Dress!" exclaimed Bartlett, who had been dazzled by her flowered green chiffon.

"Oh, I'm not going to really dress," she said. "But I couldn't wear this thing for dinner!"

"Perhaps you'd like to clean up a little, Bartlett," said Gregg. "I mean Forbes will show you your room if you want to go up."

"It might be best," said Bartlett.

Celia, in a black lace dinner gown, was rather quiet during the elaborate meal. Three or four times when Gregg addressed her, she seemed to be thinking of something else and had to ask, "What did you say, sweetheart?" Her face was red and Bartlett imagined that she had "sneaked" a drink or two besides the two helpings of Bourbon and the cocktail that had preceded dinner.

"Well, I'll leave you," said Gregg when they were in the living-room once more. "I mean the sooner I get started, the sooner I'll be back. Sweetheart, try and keep your guest awake and don't let him die of thirst. *Au revoir*, Bartlett. I'm sorry, but it can't be helped. There's a fresh bottle of the Bourbon, so go to it. I mean help yourself. It's too bad you have to drink alone."

"It *is* too bad, Mr. Bartlett," said Celia when Gregg had gone.

"What's too bad?" asked Bartlett.

"That you have to drink alone. I feel like I wasn't being a good hostess to let you do it. In fact, I refuse to let you do it. I'll join you in just a little wee sip."

"But it's so soon after dinner!"

"It's never too soon! I'm going to have a drink myself and if you don't join me, you're a quitter."

She mixed two life-sized high-balls and handed one to her guest.

"Now we'll turn on the radio and see if we can't stir things up. There! No, no! Who cares about the old baseball! Now! This is better! Let's dance."

"I'm sorry, Mrs. Gregg, but I don't dance."

"Well, you're an old cheese! To make me dance alone! 'All alone, yes, I'm all alone.'"

There was no affectation in her voice now and Bartlett was amazed at her unlabored grace as she glided around the big room.

"But it's no fun alone," she complained. "Let's shut the damn thing off and talk."

"I love to watch you dance," said Bartlett.

"Yes, but I'm no Pavlowa," said Celia as she silenced the radio. "And besides, it's time for a drink."

"I've still got more than half of mine."

"Well, you had that wine at dinner, so I'll have to catch up with you."

She poured herself another high-ball and went at the task of "catching up."

"The trouble with you, Mr.—now isn't that a scream! I can't think of your name."

"Bartlett."

"The trouble with you, Barker—do you know what's the trouble with you? You're too sober. See? You're too damn sober! That's the whole trouble, see? If you weren't so sober, we'd be better off. See? What I can't understand is how you can be so sober and me so high."

"You're not used to it."

"Not used to it! That's the cat's pajamas! Say, I'm like this half the time, see? If I wasn't, I'd die!"

"What does your husband say?"

"He don't say because he don't know. See, Barker? There's nights when he's out and there's a few nights when I'm out myself. And there's other nights when we're both in and I pretend I'm sleepy and I go up-stairs. See? But I don't go to bed. See? I have a little party all by myself. See? If I didn't, I'd die!"

"What do you mean, you'd die?"

"You're dumb, Barker! You may be sober, but you're dumb! Did you fall for all that apple sauce about the happy home and the contented wife? Listen, Barker—I'd give anything in the world to be out of this mess. I'd give anything to never see him again."

"Don't you love him any more? Doesn't he love you? Or what?"

"Love! I never did love him! I didn't know what love was! And all his love is for himself!"

"How did you happen to get married?"

"I was a kid; that's the answer. A kid and ambitious. See? He was a director then and he got stuck on me and I thought he'd make me a star. See, Barker? I married him to get myself a chance. And now look at me!"

"I'd say you were fairly well off."

"Well off, am I? I'd change places with the scum of the earth just to be free! See, Barker? And I could have been a star without any help if I'd only realized it. I had the looks and I had the talent. I've got it yet. I could be a Swanson and get myself a marquis; maybe a prince! And look what I did get! A self-satisfied, self-centered——! I thought he'd *make* me! See,

Barker? Well, he's made me all right; he's made me a chronic mother and it's a wonder I've got any looks left.

"I fought at first. I told him marriage didn't mean giving up my art, my life work. But it was no use. He wanted a beautiful wife and beautiful children for his beautiful home. Just to show us off. See? I'm part of his chattels. See, Barker? I'm just like his big diamond or his cars or his horses. And he wouldn't stand for his wife 'lowering' herself to act in pictures. Just as if pictures hadn't made him!

"You go back to your magazine tomorrow and write about our love nest. See, Barker? And be sure and don't get mixed and call it a baby ranch. Babies! You thought little Norma was pretty. Well, she is. And what is it going to get her? A rich —— of a husband that treats her like a ——! That's what it'll get her if I don't interfere. I hope I don't last long enough to see her grow up, but if I do, I'm going to advise her to run away from home and live her own life. And *be* somebody! Not a *thing* like I am! See, Barker?"

"Did you ever think of a divorce?"

"Did I ever think of one! Listen—but there's no chance. I've got nothing on him, and no matter what he had on me, he'd never let the world know it. He'd keep me here and torture me like he does now, only worse. But I haven't done anything wrong, see? The men I might care for, they're all scared of him and his money and power. See, Barker? And the others are just as bad as him. Like fat old Morris, the hotel man, that everybody thinks he's a model husband. The reason he don't step out more is because he's too stingy. But I could have him if I wanted him. Every time he gets near enough to me, he squeezes my hand. I guess he thinks it's a nickel, the tight old ——! But come on, Barker. Let's have a drink. I'm running down."

"I think it's about time you were running up—up-stairs," said Bartlett. "If I were you, I'd try to be in bed and asleep when Gregg gets home."

"You're all right, Barker. And after this drink I'm going to do just as you say. Only I thought of it before you did, see? I think of it lots of nights. And tonight you can help me out by telling him I had a bad headache."

Left alone, Bartlett thought a while, then read, and finally dozed off. He was dozing when Gregg returned.

"Well, well, Bartlett," said the great man, "did Celia desert you?"

"It was perfectly all right, Mr. Gregg. She had a headache and I told her to go to bed."

"She's had a lot of headaches lately; reads too much, I guess. Well, I'm sorry I had this date. It was about a new golf club and I had to be there. I mean I'm going to be president of it. I see you consoled yourself with some of the Bourbon. I mean the bottle doesn't look as full as it did."

"I hope you'll forgive me for helping myself so generously," said Bartlett. "I don't get stuff like that every day!"

"Well, what do you say if we turn in? We can talk on the way to town tomorrow. Though I guess you won't have much to ask me. I guess you know all about us. I mean you know all about us now."

"Yes, indeed, Mr. Gregg. I've got plenty of material if I can just handle it."

Celia had not put in an appearance when Gregg and his guest were ready to leave the house next day.

"She always sleeps late," said Gregg. "I mean she never wakes up very early. But she's later than usual this morning. Sweetheart!" he called up the stairs.

"Yes, sweetheart," came the reply.

"Mr. Bartlett's leaving now. I mean he's going."

"Oh, good-by, Mr. Bartlett. Please forgive me for not being down to see you off."

"You're forgiven, Mrs. Gregg. And thanks for your hospitality."

"Good-by, sweetheart!"

"Good-by, sweetheart!"

A Day with Conrad Green

CONRAD GREEN woke up depressed and, for a moment, could not think why. Then he remembered. Herman Plant was dead; Herman Plant, who had been his confidential secretary ever since he had begun producing; who had been much more than a secretary—his champion, votary, shield, bodyguard, tool, occasional lackey, and the butt of his heavy jokes and nasty temper. For forty-five dollars a week.

Herman Plant was dead, and this Lewis, recommended by Ezra Peebles, a fellow entrepreneur, had not, yesterday, made a good first impression. Lewis was apparently impervious to hints. You had to tell him things right out, and when he did understand he looked at you as if you were a boob. And insisted on a salary of sixty dollars right at the start. Perhaps Peebles, who, Green knew, hated him almost enough to make it fifty-fifty, was doing him another dirty trick dressed up as a favor.

After ten o'clock, and still Green had not had enough sleep. It had been nearly three when his young wife and he had left the Bryant-Walkers'. Mrs. Green, the former Marjorie Manning of the Vanities chorus, had driven home to Long Island, while he had stayed in the rooms he always kept at the Ambassador.

Marjorie had wanted to leave a good deal earlier; through no lack of effort on her part she had been almost entirely ignored by her aristocratic host and hostess and most of the guests. She had confided to her husband more than once that she was sick of the whole such-and-such bunch of so-and-so's. As far as she was concerned, they could all go to hell and stay there! But Green had been rushed by the pretty and stage-struck Joyce Brainard, wife of the international polo star, and had successfully combated his own wife's importunities till the Brainards themselves had gone.

Yes, he could have used a little more sleep, but the memory of the party cheered him. Mrs. Brainard, excited by his theatrical aura and several highballs, had been almost affectionate. She had promised to come to his office some time and talk over a stage career which both knew was impossible so long as Brainard lived. But, best of all, Mr. and Mrs. Green would be listed in the papers as among those present at the Bryant-Walkers', along with the Vanderbecks, the Suttons, and the Schuylers, and that would just about be the death of Peebles and other social sycophants of "show business." He would order all the papers now and look for his name. No; he was late and must get to his office. No telling what a mess things were in without Herman Plant. And, by the way, he mustn't forget Plant's funeral this afternoon.

He bathed, telephoned for his breakfast, and his favorite barber, dressed in a symphony of purple and gray, and set out for Broadway, pretending not to hear the "There's Conrad Green!" spoken in awed tones by two flappers and a Westchester realtor whom he passed en route.

Green let himself into his private office, an office of luxurious, exotic furnishings, its walls adorned with expensive landscapes and a Zuloaga portrait of his wife. He took off his twenty-five dollar velour hat, approved of himself in the large mirror, sat down at his desk, and rang for Miss Jackson.

"All the morning papers," he ordered, "and tell Lewis to come in."

"I'll have to send out for the papers," said Miss Jackson, a tired-looking woman of forty-five or fifty.

"What do you mean, send out? I thought we had an arrangement with that boy to leave them every morning."

"We did. But the boy says he can't leave them any more till we've paid up to date."

"What do we owe?"

"Sixty-five dollars."

"Sixty-five dollars! He's crazy! Haven't you been paying him by the week?"

"No. You told me not to."

"I told you nothing of the kind! Sixty-five dollars! He's trying to rob us!"

"I don't believe so, Mr. Green," said Miss Jackson. "He showed me his book. It's more than thirty weeks since he began, and you know we've never paid him."

"But hell! There isn't sixty-five dollars' worth of newspapers ever been printed! Tell him to sue us! And now send out for the papers and do it quick! After this we'll get them down at the corner every morning and pay for them. Tell Lewis to bring me the mail."

Miss Jackson left him, and presently the new secretary came in. He was a man under thirty, whom one would have taken for a high school teacher rather than a theatrical general's aide-de-camp.

"Good-morning, Mr. Green," he said.

His employer disregarded the greeting.

"Anything in the mail?" he asked.

"Not much of importance. I've already answered most of it. Here are a few things from your clipping bureau and a sort of dunning letter from some jeweler in Philadelphia."

"What did you open that for?" demanded Green, crossly. "Wasn't it marked personal?"

"Look here, Mr. Green," said Lewis quietly: "I was told you had a habit of being rough with your employees. I want to warn you that I am not used to that sort of treatment and don't intend to get used to it. If you are decent with me, I'll work for you. Otherwise I'll resign."

"I don't know what you're talking about, Lewis. I didn't mean to be rough. It's just my way of speaking. Let's forget it and I'll try not to give you any more cause to complain."

"All right, Mr. Green. You told me to open all your mail except the letters with that one little mark on them——"

"Yes, I know. Now let's have the clippings."

Lewis laid them on the desk.

"I threw away about ten of them that were all the same—the announcement that you had signed Bonnie Blue for next season. There's one there that speaks of a possible partnership between you and Sam Stein——"

"What a nerve he's got, giving out a statement like that. Fine chance of me mixing myself up with a crook like Stein! Peebles says he's a full stepbrother to the James boys. So is Peebles himself, for that matter. What's this long one about?"

"It's about that young composer, Casper Ettelson. It's by Deems Taylor of the *World*. There's just a mention of you down at the bottom."

"Read it to me, will you? I've overstrained my eyes lately."

The dead Herman Plant had first heard of that recent eye

strain twenty years ago. It amounted to almost total blindness where words of over two syllables were concerned.

"So far," Lewis read, "Ettelson has not had a book worthy of his imaginative, whimsical music. How we would revel in an Ettelson score with a Barrie libretto and a Conrad Green production."

"Who is this Barrie?" asked Green.

"I suppose it's James M. Barrie," replied Lewis, "the man who wrote Peter Pan."

"I thought that was written by a fella over in England," said Green.

"I guess he does live in England. He was born in Scotland. I don't know where he is now."

"Well, find out if he's in New York, and, if he is, get a hold of him. Maybe he'll do a couple of scenes for our next show. Come in, Miss Jackson. Oh, the papers!"

Miss Jackson handed them to him and went out. Green turned first to the society page of the *Herald Tribune*. His eye trouble was not so severe as to prevent his finding that page. And he could read his name when it was there to be read.

Three paragraphs were devoted to the Bryant-Walker affair, two of them being lists of names. And Mr. and Mrs. Conrad Green were left out.

"——!" commented Green, and grabbed the other papers. The *World* and *Times* were searched with the same hideous result. And the others did not mention the party at all.

"——!" repeated Green. "I'll get somebody for this!" Then, to Lewis: "Here! Take this telegram. Send it to the managing editors of all the morning papers; you'll find their names pasted on Plant's desk. Now: 'Ask your society editor why my name was not on list of guests at Bryant-Walker dinner Wednesday night. Makes no difference to me, as am not seeking and do not need publicity, but it looks like conspiracy, and thought you ought to be informed, as have always been good friend of your paper, as well as steady advertiser.' I guess that's enough."

"If you'll pardon a suggestion," said Lewis, "I'm afraid a telegram like this would just be laughed at."

"You send the telegram; I'm not going to have a bunch of cheap reporters make a fool of me!"

"I don't believe you can blame the reporters. There probably weren't reporters there. The list of guests is generally given out by the people who give the party."

"But listen——" Green paused and thought. "All right. Don't send the telegram. But if the Bryant-Walkers are ashamed of me, why the hell did they invite me? I certainly didn't want to go and they weren't under obligations to me. I never——"

As if it had been waiting for its cue, the telephone rang at this instant, and Kate, the switchboard girl, announced that the Bryant-Walkers' secretary was on the wire.

"I am speaking for Mrs. Bryant-Walker," said a female voice. "She is chairman of the committee on entertainment for the Women's Progress Bazaar. The bazaar is to open on the third of next month and wind up on the evening of the fifth with a sort of vaudeville entertainment. She wanted me to ask you —"

Green hung up with an oath.

"That's the answer!" he said. "The damn grafters!"

Miss Jackson came in again.

"Mr. Robert Blair is waiting to see you."

"Who is he?"

"You know. He tried to write some things for one of the shows last year."

"Oh, yes. Say, did you send flowers to Plant's house?"

"I did," replied Miss Jackson. "I sent some beautiful roses."

"How much?"

"Forty-five dollars," said Miss Jackson.

"Forty-five dollars for roses! And the man hated flowers even when he was alive! Well, send in this Blair."

Robert Blair was an ambitious young free lance who had long been trying to write for the stage, but with little success.

"Sit down, Blair," said Green. "What's on your mind?"

"Well, Mr. Green, my stuff didn't seem to suit you last year, but this time I think I've got a scene that can't miss."

"All right. If you want to leave it here, I'll read it over."

"I haven't written it out. I thought I'd tell you the idea first."

"Well, go ahead, but cut it short; I've got a lot of things to do today. Got to go to old Plant's funeral for one thing."

"I bet you miss him, don't you?" said Blair, sympathetically.

"Miss him! I should say I do! A lovable character and"— with a glance at Lewis—"the best secretary I'll ever have. But let's hear your scene."

"Well," said Blair, "it may not sound like much the way I tell it, but I think it'll work out great. Well, the police get a report that a woman has been murdered in her home, and they go there and find her husband, who is acting very nervous. They give him the third degree, and he finally breaks down and admits he killed her. They ask him why, and he tells them he is very fond of beans, and on the preceding evening he came home to dinner and asked her what there was to eat, and she told him she had lamb chops, mashed potatoes, spinach, and apple pie. So he says, 'No beans?' and she says, 'No beans.' So he shoots her dead. Of course, the scene between the husband and wife is acted out on the stage. Then——"

"It's no good!" said Conrad Green. "In the first place, it takes too many people, all those policemen and everybody."

"Why, all you need is two policemen and the man and his wife. And wait till I tell you the rest of it."

"I don't like it; it's no good. Come back again when you've got something."

When Blair had gone Green turned to Lewis.

"That's all for just now," he said, "but on your way out tell Miss Jackson to get a hold of Martin and say I want him to drop in here as soon as he can."

"What Martin?" asked Lewis.

"She'll know—Joe Martin, the man that writes most of our librettos."

Alone, Conrad Green crossed the room to his safe, opened it, and took out a box on which was inscribed the name of a Philadelphia jeweler. From the box he removed a beautiful rope of matched pearls and was gazing at them in admiration when Miss Jackson came in; whereupon he hastily replaced them in their case and closed the safe.

"That man is here again," said Miss Jackson. "That man Hawley from *Gay New York*."

"Tell him I'm not in."

"I did, but he says he saw you come in and he's going to wait till you'll talk to him. Really, Mr. Green, I think it would be best in the long run to see him. He's awfully persistent."

"All right; send him in," said Green, impatiently, "though I have no idea what he can possibly want of me."

Mr. Hawley, dapper and eternally smiling, insisted on shaking hands with his unwilling host, who had again sat down at his desk.

"I think," he said, "we've met before."

"Not that I know of," Green replied shortly.

"Well, it makes no difference, but I'm sure you've read our little paper, *Gay New York*."

"No," said Green. "All I have time to read is manuscripts."

"You don't know what you're missing," said Hawley. "It's really a growing paper, with a big New York circulation, and a circulation that is important from your standpoint."

"Are you soliciting subscriptions?" asked Green.

"No. Advertising."

"Well, frankly, Mr. Hawley, I don't believe I need any advertising. I believe that even the advertising I put in the regular daily papers is a waste of money."

"Just the same," said Hawley, "I think you'd be making a mistake not to take a page in *Gay New York*. It's only a matter of fifteen hundred dollars."

"Fifteen hundred dollars! That's a joke! Nobody's going to hold *me* up!"

"Nobody's trying to, Mr. Green. But I might as well tell you that one of our reporters came in with a story the other day— well, it was about a little gambling affair in which some of the losers sort of forgot to settle, and—well, my partner was all for printing it, but I said I had always felt friendly toward you and why not give you a chance to state your side of it?"

"I don't know what you're talking about. If your reporter has got my name mixed up in a gambling story he's crazy."

"No. He's perfectly sane and very, very careful. We make a specialty of careful reporters and we're always sure of our facts."

Conrad Green was silent for a long, long time. Then he said:

"I tell you, I don't know what gambling business you refer to, and, furthermore, fifteen hundred dollars is a hell of a price for a page in a paper like yours. But still, as you say, you've got the kind of circulation that might do me good. So if you'll cut down the price——"

"I'm sorry, Mr. Green, but we never do that."

"Well, then, of course you'll have to give me a few days to

get my ad fixed up. Say you come back here next Monday afternoon."

"That's perfectly satisfactory, Mr. Green," said Hawley, "and I assure you that you're not making a mistake. And now I won't keep you any longer from your work."

He extended his hand, but it was ignored, and he went out, his smile a little broader than when he had come in. Green remained at his desk, staring straight ahead of him and making semi-audible references to certain kinds of dogs as well as personages referred to in the Old and New Testaments. He was interrupted by the entrance of Lewis.

"Mr. Green," said the new secretary, "I have found a check for forty-five dollars, made out to Herman Plant. I imagine it is for his final week's pay. Would you like to have me change it and make it out to his widow?"

"Yes," said Green. "But no; wait a minute. Tear it up and I'll make out my personal check to her and add something to it."

"All right," said Lewis, and left.

"Forty-five dollars' worth of flowers," said Green to himself, and smiled for the first time that morning.

He looked at his watch and got up and put on his beautiful hat.

"I'm going to lunch," he told Miss Jackson on his way through the outer office. "If Peebles or anybody important calls up, tell them I'll be here all afternoon."

"You're not forgetting Mr. Plant's funeral?"

"Oh, that's right. Well, I'll be here from one-thirty to about three."

A head waiter at the Astor bowed to him obsequiously and escorted him to a table near a window, while the occupants of several other tables gazed at him spellbound and whispered, "Conrad Green."

A luncheon of clams, sweetbreads, spinach, strawberry ice cream, and small coffee seemed to satisfy him. He signed his check and then tipped his own waiter and the head waiter a dollar apiece, the two tips falling just short of the cost of the meal.

Joe Martin, his chief librettist, was waiting when he got back to his office.

"Oh, hello, Joe!" he said, cordially. "Come right inside. I think I've got something for you."

Martin followed him in and sat down without waiting for an invitation. Green seated himself at his desk and drew out his cigarette case.

"Have one, Joe?"

"Not that kind!" said Martin, lighting one of his own. "You've got rotten taste in everything but gals."

"And librettists," replied Green, smiling.

"But here's what I wanted to talk about. I couldn't sleep last night, and I just laid there and an idea came to me for a comedy scene. I'll give you the bare idea and you can work it out. It'll take a girl and one of the comics, maybe Fraser, and a couple of other men that can play.

"Well, the idea is that the comic is married to the girl. In the first place, I'd better mention that the comic is crazy about beans. Well, one night the comic—no, wait a minute. The police get word that the comic's wife has been murdered and two policemen come to the comic's apartment to investigate. They examine the corpse and find out she's been shot through the head. They ask the comic if he knows who did it and he says no, but they keep after him, and finally he breaks down and admits that he did it himself.

"But he says, 'Gentlemen, if you'll let me explain the circumstances, I don't believe you'll arrest me.' So they tell him to explain, and he says that he came home from work and he was very hungry and he asked his wife what they were going to have for dinner. So she tells him—clams and sweetbreads and spinach and strawberry ice cream and coffee. So he asks her if she isn't going to have any beans and she says no, and he shoots her. What do you think you could do with that idea?"

"Listen, Connie," said Martin: "You've only got half the scene, and you've got that half wrong. In the second place, it was played a whole season in the Music Box and it was written by Bert Kalmar and Harry Ruby. Otherwise I can do a whole lot with it."

"Are you sure you're right?"

"I certainly am!"

"Why, that damn little thief! He told me it was his!"

"Who?" asked Martin.

"Why, that Blair, that tried to butt in here last year. I'll fix him!"

"I thought you said it was your own idea."

"Hell, no! Do you think I'd be stealing stuff, especially if it was a year old?"

"Well," said Martin, "when you get another inspiration like this, give me a ring and I'll come around. Now I've got to hurry up to the old Stadium and see what the old Babe does in the first inning."

"I'm sorry, Joe. I thought it was perfectly all right."

"Never mind! You didn't waste much of my time. But after this you'd better leave the ideas to me. So long!"

"Good-by, Joe; and thanks for coming in."

Martin went and Green pressed the button for Miss Jackson.

"Miss Jackson, don't ever let that young Blair in here again. He's a faker!"

"All right, Mr. Green. But don't you think it's about time you were starting for the funeral? It's twenty minutes of three."

"Yes. But let's see: where is Plant's house?"

"It's up on One Hundred and Sixtieth street, just off Broadway."

"My God! Imagine living there! Wait a minute, Miss Jackson. Send Lewis here."

"Lewis," he said, when the new secretary appeared, "I ate something this noon that disagreed with me. I wanted to go up to Plant's funeral, but I really think it would be dangerous to try it. Will you go up there, let them know who you are, and kind of represent me? Miss Jackson will give you the address."

"Yes, sir," said Lewis, and went out.

Almost immediately the sanctum door opened again and the beautiful Marjorie Green, née Manning, entered unannounced. Green's face registered not altogether pleasant surprise.

"Why, hello, dear!" he said. "I didn't know you were coming to town today."

"I never told you I wasn't," his wife replied.

They exchanged the usual connubial salutations.

"I supposed you noticed," said Mrs. Green, "that our names were not on the list of guests at the party."

"No; I haven't had time to look at the papers. But what's the difference?"

"No difference at all, of course. But do you know what I think? I think we were invited just because those people want to get something out of you, for some benefit or something."

"A fine chance! I hope they try it!"

"However, that's not what I came to talk about."

"Well, dear, what is it?"

"I thought maybe you'd remember something."

"What, honey?"

"Why—oh, well, there's no use talking about it if you've forgotten."

Green's forehead wrinkled in deep thought; then suddenly his face brightened.

"Of course I haven't forgotten! It's your birthday!"

"You just thought of it now!"

"No such a thing! I've been thinking of it for weeks!"

"I don't believe you! If you had been, you'd have said something, and"—his wife was on the verge of tears—"you'd have given me some little thing, just any little thing."

Once more Green frowned, and once more brightened up.

"I'll prove it to you," he said, and walked rapidly to the safe.

In a moment he had placed in her hands the jewel box from Philadelphia. In another moment she had opened it, gasped at the beauty of its contents, and thrown her arms around his neck.

"Oh, dearest!" she cried. "Can you ever forgive me for doubting you?"

She put the pearls to her mouth as if she would eat them.

"But haven't you been terribly extravagant?"

"I don't consider anything too extravagant for you."

"You're the best husband a girl ever had!"

"I'm glad you're pleased," said Green.

"Pleased! I'm overwhelmed. And to think I imagined you'd forgotten! But I'm not going to break up your whole day. I know you want to get out to poor old Plant's funeral. So I'll run along. And maybe you'll take me to dinner somewhere tonight."

"I certainly will! You be at the Ambassador about six-thirty and we'll have a little birthday party. But don't you want to leave the pearls here now?"

"I should say not! They're going to stay with me forever! Anyone that tries to take them will do it over my dead body!"

"Well, good-by, then, dear."

"Till half past six."

Green, alone again, kicked shut the door of his safe and returned to his desk, saying in loud tones things which are not ordinarily considered appropriate to the birthday of a loved one. The hubbub must have been audible to Miss Jackson outside, but perhaps she was accustomed to it. It ceased at another unannounced entrance, that of a girl even more beautiful than the one who had just gone out. She looked at Green and laughed.

"My God! You look happy!" she said.

"Rose!"

"Yes, it's Rose. But what's the matter with you?"

"I've had a bad day."

"But isn't it better now?"

"I didn't think you were coming till tomorrow."

"But aren't you glad I came today?"

"You bet I am!" said Green. "And if you'll come here and kiss me I'll be all the gladder."

"No. Let's get our business transacted first."

"What business?"

"You know perfectly well! Last time I saw you you insisted that I must give up everybody else but you. And I promised you it would be all off between Harry and I if—— Well, you know. There was a little matter of some pearls."

"I meant everything I said."

"Well, where are they?"

"They're all bought and all ready for you. But I bought them in Philadelphia and for some damn reason they haven't got here yet."

"Got here yet! Were they so heavy you couldn't bring them with you?"

"Honest, dear, they'll be here day after tomorrow at the latest."

"'Honest' is a good word for you to use! Do you think I'm dumb? Or is it that you're so used to lying that you can't help it?"

"If you'll let me explain——"

"Explain hell! We made a bargain and you haven't kept your end of it. And now——"

"But listen——"

"I'll listen to nothing! You know where to reach me and when you've kept your promise you can call me up. Till then—Well, Harry isn't such bad company."

"Wait a minute, Rose!"

"You've heard all I've got to say. Good-by!"

And she was gone before he could intercept her.

Conrad Green sat as if stunned. For fifteen minutes he was so silent and motionless that one might have thought him dead. Then he shivered as if with cold and said aloud:

"I'm not going to worry about them any more. To hell with all of them!"

He drew the telephone to him and took off the receiver.

"Get me Mrs. Bryant-Walker."

And after a pause:

"Is this Mrs. Bryant-Walker? No, I want to speak to her personally. This is Conrad Green. Oh, hello, Mrs. Walker. Your secretary called me up this morning, but we were cut off. She was saying something about a benefit. Why, yes, certainly, I'll be glad to. As many of them as you want. If you'll just leave it all in my hands I'll guarantee you a pretty good entertainment. It's no bother at all. It's a pleasure. Thank you. Good-by."

Lewis came in.

"Well, Lewis, did you get to the funeral?"

"Yes, Mr. Green, and I saw Mrs. Plant and explained the circumstances to her. She said you had always been very kind to her husband. She said that during the week of his illness he talked of you nearly all the time and expressed confidence that if he died you would attend his funeral. So she wished you had been there."

"Good God! So do I!" said Conrad Green.

Who Dealt?

YOU KNOW, this is the first time Tom and I have been with real friends since we were married. I suppose you'll think it's funny for me to call you *my* friends when we've never met before, but Tom has talked about you so much and how much he thought of you and how crazy he was to see you and everything—well, it's just as if I'd known you all my life, like he has.

We've got our little crowd out there, play bridge and dance with them; but of course we've only been there three months, at least I have, and people you've known that length of time, well, it isn't like knowing people all your life, like you and Tom. How often I've heard Tom say he'd give any amount of money to be with Arthur and Helen, and how bored he was out there with just poor little me and his new friends!

Arthur and Helen, Arthur and Helen—he talks about you so much that it's a wonder I'm not jealous; especially of you, Helen. You must have been his real pal when you were kids.

Nearly all of his kid books, they have your name in front—to Thomas Cannon from Helen Bird Strong. This is a wonderful treat for him to see you! And a treat for me, too. Just think, I've at last met the wonderful Helen and Arthur! You must forgive me calling you by your first names; that's how I always think of you and I simply can't say Mr. and Mrs. Gratz.

No, thank you, Arthur; no more. Two is my limit and I've already exceeded it, with two cocktails before dinner and now this. But it's a special occasion, meeting Tom's best friends. I bet Tom wishes he could celebrate too, don't you, dear? Of course he could if he wanted to, but when he once makes up his mind to a thing, there's nothing in the world can shake him. He's got the strongest will power of any person I ever saw.

I do think it's wonderful, him staying on the wagon this long, a man that used to—well, you know as well as I do; probably a whole lot better, because you were with him so much in the old days, and all I know is just what he's told me. He told me about once in Pittsburgh—— All right, Tommie; I won't say another word. But it's all over now, thank heavens! Not a drop since we've been married; three whole months! And he says it's forever, don't you, dear? Though I don't mind a person drinking if they do it in moderation. But you know Tom! He goes the limit in everything he does. Like he used to in athletics——

All right, dear; I won't make you blush. I know how you hate the limelight. It's terrible, though, not to be able to boast about your own husband; everything he does or ever has done seems so wonderful. But is that only because we've been married such a short time? Do you feel the same way about Arthur, Helen? You do? And you married him four years ago, isn't that right? And you eloped, didn't you? You see I know all about you.

Oh, are you waiting for me? Do we cut for partners? Why can't we play families? I don't feel so bad if I do something dumb when it's Tom I'm playing with. He never scolds, though he does give me some terrible looks. But not very often lately; I don't make the silly mistakes I used to. I'm pretty good now, aren't I, Tom? You better say so, because if I'm not, it's your fault. You know Tom had to teach me the game. I never played at all till we were engaged. Imagine! And I guess I was pretty awful at first, but Tom was a dear, so patient! I know he thought I never would learn, but I fooled you, didn't I, Tommie?

No, indeed, I'd rather play than do almost anything. But you'll sing for us, won't you, Helen? I mean after a while. Tom has raved to me about your voice and I'm dying to hear it.

What are we playing for? Yes, a penny's perfectly all right. Out there we generally play for half a cent a piece, a penny a family. But a penny apiece is all right. I guess we can afford it now, can't we, dear? Tom hasn't told you about his raise. He was—— All right, Tommie; I'll shut up. I know you hate to be talked about, but your wife can't help being just a teeny bit proud of you. And I think your best friends are interested in your affairs, aren't you, folks?

But Tom is the most secretive person I ever knew. I believe he even keeps things from me! Not very many, though. I can usually tell when he's hiding something and I keep after him till he confesses. He often says I should have been a lawyer or a detective, the way I can worm things out of people. Don't you, Tom?

For instance, I never would have known about his experience with those horrid football people at Yale if I hadn't just made him tell me. Didn't you know about that? No, Tom, I'm going to tell Arthur even if you hate me for it. I know you'd be interested, Arthur, not only because you're Tom's friend, but on account of you being such a famous athlete yourself. Let me see, how was it, Tom? You must help me out. Well, if I don't get it right, you correct me.

Well, Tom's friends at Yale had heard what a wonderful football player he was in high school so they made him try for a place on the Yale nine. Tom had always played half-back. You have to be a fast runner to be a half-back and Tom could run awfully fast. He can yet. When we were engaged we used to run races and the prize was—— All right, Tommie, I won't give away our secrets. Anyway, he can beat me to pieces.

Well, he wanted to play half-back at Yale and he was getting along fine and the other men on the team said he would be a wonder and then one day they were having their practice and Tex Jones, no, Ted Jones—he's the main coach—he scolded Tom for having the signal wrong and Tom proved that Jones was wrong and he was right and Jones never forgave him. He made Tom quit playing half-back and put him tackle or end or some place like that where you can't do anything and being a fast runner doesn't count. So Tom saw that Jones had it in for him and he quit. Wasn't that it, Tom? Well, anyway, it was something.

Oh, are you waiting for me? I'm sorry. What did you bid, Helen? And you, Tom? You doubled her? And Arthur passed? Well, let's see. I wish I could remember what that means. I know that sometimes when he doubles he means one thing and sometimes another. But I always forget which is which. Let me see; it was two spades that he doubled, wasn't it? That means I'm to leave him in, I'm pretty sure. Well, I'll pass. Oh, I'm sorry, Tommie! I knew I'd get it wrong. Please forgive me. But maybe we'll set them anyway. Whose lead?

I'll stop talking now and try and keep my mind on the game. You needn't look that way, Tommie. I *can* stop talking if I try. It's kind of hard to concentrate though, when you're, well, excited. It's not only meeting you people, but I always get excited traveling. I was just terrible on our honeymoon, but then I guess a honeymoon's enough to make anybody nervous. I'll never forget when we went into the hotel in Chicago—— All right, Tommie, I won't. But I can tell about meeting the Bakers.

They're a couple about our age that I've known all my life. They were the last people in the world I wanted to see, but we ran into them on State Street and they insisted on us coming to their hotel for dinner and before dinner they took us up to their room and Ken—that's Mr. Baker—Ken made some cocktails, though I didn't want any and Tom was on the wagon. He said a honeymoon was a fine time to be on the wagon! Ken said.

"Don't tempt him, Ken," I said. "Tom isn't a drinker like you and Gertie and the rest of us. When he starts, he can't stop." Gertie is Mrs. Baker.

So Ken said why should he stop and I said there was good reason why he should because he had promised me he would and he told me the day we were married that if I ever saw him take another drink I would know that——

What did you make? Two odd? Well, thank heavens that isn't a game! Oh, that does make a game, doesn't it? Because Tom doubled and I left him in. Isn't that wicked! Oh, dearie, please forgive me and I'll promise to pay attention from now on! What do I do with these? Oh, yes, I make them for Arthur.

I was telling you about the Bakers. Finally Ken saw he couldn't make Tom take a drink, so he gave up in disgust. But imagine meeting them on our honeymoon, when we didn't want to see anybody! I don't suppose anybody does unless they're already tired of each other, and we certainly weren't, were we, Tommie? And aren't yet, are we, dear? And never will be. But I guess I better speak for myself.

There! I'm talking again! But you see it's the first time we've been with anybody we really cared about; I mean, you're Tom's best friends and it's so nice to get a chance to talk to somebody who's known him a long time. Out there the people we run around with are almost strangers and they don't talk about anything but themselves and how much money their husbands make. You never can talk to them about things that are worth while, like books. I'm wild about books, but I honestly don't believe half the women we know out there can read. Or at least they don't. If you mention some really worth while novel like, say, "Black Oxen," they think you're trying to put on the Ritz.

You said a no-trump, didn't you, Tom? And Arthur passed. Let me see; I wish I knew what to do. I haven't any five-card—it's terrible! Just a minute. I wish somebody could—I know I ought to take—but—well, I'll pass. Oh, Tom, this is the worst you ever saw, but I don't know what I could have done.

I do hold the most terrible cards! I certainly believe in the saying, "Unlucky at cards, lucky in love." Whoever made it up must have been thinking of me. I hate to lay them down, dear. I know you'll say I ought to have done something. Well, there they are! Let's see your hand, Helen. Oh, Tom, she's—but I mustn't tell, must I? Anyway, I'm dummy. That's one comfort. I can't make a mistake when I'm dummy. I believe Tom over-bids lots of times so I'll be dummy and can't do anything ridiculous. But at that I'm much better than I used to be, aren't I, dear?

Helen, do you mind telling me where you got that gown? Crandall and Nelsons's? I've heard of them, but I heard they were terribly expensive. Of course a person can't expect to get a gown like that without paying for it. I've got to get some things while I'm here and I suppose that's where I better go, if their things aren't too horribly dear. I haven't had a thing new since I was married and I've worn this so much I'm sick of it.

Tom's always after me to buy clothes, but I can't seem to get used to spending somebody else's money, though it was dad's money I spent before I did Tom's, but that's different, don't you think so? And of course at first we didn't have very much to spend, did we, dear? But now that we've had our raise——All right, Tommie, I won't say another word.

Oh, did you know they tried to get Tom to run for mayor? Tom is making faces at me to shut up, but I don't see any harm in telling it to his best friends. They know we're not the kind that brag, Tommie. I do think it was quite a tribute; he'd only lived there a little over a year. It came up one night when the Guthries were at our house, playing bridge. Mr. Guthrie—that's A. L. Guthrie—he's one of the big lumbermen out there. He owns—just what does he own, Tom? Oh, I'm sorry. Anyway, he's got millions. Well, at least thousands.

He and his wife were at our house playing bridge. She's the queerest woman! If you just saw her, you'd think she was a janitor or something; she wears the most hideous clothes. Why, that night she had on a—honestly you'd have sworn it was a maternity gown, and for no reason. And the first time I met her—well, I just can't describe it. And she's a graduate of Bryn Mawr and one of the oldest families in Philadelphia. You'd never believe it!

She and her husband are terribly funny in a bridge game. He doesn't think there ought to be any conventions; he says a person might just as well tell each other what they've got. So he won't pay any attention to what-do-you-call-'em, informatory, doubles and so forth. And she plays all the conventions, so you can imagine how they get along. Fight! Not really fight, you know, but argue. That is, he does. It's horribly embarrassing to whoever is playing with them. Honestly, if Tom ever spoke to me like Mr. Guthrie does to his wife, well—aren't they terrible, Tom? Oh, I'm sorry!

She was the first woman in Portland that called on me and I thought it was awfully nice of her, though when I saw her at the door I would have sworn she was a book agent or maybe a cook looking for work. She had on a—well, I can't describe it. But it was sweet of her to call, she being one of the real people there and me—well, that was before Tom was made a vice-president. What? Oh, I never dreamed he hadn't written you about that!

But Mrs. Guthrie acted just like it was a great honor for her to meet me, and I like people to act that way even when I know it's all apple sauce. Isn't that a funny expression, "apple sauce"? Some man said it in a vaudeville show in Portland the Monday night before we left. He was a comedian—Jack Brooks or Ned Frawley or something. It means—well, I don't know how to describe it. But we had a terrible time after the first few minutes. She is the silentest person I ever knew and I'm kind of bashful myself with strangers. What are you grinning about, Tommie? I am, too, bashful when I don't know people. Not exactly bashful, maybe, but, well, bashful.

It was one of the most embarrassing things I ever went through. Neither of us could say a word and I could hardly help from laughing at what she had on. But after you get to know her you don't mind her clothes, though it's a terrible temptation all the time not to tell her how much nicer—— And her hair! But she plays a dandy game of bridge, lots better than her husband. You know he won't play conventions. He says it's just like telling you what's in each other's hand. And they have awful arguments in a game. That is, he does. She's nice and quiet and it's a kind of mystery how they ever fell in love. Though there's a saying or a proverb or something, isn't there, about like not liking like? Or is it just the other way?

But I was going to tell you about them wanting Tom to be mayor. Oh, Tom, only two down? Why, I think you did splendidly! I gave you a miserable hand and Helen had—what didn't you have, Helen? You had the ace, king of clubs. No, Tom had the king. No, Tom had the queen. Or was it spades? And you had the ace of hearts. No, Tom had that. No, he didn't. What *did* you have, Tom? I don't exactly see what you bid on. Of course I was terrible, but—what's the difference anyway?

What was I saying? Oh, yes, about Mr. and Mrs. Guthrie. It's funny for a couple like that to get married when they are so different in every way. I never saw two people with such different tastes. For instance, Mr. Guthrie is keen about motoring and Mrs. Guthrie just hates it. She simply suffers all the time she's in a car. He likes a good time, dancing, golfing, fishing, shows, things like that. She isn't interested in anything but church work and bridge work.

"Bridge work." I meant bridge, not bridge work. That's funny, isn't it? And yet they get along awfully well; that is when they're not playing cards or doing something else together. But it does seem queer that they picked each other out. Still, I guess hardly any husband and wife agree on anything.

You take Tom and me, though, and you'd think we were made for each other. It seems like we feel just the same about everything. That is, almost everything. The things we don't agree on are little things that don't matter. Like music. Tom is wild about jazz and blues and dance music. He adores Irving Berlin and Gershwin and Jack Kearns. He's always after those kind of things on the radio and I just want serious, classical things like "Humoresque" and "Indian Love Lyrics." And then there's shows. Tom is crazy over Ed Wynn and I can't see anything in him. Just the way he laughs at his own jokes is enough to spoil him for me. If I'm going to spend time and money on a theater I want to see something worth while— "The Fool" or "Lightnin'."

And things to eat. Tom insists, or that is he did insist, on a great big breakfast—fruit, cereal, eggs, toast, and coffee. All I want is a little fruit and dry toast and coffee. I think it's a great deal better for a person. So that's one habit I broke Tom of, was big breakfasts. And another thing he did when we were first married was to take off his shoes as soon as he got home from the office and put on bedroom slippers. I believe a person ought not to get sloppy just because they're married.

But the worst of all was pajamas! What's the difference, Tommie? Helen and Arthur don't mind. And I think it's kind of funny, you being so old-fashioned. I mean Tom had always worn a nightgown till I made him give it up. And it was a struggle, believe me! I had to threaten to leave him if he didn't buy pajamas. He certainly hated it. And now he's mad at me for telling, aren't you, Tommie? I just couldn't help it. I think it's so funny in this day and age. I hope Arthur doesn't wear them; nightgowns, I mean. You don't, do you, Arthur? I knew you didn't.

Oh, are you waiting for me? What did you say, Arthur? Two diamonds? Let's see what that means. When Tom makes an original bid of two it means he hasn't got the tops. I wonder— but of course you couldn't have the—heavens! What am I saying! I guess I better just keep still and pass.

But what was I going to tell you? Something about—oh, did I tell you about Tom being an author? I had no idea he was talented that way till after we were married and I was unpacking his old papers and things and came across a poem he'd written, the saddest, mushiest poem! Of course it was a long time ago he wrote it; it was dated four years ago, long before he met me, so it didn't make me very jealous, though it was about some other girl. You didn't know I found it, did you, Tommie?

But that wasn't what I refer to. He's written a story, too, and he's sent it to four different magazines and they all sent it back. I tell him though, that that doesn't mean anything. When you see some of the things the magazines do print, why, it's an honor to have them *not* like yours. The only thing is that Tom worked so hard over it and sat up nights writing and rewriting, it's a kind of a disappointment to have them turn it down.

It's a story about two men and a girl and they were all

brought up together and one of the men was awfully popular and well off and good-looking and a great athlete—a man like Arthur. There, Arthur! How is that for a T. L.? The other man was just an ordinary man with not much money, but the girl seemed to like him better and she promised to wait for him. Then this man worked hard and got money enough to see him through Yale.

The other man, the well-off one, went to Princeton and made a big hit as an athlete and everything and he was through college long before his friend because his friend had to earn the money first. And the well-off man kept after the girl to marry him. He didn't know she had promised the other one. Anyway she got tired waiting for the man she was engaged to and eloped with the other one. And the story ends up by the man she threw down welcoming the couple when they came home and pretending everything was all right, though his heart was broken.

What are you blushing about, Tommie? It's nothing to be ashamed of. I thought it was very well written and if the editors had any sense they'd have taken it.

Still, I don't believe the real editors see half the stories that are sent to them. In fact I know they don't. You've either got to have a name or a pull to get your things published. Or else pay the magazines to publish them. Of course if you are Robert Chambers or Irving R. Cobb, they will print whatever you write whether it's good or bad. But you haven't got a chance if you are an unknown like Tom. They just keep your story long enough so you will think they are considering it and then they send it back with a form letter saying it's not available for their magazine and they don't even tell why.

You remember, Tom, that Mr. Hastings we met at the Hammonds'. He's a writer and knows all about it. He was telling me of an experience he had with one of the magazines; I forget which one, but it was one of the big ones. He wrote a story and sent it to them and they sent it back and said they couldn't use it.

Well, some time after that Mr. Hastings was in a hotel in Chicago and a bell-boy went around the lobby paging Mr.——— I forget the name, but it was the name of the editor of this magazine that had sent back the story, Runkle, or Byers, or some such name. So the man, whatever his name was, he was really there and answered the page and afterwards Mr. Hastings went up to him and introduced himself and told the man about sending a story to his magazine and the man said he didn't remember anything about it. And he was the editor! Of course he'd never seen it. No wonder Tom's story keeps coming back!

He says he is through sending it and just the other day he was going to tear it up, but I made him keep it because we may meet somebody some time who knows the inside ropes and can get a hearing with some big editor. I'm sure it's just a question of pull. Some of the things that get into the magazines sound like they had been written by the editor's friends or relatives or somebody whom they didn't want to hurt their feelings. And Tom really can write!

I wish I could remember that poem of his I found. I memorized it once, but—wait! I believe I can still say it! Hush, Tommie! What hurt will it do anybody? Let me see; it goes:

> "I thought the sweetness of her song
>   Would ever, ever more belong
>   To me; I thought (O thought divine!)
>   My bird was really mine!

> "But promises are made, it seems,
>   Just to be broken. All my dreams
>   Fade out and leave me crushed, alone.
>   My bird, alas, has flown!"

Isn't that pretty. He wrote it four years ago. Why, Helen, you revoked! And, Tom, do you know that's Scotch you're drinking? You said—— *Why, Tom!*

Rhythm

THIS STORY is slightly immoral, but so, I guess, are all stories based on truth. It concerns, principally, Harry Hart,
whose frankness and naturalness were the traits that endeared
him to fellow members of the Friars' Club and all red-blooded
she-girls who met him in and out of show business. Music
writers have never been noted for self-loathing and Harry was
a refreshing exception to the general run. That was before
"Upsy Daisy" began its year's tenancy of the Casino.

You can judge what sort of person he was by listening in on
a talk he had at the club one night with Sam Rose, lyricist of
"Nora's Nightie," "Sheila's Shirt" and a hundred popular
songs. They were sitting alone at the table nearest the senile
piano.

"Sam," said Harry, "I was wondering if they's a chance of
you and I getting together."

"What's happened to Kane?" asked Sam.

"It's off between he and I," Harry replied. "That dame
ruined him. I guess she married him to make an honest man of
him. Anyways, he got so honest that I couldn't stand it no
more. You know how I am, Sam—live and let live. I don't
question nobody's ethics or whatever you call them, as long as
they don't question mine. We're all trying to get along; that's
the way I look at it. At that, I've heard better lyrics than he
wrote for those two rhythm numbers of mine in 'Lottie'; in
fact, between you and I, I thought he made a bum out of
those two numbers. They sold like hymns, so I was really able
to bear up when we reached the parting of the ways.

"But I'll tell you the climax just to show you how silly a guy
can get. You remember our 'Yes, Yes, Eulalie.' Well, they was a
spot for a swell love duet near the end of the first act and I had
a tune for it that was a smash. You know I'm not bragging
when I say that; I don't claim it as my tune, but it was and is a
smash. I mean the 'Catch Me' number."

"I'll say it's a smash!" agreed Sam.

"But a smash in spite of the words," said Harry.

"You're right," said Sam.

"Well, the first time I played this tune for him, he went nuts over it and I gave him a lead sheet and he showed it to his wife. It seems she plays piano a little and she played this melody and she told him I had stole it from some opera; she thought it was 'Gioconda,' but she wasn't sure. So the next day Kane spoke to me about it and I told him it wasn't 'Gioconda'; it was Donizetti's 'Linda di Chamounix.' Well, he said he didn't feel like it was right to work on a melody that had been swiped from somewhere. So I said, 'Ain't it kind of late for you to be having all those scruples?' So he said, 'Maybe it is, but better late than never.' So I said, 'Listen, Benny—this is your wife talking, not you.' And he said, 'Let's leave her out of this,' and I said, 'I wished to heaven we could.'

"I said, 'Benny, you'll admit that's a pretty melody,' and he said yes, he admitted it. So I said: 'Well, how many of the dumb-bells that goes to our shows has ever heard "Linda di Chamounix" or ever will hear it? When I put this melody in our troupe I'm doing a million people a favor; I'm giving them a chance to hear a beautiful piece of music that they wouldn't never hear otherwise. Not only that, but they'll hear it at its best because I've improved it.' So Benny said, 'The first four bars is exactly the same and that's where people will notice.'

"So then I said: 'Now listen here, Benny—up to the present you haven't never criticized my music and I haven't criticized your lyrics. But now you say I'm a tune thief. I don't deny it, but if I wasn't, you'd of had a sweet time making a living for yourself, let alone get married. However, laying that to one side, I was over to my sister's house the other night and she had a soprano singer there and she sung a song something about "I love you, I love you; 'tis all my heart can say." It was a mighty pretty song and it come out about twenty or thirty years ago.'

"So then Benny said, 'What of it?' So I said, 'Just this: I can recall four or five lyrics of yours where "I love you" comes in and I bet you've used the words "heart" and "say" and "all" at least twice apiece during your remarkable career as a song writer. Well, did you make those words up or did you hear them somewhere?' That's what I said to him and of course he was stopped. But his ethics was ravaged just the same and it was understood we'd split up right after 'Eulalie.' And as I say, his words wasn't no help to my Donizetti number; they'd of slayed it if it could of been slayed."

"Well?" said Sam.

"Well," said Harry, "Conrad Green wired me yesterday to come and see him, so I was up there today. He's so dumb that he thinks I'm better than Friml. And he's got a book by Jack Prendergast that he wanted Kane and I to work on. So I told him I wouldn't work with Kane and he said to get who I wanted. So that's why I gave you a ring."

"It sounds good to me," said Sam. "How is the book?"

"I only skimmed it through, but I guess it's all right. It's based on 'Cinderella,' so what with that idear combined with your lyrics and my tunes, it looks like we ought to give the public a novelty at least."

"Have you got any new tunes?"

"New?" Hart laughed. "I'm dirty with them." He sat down at the piano. "Get this rhythm number. If it ain't a smash, I'm Gatti-Casazza!"

He played it, beautifully, first in F sharp—a catchy refrain that seemed to be waltz time in the right hand and two-four in the left.

"It's pretty down here, too," he said, and played it again, just as surely, in B natural, a key whose mere mention is henbane to the average pianist.

"A wow!" enthused Sam Rose. "What is it?"

"Don't you know?"

"The Volga boat song."

"No," said Hart. "It's part of Aïda's number when she finds out the fella is going to war. And nobody that comes to our shows will spot it except maybe Deems Taylor and Alma Gluck."

"It's so pretty," said Sam, "that it's a wonder it never goes popular."

"The answer is that Verdi didn't know rhythm!" said Hart.

Or go back and observe our hero at the Bucks' house on Long Island. Several of the boys and girls were there and thrilled to hear that Harry Hart was coming. He hardly had time to taste his first cocktail before they were after him to play something.

"Something of your own!" pleaded the enraptured Helen Morse.

"If you mean something I made up," he replied with engaging frankness, "why, that's impossible; not exactly impossible, but it would be the homeliest tune you ever listened to. However, my name is signed to some mighty pretty things and I'll play you one or two of those."

Thus, without the conventional show of reluctance, Harry played the two "rhythm numbers" and the love-song that were making Conrad Green's "Upsy Daisy" the hit of the season. And he was starting in on another, a thing his informal audience did not recognize, when he overheard his hostess introducing somebody to Mr. Rudolph Friml.

"Good night!" exclaimed Hart. "Let somebody play that can play!" And he resigned his seat at the piano to the newcomer and moved to a far corner of the room.

"I hope Friml didn't hear me," he confided to a Miss Silloh. "I was playing a thing he wrote himself and letting you people believe it was mine."

Or catch him in the old days at a football game with Rita Marlowe of Goldwyn. One of the college bands was playing "Yes, Sir! That's My Baby!"

"Walter Donaldson. There's the boy that can write the hits!" said Hart.

"Just as if you couldn't!" said his companion.

"I don't class with him," replied her modest escort.

Later on, Rita remarked that he must have been recognized by people in the crowd. Many had stared.

"Let's not kid ourselves, girlie," he said. "They're staring at you, not me."

Still later, on the way home from the game, he told her he had saved over $25,000 and expected to average at least $40,000 a year income while his vogue lasted.

"I'm good as long as I don't run out of pretty tunes," he said, "and they's no reason why I should with all those old masters to draw from. I'm telling you my financial status because—well, I guess you know why."

Rita did know, and it was the general opinion, shared by the two principals, that she and Harry were engaged.

When "Upsy Daisy" had been running two months and its hit numbers were being sung, played, and whistled almost to cloyment, Hart was discovered by Spencer Deal. That he was the pioneer in a new American jazz, that his rhythms would revolutionize our music—these things and many more were set forth by Deal in a four-thousand-word article called "Harry Hart, Harbinger," printed by the erudite Webster's Weekly. And Harry ate it up, though some of the words nearly choked him.

Interesting people were wont to grace Peggy Leech's drawing-room on Sunday afternoons. Max Reinhardt had been there. Reinald Werrenrath had been there. So had Heifetz and Jeritza and Michael Arlen, and Noel Coward and Dudley Malone. And Charlie Chaplin, and Gene Tunney. In fact, Peggy's Sunday afternoons could be spoken of as salons and her apartment as a hotbed of culture.

It was to Peggy's that Spencer Deal escorted Hart a few weeks after the appearance of the article in Webster's. Deal, in presenting him, announced that he was at work on a "blue" symphony that would make George Gershwin's ultra rhythms and near dissonants sound like the doxology. "Oh!" exclaimed pretty Myra Hampton. "Will he play some of it for us?"

"Play, play, play!" said Hart querulously. "Don't you think I ever want a rest! Last night it was a party at Broun's and they kept after me and wouldn't take 'No' and finally I played just as rotten as I could, to learn them a lesson. But they didn't even know it was rotten. What do you do for a living?"

"I'm an actress," confessed the embarrassed young lady.

"Well, would you like it if, every time you went anywhere socially, people asked you to act?"

"Yes," she answered, but he had moved away.

He seemed to be seeking seclusion; sat down as far as possible from the crowd and looked hurt. He accepted a highball proffered by his hostess, but neglected to thank her. Not a bit discouraged, she brought him Signor Parelli of the Metropolitan.

"Mr. Hart," she said, "this is Mr. Parelli, one of the Metropolitan's conductors."

"Yay?" said Hart.

"Perhaps some day Mr. Parelli will conduct one of your operas."

"I hope so," said the polite Parelli.

"Do you?" said Hart. "Well, if I ever write an opera, I'll

conduct it myself, or at least I won't take no chance of having it ruined by a foreigner."

The late war increased people's capacity for punishment and in about twenty minutes Peggy's guests began to act as if they would live in spite of Harry's refusal to perform. In fact, one of them, Roy Lattimer, full of Scotch courage and not so full of musical ability, went to the piano himself and began to play.

"Began" is all, for he had not completed four bars before Hart plunged across the room and jostled him off the bench.

"I hope you don't call yourself a pianist!" he said, pronouncing it as if it meant a cultivator of, or dealer in, peonies. And for two hours, during which everybody but Spencer Deal and the unfortunate hostess walked out on him, Harry played and played and played. Nor in all that time did he play anything by Kern, Gershwin, Stephen Jones, or Isham Jones, Samuels, Youmans, Friml, Stamper, Tours, Berlin, Tierney, Hubbell, Hein, or Gitz-Rice.

It was during this epoch that Harry had occasion one day to walk up Fifth Avenue from Forty-fifth Street to the Plaza. He noticed that almost everyone he passed on the line of march gazed at him intently. He recalled that his picture had been in two rotogravure sections the previous Sunday. It must have been a better likeness than he had thought.

New York was burning soft coal that winter and when Hart arrived in the Plaza wash-room he discovered a smudge on the left side of his upper lip. It made him look as if he had had a mustache, had decided to get it removed and then had changed his mind when the barber was half through.

Harry's date at the Plaza was with Rita Marlowe. He had put it off as long as he could. If the girl had any pride or sense, she'd have taken a hint. Why should he waste his time on a second-rate picture actress when he was hobnobbing with women like Elinor Deal and Thelma Warren and was promised an introduction to Mrs. Wallace Gerard? Girls ought to know that when a fella who has been taking them out three and four times a week and giving them a ring every morning, night and noon between whiles—they ought to know that when a fella stops calling them up and taking them out and won't even talk to them when they call up, there is only one possible answer.

Yet this dame insists on you meeting her and probably having a scene. Well, she'll get a scene. No, she won't. No use being brutal. Just make it apparent in a nice way that things ain't like they used to be and get it over as quick as possible.

"Where can we go?" asked Rita. "I mean, to talk."

"Nowheres that'll take much time," said Harry. "I've got a date with Paul Whiteman to look over part of my symphony."

"I don't want to interrupt your work," said Rita. "Maybe it would be better if you came up to the house tonight."

"I can't tonight," he told her.

"When can you?"

"I'll give you a ring. It's hard to get away. You see——"

"I think I do," said Rita, and left him.

"About time," said Harry to himself.

His symphony went over fairly "big." The critics seemed less impressed than with the modern compositions of Gershwin and Deems Taylor. "But then," Harry reflected, "Gershwin was ahead of me and of course Taylor has friends on the paper."

A party instigated by Spencer Deal followed the concert and Harry met Mrs. Wallace Gerard, who took a great interest in young composers and had been known to give them substantial aid. Hart accepted an invitation to play to her at her Park Avenue apartment. He made the mistake of thinking she wanted to be petted, not played to, and his first visit was his last.

He had been engaged by Conrad Green to do the music for a new show, with a book by Guy Bolton. He balked at working again with Sam Rose, whose lyrics were hopelessly proletarian. Green told him to pick his own lyricist and Harry chose Spencer Deal. The result of the collaboration was a score that required a new signature at the beginning of each bar, and a collection of six-syllable rhymes that has as much chance of being unriddled, let alone sung, by chorus girls as a pandect on biotaxy by Ernest Boyd.

"Terrible!" was Green's comment on advice of his musical adviser, Frank Tours.

"You're a fine judge!" said Hart. "But it don't make no difference what you think. Our contract with you is to write music and lyrics for this show and that's what we've done. If you don't like it, you can talk to my lawyer."

"Your lawyer is probably one of mine, too," replied Green. "He must be if he practises in New York. But that is neither here or there. If you think you can compel me to accept a score which Tours tells me that if it was orchestrated, Stokowski himself couldn't even read the triangle part, to say nothing of lyrics which you would have to ring up every night at seven o'clock to get the words in the opening chorus all pronounced in time for Bayside people to catch the one-twenty train—well, Hart, go along home now, because you and I are going to see each other in court every day for the next forty years."

A year or so later, Harry's total cash on hand and in bank amounted to $214.60, including the $56 he had cleaned up on the sale of sheet music and mechanical records of his symphony. He read in the Sunday papers that Otto Harbach had undertaken a book for Willis Merwin and the latter was looking around for a composer. Merwin was one of the younger producers and had been a pal of Harry's at the Friars'. Hart sought him there. He found Merwin and came to the point at once.

"It's too late," said the young entrepreneur. "I did consider you at first, but—well, I didn't think you were interested now in anything short of oratorio. The stuff you used to write would have been great, but this piece couldn't stand the ponderous junk you've been turning out lately. It needs light treatment and I've signed Donaldson and Gus Kahn."

"Maybe I could interpolate——" Harry began.

"I don't believe so," Merwin interrupted. "I don't recall a spot where we could use either a fugue or a dirge."

On his way out, Hart saw Benny Kane, his collaborator of other years. Benny made as if to get up and greet him, but changed his mind and sank back in his sequestered chair.

"He don't look as cocky as he used to," thought Harry, and wished that Kane had been more cordial. "What I'll have to do is turn out a hit song, just to tide me over. Of course I can write the words myself, but Benny had good idears once in a while."

Hart stopped in at his old publishers' where, in the halcyon days, he had been as welcome as more beer at the Pastry

Cooks' Ball. He had left them for a more esthetic firm at the suggestion of Spencer Deal.

"Well, Harry," said Max Wise, one of the partners, "you're quite a stranger. We don't hear much of you lately."

"Maybe you will again," said Hart. "What would you say if I was to write another smash?"

"I'd say," replied Wise, "that it wasn't any too soon."

"How would you like to have me back here?"

"With a smash, yes. Go get one and you'll find the door wide open. Who are you working with?"

"I haven't nobody."

"You could do a lot worse," said Wise, "than team up again with Benny Kane. You and him parting company was like separating Baltimore and Ohio or pork and beans."

"He hasn't done nothing since he left me," said Hart.

"No," replied Wise, "but you can't hardly claim to have been glutting the country with sensations yourself!"

Hart went back to his hotel and wished there was no such thing as pride. He'd like to give Benny a ring.

He answered the telephone and recognized Benny's voice.

"I seen you at the Friars' today," said Benny, "and it reminded me of an idear. Where could we get together?"

"At the club," Harry replied. "I'll be there in a half-hour."

"I was thinking," said Benny, when they were seated at the table near the piano, "that nobody has wrote a rhythm song lately about 'I love you'; that is, not in the last two or three months. And one time you was telling me about being over to your sister's and they was a soprano there that sung a song that went 'I love you, I love you; 'tis all my heart can say.'"

"What of it?"

"Well," said Benny, "let's take that song and I'll just fix up the words a little and you can take the tune and put it into your rhythm and we're all set. That is, if the tune's o. k. What is it like?"

"Oh, 'Arcady' and 'Marcheta' and maybe that 'Buzz Around' song of Dave Stamper's. But then, what ain't?"

"Well, let's go to it."

"Where is your ethics?"

"Listen," said Benny Kane—"I and Rae was talking this

afternoon, and we didn't disgust ethics. She was just saying she thought that all God's children had shoes except her."

"All right," said Hart. "I can remember enough of the tune. But I'll look the song up tomorrow and give it to you and you can rewrite the words."

"Fine! And now how about putting on the feed bag?"

"No," said Harry. "I promised to call up a dame."

Whereupon he kept his ancient promise.

"You've got a lot of nerve," said Rita at the other end of the wire, "imagining a girl would wait for you this long. And I'd say 'No' and say it good and loud, except that my piano has just been tuned and you've never played me your symphony."

"I ain't going to, neither," said Harry. "But I want to try out a new rhythm number that ought to be a smash. It starts off 'I love you, I love you.'"

"It sounds wonderful!" said Rita.

FROM

ROUND UP

Travelogue

THEY MET for the first time at luncheon in the diner of the westbound limited that had left Chicago the night before. The girls, it turned out, were Hazel Dignan and her friend Mildred Orr. The man was Dan Chapman.

He it was who broke the ice by asking if they minded riding backwards. It was Hazel who answered. She was a seasoned traveler and knew how to talk to strangers. Mildred had been hardly anywhere and had little to say, even when she knew people.

"Not at all," was Hazel's reply to his polite query. "I'm so used to trains that I believe I could ride on top of them and not be uncomfortable."

"Imagine," put in Mildred, "riding on top of a train!"

"Many's the time I've done it!" said their new acquaintance. "Freight-trains, though; not passenger-trains. And it was when I was a kid."

"I don't see how you dared," said Mildred.

"I guess I was a kind of a reckless, wild kid," he said. "It's a wonder I didn't get killed, the chances I took. Some kids takes lots of chances; that is, boys."

"Girls do, too," said Hazel quickly. "Girls take just as many chances as boys."

"Oh, no, Hazel!" remonstrated her friend, and received an approving look from the male.

"Where are you headed for?" he asked.

"Frisco first and then Los Angeles," Hazel replied.

"Listen—let me give you a tip. Don't say 'Frisco' in front of them native sons. They don't like that nickname."

"I should worry what they like and don't like!" said Hazel, rather snootily, Mildred thought.

"This your first trip out there?" Chapman inquired.

"No," Hazel answered to Mildred's surprise, for the purpose of the journey, she had been led to believe, was to give Hazel a glimpse of one of the few parts of America that she had never visited.

"How long since you was out there last?" asked Chapman.

"Let's see," said Hazel. "It's been——" She was embarrassed by Mildred's wondering look. "I don't know exactly. I've forgotten."

"This is about my fiftieth trip," said Chapman. "If you haven't been——"

"I like Florida better," interrupted Hazel. "I generally go there in the winter."

"'Generally!'" thought Mildred, who had reliable information that the previous winter had been her friend's first in the South.

"I used to go to Palm Beach every year," said Chapman, "but that was before it got common. It seems to be that the people that goes to Florida now, well, they're just riffraff."

"The people that go to Tampa aren't riffraff," said Hazel. "I met some lovely people there last winter, especially one couple, the Babcocks. From Racine. They were perfectly lovely to me. We played Mah Jongg nearly every evening. They wanted me to come up and visit them in Racine this last summer, but something happened. Oh, yes; Sis's nurse got married. She was a Swedish girl. Just perfect! And Sis had absolute confidence in her.

"I always say that when a Swede is good, they're *good!* Now she's got a young girl about nineteen that's wild about movie actors and so absent-minded that Sis is scared to death she'll give Junior coffee and drink his milk herself. Just crazy! Jennie, her name is. So I didn't get up to Racine."

"Ever been out to Yellowstone?"

"Oh, isn't it wonderful!" responded Hazel. "Isn't 'Old Faithful' just fascinating! You see," she explained to Mildred, "it's one of the geysers and they call it 'Old Faithful' because it spouts every hour and ten minutes or something, just as regular as clockwork. Wonderful! And the different falls and canyons! Wonderful! And what a wonderful view from Inspiration Point!"

"Ever been to the Thousand Islands?" asked Chapman.

"Wonderful! And I was going up there again last summer with a girl friend of mine, Bess Eldridge. She was engaged to a man named Harley Bateman. A wonderful fellow when he wasn't drinking, but when he'd had a few drinks, he was just terrible. So Bess and I were in Chicago and we went to a show;

Eddie Cantor. It was the first time I ever saw him when he wasn't blacked up. Well, we were walking out of the theater that night and who should we run into but Harley Bateman, terribly boiled, and a girl from Elkhart, Joan Killian. So Bess broke off her engagement and last fall she married a man named Wannop who's interested in flour-mills or something up in Minneapolis. So I didn't get to the Thousand Islands after all. That is, a second time.

"But I always think that if a person hasn't taken that trip, they haven't seen anything. And Bess would have certainly enjoyed it. She used to bite her finger-nails till she didn't have any left. But she married this man from Minneapolis."

After luncheon the three moved to the observation-car and made a brave effort to be interested in what passes for scenery in Nebraska.

For no possible reason, it reminded Chapman of Northern Michigan.

"Have you ever been up in Northern Michigan?"

"Yes, indeed," said Hazel. "I visited a week once in Petoskey. Some friends of mine named Gilbert. They had their own launch. Ina Gilbert—that's Mrs. Gilbert—her hair used to be the loveliest thing in the world and she had typhoid or something and lost nearly all of it. So we played Mah Jongg every afternoon and evening."

"I mean 'way up," said Chapman. "Mackinac Island and the Upper Peninsula, the Copper Country."

"Oh, wonderful!" said Hazel. "Calumet and Houghton and Hancock! Wonderful! And the boat trip is wonderful! Though I guess I was about the only one that thought so. Everybody else was sick. The captain said it was the roughest trip he'd ever been on, and he had lived on the Great Lakes for forty years. And another time I went across from Chicago to St. Joseph. But that wasn't so rough. We visited the House of David in Benton Harbor. They wear long beards. We were almost in hysterics, Marjorie Trumbull and I. But the time I went to Petoskey, I went alone."

"You see a lot of Finns up in that Northern Peninsula," remarked Chapman.

"Yes, and Sis had a Finnish maid once. She couldn't hardly

understand a word of English. She was a Finn. Sis finally had to let her go. Now she has an Irish girl for a maid and Jennie takes care of the kiddies. Poor little Dickie, my nephew, he's nearly seven and of course he's lost all his front teeth. He looks terrible! Teeth do make such a difference! My friends always say they envy me my teeth."

"Talking about teeth," said Chapman, "you see this?" He opened his mouth and pointed to a large, dark vacancy where once had dwelt a molar. "I had that one pulled in Milwaukee the day before yesterday. The fella said I better take gas, but I said no. So he said, 'Well, you must be pretty game.' I said I faced German shell-fire for sixteen months and I guess I ain't going to be a-scared of a little forceps. Well, he said afterwards that it was one of the toughest teeth he ever pulled. The roots were the size of your little finger. And the tooth itself was full of——"

"I only had one tooth pulled in my life," said Hazel. "I'd been suffering from rheumatism and somebody suggested that it might be from a tooth, but I couldn't believe it at first because my teeth are so perfect. But I hadn't slept in months on account of these pains in my arms and limbs. So finally, just to make sure, I went to a dentist, old Doctor Platt, and he pulled this tooth"—she showed him where it had been—"and my rheumatism disappeared just like that. It was terrible not to be able to sleep because I generally sleep like a log. And I do now, since I got my tooth pulled."

"I don't sleep very good on trains," said Chapman.

"Oh, I do. Probably on account of being so used to it. I slept just beautifully last night. Mildred here insisted on taking the upper. She said if she was where she could look out the window, she never would go to sleep. Personally, I'd just as lief have the upper. I don't mind it a bit. I like it really better. But this is Mildred's first long trip and I thought she ought to have her choice. We tried to get a compartment or drawing-room, but they were all gone. Sis and I had a compartment the time we went to New Orleans. I slept in the upper."

Mildred wished she had gone places so she could take part in the conversation. Mr. Chapman must think she was terribly dumb.

She had nothing to talk about that people would care to hear, and it was kind of hard to keep awake when you weren't talking yourself, even with such interesting, traveled people to listen to as Mr. Chapman and Hazel. Mr. Chapman was a dandy-looking man and it was terrible to have to appear dumb in front of him.

But after all, she *was* dumb and Hazel's erudition made her seem all the dumber. No wonder their new acquaintance had scarcely looked at her since luncheon.

"Have you ever been to San Antone?" Chapman asked his companions.

"Isn't it wonderful!" Hazel exclaimed. "The Alamo! Wonderful! And those dirty Mexicans! And Salt Lake City is wonderful, too! That temple! And swimming in the lake itself is one of the most fascinating experiences! You know, Mildred, the water is so salt that you can't sink in it. You just lie right on top of it like it was a floor. You can't sink. And another wonderful place is Lake Placid. I was going back there last summer with Bess Eldridge, but she was engaged at the time to Harley Bateman, an awfully nice boy when he wasn't drinking, but perfectly terrible when he'd had a few drinks. He went to college with my brother, to Michigan. Harley tried for the football nine, but the coach hated him. His father was a druggist and owned the first automobile in Berrien County. So we didn't go to Placid last summer, but I'm going next summer sure. And it's wonderful in winter, too!"

"It feels funny, where that tooth was," said Chapman.

"Outside of one experience," said Hazel, "I've never had any trouble with my teeth. I'd been suffering from rheumatism and somebody suggested it might be a bad tooth, but I couldn't believe it because my teeth are perfect——"

"This was all shot to pieces," said Chapman.

"But my friends always say they envy me my teeth; my teeth and my complexion. I try to keep my mouth clean and my face clean, and I guess that's the answer. But it's hard to keep clean on a train."

"Where are you going? Out to the coast?"

"Yes. Frisco and then Los Angeles."

"Don't call it Frisco in front of them Californians. They

don't like their city to be called Frisco. Is this your first trip out there?"

"No. I was there a good many years ago."

She turned to Mildred.

"You didn't know that, did you?" she said. But Mildred was asleep. "Poor Mildred! She's worn out. She isn't used to traveling. She's quite a pretty girl, don't you think so?"

"Very pretty!"

"Maybe not exactly pretty," said her friend, "but kind of sweet-looking, like a baby. You'd think all the men would be crazy about her, but they aren't. Lots of people don't even think she's pretty and I suppose you can't be really pretty unless you have more expression in your face than she's got. Poor Mildred hasn't had many advantages."

"At this time of year, I'd rather be in Atlantic City than San Francisco."

"Oh, isn't Atlantic City wonderful! There's only one Atlantic City! And I really like it better in the winter. Nobody but nice people go there in the winter. In the summer-time it's different. I'm no snob, but I don't mind saying that I hate to mix up with some people a person has to meet at these resort places. Terrible! Two years ago I went to Atlantic City with Bess Eldridge. Like a fool I left it to her to make the reservations and she wired the Traymore, she says, but they didn't have anything for us. We tried the Ritz and the Ambassador and everywhere else, but we couldn't get in anywhere, that is, anywhere a person would want to stay. Bess was engaged to Harley Bateman at the time. Now she's married a man named Wannop from Minneapolis. But this time I speak of, we went to Philadelphia and stayed all night with my aunt and we had scrapple and liver and bacon for breakfast. Harley was a dandy boy when he wasn't drinking. But give me Atlantic City any time of the year!"

"I've got to send a telegram at Grand Island."

"Oh, if I sent one from there, when would it get to Elkhart?"

"Tonight or tomorrow morning."

"I want to wire my sister."

"Well, wire her from Grand Island."

"I think I'll wait and wire her from Frisco."

"But we won't be in San Francisco for over two days yet."

"But we change time before then, don't we?"

"Yes, we change at North Platte."

"Then I think I'll wire her from Grand Island."

"Your sister, you say?"

"Yes. My sister Lucy. She married Jack Kingston, the King-ston tire people."

"It certainly feels empty, where that tooth was," said Chap-man.

As the train pulled out of North Platte, later in the afternoon, Chapman rejoined the two girls in the observation-car.

"Now, girls," he said, "you can set your watches back an hour. We change time here. We were Central time and now we're Mountain time."

"Mountain time," repeated Mildred. "I suppose that's where the expression started, 'it's high time.'"

Hazel and Chapman looked blank and Mildred blushed. She felt she had made a mistake saying anything at all. She opened her book, "Carlyle on Cromwell and Others," which Rev. N. L. Veach had given her for Christmas.

"Have you ever been to Washington?" Chapman asked Hazel.

"Oh, isn't it beautiful! 'The City of Magnificent Distances.' Wonderful! I was there two years ago with Bess Eldridge. We were going to meet the President, but something happened. Oh, yes; Bess got a wire from Harley Bateman that he was going to get in that afternoon. And he never came at all. He was awfully nice when he wasn't drinking, and just terrible when he drank. Bess broke off her engagement to him and married a man named Wannop, who owned some flour-mills in Minneapolis. She was a dandy girl, but bit her finger-nails just terribly. So we didn't get to see the President, but we sat through two or three sessions of the Senate and House. Do you see how they ever get anything done? And we went to Rock Creek Park and Mount Vernon and Arlington Cemetery and Keith's.

"Moran and Mack were there; you know, the black-face co-medians. Moran, or maybe it's Mack, whichever is the little one, he says to the other—I've forgotten just how it went, but they were simply screaming and I thought Bess and I would be put out. We just howled. And the last night we were there we saw Thomas Meighan in 'Old Home Week.' Wonderful! Harley Bateman knows Thomas Meighan personally. He's got a beautiful home out on Long Island. He invited Harley out there to dinner one night, but something happened. Oh, yes; Harley lost a front tooth once and he had a false one put in and this day he ate some caramels and the tooth came out——"

"Look here," said Chapman, opening his month and pointing in it. "I got that one pulled in Milwaukee——"

"Harley was a perfect peach when he was sober, but terrible when——"

It occurred to Mildred that her presence might be embarrassing. Here were evidently kindred spirits, two people who had been everywhere and seen everything. But of course they couldn't talk anything but geography and dentistry before her.

"I think I'll go to our car and take a little nap," she said.

"Oh, don't——" began Chapman surprisingly, but stopped there.

She was gone and the kindred spirits were alone.

"I suppose," said Chapman, "you've been to Lake Louise."

"Wonderful!" Hazel responded. "Did you ever see anything as pretty in your life? They talk about the lakes of Ireland and Scotland and Switzerland, but I don't believe they can compare with Lake Louise. I was there with Bess Eldridge just before she got engaged to Harley Bateman. He was——"

"Your friend's a mighty pretty girl."

"I suppose some people would think her pretty. It's a matter of individual taste."

"Very quiet, isn't she?"

"Poor Mildred hasn't much to say. You see, she's never had any advantages and there's really nothing she can talk about. But what was I saying? Oh, yes; about Harley Bateman——"

"I think that's a good idea, taking a little nap. I believe I'll try it, too."

Hazel and Chapman lunched alone next day.

"I'm afraid Mildred is a little train sick," said Hazel. "She says she is all right but just isn't hungry. I guess the trip has been a little too much for her. You see, this is the first time she's ever been anywhere at all."

The fact was that Mildred did not like to be stared at and Chapman had stared at her all through dinner the night before, stared at her, she thought, as if she were a curiosity, as if he doubted that one so dumb could be real. She liked him, too, and it would have been so nice if she had been more like Hazel, never at a loss for something to say and able to interest him in her conversation.

"We'll be in Ogden in half an hour," said Chapman. "We stay there twenty-five minutes. That ought to give your friend a chance to get over whatever ails her. She should get out and walk around and get some air."

"You seem quite interested in Mildred," Hazel said.

"She's a mighty attractive girl," he replied. "And besides, I feel sorry for anybody that——"

"Men don't usually find her attractive. She's pretty in a way, but it's a kind of a babyish face."

"I don't think so at all——"

"We change time here again, don't we?"

"Yes. Another hour back. We've been on Mountain time and now we go to Pacific time. Some people say it's bad for a watch to turn it backwards, but it never seemed to hurt mine any. This watch——"

"I bought this watch of mine in New York," said Hazel. "It was about two years ago, the last time Bess Eldridge and I went East. Let's see; was that before or after she broke her engagement to Harley Bateman? It was before. But Harley said he knew the manager of the Belmont and he would wire him and get us a good room. Well, of course, he forgot to wire, so we finally got into the Pennsylvania, Room 1012. No, Room 1014. It was some people from Pittsburgh, a Mr. and Mrs. Bradbury, in 1012. He was lame. Bess wanted to see Jeanne Eagels in 'Rain' and we tried to get tickets at the newsstand, but they said fifteenth row. We finally went to the Palace that night. Ina Claire was on the bill. So the next morning we came down to breakfast and who should we run into but Dave Homan! We'd met him at French Lick in the spring. Isn't French Lick wonderful!

"Well, Dave insisted on 'showing' us New York, like we didn't know it backwards. But we did have a dandy time. Dave kept us in hysterics. I remember he took us to the Aquarium and of course a lot of other people were in there and Dave gave one of the attendants a quarter to page Mr. Fish. I thought they'd put us out, we screamed so! Dave asked me to marry him once, just jokingly, and I told him I wouldn't think of it because I had heard it made people fat to laugh and if I lived with him I would soon have to buy my clothes from a tent-maker. Dave said we would make a great pair as we both have such a keen sense of humor. Honestly, I wouldn't give up my sense of humor for all the money in the world. I don't see how people can live without a sense of humor. Mildred, for instance; she never sees the funny side of things unless you make her a diagram and even then she looks at you like she thought you were deranged.

"But I was telling you about Dave Homan. We were talking along about one thing and another and I happened to mention Harley Bateman and Dave said, 'Harley Bateman! Do you know Harley Bateman?' and Bess and I smiled at each other and I said I guessed we did. Well, it seems that Dave and Harley had been at Atlantic City together at a Lions' convention or something and they had some drinks and Dave had a terrible time keeping a policeman from locking Harley up. He's just as different when he's drinking as day and night. Dave got him out of it all right and they met again later on, in Chicago. Or was it Duluth? So the next day was Wednesday and Dave asked Bess and I to go to the matinée of 'Rain,' but Bess had an engagement with a dentist——"

"Do you see this?" interrupted Chapman, opening his mouth wide.

"So Dave took me alone and he said he had been hoping for that chance right along. He said three was a crowd. I believe if I had given him any encouragement—— But the man I marry must be something more than clever and witty. I like men that have been around and seen things and studied human nature and have a background. Of course they must see the funny side, too. That's the trouble with Dave Homan—he can't be serious. Harley Bateman is twice as much of a man if he wouldn't drink. It's like two different people when he drinks. He's terrible! Bess Eldridge was engaged to him, but she broke it off after we happened to see him in Chicago one time with Joan Killian, from Elkhart. Bess is married now, to a man named Wannop, a flour man from Minneapolis. So after the matinée we met Bess. She'd been to the dentist——"

"Three days ago, in Milwaukee——" began Chapman.

"So the next afternoon we were taking the boat for Boston. I'd been to Boston before, of course, but never by boat. Harley Bateman told us it was a dandy trip, so we decided to try it. Well, we left New York at five o'clock and Bess and I were up on deck when somebody came up behind us and put their hands over my eyes and said, 'Guess who it is?' Well, I couldn't have guessed in a hundred years. It was Clint Poole from South Bend. Imagine! Harley Bateman's brother-in-law!"

"Here's Ogden," said Chapman as the train slowed down.

"Oh, and I've got to send Sis a telegram! My sister Lucy Kingston."

"I think I'll get out and get some air," said Chapman, but he went first to the car where Mildred sat reading.

"Miss Mildred," he said, "suppose you have breakfast with me early tomorrow morning. I'd like to show you the snow-sheds."

"That would be wonderful!" said Mildred. "I'll tell Hazel."

"No," said Chapman. "Please don't tell Hazel. I'd like to show them to you alone."

Well, even if Mildred had been used to trains, that remark would have interfered seriously with her night's sleep.

Mildred found Chapman awaiting her in the diner next morning, an hour west of Truckee.

"Are those the snow-sheds you spoke of?"

"Yes," he replied, "but we'll talk about them later. First I want to ask you a few questions."

"Ask *me* questions!" said Mildred. "Well, they'll have to be simple ones or I won't be able to answer them."

"They're simple enough," said Chapman. "The first one is, do you know Harley Bateman?"

"I know *of* him, but I don't know him."

"Do you know Bess Eldridge?"

"Just to speak to; that's all."

"What other trips have you taken besides this?"

"None at all. This is really the first time I've ever been anywhere."

"Has your friend ever been engaged?"

"Yes; twice. It was broken off both times."

"I bet I know why. There was no place to take her on a honeymoon."

"What do you mean?"

"Oh, nothing. Say, did I tell you about getting my tooth pulled in Milwaukee?"

"I don't believe so," said Mildred.

"Well, I had a terrible toothache. It was four days ago. And I thought there was no use fooling with it, so I went to a dentist and told him to pull it. He said I'd better take gas, but I wouldn't. So he pulled it and it pretty near killed me, but I never batted an eye. He said it was one of the toughest teeth he'd ever seen; roots as big as your little finger. And the tooth itself full of poison."

"How terrible! You must be awfully brave!"

"Look here, at the hole," said Chapman, opening his mouth.

"Why, Mr. Chapman, it must have hurt horribly!"

"Call me Dan."

"Oh, I couldn't."

"Well, listen—are you going to be with Miss Hazel all the time you're in San Francisco?"

"Why, no," said Mildred. "Hazel is going to visit her aunt in Berkeley part of the time. And I'm going to stop at the Fairmont."

"When is she going to Berkeley?"

"Next Tuesday, I think."

"Can I phone you next Wednesday?"

"But Hazel will be gone then."

"Yes, I know," said Chapman, "but if you don't mind, I'll phone you just the same. Now about these snow-sheds——"

I Can't Breathe

I AM staying here at the Inn for two weeks with my Uncle Nat and Aunt Jule and I think I will keep a kind of a diary while I am here to help pass the time and so I can have a record of things that happen though goodness knows there isn't lightly to anything happen, that is anything exciting with Uncle Nat and Aunt Jule making the plans as they are both at least 35 years old and maybe older.

Dad and mother are abroad to be gone a month and me coming here is supposed to be a recompence for them not taking me with them. A fine recompence to be left with old people that come to a place like this to rest. Still it would be a heavenly place under different conditions, for instance if Walter were here, too. It would be heavenly if he were here, the very thought of it makes my heart stop.

I can't stand it. I won't think about it.

This is our first seperation since we have been engaged, nearly 17 days. It will be 17 days tomorrow. And the hotel orchestra at dinner this evening played that old thing "Oh how I miss you tonight" and it seemed as if they must be playing it for my benefit though of course the person in that song is talking about how they miss their mother though of course I miss mother too, but a person gets used to missing their mother and it isn't like Walter or the person you are engaged to.

But there won't be any more seperations much longer, we are going to be married in December even if mother does laugh when I talk to her about it because she says I am crazy to even think of getting married at 18.

She got married herself when she was 18, but of course that was "different," she wasn't crazy like I am, she knew whom she was marrying. As if Walter were a policeman or a foreigner or something. And she says she was only engaged once while I have been engaged at least five times a year since I was 14, of course it really isn't as bad as that and I have really only been really what I call engaged six times altogether, but is getting engaged my fault when they keep insisting and hammering at you and if you didn't say yes they would never go home.

But it is different with Walter. I honestly believe if he had not asked me I would have asked him. Of course I wouldn't have, but I would have died. And this is the first time I have ever been engaged to be really married. The other times when they talked about when should we get married I just laughed at them, but I hadn't been engaged to Walter ten minutes when he brought up the subject of marriage and I didn't laugh. I wouldn't be engaged to him unless it was to be married. I couldn't stand it.

Anyway mother may as well get used to the idea because it is "No Foolin'" this time and we have got our plans all made and I am going to be married at home and go out to California and Hollywood on our honeymoon. December, five months away. I can't stand it. I can't wait.

There were a couple of awfully nice looking boys sitting together alone in the dining-room tonight. One of them wasn't so much, but the other was cute. And he——

There's the dance orchestra playing "Always," what they played at the Biltmore the day I met Walter. "Not for just an hour not for just a day." I can't live. I can't breathe.

July 13

This has been a much more exciting day than I expected under the circumstances. In the first place I got two long night letters, one from Walter and one from Gordon Flint. I don't see how Walter ever had the nerve to send his, there was everything in it and it must have been horribly embarrassing for him while the telegraph operator was reading it over and counting the words to say nothing of embarrassing for the operator.

But the one from Gordon was a kind of a shock. He just got back from a trip around the world, left last December to go on it and got back yesterday and called up our house and Helga gave him my address, and his telegram, well it was nearly as bad as Walter's. The trouble is that Gordon and I were engaged when he went away, or at least he thought so and he wrote to me right along all the time he was away and sent cables and things and for a while I answered his letters, but then I lost track of his itinery and couldn't write to him any more and when I got really engaged to Walter I couldn't let Gordon know because I had no idea where he was besides not wanting to spoil his trip.

And now he still thinks we are engaged and he is going to call me up tomorrow from Chicago and how in the world can I explain things and get him to understand because he is really serious and I like him ever and ever so much and in lots of ways he is nicer than Walter, not really nicer but better looking and there is no comparison between their dancing. Walter simply can't learn to dance, that is really dance. He says it is because he is flat footed, he says that as a joke, but it is true and I wish to heavens it wasn't.

All forenoon I thought and thought and thought about what to say to Gordon when he calls up and finally I couldn't stand thinking about it any more and just made up my mind I wouldn't think about it any more. But I will tell the truth though it will kill me to hurt him.

I went down to lunch with Uncle Nat and Aunt Jule and they were going out to play golf this afternoon and were insisting that I go with them, but I told them I had a headache and then I had a terrible time getting them to go without me. I didn't have a headache at all and just wanted to be alone to think about Walter and besides when you play with Uncle Nat he is always correcting your stance or your swing or something and always puts his hands on my arms or shoulders to show me the right way and I can't stand it to have old men touch me, even if they are your uncle.

I finally got rid of them and I was sitting watching the tennis when that boy that I saw last night, the cute one, came and sat right next to me and of course I didn't look at him and I was going to smoke a cigarette and found I had left my lighter upstairs and I started to get up and go after it when all of a sudden he was offering me his lighter and I couldn't very well refuse it without being rude. So we got to talking and he is even cuter than he looks, the most original and wittiest person I believe I ever met and I haven't laughed so much in I don't know how long.

For one thing he asked me if I had heard Rockefeller's song and I said no and he began singing "Oil alone." Then he asked me if I knew the orange juice song and I told him no again and he said it was "Orange juice sorry you made me cry." I was in hysterics before we had been together ten minutes.

His name is Frank Caswell and he has been out of Darth-mouth a year and is 24 years old. That isn't so terribly old, only two years older than Walter and three years older than Gordon. I hate the name Frank, but Caswell is all right and he is so cute.

He was out in California last winter and visited Hollywood and met everybody in the world and it is fascinating to listen to him. He met Norma Shearer and he said he thought she was the prettiest thing he had ever seen. What he said was "I did think she was the prettiest girl in the world, till today." I was going to pretend I didn't get it, but I finally told him to be sensible or I would never be able to believe anything he said.

Well, he wanted me to dance with him tonight after dinner and the next question was how to explain how we had met each other to Uncle Nat and Aunt Jule. Frank said he would fix that all right and sure enough he got himself introduced to Uncle Nat when Uncle Nat came in from golf and after dinner Uncle Nat introduced him to me and Aunt Jule too and we danced together all evening, that is not Aunt Jule. They went to bed, thank heavens.

He is a heavenly dancer, as good as Gordon. One dance we were dancing and for one of the encores the orchestra played "In a cottage small by a waterfall" and I simply couldn't dance to it. I just stopped still and said "Listen, I can't bear it, I can't breathe" and poor Frank thought I was sick or something and I had to explain that that was the tune the orchestra played the night I sat at the next table to Jack Barrymore at Barney Gallant's.

I made him sit out that encore and wouldn't let him talk till they got through playing it. Then they played something else and I was all right again and Frank told me about meeting Jack Barrymore. Imagine meeting him. I couldn't live.

I promised Aunt Jule I would go to bed at eleven and it is way past that now, but I am all ready for bed and have just been writing this. Tomorrow Gordon is going to call up and what will I say to him? I just won't think about it.

July 14

Gordon called up this morning from Chicago and it was

wonderful to hear his voice again though the connection was terrible. He asked me if I still loved him and I tried to tell him no, but I knew that would mean an explanation and the connection was so bad that I never could make him understand so I said yes, but I almost whispered it purposely, thinking he wouldn't hear me, but he heard me all right and he said that made everything all right with the world. He said he thought I had stopped loving him because I had stopped writing.

I wish the connection had been decent and I could have told him how things were, but now it is terrible because he is planning to get to New York the day I get there and heaven knows what I will do because Walter will be there, too. I just won't think about it.

Aunt Jule came in my room just after I was through talking to Gordon, thank heavens. The room was full of flowers. Walter had sent me some and so had Frank. I got another long night letter from Walter, just as silly as the first one. I wish he would say those things in letters instead of night letters so everybody in the world wouldn't see them. Aunt Jule wanted me to read it aloud to her. I would have died.

While she was still in the room, Frank called up and asked me to play golf with him and I said all right and Aunt Jule said she was glad my headache was gone. She was trying to be funny.

I played golf with Frank this afternoon. He is a beautiful golfer and it is thrilling to watch him drive, his swing is so much more graceful than Walter's. I asked him to watch me swing and tell me what was the matter with me, but he said he couldn't look at anything but my face and there wasn't anything the matter with that.

He told me the boy who was here with him had been called home and he was glad of it because I might have liked him, the other boy, better than himself. I told him that couldn't be possible and he asked me if I really meant that and I said of course, but I smiled when I said it so he wouldn't take it too seriously.

We danced again tonight and Uncle Nat and Aunt Jule sat with us a while and danced a couple of dances themselves, but they were really there to get better acquainted with Frank and see if he was all right for me to be with. I know they certainly couldn't have enjoyed their own dancing, no old people really can enjoy it because they can't really *do* anything.

They were favorably impressed with Frank I think, at least Aunt Jule didn't say I must be in bed at eleven, but just not to stay up too late. I guess it is a big surprise to a girl's parents and aunts and uncles to find out that the boys you go around with are all right, they always seem to think that if I seem to like somebody and the person pays a little attention to me, why he must be a convict or a policeman or a drunkard or something queer.

Frank had some more songs for me tonight. He asked me if I knew the asthma song and I said I didn't and he said "Oh, you must know that. It goes yes, sir, asthma baby." Then he told me about the underwear song, "I underwear my baby is tonight." He keeps you in hysterics and yet he has his serious side, in fact he was awfully serious when he said good night to me and his eyes simply shown. I wish Walter were more like him in some ways, but I mustn't think about that.

July 15

I simply can't live and I know I'll never sleep tonight. I am in a terrible predicament or rather I won't know whether I really am or not till tomorrow and that is what makes it so terrible.

After we had danced two or three dances, Frank asked me to go for a ride with him and we went for a ride in his car and he had had some cocktails and during the ride he had some drinks out of a flask and finally he told me he loved me and I said not to be silly, but he said he was perfectly serious and he certainly acted that way. He asked me if I loved anybody else and I said yes and he asked if I didn't love him more than anybody else and I said yes, but only because I thought he had probably had too much to drink and wouldn't remember it anyway and the best thing to do was humor him under the circumstances.

Then all of a sudden he asked me when I could marry him and I said, just as a joke, that I couldn't possibly marry him before December. He said that was a long time to wait, but I was certainly worth waiting for and he said a lot of other things and maybe I humored him a little too much, but that is just the trouble, I don't know.

I was absolutely sure he was tight and would forget the whole thing, but that was early in the evening, and when we said good night he was a whole lot more sober than he had been and now I am not sure how it stands. If he doesn't remember anything about it, of course I am all right. But if he does remember and if he took me seriously, I will simply have to tell him about Walter and maybe about Gordon, too. And it isn't going to be easy. The suspense is what is maddening and I know I'll never live through this night.

July 16

I can't stand it, I can't breathe, life is impossible. Frank remembered everything about last night and firmly believes we are engaged and going to be married in December. His people live in New York and he says he is going back when I do and have them meet me.

Of course it can't go on and tomorrow I will tell him about Walter or Gordon or both of them. I know it is going to hurt him terribly, perhaps spoil his life and I would give anything in the world not to have had it happen. I hate so to hurt him because he is so nice besides being so cute and attractive.

He sent me the loveliest flowers this morning and called up at ten and wanted to know how soon he could see me and I hope the girl wasn't listening in because the things he said were, well, like Walter's night letters.

And that is another terrible thing, today I didn't get a night letter from Walter, but there was a regular letter instead and I carried it around in my purse all this afternoon and evening and never remembered to read it till ten minutes ago when I came up in the room. Walter is worried because I have only sent him two telegrams and written him one letter since I have been here, he would be a lot more worried if he knew what has happened now, though of course it can't make any difference because he is the one I am really engaged to be married to and the one I told mother I was going to marry in December and I wouldn't dare tell her it was somebody else.

I met Frank for lunch and we went for a ride this afternoon and he was so much in love and so lovely to me that I simply did not have the heart to tell him the truth, I am surely going to tell him tomorrow and telling him today would have just meant one more day of unhappiness for both of us.

He said his people had plenty of money and his father had

offered to take him into partnership and he might accept, but he thinks his true vocation is journalism with a view to eventually writing novels and if I was willing to undergo a few hardships just at first we would probably both be happier later on if he was doing something he really liked. I didn't know what to say, but finally I said I wanted him to suit himself and money wasn't everything.

He asked me where I would like to go on my honeymoon and I suppose I ought to have told him my honeymoon was all planned, that I was going to California, with Walter, but all I said was that I had always wanted to go to California and he was enthusiastic and said that is where we would surely go and he would take me to Hollywood and introduce me to all those wonderful people he met there last winter. It nearly takes my breath away to think of it, going there with someone who really knows people and has the entrée.

We danced again tonight, just two or three dances, and then went out and sat in the tennis-court, but I came upstairs early because Aunt Jule had acted kind of funny at dinner. And I wanted to be alone, too, and think, but the more I think the worse it gets.

Sometimes I wish I were dead, maybe that is the only solution and it would be best for everyone concerned. I *will* die if things keep on the way they have been. But of course tomorrow it will be all over, with Frank I mean, for I must tell him the truth no matter how much it hurts us both. Though I don't care how much it hurts me. The thought of hurting him is what is driving me mad. I can't bear it.

July 18

I have skipped a day. I was busy every minute of yesterday and so exhausted when I came upstairs that I was tempted to fall into bed with all my clothes on. First Gordon called me up from Chicago to remind me that he would be in New York the day I got there and that when he comes he wants me all to himself all the time and we can make plans for our wedding. The connection was bad again and I just couldn't explain to him about Walter.

I had an engagement with Frank for lunch and just as we were going in another long distance call came, from Walter this time. He wanted to know why I haven't written more letters and sent him more telegrams and asked me if I still loved him and of course I told him yes because I really do. Then he asked if I had met any men here and I told him I had met one, a friend of Uncle Nat's. After all it was Uncle Nat who introduced me to Frank. He reminded me that he would be in New York on the 25th which is the day I expect to get home, and said he would have theater tickets for that night and we would go somewhere afterwards and dance.

Frank insisted on knowing who had kept me talking so long and I told him it was a boy I had known a long while, a very dear friend of mine and a friend of my family's. Frank was jealous and kept asking questions till I thought I would go mad. He was so serious and kind of cross and gruff that I gave up the plan of telling him the truth till some time when he is in better spirits.

I played golf with Frank in the afternoon and we took a ride last night and I wanted to get in early because I had promised both Walter and Gordon that I would write them long letters, but Frank wouldn't bring me back to the Inn till I had named a definite date in December. I finally told him the 10th and he said all right if I was sure that wasn't a Sunday. I said I would have to look it up, but as a matter of fact I know the 10th falls on a Friday because the date Walter and I have agreed on for our wedding is Saturday the 11th.

Today has just been the same thing over again, two more night letters, a long distance call from Chicago, golf and a ride with Frank, and the room full of flowers. But tomorrow I am going to tell Frank and I am going to write Gordon a long letter and tell him, too, because this simply can't go on any longer. I can't breathe. I can't live.

July 21

I wrote to Gordon yesterday, but I didn't say anything about Walter because I don't think it is a thing a person ought to do by letter. I can tell him when he gets to New York and then I will be sure that he doesn't take it too hard and I can promise him that I will be friends with him always and make him promise not to do anything silly, while if I told it to him in a letter there is no telling what he would do, there all alone.

And I haven't told Frank because he hasn't been feeling well, he is terribly sunburned and it hurts him terribly so he can hardly play golf or dance, and I want him to be feeling his best when I do tell him, but whether he is all right or not I simply must tell him tomorrow because he is actually planning to leave here on the same train with us Saturday night and I can't let him do that.

Life is so hopeless and it could be so wonderful. For instance how heavenly it would be if I could marry Frank first and stay married to him five years and he would be the one who would take me to Hollywood and maybe we could go on parties with Norman Kerry and Jack Barrymore and Buster Collier and Marion Davies and Lois Moran.

And at the end of five years Frank could go into journalism and write novels and I would only be 23 and I could marry Gordon and he would be ready for another trip around the world and he could show me things better than someone who had never seen them before.

Gordon and I would separate at the end of five years and I would be 28 and I know of lots of women that never even got married the first time till they were 28 though I don't suppose that was their fault, but I would marry Walter then, for after all he is the one I really love and want to spend most of my life with and I wouldn't care whether he could dance or not when I was that old. Before long we would be as old as Uncle Nat and Aunt Jule and I certainly wouldn't want to dance at their age when all you can do is just hobble around the floor. But Walter is so wonderful as a companion and we would enjoy the same things and be pals and maybe we would begin to have children.

But that is all impossible though it wouldn't be if older people just had sense and would look at things the right way.

It is only half past ten, the earliest I have gone to bed in weeks, but I am worn out and Frank went to bed early so he could put cold cream on his sunburn.

Listen, diary, the orchestra is playing "Limehouse Blues." The first tune I danced to with Merle Oliver, two years ago. I can't stand it. And how funny that they should play that old tune tonight of all nights, when I have been thinking of Merle off and on all day, and I hadn't thought of him before in weeks and weeks. I wonder where he is, I wonder if it is just an accident or if it means I am going to see him again. I simply mustn't think about it or I'll die.

July 22

I knew it wasn't an accident. I knew it must mean something, and it did.

Merle is coming here today, here to this Inn, and just to see me. And there can only be one reason. And only one answer. I knew that when I heard his voice calling from Boston. How could I ever had thought I loved anyone else? How could he ever have thought I meant it when I told him I was engaged to George Morse?

A whole year and he still cares and I still care. That shows we were always intended for each other and for no one else. I won't make *him* wait till December. I doubt if we even wait till dad and mother get home. And as for a honeymoon I will go with him to Long Beach or the Bronx Zoo, wherever he wants to take me.

After all this is the best way out of it, the only way. I won't have to say anything to Frank, he will guess when he sees me with Merle. And when I get home Sunday and Walter and Gordon call me up, I will invite them both to dinner and Merle can tell them himself, with two of them there it will only hurt each one half as much as if they were alone.

The train is due at 2:40, almost three hours from now. I can't wait. And what if it should be late? I can't stand it.

Sun Cured

IT SEEMS there were two New Yorkers, C. L. Walters and Ernie Fretts. They met on a train Florida bound. Fretts was in the insurance business, over in Brooklyn.

"I'm in the insurance business, over in Brooklyn," said Fretts. "Handle all kinds of insurance. I started when I was just a kid, twenty years ago, and now I've got it built up so's I don't need to worry. It runs itself. I guess that's the trouble. I mean I got too much time on my hands, and I play around too much. Why, say, it's a wonder I ain't dead, the way I been going. I bet I ain't been to bed before two, three o'clock the last six months. You can't go that pace and not feel it."

"It's bound to tell on a man after a w'ile," said Walters. "Now you take me——"

"So I'm about all in," said Fretts. "And the funny part of it is I didn't realize it. I wouldn't of thought nothing about it only for the girl I got in my office. You couldn't hardly call her a girl, either; she's a woman about fifty-three and looks like a Channel swimmer. That's the kind to have in your office. I had a regular Miss America once, the first year I was in business for myself, and we were so busy petting each other that we couldn't even answer the phone. I didn't sell enough insurance that year to keep her in typewriter erl. The smartest play I ever made in my life was getting rid of her.

"This woman I got now—well, you'd about as soon think of making love to a horse. And she's as smart as a man; you don't have to tell her nothing. And where do you think I got her? In an emplerment agency."

"Now you take me——" said Walters.

"So as I was telling you, I come in the office one day last week, along about noon, and hadn't been to bed in thirty-six hours, and Miss Clancy—that's the woman I got in the office—she give me one look and said, 'Mr. Fretts,' she said, 'don't think I am butting in on your private affairs, but you better be careful or you will kill yourself. If you will take my advice,' she said, 'lay off for a month or two and go to Florida or somewheres and rest up. Get away from these friends of yours for a w'ile.'

668

"She said, 'You know you can trust me to handle the business,' she said, 'and if you will take a vacation for a month or two, you will feel like a new man. You use' to play golf and tennis and enjer yourself in things that was good for you,' she said, 'and now look at you! I bet you ain't taken no real exercise in four years. And you don't sleep and you don't eat. Just pack up and go down to Palm Beach or Miami or some place and take a little exercise and lay around in the sun and read, or just lay there and relax yourself. You got nothing in the world to worry about and if something does come up that needs your personal attention, I will let you know. But I won't anner you,' she said, 'unless it's absolutely necessary and I don't think it will be.'

"She knows me so well that she could see what kind of shape I was in. I tell you I was a wreck, but wouldn't of thought nothing of it only for her calling my attention. I tell you I was a wreck."

"You and me both," said Walters. "Now in my case——"

"So I promised her I'd think it over and that night I went on another party—without a wink of sleep, mind you—and I told a pal of mine, Ben Drew—he's in the furniture business in Brooklyn, in partners with his brother, and a great pal of mine—I told him what Miss Clancy had said, and they was a couple of girls with us. Bonnie Werner, the girl I been going around with, she was with us, and a girl named Stevens that Ben had picked up somewhere; they were both along on the party.

"The Werner girl thinks I'm going to marry her. Fine chance!

"Anyway, she overheard me telling Ben about this Florida idear and she was all ears. She made some crack about Palm Beach being a grand place for a honeymoon. I guess she thought I was stewder than I really was. I kept right on talking to Ben and he was cock-eyed and got all steamed up over the idear and said he would go along with me. He would of been right on this train, too, only for his brother getting sick. But he's going to jern me next week."

"I tried to persuade a friend of mine——"

"We got rid of the girls and sat up all that night in a poker game and I was half asleep, and at that I win over seven hundred dollars. We was playing deuces wild and they was one hand where I had three deuces and drew to them and caught a five and nine of clubs. Well, I and a fella named Garvey bet back and forth and he finally called me and laid down a deuce and three tens. I was so gone by this time that I couldn't talk, so I just throwed down my hand face up and somebody said, 'My Lord! A straight flush!' So they give me the pot and I thought all the w'ile that what I had was four nines. That shows——"

"I don't like deuces wild," said Walters. "What's the——"

"I finally got home about noon and called up the office and then slept five or six hours and by that time I was ready for another party. But when I showed up at the office on Wednesday, Miss Clancy bawled me out again and I promised I'd take her advice. Well, I hadn't played golf or tennis for years and meanw'ile I'd moved three or four times and when I come to look for my golf-clubs and tennis racket, well, they'd disappeared. And I couldn't find a bathing-suit either, or my fishing-tackle. So all this stuff I'm taking along, it's all new; I had to buy an entire new outfit—seventy-some dollars for a set of golf-clubs and a bag, fourteen dollars for a tennis racket, and thirty-odd dollars for fishing-tackle. And besides that, a bathing-suit that I paid thirty-two dollars for it, but it'll knock 'em dead.

"I don't know how my golf game will be after laying off so long; I expect it'll come back to me after the first couple of days. The last time I played was out on Long Island, at the Engineers'; must of been four, five years ago. I remember I shot an eighty-seven and win over a hundred dollars. Tennis is my game, though, and I can't hardly wait to get at it again. What I'm planning to do is get up early in the morning, have breakfast, play two or three sets of tennis, then go swimming and maybe lay around on the beach for an hour; have lunch and then get in eighteen holes of golf and another little swim; then have my dinner, probably up in my room, and go to bed around nine, ten o'clock. Three weeks and I'll be in the pink!"

"Now you take me," said Walters, "and——"

"Yes," said Fretts, "but you probably use some judgment, or maybe you're married and don't——"

"No, I'm——"

"I don't believe they's a man living could of went the pace I been going and stood up under it. Ben Drew—he's a pal of mine—he says I'm a marvel. He said, 'Ernie, you're a marvel!' Why listen: Here's what I did three weeks ago, just for an example. That was right after New Year's eve. Of course I was on parties morning, night and noon all through the holidays and wound up with a bat that started New Year's eve and lasted till Monday morning, the third. I slept a w'ile Monday forenoon and showed up at the office about three o'clock. Miss Clancy—the girl I got in the office—she give me a message to call up a pal of mine, Ben Drew.

"I called him up and he had a date with a girl he had picked up somewhere named Stevens, and would I and my girl come along. That's a girl named Bonnie Werner that I been going with. She thinks I'm going to marry her, and I suppose everybody's entitled to their opinion. Anyway, I couldn't leave Ben in a hole so I said all right and he and I got together around five o'clock and loaded up on cocktails and later we jerned the girls and made the rounds and wound up at a Black and Tan, and I and Ben both got pie-eyed and finally sent the girls home mad and we stayed and got in a crap game and I win two three hundred dollars. The game broke up at noon.

"I went straight to the office and Miss Clancy give me a message to call up Miss Werner; that's the girl I was with the night before, Monday. She was sore on account of me not seeing her home and said if I didn't take her out this night—Tuesday—why, it was all off between her and I. Well, Tuesday nights we always have a big poker game and I told her I couldn't get out of the game, but I would see her Wednesday night. I was praying she'd stay sore and carry out her threat and I wouldn't have to bother with her no more. But no; she backed down and said Wednesday would be k. o.

"So I got in the poker game and it not only lasted all Tuesday night and all day Wednesday, but all night Wednesday night. I got outside of five, six bottles of Ben Drew's Scotch and win a hundred and seventy dollars. I snatched three, four hours sleep Thursday forenoon and when I showed up at the office, the girl, the Werner girl, was waiting for me.

"To keep her from making a scene I had to promise to devote the rest of the week to her, and the next three nights, we made the rounds of all the different jernts, dancing and drinking rat-poison. Now that's just one week, but it's like all the other weeks. No wonder Miss Clancy said I looked terrible!"

"A man can't go that pace and not feel it. I know in my case———"

"So I need just this kind of a trip—go down there where I don't know nobody and no girls pestering me all the w'ile, and be outdoors all day and exercise and breathe God's fresh air. Three, four weeks of that life and the boys in Brooklyn and New York won't recognize me. And besides that, I never been to Florida and I'm anxious to look it over and see if it's all they claim. They tell me a man can pick up some great bargains there now and if I find something I like, I'm liable to grab off a piece of it, not for speculation, but maybe build myself a little place to spend the winter months. I hate cold weather and snow and they's no sense in a man in my position hanging around New York and freezing to death when I could just as well be enjering myself in a clean, wholesome way, in the sunshine."

"You take me, now———"

"You're probably a fella that uses some judgment and eat regular, or maybe you got a wife and family to make you behave. But I got nobody only my friends, though I guess I got more of them than any man in Brooklyn. That's one of my troubles, having too many friends, but only for them, I wouldn't be where I am, I mean in business. A man in my business has got to have friends, or they wouldn't have no business."

"In my business, too. I'm———"

"This must be Fayetteville we're coming to," said Fretts. "I've got to send a wire to a pal of mine, Ben Drew. He's in Brooklyn now, but he's going to jern me next week down in Miami."

It seems that the two New Yorkers happened to be on the same train a month later, northward bound from Jacksonville.

"Hello, there," said Walters.

"Fine," replied Fretts, regarding the other somewhat vaguely.

"I come down on the same train with you a month ago," said Walters.

"That's right," said Fretts. "We come down on the same train together."

"Well, what do you think of Florida?"

"No place like it in the world!" said Fretts, warming up. "Say, I could write a book! I wished I'd kept a diary of the month I been there. Only nobody would believe it."

"Where was you? Palm Beach?"

"No, Miami. That is, I guess we drove up to Palm Beach one night. I don't know."

"Where did you stop in Miami?"

"Over at the Beach, at the Flamingo."

"What did they charge you there?"

"I've got no idear. I paid them with a check," said Fretts.

"It's American plan, ain't it?"

"No. Yes, yes, it's American plan."

"And how was the meals?"

"Meals! I don't know. I didn't hear anybody say anything about them."

"I thought——"

"After this, I'm going to take all my vacations in the winter and spend them right there. That's the Garden Spot of God's Green Footstool!"

"So you bought yourself a place?"

"No, I didn't buy nothing; that is, no real estate. I met some guy the second day that was talking about a big bargain in some development he was interested in, and I promised I'd go out and look at it. He called up a couple of times to remind me of my promise, so to keep him from pestering me, I finally did go out there, but they was no moon, so I couldn't tell much about it."

"I thought——"

"Listen till you hear something funny. When I got to the hotel, they told me my room was still occupied, but the guy was just moving out and I could move in inside of an hour. Well, they made the fella pack up in a hurry and he overlooked two bottles of Plymouth gin. So there was the two bottles staring me in the eye and I was afraid he'd come back after them, so I phoned up to another fella's room that had rode over with me in the taxi from the station and he come down and we had ten, eleven Tom Collinses just as fast as we could drink them.

"Then we filled up the both bottles with water and fixed them like they hadn't been opened, and sure enough, the bird come back for his treasure. He said he was on his way to Key West and had got clear over near to Miami station when he recalled leaving the gin and he had enough time to come back for it and still catch his train yet. That's one thing about Florida trains—you can't miss them no matter what time you get there. He said it was a good thing for him that his room had been inherited by an honest man. I'd like to heard what he said when he took his first swig out of those bottles.

"Well, I and the other fella, the fella that split the gin with me—he's a fella named Leo Hargrave, from Cleveland; got a foundry there or something—the two of us went up in his room and polished off a bottle of Scotch and then it was time to dress for dinner. That's all I done about dinner the whole month I was in Miami—I dressed for it, but I never got it. Hargrave said he knew a swell jernt out near Hialeah and we hired a car and drove out there and it was a place where you dined and danced, but we wasn't hungry and we didn't have nobody to dance with. So we just ordered some drinks——"

"Did you have any trouble getting drinks?"

"Yes. You had to call a waiter. Well, we stayed there till pretty close to midnight and then drove back towards the beach and stopped at another jernt where you play roulette. There's a game I always been wild about and I'd of been satisfied to send for my baggage and settle right down for the month. But Hargrave was dance mad and he said we would have to find some girls to travel around with. He said he knew one girl; he would call her up in the morning, and maybe she had a friend.

"I told him to never mind about a friend, because it's been my experience that when you ask a girl to bring along a girl friend, the girl friend generally always looks like she had charge of the linen room at a two dollar hotel. So we stayed up till the telegraph office was open and then I sent a letter to New York, to a girl I been going around with, a girl named Bonnie Werner, and told her to jump in an upper and jern me."

"Did she come?"

"Sure, she come. She thinks I'm going to marry her. But she

couldn't get there till two, three days later and in the meanwhile, I run around with Hargrave and his dame. I wasn't lonesome, though; not as long as they was plenty of Scotch and a roulette w'eel, and besides that, I found a poker game, to say nothing about a couple dandy fellas lives there at the Beach and love to just sit around and hit up the old barber shop harmony—Jim Allison and Jess Andrew.

"But I didn't really strike my stride till Miss Werner got in. From that time on, I went some pace! And of course it was even worse when Ben Drew showed up. He's a pal of mine, in partners with his brother in the furniture business in Brooklyn. He was going to come down with me, but his brother got sick and held him up a week. He brought a girl named Stevens that he picked up somewheres, and with Miss Werner and I, and Ben Drew and the Stevens dame, and Hargrave and his girl, that made six of us that stuck together all the w'ile; that is, for the first few nights. After that, we'd get the girls all wore out by one, two o'clock and chase them home and then I and Ben and Hargrave, we'd play the w'eel or sit in a game of stud.

"It was the same schedule, day after day, the whole time I was there. The party would start out along about seven, eight o'clock in the evening and go to whatever place we hadn't been to the night before. We'd dance till, say, one o'clock and then chase the women home and do a little serious gambling. The poker game generally broke up a little before noon. That would give us fellas the afternoon to sleep, w'ile the girls would do their shopping or go to the polo or waste their time some way another. About six o'clock, I'd get up and have the barber come in and shave me and then I'd dress and be all set for the roll-call."

"But I thought——"

"From the first day, I didn't wear nothing but dinner clothes. And I brought along a trunk full of white pants and knickers that I never even unpacked.

"You'd have to get Miss Werner or one of the other girls to tell you the different places we went. They all looked alike to me—just jernts, with tables and waiters and an orchestra."

"But the weather was beautiful——"

"So I heard somebody say. I guess it's a great climate, if that's what a man is looking for. They say California's another garden spot and that's another place I've always intended to go. But of course it takes longer."

"The California climate," said Walters, "is probably just as good——"

"I've always intended to go out there. But of course it takes longer. Four, five days on a train is too much. A fella don't get no sun or air. I always feel cooped up on a train."

"How was the golf?"

"I didn't get to play golf; never had my clubs out of the bag. But I heard somebody telling Ben Drew that they had four, five fine courses around Miami."

"Play any tennis?"

"No, I didn't have time for tennis. They got some swell courts right by the hotel, but even at that, when you change into your tennis clothes and play four, five sets and then take a bath and dress again, why, it means a waste of two hours."

"Go fishing?"

"Fishing! That's a whole day! And as far as bathing is concerned, why, it looks like they was a law that you couldn't swim only at noon time, just when a man's ready for the hay."

"How far is the ocean from the hotel where you stopped?"

"I don't know. I didn't get over there. You see you can't do everything at a place like that. It would wear you out. I'm thirty-eight years old and when a man gets that age, you've got to watch your step. You can't go in for athaletics like you was a kid.

"I'm in the insurance business in Brooklyn, and one of the things we learn in our business is that a man is taking chances if he goes in too strong for sports after a certain age. You can't be a youngster all your life."

"Did your friends go home ahead of you?"

"Do you mean Ben Drew and Miss Werner and the Stevens girl? No, Ben, he's back there in a compartment dead to the world and he said he'd shoot anybody that woke him up this side of Manhattan Transfer.

"And the girls—they look like they'd just stepped out of a waste-pipe."

"You look pretty good yourself, better than last time I seen you."

"I should! A trip like this was just what I needed—away from the office a whole month and longer and ain't even given business a thought.

"That's where so many men make mistakes—not taking a vacation; or if they do take one, they keep in touch with their office all the time and sperl the whole trip, worrying. I got a girl that can run my business pretty near as good as I can myself—not a girl, either; a woman about fifty-three years old; a Miss Clancy.

"She's the one that realized the shape I was in and insisted on me taking this trip. And how her face will light up when I walk in that office Monday morning—or maybe Monday afternoon—and she sees what this has done for me!"

Liberty Hall

M Y HUSBAND is in Atlantic City, where they are trying out "Dear Dora," the musical version of "David Copperfield." My husband wrote the score. He used to take me along for these out-of-town openings, but not any more.

He, of course, has to spend almost all his time in the theater and that leaves me alone in the hotel, and pretty soon people find out whose wife I am and introduce themselves, and the next thing you know they are inviting us for a week or a week-end at Dobbs Ferry or Oyster Bay. Then it is up to me to think of some legitimate-sounding reason why we can't come.

In lots of cases they say, "Well, if you can't make it the twenty-second, how about the twenty-ninth?" and so on till you simply have to accept. And Ben gets mad and stays mad for days.

He absolutely abhors visiting and thinks there ought to be a law against invitations that go beyond dinner and bridge. He doesn't mind hotels where there is a decent light for reading in bed and one for shaving, and where you can order meals, with coffee, any time you want them. But I really believe he would rather spend a week in the death house at Sing Sing than in somebody else's home.

Three or four years ago we went around quite a lot with a couple whom I will call the Buckleys. We liked them and they liked us. We had dinner together at least twice a week and after dinner we played bridge or went to a show or just sat and talked.

Ben never turned down their invitations and often actually called them up himself and suggested parties. Finally they moved to Albany on account of Mr. Buckley's business. We missed them a great deal, and when Mrs. Buckley wrote for us to come up there for the holidays we were tickled pink.

Well, their guest-room was terribly cold; it took hours to fill the bathtub; there was no reading-lamp by the bed; three reporters called to interview Ben, two of them kittenish young girls; the breakfasts were just fruit and cereal and toast; coffee was not served at luncheon; the faucets in the wash-basin were the kind that won't run unless you keep pressing them; four important keys on the piano were stuck and people were invited in every night to hear Ben play, and the Buckley family had been augmented by a tremendous police dog, who was "just a puppy and never growled or snapped at anyone he knew," but couldn't seem to remember that Ben was not an utter stranger.

On the fourth awful day Ben gave out the news—news to him and to me as well as to our host and hostess—that he had lost a filling which he would not trust any but his own New York dentist to replace. We came home and we have never seen the Buckleys since. If we do see them it will be an accident. They will hardly ask us there unless we ask them here, and we won't ask them here for fear they would ask us there. And they were honestly the most congenial people we ever met.

It was after our visit to the Craigs at Stamford that Ben originated what he calls his "emergency exit." We had such a horrible time at the Craigs' and such a worse time getting away that Ben swore he would pay no more visits until he could think up a graceful method of curtailing them in the event they proved unbearable.

Here is the scheme he hit on: He would write himself a telegram and sign it with the name Ziegfeld or Gene Buck or Dillingham or George M. Cohan. The telegram would say that he must return to New York at once, and it would give a reason. Then, the day we started out, he would leave it with Irene, the girl at Harms', his publishers, with instructions to have it sent to him twenty-four hours later.

When it arrived at whatever town we were in, he would either have the host or hostess take it over the telephone or ask the telegraph company to deliver it so he could show it around. We would put on long faces and say how sorry we were, but of course business was business, so good-by and so forth. There was never a breath of suspicion even when the telegram was ridiculous, like the one Ben had sent to himself at Spring Lake, where we were staying with the Marshalls just after "Betty's Birthday" opened at the Globe. The Marshalls loved musical shows, but knew less than nothing about music and swallowed this one whole:

Shaw and Miss Miller both suffering from laryngitis Stop Entire score must be rewritten half tone lower Stop Come at once Stop.

C. B. Dillingham.

If, miraculously, Ben had ever happened to be enjoying himself, he would, of course, have kept the contents of his message a secret or else displayed it and remarked swaggeringly that he guessed he wasn't going to let any so-and-so theatrical producer spoil his fun.

Ben is in Atlantic City now and I have read every book in the house and am writing this just because there doesn't seem to be anything else to do. And also because we have a friend, Joe Frazier, who is a magazine editor and the other day I told him I would like to try my hand at a short story, but I was terrible at plots, and he said plots weren't essential; look at Ernest Hemingway; most of his stories have hardly any plot; it's his style that counts. And he—I mean Mr. Frazier—suggested that I write about our visit to Mr. and Mrs. Thayer in Lansdowne, outside of Philadelphia, which Mr. Frazier said, might be termed the visit that ended visits and which is the principal reason why I am here alone.

Well, it was a beautiful night a year ago last September. Ben was conducting the performance—"Step Lively"—and I was standing at the railing of the Boardwalk in front of the theater, watching the moonlight on the ocean. A couple whom I had noticed in the hotel dining-room stopped alongside of me and pretty soon the woman spoke to me, something about how pretty it was. Then came the old question, wasn't I Mrs. Ben Drake? I said I was, and the woman went on:

"My name is Mrs. Thayer—Hilda Thayer. And this is my husband. We are both simply crazy about Mr. Drake's music and just dying to meet him personally. We wondered if you and he would have supper with us after the performance tonight."

"Oh, I'm afraid that's impossible," I replied. "You see when they are having a tryout, he and the librettists and the lyric writers work all night every night until they get everything in shape for the New York opening. They never have time for more than a sandwich and they eat that right in the theater."

"Well, how about luncheon tomorrow?"

"He'll be rehearsing all day."

"How about dinner tomorrow evening?"

"Honestly, Mrs. Thayer, it's out of the question. Mr. Drake never makes engagements during a tryout week."

"And I guess he doesn't want to meet us anyway," put in Mr. Thayer. "What use would a genius like Ben Drake have for a couple of common-no-account admirers like Mrs. Thayer and myself! If we were 'somebody' too, it would be different!"

"Not at all!" said I. "Mr. Drake is perfectly human. He loves to have his music praised and I am sure he would be delighted to meet you if he weren't so terribly busy."

"Can you lunch with us yourself?"

"Tomorrow?"

"Any day."

Well, whatever Ben and other husbands may think, there is no decent way of turning down an invitation like that. And besides I was lonesome and the Thayers looked like awfully nice people.

I lunched with them and I dined with them, not only the next day but all the rest of the week. And on Friday I got Ben to lunch with them and he liked them, too; they were not half as gushing and silly as most of his "fans."

At dinner on Saturday night, they cross-examined me about our immediate plans. I told them that as soon as the show was "over" in New York, I was going to try to make Ben stay home and do nothing for a whole month.

"I should think," said Mrs. Thayer, "it would be very hard for him to rest there in the city, with the producers and publishers and phonograph people calling him up all the time."

I admitted that he was bothered a lot.

"Listen, dearie," said Mrs. Thayer. "Why don't you come to Lansdowne and spend a week with us? I'll promise you faithfully that you won't be disturbed at all. I won't let anyone know you are there and if any of our friends call on us I'll pretend we're not at home. I won't allow Mr. Drake to even touch the piano. If he wants exercise, there are miles of room in our yard to walk around in, and nobody can see him from the street. All day and all night, he can do nothing or anything, just as he pleases. It will be 'Liberty Hall' for you both. He needn't tell anybody where he is, but if some of his friends or business acquaintances find out and try to get in touch with him, I'll frighten them away. How does that sound?"

"It sounds wonderful," I said, "but——"

"It's settled then," said Mrs. Thayer, "and we'll expect you on Sunday, October eleventh."

"Oh, but the show may not be 'set' by that time," I remonstrated.

"How about the eighteenth?" said Mr. Thayer.

Well, it ended by my accepting for the week of the twenty-fifth and Ben took it quite cheerfully.

"If they stick to their promise to keep us under cover," he said, "it may be a lot better than staying in New York. I know that Buck and the Shuberts and Ziegfeld want me while I'm 'hot' and they wouldn't give me a minute's peace if they could find me. And of course if things aren't as good as they look, Irene's telegram will provide us with an easy out."

On the way over to Philadelphia he hummed me an awfully pretty melody which had been running through his head since we left the apartment. "I think it's sure fire," he said. "I'm crazy to get to a piano and fool with it."

"That isn't resting, dear."

"Well, you don't want me to throw away a perfectly good tune! They aren't so plentiful that I can afford to waste one. It won't take me five minutes at a piano to get it fixed in my mind."

The Thayers met us in an expensive-looking limousine.

"Ralph," said Mrs. Thayer to her husband, "you sit in one of the little seats and Mr. and Mrs. Drake will sit back here with me."

"I'd really prefer one of the little seats myself," said Ben and he meant it, for he hates to get his clothes mussed and being squeezed in beside two such substantial objects as our hostess and myself was bound to rumple him.

"No, sir!" said Mrs. Thayer positively. "You came to us for a rest and we're not going to start you off uncomfortable."

"But I'd honestly rather——"

It was no use. Ben was wedged between us and throughout the drive maintained a morose silence, unable to think of anything but how terrible his coat would look when he got out.

The Thayers had a very pretty home and the room assigned to us was close to perfection. There were comfortable twin beds with a small stand and convenient reading-lamp between; a big dresser and chiffonier; an ample closet with plenty of hangers; a bathroom with hot water that was hot, towels that were not too new and faucets that stayed on when turned on, and an ash-tray within reach of wherever you happened to be. If only we could have spent all our time in that guest-room, it would have been ideal.

But presently we were summoned downstairs to luncheon. I had warned Mrs. Thayer in advance and Ben was served with coffee. He drinks it black.

"Don't you take cream, Mr. Drake?"

"No. Never."

"But that's because you don't get good cream in New York."

"No. It's because I don't like cream in coffee."

"You would like our cream. We have our own cows and the cream is so rich that it's almost like butter. Won't you try just a little?"

"No, thanks."

"But just a little, to see how rich it is."

She poured about a tablespoonful of cream into his coffee-cup and for a second I was afraid he was going to pick up the cup and throw it in her face. But he kept hold of himself, forced a smile and declined a second chop.

"You haven't tasted your coffee," said Mrs. Thayer.

"Yes, I have," lied Ben. "The cream is wonderful. I'm sorry it doesn't agree with me."

"I don't believe coffee agrees with anyone," said Mrs. Thayer. "While you are here, not doing any work, why don't you try to give it up?"

"I'd be so irritable you wouldn't have me in the house. Besides, it isn't plain coffee that disagrees with me; it's coffee with cream."

"Pure, rich cream like ours couldn't hurt you," said Mrs. Thayer, and Ben, defeated, refused to answer.

He started to light a Jaguar cigaret, the brand he had been smoking for years.

"Here! Wait a minute!" said Mr. Thayer. "Try one of mine."

"What are they?" asked Ben.

"Trumps," said our host, holding out his case. "They're mild and won't irritate the throat."

"I'll sample one later," said Ben.

"You've simply got to try one now," said Mrs. Thayer. "You may as well get used to them because you'll have to smoke them all the time you're here. We can't have guests providing their own cigarets." So Ben had to discard his Jaguar and smoke a Trump, and it was even worse than he had anticipated.

After luncheon we adjourned to the living-room and Ben went straight to the piano.

"Here! Here! None of that!" said Mrs. Thayer. "I haven't forgotten my promise."

"What promise?" asked Ben.

"Didn't your wife tell you? I promised her faithfully that if you visited us, you wouldn't be allowed to touch the piano."

"But I want to," said Ben. "There's a melody in my head that I'd like to try."

"Oh, yes, I know all about that," said Mrs. Thayer. "You just think you've got to entertain us! Nothing doing! We invited you here for yourself, not to enjoy your talent. I'd be a fine one to ask you to my home for a rest and then make you perform."

"You're not making me," said Ben. "Honestly I want to play for just five or ten minutes. I've got a tune that I might do something with and I'm anxious to run it over."

"I don't believe you, you naughty man!" said our hostess. "Your wife has told you how wild we are about your music and you're determined to be nice to us. But I'm just as stubborn as you are. Not one note do you play as long as you're our guest!"

Ben favored me with a stricken look, mumbled something about unpacking his suitcase—it was already unpacked—and went up to our room, where he stayed nearly an hour, jotting down his new tune, smoking Jaguar after Jaguar and wishing that black coffee flowed from bathtub faucets.

About a quarter of four Mr. Thayer insisted on taking him around the place and showing him the shrubbery, something that held in Ben's mind a place of equal importance to the grade of wire used in hairpins.

"I'll have to go to business tomorrow," said Mr. Thayer, "and you will be left to amuse yourself. I thought you might enjoy this planting more if you knew a little about it. Of course it's much prettier in the spring of the year."

"I can imagine so."

"You must come over next spring and see it."

"I'm usually busy in the spring," said Ben.

"Before we go in," said Mr. Thayer, "I'd like to ask you one question: Do tunes come into your mind and then you write them down, or do you just sit at the piano and improvise until you strike something good?"

"Sometimes one way and sometimes the other," said Ben.

"That's very interesting," said Mr. Thayer. "I've often wondered how it was done. And another question: Do you write the tunes first and then give them to the men who write the words, or do the men write the words first and then give them to you to make up the music to them?"

"Sometimes one way and sometimes the other," said Ben.

"That's very interesting," said Mr. Thayer. "It's something I'm glad to know. And now we'd better join the ladies or my wife will say I'm monopolizing you."

They joined us, much to my relief. I had just reached a point where I would either have had to tell "Hilda" exactly how much Ben earned per annum or that it was none of her business.

"Well!" said Mrs. Thayer to Ben. "I was afraid Ralph had kidnapped you."

"He was showing me the shrubbery," said Ben.

"What did you think of it?"

"It's great shrubbery," said Ben, striving to put some warmth into his voice.

"You must come and see it in the spring."

"I'm usually busy in the spring."

"Ralph and I are mighty proud of our shrubbery."

"You have a right to be."

Ben was taking a book out of the bookcase.

"What book is that?" asked Mrs. Thayer.

"'The Great Gatsby,'" said Ben. "I've always wanted to read it but never got around to it."

"Heavens!" said Mrs. Thayer as she took it away from him. "That's old! You'll find the newest ones there on the table. We keep pretty well up to date. Ralph and I are both great readers. Just try any one of those books in that pile. They're all good."

Ben glanced them over and selected "Chevrons." He sat down and opened it.

"Man! Man!" exclaimed Mrs. Thayer. "You've picked the most uncomfortable chair in the house!"

"He likes straight chairs," I said.

"That's on the square," said Ben.

"But you mustn't sit there," said Mrs. Thayer. "It makes me uncomfortable just to look at you. Take this chair here. It's the softest, nicest chair you've ever sat in."

"I like hard straight chairs," said Ben, but he sank into the soft, nice one and again opened his book.

"Oh, you never can see there!" said Mrs. Thayer. "You'll ruin your eyes! Get up just a minute and let Ralph move your chair by that lamp."

"I can see perfectly well."

"I know better! Ralph, move his chair so he can see."

"I don't believe I want to read just now anyway," said Ben, and went to the phonograph. "Bess," he said, putting on a record, "here's that 'Oh! Miss Hannah!' by the Revelers."

Mrs. Thayer fairly leaped to his side, and herded Miss Hannah back into her stall.

"We've got lots later ones than that," she said. "Let me play you the new Gershwins."

It was at this juncture that I began to suspect our hostess of a lack of finesse. After all, Gershwin is a rival of my husband's and, in some folks' opinion, a worthy one. However, Ben had a word of praise for each record as it ended and did not even hint that any of the tunes were based on melodies of his own.

"Mr. Drake," said our host at length, "would you like a gin cocktail or a Bacardi?"

"I don't like Bacardi at all," said Ben.

"I'll bet you will like the kind I've got," said Mr. Thayer. "It was brought to me by a friend of mine who just got back from Cuba. It's the real stuff!"

"I don't like Bacardi," said Ben.

"Wait till you taste this," said Mr. Thayer.

Well, we had Bacardi cocktails. I drank mine and it wasn't so good. Ben took a sip of his and pretended it was all right. But he had told the truth when he said he didn't like Bacardi.

I won't go into details regarding the dinner except to relate that three separate items were highly flavored with cheese, and Ben despises cheese.

"Don't you care for cheese, Mr. Drake?" asked Mr. Thayer, noticing that Ben was not exactly bolting his food.

"No," replied the guest of honor.

"He's spoofing you, Ralph," said Mrs. Thayer. "Everybody likes cheese."

There was coffee, and Ben managed to guzzle a cup before it was desecrated with pure cream.

We sat down to bridge.

"Do you like to play families or divide up?"

"Oh, we like to play together," said I.

"I'll bet you don't," said Mrs. Thayer. "Suppose Ralph and you play Mr. Drake and me. I think it's a mistake for husbands and wives to be partners. They're likely to criticize one another and say things that leave a scar."

Well, Mr. Thayer and I played against Ben and Mrs. Thayer and I lost sixty cents at a tenth of a cent a point. Long before the evening was over I could readily see why Mrs. Thayer thought it was a mistake to play with her husband and if it had been possible I'd have left him a complete set of scars.

Just as we were getting to sleep, Mrs. Thayer knocked on our door.

"I'm afraid you haven't covers enough," she called. "There are extra blankets on the shelf in your closet."

"Thanks," I said. "We're as warm as toast."

"I'm afraid you aren't," said Mrs. Thayer.

"Lock the door," said Ben, "before she comes in and feels our feet."

All through breakfast next morning we waited in vain for the telephone call that would yield Irene's message. The phone rang once and Mrs. Thayer answered, but we couldn't hear what she said. At noon Ben signalled me to meet him upstairs and there he stated grimly that I might do as I choose, but he was leaving Liberty Hall ere another sun had set.

"You haven't any excuse," I reminded him.

"I'm a genius," he said, "and geniuses are notoriously eccentric."

"Geniuses' wives sometimes get eccentric, too," said I, and began to pack up.

Mr. Thayer had gone to Philadelphia and we were alone with our hostess at luncheon.

"Mrs. Thayer," said Ben, "do you ever have premonitions or hunches?"

She looked frightened. "Why, no. Do you?"

"I had one not half an hour ago. Something told me that I positively must be in New York tonight. I don't know whether it's business or illness or what, but I've just got to be there!"

"That's the strangest thing I ever heard of," said Mrs. Thayer. "It scares me to death!"

"It's nothing you need be scared of," said Ben. "It only concerns me."

"Yes, but listen," said Mrs. Thayer. "A telegram came for you at breakfast time this morning. I wasn't going to tell you about it because I had promised that you wouldn't be disturbed. And it didn't seem so terribly important. But this hunch of yours puts the matter in a different light. I'm sorry now that I didn't give you the message when I got it, but I memorized it and can repeat it word for word: 'Mr. Ben Drake, care of Mr. Ralph Thayer, Lansdowne, Pennsylvania. In Nile song, second bar of refrain, bass drum part reads A flat which makes discord. Should it be A natural? Would appreciate your coming to theater tonight to straighten this out as harmony must be restored in orchestra if troupe is to be success. Regards, Gene Buck.'"

"It sounds silly, doesn't it?" said Ben. "And yet I have known productions to fail and lose hundreds of thousands of dollars just because an author or composer left town too soon. I can well understand that you considered the message trivial. At the same time I can thank my stars that this instinct, or divination, or whatever you want to call it, told me to go home."

Just as the trainmen were shouting "Board!" Mrs. Thayer said:

"I have one more confession to make. I answered Mr. Buck's telegram. I wired him. 'Mr. Ben Drake resting at my home. Must not be bothered. Suggest that you keep bass drums still for a week.' And I signed my name. Please forgive me if I have done something terrible. Remember, it was for you."

Small wonder that Ben was credited at the Lambs' Club with that month's most interesting bender.

There Are Smiles

A T THE busy corner of Fifth Avenue and Forty-sixth Street there was, last summer, a traffic policeman who made you feel that he didn't have such a terrible job after all. Lots of traffic policemen seem to enjoy abusing you, sadistic complex induced by exposure to bad weather and worse drivers, and, possibly, brutal wives. But Ben Collins just naturally appeared to be having a good time whether he was scolding you or not; his large freckled face fairly beamed with joviality and refused to cloud up even under the most trying conditions.

It heartened you to look at him. It amused you to hear him talk. If what he said wasn't always so bright, the way he said it was.

Ben was around thirty years old. He was six feet four inches tall and weighed two hundred and eighteen pounds. This describes about eighty per cent of all the traffic officers between Thirty-second Street and the Park. But Ben was distinguished from the rest by his habitual good humor and—well, I guess you'd have to call it his subtlety.

For example, where Noonan or Wurtz or Carmody was content with the stock "Hey! Get over where you belong!" or "Where the hell do you think you're going?" Ben was wont to finesse.

"How are you, Barney?" he would say to a victim halted at the curb.

"My name isn't Barney."

"I beg your pardon. The way you was stepping along, I figured you must be Barney Oldfield."

Or, "I suppose you didn't see that red light."

"No."

"Well, what did you think the other cars was stopped for? Did you think they'd all ran out of gas at once?"

Or, "What business are you in?"

"I'm a contractor."

"Well, that's a good, honorable business and, if I was you, I wouldn't be ashamed of it. I'd quit trying to make people believe I was in the fire department."

Or, "How do you like London?"

"Me? I've never been there."

"I thought that's where you got the habit of driving on the wrong side of the street."

Transgressions at Ben's corner, unless they resulted seriously, were seldom punished beyond these sly rebukes, which were delivered in such a nice way that you were kind of glad you had done wrong.

Off duty he was "a big good-natured boy," willing to take Grace to a picture, or go over to the Arnolds' and play cards, or just stay at home and do nothing.

And then one morning in September, a dazzlingly new Cadillac roadster, blue with yellow trimmings, flashed down from the north, violating all the laws of common sense and of the State and City of New York. Shouts and whistles from Carmody and Noonan, at Forty-eighth and Forty-seventh, failed to check its crazy career, but Ben, first planting his huge bulk directly in its path, giving the driver the choice of slackening speed or running into him, and then, with an alertness surprising in one so massive, sidestepping and jumping onto the running-board, succeeded in forcing a surrender at the curb half-way between his post and Forty-fifth Street.

He was almost mad and about to speak his mind in words beginning with capitals when he got his first look at the miscreant's face. It was the prettiest face he had ever seen and it wore a most impudent, ill-timed, irresistible smile, a smile that spoiled other smiles for you once for all.

"Well—" Ben began falteringly; then recovering something of his stage presence: "Where's your helmet?"

She made no reply, but continued to smile.

"If you're in the fire department," said Ben, "you ought to wear a helmet and a badge. Or paint your car red and get a sireen."

Still no reply.

"Maybe I look like a bobby. Maybe you thought you was in London where they drive on the left side of the street."

"You're cute," she said, and her voice was as thrilling as her smile. "I could stay here all morning and listen to you. That is I could, but I can't. I've got a date down on Eighth Street and I'm late for it now. And I know you're busy, too. So we mustn't keep each other any longer now. But I'd like to hear your whole line some day."

"Oh, you would!"

"Where do you live?"

"At home."

"That isn't very polite, is it? I was thinking you might live in the Bronx——"

"I do."

"—and that's on the way to Rye, where I live, so I might drive you."

"Thanks. When I die, I want to die of old age."

"Oh, I'm not a bad driver, really. I do like to go fast, but I'm careful. In Buffalo, where we lived before, the policemen all knew I was careful and they generally let me go as fast as I wanted to."

"This ain't Buffalo. And this ain't no speedway. If you want to go fast, stay off Fifth Avenue."

The girl looked him right in the eye. "Would you like that?"

"No," said Ben.

She smiled at him again. "What time are you through?"

"Four o'clock," said Ben.

"Well," said the girl, "some afternoon I may be going home about then——"

"I told you I wasn't ready to die."

"I'd be extra careful."

Ben suddenly realized that they were playing to a large staring audience and that, for once, he was not the star.

"Drive on!" he said in his gruffest tone. "I'm letting you go because you're a stranger, but you won't get off so easy next time."

"I'm very, very grateful," said the girl. "Just the same I don't like being a stranger and I hope you won't excuse me on that ground again."

Which remark, accompanied by her radiant smile, caused Mr. Collins, hitherto only a bathroom singer, to hum quite loudly all the rest of his working day snatches of a gay Ohman and Arden record that his wife had played over and over the night before.

His relief, Tim Martin, appeared promptly at four, but Ben seemed in no hurry to go home. He pretended to listen to two new ones Tim had heard on the way in from Flushing, one about a Scotchman and some hotel towels and one about two Heebs in a night club. He managed to laugh in the right place, but his attention was on the northbound traffic, which was now none of his business.

At twenty minutes past four he said good-by to Martin and walked slowly south on the east side of the street. He walked as far as Thirty-sixth, in vain. Usually he caught a ride home with some Bronx or north suburban motorist, but now he was late and had to pay for his folly by hurrying to Grand Central and standing up in a subway express.

"I was a sucker!" he thought. "She probably drove up some other street on purpose to miss me. Or she might have came in on one of them cross streets after I'd walked past it. I ought to stuck at Forty-fourth a while longer. Or maybe some other fella done his duty and had her locked up. Not if she smiled at him, though."

But she wouldn't smile like that at everybody. She had smiled at him because she liked him, because she really thought he was cute. Yes, she did! That was her regular line. That was how she had worked on them Buffalo fellas. "Cute!" A fine word to use on a human Woolworth Building. She was kidding. No, she wasn't; not entirely. She'd liked his looks as plenty other gals had, and maybe that stuff about the fire department and London had tickled her.

Anyway, he had seen the most wonderful smile in the world and he still felt warm from it when he got home, so warm that he kissed his wife with a fervor that surprised her.

When Ben was on the day shift, he sometimes entertained Grace at supper with an amusing incident or two of his work. Sometimes his stories were pure fiction and she suspected as much, but what difference did it make? They were things that ought to have happened even if they hadn't.

On this occasion he was wild to talk about the girl from Rye, but he had learned that his wife did not care much for anecdotes concerning pretty women. So he recounted one-sided arguments with bungling drivers of his own sex which had very little foundation in fact.

"There was a fella coming south in a 1922 Buick and the

light changed and when it was time to go again, he thought he was starting in second, and it was reverse instead, and he backed into a big Pierce from Greenwich. He didn't do no damage to the Pierce and only bent himself a little. But they'd have held up the parade ten minutes talking it over if I hadn't bore down.

"I got the Buick fella over to the curb and I said to him, 'What's the matter? Are you homesick?' So he said what did I mean, homesick, and I said, 'Well, you was so anxious to get back to wherever you come from that you couldn't even wait to turn around.'

"Then he tried to explain what was the matter, just like I didn't know. He said this was his first trip in a Buick and he was used to a regular gear shift.

"I said, 'That's fine, but this ain't no training-camp. The place to practice driving is four blocks farther down, at Forty-second. You'll find more automobiles there and twicet as many pedestrians and policemen, and besides, they've got street-cars and a tower to back into.'

"I said, 'You won't never learn nothing in a desert like this.' You ought to heard the people laugh."

"I can imagine!" said Grace.

"Then there was a Jordan, an old guy with a gray beard. He was going to park right in front of Kaskel's. He said he wouldn't be more than half an hour. I said, 'Oh, that's too bad! I wished you could spend the weekend.' I said, 'If you'd let us knew you was coming, we'd have arranged some parties for you.' So he said, 'I've got a notion to report you for being too fresh.'

"So I said, 'If you do that, I'll have you arrested for driving without your parents' consent.' You ought to have heard them laugh. I said, 'Roll, Jordan, roll!' You ought to have heard them."

"I'll bet!" said Grace.

Ben fell into a long, unaccustomed silence.

"What are you thinking about?"

It came out against his better judgment. "There was a gal in a blue Cadillac."

"Oh! There was! What about her?"

"Nothing. Only she acted like it was her Avenue and I give her hell."

"What did you say to her?"

"I forget."

"Was she pretty?"

"I didn't notice. I was sore."

"You!"

"She all but knocked me for a corpse."

"And you probably just smiled at her."

"No. She done the smiling. She smiled——" He broke off and rose from the table. "Come on, babe. Let's go to the Franklin. Joe Frisco's there. And a Chaplin picture."

Ben saw nothing of the blue Cadillac or its mistress the rest of that week, but in all his polemics he was rehearsing lines aimed to strengthen her belief in his "cuteness." When she suddenly appeared, however, late on the following Tuesday afternoon, he was too excited to do anything but stare, and he would have lost an opportunity of hearing her enchanting voice if she hadn't taken the initiative. Northbound, she stopped at the curb a few feet above his corner and beckoned to him.

"It's after four," she said. "Can't I drive you home?"

What a break! It was his week on the late shift.

"I just come to work. I won't be off till midnight."

"You're mean! You didn't tell me you were going to change."

"I change every week. Last week, eight to four; this week, four to twelve."

"And next week eight to four?"

"Yes'm."

"Well, I'll just have to wait."

He couldn't say a word.

"Next Monday?"

He made an effort. "If you live."

She smiled that smile. "I'll live," she said. "There's an incentive."

She was on her way and Ben returned to his station, dizzy.

"Incentive, incentive, incentive," he repeated to himself, memorizing it, but when he got home at half past one, he couldn't find it in Grace's abridged Webster; he thought it was spelled with an *s*.

The longest week in history ended. A little before noon on Monday the Cadillac whizzed past him going south and he caught the word "later." At quitting time, while Tim Martin was still in the midst of his first new one about two or more Heebs, Ben was all at once aware that she had stopped right beside him, was blocking the traffic, waiting for him.

Then he was in her car, constricting his huge bulk to fit it and laughing like a child at Tim's indelicate ejaculation of surprise.

"What are you laughing at?"

"Nothing. I just feel good."

"Are you glad to be through?"

"Yes. Today."

"Not always?"

"I don't generally care much."

"I don't believe you do. I believe you enjoy your job. And I don't see how you can because it seems to me such a hard job. I'm going to make you tell me all about it as soon as we get out of this jam."

A red light stopped them at Fifty-first Street and she turned and looked at him amusedly.

"It's a good thing the top is down," she said. "You'd have been hideously uncomfortable in one more fold."

"When I get a car of my own," said Ben, "it'll have to be a Mack, and even then I'll have to hire a man to drive it."

"Why a man?"

"Men ain't all crazy."

"Honestly, I'm not crazy. Have I come near hitting anything?"

"You've just missed everything. You drive too fast and you take too many chances. But I knew it before I got in, so I can't kick."

"There isn't room for you to, anyway. Do you want to get out?"

"No."

"I doubt if you could. Where do you live?"

"Hundred and sixty-fourth, near the Concourse," said Ben.

"How do you usually go home?"

"Like this."

"And I thought I was saving you from a tiresome subway ride or something. I ought to have known you'd never lack invitations. Do you?"

"Hardly ever."

"Do the people ask you all kinds of questions?"

"Yes."

"I'm sorry. Because I wanted to and now I can't."

"Why not?"

"You must be tired of answering."

"I don't always answer the same."

"Do you mean you lie to people, to amuse yourself?"

"Sometimes."

"Oh, that's grand! Come on, lie to me! I'll ask you questions, probably the same questions they all ask, and you answer them as if I were a fool. Will you?"

"I'll try."

"Well, let's see. What shall I ask first? Oh, yes. Don't you get terribly cold in winter?"

He repeated a reply he had first made to an elderly lady, obviously a visitor in the city, whose curiosity had prompted her to cross-examine him for over twenty minutes on one of the busiest days he had ever known.

"No. When I feel chilly, I stop a car and lean against the radiator."

His present interviewer rewarded him with more laughter than was deserved.

"That's wonderful!" she said. "And I suppose when your ears are cold, you stop another car and borrow its hood."

"I'll remember that one."

"Now what next? Do you ever get hit?"

"Right along, but only glancing blows. I very seldom get knocked down and run over."

"Doesn't it almost kill you, standing on your feet all day?"

"It ain't near as bad as if it was my hands. Seriously, Madam, I get so used to it that I sleep that way nights."

"Don't the gasoline fumes make you sick?"

"They did at first, but now I can't live without them. I have an apartment near a public garage so I can run over there any time and re-fume myself."

"How tall are you?"

"Six feet ten."

"Not really!"

"You know better, don't you? I'm six feet four, but when women ask me, I tell them anything from six feet eight to seven feet two. And they always say, 'Heavens!'"

"Which do you have the most trouble with, men drivers or women drivers?"

"Men drivers."

"Honestly?"

"Sure. There's fifty times as many of them."

"Do lots of people ask you questions?"

"No. You're the first one."

"Were you mad at me for calling you cute the other day?"

"I couldn't be mad at you."

A silence of many blocks followed. The girl certainly did drive fast and Ben might have been more nervous if he had looked ahead, but mostly his eyes were on her profile which was only a little less alluring than her smile.

"Look where we are!" she exclaimed as they approached Fordham Road. "And you live at a Hundred and sixty-fourth! Why didn't you tell me?"

"I didn't notice."

"Don't get out. I'll drive you back."

"No, you won't. I'll catch a ride. There's a fella up this way I want to see."

"You were nice to take a chance with me and not to act scared. Will you do it again?"

"Whenever you say."

"I drive in once a week. I go down to Greenwich Village to visit my sister. Generally on Mondays."

"Next Monday I'll be on the late shift."

"Let's make it the Monday after."

"That's a long ways off."

"The time will pass. It always does."

It did, but so haltingly! And the day arrived with such a threat of rain that Ben was afraid she wouldn't come in. Later on, when the threat was fulfilled and the perils of motoring trebled by a steady drizzle and slippery pavements, he was afraid she would. Prudence, he knew, was not in her make-up and if she had an engagement with her sister, nothing short of a flood would prevent her keeping it.

Just before his luncheon time, the Cadillac passed, going south. Its top was up and its squeegee flying back and forth across the front glass.

Through the rain he saw the girl smile and wave at him briefly. Traffic was thick and treacherous and both must keep their minds on it.

It was still drizzling when she reappeared and stopped for him at four.

"Isn't this a terrible day?" she said.

"Not now!"

She smiled, and in an instant he forgot all the annoyance and discomfort of the preceding hours.

"If we leave the top up, you'll get stoop-shouldered, and if we take it down, we'll be drowned."

"Leave it up. I'm all right."

"Do you mind if we don't talk much? I feel quiet."

He didn't answer and nothing more was said until they turned east at Mount Morris Park. Then:

"I could find out your name," she said, "by remembering your number and having somebody look it up. But you can save me the trouble by telling me."

"My name is Ben Collins. And I could learn yours by demanding to see your driver's license."

"Heavens! Don't do that! I haven't any. But my name is Edith Dole."

"Edith Dole. Edith Dole," said Ben.

"Do you like it?"

"It's pretty."

"It's a funny combination. Edith means happiness and Dole means grief."

"Well," said Ben, "you'll have plenty of grief if you drive without a license. You'll have it anyway if you drive fast on these kind of streets. There's nothing skiddier than car-tracks when it's raining."

They were on upper Madison and the going was dangerous. But that was not the only reason he wanted her to slow down.

Silence again until they were on the Concourse.

"Are you married?" she asked him suddenly.

"No," he lied. "Are you?"

"I will be soon."

"Who to?"

"A man in Buffalo."

"Are you stuck on him?"

"I don't know. But he wants me and my father wants him to have me."

"Will you live in Buffalo?"

"No. He's coming here to be my father's partner."

"And yours."

"Yes. Oh, dear! Here's a Hundred and sixty-fourth and I mustn't take you past it today, not in this weather. Do you think you can extricate yourself?"

He managed it with some difficulty.

"I don't suppose I'll see you again for two weeks."

"I'm afraid not," she said.

He choked down the words that wanted to come out. "Miss Dole," he said, "take my advice and don't try for no records getting home. Just loaf along and you'll be there an hour before your supper's ready. Will you? For that guy's sake in Buffalo?"

"Yes."

"And my sake, too."

Gosh! What a smile to remember!

He must walk slow and give himself a chance to calm down before he saw Grace. Why had he told the girl he wasn't married? What did she care?

Grace's greeting was a sharp command. "Take a hot bath right away! And wear your bath-robe afterwards. We won't be going anywhere tonight."

She and Mary Arnold had been in Mount Vernon at a card-party. They had got soaked coming home. She talked about it all through supper, thank the Lord!

After supper he tried to read, but couldn't. He listened awhile to the Ohman and Arden record which his wife couldn't get enough of. He went to bed, wishing he could sleep and dream, wishing he could sleep two weeks.

He was up early, early enough to look at the paper before breakfast. "Woman Motorist Killed By Street-Car in Bronx." His eyes felt funny as he read: "Miss Edith Dole, twenty-two, of Rye, was instantly killed when the automobile she was driving skidded and struck a street-car at the corner of Fordham Road and Webster Avenue, the Bronx, shortly after four-thirty yesterday afternoon."

"Grace," he said in a voice that was not his own, "I forgot. I'm supposed to be on the job at seven this morning. There's some kind of a parade."

Out of the house, alone, he talked aloud to himself for the first time since he was a kid.

"I can't feel as bad as I think I do. I only seen her four or five times. I can't really feel this bad."

Well, on an afternoon two or three weeks later, a man named Hughes from White Plains, driving a Studebaker, started across Forty-sixth Street out of turn and obeyed a stern order to pull over to the curb.

"What's your hurry?" demanded the grim-faced traffic policeman. "Where the hell do you think you're going? What's the matter with you, you so-and-so!"

"I forgot myself for a minute. I'm sorry," said Mr. Hughes. "If you'll overlook it, I'll pick you up on my way home and take you to the Bronx. Remember, I give you a ride home last month? Remember? That is, it was a fella that looked like you. That is, he looked something like you. I can see now it wasn't you. It was a different fella."

Ex Parte

MOST ALWAYS when a man leaves his wife, there's no excuse in the world for him. She may have made whoop-whoop-whoopee with the whole ten commandments, but if he shows his disapproval to the extent of walking out on her, he will thereafter be a total stranger to all his friends excepting the two or three bums who will tour the night clubs with him so long as he sticks to his habits of paying for everything.

When a woman leaves her husband, she must have good and sufficient reasons. He drinks all the time, or he runs around, or he doesn't give her any money, or he uses her as the heavy bag in his home gymnasium work. No more is he invited to his former playmates' houses for dinner and bridge. He is an outcast just the same as if he had done the deserting. Whichever way it happens, it's his fault. He can state his side of the case if he wants to, but there is nobody around listening.

Now I claim to have a little chivalry in me, as well as a little pride. So in spite of the fact that Florence has broadcast her grievances over the red and blue network both, I intend to keep mine to myself till death do me part.

But after I'm gone, I want some of my old pals to know that this thing wasn't as lopsided as she has made out, so I will write the true story, put it in an envelope with my will and appoint Ed Osborne executor. He used to be my best friend and would be yet if his wife would let him. He'll have to read all my papers, including this, and he'll tell everybody else about it and maybe they'll be a little sorry that they treated me like an open manhole.

(Ed, please don't consider this an attempt to be literary. You know I haven't written for publication since our days on "The Crimson and White," and I wasn't so hot then. Just look on it as a statement of facts. If I were still alive, I'd take a bible oath that nothing herein is exaggerated. And whatever else may have been my imperfections, I never lied save to shield a woman or myself.)

Well, a year ago last May I had to go to New York. I called up Joe Paxton and he asked me out to dinner. I went, and met

Florence. She and Marjorie Paxton had been at school together and she was there for a visit. We fell in love with each other and got engaged. I stopped off in Chicago on the way home, to see her people. They liked me all right, but they hated to have Florence marry a man who lived so far away. They wanted to postpone her leaving home as long as possible and they made us wait till April this year.

I had a room at the Belden and Florence and I agreed that when we were married, we would stay there awhile and take our time about picking out a house. But the last day of March, two weeks before the date of our wedding, I ran into Jeff Cooper and he told me his news, that the Standard Oil was sending him to China in some big job that looked permanent.

"I'm perfectly willing to go," he said. "So is Bess. It's a lot more money and we think it will be an interesting experience. But here I am with a brand-new place on my hands that cost me $45,000, including the furniture, and no chance to sell it in a hurry except at a loss. We were just beginning to feel settled. Otherwise we would have no regrets about leaving this town. Bess hasn't any real friends here and you're the only one I can claim."

"How much would you take for your house, furniture and all?" I asked him.

"I'd take a loss of $5,000," he said. "I'd take $40,000 with the buyer assuming my mortgage of $15,000, held by the Phillips Trust and Mortgage Company in Seattle."

I asked him if he would show me the place. They had only been living there a month and I hadn't had time to call. He said, what did I want to look at it for and I told him I would buy it if it looked o. k. Then I confessed that I was going to be married; you know I had kept it a secret around here.

Well, he took me home with him and he and Bess showed me everything, all new and shiny and a bargain if you ever saw one. In the first place, there's the location, on the best residential street in town, handy to my office and yet with a whole acre of ground, and a bed of cannas coming up in the front yard that Bess had planted when they bought the property last fall. As for the house, I always liked stucco, and this one is *built!* You could depend on old Jeff to see to that.

But the furniture was what decided me. Jeff had done the

smart thing and ordered the whole works from Wolfe Brothers, taking their advice on most of the stuff, as neither he nor Bess knew much about it. Their total bill, furnishing the entire place, rugs, beds, tables, chairs, everything, was only $8,500, including a mahogany upright player-piano that they ordered from Seattle. I had my mother's old mahogany piano in storage and I kind of hoped Jeff wouldn't want me to buy this, but it was all or nothing, and with a bargain like that staring me in the face, I didn't stop to argue, not when I looked over the rest of the furniture and saw what I was getting.

The living-room had, and still has, three big easy chairs and a couch, all over-stuffed, as they call it, to say nothing of an Oriental rug that alone had cost $500. There was a long mahogany table behind the couch, with lamps at both ends in case you wanted to lie down and read. The dining-room set was solid mahogany—a table and eight chairs that had separated Jeff from $1,000.

The floors downstairs were all oak parquet. Also he had blown himself to an oak mantelpiece and oak woodwork that must have run into heavy dough. Jeff told me what it cost him extra, but I don't recall the amount.

The Coopers were strong for mahogany and wanted another set for their bedroom, but Jake Wolfe told them it would get monotonous if there was too much of it. So he sold them five pieces—a bed, two chairs, a chiffonier and a dresser—of some kind of wood tinted green, with flowers painted on it. This was $1,000 more, but it certainly was worth it. You never saw anything prettier than that bed when the lace spreads were on.

Well, we closed the deal and at first I thought I wouldn't tell Florence, but would let her believe we were going to live at the Belden and then give her a surprise by taking her right from the train to our own home. When I got to Chicago, though, I couldn't keep my mouth shut. I gave it away and it was I, not she, that had the surprise.

Instead of acting tickled to death, as I figured she would, she just looked kind of funny and said she hoped I had as good taste in houses as I had in clothes. She tried to make me describe the house and the furniture to her, but I wouldn't do it. To appreciate a layout like that, you have to see it for yourself.

We were married and stopped in Yellowstone for a week on

our way here. That was the only really happy week we had to-gether. From the minute we arrived home till she left for good, she was a different woman than the one I thought I knew. She never smiled and several times I caught her crying. She wouldn't tell me what ailed her and when I asked if she was just homesick, she said no and choked up and cried some more.

You can imagine that things were not as I expected they would be. In New York and in Chicago and Yellowstone, she had had more *life* than any girl I ever met. Now she acted all the while as if she were playing the title rôle at a funeral.

One night late in May the telephone rang. It was Mrs. Dwan and she wanted Florence. If I had known what this was going to mean, I would have slapped the receiver back on the hook and let her keep on wanting.

I had met Dwan a couple of times and had heard about their place out on the Turnpike. But I had never seen it or his wife either.

Well, it developed that Mildred Dwan had gone to school with Florence and Marjorie Paxton, and she had just learned from Marjorie that Florence was my wife and living here. She said she and her husband would be in town and call on us the next Sunday afternoon.

Florence didn't seem to like the idea and kind of discour-aged it. She said we would drive out and call on them instead. Mrs. Dwan said no, that Florence was the newcomer and it was her (Mrs. Dwan's) first move. So Florence gave in.

They came and they hadn't been in the house more than a minute when Florence began to cry. Mrs. Dwan cried, too, and Dwan and I stood there first on one foot and then the other, trying to pretend we didn't know the girls were crying. Finally, to relieve the tension, I invited him to come and see the rest of the place. I showed him all over and he was quite enthusiastic. When we returned to the living-room, the girls had dried their eyes and were back in school together.

Florence accepted an invitation for one-o'clock dinner a week from that day. I told her, after they had left, that I would go along only on condition that she and our hostess would both control their tear-ducts. I was so accustomed to solo sobbing that I didn't mind it any more, but I couldn't stand a duet of it either in harmony or unison.

Well, when we got out there and had driven down their private lane through the trees and caught a glimpse of their house, which people around town had been talking about as something wonderful, I laughed harder than any time since I was single. It looked just like what it was, a reorganized barn. Florence asked me what was funny, and when I told her, she pulled even a longer face than usual.

"I think it's beautiful," she said.

Tie that!

I insisted on her going up the steps alone. I was afraid if the two of us stood on the porch at once, we'd fall through and maybe founder before help came. I warned her not to smack the knocker too hard or the door might crash in and frighten the horses.

"If you make jokes like that in front of the Dwans," she said, "I'll never speak to you again."

"I'd forgotten you ever did," said I.

I was expecting a hostler to let us in, but Mrs. Dwan came in person.

"Are we late?" said Florence.

"A little," said Mrs. Dwan, "but so is dinner. Helga didn't get home from church till half past twelve."

"I'm glad of it," said Florence. "I want you to take me all through this beautiful, beautiful house right this minute."

Mrs. Dwan called her husband and insisted that he stop in the middle of mixing a cocktail so he could join us in a tour of the beautiful, beautiful house.

"You wouldn't guess it," said Mrs. Dwan, "but it used to be a barn."

I was going to say I had guessed it. Florence gave me a look that changed my mind.

"When Jim and I first came here," said Mrs. Dwan, "we lived in an ugly little rented house on Oliver Street. It was only temporary, of course; we were just waiting till we found what we really wanted. We used to drive around the country Saturday afternoons and Sundays, hoping we would run across the right sort of thing. It was in the late fall when we first saw this place. The leaves were off the trees and it was visible from the Turnpike.

"'Oh, Jim!' I exclaimed. 'Look at that simply gorgeous old barn! With those wide shingles! And I'll bet you it's got hand-hewn beams in that middle, main section.' Jim bet me I was wrong, so we left the car, walked up the driveway, found the door open and came brazenly in. I won my bet as you can see."

She pointed to some dirty old rotten beams that ran across the living-room ceiling and looked as if five or six generations of rats had used them for gnawing practise.

"They're beautiful!" said Florence.

"The instant I saw them," said Mrs. Dwan, "I knew this was going to be our home!"

"I can imagine!" said Florence.

"We made inquiries and learned that the place belonged to a family named Taylor," said Mrs. Dwan. "The house had burned down and they had moved away. It was suspected that they had started the fire themselves, as they were terribly hard up and it was insured. Jim wrote to old Mr. Taylor in Seattle and asked him to set a price on the barn and the land, which is about four acres. They exchanged several letters and finally Mr. Taylor accepted Jim's offer. We got it for a song."

"Wonderful!" said Florence.

"And then, of course," Mrs. Dwan continued, "we engaged a house-wrecking company to tear down the other four sections of the barn—the stalls, the cow-shed, the tool-shed, and so forth—and take them away, leaving us just this one room. We had a man from Seattle come and put in these old pine walls and the flooring, and plaster the ceiling. He was recommended by a friend of Jim's and he certainly knew his business."

"I can see he did," said Florence.

"He made the hay-loft over for us, too, and we got the wings built by day-labor, with Jim and me supervising. It was so much fun that I was honestly sorry when it was finished."

"I can imagine!" said Florence.

Well, I am not very well up in Early American, which was the name they had for pretty nearly everything in the place, but for the benefit of those who are not on terms with the Dwans I will try and describe from memory the *objets d'art* they bragged of the most and which brought forth the loudest squeals from Florence.

The living-room walls were brown bare boards without a picture or scrap of wall-paper. On the floor were two or three "hooked rugs," whatever that means, but they needed five or six more of them, or one big carpet, to cover up all the knots in the wood. There was a maple "low-boy"; a "dough-trough" table they didn't have space for in the kitchen; a pine "stretcher" table with sticks connecting the four legs near the bottom so you couldn't put your feet anywhere; a "Dutch" chest that looked as if it had been ordered from the undertaker by one of Singer's Midgets, but he got well; and some "Windsor" chairs in which the only position you could get comfortable was to stand up behind them and lean your elbows on their back.

Not one piece that matched another, and not one piece of mahogany anywhere. And the ceiling, between the beams, had apparently been plastered by a workman who was that way, too.

"Some day soon I hope to have a piano," said Mrs. Dwan. "I can't live much longer without one. But so far I haven't been able to find one that would fit in."

"Listen," I said. "I've got a piano in storage that belonged to my mother. It's a mahogany upright and not so big that it wouldn't fit in this room, especially when you get that 'trough' table out. It isn't doing me any good and I'll sell it to you for $250. Mother paid $1,250 for it new."

"Oh, I couldn't think of taking it!" said Mrs. Dwan.

"I'll make it $200 even just because you're a friend of Florence's," I said.

"Really, I couldn't!" said Mrs. Dwan.

"You wouldn't have to pay for it all at once," I said.

"Don't you see," said Florence, "that a mahogany upright piano would be a perfect horror in here? Mildred wouldn't have it as a gift, let alone buy it. It isn't in the period."

"She could get it tuned," I said.

The answer to this was, "I'll show you the up-stairs now and we can look at the dining-room later on."

We were led to the guest-chamber. The bed was a maple four-poster, with pineapple posts, and a "tester" running from pillar to post. You would think a "tester" might be a man that went around trying out beds, but it's really a kind of frame that holds a canopy over the bed in case it rains and the roof leaks. There was a quilt made by Mrs. Dwan's great-grandmother, Mrs. Anthony Adams, in 1859, at Lowell, Mass. How is that for a memory?

"This used to be the hay-loft," said Mrs. Dwan.

"You ought to have left some of the hay so the guests could hit it," I said.

The dressers, or chests of drawers, and the chairs were all made of maple. And the same in the Dwans' own room; everything maple.

"If you had maple in one room and mahogany in the other," I said, "people wouldn't get confused when you told them that so and so was up in Maple's room."

Dwan laughed, but the women didn't.

The maid hollered up that dinner was ready.

"The cocktails aren't ready," said Dwan.

"You will have to go without them," said Mrs. Dwan. "The soup will be cold."

This put me in a great mood to admire the "sawbuck" table and the "slat back" chairs, which were evidently the *chef-d'œuvre* and the *pièce de résistance* of the *chez Dwan*.

"It came all the way from Pennsylvania," said Mildred, when Florence's outcries, brought on by her first look at the table, had died down. "Mother picked it up at a little place near Stroudsburg and sent it to me. It only cost $550, and the chairs were $45 apiece."

"How reasonable!" exclaimed Florence.

That was before she had sat in one of them. Only one thing was more unreasonable than the chairs, and that was the table itself, consisting of big planks nailed together and laid onto a railroad tie, supported underneath by a whole forest of cross-pieces and beams. The surface was as smooth on top as the trip to Catalina Island and all around the edges, great big divots had been taken out with some blunt instrument, probably a bayonet. There were stains and scorch marks that Florence fairly crowed over, but when I tried to add to the general ensemble by laying a lighted cigaret right down beside my soup-plate, she and both the Dwans yelled murder and made me take it off.

They planted me in an end seat, a location just right for a man who had stretched himself across a railway track and had both legs cut off at the abdomen. Not being that kind of man, I had to sit so far back that very few of my comestibles carried more than half-way to their target.

After dinner I was all ready to go home and get something to eat, but it had been darkening up outdoors for half an hour and now such a storm broke that I knew it was useless trying to persuade Florence to make a start.

"We'll play some bridge," said Dwan, and to my surprise he produced a card-table that was nowhere near "in the period."

At my house there was a big center chandelier that lighted up a bridge game no matter in what part of the room the table was put. But here we had to waste forty minutes moving lamps and wires and stands and when they were all fixed, you could tell a red suit from a black suit, but not a spade from a club. Aside from that and the granite-bottomed "Windsor" chairs and the fact that we played "families" for a cent a point and Florence and I won $12 and didn't get paid, it was one of the pleasantest afternoons I ever spent gambling.

The rain stopped at five o'clock and as we splashed through the puddles of Dwan's driveway, I remarked to Florence that I had never known she was such a kidder.

"What do you mean?" she asked me.

"Why, your pretending to admire all that junk," I said.

"Junk!" said Florence. "That is one of the most beautifully furnished homes I have ever seen!"

And so far as I can recall, that was her last utterance in my presence for six nights and five days.

At lunch on Saturday I said: "You know I like the silent drama one evening a week, but not twenty-four hours a day every day. What's the matter with you? If it's laryngitis, you might write me notes."

"I'll tell you what's the matter!" she burst out. "I hate this house and everything in it! It's too new! Everything shines! I loathe new things! I want a home like Mildred's, with things in it that I can look at without blushing for shame. I can't invite anyone here. It's too hideous. And I'll never be happy here a single minute as long as I live!"

Well, I don't mind telling that this kind of got under my

skin. As if I hadn't intended to give her a pleasant surprise! As if Wolfe Brothers, in business thirty years, didn't know how to furnish a home complete! I was pretty badly hurt, but I choked it down and said, as calmly as I could:

"If you'll be a little patient, I'll try to sell this house and its contents for what I paid for it and them. It oughtn't to be much trouble; there are plenty of people around who know a bargain. But it's too bad you didn't confess your barn complex to me long ago. Only last February, old Ken Garrett had to sell his establishment and the men who bought it turned it into a garage. It was a livery-stable which I could have got for the introduction of a song, or maybe just the vamp. And we wouldn't have had to spend a nickel to make it as nice and comfortable and homey as your friend Mildred's dump."

Florence was on her way upstairs before I had finished my speech.

I went down to Earl Benham's to see if my new suit was ready. It was and I put it on and left the old one to be cleaned and pressed.

On the street I met Harry Cross.

"Come up to my office," he said. "There's something in my desk that may interest you."

I accepted his invitation and from three different drawers he pulled out three different quart bottles of Early American rye.

Just before six o'clock I dropped in Kane's store and bought myself a pair of shears, a blow torch and an ax. I started home, but stopped among the trees inside my front gate and cut big holes in my coat and trousers. Alongside the path to the house was a sizable mud puddle. I waded in it. And I bathed my gray felt hat.

Florence was sitting on the floor of the living-room, reading. She seemed a little upset by my appearance.

"Good heavens! What's happened?"

"Nothing much," said I. "I just didn't want to look too new."

"What are those things you're carrying?"

"Just a pair of shears, a blow torch and an ax. I'm going to try and antique this place and I think I'll begin on the dining-room table."

Florence went into her scream, dashed upstairs and locked

herself in. I went about my work and had the dinner-table looking pretty Early when the maid smelled fire and rushed in. She rushed out again and came back with a pitcher of water. But using my vest as a snuffer, I had had the flames under control all the while and there was nothing for her to do.

"I'll just nick it up a little with this ax," I told her, "and by the time I'm through, dinner ought to be ready."

"It will never be ready as far as I'm concerned," she said. "I'm leaving just as soon as I can pack."

And Florence had the same idea—vindicating the old adage about great minds.

I heard the front door slam and the back door slam, and I felt kind of tired and sleepy, so I knocked off work and went up to bed.

That's my side of the story, Eddie, and it's true so help me my bootlegger. Which reminds me that the man who sold Harry the rye makes this town once a week, or did when this was written. He's at the Belden every Tuesday from nine to six and his name is Mike Farrell.

Old Folks' Christmas

Tom and Grace Carter sat in their living-room on Christmas Eve, sometimes talking, sometimes pretending to read and all the time thinking things they didn't want to think. Their two children, Junior, aged nineteen, and Grace, two years younger, had come home that day from their schools for the Christmas vacation. Junior was in his first year at the university and Grace attending a boarding-school that would fit her for college.

I won't call them Grace and Junior any more, though that is the way they had been christened. Junior had changed his name to Ted and Grace was now Caroline, and thus they insisted on being addressed, even by their parents. This was one of the things Tom and Grace the elder were thinking of as they sat in their living-room Christmas Eve.

Other university freshmen who had lived here had returned on the twenty-first, the day when the vacation was supposed to begin. Ted had telegraphed that he would be three days late owing to a special examination which, if he passed it, would lighten the terrific burden of the next term. He had arrived at home looking so pale, heavy-eyed and shaky that his mother doubted the wisdom of the concentrated mental effort, while his father secretly hoped the stuff had been non-poisonous and would not have lasting effects. Caroline, too, had been behind schedule, explaining that her laundry had gone astray and she had not dared trust others to trace it for her.

Grace and Tom had attempted, with fair success, to conceal their disappointment over this delayed home-coming and had continued with their preparations for a Christmas that would thrill their children and consequently themselves. They had bought an imposing lot of presents, costing twice or three times as much as had been Tom's father's annual income when Tom was Ted's age, or Tom's own income a year ago, before General Motors' acceptance of his new weather-proof paint had enabled him to buy this suburban home and luxuries such as his own parents and Grace's had never dreamed of, and to give Ted and Caroline advantages that he and Grace had perforce gone without.

Behind the closed door of the music-room was the elaborately decked tree. The piano and piano bench and the floor around the tree were covered with beribboned packages of all sizes, shapes and weights, one of them addressed to Tom, another to Grace, a few to the servants and the rest to Ted and Caroline. A huge box contained a sealskin coat for Caroline, a coat that had cost as much as the Carters had formerly paid a year for rent. Even more expensive was a "set" of jewelry consisting of an opal brooch, a bracelet of opals and gold filigree, and an opal ring surrounded by diamonds.

Grace always had preferred opals to any other stone, but now that she could afford them, some inhibition prevented her from buying them for herself; she could enjoy them much more adorning her pretty daughter. There were boxes of silk stockings, lingerie, gloves and handkerchiefs. And for Ted, a three-hundred-dollar watch, a de-luxe edition of Balzac, an expensive bag of shiny, new steel-shafted golf-clubs and the last word in portable phonographs.

But the big surprise for the boy was locked in the garage, a black Gorham sedan, a model more up to date and better-looking than Tom's own year-old car that stood beside it. Ted could use it during the vacation if the mild weather continued and could look forward to driving it around home next spring and summer, there being a rule at the university forbidding undergraduates the possession or use of private automobiles.

Every year for sixteen years, since Ted was three and Caroline one, it had been the Christmas Eve custom of the Carters to hang up their children's stockings and fill them with inexpensive toys. Tom and Grace had thought it would be fun to continue the custom this year; the contents of the stockings—a mechanical negro dancing doll, music-boxes, a kitten that meowed when you pressed a spot on her back, et cetera—would make the "kids" laugh. And one of Grace's first pronouncements to her returned offspring was that they must go to bed early so Santa Claus would not be frightened away.

But it seemed they couldn't promise to make it so terribly early. They both had long-standing dates in town. Caroline

was going to dinner and a play with Beatrice Murdock and
Beatrice's nineteen-year-old brother Paul. The latter would
call for her in his car at half past six. Ted had accepted an invitation to see the hockey match with two classmates, Herb
Castle and Bernard King. He wanted to take his father's
Gorham, but Tom told him untruthfully that the foot-brake
was not working; Ted must be kept out of the garage till to-
morrow morning.

Ted and Caroline had taken naps in the afternoon and gone
off together in Paul Murdock's stylish roadster, giving their
word that they would be back by midnight or a little later and
that tomorrow night they would stay home.

And now their mother and father were sitting up for them,
because the stockings could not be filled and hung till they
were safely in bed, and also because trying to go to sleep is a
painful and hopeless business when you are kind of jumpy.

"What time is it?" asked Grace, looking up from the third
page of a book that she had begun to "read" soon after dinner.

"Half past two," said her husband. (He had answered the
same question every fifteen or twenty minutes since midnight.)

"You don't suppose anything could have happened?" said
Grace.

"We'd have heard if there had," said Tom.

"It isn't likely, of course," said Grace, "but they might have
had an accident some place where nobody was there to report
it or telephone or anything. We don't know what kind of a
driver the Murdock boy is."

"He's Ted's age. Boys that age may be inclined to drive too
fast, but they drive pretty well."

"How do you know?"

"Well, I've watched some of them drive."

"Yes, but not all of them."

"I doubt whether anybody in the world has seen every
nineteen-year-old boy drive."

"Boys these days seem so kind of irresponsible."

"Oh, don't worry! They probably met some of their young
friends and stopped for a bite to eat or something." Tom got
up and walked to the window with studied carelessness. "It's a
pretty night," he said. "You can see every star in the sky."

But he wasn't looking at the stars. He was looking down the

road for headlights. There were none in sight and after a few moments he returned to his chair.

"What time is it?" asked Grace.

"Twenty-two of," he said.

"Of what?"

"Of three."

"Your watch must have stopped. Nearly an hour ago you told me it was half past two."

"My watch is all right. You probably dozed off."

"I haven't closed my eyes."

"Well, it's time you did. Why don't you go to bed?"

"Why don't *you*?"

"I'm not sleepy."

"Neither am I. But honestly, Tom, it's silly for you to stay up. I'm just doing it so I can fix the stockings, and because I feel so wakeful. But there's no use of your losing your sleep."

"I couldn't sleep a wink till they're home."

"That's foolishness! There's nothing to worry about. They're just having a good time. You were young once yourself."

"That's just it! When I was young, I was young." He picked up his paper and tried to get interested in the shipping news.

"What time is it?" asked Grace.

"Five minutes of three."

"Maybe they're staying at the Murdocks' all night."

"They'd have let us know."

"They were afraid to wake us up, telephoning."

At three-twenty a car stopped at the front gate.

"There they are!"

"I told you there was nothing to worry about."

Tom went to the window. He could just discern the outlines of the Murdock boy's roadster, whose lighting system seemed to have broken down.

"He hasn't any lights," said Tom. "Maybe I'd better go out and see if I can fix them."

"No, don't!" said Grace sharply. "He can fix them himself. He's just saving them while he stands still."

"Why don't they come in?"

"They're probably making plans."

"They can make them in here. I'll go out and tell them we're still up."

"No, don't!" said Grace as before, and Tom obediently remained at the window.

It was nearly four when the car lights flashed on and the car drove away. Caroline walked into the house and stared dazedly at her parents.

"Heavens! What are you doing up?"

Tom was about to say something, but Grace forestalled him.

"We were talking over old Christmases," she said. "Is it very late?"

"I haven't any idea," said Caroline.

"Where is Ted?"

"Isn't he home? I haven't seen him since we dropped him at the hockey place."

"Well, you go right to bed," said her mother. "You must be worn out."

"I am, kind of. We danced after the play. What time is breakfast?"

"Eight o'clock."

"Oh, Mother, can't you make it nine?"

"I guess so. You used to want to get up early on Christmas."

"I know, but——"

"Who brought you home?" asked Tom.

"Why, Paul Murdock—and Beatrice."

"You look rumpled."

"They made me sit in the 'rumple' seat."

She laughed at her joke, said good night and went upstairs. She had not come even within hand-shaking distance of her father and mother.

"The Murdocks," said Tom, "must have great manners, making their guest ride in that uncomfortable seat."

Grace was silent.

"You go to bed, too," said Tom. "I'll wait for Ted."

"You couldn't fix the stockings."

"I won't try. We'll have time for that in the morning; I mean, later in the morning."

"I'm not going to bed till you do," said Grace.

"All right, we'll both go. Ted ought not to be long now. I suppose his friends will bring him home. We'll hear him when he comes in."

There was no chance not to hear him when, at ten minutes

before six, he came in. He had done his Christmas shopping late and brought home a package.

Grace was downstairs again at half past seven, telling the servants breakfast would be postponed till nine. She nailed the stockings beside the fireplace, went into the music-room to see that nothing had been disturbed and removed Ted's hat and overcoat from where he had carefully hung them on the hall floor.

Tom appeared a little before nine and suggested that the children ought to be awakened.

"I'll wake them," said Grace, and went upstairs. She opened Ted's door, looked, and softly closed it again. She entered her daughter's room and found Caroline semiconscious.

"Do I have to get up now? Honestly I can't eat anything. If you could just have Molla bring me some coffee. Ted and I are both invited to the Murdocks' for breakfast at half past twelve, and I could sleep for another hour or two."

"But dearie, don't you know we have Christmas dinner at one?"

"It's a shame, Mother, but I thought of course our dinner would be at night."

"Don't you want to see your presents?"

"Certainly I do, but can't they wait?"

Grace was about to go to the kitchen to tell the cook that dinner would be at seven instead of one, but she remembered having promised Signe the afternoon and evening off, as a cold, light supper would be all anyone wanted after the heavy midday meal.

Tom and Grace breakfasted alone and once more sat in the living-room, talking, thinking and pretending to read.

"You ought to speak to Caroline," said Tom.

"I will, but not today. It's Christmas."

"And I intend to say a few words to Ted."

"Yes, dear, you must. But not today."

"I suppose they'll be out again tonight."

"No, they promised to stay home. We'll have a nice cozy evening."

"Don't bet too much on that," said Tom.

At noon the "children" made their entrance and responded to their parents' salutations with almost the proper warmth. Ted declined a cup of coffee and he and Caroline apologized for making a "breakfast" date at the Murdocks'.

"Sis and I both thought you'd be having dinner at seven, as usual."

"We've always had it at one o'clock on Christmas," said Tom.

"I'd forgotten it was Christmas," said Ted.

"Well, those stockings ought to remind you."

Ted and Caroline looked at the bulging stockings.

"Isn't there a tree?" asked Caroline.

"Of course," said her mother. "But the stockings come first."

"We've only a little time," said Caroline. "We'll be terribly late as it is. So can't we see the tree now?"

"I guess so," said Grace, and led the way into the music-room.

The servants were summoned and the tree stared at and admired.

"You must open your presents," said Grace to her daughter.

"I can't open them all now," said Caroline. "Tell me which is special."

The cover was removed from the huge box and Grace held up the coat.

"Oh, Mother!" said Caroline. "A sealskin coat!"

"Put it on," said her father.

"Not now. We haven't time."

"Then look at this!" said Grace, and opened the case of jewels.

"Oh, Mother! Opals!" said Caroline.

"They're my favorite stone," said Grace quietly.

"If nobody minds," said Ted, "I'll postpone my personal investigation till we get back. I know I'll like everything you've given me. But if we have no car in working order, I've got to call a taxi and catch a train."

"You can drive in," said his father.

"Did you fix the brake?"

"I think it's all right. Come up to the garage and we'll see."

Ted got his hat and coat and kissed his mother good-by.

"Mother," he said, "I know you'll forgive me for not having any presents for you and Dad. I was so rushed the last three days at school. And I thought I'd have time to shop a little when we got in yesterday, but I was in too much of a hurry to be home. Last night, everything was closed."

"Don't worry," said Grace. "Christmas is for young people. Dad and I have everything we want."

The servants had found their gifts and disappeared, express-ing effusive Scandinavian thanks.

Caroline and her mother were left alone.

"Mother, where did the coat come from?"

"Lloyd and Henry's."

"They keep all kinds of furs, don't they?"

"Yes."

"Would you mind horribly if I exchanged this?"

"Certainly not, dear. You pick out anything you like, and if it's a little more expensive, it won't make any difference. We can go in town tomorrow or next day. But don't you want to wear your opals to the Murdocks'?"

"I don't believe so. They might get lost or something. And I'm not—well, I'm not so crazy about——"

"I think they can be exchanged, too," said Grace. "You run along now and get ready to start."

Caroline obeyed with alacrity, and Grace spent a welcome moment by herself.

Tom opened the garage door.

"Why, you've got two cars!" said Ted.

"The new one isn't mine," said Tom.

"Whose is it?"

"Yours. It's the new model."

"Dad, that's wonderful! But it looks just like the old one."

"Well, the old one's pretty good. Just the same, yours is bet-ter. You'll find that out when you drive it. Hop in and get started. I had her filled with gas."

"I think I'd rather drive the old one."

"Why?"

"Well, what I really wanted, Dad, was a Barnes sport road-ster, something like Paul Murdock's, only a different color scheme. And if I don't drive this Gorham at all, maybe you could get them to take it back or make some kind of a deal with the Barnes people."

Tom didn't speak till he was sure of his voice. Then: "All right, son. Take my car and I'll see what can be done about yours."

Caroline, waiting for Ted, remembered something and called to her mother. "Here's what I got for you and Dad," she said. "It's two tickets to 'Jolly Jane,' the play I saw last night. You'll love it!"

"When are they for?" asked Grace.

"Tonight," said Caroline.

"But dearie," said her mother, "we don't want to go out tonight, when you promised to stay home."

"We'll keep our promise," said Caroline, "but the Murdocks may drop in and bring some friends and we'll dance and there'll be music. And Ted and I both thought you'd rather be away somewhere so our noise wouldn't disturb you."

"It was sweet of you to do this," said her mother, "but your father and I don't mind noise as long as you're enjoying yourselves."

"It's time anyway that you and Dad had a treat."

"The real treat," said Grace, "would be to spend a quiet evening here with just you two."

"The Murdocks practically invited themselves and I couldn't say no after they'd been so nice to me. And honestly, Mother, you'll love this play!"

"Will you be home for supper?"

"I'm pretty sure we will, but if we're a little late, don't you and Dad wait for us. Take the seven-twenty so you won't miss anything. The first act is really the best. We probably won't be hungry, but have Signe leave something out for us in case we are."

Tom and Grace sat down to the elaborate Christmas dinner and didn't make much impression on it. Even if they had had any appetite, the sixteen-pound turkey would have looked almost like new when they had eaten their fill. Conversation was intermittent and related chiefly to Signe's excellence as a cook and the mildness of the weather. Children and Christmas were barely touched on.

Tom merely suggested that on account of its being a holiday and their having theatre tickets, they ought to take the six-ten and eat supper at the Metropole. His wife said no; Ted and Caroline might come home and be disappointed at not finding them. Tom seemed about to make some remark, but changed his mind.

The afternoon was the longest Grace had ever known. The children were still absent at seven and she and Tom taxied to the train. Neither talked much on the way to town. As for the play, which Grace was sure to love, it turned out to be a rehash of "Cradle Snatchers" and "Sex," retaining the worst features of each.

When it was over, Tom said: "Now I'm inviting you to the Cove Club. You didn't eat any breakfast or dinner or supper and I can't have you starving to death on a feast-day. Besides, I'm thirsty as well as hungry."

They ordered the special *table d'hôte* and struggled hard to get away with it. Tom drank six high-balls, but they failed to produce the usual effect of making him jovial. Grace had one high-ball and some kind of cordial that gave her a warm, contented feeling for a moment. But the warmth and contentment left her before the train was half way home.

The living-room looked as if Von Kluck's army had just passed through. Ted and Caroline had kept their promise up to a certain point. They had spent part of the evening at home, and the Murdocks must have brought all their own friends and everybody else's, judging from the results. The tables and floors were strewn with empty glasses, ashes and cigaret stubs. The stockings had been torn off their nails and the wrecked contents were all over the place. Two sizable holes had been burnt in Grace's favorite rug.

Tom took his wife by the arm and led her into the music-room.

"You never took the trouble to open your own present," he said.

"And I think there's one for you, too," said Grace. "They didn't come in here," she added, "so I guess there wasn't much dancing or music."

Tom found his gift from Grace, a set of diamond studs and cuff buttons for festive wear. Grace's present from him was an opal ring.

"Oh, Tom!" she said.

"We'll have to go out somewhere tomorrow night, so I can break these in," said Tom.

"Well, if we do that, we'd better get a good night's rest."

"I'll beat you upstairs," said Tom.

UNCOLLECTED STORIES

Second-Act Curtain

THEY WERE trying out a play in Newark. The play was to open in New York the following week. Washington had liked it pretty well and business had been picking up in the big New Jersey metropolis until a full house at a rainy Wednesday matinée had just about convinced the authors and the manager that they had something.

The three were standing in the lobby before the evening performance.

"We'd be all set," said Mr. Rose, the manager, "if we just had a curtain for the second act."

The authors, Mr. Chambers and Mr. Booth, walked away from him as fast as they could go. Neither of them wanted the blood, even of a manager, on his hands; and they had been told so often—by the manager, the company manager, various house managers, the entire office staff, every member of the cast and the citizens of New Jersey and the District of Columbia—that they lacked a second-act curtain (just as if it were news to them), that both had spent most of their prospective profits on scimitars, stiletti, grenades and sawed-off shotguns, and it was only a question of time before some of these trinkets would be brought into play.

After a while the good folks from the Oranges and Montclair began looming up in such numbers that Chambers and Booth thought Mr. Rose's mind might be on some other subject and they ventured back into the lobby.

"Boys," said Mr. Rose, "we've got a hit. If we only—"

Chambers grabbed Booth by the arm.

"Come here a minute," he commanded, and Booth obeyed.

"Now, listen," said Chambers, "we're not going to find a second-act curtain by watching another performance of this clambake. Let's leave it flat for tonight and go to our respective homes and do a little real thinking."

Chambers' respective home was a mansion in the lower sixties. Booth's was a hotel room in which he had spent nearly all of the summer working, because he found it impossible to work out on Long Island where everybody else was having a good time. The collaborators parted at the Thirty-third Street terminal of the Hudson Tube and Booth went first to a speakeasy to buy himself some thinking powders and then to his room—the number doesn't make any difference because each is equipped with radio, and all you have to do to avoid it is not open the drawer of the table by the bed.

Booth's room was not an expensive room. It was a $4.00 room and opened on a court, and the people in the other rooms opening on the court were nice and friendly and hardly ever pulled down their window shades, no matter what they were doing. For three days the room right across the court from Booth's had been occupied by a comely and frank lady of about twenty-six, so Booth took a powder before settling down to real thinking. The room across the court was dark. Booth got into his thinking costume, consisting of pajamas, slippers and bathrobe, had another powder and decided he had better eat something.

While waiting for the food, he began a letter to somebody at Syracuse University who didn't know him and wanted him to make a speech. He discovered that the *I* key on the typewriter had gone blooey from overwork, rendering him mute. The food came and he sat on the bed to eat it. There was a knock at the door and in scampered a chambermaid not a day over fifty.

"Are you sick?" she said.

"No," said Booth. "Why?"

"Well," said the chambermaid, "there was a woman sick in this room a couple of weeks ago and I thought maybe she was still here."

"You're the only woman in this room," said Booth, "and I hope you're not too sick to leave."

"It's a funny thing," said the chambermaid, "but I came in a room along this hall one time, it must have been last spring, and there was a man and a woman both in there, both sick. And they knew me because I worked in a hospital once and they were both there, too."

"Marriage might regain something of its former sanctity," observed Booth, "if husbands and wives were always both sick together."

"I'll just turn down your bed."

"No. Let it alone. I'll fix it when I get ready."

"Well, I wouldn't sit around like that or you'll catch cold."

"Good night."

Booth finished eating and looked around the room for reading matter. There were three books—Heart Throbs, a collection, by Joe Mitchell Chapple of Boston, of favorite bits of verse or prose of well-known Americans; Holy Bible, anonymous, but a palpable steal of Gideon's novel of the same name, and the Insidious Dr. Fu Manchu, by Sax Rohmer. Booth had seen them on the desk all summer, but had been too busy to read when the *I* key was working.

He took another powder and started in on the insidious Chink, but the author's quaint method of handling direct discourse ("Too small by inches!" he jerked; "The pigtail again!" rapped Weymouth; "Is 'Parson Dan'?" rapped Smith; "But," rapped Smith; "Got any theory?" he jerked) was a little too much for frayed nerves. "It is all right," he rapped to himself, "for a guest to bring a book like this with him, but there certainly ought to be a penalty for leaving it in the room."

Holy Bible began too slow and after another powder Booth dived into Heart Throbs, only to be confronted by the complete text of Home, Sweet Home. Now out in the town where Booth's family was spending the summer the natives had pointed with pride to the house where Mr. Payne, who wrote this famous lyric, used to live. If the natives had ever read the whole thing, they probably would have burned the house instead of pointing to it.

Turning over a few pages, however, Booth came across a poem that soon had him fighting to keep back the tears. It told about a mother who often cried at the memory of the good times she used to have, before she was married and gave birth to a little one, but who felt all right again when the little one reminded her of her present blessings by climbing on her knee—

> *And she says and twists a curl:*
> *"I am Mamma's baby dirl!"*
> *And the while I bless my lot*
> *Whispers: "Mamma had fordot!"*

And another whose first stanza ran:

When you see a man in woe,
Walk right up and say, "Hello!"
Say, "Hello!" and "How d'ye do?
How's the world been using you?"
Slap the fellow on his back,
Bring your hand down with a whack;
Waltz straight up and don't go slow,
Shake his hand and say, "Hullo!"

For a brief moment Booth considered dressing again, engaging a taxi, driving to Chambers' house, waltzing straight up to Chambers' room, bringing his hand down with a whack on Chambers' shoulder and saying, "Hullo, and how d'ye do, and how's your second-act curtain?" But he hadn't had enough powders.

While the waiter was removing the tray, he took another one and looked across at the opposite room. Strangely, the shade was down.

Booth lay on his bed, with glass and bottle beside him, for half an hour. Inspiration came to him. The second act should end with a song. But he'd better call up Chambers and get his approval.

"Why, sure," said Chambers. "Only it's got to be damn' funny."

"Have you had any ideas yourself?"

"Not yet. I've been reading. You realize, of course, that a line or a piece of business would be better than a song unless the song's damn' funny."

"But I can't think of a line or a piece of business."

"Then go ahead with your song, and be sure it's damn' funny."

Booth hung up and took a drink. In a room devoid of musical instruments he had to compose a song that would be a curtain, would make an audience laugh, would be damn' funny.

He looked across the court and saw the light in the girl's room flash on and then off.

He pictured her as a buyer from St. Louis or Cincinnati. She worked hard all day while he attended rehearsals, or while he sat there in his own room and attempted to think up lines dumb audiences would laugh at, as substitutes for lines that they wouldn't. He wondered whether she was dumb.

In the evening she came back to her $4.00 cell, and perhaps changed her clothes and went to a picture, or sat in the grill or on the roof and dined alone and wished there were someone for her to dance with when the orchestra played Here Am I.

After her solitary dinner or the pictures, she probably went to bed and read the confessions of John Gilbert and Rudy Vallée until she fell asleep.

It was a shame, thought Booth, that the conventions and his arduous work kept him from calling her up and perhaps taking her to dinner or a show, or merely carrying on friendly conversations with her so she would not be quite so homesick.

He fell asleep and was awakened by the telephone at half past two.

"Listen," said the voice of Mr. Rose, "we've got a show if we find a curtain for that second act. They liked everything but that tonight. You fellas have got to dig up a curtain by tomorrow."

"I think I've got an idea."

"Well, I hope it's good."

Booth began to hum different people's tunes to himself. Tunes lots of times suggest words; it's customary and much more satisfactory to get the tune first—

He looked across the court once more. The lights were on, only the thin shade was down, and he could see a man in shirt sleeves standing in the middle of the room.

"Well," thought Booth, "she's married and I've been wasting all my sympathy. A girl that's married may not be having a good time, but at least she isn't alone."

For some reason, however, he felt resentful and the drink he took was three times as big as its predecessors. So, she was married—

Suddenly there flashed into his head one of the prettiest tunes he had ever heard. He grabbed a piece of music manuscript paper and wrote a lead sheet of half the refrain.

"It will be all the better," he thought, "if I can get some silly, incongruous words to such a pretty melody as this."

He set down what he considered an amusing line and was at work on a second when the telephone rang again.

"This is Rose. I was thinking maybe you'd better tell me something about your idea for a curtain."

"It's a song. I've got it half done."

"You might just as well quit working on it. We can't drop on a song. It's got to be a gag."

"But suppose the song is a gag—"

"No, I tell you we can't ring down on a song. We've got too many of them. This is no musical. Just forget that idea and work on another."

Booth tried to answer, but Mr. Rose had hung up.

"Whether we ring down on it or not," Booth said to the bottle, "we can use it somewhere."

But in the middle of the third line of the lyric a terrible hunch came to him. He had heard the tune before. Where? Why, back at home in the Episcopal church choir. Only there it had been in nine-eight or something, and now it was four-four. "The strife is o'er, the battle done."

"I won't give up till I'm sure," he said to himself.

There was one composer in town who, chances were, would be up at this time of night, five or ten minutes past three. It was quite a job to grab hold of the telephone, but Booth finally managed it.

"Well, whistle it or hum it, but do it quick because I'm working," said Mr. Youmans.

Booth whistled the refrain, though whistling was difficult.

"I like it very much," said Mr. Youmans.

"But isn't it a hymn? I seem to have heard it in church."

"It's a hymn all right," said Mr. Youmans, "but I don't think you heard it in church. I'm sure I never did."

"No. I can imagine that."

"But I can tell you where you did hear it."

"Where?"

"Do you remember the morning you came to my Great Day rehearsal? That's where you heard it. It's the Negroes' hymn that opens the second act."

Booth tore up his sheet of music paper and looked across the court. Clearly visible was the silhouette of the gentleman putting on his coat and hat.

Booth lunged for the telephone again.

"I'll call her up," he thought. "I'll tell her I'm sorry her husband has to go to work so early."

The operator answered in a voice as thick and sleepy as his own.

"Listen," he said, "what's the number of the room right across the court from me?"

"I don't know, and if I did I wouldn't tell you."

"But I've got something important to say."

"You sound like it. Anyway, you tell it to me and I'll deliver the message."

"All right," said Booth. "You tell her I've been in my room alone all evening, trying to think up a second-act curtain. And I can't think of one."

At seven in the morning he was aroused by strange noises that issued forth from the telephone receiver, which was off the hook, and the cord of which was looped around his neck.

"Will you please hang up your receiver?" said the operator.

"I will if you'll send me the house detective."

"All right."

A house detective appeared before Booth had a chance to get back to sleep.

"Officer," said the latter, "there was somebody in this room last night."

"It looks it."

"When I came in, I brought a full bottle of pretty good stuff. I had my dinner, I worked a little and read a little, and then I went to sleep. Ten minutes ago I woke up to find the bottle empty and the telephone cord twisted around my neck as if someone had tried to strangle me."

"Go back to sleep," said the detective, "and give me time to run down clues. I think we will find that both crimes—the emptying of the bottle and the displacement of the telephone receiver—were the work of one man."

Bob's Birthday

THIS IS my first attempt at writing a story, and I would not have courage to make the attempt only for a friend of Bob's who is editor of a magazine named Mr. Bishop encouraging me to make the attempt, and also because there is nothing I would stoop so low as to make money in order to relieve some of the burden from Bob's shoulders as he seems to be carrying everybody in the world's burden on his shoulders. At first I thought I would try and write a detective story about a mystery, but he said to write about a subject I am more conversant, I mean Mr. Bishop, and he suggested a story about some incident in my home life. So he being the editor, I am taking his advice and writing a story about an incident in my home life, and I only wish it could be more exciting, but all I can do is hope that we will soon have a murder in the family or somebody will die so that when I write my next (?) story it will be really exciting with a murder or at least an inquest in the plot.

Our name is Tyler and my bother Bob is 17 years of age and a born musician and plays the saxophone and clarinet in Belden's Orchestra and makes arrangements for the orchestra of new pieces and Mr. Belden pays him a salary of $150.00 per week. How is that for only 17 years of age? But it is just awful the way he has to work and has been supporting the family for two years, ever since my father lost his position with Kemp and Warren. During the daytime Bob is either making records or writing arrangements or attending rehearsals, and from dinner time on they play engagements at some restaurant till 3 or 4 o'clock in the morning, and they broadcast every Wednesday night and several weeks every year they play engagements at some theater like the Paramount or Capitol or Palace.

It is funny sometimes how different a person's plans turn out than the way they planned them. Two years ago Bob was a junior in high school and desperately in love with Kathleen Dennis, whose father is president of Dennis & Co. and has a chair in the Stock Exchange Market. No girl could help loving Bob, and Kathleen loved him and they were engaged, but her father did not like him just being a musician though even at that time Bob had offers from Mr. Belden and other good orchestras to join their orchestras. But in order to please Mr. Dennis, Bob said he would graduate from high school and then work his way through Yale or some big university by forming an orchestra like Rudy Vallée and would learn some profession like medicine or a lawyer, and Mr. Dennis liked this idea because he said it showed that Bob had the right stuff in him, and he said that it would take 8 or 9 years for Bob to carry out this idea and by that time I guess he thought Bob and Kathleen would be tired of each other, though I am 14 years of age myself and have lived with Bob all that time and never got tired of him. But Kathleen said that was different because a sister might get so she could not bear the sight of her brother and what could she do about it, but if it was her husband she could get rid of him.

Anyways my father lost his position and Bob not only had to give up his plans for college, but also quit high school and go with Belden's Orchestra, and he has been supporting my mother and father and myself ever since because my father does not seem able to secure another position and Bob says positions are very hard to secure these days especially when a person tries to secure them by playing contract every afternoon and spending all their evenings at the club like my mother and father and my Aunt Lucille and Uncle George. They say they go there to forget and pretend things are like they used to be, and I would say there is very little difference at that, judging from the noise when they come home.

I forgot to tell you about my uncle and aunt. Their name is Marshall and Uncle George is my mother's brother. He lost his position about the same time my father did his, and every time they cannot think of anything else to quarrel over, they quarrel over who lost his position first. My father claims he did and Uncle George claims he did and you would think that Congress was going to award the Legend of Honor to whomever could prove they had been out of work the longest time.

Anyways it was 3 or 4 months ago when my mother told Bob she had good news for him, that Uncle George and Aunt Lucille had decided to come and live with us and they would pay $25.00 per week, and though it meant that Bob would have to sleep on the divan in the living-room, he did not mind that as he never has time to sleep more than 2 or 3 hours and he is so dog tired that he says he could sleep on an arpeggio. He knew Uncle George's habits and rightly figured that he would not add much to our grocery bill because when he was out of a job he would only eat a light breakfast at home around noontime and go to the club for dinner and take Aunt Lucille with him the same as my father and mother or anyone else when they are drinking. But what Bob did not know was that Uncle George came to live with us because the people where he rented his apartment put him out for not paying his rent and he had no more money than my father himself, and like my father, he picked up the habit of borrowing gin money and taxi money from Bob, so that at the end of 3 months he had actually borrowed more than he owed us for board and lodging.

During the week before last, Belden's Orchestra had their first vacation in over a year and a half, due to them ending an engagement at the Crawford, and Mr. Belden arranged for them to take a week off before they begun their new engagement at the Maples. It was not really a vacation for Bob because he had to make arrangements for 5 new numbers and rehearse, and they did their regular broadcast on Wednesday night, but at least he was able to be home almost every other evening except Wednesday, and Mother promised that she and Dad would stay home for dinner 5 evenings that week just so we could get acquainted again. I can remember when they used to stay home 2 or 3 evenings a week and play backgammon or even read, and it was fun having them because they acted as if they liked us and enjoyed our company even though we were only their children. But that was a long time ago.

Secretly I hoped to myself that Aunt Lucille and Uncle George would keep on going out as usual. It only takes 1 drink now to make Uncle George as bad as he was the night before, and his conversation is always on 1 of 3 subjects, none of which are likely to add to the gayety of the occasion. Either he is asking Bob for $10.00 more or he is bragging about how long since he lost his job or he is quoting some violinist friend of his who says that real musicians look down on people who play the saxophone or clarinet. Bob is one of the best-natured persons in the world, but it is awfully hard for him to just laugh and take that last crack without replying when there are so many things he could say, especially to Uncle George. He admits that a saxophone is a kind of a mongrel instrument as he calls it, but nobody can play a clarinet as Bob plays it by just greasing their hair like Rudy Vallée. Besides, where would Uncle George and Dad get their gin if Bob had decided to spend these years in Europe learning to be a second Kreisler?

Well, my mother begged off for Monday evening, saying that she and my father and the Marshalls had been invited to the club by Mr. Gaines and they could not afford to refuse because there was a chance that Mr. Gaines might offer Dad a position. I did not see how he could very well do this as Mr. Gaines has no position himself, but there is no use arguing with Mother. They gave the same excuse for Tuesday night, only this time Mr. Sterrett was host and it was Uncle George who might get the job. No alibi was necessary for Wednesday, when Bob had his broadcast date, and on Thursday, Mother just said I would have to forgive her again, she had forgotten Bob and me and made an engagement at the club with the Lavelles. But I insisted on no excuses for Friday because it was Bob's birthday, and I also made her give me her word that she and Dad would buy him some kind of a present, even if it only cost them a dime of all the money he had loaned them in the past 2 years.

Personally I took some money of my own which I had saved up towards some clothes that I would simply have to have if Kathleen Dennis invited me for a week-end at Southampton as she promised, and I bought Bob a copy of the Life of Richard Wagner, a great German composer, and got Olga to make him a birthday cake.

There is two items that I have forgotten to mention, which shows how unexperienced I am as an authoress, and one of them is that Kathleen and Bob were still in love with each other all this time, but Mr. Dennis would not permit Kathleen to call it an engagement on account of the uncertainty of Bob's plans and you can hardly blame him as it looked like Bob would hardly be able to support a wife for some time to come in addition to Mother and Dad and myself and Uncle George and Aunt Lucille. The other item is my grandfather, who had a position as book-keeper with Silvers & Co. which paid him enough to pay for his room and board at Mrs. Hackley's, and he was still able to put a little in the savings bank every week so he would have enough to keep him when he was no longer able to work. That is, we thought he was one person whom we would not have to worry about, but it turned out different.

Well, the rest of my story is kind of embarrassing for me to put down in black and white. My father and mother and the Marshalls did not get home from their Thursday night party till 8 o'clock Friday morning. Mother and Aunt Lucille spent Friday in bed and came to Bob's birthday dinner in their kimona. Dad and Uncle George got up late in the afternoon and went out somewhere, Dad first borrowing $10.00 from Bob. I did not expect either of them to come home, but they did, at 8 o'clock, when the dinner was completely spoiled, and they brought Bob two presents, a bottle of gin and Grandfather.

Well, if there was ever a "happy birthday," Bob's was it. There was Aunt Lucille in her kimona and Uncle George with two days growth of beard neither of which were expected or wanted. There was Mother and Dad, who were welcome heaven knows, but not the way they felt or looked. There was Grandfather, who must have been rooming a couple of nights in a coal chute and celebrating some occasion of his own, because all he could do was take a drink of gin whenever they passed him Bob's "present," and no matter what you said to him, his answer was "Hotcha!"

If anybody had been hungry there would not have been nearly enough to go around, but even before the meal started, Bob and I were the only ones who could look at food without getting sick, and it was not long before our appetites were gone too. When Olga brought in the birthday cake, everyone suddenly remembered that it was Bob's birthday and congratulated him, that is if you could call Grandfather's "Hotcha!" a congratulation, and Dad got up and made a speech which was news to us and not good news either. He told us that Grandfather had joined the ranks of the unemployed three months ago, of which he and Uncle George were charter members, and that all of his savings had been spent paying for his room and board while he had sought in vain for a new position, that his landlady would give him no more credit and finally, to make a long story short, he (Dad) was giving him (Grandfather) to Bob for a birthday present. He added that it would only be for a little while as Grandfather is now 62 years of age and very few of the Tylers live much beyond eighty.

Almost before my father had finished speaking the doorbell rang. Well, it was Mr. Dennis and Kathleen.

They had come, so Mr. Dennis said, to wish Bob a happy birthday, and Kathleen had brought him a box of fudge which she had made herself. I knew that they had really come to spy on us, I mean Mr. Dennis, not Kathleen. To spy on us and to let Kathleen see what a mess she would be getting into if she ever married Bob.

She saw and she heard, and it did not take more than a minute. Mother and Aunt Lucille, sitting there in dirty kimonas, looking as if they had forgotten to brush their hair or even wash their hands. Dad and Uncle George and Grandfather, all of them dirty and unshaven and much the worse for gin. Bob standing up, trying and failing not to look ashamed.

"You are lucky to catch us all home at once," said my father. "It would not happen only for it being Bob's birthday."

"Bob is a fine young man," said Mr. Dennis. "You are fortunate in having such a good son."

"And you will be fortunate in getting such a good son-in-law," said my father.

"I hardly think it will come to that," said Mr. Dennis. "I would not ask Bob to assume any more financial responsibilities than he has already."

"If you were half a man," said my father, "you would relieve him of those responsibilities. Here is my brother-in-law, George Marshall, and myself and my father, all out of jobs through no fault of our own and all capable of filling any position that may be vacant in your office or any position you might create for us. It is men like you who are to blame for present conditions in this country. And now you come around here and hint that you are not going to allow your daughter to marry my son. Well, listen, Mr. Dennis, I will beat you to it. I would not allow my son to marry your daughter, not if she was the last girl in the world."

"That's talking!" said Uncle George.

"Hotcha!" said Grandfather.

"Come on, Kathie," said Mr. Dennis. "I think we have stayed at least long enough."

They went without saying good-night to anyone, not even Bob. Dad seemed to think he had done something wonderful and both Uncle George and Grandfather were praising him for what they called "speaking up."

When I could not stand it any longer, I ran into the living-room and threw myself on the divan. Bob followed me and patted me on the shoulder and told me not to worry.

"Worry!" I said. "But with Grandfather here, where will you sleep?"

"Well," he said, "it will hardly matter tonight because I do not expect to feel like sleeping. And thanks to you I have got Old Man Wagner, so I would rather read than sleep."

That is the story of Bob's birthday and I could go on and tell you what we did about the sleeping arrangements with my grandfather added to the family, but I am afraid the story is already like what Mr. Dennis said about his stay at our house, it is "at least long enough."

Poodle

Now, I won't tell you who I am, but if you want to ferret it out for yourself, call up Information and inquire for a fella that's married to a woman named Mary who says that when her husband's drinking, he talks a great deal too much. When he ain't drinking, he won't talk at all. Mary always gets mad at him when he's drinking, so she must figure that if he talks at all, it's too much. Like a Vice-President or something. I don't mean to imply that Vice-Presidents drink; in fact, I understand that their parents have warned the saloons not to sell it to them because statistics show that we're losing thousands of shade trees every year on account of kids, coming home from late parties, driving into big maples and elms to save their brake bands.

Where were we? Oh, yes, I was going to say that Mary's got all the best of it in our team. I have no objection to her drinking. I'm in favor of it, up to a certain point. If she stops before she comes to this point, why it don't do any good. But if she keeps on till she gets there, she falls asleep and quits talking.

Outside of me, the great sorrow in Mary's life is not having insomnia. It just about kills her to think that there's seven or eight hours out of the twenty-four when she ain't talking. I've tried to tell her that she talks in her sleep. She won't believe it because she always wakes up depressed.

I'm certainly out of talking practise; I keep wandering off the subject, if I was ever on it. Well, let's begin all over. I meant to say that every Christmas up to last Christmas, Waldron's always gave their employees a bonus of ten percent, and believe it or not, that meant six hundred dollars to the fella that's promised to rock you to sleep. As a matter of fact, it didn't really mean a dime; I just kept the check till I got home, and then I endorsed it and turned it over to Mary and she went ahead and spent it whatever way she wanted to, which was to help pay for a new car because the one she bought last year had cigaret ashes on the running board.

But when we girls and boys opened our envelops on the twenty-fourth of December this last ult., we got a big surprise.

It seems the old man had received a mash note from the Secretary of the Treasury and he'd read between the lines and found out that there was a temporary slump in business, and the only way to offset it was to turn over our bonus checks to some deserving charity on Wall Street. He enclosed a substitute for same in the form of an order on a couple of haberdashers, one for women and one for men, calling for fifty dollars' worth of pearl-handled suspenders for the high-salaried guys like myself and scaling all the way down to five-dollar certificates for the office boys and the little blond kid who had been playing guessing games with the telephone switchboard for three weeks.

Well, during the first week of my married life I'd passed a resolution to never tell Mary any bad news, and the result was that I'd practically become a mute except when I made a few local stops on the way home from the office. But this time there was no way of concealing the facts or even stalling long enough to not spoil the spirit of the occasion. Mary never made much of just an ordinary homecoming. Other days of the year, she generally managed to suppress a wife's natural urge to rush to the door when she heard her handsome husband's hoof-beats crunching up the gravel walk. On Christmas Eve, however, she always risked the danger of taking cold by waiting for me on the front steps.

Maybe it would have been better this time to telephone before I left town and give her a hint of what had happened. I know that nothing could have been worse than the way it was. I handed her the envelop without a word of warning and when she'd read the contents often enough to realize that it wasn't a joke, she let out a yell that would have waked up a porter and looked so much like she was going to faint that I went in the kitchen and told the girl to let the cold water run.

I won't attempt to remember all the bright ideas she had when the first shock was over. One was to hire a lawyer and sue Mr. Waldron for the six hundred on the grounds that he had given it to me so many Christmases that it was really part of my salary. Another one was to threaten him that if he didn't come across, I would spread a report that we were saving money by buying an inferior grade of raw materials. Still another one was to appoint myself head man among the employees and organize a strike, which we wouldn't have to go through with, of course, because it's pretty near impossible these days to fill vacancies in a high-class establishment like Waldron's.

When you've been Mary's husband eight years, you know that the only way to win an argument, or stop one, is to agree with everything she says. After you've yes-ed her a couple of times, she'll change sides. Then you change with her. If she jumps back, you jump, too, and if she goes neutral, you do the same. She finally gets disgusted and picks out another subject, but whatever subject she switches to, it's bound to be better than the one she was on.

She gave up plotting how to fleece Mr. Waldron after I'd cheered every suggestion she could think of, and the next problem was what to do with my fifty-dollar order on Norton's Store for Men; that is, what to do besides what the old man intended for me to do.

It was a long while before Mary convinced herself that the certificate wouldn't do her any good. It said right on it that you couldn't turn it in for cash, and Morton's is one place a woman might as well stay out of unless she's got a boy friend. She had already bought me a carton of her kind of cigarets and she was giving a record of "Tea for Two" to Jack Ingram. It's her favorite piece and the Ingrams have got a phonograph and we're over there three or four nights a week. Anyway, she finally decided to give me my certificate, and if I only had a new suit of clothes to go with this shirt and tie, I'd be a pretty good-looking fella.

The Ingrams were the first people we met when we came to New York. As far as I know, they're the only people Mary ever met outside of the man that's got the Bayside agency for Parker automobiles. We were going to rent an apartment in town till we could afford a little home in some suburb, and the idea was to stay at a hotel while Mary looked the place over. We happened to pick the Hotel Lindsay, and that's where the Ingrams were living, waiting for their house to be finished out in Bayside.

Well, it only took Mary and Edith Ingram twenty minutes to cement a beautiful friendship and I'd have had to like Jack even if he was a Collector of Internal Revenue. Instead of that he's a harmless kind of a fella and a good talker if you're interested in blooded cattle. He never owned any and it looks now like he never would, but he subscribed to a couple of maga-zines that tell you how to bring up an ox and you can get along with him if you say "Wonderful!" in the right spot and don't keep dozing off the way you've been doing.

Jack had a good job with the Boland Drug Company, which paid him for knowing something about chemistry, not cows. He was getting seven thousand when we met him and they boosted him to seventy-five hundred before the crash. Edith had some money of her own and when their house was ready, they owned it clear.

Of course, Mary went along two or three times to help Edith superintend the finishing touches and we spent the first week-end with them after they moved in. Right then and there Mary lost all interest in New York apartments. It was Bayside or bust, and maybe both. She knew we couldn't buy or build, but she found a place for rent and we've been there ever since. Evenings when we didn't go to the Ingrams' house, they'd come to ours. Sundays in the winter time, they just meant six or seven hours' extra gayety, and in the summer, a drive in the latest model Parker sedan, with me and Jack in the back seat and Mary at the wheel, on whatever road she thought we'd find the worst jam; me jealous of Edith for being able to sleep; Jack always wishing we'd get stalled in front of a stock farm, and never getting his wish, and everybody but Mary hoping there'd be a cloudburst next Sunday at a quarter to two.

When the Ingrams built their house, they didn't build a ga-rage. They decided to wait till they could buy a car. Mary de-cided to buy a car because the place we rented had a garage and the rent would have been lower if it hadn't had one, so if we didn't use it we were cheating ourselves. This saved the Ingrams a lot of trouble and expense. I had to get to New York earlier than Jack and my train left Bayside a half hour ahead of his. But after Mary had driven me to the station, she'd go and get him. Then, during the rest of the day, she'd taxi Edith around the village or wherever else she had errands to do. For all that, I'll bet there was many a time when Jack and Edith wished they had their own car so they could stay home Sundays.

Christmas Eve, it was the Ingrams' turn to come and see us. Mary said I mustn't tell them about our little surprise; they liked us so much that they'd feel pretty near as bad as we did, especially Edith, who could be so sympathetic sometimes that it was almost impossible not to get up and sock her in the jaw. You see, the difference between my regular salary and Jack's was fifteen hundred dollars, but his firm had never even given him a pocket comb for Christmas, let alone a check, so if Edith didn't know our secret, Mary could still take advantage of her only annual chance to gloat, and I will state in behalf of my Mary that she can outgloat any two women I ever met, and doesn't need to speak a word. Twice during the evening Edith brought up the subject herself. She asked me how it felt to be a millionaire. I said I wished I knew, but Mary flashed a smile that would have fooled a whole lot less dumber dame than Edie. Mr. Waldron had raised the bonus instead of repealing it—that's what you'd have thought, seeing Mary smile. She acted like a child with a new flask, except every so often some speech of Edith's would remind her that the Boland Drug people didn't believe in Santa Claus; then she'd sober up for a minute and look ashamed, as if she'd laughed out loud at a disarmament conference.

Well, Jack's concern remembered him the last day of the year. They gave him his freedom and a nice note telling him how sorry they were to lose his services; they knew he wouldn't have any trouble finding another job and not to hesitate to call on them if his future employers wanted a recommendation. Jack realized that there wasn't a chance of him landing anything in his line at even half what the Boland people had paid him, so he and Edith moved out to Chicago where his brother owns a couple of hotels and he's going to run one of them, or maybe it's the elevator. They left their house with a real estate man, and he's supposed to hold onto it till he can get what it cost them; in other words, he's supposed to hold onto it.

Mary felt terrible losing Edith, but she did have the satisfaction of one final gloat the night before they went away. That happened to be the seventh of January and the seventh of January happened to be my birthday. And without knowing anything about it being my birthday, Mr. Waldron called me in his office that afternoon and made a speech which I'm still wondering why he made it. He said he understood what a blow the bonus thing must have been to the employees; it had probably spoiled their Christmas; it had spoiled his Christmas worrying about it; he hated not showing his appreciation of our loyalty in the usual way, but business conditions didn't warrant his keeping everybody on the payroll, let alone giving us a bonus of ten percent. However, I was the most valuable man in his employ and it wasn't fair for me to be treated like the riffraff and he intended to more than make up to me for the six hundred dollars I hadn't got; it wouldn't be in the form of a bonus, but my salary check would be different from now on; and finally I must treat this as strictly confidential.

Well, I gulped and thanked him and went back to my desk, where I spent the rest of the afternoon trying to guess what for and how much. I was so baffled that when it came time to quit, I happened to go to a saloon instead of the station, and I caught the six-fifteen instead of the five-twelve.

As I told you before, and maybe you believe me by now: when I drink, I talk too much. And when I drink, Mary gets mad. On this particular evening, she wasn't any too good-natured to start with; she doesn't like for me to come home one train late, to say nothing of two, and Edith always felt so sorry for her when I'd had a couple of drinks that it looked like the gals' last evening together would find the sympathy all on the wrong side. But the reception I got broke down my morale and I took three drinks before dinner in place of the two I intended to take, and that extra drink was what made me tell Mary everything Waldron had said and put her in a position to send her best friend away thoroughly whipped.

The old man hadn't stated how much my raise was to be; just that it would more than equal six hundred dollars. Mary insisted on me guessing and I guessed seven hundred. That didn't satisfy her at all, so I made it eight hundred and fifty. But she's the kind that you give her an inch and she'll take the Lincoln Highway, and by the time the Ingrams showed up, she had me getting eight thousand a year, five hundred more than Bolands were paying Jack before they fired him. Not only that, but she appointed me general manager and if the Ingrams had stayed an hour longer, she probably would have made me Waldron's partner. Edith was the silentest I ever saw her. If she'd opened her mouth she'd have screamed.

You've been drowsing and not listening, but I'm going to tell you the rest of it just the same. My pay checks for the last three weeks in January were no different from what they had been before the old man spoke his piece. Mary had told the Ingrams that the new scale was to become effective on the fourteenth. When it didn't, and when the twenty-first and the twenty-eighth went by and still no signs of action, she said the old boy must have forgot all about it and I ought to remind him. I convinced her that this wasn't the year when the best people considered it stylish to insist on raises in salary; the thing for me to do was keep my mouth shut and indulge in silent prayer.

That brings us to the comedy relief, or the love interest, or something. Waldron left for Florida Monday night, the thirtieth of January. He didn't call me in to bid him goodbye, but when I got to the office Tuesday morning, there was a mash note from him saying he regretted that a sudden change in plans had prevented him seeing me in person, and a sudden change in the business outlook had rendered it necessary to reduce expenses fifty per cent; I was the highest salaried man in his employ and it was simply impossible to pay me what I'd been getting; on the other hand, or maybe the same one, he wouldn't insult such a valuable and important employee by asking me to take a cut, so this was a notice that he would have to worry along without my services after February the fourth, and he hoped I'd understand that he, and not I, was the one who would really suffer.

You must bear in mind that I hadn't squawked about the Christmas surprise and I hadn't asked for a raise or ever hinted that I thought I was worth more than he was paying me. He had made his speech and his promise without any threat or suggestion from me. That's why the entire proceedings are a jigsaw puzzle with all the pieces missing; that's why I haven't averaged two hours' sleep per night from the last day of January till now, and I envy you every cat-nap you've enjoyed since I began this monolog.

Now I may as well admit that I was afraid to break the news to Mary. She was already in convulsions over the salary proposition. To report that my future earnings would be nothing per annum instead of seven thousand, or eight, or ten—well, you don't go up to a ravenous wolf and tell him they took the diner off at Jackson.

I was in a tough spot and it was necessary to practise deception, which is as foreign to my nature as rolling on a duck's back. The system in our family has always been for me to give Mary my check and for her to give me ten dollars a week for subway fare and lunch and side trips to the old Spanish missions. At the end of the month, she makes out a check for the next month's railroad ticket, but she makes it out to the Long Island Railroad Company. That didn't matter anyway, because if my secret was to be a secret, I had to go to town and come home on my regular train, job or no job; besides, I could think of many a more economical way of spending the winter than to hang around the house all day long and wait for Mary to run out of hallelujahs.

If I hadn't been scared of rousing suspicion, I'd have done at least one thing different: I'd have changed morning trains. The train I always take is like most trains—it carries more than one passenger—and there's a fella that's been getting on with me at Bayside every morning since the Boer War, who I never knew his name and don't know it yet and don't want to know it, but he got the idea somewhere that he and I were old schoolmates and he must sit by me or behind me or in front of me, or stand in the aisle alongside of my seat, and keep up a conversation every minute of the trip or I would feel neglected and lonesome. Years ago I gave up trying to shake him off: silence and cold stares and insults, they just seemed to draw us closer together.

I've got nothing against the fella except that I do like to read the papers in the morning, even when there's no news. With him always asking questions and expecting answers, I didn't find out till a couple of weeks ago that Byrd was back home or Mussolini had swum the Channel.

Another risk I couldn't afford to take was in regards to being called up at the office; I mean, after February fourth. Mary hardly ever phoned, but she might. I had to fix it with the switchboard gal to say I was out or in conference and couldn't be disturbed, and was there any message? The gal was as dumb as they come, but she would lie for me because I never squawked when she made a mistake, which was every day from eight-thirty to five, with a half hour off for lunch, where she probably got somebody else's order.

When Mary gave me my allowance the morning of the sixth, I realized I'd better go light on lunch myself; it don't take more than two or three hours to answer all the help-wanted ads, and in the middle of winter, with the kind of weather we've had, you get bored waiting for time to go home. You ain't in any frame of mind to read, except the ads, so the Public Library is no good. The waiting room in the Long Island station, or any other station, or the lobby of a hotel—any place that's indoors and free—they all lose their kick after a few days. Twice I spent a nickel riding to the end of the subway and back; it gave me a headache and it wasn't much fun and it didn't take long enough. It came down to a choice between the talkies and the speakies, though there wasn't really a choice. Ten dollars don't last forever in a place like this, and in my case, the explanation when I got home would have lasted the rest of my life. Well, I've seen every cheap talkie in town and most of them twice in one day.

When I got home at the end of the first week of "vacation" I didn't have to excuse myself for the check not being bigger than usual, but I had to explain why there was no check at all. As I've already said, I'm not an expert at deception; just the same, Mary believed my story and liked it better than anything I'd told her since the night I broke the news of the phantom raise.

It appears that Mr. Waldron had decided to pay me my new salary monthly instead of weekly. I would receive my next check the first of March and another the first of April, and so on. This was the orders he'd left with the cashier, but the cashier hadn't stated how much the monthly check would be and I hadn't had the nerve to ask. He probably took it for granted I knew and I would feel silly admitting that I didn't.

I was afraid Mary would be sore about this. She was just the opposite. I never saw her enjoy herself as much as she did that night, dividing different amounts by twelve and then multiplying to see if they came out the same way. Of course it couldn't be as little as five hundred a month because that would only mean the six thousand I'd been getting without the ten percent bonus and he'd promised me more than six thousand plus the ten percent. The lowest it could possibly be was six hundred a month or seventy-two hundred a year. If it was any figure between sixty-six hundred and seventy-two hundred, what was the sense in paying me by the month instead of by the week? But even seventy-two hundred wasn't much more than sixty-six, and the chances were that it would be seven hundred a month, which made eighty-four hundred a year, or nine hundred more than Jack Ingram got before he got fired.

She had money in the bank and she didn't mind advancing me ten dollars every Monday morning till the new deal went into effect.

Maybe I ought to have felt mean, filling her full of hopes that were headed for a nose dive. But it was fun for her while it lasted, and temporary peace for me. Maybe I *did* feel mean, but if you knew Mary—anyway, I don't feel mean now.

I wish I'd kept a list of the jobs I tried to get and didn't get and couldn't have held onto them if I'd got them. "General sales manager, protected territory, photographic equipment— probable earnings twenty thousand for the right man"; "Tall American headwaiter, maintenance and a hundred a month, must speak German"; "Silk examiner and analyst, thoroughly experienced, thirty dollars a week"; "Manager for a New York City credit clothing store, large city experience essential"; "Photo retoucher," and I hardly ever touch a photo, let alone doing it twice; "Young man for exterminating, must live in Westchester and own an auto"; "Superintendent-gardener for 75-acre Nassau County estate"; "Experienced travel-bureau manager with following"; "Mechanic, typewriters, all-around man, inside or outside, thirty-five dollars per week." I'm pretty sure I'd rather be outside a typewriter than in one, but they didn't give me a chance to choose; they hired the second all-around man that was after the place, and I was about Number 27 in a line of forty.

I applied for positions that I don't even know what the words mean: "Galalith" for instance, if that's how you pro- nounce it; and "Furniture tracer, to locate furniture skips"; and "Fanfold biller," "Silk disponent," and "Beveler." I even went to an address in Twenty-first Street where they wanted a man to cut boudoir dolls; if they'd engaged me, I wouldn't have known whether to use a razor or an ax. But I needn't have worried; at least twenty guys were waiting when I got there and they took one of the first four or five.

Now try and stay awake long enough to listen to what happened today. I came in town as usual, with my boy friend sitting in the seat in front of me, but with his neck twisted around so he could face me while he asked what I thought of free wheeling and relativity and a half dozen other subjects that a year-old child could tell you all about. The papers only had three new want ads I could answer in person and I wasn't qualified for any of the jobs they offered even if they gave me a trial. Just the same I answered them so as not to spoil my record. The first place I went was on West Thirty-fourth Street, where a watch company wanted a collector. They had him before I arrived on the scene, but I wouldn't have stood a chance anyway; I'd have to admit that I'm thirty-four years old and haven't collected a watch since I graduated from high school. I was also too late at the next stop, on Third Avenue, 'way uptown, where a German had advertised for a private tutor to learn him to speak English. The fella he had engaged was talking to him in German and they were getting along so well that they'll probably wind up by not fooling with English at all.

Finally I lost out with a concern that was looking for an intelligent young man to operate addressograph and graphotype machines, laundry experience preferred. The position was no longer open—they never are. Outside of that, and not being young or intelligent, or having any idea which machine was which, the job was right up my street. I've had plenty of experience with laundries.

This part of the performance was finished at ten and I spent the next two hours writing to people who wanted their ads answered by mail. That's really the best way to go job-hunting. You don't have to listen to thirty or forty hard-luck stories from bozos that are as bad off as you are, or pretend you're pulling for them to land the same job that you hope to land for yourself. You don't have to act indifferent or force a smile when the master of ceremonies announces that "there's no need detaining you gentlemen; the vacancy has been filled." And when you've written your letter and dropped it in the box, the suspense is over. You know you'll never hear from it again and some lucky fifteen-dollar-a-week secretary will soon be tossing it in the waste-basket.

It was a little past noon, hardly twelve hours ago, I got

through with my day's "work" and nothing to do till train time, and I was headed for Felton's Restaurant where the Fifty-Cent Blue Plate Lunch is just as bad as other places, but it takes them a lot longer to serve it, and crossing Forty-second Street I heard a couple of women say, "Oh, let's go to the Paramount! Paul Whiteman's there this week," only I guess they didn't both say it, but one was enough—I'm a sucker for Whiteman's music—and the other woman said, "If we go now, we can hear him twice"; I certainly had no right to overlook a bargain, and it was a safe bet that no matter how long you hung around Felton's, they wouldn't serve you two blue plate lunches for one fifty cents. Next thing you know I was settling myself in a seat that alone was bigger than the theaters I've been haunting, and though I didn't get to hear Whiteman twice or even pay proper attention to him the first time, I can't complain of my bargain, and I only wish some of my brother unemployed, who I've chummed with mornings for pretty near a month—I only wish they could get the same kind of a break.

A newsreel was showing a bunch of Greeks, all twins, fishing for sponges at Tarpon Springs, Florida, when the guy next to me nudged me in the elbow and said, "Well, Poodle, how do you like the big town?"

I gave him a dirty look, never having seen him before in my life, but he just smiled and came at me again.

He said, "Are you too proud to talk to the home folks?" he said. "Or don't you like being called your old nickname?"

So I said, "Listen, Cuckoo," I said, "you've got me mixed up with some other dog. You and I are strangers," I said, "and it suits me fine to continue the relationship."

So he said, "Your parents would hate to see the change in you," he said. "They came of a good family, but they weren't too good for other people," he said. "They never would have got the swell head just because they live in New York."

This didn't go so good with me; I just had to set him right on my opinion in regards to the metropolis. I said, "People don't get the swell head on account of living in New York. They get embarrassed, unless they're crazy, like you."

So he said, "I'm not crazy, Poodle," he said, "but I *am* under observation."

"Why not?" I said. "You're talking as loud as a Congress-man and even sillier."

So he said, "I mean I'm under observation at Graves' Hospital, on Fifty-seventh," he said. "I don't want you to mention that when you write home."

"I'm not liable to," I said. "I don't write home because there's nobody left to write to, and if I did, I couldn't mention you because I don't know your name."

He dropped his voice to a shout.

"I'll tell you my name," he said, "though you know it as well as I do. I'm Phil Hughes. There!" he said. "How does that strike you?"

"It's prettier than Poodle," I said, "but it's the first time I ever heard it."

So he said, "I haven't any idea why you want to keep up this sham. Your mother's son couldn't be very bad, but if you're mixed up in a shady business of any kind, I won't squeal on you," he said. "I won't even say I saw you if I ever go back to Oconomowoc."

I asked him if that was where we came from and he said, "Just as if you didn't know!" So I asked him what was my name and he said, "Ben Collins, the same as your dad's, but everybody called you Poodle because you looked like a poodle and still do." I thanked him and then I said, "Now listen once more: my real name is none of your business. But it ain't Ben Collins and nobody but you calls me Poodle or ever called me Poodle much as I may look like one, and besides that, the only Oconomowoc I ever heard of is in Wisconsin—there couldn't be two of them—and I was never west of Parkesburg, Pennsylvania, in all my life."

So he said, "You better not talk so loud, Poodle, or they'll put you out," he said. "You've got some reason for changing your identity. I don't like to pry into your affairs, though I'd like to know what you're doing and I hope it's honest for your mother's sake."

So I said, "I'll tell you. I'm making an honest effort to hear Whiteman's band, but the competition has got me licked." So he said, "I'd like to know what you're doing for a living," and I said, "I'll tell you another piece of truth: I was making an honest living, but I ain't making any living at all right now because I lost my job." So he said, "If that's true and you can prove it's true, I'll give you a job, but we'll have to leave here and go somewhere else to discuss it." And as the ushers reached the same decision at the same time, my pal, Phil Hughes, and his pal, Poodle, marched out of the theater to the strains of "Rhapsody in Blue."

If the fella wasn't old, close to sixty; if I wasn't convinced that he really thought he knew me, or if he'd talked like a bum or dressed like one, I'd have shaken him off when he first started talking, and I'd have alibi-ed myself to the ushers and stayed in and seen the show. But he wasn't trying to put anything over and he had me pegged for somebody who he was acquainted with, just like the fella that shadows me mornings on the train; only this new fella is crazy enough to be interesting, and not a pest that drives you crazy yourself with childish questions and remarks.

I'll be through in a few minutes; I want to get some sleep, too. I thought that when he saw me in broad daylight, he might realize his mistake and admit it. But no; I was still Poodle on Seventh Avenue and still Poodle when we got out of the taxi at Grave's Hospital on Fifty-seventh Street. He took me up to the seventh floor and introduced me to a nurse as Mr. Collins, a young man he used to know in Oconomowoc. He asked the nurse to send for Dr. Gregory. The nurse said that the doctor was somewhere in the hospital, and he said to send him to his room. The room is a nice, big room and full of books about travel in this country and Europe.

While he waited, Mr. Hughes said that he was allowed to go out alone after nine in the morning provided he reported at the hospital for lunch and was in for good by five in the afternoon. The doctor had been after him to employ a companion to go around with him daytimes, not because there was danger of him doing anything rash, but to keep him from spending too much money. If I wanted the job, I could have it because it would make him feel good to think he was helping my mother's son. I told him again that he had never seen my mother, that my name wasn't Ben Collins or Poodle Collins and didn't even begin with a C, and that Pennsylvania was the closest I'd ever been to Oconomowoc. He said, "Some day you'll trust me with your secret, but you can't fool me and we'll just let it go at that." I told him what I had been getting at Waldron's and he said he would pay me seventy-two hundred dollars a year, and the first month in advance. In my pocket right now I've got his check for five hundred, and the money I've been spending tonight is part of a hundred-dollar bill he gave me in case I needed cash, as I certainly did. It wasn't the doctor's business how much he paid me, but he wanted the doctor's approval of me as a man.

Finally the doctor showed up and Mr. Hughes introduced me to him: "Dr. Gregory, this is a boy from my home town. We used to call him Poodle Collins and now he resents the nickname and denies the rest of it. But if he meets with your approval, I'll take him as a companion, and we've already agreed on terms."

The doctor said he would like to talk to me alone, and we went out to some visitors' room or something and I thought that as soon as I told him the truth, Poodle would die the death of a dog and I'd be as far out of a job as I was this morning. But get this: the doctor said his own name was Tyson, not Gregory, only Mr. Hughes insisted that he was Dr. Gregory and that he'd known him in Cleveland, where Dr. Tyson has never been. Mr. Hughes makes Dr. Tyson's checks to cash because Dr. Tyson doesn't like to endorse them with the name Gregory. This check I've got is made out to cash because I'd have trouble establishing myself as Ben Collins or Poodle and Mr. Hughes won't believe my name is anything else. Dr. Tyson said that if I was on the level it didn't make any difference what my name was or where I came from; he wanted Mr. Hughes to have somebody with him when he's wandering around, to prevent him buying the corner of Forty-Second and Fifth Avenue and starting a rival Radio City. He gets a big monthly check from a trust fund and he tries to get rid of it as fast as he can. My six hundred a month may save him six times that amount and spare Dr. Tyson a lot of worry.

The fella is harmless and no bad habits. He likes to go to matinees and picture shows and baseball in the summer. Won't that be tough, if Poodle can hold his job! And Dr. Tyson thinks I can if I pretend I came from Oconomowoc and know everybody I'm supposed to know, though the doctor says their records show that Mr. Hughes didn't live in Oconomowoc and only spent a couple of summers there.

The doctor naturally wanted references and the only one I could give him was Waldron's, with the old man still in Palm Beach. But he telephoned to the treasurer and the vice-president, and what they said must have satisfied him. If it hadn't, I'd have gone down there and shot up the joint. I was the best man they had; so Mr. Waldron told me himself—three weeks before he canned me.

So that's about all. I'm a seventy-two-hundred-dollar day nurse named Poodle. I spend eight hours a day with a crazy person that pays me and the rest of the time with one that doesn't. Only she ain't around just now, and maybe she won't be for quite a while. Because it seems that she called up Waldron's a half hour before my regular lunch hour today and Waldron's had a new switchboard gal, which I don't blame them for, but the gal they fired had forgotten to leave instructions with the new one protecting me, and the new one had never heard my name, but said to wait and she would make inquiries. Evidently she told Mary the truth, which was that I hadn't been connected with the place since February fourth. So when I got to Bayside this evening, there was no Parker sedan to meet me at the station and for the first time in months I had to use my key to open the Love Nest door. On the table in the hall there was twenty dollars and a note. It's short and I'll read it to you:

"I am going home to my mother and I wish I had never left her and never had met a man like you. I did not know there was such people in the world, people who can deliberately lie and lie to the person they have promised to love and cherish and who have made as many sacrifices for you as I. I do not know and certainly don't wish to know the name of the woman with whom you have been associating all the weeks when you pretended you were still at work. When you have given her up and when you have secured a position and can support a true and loyal wife as she should be supported and when you have convinced me that you are through once and for all with the lies and deceptions and frauds and infidelity which you have been practising and laughing in your sleeve at the loving wife who has sacrificed her whole life to make you happy, perhaps then and only then I may perhaps come back and resume my own humiliating position as your slave whom you have treated worse than the harems of Italy and Europe. Until that time I ask for you to not communicate with me in any way, shape or manner as you will receive no reply. Kindly be careful not to throw ashes and lighted cigarets on the floor and I imagine that when this money which I am giving you runs out your huzzy will gladly supply you with ample to supply your needs extravagant as they may be and as I know they are. Please do not insult me further by bringing that woman into this house."

Well, I guess Mary deserves a vacation and I'm going to let her have one at least as long as the one I've enjoyed; maybe a couple of months longer.

I've told you that when I drink, I talk too much. And it works the other way, too. When I talk too much, I drink. So let's not quit just yet. Get rid of those four in front of you and take a fresh one on old Poodle. Every dog must have his night.

Widow

J OHN WINSLOW was sick for only two days before he died. That is, he was sick in bed for only two days. His heart had been bothering him for a long while, racing at an alarming speed if he drank too much coffee, or smoked too many cigarettes, or went upstairs in a hurry. He had spoken of it to his doctor, to his brother and to his wife. But he had always told everyone else he felt fine—being rather reticent, for one thing, and for another, knowing that the inquirers into the state of his health would not be listening to his reply.

He took to his bed early on a Sunday evening, feeling anything but fine. He died Tuesday night. Mrs. Winslow telephoned to his brother Ed; and Ed and Mrs. Ed came over and stayed in the house with her. Mrs. Ed kept saying: "Keep hold of yourself, Margaret." She said it so many times that Mrs. Winslow was at last unable to keep hold of herself any longer, and cried on Mrs. Ed's shoulder for several hours. Mrs. Ed (Alice) told her husband that it was a good thing Margaret had "cried it out"—crying was so much better than suppressing your grief. Ed wondered why, if that were true, Alice had said, "Keep hold of yourself, Margaret," so often; but Ed had the Winslow reticence and wondered in silence.

Ed called up his office Wednesday morning and announced he would be unable to come to work the rest of the week. He assumed the management of the funeral and notified the papers. Margaret and Alice received many sympathetic visitors Wednesday afternoon and Thursday. Most of the visitors told Alice, as they were leaving, that Margaret was one of the bravest women they had ever seen, and was bearing up beautifully. Alice explained that Margaret had cried it out on her shoulder for several hours and had got it over with, which was much better than trying to hold yourself in.

"She may break down at the cemetery," said Alice, "but I don't believe she will even then, because she has already cried it out on my shoulder."

There were a few men among the visitors. They awkwardly expressed their sympathy to Margaret, shook her hand and they went into another room to talk to Ed, with whom they felt more at home. The women were sorry Alice was there. They felt they would have had a much better chance of making Margaret cry if they had caught her alone.

"You're perfectly wonderful to be up and seeing people," said Mrs. Hastings to Margaret. "If anything happened to Frank—I mean if he was taken away from me—well, I'd want to die too, or disappear and never see anybody again."

"I should think," said Mrs. Somers, "you ought to be in bed resting; you'll need all your strength for Friday. I know that if anything happened to Paul, I'd refuse myself to everybody and just hide. But I suppose things affect different people in different ways."

"I'm only going to stay a minute," said Mrs. Gordon. "I just wanted to tell you that you have all of my and Joe's sympathy, and we only wish there was something we could do. But there isn't anything, is there, dear?"

"No, thank you," said Margaret. "Ed and Alice are attending to everything. They're wonderful. But it's nice of you to offer just the same."

"You're lucky to have Alice and Ed," said Mrs. Gordon. "My sister Julia was all alone when her husband died, and she lived up in Minneapolis, so it was two days before I could get there. You never met Julia, I guess. You were away when she visited me. She had friends, of course; but friends aren't like your own family. Bert—that was Julia's husband—he was a wealthy man, had a half-interest in a big garage, and he left Julia comfortably off. But a person doesn't think of money at a time like this."

And when Mrs. Gordon was leaving, half an hour later, she said: "If there *is* anything I can do, or Joe either, don't hesitate to let me know."

Mrs. Bishop, failing to make Margaret break down, did it herself, and had to be consoled out of the house by Alice.

Mrs. Milburn had buried one husband and spoke with more authority than the rest.

"You will find that time is a great healer. When Archie died, I felt like life just couldn't go on for me. If it hadn't been for my religion, I believe I would have made away with myself. I honestly mean it. I would have. For weeks and weeks, when people talked to me, I simply didn't hear what they said. I was in another world. I couldn't think of anything but Archie, and how much his passing meant to me. I couldn't reconcile myself to living without him. My friends did everything they could to keep my mind off; they were afraid I would go crazy or have a breakdown. Finally I did get really sick and had to have a doctor. It was Dr. Sampson, in Louisville so of course you don't know him. He was perfectly wonderful to me; he seemed to understand things, and he gave me perfectly wonderful advice. He told me my illness was partly physical, because I wasn't eating or sleeping, but it was mostly mental, and he recommended me to travel and get away from home. He said a change of scene would be my salvation—that, and getting away from things that were constantly reminding me of Archie.

"Fortunately, I had money enough to do what he said, and I went to Miami, and that was where I met Fred. I really went there on account of the climate more than anything else— I hate cold weather; and I had no intention of seeing people or going out, though it was nearly five months after I had buried Archie; but there was a married couple stopping in the same hotel where I was stopping—I mean some people I knew, the Beldens, from Frankfort, Kentucky, and they simply insisted on me going to a party at the Casino. They had a terrible time coaxing me into it; I made every possible excuse; for one thing, I'd only brought two evening gowns. But they insisted and insisted till—well, Flora Belden acted like she was going to be mad at me if I didn't say yes. So I went with them and met Fred—it was the beginning of a new life. Archie still has his place in my memory and in my heart, but there is room for Fred too. So you mustn't give up, Margaret. Time will do wonders for you, and a year from now this may all seem like a bad dream that never really happened."

Several ladies besides Mrs. Gordon and Mrs. Milburn mentioned money in the course of their condolences, and an outsider might have thought there was some curiosity regarding how much John Winslow had left. Margaret knew, but did not tell. There was eleven hundred dollars in a checking-account, eight hundred in a savings-bank, and twenty-five thousand dollars' life insurance. He had also carried an accident policy for fifteen thousand dollars, which was now, of course, worthless.

Mr. and Mrs. Fleming called together. Mrs. Fleming said the news had shocked her, that she had no idea there'd been anything the matter with Mr. Winslow—he had always looked so well.

"I had no idea myself," said Margaret. "He never told me anything. I guess the suddenness of it was what makes it so hard."

"Just what did the doctor say it was?"

"Heart trouble was all he called it. And it was a surprise to him too. John had seen him about other things, things like sinus and head colds, but had never mentioned his heart, though Dr. Hyland says he must have known about it for years."

Mr. Fleming sneaked, as soon as he could, into the room where Ed was handling the male contingent. He got there in time to hear Ed replying to a query by Mr. Somers:

"Oh, yes. Jack knew his heart was wrong. He often spoke of it to Margaret and me. And he consulted Doc Hyland. Doc told him to cut down on smoking and coffee and lay off whisky entirely. And rest all he could. Well, Jack did quit drinking; he never drank much, anyway. But he wasn't the kind of a fella that would rest or take any care of himself. He couldn't even walk slow, no matter if there was no hurry about him getting places. He was like a three-year-old colt, nervous and high-strung."

The mention of a three-year-old colt reminded Frank Hastings of the pathetic story of his visit to Saratoga the summer before. A drunken man had given him a tip on Jim Dandy in the race that was supposed to be a duel between Gallant Fox and Whichone. Frank, it seemed, had been inclined to bet on Jim Dandy because of the odds, but the drunk was such a pest that he had changed his mind.

The other men in the room had heard the story many times and had laughed at Frank's serio-comic way of telling it. They laughed at it now; in fact, they were putting on a show of light-heartedness that was in decided contrast to the scene in Margaret's stronghold. The men did a lot of laughing, and seldom mentioned John Winslow's death. There was no concerted or individual attempt to make his brother cry. . . .

Funeral services were held in the house on Friday. Alice protested at first, saying it was bad luck for anyone to go away on Friday, but Margaret pointed out that John had really gone away on Tuesday night.

The casket was much too small to hold all the floral tributes. Alice told Ed that the one which probably cost most was what she called a "Gates Ajar," sent by the Fred Milburns, though a spray of roses embellished with ferns must have set the Gordons back twenty dollars. There were other rose sprays, of course, and a plethora of lilies and carnations.

A mixed quartet from the Winslows' church sang two hymns; rather, they sang "Just As I Am" as well as a mixed quartet can sing anything when there is no piano or organ to accompany them and they fought a losing battle with "In the Hour of Trial," owing to the fact that Miss Wells, the soprano, pitched it three tones too high for her own good or that of Mr. Standing, the tenor. It was abruptly decided by a vote of four to nothing to put the Amen after the second verse.

The Rev. Miles Langdon read the service and toasted the deceased in a twenty-five-minute talk. One of his paragraphs was to the effect that nobody ought to feel sorry for John, who had gone to his reward and finally attained happiness, a statement that may have been true but was not very complimentary to Margaret. Mr. Gordon and Mr. Hastings, two of the bearers, were dying for a smoke, and heartily wished the Rev. Langdon could be muzzled.

Margaret knew that tears were expected of her, and two or three times she was close to them; she and John had lived together for six years; she would miss him. But she managed to keep hold of herself by thinking of other things—how had the local florists managed to corner the world's carnations in so short a time? Was Mrs. Hastings crying because it was John's funeral and not Frank's? And why hadn't Dick Randall called or written or telephoned? Perhaps he had telephoned and Alice had just not told her. Did Alice suspect something? She couldn't *know* anything, because there wasn't anything to know. At least, not much.

Twelve cars were in the procession that went to the cemetery. Margaret had a hard time there, because Ed cried, and so did two of John's men friends. John must have been nice if men liked him that well. She felt sorrier for them than for herself. And she had always hated to see men cry. . . .

She was home at last, and Alice and Ed were still with her. She had hoped they would go to their own house and leave her alone, but it was useless to suggest this to Alice. The latter was one of a large majority of human beings who believed that when you have lost one near to you, you must not be allowed to seclude yourself for at least a week.

On Saturday, Margaret inquired whether it was necessary to reply to the letters and telegrams of condolence she had received.

"Yes," said Alice, "but not for another day or two. Wait till you feel more like it. They are all there together in the top drawer. I wish I could answer them for you, but that wouldn't do."

In the end, they were all there together in the waste-basket, and Margaret had not answered any of them.

On Sunday, Alice persuaded Ed that it was time to talk to his sister-in-law about her future.

"Your rent," said Ed, "is paid up till the first of next month, and there won't be any trouble getting you out of your lease after that. Of course you don't want to stay on here; you can't afford to, anyway."

"No."

"You'll have to rent a room at Miss Brent's or Mrs. Logan's or some other place where they're reasonable."

"Yes."

"John didn't leave hardly any debts. When you've paid off the few he did leave, you'll have somewhere around twenty-six thousand dollars. What you've got to do is invest it in high-grade bonds or maybe first mortgages. You can get six per cent and be perfectly safe. Let's see: Six per cent on twenty-six thousand is—six times six is thirty-six, and six times two is twelve, and three to carry makes fifteen. That gives you an income of fifteen hundred and sixty dollars a year, or twelve into fifteen is—let's see—one hundred and thirty. You'll have a hundred and thirty dollars a month, and that's enough to live on and save a little besides if you're careful."

"It's just as well you haven't any children," said Alice, who had remarked two days previously that it was too bad Margaret had no children, because they would have been such a comfort and given her something to live for.

"I forgot about the State tax," said Ed. "The State will take a small percentage of your inheritance, but not enough to make any difference. If the amount was a hundred thousand or more, the Federal Government would cut in."

"Well, then," thought Margaret, "I ought to get consolation out of the amount not being four times as much as it is, but it seems odd the State should punish me because John had heart trouble."

"If you want me to," said Ed, "I'll look up possible investments and attend to all that part of it for you."

"I wish you would," said Margaret. "I'm helpless when it comes to business."

"And I," said Alice, "will see Miss Brent and Mrs. Logan and try to get you a decent room at a decent price."

"You're awfully good to me, but please don't make anything too definite. I may want to go away for a while."

"Where would you go?"

"I have no idea. I just think maybe a change of scene will help me. Don't worry. I'm not planning an expensive trip."

"Well, I hope not," said Alice. "You must remember that every cent counts from now on."

Ed went back to work Monday, and he and Alice returned to their own home Wednesday evening, having decided that Margaret could be safely left alone. Margaret, lying awake after they had gone, did a lot of thinking. She thought a little about John, and how nice he must have been to win those men's love and respect. She recalled his having often spoken of his heart, and she wondered vaguely why she had paid so little attention, or been unable to believe he was not feeling all right.

She thought regretfully of next Saturday night's costume party at the Hamlins', a party which was an annual affair, but to which she and John had never been invited till this year. She thought of the Elizabethan costume she had rented, and how pretty she looked in it and how pretty Dick Randall would have told her she looked in it. If John could have postponed his death for two weeks!

And she thought if it were ordained that John was to die, he might just as well have died by accident. That would have meant fifteen thousand dollars more in insurance, or about forty thousand dollars altogether. Six times four is twenty-four

—twenty-four hundred dollars a year instead of fifteen hundred and sixty, or two hundred dollars a month instead of a hundred and thirty. . . .

But she thought most of Dick Randall: of the first time they had danced together, and he had said things that made her warm inside; of the first time he had kissed her, and she had pretended to be shocked but was thrilled; of the other times he had kissed her as she had not been kissed for years and years; of how he had said over and over again: "If you were only free!"

Well, she was free now, and had been free a week, and she had not seen him or heard from him, though she knew he was in town. Perhaps it was delicacy of feeling that was holding him back. Perhaps it was fear of Alice and Ed. Or fear of what people would say.

He would know tomorrow that she was alone, and he would telephone, or come to her, or something. There was nothing for her to do but wait.

She waited a day, a long day, and then called him.

"Dick, what's been the matter?"

"What do you mean?"

"I thought I would see you or hear from you at least."

"Listen, Margaret: I hate funerals, and I figured you would have enough people bothering you without me. I did send flowers."

"Yes. They were lovely."

"I just don't know what to say in a case like this. There's nothing I *can* say. If there was anything I could do for you, I'd do it."

"You might come and see me. I'm all alone."

"Well, I'll try to, sometime."

"I don't mean 'sometime.' I mean now."

"I've got a lodge meeting tonight."

"All right, if your lodge is more important than I am."

"Of course it isn't. But I've got to be there. It's an installation."

"You could come here for a few minutes first."

"Well, if you want me to. But it can only be for a few minutes."

"All right."

"Are you sure you're alone?"

"Very sure."

Dick waited till it was quite dark before he rang the Winslow bell. Margaret opened the door, and he came in and shook hands. They sat down in the living-room.

"As I told you, I never know what to say in a case like this. About all there is to say is that I'm sorry, Margaret—terribly sorry," said Dick.

Margaret made no reply, and there was an awkward silence.

"I've only got a minute to stay," said Dick.

"Before you go," said Margaret, "I wish you'd tell me why you're acting so funny."

"What do you mean, funny?"

"Well, Dick, two weeks ago, at the Flemings', we were on different terms than we seem to be on now."

"I don't think so."

"You know so. And I just want to know why."

There was another silence. Then Dick looked at his watch and then he said:

"I guess you must have got me wrong, Margaret. You and I had some pretty good times; we flirted a little, and we both enjoyed it; I did, anyway. But it's all different now. I should think you'd understand that."

"I'm trying to, but I can't."

"I may as well make myself clear, then: John and I were in the Rotary together, and I got to know him pretty well. I got to like him pretty well, too. There's no man in this town I like better than I liked John. He was twice the man that I am. It broke me all up when I heard he was dead. I cried for the first time in twenty years. And as for you and me, why, now that he's gone, of course there can't be anything between us like there was before. I'd always be thinking of him, and—"

"You'll be late for your lodge, Dick."

Margaret, alone again, did some more thinking. The insurance money would be paid to her, not to Ed. She could give Ed as much or as little of it as she liked. She could keep what she wanted for a trip. She thought that Mrs. Milburn's doctor's advice about a change of scene was very sensible. But she certainly did not want to discover another Fred Milburn, and she would steer as far away from Miami as possible. She wondered how much it would cost to go to Los Angeles.

SKETCHES AND REPORTING

Tyrus

S IT DOWN here a while, kid, and I'll give you the dope on
this guy. You say you didn't see him do nothin' wonderful?
But you only seen him in one serious. Wait till you been in the
league more'n a week or two before you go judgin' ball players. He may of been sick when you played agin him. Even
when he's sick, though, he's got everybody I ever seen skun,
and I've saw all the best of 'em.

Say, he ain't worth nothin' to that club; no, nothin'! I don't
know what pay he's gettin', but whatever it is, it ain't enough.
If they'd split the receipts fifty-fifty with that bird, they
wouldn't be gettin' none the worst of it. That bunch could
get along just as well without him as a train could without no
engine.

He's twicet the ball player now that he was when he come
up. He didn't seem to have no sense when he broke in; he run
bases like a fool and was a mark for a good pitcher or catcher.
They used to just lay for him when he got on. Sully used to tell
the pitchers to do nothin' but waste balls when he was on first
or second base. It was pretty near always good dope, too, because they'd generally nail him off one base or the other, or
catch him tryin' to go to the next one. But Sully had to make
perfect pegs to get him even when he knowed beforehand that
he was goin'. Sully was the boy that could make them perfect
pegs, too. Don't forget that.

Cobb seemed to think they was only one rule in the book,
and that was a rule providin' that nobody could stay on one
base more'n one second. They tell me that before he got into
the South Atlantic League he was with a club down there in
Georgia called the Royston Rompers. Maybe he thought he
had to keep on rompin' up here.

Another thing was that he couldn't hit a left-hander very
good. Doc W'ite used to make him look like a sucker. Doc was
a fox to begin with, and he always give you just what you
wasn't lookin' for. And then, his curve ball was somethin' Ty
hadn't never saw before and it certainly did fool him. He'd
hand Cobb a couple o' curves and the baby'd miss 'em a foot.

Then, when he was expectin' another one, Doc'd shoot his fast one right past his chin and make a monkey out of him.

That was when he first come up here. But Ty ain't the guy that's goin' to stay fooled all the time. When he wises up that somebody's got somethin' on him, he don't sleep nor do nothin' till he figures out a way to get even. It's a good thing Doc had his chancet to laugh when he did, because Cobb did most o' the laughin' after a couple o' seasons of it. He seen he couldn't hit the curve when it was breakin', so he stood way back in the box and waited till it'd broke. Then he nailed it. When Ty'd learned that trick, Doc got so's he was well pleased when the balls this guy hit off'n him stayed in the park.

It was the same way with every pitcher that had his number when he first busted in. He got to 'em in short order and, before long, nobody was foolin' him so's you could notice it. Right now he's as good agin left-handers as he is agin regular fellas. And if they's any pitcher in baseball that's got him fooled, he's keepin' the fact well concealed.

I was tellin' you what a wild base-runner he was at first. Well, he's still takin' chances that nobody else takes, but he's usin' judgment with it. He don't run no more just for the sake o' runnin'. They was a time when the guy on the base ahead of him was afraid all the time that he'd get spiked in the heels. But no more o' that. They's no more danger of him causin' a rear end collision, providin' the guy ahead don't blockade the right o' way too long.

You may not believe it, but I'll bet most o' these here catchers would rather have somebody on second base when Ty's on first base than to have him on first base alone. They know he ain't goin' to pull no John Anderson and they feel pretty safe when he can't steal without bumpin' into one of his own teammates. But when the track's all clear, look out!

All my life I been hearin' about the slow, easy-goin' Southerner. Well, Ty's easy-goin' all right—like a million-dollar tourin' car. But if Southerners is slow, he must be kiddin' us when he says he was born down South. He must of came from up there where Doc Cook pretty near got to.

You say you've heard ball players talk about how lucky he was. Yes, he is lucky. But it's because he makes his own luck. If he's got horseshoes, he's his own blacksmith. You got to have

the ability first, and the luck'll string along with you. Look at
Connie Mack and John D. and some o' them fellas.

You know I ain't played no ball for the last few years, but I
seen a lot of it played. And I don't overlook no chancet to
watch this here Tyrus. I've saw him agin every club in the
American League and I've saw him pull more stuff than any
other guy ever dreamed of. Lots o' times, after seein' him get
away with somethin', I've said to myself: "Gosh, he's a lucky
stiff!" But right afterward, I've thought: "Yes, and why don't
nobody else have that luck? Because they don't go out and
get it."

I remember one time in Chi, a year or two ago. The Sox was
two to the bad and it was the ninth innin'. They was two men
down. Bodie was on second base and somebody hits a single
to center field. Bodie tries to score. It wasn't good baseball to
take the chancet, because that run wasn't goin' to do no good
without another one to put with it. Cobb pegs to the plate and
the umps calls Bodie out, though it looked to everybody like
he was safe. Well, it was a bad play of Bodie's, wasn't it? Yes.
Well then, it was a bad play o' Cobb's to make the throw. If
Detroit hadn't of got the best o' that decision, the peg home
would of let the man that hit the ball go to second and be
planted there in position to score the tyin' run on another base
hit. Where if Ty had of played it safe, like almost anybody
would, the batter'd of been held on first base where it would
take two base hits or a good long wallop to score him. It was
lucky for Ty that the umps happened to guess wrong. But say,
I think that guy's pretty near smart enough to know when a
umpire's goin' to make a rotten decision.

O' course you know that Ty gets to first base more'n anybody in the world. In the first place, he always manages to hit
better'n anybody. And when he don't hit safe, but just bounds
one to some infielder, the bettin's 2 to 1 that the ball will be
booted or throwed wild. That's his luck, is it? No, sir. It's no
such a thing. It's his speed. The infielder knows he ain't got no
time to spare. He's got to make the play faster'n he would for
anybody else, and the result is that he balls it all up. He tries to
throw to first base before he's got the pill to throw, or else he
hurries the throw so much that he don't have no time to aim.
Some o' the ball players round the league says that the scorers

favor Ty and give him a base hit on almost anything. Well, I think they ought to. I don't believe in handin' a error to a fella when he's hurried and worried to death. If you tried to make the play like you do for other guys, Ty'd beat the ball to first base and then you'd get a hot call from the bench for loafin'.

If you'd saw him play as much baseball as I have, you wouldn't be claimin' he was overrated. I ain't goin to come right out and say he's the best ever, because they was some old-timers I never seen. (Comiskey, though, who's saw 'em all, slips it to him.) I just want to tell you some o' the things he's did, and if you can show me his equal, lead me to him and I'll take off my hat.

Detroit was playin' the Ath-a-letics oncet. You know they ain't no club that the Tigers looks better agin than the Ath-a-letics, and Cobb's more of a devil in Philly than anywheres else. Well, this was when he was battin' fourth and Jim Dela-hanty was followin' him. Ty singles and Del slips him the hit and run sign on the first ball. The ball was pitched a little out-side, and Del cuts it down past Harry Davis for a single to right field. Do you know what Cobb done? He scored; that's all. And they wasn't no boot made, neither. Danny Murphy picked the ball up clean and pegged it to Davis and Davis re-lays it straight home to Ira Thomas. Ty was there ahead of it. If I hadn't o' been watchin' close, I'd o' thought he forgot to touch two or three bases. But, no, sir. He didn't miss none of 'em. They may be other guys that could do that if they tried, but the diff'rence between them and Cobb is that he done it and they didn't. Oh, I guess other fellas has scored from first base on a long single in the hit and run, but not when the ball was handled perfectly clean like this one.

Well, here's another one: I forget the exact details, except that the game was between the White Sox and Detroit and that Tannehill was playin' third base at the time, and that the score was tied when Cobb pulled it. It was the eighth innin'. He was on first base. The next guy hits a single to left field. Ty, o' course, rounds second and starts for third. The left fielder makes a rotten peg and the pill comes rollin' in. Ty has the play beat a mile and they ain't no occasion for him to slide. But he slid, and do you know what he done? He took a healthy kick at that rollin' ball and sent it clear over to the grand stand. Then he jumped to his feet and kept on goin'. He was acrost the plate with the winnin' run before nobody'd realized what he'd did. It's agin the rules, o' course, to kick the ball a-purpose, but how could the umps prove that this wasn't a accident? Ty could of told him that he thought the play was goin' to be close and he'd better slide. I might o' thought it was a accident, too, if that had of been the only time I seen him do it. I can't tell you how many times he's pulled it, but it's grew to be a habit with him. When it comes to scorin' on kicks, he's got this here What's-His-Name—Brickley—tied.

I've saw him score from second base on a fly ball, too; a fly ball that was catched. Others has did it, but not as regular as this guy. He come awful near gettin' away with it agin a little while ago, in Chi. They was also somebody on third when the ball was hit. The guy on third started home the minute Bodie catched the ball and Ping seen they was no chancet to get him. So he pegs toward Weaver, who's down near third base. Cobb's at third before the ball gets to the infield. He don't never hesitate. He keeps right on goin' for the plate. Now, if Weaver'd of been able to of intercepeted the ball, Ty'd of been out thirty feet. But the throw goes clear through to the third baseman. Then it's relayed home. The gang sittin' with me all thought Ty was safe. I don't know about it, but anyway, he was called out. It just goes to show you what this guy's liable to do. You can't take no afternoon nap when he's around. They's lots of other fast guys, but while they're thinkin' about what they're goin' to do, he's did it. He's figurin' two or three bases ahead all the while. So, as I say, you don't get no sleep with him in the game.

Fielder Jones used to tell us: "When that bird's runnin', throw the ball somewheres just's soon as you get a-hold of it. I don't care where you throw it, but throw it somewheres. Don't hold onto it."

I seen where the papers says the other day that you out-guessed him. I wasn't out to that game. I guess you got away with somethin' all right, but don't feel too good about it. You're worse off now than you was before you done it because he won't never rest till he shows you up. You stopped him oncet, and just for that he'll make you look like a rummy next time he plays agin you. And after he's did it oncet and got even, he'll do it agin. And then he'll do it agin. They's a lot o' fellas round this league that's put over a smart play on Tyrus and most of 'em has since wished they hadn't. It's just like as if I'd go out and lick a policeman. I'd live to regret it.

We had a young fella oncet, a catcher, that nailed him flat-footed off'n first base one day. It was in the first game of a seri-ous. Ty didn't get on no more that day, but he walked the first time up the followin' afternoon. They was two out. He takes a big lead and the young fella pegs for him agin. But Tyrus was off like a streak when the ball was throwed, and about the time the first baseman was catchin' it, he was slidin' into second. Then he gets a big lead off'n second and the young catcher takes a shot for him there. But he throws clear to center field and Ty scores. The next guy whiffs, so they wouldn't of been no run if the young guy hadn't of got so chesty over the precedin' day's work. I'm tellin' you this so's you won't feel too good.

They's times when a guy does try to pull something on this Cobb, and is made to look like a sucker without deservin' it. I guess that's because the Lord is for them that helps themselves and don't like to see nobody try to show 'em up.

I was sittin' up in the stand in Cleveland one day. Ty was on second base when somebody hits a fly ball, way out, to Bir-mingham. At that time, Joe had the best throwin' arm you ever see. He could shoot like a rifle. Cobb knowed that, o' course, and didn't feel like takin' no chancet, even though Joe was pretty far out there. Ty waits till the ball's catched and then makes a bluff to go to third, thinkin' Birmy'd throw and that the ball might get away. Well, Joe knows that Cobb knows what kind of arm he's got and figures that the start from second is just a bluff; that he ain't really got no intention o' goin'. So, instead o' peggin' to third, he takes a quick shot for second, hopin' to nail Cobb before he can get back. The throw's perfect and Cobb sees where he's trapped. So he hikes for third. And the second sacker—I don't think the big Frenchman was playin' that day—drops the ball. If he'd of held it, he'd of had plenty of time to relay to third and nail Ty by a block. But no. He drops the ball. See? Birmy'd outguessed Ty, but all it done for him was to make him look bad and make Ty look good.

Another time, a long while ago, Detroit needed a run to win

from the Sox. Ty gets to first base with one out. Sully was catchin'. Sully signs for a pitch-out and then snaps the ball to first base. Ty wasn't lookin' for it and he was caught clean. He couldn't get back to first base, so he goes for second. Big Anderson was playin' first base and he makes a bum peg. The ball hits Cobb on the shoulder and bounds so far out in left center that he didn't even have to run to get home. You see, Sully'd outguessed Ty and had pulled a play that ought to of saved the game. Instead o' that, it give the game to Detroit. That's what hurts and discourages a fella from tryin' to pull anything on him.

Sometimes I pretty near think they's nothin' he couldn't do if he really set out to do it. Before you joined the club, some o' the boys was kiddin' him over to Detroit. Callahan was tellin' me about it. Cobb hadn't started hittin'. One o' the players clipped the averages out o' the paper and took 'em to the park. He showed the clippin' to Ty.

"You're some battin' champ, Ty," he says. "Goin' at a .225 clip, eh?"

Tyrus just laughed at him.

"I been playin' I was one o' you White Sox," he says. "But wait till a week from to-day. It'll be .325 then."

Well, it wasn't. No, sir! It was .326.

One time, in 1912 I think it was, I happened to be goin' East, lookin' for a job of umpirin', and I rode on the train with the Tigers. I and Cobb et breakfast together. I had a Sunday paper with me and was givin' the averages the oncet over.

"Read 'em to me," says Ty.

"You don't want 'em all, do you?" I says.

"No, no. Just the first three of us," he says. "I know about where I'm at, but not exactly."

So I read it to him:

"Jackson's first with .412. Speaker's second with .400. You're third with .386."

"Well," says Ty, "I reckon the old boy'd better get busy. Watch me this trip!"

I watched him, through the papers. In the next twenty-one times at bat, he gets exactly seventeen hits, and when the next averages was printed, he was out in front. He stayed there, too.

So I don't know, but I believe that if Jackson and Speaker

and Collins and Lajoie and Crawford was to go crazy and hit .999, this Cobb would come out on top with 1,000 even.

He's got a pretty good opinion of himself, but he ain't no guy to really brag. He's just full o' the old confidence. He thinks Cobb's a good ball player, and a guy's got to think that way about himself if he wants to get anywheres. I know a lot o' ball players that gets throwed out o' the league because they think the league's too fast for 'em. It's diff'rent with Tyrus. If they was a league just three times as fast as the one he's in and if he was sold up there, he'd go believin' he could lead it in battin'. And he'd lead it too!

Yes, sir, he's full o' that old stuff, and the result is that lots o' people that don't know him think he's a swell-head, and don't like him. But I'm tellin' you that he's a pretty good guy now, and the rest o' the Tigers is strong for him, which is more'n they used to be. He busted in with a chip on his shoulder, and he soon become just as popular as the itch. Everybody played him for a busher and started takin' liberties with him. He was a busher, too, but he was one o' the kind that can't take a joke. You know how they's young fellas that won't stand for nothin'. Then they's them that stands for too much. Then they's the kind that's just about half way. You can go a little ways with 'em, but not too far. That's the kind that's popular.

Cobb wouldn't stand for nothin'. If somebody poured ketchup in his coffee, he was liable to pick up the cup and throw it at the guy nearest to him. If you'd stepped on his shine, he'd of probably took the other foot and aimed it at you like he does now at the ball when it's lyin' loose on the ground. If you'd called him some name on the field, he'd of walloped you with a bat, even if you was his pal. So they was all stuck on him, was they not?

He got trimmed a couple o' times, right on his own club, too. But when they seen what kind of a ball player he was goin' to be, they decided they'd better not kill him. It's just as well for 'em they didn't. I'd like to know where their club would of finished—in 1907 and 1908, for instance—if it hadn't of been for him. It was nobody but him that beat us out in 1908. I'll tell you about it later on.

I says to him one day not long ago, I says:

"You wasn't very strong with the boys when you first come up. What was the trouble?"

"Well," he says, "I didn't understand what was comin' off. I guess they meant it all right, but nobody'd tipped me that a busher's supposed to be picked on. They were hazin' me; that's what they were doin', hazin' me. I argued with 'em because I didn't know better."

"You learned, though, didn't you?" I says.

"Oh, yes," says Ty, "I learned all right."

"Maybe you paid for your lessons, too," I says.

"Maybe I did," he says.

"Well," I says, "would you act just the same way if you had it to do over again?"

"I reckon so," he says.

And he would, too, because if he was a diff'rent kind o' guy, he wouldn't be the ball player he is.

Say, maybe you think I didn't hate him when I was playin' ball. I didn't know him very well, see? But I hated him on general principles. And I never hated him more'n I did in 1908. That was the year they beat us out o' the big dough the last day o' the season, and it come at a time when I needed that old dough, because I knowed darn well that I wasn't goin' to last no ten years more or nothin' like that.

You look over the records now, and you'll see that the Detroit club and us just about broke even on the year's serious agin each other. I don't know now if it was exactly even or not, or, if it wasn't, which club had the best of it. But I do know one thing, and that is that they beat us five games that we'd ought to of copped from 'em easy and they beat us them games for no other reason than that they had this here Georgia Peach.

The records don't show no stuff like that, but I can remember most o' them games as if they was played yesterday; that is, Cobb's part in 'em. In them days, they had Crawford hittin' third and Cobb fourth and Rossman fifth. Well, one day we had 'em licked by three runs in the seventh innin'. Old Nick was pitchin' for us and Sully was catchin'. Tannehill was at third base and Hahn was switched from right to left field because they was somethin' the matter with Dougherty. Well, this seventh innin' come, as I was sayin', and we was three runs to the good. Crawford gets on someway and Cobb singles. Jones thought Nick was slippin', so he hollered for Smitty. Smitty comes in and pitches to big Rossman and the big guy hits one back at him. Smitty had the easiest kind of a double play starin' him in the face—a force play on Crawford at third and then the rest of it on Rossman, who wasn't no speed marvel. But he makes a bad peg to Tannie and the ball gets by him. It didn't look like as if Crawford could score, and I guess he was goin' to stop at third.

But Tyrus didn't pay no attention to Crawford. He'd saw the wild peg and he was bound to keep right on comin'. So Crawford's got to start home to keep from gettin' run over. Hahn had come in to get the ball and when he seen Crawford startin' home, he cut loose a wild peg that went clear to the bench. Crawford and Cobb both scored, o' course, and what does Ty do but yell at Rossman to follow 'em in, though it looked like sure death. Sully has the ball by that time, but it's just our luck that he has to peg wild too. The ball sailed over Smitty, who'd came up to cover the plate. The score's tied and for no reason but that Tyrus had made everybody run. The next three was easy outs, but they went on and licked us in extra innin's.

Well, they was another game, in that same serious I think it was, when Big Ed had 'em stopped dead to rights. They hadn't no more business scorin' off'n him than a rabbit. I don't think they hit two balls hard all day. We wasn't the best hittin' club in the world, but we managed to get one run for the Big Moose in the first innin' and that had ought to of been a-plenty.

Up comes Cobb in the fourth and hits one that goes in two bounds to Davis or whoever was playin' short. If he could of took his time, they'd of been nothin' to it. But he has to hurry the play because it's Cobb runnin', and he pegs low. Izzy gets the ball off'n the ground all right, but juggles it, and then Ty's safe.

They was nobody out, so Rossman bunts. He's throwed out a mile at first base, but Ty goes all the way to third. Then the next guy hits a fly ball to Hahn that wouldn't of been worth a nickel if Cobb'd of went only to second on the sacrifice, like a human bein'. He's on third, though, and he scores on the fly ball. The next guy takes three swings and the side's out, but we're tied up.

Then we go along to the ninth innin' and it don't look like they'd score agin on Big Ed if they played till Easter. But

Cobb's up in the ninth with one out. He gets the one real healthy hit that they'd made all day. He singled to right field. I say he singled, because a single's what anybody else would of been satisfied with on the ball he hit. But Ty didn't stop at first base. He lights out for second and whoever was in right field made a good peg. The ball's there waitin' for Ty, but he slides away from it. Jake thought he had him, but the umps called him safe. Well, Jake gets mad and starts to kick. They ain't no time called or nothin'. The umps turns away and Jake slams the ball on the ground and before anybody could get to it, Cobb's on third. We all hollered murder, but it done us no good. Rossman then hit a fly ball and the game's over.

I remember another two to one game that he win from us. I don't recall who was pitchin'—one o' the left-handers, I guess. Whoever it was had big Rossman on his staff that day. He whiffed him twicet and made him pop out another time. They was one out in the eighth when Cobb beats out a bunt. We was leadin' by one run at the time, so naturally we wanted to keep him on first base. Well, whoever it was pitchin' wasted three balls tryin' to outguess Tyrus, and he still stood there on first base, laughin' at us. Rossman takes one strike and the pitcher put the next one right over and took a chancet, instead o' runnin' the risk o' walkin' him. Rossman has a toe-hold and he meets the ball square and knocks it clear out o' the park. We're shut out in the ninth and they've trimmed us. You'll say, maybe, it was Rossman that beat us. It was his wallop all right, but our pitcher wouldn't of wasted all them balls and got himself in the hole if anybody but Cobb'd of been on first base.

One day we're tied in the ninth, four to four, or somethin' like that. Cobb doubled and Rossman walked after two was out. Jones pulled Smitty out o' the game and put in Big Ed. Now, nobody was lookin' for Ty to steal third with two out. It's a rotten play when anybody else does it. This ain't no double steal, because Rossman never moved off'n first base. Cobb stole third all right and then, on the next pitch, Rossman starts to steal second. Our catcher oughtn't to of paid no attention to him because Walsh probably could of got the batter and retired the side. It wasn't Sully catchin' or you can bet no play'd of been made. But this catcher couldn't see

nobody run without peggin', so he cut loose. Rossman stopped
and started back for first base. The shortstop fired the ball back
home, but he was just too late. Cobb was acrost already and it
was over. Now in that case, our catcher'd ought to of been
killed, but if Tyrus hadn't did that fool stunt o' stealin' third
with two out, they'd of been no chancet for the catcher to pull
the boner.

How many did I say he beat us out of? Five? Oh, yes, I remember another one. I can make it short because they wasn't
much to it. It was another one o' them tied up affairs, and
both pitchers was goin' good. It was Smitty for us and, I think,
Donovan for them. Cobb gets on with two down in the tenth
or 'leventh and steals second while Smitty stands there with
the ball in his hand. Then Rossman hits a harmless lookin'
ground ball to the shortstop. Cobb runs down the line and
stops right in front o' where the ball was comin', so's to bother
him. But Ty pretends that he's afraid the ball's goin' to hit him.
It worked all right. The shortstop got worried and juggled the
ball till it was too late to make a play for Rossman. But Cobb's
been monkeyin' so long that he ain't nowheres near third base
and when the shortstop finally picks up the ball and pegs there,
Cobb turns back. Well, they'd got him between 'em and
they're tryin' to drive him back toward second. Somebody
butts in with a muff and he goes to third base. And when
Smitty starts to pitch agin, he steals home just as clean as a
whistle.

The last game o' the season settled the race, you know. I
can't say that Tyrus won that one for 'em. They all was due to
hit and they sure did hit. Cobb and Crawford both murdered
the ball in the first innin' and won the game right there, because Donovan was so good we didn't have no chancet. But if
he hadn't of stole them other games off'n us, this last one
wouldn't of did 'em no good. We could of let our young fellas
play that one while we rested up for the world's serious.

I don't say our club had a license to be champions that year.
We was weak in spots. But we'd of got the big dough if it
hadn't of been for Tyrus. You can bet your life on that.

You can easy see why I didn't have no love for him in them
days. And I'll bet the fellas that was on the Ath-a-letics in 1907
felt the same toward him, because he was what kept 'em from

coppin' that year. I ain't takin' nothin' away from Jennin's and Crawford and Donovan and Bush and Mullin and McIntire and Rossman and the rest of 'em. I ain't tryin' to tell you that them fellas ain't all had somethin' to do with Detroit's winnin' in diff'rent years. Jennin's has kept 'em fightin' right along, and they's few guys more valuable to their club than Crawford. He busted up a lot o' games for 'em in their big years and he's doin' it yet. And I consider Bush one o' the best infielders I ever see. The others was all right, too. They all helped. But this guy I'm tellin' you about knocked us out o' the money by them stunts of his that nobody else can get by with.

It's all foolishness to hate a fella because he's a good ball player, though. I realize that now that I'm out of it. I can go and watch Tyrus and enjoy watchin' him, but in them days it was just like pullin' teeth whenever he come up to the plate or got on the bases. He was reachin' right down in my pocket and takin' my money. So it's no wonder I was sore on him.

If I'd of been on the same club with him, though, I wouldn't never of got sore at him no matter how fresh he was. I'd of been afraid that he might get so sore at me that he'd quit the club. He could of called me anything he wanted to and got away with it or he could have took me acrost his knee and spanked me eighty times a day, just so's he kept on puttin' money in my kick instead o' beatin' me out of it.

As I was sayin', I enjoy seein' him play now. If the game's rotten or not, it don't make no diff'rence, and it don't make a whole lot even if he's havin' a bad day. They's somethin' fascinatin' in just lookin' at the baby.

I ain't alone in thinkin' that, neither. I don't know how many people he draws to the ball parks in a year, but it's enough to start a big manufacturin' town and a few suburbs. You heard about the crowd that was out to the Sox park the Sunday they was two rival attractions in town? It was in the spring, before you come. Well, it was some crowd. Now, o' course, the Sox draw good at home on any decent Sunday, but I'm tellin' you they was a few thousands out there that'd of been somewheres else if Cobb had of stayed in Georgia.

I was in Boston two or three years ago this summer and the Tigers come along there for a serious o' five games, includin' a double-header. The Detroit club wasn't in the race and neither was the Red Sox. Well, sir, I seen every game and I bet they was seventy thousand others that seen 'em, or better'n fifteen thousand a day for four days. They was some that was there because they liked baseball. They was others that was stuck on the Red Sox. They was still others that was strong for the Detroit club. And they was about twenty-five or thirty thousand that didn't have no reason for comin' except this guy I'm tellin' you about. You can't blame him for holdin' out oncet in awhile for a little more money. You can't blame the club for slippin' it to him, neither.

They's a funny thing I've noticed about him and the crowds. The fans in the diff'rent towns hates him because he's beat their own team out o' so many games. They hiss him when he pulls off somethin' that looks like dirty ball to 'em. Sometimes they get so mad at him that you think they're goin' to tear him to pieces. They holler like a bunch of Indians when some pitcher's good enough or lucky enough to strike him out. And at the same time, right down in their hearts, they're disappointed because he did strike out.

How do I know that? Well, kid, I've felt it myself, even when I was pullin' agin Detroit. I've talked to other people and they've told me they felt the same way. When they come out to see him, they expect to see him do somethin'. They're glad if he does and glad if he don't. They're sore at him if he don't beat their team and they're sore if he does. It's a funny thing and I ain't goin' to sit here all night tryin' to explain it.

But, say, I wisht I was the ball player he is. They could throw pop bottles and these here bumbs at me, and I wouldn't kick. They could call me names from the stand, but I wouldn't care. If the whole population o' the United States hated me like they think they hate him, I wouldn't mind, so long's I could just get back in that old game and play the ball he plays. But if I could, kid, I wouldn't have no time to be talkin' to you.

The other day, I says to Callahan:

"What do you think of him?"

"Think of him!" says Cal. "What could anybody think of him? I think enough of him to wish he'd go and break a leg. And I'm not sore on him personally at that."

"Don't you like to see him play ball?" I says.

"I'd love to watch him," says Cal, "if I could just watch him when he was playin' Philadelphia or Washington or any club but mine."

"I guess you'd like to have him, wouldn't you?" I says.

"Me?" says Cal. "All I'd give for him is my right eye."

"But," I says, "he must keep a manager worried some, in one way and another; you'd always be afraid he was goin' to break his own neck or cut somebody else's legs off or jump to the Fed'rals or somethin'."

"I'd take my chances," says Cal. "I believe I could even stand the worry for a few days."

I seen in the papers where McGraw says Eddie Collins is the greatest ball player in the world. I ain't goin' to argue with him about it, because I got nothin' but admiration for Collins. He's a bear. But, kid, I wisht McGraw had to play twenty-two games a year agin this Royston Romper. No, I don't, neither. McGraw never done nothin' to me.

from *My Four Weeks in France*

Friday, August 24. Paris.

An American major—it is interdict by the censor to mention the names of any officers save General Sibert and General Pershing—asked a friend in London to buy him an automobile and ship it here for his use. The Londoner was able, after much difficulty, to purchase one of those things that grow so rapidly in Detroit. He packed it up and mailed it to Le Havre. From there it had to be driven to Paris.

The major had never learned to drive this particular brand. In fact, his proportions are such that not even a shoehorn could coax him into the helmsman's seat. He asked me to go up and get it for him. I declined on grounds of neutrality. That was a week ago.

Well, yesterday one Mr. Kiley, who has been over here some time in the ambulance service, came back to town with the car and four flat tires, which, evidently, were far past the draft age when the sale was made in London. Mr. Kiley helped himself to a stimulant and then told me about his trip.

He reached Le Havre last Saturday afternoon. He had in his pockets no papers except an order for the car. He had been in Le Havre about two minutes when a gentleman attacked him from behind with a tap on the shoulder. The gentleman pulled back his coat lapel and flashed a star bearing the insignia of the British Intelligence Department. He was curious as to Mr. Kiley's name and business. Mr. Kiley told him. Then he wanted to see Mr. Kiley's papers. Mr. Kiley showed him the order for the car.

"I'm afraid that won't do," said the officer. "I'd advise you to leave town."

"Give me just an hour," pleaded Mr. Kiley, "just time enough to get the car and get out."

"All right," said the officer, "and be sure it's only an hour."

Mr. Kiley hastened to where the car was reposing, displayed the order, and started joyously to wind her up. He cranked and he cranked and he cranked. Nothing doing. He gave her a push downhill and tried to throw her into speed. Nothing doing. It occurred to him that something must be the matter. A thorough examination resulted in a correct diagnosis. There was no gas.

Next to getting a drink of ice-water in Paris, the hardest job for a stranger is buying gasoline in any French town. Mr. Kiley was turned down five times before eighteen o'clock, when all the garages closed for the day.

He registered at a hotel and went into the café for dinner. He was just picking up the carte du jour when his friend, the officer, horned in.

"Mr. Kiley," says this guy, "you have been in town more than an hour."

"Yes, sir," said Mr. Kiley. "But I've had trouble. I found my car, but I can't run it because there's no essence."

"I think you'd better leave town," said the officer.

"If you don't mind," said Mr. Kiley, "I'll leave early in the morning."

"I wouldn't mind if you left right now," said he.

There followed a long discussion and a cross-examination even crosser than mine in Bordeaux. Mr. Kiley revealed his whole family history and won the right to stay overnight, provided he remained indoors and departed from town first thing in the morning.

But France is like America in that Saturday is usually succeeded by Sunday, and when Mr. Kiley arose from his hotel bed and resumed his search for gas he found every garage in town shut up tight. As I remember the United States, garages do not keep holy the Sabbath Day nor any other day. Over here, however, everything closes on Sunday except churches, theaters and saloons.

Mr. Kiley took in the situation and returned to his room to hide. Shortly before midi there was a knock at his door and a new officer appeared.

"You seem to like our town, Mr. Kiley," said he.

"I'll leave it as soon as I can get away," said Mr. Kiley.

"No doubt," replied the officer. "But I believe you will be here a long while."

Mr. Kiley tried to look calm.

"Bone," he said in perfectly good French.

"For the present," said the officer, "you must not leave the hotel. Later on we'll talk things over."

In the café on Sunday night Mr. Kiley met an American and told him his troubles. The American had a car of his own in Le Havre and plenty of gasoline. He would be glad to give Mr. Kiley enough to start him on his way.

"But I can't go," said Mr. Kiley, "till I've fixed it with the police. I'll have to look for them."

He didn't have far to look. No. 2 was in the lobby.

"Yes," said No. 2, "you can leave town if you leave quick. There must be no more foolishness. The only thing that saves you from arrest is your uniform."

Mr. Kiley left town and left quick, and, aside from his four blow-outs, had an uneventful trip to Paris.

But what if I had taken that assignment—I with no uniform except one willed me by the Chicago Cubs? O Boy!

Ring Lardner—Himself

Remarks By Himself

THE PUBLIC will doubtless be dumfounded to learn that I recently celebrated my thirty-second birthday anniversary. We had a cake and candles.

CHRONOLOGY

1885
   Began to eat at Niles, Mich.

1889
   Could tell by the sound of the whistle the number of the engine that was passing on the Cincinnati, Wabash & Michigan's main and only track, which lay across the street and down the hill from our house.

1895
   Determined to be a brakeman.

1896
   Determined not to be a brakeman. Smoked a cigarette.

1897
   Decided not to be a clergyman.

1901
   Was graduated from the Niles High School.
   "And so young!" said they.
   Accepted an office boy's portfolio with the Harvester Company in Chicago. Canned.
   Served a prominent Chicago real-estate firm in the same capacity. Canned.
   Was appointed third assistant freight hustler at the Michigan Central in Niles. Canned for putting a box of cheese in the through Jackson car, when common sense should have told me that it ought to go to Battle Creek.

1902
   "Studied" mechanical engineering at Armour Institute,

Chicago. Passed in rhetoric. Decided not to become a mechanical engineer.

1903
   Rested. Recovered from the strain which had wrought havoc with my nervous system.

1904 and Part of 1905
   Became bookkeeper for the Niles Gas Company.

Part of 1905, 1906 and Part of 1907
   Society reporter, court-house man, dramatic critic and sporting editor for the South Bend, Indiana, Times.

Part of 1907
   Sports reporter for the Chicago Inter Ocean.

1908 to 1912
   Baseball writer on the Chicago Examiner, the Chicago Tribune, St. Louis Sporting News, Boston American, and copy reader on the Chicago American.

1913——
   Resting on the Chicago Tribune.

1914——
   Started writing for THE SATURDAY EVENING POST. Its circulation was then only a little over a million.

19??
   Died intestate.

TASTES

Favorite author—Ring W. Lardner.
Favorite actor—Bert A. Williams.
Favorite actress—Ina Claire.
Favorite composer—Jerome Kern.
Favorite flower—Violet.
Favorite bird—Buzzard.
Favorite recreation—Bronco busting.

SUMMARY	Jobs	W.	L.	Pct.
	13	8	5	.616

A Literary Diary

Y OU DON'T hardly ever pick up a Sunday paper now days but what some high brow writer has got their dairy in there for the past wk. or in other wds. a record of who they seen and talked to and what they done since the last time we heard from them.

Well naturly they's a good many famous names broughten into these here dairys who the public is interested in reading about them, but the public is also interested in reading about the writers themselfs provided they are famous enough and any way the idear has been suggested that my own dairy for a wk. would make interesting reading even though I don't take lunch very often with men like Babe Ruth, H. G. Wells and Suzanne Lenglen so any way I am going to write down my journal for Aug. 6–13 inclusive and anybody that is bored by the same can lay it to 1 side and no hard feelings.

Aug. 6

Everybody was cooking their Sunday dinner at once and Great Neck seemed to run out of gas so we had to finnish up the chicken in the coal range and didn't get nothing to eat till after 3 P.M. My sister-in-law Dorothy and husband H. Kitchell and 2 babies come to pay us a visit though they didn't owe us none but at lease they ain't going to stay long. President Harding called up long distants to say hello. The Mrs. talked to him as I was playing with the cat.

Aug. 7

Went to N.Y. city to get a hair cut and was walking along 7th. ave. and seen a man teaseing a musk rat so I went up to the man and busted him in the jaw and knocked him down. A policeman come along and picked the man up and asked him who he was. It turned out that he was Jack Dempsey. I went over to the athletic club and exercised as I ain't been getting none lately.

Aug. 8

Peggy Hopkins called up and wanted we should go for a sail

but I had a date to play golf with Sarazen, Hagen and Barnes. I and Hagen played the other two best ball and added score for a $25.00 nassua but only beat them by about 7 pts. as Hagen wasn't putting good. I had 12 eagles but only managed to get a couple of ones. When I got home Sousa was there and we played some Brahms and Grieg with me at the piano and him at one end of a cornet. "How well you play Lardy," was Sousa's remark. Brahms called up in the evening and him and his wife come over and played rummy.

Aug. 9

David Wark Griffith drove up to the house in his Ford so silently that he caught me setting on the porch before the butler could tell him I was out. He says he was getting up a new picture based on the story of "The Prisoner of Zenda," and it laid between Jack Barrymore, Richard Barthelmess and I which one of us should play the lead. "It is yours if you want it," he said to me. "I am sorry, Dave," I says, "but I promised the little woman to not work this summer." "I am sorry, too, Lardy," he said, and drove off. Took a ride on the Long Island R.R. to study human nature. They was a man quarrelling with the conductor and the conductor seemed to be getting the worst of it so I throwed the man off of the train. Found out afterwards it was Stanislaus Zbyszko. Felt bored and sleepy so went home.

Aug. 10

Went to the Follies but a lot of people seen me come in and begun hollering author, author, till it become so embarrassing I had to duck. Had lunch with Beethoven and Bach, and they wanted to know what I was doing in the evening. "Well, boys," I said. "I am at your disposal." They acted tickled to death and we spent the evening in the Lambs playing trios. Amongst other pieces we tried out Bach's new sonata for 2 pianos and a cuspidor.

Aug. 11

Had breakfast with Mayor Hylan and Senator Lodge. After breakfast the senator says "Lardy tear us off some Chopin." After I had played them a few pieces I drove the boys down town and I went to the club and played billiards with Willie Hoppe and had a narrow escape from him beating me as I was off my game. "Well," he said when it was over, "I come pretty near beating you that time Lardy." "Yes you did, Willie," I told him with a smile. Went to dinner with Wm. M. Thackeray a English author and he suggested that we should eat crow's knuckles meuniere which I hadn't never tried but it tasted O.K. and reminded a good deal like pelican's finger nails a la creole. "How do you like it Lardy," asked my host. "All right Thack," was my smiling reply. Went home and played some Rubinstein on the black keys.

Aug. 12

This was Saturday and the banks close at noon on Saturdays so I visited them all dureing the forenoon and found everything lovely. Everywhere I went it was hello Lardy how is everything Lardy. Played 4 or 5 rounds of Beethoven and had lunch with Gatti-Casazza and Gen. Pershing. Went home to practice on my harp and the phone rung and it was Madame Jeritska who wanted I should take her to dinner but I pretended like I was busy. Scotti and Gerry Farrar called up in the evening and wanted a game of bridge but I and the Mrs. was invited over to Luccini's to try out their new piano. "Well Lardy we will half to make it some other time," said Gerry. "You said a mouthfull Gerry" was my smileing reply.

The Dames

IT MAY not be generally known west of the river, but the present writer, who will state by way of alibi that he is writing this with the aid of a violent toothache, was the author of a few scenes in a certain edition of a revue which has been a annual headliner on the American stage for the past 16 years and which I am not allowed to mention the name of same but you will probably guess before I am through that I refer to the Ziegfeld Follies.

Well, a great many people in this part of the country seems to envy me the position not on acct. of how the royalties rolls in but because being a author, a person can go backstage any time they want to and talk to Bill Rogers and the chorus gals. About the same number of people has asked me why didn't I tell some of my personal experiences during the rehearsals of the show and etc. because they was wild to hear about same, so I am taking this opportunity to satisfy a public craving that almost amounts to a fever you might say.

In the 1st. place will state that I never seen nobody, be he author or mayor or inspector of ashcans, who couldn't talk to Mr. Rogers provided they caught Bill at a time when he himself had momentarily ran out of words. In the 2d. place I don't know only a few of the chorus gals who you yourself couldn't talk to them all you wanted to and when you got through talking to them you would find out like I did that they hadn't listened to nothing you said and didn't care a damn anyway.

But I will admit that they's 1 or 2 privileges which a author enjoys and which is not open to the gen. public and 1 of these is to attend chorus rehearsals and observe the practice costumes worn by the gals during the same. These costumes beggars description at least on my part and can only say that the most of them looks like their occupants had been drove out of their home by a alarm of fire 4 minutes after they started up to bed.

Along these lines I will relate a incidence which took place about the 4th. day of rehearsals and which I would entitle "My Most Embarrassing Moment" if that title had not of all

ready been used as a caption for a well-known newspaper feature and besides it didn't seem like a moment to me but years.
Well, I was standing out by the stage-door on 41st. St. smoking and they was a lull in the dancing rehearsal inside and one
of the prettiest of the dames as I have nicknamed them come
up to me and says have you got a cigarette. Will state that this
dame has been in the chorus long enough to know what to
wear in order to have perfect freedom during dancing rehearsals. But anyway I offered her a cigarette and she looked at it
and says Oh I can't smoke those kind.

"Would you mind," she says, "going down to that little store
this side of the corner and getting me some——?" (Naming
her brand.)

So I says I would like nothing better and she made a heart
rendering attempt to give me a ¼ to pay for same but I need
not tell my friends that I refused the ¼ as I don't take no
money from ladies save at the gaming table or at home.

Well, I started toward 7th. Ave. but I had not went more
than 3 or 4 steps when she says wait a minute, I think I will go
along with you and get a orangeade. I can only add that this
was about 2 o'clock on a May P.M. and the sun was high in the
heavens and the distance from the stage-door to the little store
and back to the stage-door amounts to about 1 city block, but
when the round trip was over I felt like a Cornell harrier crossing the finishing line exhausted but winner. Winner because in
the throngs that quickly gathered to watch us en route I hadn't
recognized none of my relatives by marriage.

I am not the hero of the next pathetic incidence which I will
relate, but am setting it down to show that a chorus dame has
got idears on subjects outside of their looks, their salary and
who is the next meal coming from. On this occasion the rehearsal was being held on "The Roof" and your correspondent
and Gene Buck the rhyme writer was setting near the piano,
watching and listening to young Dave Stamper, who don't
know if E flat is black, white or mulatto but plays like he was
born in a piano box.

Well, all the gals was there and a man was learning them
some new steps if any and all of a sudden another man come in
and whispered to him and went out again and the first man
clapped his hands twice which means stop dancing and he sent

the gals to their corners and made the following remarks in part:

"Everybody quiet. I'm afraid I've got some bad news. A package was just delivered at the stage-door downstairs. It was addressed to Miss ——. The package looked suspicious and was opened by Mr. ——. It was a bottle of ——. Now, you know, everybody knows that there is a strict rule against bringing —— into this theatre. Miss —— is therefore dismissed."

Miss —— left her place in line and took the air amidst a dead silence. The last named was broken in our vicinity by a gal who turned around and whispered:

"Say, listen: suppose I was to take it into my head to send a big box of flowers to one of you fellas and I would put a card in it saying with lots of love. And maybe not sign it or just sign my first name or something. And maybe you might not even know who they come from. But your Mrs. went to the door and got the package and opened it. What would happen to you? Would you get the air?"

After some deep thinking one of us said he didn't know what would happen to him but he thought the flowers would be blighted by the frost.

And that reminds me that they was 16 young English ladies in the troupe that hadn't seen dear old London since last April and you would think by this time they would be homesick enough to bark and snarl at everybody within reason. But the impression you got by talking to them was that they are the calmest and most contentedest gals on either side of the old pond and I never noticed one of them even excited except once. That was after the show had been running a long wile and I went in one night to see how many more of my lines had called for replacements and it just happened that amongst the audience was a man named Valentino. Well, the rumor that he was out front soon got backstage and when I drifted there the first person I met was one of these Tiller gals from London.

"Is that right?" she says. "Is Valentino really out there?"

So I told her it was right and where he was setting.

"What does he look like?" she says.

"I can't describe male beauty," I says, "but I am often taken for him on the street."

It was at this point that she give vent to strong emotion which I will not repeat the words of same.

I suppose that wile we are talking about it I may as well report another incidence that come off on this special night though this time a star is the heroine instead of a chorus dame. It was about the middle of the 2d act and Rodolph was the sole topic of conversation backstage. The star, dressed or vice versa for her next number, strolled up into the bunch and stood silent till the beautiful screen artist's name had been uttered 3 or 4 times. Then she spoke.

"——," she says, mentioning a biblical character, "just imagine a few years ago he was getting fifty bills a week dancing around tearooms and cabarets here in New York. And now look at him. That shows what a pretty face will do for you."

"Well," says somebody, "look what yours done for you."

"Mine!" she says. "I could cut off my head and the audience would never miss it."

Bed-Time Stories

HOW TO TELL A TRUE PRINCESS

WELL MY little boys and gals this is the case of a prince who his father had told him he must get married but the gal he married must be a true princess. So he says to the old man how do you tell if a princess is a true princess or a phony princess. So the old man says why if she is a true princess she must be delicate.

Yes said the prince but what is the true test of delicate.

Why said the old man who was probably the king if she is delicate why she probably can't sleep over 49 eiderdown quilts and 28 mattresses provided they's a pea parked under same which might disturb her. So they made her bed this day in these regards. They put a single green pea annext the spring and then piled 28 mattresses and 49 eider quilts on top of same and says if she can sleep on this quantity of bed clothing and not feel disturbed, why she can't possibly be delicate and is therefore not a princess.

Well the princess went to bed at 10 o'clock on acct. of having called up everybody and nobody would come over and play double Canfield with her and finely she give up and went to bed and hadn't been asleep more than 3 hrs. when she woke up and says I am very uncomfortable, they must be a pea under all these quilts. So they looked it up and sure enough they was a green pea under the quilts and mattresses. It made her miserable. She was practally helpless.

But the next day when she woke up they didn't know if she was a princess or the reverse. Because lots of people had slept under those conditions and maybe it was the mattress or the springs that had made them miserable. So finely the king suggested why not give her a modern trial.

So the next evening but one they sent her to bed under these conditions:

The counterpane was concrete and right under it was 30 layers of tin plate and then come 4 bales of cotton and beneath that 50 ft. of solid rock and under the entire layout a canary's feather.

"Now Princess," they said to her in a friendly way, "if you can tell us the name of the bird which you are sleeping on under all these condiments, why then we will know you are a true princess and worthy to marry the prince."

"Prince!" she said. "Is that the name of a dog?"

They all laughed at her in a friendly way.

"Why yes," she said, "I can tell you the name of that bird. His name is Dickie."

This turned the laugh on them and at the same time proved she was a true princess.

To-morrow night I will try to tell you the story of how 6 men travelled through the wide world and the story will begin at 6:30 and I hope it won't keep nobody up.

CINDERELLA

Once upon a time they was a prominent clubman that killed his wife after a party where she doubled a bid of four diamonds and the other side made four odd, giving them game and a $26.00 rubber. Well, she left him a daughter who was beginning to run absolutely hog wild and he couldn't do nothing with her, so he married again, this time drawing a widow with two gals of her own, Patricia and Micaela.

These two gals was terrible. Pat had a wen, besides which they couldn't nobody tell where her chin started and her neck left off. The other one, Mike, got into a brawl the night she come out and several of her teeth had came out with her. These two gals was impossible.

Well, the guy's own daughter was a pip, so both her stepmother and the two stepsisters hated her and made her sleep in the ashcan. Her name was Zelda, but they called her Cinderella on account of how the ashes and clinkers clang to her when she got up noons.

Well, they was a young fella in the town that to see him throw his money around, you would of thought he was the Red Sox infield trying to make a double play. So everybody called him a Prince. Finally he sent out invitations to a dance for just people that had dress suits. Pat and Mike was invited, but not Cinderella, as her best clothes looked like they worked in a garage. The other two gals made her help them doll up and they kidded her about not going, but she got partly even by garnisheeing their hair with eau de garlic.

Well, Pat and Mike started for Webster Hall in a bonded taxi and they hadn't much sooner than went when a little bit of an old dame stepped out of the kitchen sink and stood in front of Cinderella and says she was her fairy godmother.

"Listen," says Cinderella: "don't mention mother to me! I've tried two different kinds and they've both been a flop!"

"Yes, but listen yourself," says the godmother: "wouldn't you like to go to this here dance?"

"Who and the h—l wouldn't!" says Cinderella.

"Well, then," says the godmother, "go out in the garden and pick me a pumpkin."

"You're pie-eyed," was Cinderella's criticism, but anyway she went out and got a pumpkin and give it to the old dame and the last named touched it with her wand and it turned into a big, black touring car like murderers rides in.

Then the old lady made Cinderella go to the mouse-trap and fetch her six mice and she prodded them with her wand and they each became a cylinder. Next she had her bring a rat from the rat trap and she turned him into a big city chauffeur, which wasn't hardly any trouble.

"Now," says the godmother, "fetch me a couple lizards."

So Cinderella says, "What do you think this is, the zoo?" But she went in the living-room and choose a couple lizards off the lounge and the old lady turned them into footmen.

The next thing the old godmother done was tag Cinderella herself with the wand and all of a sudden the gal's rags had become a silk evening gown and her feet was wrapped up in a pair of plate-glass slippers.

"How do you like them slippers?" asked the old dame.

"Great!" says Cinderella. "I wished you had of made the rest of my garments of the same material."

"Now, listen," says the godmother: "don't stay no later than midnight because just as soon as the clock strikes twelve, your dress will fall off and your chauffeur and so forth will change back into vermin."

Well, Cinderella clumb in the car and they was about to start when the chauffeur got out and went around back of the tonneau.

"What's the matter?" says Cinderella.

"I wanted to be sure my tail-light was on," says the rat.

Finally they come to Webster Hall and when Cinderella entered the ballroom everybody stopped dancing and looked at her pop-eyed. The Prince went nuts and wouldn't dance with nobody else and when it come time for supper he got her two helpings of stewed rhubarb and liver and he also had her laughing herself sick at the different wows he pulled. Like for instance they was one occasion when he looked at her feet and asked her what was her shoes made of.

"Plate glass," says Cinderella.

"Don't you feel no pane?" asked the Prince.

Other guests heard this one and the laughter was general.

But finally it got to be pretty near twelve o'clock and Cinderella went home in her car and pretty soon Pat and Mike blowed in and found her in the ashcan and told her about the ball and how the strange gal had come and stole the show.

"We may see her again to-morrow night," says Pat.

"Oh," says Cinderella, "is they going to be another ball?"

"Why, no, you poor sap!" says Mike. "It's a Marathon."

"I wished I could go," says Cinderella. "I could if you would leave me take your yellow dress."

The two stepsisters both razzed her, little wreaking that it was all as she could do to help from laughing outright.

Anyway they both went back to the dance the next night and Cinderella followed them again, but this time the gin made her drowsy and before she realized it, the clock was striking twelve. So in her hurry to get out she threw a shoe and everybody scrambled for it, but the Prince got it. Meanw'ile on account of it being after midnight, the touring car had disappeared and Cindy had to walk home and her former chauffeur kept nibbling at her exposed foot and annoying her in many other ways.

Well, the Prince run a display ad the next morning that he would marry the gal who could wear the shoe and he sent a trumpeter and a shoe clerk to make a house to house canvass of Greater New York and try the shoe on all the dames they could find and finally they come to the clubman's house and the trumpeter woke up the two stepsisters for a fitting. Well, Pat took one look at the shoe and seen they was no use. Mike

was game and tried her best to squeeze into it, but flopped, as
her dogs was also mastiffs. She got sore and asked the trumpeter why hadn't he broughten a shoe horn instead of that
bugle. He just laughed.

All of a sudden him and the shoe clerk catched a glimpse of
Cinderella and seen that she had small feet and sure enough,
the slipper fitted her and they run back to the Prince's apartment to tell him the news.

"Listen, Scott," they says, for that was the Prince's name:
"we have found the gal!"

So Cinderella and the Prince got married and Cinderella
forgive her two stepsisters for how they had treated her and
she paid a high-price dentist to fix Mike up with a removable
bridge and staked Pat to a surgeon that advertised a new, safe
method of exterminating wens.

That is all of the story, but it strikes me like the plot—with
the poor, ragged little gal finally getting all the best of it—
could be changed around and fixed up so as it would make a
good idear for a play.

RED RIDING HOOD

Well, children, here is the story of little Red Riding Hood
like I tell it to my little ones when they wake up in the morning with a headache after a tough night.

Well, one or two times they was a little gal that lived in the
suburbs who they called her little Red Riding Hood because
she always wore a red riding hood in the hopes that sometime
a fresh guy in a high power roadster would pick her up and
take her riding. But the rumor had spread the neighborhood
that she was a perfectly nice gal, so she had to walk.

Red had a grandmother that lived over near the golf course
and got in on most of the parties and one noon she got up and
found that they wasn't no gin in the house for her breakfast so
she called up her daughter and told her to send Red over with
a bottle of gin as she was dying.

So Red starts out with a quart under her arm but had not
went far when she met a police dog. A good many people
has police dogs, and brags about them and how nice they
are for children and etc. but personly I would just as leaf

have my kids spend their week-end swimming in the State Shark Hatchery.

Well, this special police dog was like the most of them and hated everybody. When he seen Red he spoke to her and she answered him. Even a dog was better than nothing. She told him where she was going and he pertended like he wasn't paying no tension but no sooner had not she left him when he beat it up a alley and got to her grandmother's joint ahead of her.

Well the old lady heard him knock at the door and told him to come in, as she thought he must either be Red or a bootlegger. So he went in and the old lady was in bed with this hangover and the dog eat her alive.

Then he put on some pajamas and laid down in the bed and pertended like he was her, so pretty soon Red come along and knocked at the door and the dog told her to come in and she went up to the bed to hand him the quart. She thought of course it would be her grandmother laying in the bed and even when she seen the dog she still figured it was her grandmother and something she had drank the night before must of disagreed with her and made her look different.

"Well, grandmother," she says, "you must of hit the old hair tonic last night. Your arms looks like Luis Firpo."

"I will Firpo you in a minute," says the dog.

"But listen grandmother," says Red, "don't you think you ought to have your ears bobbed?"

"I will ear you in a minute," says the dog.

"But listen grandmother," says Red, "you are cock-eyed."

"Listen," says the dog, "if you had of had ½ of what I had last night you would of been stone blind."

"But listen grandmother," says Red, "where did you get the new store teeth?"

"I heard you was a tough egg," says the dog, "so I bought them to eat you with."

So then the dog jumped out of bed and went after Red and she screamed.

In the mean w'ile Red's father had been playing golf for a quarter a hole with a couple of guys that conceded themselfs all putts under 12 ft. and he was $.75 looser coming to the 10th. tee.

The 10th. hole is kind of tough as your drive has to have a carry of 50 yards or it will fall in a garbage incinerating plant. You can either lift out with a penalty of two strokes or else play it with a penalty of suffocation. Red's old man topped his drive and the ball rolled into the garbage. He elected to play it and made what looked like a beautiful shot, but when they got up on the green they found that he had hit a white radish instead of a golf ball.

A long argument followed during which the gallery went home to get his supper. The hole was finely conceded.

The 11th. hole on the course is probably the sportiest hole in golfdom. The tee and green are synonymous and the first shot is a putt, but the rules signify that the putt must be played off a high tee with a driver. Red's father was on in two and off in three more and finely sunk his approach for a birdie eight, squaring the match.

Thus the match was all square coming to the home hole which is right close to grandmother's cottage. Red's father hooked his drive through an open window in his mother-in-law's house and forced his caddy to lend him a niblick. He entered the cottage just as the dog was beginning to eat Red.

"What hole are you playing father?" asked Red.

"The eighteenth," says her father, "and it is a dog's leg."

Where-at he hit the police dog in the leg with his niblick and the dog was so surprised that he even give up the grandmother.

"I win, one up," says Red's father and he went out to tell the news to his two opponents. But they had quit and went home to dress for the Kiwanis Club dance.

"In Conference"

HARVEY HESTER entered the outer office of Kramer & Company, Efficiency Engineers. He approached the girl at the desk.

"I want to see Mr. Lansing," he said.

"A. M. or A. T.?" inquired the girl.

"Mr. A. T. Lansing," Hester replied.

"What is your name?"

"Harvey Hester."

The girl pressed a button and wrote something on a slip of paper. A boy appeared. She gave him the paper.

"For Mr. A. T. Lansing," she said.

The boy went away. Presently a young lady in mannish attire came out.

"I am Mr. Lansing's secretary," she said. "Did you want to see him personally?"

"I did and do," said Hester.

"Well, just now he's in conference," said the secretary. "Perhaps you would like to wait."

"Listen. This is pretty important——"

"I'm sorry, but it's against the rules to disturb any of the officers in conference."

"How long will the conference last?"

"It's hard to say," replied the secretary. "They just got through one conference and they're beginning another. It may be ten minutes and it may be an hour."

"But listen——"

"I'm sorry, but there's nothing for you to do but call again, or else wait."

"I'll wait," snapped Hester, "but I won't wait long!"

The conferees were sitting around the big table in the conference room. At the head of the table was J. H. Carlisle, president of the firm.

"Where is L. M.?" he inquired crossly. "This is the fifth conference he's been late to this morning. And we've had only six."

"Well, J. H. C.," said R. L. Jamieson, a vice-president, "I

don't think we ought to wait for him. If we drag along this way we won't be able to get in a dozen conferences all day. And a dozen was the absolute minimum agreed on."

"That's all right, R. L.," said K. M. Dewey, another vice-president, "but it happens that L. M. is the one that asked for this conference, and he's the only one that knows what it's about. So we'd——"

At this moment the door opened and the tardy one entered. He was L. M. Croft, one of the vice-presidents.

"I'm sorry to be late," he apologized, addressing J. H. C.

"I was talking over the phone to J. P. The reason I asked for this conference," he continued, "was to get your thought on a proposition that came up about twenty minutes ago. There was a post-card in the mail addressed to the firm. It was from the main post-office. It says they are holding a letter for us which reached them unstamped. If we sign the card and send it to them, together with a two-cent stamp, they will forward us the letter. Otherwise they will send it to the Dead Letter Office. The question is, Is the letter worth the time and expense of sending for it?"

"Who is the letter from, L. M.?" The inquirer was S. P. Daniels, one of the vice-presidents.

"The card didn't say, S. P.," replied Croft.

"My suggestion, J. H. C. and gentlemen," said A. M. Lansing, a vice-president, "is to write to whoever is in charge of that office, authorize him to open the letter, see who it's from and what it's about, and if he thinks it important, to let us know, and then we can mail the required stamp."

"It's a mighty ticklish business, gentlemen," ventured Vice-President T. W. Havers. "I have a brother, G. K. Havers. He's a pharmaceutical dispenser at a drug store on upper Broadway. He received a card like this from a branch post-office. He signed the card and sent the stamp, and the letter turned out to be nothing but advertising matter from a realtor."

"Why, T. W.," said A. T. Lansing, "you never told any one of us you had a brother."

"Oh, yes, A. T.," replied Havers. "I've got two other brothers besides G. K. One of them, N. D., is a mortuary artisan and the other, V. F., is a garbage practitioner in Harrisburg."

"I'm one of a family of seven boys," put in Vice-President B. B. Nordyke.

"I was born in Michigan," said H. J. Milton, the firm's secretary, "in a little bit of town called Watervliet."

"I'm a Yankee myself," said S. P. Daniels, "born and raised in Hingham, Massachusetts."

"How far is that from North Attleboro?" asked K. M. Dewey.

"It's right near Boston, K. M.," answered S. P. "It's a suburb of Boston."

"Philadelphia has some mighty pretty suburbs," said A. M. Lansing. "Don't you think so, R. L.?"

"I haven't been there for fifteen years, A. M.," replied R. L. Jamieson. "Last time I was there was in 1909."

"That was fifteen years ago, R. L.," remarked T. W. Havers.

"That's what I say, T. W., fifteen years," said Jamieson.

"I thought you said fourteen years," rejoined Havers.

"Let's see," put in C. T. Miller, treasurer of the firm. "Where was I fifteen years ago? Oh, yes, I was a bibliopolistic actuary in southern Ohio. I was selling Balzac complete for twenty-six dollars."

"Did you read Jimmie Montague's poem in the Record this morning, Z. H.?" inquired F. X. Murphy of Z. H. Holt.

"No, F. X.," replied Holt. "I don't go in for that highbrow stuff and anyways, when I get through my day's work here, I'm too tired to read."

"What do you do with yourself evenings, Z. H.?" asked A. T., the younger of the Lansings.

"Oh, maybe play the player piano or go to a movie or go to bed," said Holt.

"I bet there's none of you spends your evenings like I do," said young Lansing. "Right after dinner, the wife and I sit down in the living room and I tell her everything that I've done down here during the day."

"Don't she get bored?" asked S. P. Daniels.

"I should say not, S. P.!" replied young Lansing. "She loves it!"

"My sister Minnie—she married L. F. Wilcox, the tire people—she was over to the house last night," announced L. M. Croft. "She was reading us a poem by this Amy Leslie, the woman that got up this free verse. I couldn't make much out of it."

"Gentlemen," said J. H. C. at this juncture, "have you any more suggestions in regards to this unstamped letter? How about you, Z. H.?" he added, turning to Holt.

"Well, I'll tell you, J. H. C.," replied Holt, "a thing like this has got to be handled mighty careful. It may be all right, and it may be a hoax, and it may be out and out blackmail. I remember a somewhat similar case that occurred in my home town, Marengo, Illinois."

"Did you know the Lundgrens there?" asked L. M. Croft.

"Yes, indeed, L. M.," answered Holt. "I used to go into Chicago to see Carl pitch. He was quite a card player, too. But this case I speak of, why, it seems that S. W. Kline—he was a grass truncater around town—why, he received an anonymous post-card with no name signed to it. It didn't even say who it was from. All it said was that if he would be at a certain corner at a certain hour on a certain day, he would find out something that he'd like to know."

"What?" interrupted the elder Lansing.

"I was saying," said Holt, "that in my home town, Marengo, Illinois, there was a man named S. W. Kline who got an anonymous post-card with no name signed to it, and it said that if he would be at a certain corner at a certain hour on a certain day, he would find out something that he'd like to know."

"What?" repeated the elder Lansing.

"Never mind, Z. H.," said J. H. C. "Tell us what happened."

"Nothing," said Holt. "Kline never went near the place."

"That reminds me," put in K. M. Dewey, "of a funny thing that came off in St. Louis. That's when I was with the P. D. advertising department. One afternoon the postman brought the mail to our house and my wife looked it over and found a letter addressed to some name like Jennings or Galt or something like that. It wasn't for us at all. So she laid for the postman next day and gave him back the letter. She said, 'Look here, here's a letter that don't belong to us at all. It's for somebody else.' I forget now just what the name was. Anyway, he took the letter and I guess he delivered it to the right people."

"I got some pretty good Scotch myself for fifty-six dollars a case," said S. P. Daniels. "It's old James Buchanan."

"Where did you get it, S. P.?" inquired Paul Sickles.

"I've got the phone number home," replied Daniels. "I'll bring it to you to-morrow, Paul."

Sickles was the only man in the outfit who was not an officer, so they called him Paul instead of by his initials.

"Prohibition's a joke!" said T. W. Havers.

"People drink now'days that never drank before," said S. P. Daniels.

"Even nice women are drinking," said L. M. Croft.

"I think you'll see light wines and beer before it's over," said K. M. Dewey.

J. H. C. spoke again.

"But what about this letter?"

"It seems funny to me," said A. T. Lansing, "that the people in the post-office don't open it and find out what it's all about. Why, my wife opens my personal mail, and when I'm home I open hers."

"Don't she care?" asked S. P. Daniels.

"No, S. P.," said the younger Lansing. "She thinks everything I do is all right."

"My wife got a letter last week with no stamp on it at all," said Sickles. "The stamp must have dropped off. All it was anyways was a circular about mah jongg sets."

"Do you play with flowers, Paul?" asked K. M. Dewey.

"Why——"

Harvey Hester, in the outer office, looked at his watch for the twentieth time; then got up and went to the girl at the desk.

"Please have Mr. Lansing's secretary come out here again," he said.

"A. M. or A. T.?" asked the girl.

"A. T.," said Hester.

The secretary came out.

"Listen," said Hester. "If I can't see Mr. Lansing right this minute it'll be too late."

"I'm sorry, but I can't interrupt him when he's in conference."

"All right," said Hester. "Will you please give him this message? You've got my name. Mr. Lansing and I were in school together and were more or less friendly. Well, I was tipped off this morning—I don't need to tell you how—I was tipped off that

Mrs. Lansing is leaving for Chicago on the 12:05 train. And she isn't leaving alone. She's eloping. I thought Mr. Lansing might want to try to stop her."

"What time is it now?"

"Seven minutes of twelve," said Hester. "He can just make it."

"But he's still in conference," said the secretary.

Prohibition

CONGRESSMAN VOLSTEAD of the lowest house yesterday issued a proclamation declaring January 16th. a legal holiday as it is the glass wedding anniversary of the date when his act preventing the sale or manufacture of liquor went into such good and lasting effect. Everything will be closed on this date but the saloons.

Some of us is old enough to remember back 5 yrs. ago last New Years eve when the papers all come out and said that the celebration would be the wildest that ever took place in the U. S. as it was in the nature of a farewell to hootch which by next New Years eve, meaning Dec. 31, 1920, would be a thing of the past. The boys that made this prediction was as near right as Bernard Shaw on pugilism. The last New Years eve I heard of was New Years eve 1924 and I gather from hearsay that never before in history was they more and better people that had to be poured home.

I can also remember disgusting the prohibition question in the privacy of the household the day after it was made law and I made the remark that wile I might not approve of the proposition on principle, still and all I was glad it had went through on one acct. at lease, namely that by the time my boys growed up to college age they wouldn't be no chance for them to run wild as they wouldn't be nothing left to run wild on. This was another great prediction and judging by the increasing numbers of rah rah boys that staggers to classes, why in 6 or 7 yrs. when the first of my kiddies is ready to die for old Rutgers why they won't no football player think of going into a big game without a qt. on the hip.

It seems like about the biggest difference between now and 7 or 8 yrs. ago in big cities at least is that in them days most cities had a law that you must close your saloon at 11 o'clock or 12 o'clock or 1 o'clock. Now days according to the law, they ain't no saloons so they can and do stay open as long as they feel like. In this connection however I might relate a little incidence that come off near where I live and they was a couple of boys going home from a dance at their golf club and they stopped in at a road-house just as the prop. of same was turning out the lights and the door was locked but they knocked and a waiter left them come in and they said they would like a drink.

"He won't leave me serve you nothing," says the waiter referring to the prop.

Well the 2 boys hadn't never been in there before so they thought it was on acct. of the prop. not knowing them as they begin mentioning a lot of names of people that was regular customers of the place and had recommended it to them.

"Oh that is all right," says the waiter. "You gents looks all right, but he won't leave me serve you because it is 10 minutes after 1 o'clock."

"What has that got to do with it?" says one of the thirsty ones. "Under the Volstead act it's just as much vs. the law to sell drinks one time as another time."

"That may all be," says the waiter, "but the boss don't know they is a Volstead act. He has been stone deaf for 10 yrs."

The pastime of raiding is conducted on a whole lot more sensible lines now than in the old days. When the law allowed saloons but said they must close up at some certain time of night, why every little wile you would read in the paper where So and So had been raided the night before and him and all his help arrested just because they had been surprised at 3 A. M. with their bar open.

Compare this proceedings with the way things is handled under absolute prohibition. Like for inst. I was in a certain town in Jersey a wile ago and was setting in a cafe talking to the mgr. of same and all of a sudden a man come in and come to our table and whispered something to the mgr. and went right out again and then the mgr. called the head bartender and told him to take all the hard stuff upstairs and put it in the rm. under the roof and be sure and have this done by 8 o'clock and leave it there till 8.30.

Well I asked the mgr. what was the idear and he says that the man had broughten him word that the federal officers was on a raiding party and his place was scheduled for 8 o'clock. He says that the man who had just been in and warned him was employed by all the places in the town to do just that thing and he was now making his rounds telling the mgr. of each place just what time the raiders would call at that particular place.

"We only been caught once," says the mgr. "On that occasion the enforcement boys dropped in on us without sending no advance word or nothing and of course they found all kinds of stuff in the bar. It was a raw deal and we certainly told them what we thought of that kind of monkey business and they ain't never tried it since."

All and all it is no wonder that the congressman felt like the holiday should ought to be proclaimed as prohibition has sure been a godsend in a whole lot of ways. It has given lucrative employment to a great many men that did not have nothing before only their courage. It has cemented the friendship between the U. S. and Canada. It has give gals and women a new interest in life and something to talk about besides hair and children. And it has made our govt. appreciate the enormous extent of our coast line and how tough it would be to defend same vs. invasion.

As far as it affecting the present and future consumption of alcohol is conserned, why a person that said that drinking in the U. S. was still in its infancy would be just about hitting the nail on the hammer.

Tennis by Cable

HERE IS a idea that was suggested by my 2d. son Jimmie as we was setting at some meal the day after the tennis boys played for the east and west championship. I made the remark that Vincent Richards had beat Bill Johnston in straight sets and he says where was the matches played and I says right here on Long Island and he says well was he here on Long Island yesterday.

So I give him a sarcastic answer, namely Oh no, he was out in San Francisco and they played by telegraph like they play the international chess matches sometimes. So then I had to exclaim to him about the international chess matches that is sometimes played by cable and he says why don't they play the international golf matches and tennis matches and etc. by cable instead of them all taking the trouble to make the trips back and forth.

So I thought it over a long wile and come to the conclusion that maybe after all he was right and why should people cross the ocean just for a friendly game that they don't get no money out of it and we will take for inst. the Australian tennis team who I have nicknamed the anzacs and it must cost them a mint of money to come here from clear over there and what does it get them outside of the exercise which they could just as well of had over there and not take no chances of being seasick and I don't know how much it costs to get here from Australia, but it certainly would not cost nowheres near as much if they played by cable.

For example suppose Tilden was playing Gerald Patterson and it happened to be Tilden's first serve, why he would cable to Patterson that he had got his first service over and it was a terrific hard hit ball and what are you going to do about it, why Patterson would cable back, it did not look so hard hit to me. I returned it way into the upper corner of the court on your back-hand where it was pretty near impossible for you to get it. Then Tilden would reply, well I did get it on my back-hand and you was up close to the net, I made a passing shot which you couldn't possibly get. Then Patterson would reply, it may of seemed to you like I couldn't possibly get it, but as a matter of fact I did get it by a phenomenal stab and I returned it where you couldn't get it in a week.

Then Tilden would wait a wile and send back the following answer. It ain't only five days since your last shot came back and I managed to get a hold of it and lob it over your head to pretty close to the base line where I doubt if you could get your racket on it unless you used a airship.

Patterson's reply would be, I bought a airship as soon as I received your cable and managed to get back and hit that ball and I hit it with such force that even if you do get your racket on it, it will probably break your racket. Tilden would answer: Well, I seen that ball was going to break my racket as the last named is a old racket that has stood lots of wear and tear, so I bought myself a new racket and returned your shot to one inch from the base line where no living being could get their racket on it.

In this way the game could be carried on indefinitely and would probably be the closest tennis game ever played and still not cost near as much as if Mr. Patterson had came over here to play it and further and more we would not half to set out in a boiling sun on hot seats to watch it. To say nothing about how much more chance Patterson would have to win.

The Olympic games could be pulled off in the same way. Like for inst. Hubbard of Michigan was broad jumping vs. who ever broad jumps for France who we will call Lafayette and Hubbard makes the first jump and cables I just jumped 26 ft., try and laugh that off. So Lafayette wires back, you look silly to me, I just took my first leap and done 27 ft. They could keep this up till all records was broke and themselfs too.

But the best game that could be played by cable would be a bridge game because a person could bid pretty near as high as they wanted to and for inst. say they was bidding 6 spades, why when they come to play the hand the declarer could say I have got 12 spades in my hand and the ace of diamonds and the dummy has got the other spade and no diamonds and of course the oppts. could not see what was in either hand and it is bound to be a grand slam.

Who's Who

NOT SINCE I got through with the Telephone Directory has they been a book that give me so many thrills as Who's Who in America for 1924–25 and have just finished reading same and could hardly lay same down or hold it up either on acct. of it weighing pretty near as much as a grand opera chorus gal. Who's Who is published every other yr. by a guy out in Chi and before the guy goes to press he writes you a letter and asks if the dope on you in the last issue is still O. K. or have you moved or joined any new clubs etc. It looks like the more clubs you belong to the better chance you got of being in Who's Who, so I been joining a new club every couple of months since I come to N. Y. and just before this new Who's Who come out I joined the Friars which give me a total of 11 clubs all told not counting the Cooks and Pastry Cooks assn. of St. Louis which I was made a member in 1909 when it was the only place you could get a drink on Sunday.

But my entrée into the Friars come too late to get into this edition but the 10 other clubs got me by O. K. and then I begin wondering if they was anybody else in the U. S. that belonged to as many as 10 clubs so I started reading the book and had not got no distants at all before I found out that I am still in my nonage as far as joining clubs is concerned.

I will pass over the boys that tops me by a margin of 2 or 3 clubs and lead right up to the climax of the book which is Reginald C. Vanderbilt whom I might state at this junction was a fellow passenger on the board of the Paris the last and 2d. time I crossed the old pond. Well, here in part is a list of Reginald's clubs and will half to admit that they make me look like a hermit:

Knickerbocker, Brook, Metropolitan, Coaching, Turf, and Field, Riding and Driving, Racquet and Tennis, Automobile of America, Newport Reading Room, Newport Casino, Travelers (Paris), Meadowbrook, Four-in-hand (Philadelphia), Massachusetts Auto, Westchester Polo, American Kennel, Dalmatian, Russian Wolfhound, American Fox Terrier, French Bulldog, and Old English Sheepdog.

It will be noted that amongst the bunch is one foreign club and one Philadelphia club and 3 or 4 New England clubs to say nothing about all them dog clubs which I can't belong to none of them on acct. of us not having no dog, but I am eligible for a Orange and Black Striped Cat club if they is such a thing and also a Black Milch Cow club and a Green and Red Parrot club and a couple of exclusive Rodent societies. However I ain't got no hopes of catching up with Mr. Vanderbilt as he is still a young man and in a few years time they may half to get out a individual edition of Who's Who which the exclusive contents of same will be just his clubs.

But of course I don't mean to insinuate that clubs in quantity lots is enough to get you into the book. If it was they would half to devote a paragraph to Casey Stengel who in the National League alone has belonged to the Brooklyn, Pittsburgh, Philadelphia, New York and Boston clubs or pretty close to a clean sweep. The qualifications for honorable mention in the volume is printed right after the preface and in a nutshell is as follows:

(1) You either half to be a success in some creditable line of effort, making you the subject of extensive interest, inquiry or discussion in this country, or (2) you half to hold a high up civil, military, naval, religious or educational position. Well, on acct. of the last named rule, the book is pretty well messed up with the names of congressmen to say nothing about former Secretary Fall.

As for the boys that has succeeded in creditable lines of effort, why it ain't no trouble to run acrost a few names in the book which you can't help from wondering what their creditable lines of effort was unless it was their efforts to keep track of the clubs they belonged to. On the other hand they's some names which it would amaze you what they have accomplished out of a clear sky you might say, and no wonder they have win a nitch in Who's Who.

Like for inst. we will take A. P. Derby of Gardner, Mass. He went to Williams College for 2 yrs. and just as soon as he got out of college he begin to manufacture chairs and aptly enough, from 1921 to 1923, he was chairman of the Nat. Council Furniture associations. Mr. Derby is a Republican and a Congregationalist and a Mason and a Deke and is still living in Gardner, Mass., and manufacturing chairs. A record not to be sneezed at. Or take W. M. Hepburn of West Lafayette, Ind. He was born in Nova Scotia and went to Dalhousie University in Halifax and then to a library school in Albany and now he is librarian at Purdue and a Presbyterian.

That is just a couple samples of what it takes to get into Who's Who if you don't belong to plenty clubs, but it seems to me like the editor overlooked successes in a few creditable lines of effort when he left out Walter Johnson, Babe Ruth, Rogers Hornsby, Jack Dempsey, Bobby Jones, Walter Hagen, Ty Cobb, Jim Thorpe, Red Grange, Knute Rockne and the entire Notre Dame backfield. Just the same the book is well worth reading if it didn't learn you nothing except that they's 2 men in this country named Goodnight, both of them college professors.

On Conversation

THE OTHER night I happened to be comeing back from
Wilmington, Del. to wherever I was going and was setting
in the smokeing compartment or whatever they now call the
wash room and overheard a conversation between two fellows
who we will call Mr. Butler and Mr. Hawkes. Both of them
seemed to be from the same town and I only wished I could
repeat the conversation verbatim but the best I can do is report it from memory. The fellows evidently had not met for
some three to fifteen years as the judges say.

"Well," said Mr. Hawkes, "if this isn't Dick Butler!"

"Well," said Mr. Butler, "if it isn't Dale Hawkes."

"Well, Dick," said Hawkes, "I never expected to meet you
on this train."

"No," replied Butler. "I genally always take Number 28. I
just took this train this evening because I had to be in Wilmington today."

"Where are you headed for?" asked Hawkes.

"Well, I am going to the big town," said Butler.

"So am I, and I am certainly glad we happened to be in the
same car."

"I am glad too, but it is funny we happened to be in the
same car."

It seemed funny to both of them but they successfully concealed it so far as facial expression was conserned. After a pause
Hawkes spoke again:

"How long since you been back in Lansing?"

"Me?" replied Butler. "I ain't been back there for 12 years."

"I ain't been back there either myself for ten years. How
long since you been back there?"

"I ain't been back there for twelve years."

"I ain't been back there myself for ten years. Where are you
headed for?"

"New York," replied Butler. "I have got to get there about
once a year. Where are you going?"

"Me?" asked Hawkes. "I am going to New York too. I have
got to go down there every little wile for the firm."

"Do you have to go there very often?"

"Me? Every little while. How often do you have to go there?"

"About once a year. How often do you get back to Lansing?"

"Last time I was there was ten years ago. How long since you was back?"

"About twelve years ago. Lot of changes there since we left there."

"That's the way I figured it. It makes a man seem kind of old to go back there and not see nobody you know."

"You said something. I go along the streets there now and don't see nobody I know."

"How long since you was there?"

"Me?" said Hawkes. "I only get back there about once every ten years. By the way what become of old man Kelsey?"

"Who do you mean, Kelsey?"

"Yes, what become of him?"

"Old Kelsey? Why he has been dead for ten years."

"Oh, I didn't know that. And what become of his daughter? I mean Eleanor."

"Why Eleanor married a man named Forster or Jennings or something like that from Flint."

"Yes, but I mean the other daughter, Louise."

"Oh, she's married."

"Where are you going now?"

"I am headed for New York on business for the firm."

"I have to go there about once a year myself—for the firm."

"Do you get back to Lansing very often?"

"About once in ten or twelve years. I hardly know anybody there now. It seems funny to go down the street and not know nobody."

"That the way I always feel. It seems like it was not my old home town at all. I go up and down the street and don't know anybody and nobody speaks to you. I guess I know more people in New York now than I do in Lansing."

"Do you get to New York often?"

"Only about once a year. I have to go there for the firm."

"New York isn't the same town it used to be neither."

"No, it is changeing all the time. Just like Lansing. I guess they all change."

"I don't know much about Lansing any more. I only get there about once in ten or twelve years."

"What are you reading there?"

"Oh, it is just a little article in Asia. They's a good many interesting articles in Asia."

"I only seen a couple copies of it. This thing I am reading is a little article on 'Application' in the American."

"Well, go ahead and read and don't let me disturb you."

"Well I just wanted to finish it up. Go ahead and finish what you're reading yourself."

"All right. We will talk things over later. It is funny we happened to get on the same car."

from *The Other Side*

I SUPPOSE you people wants to hear about my trip acrost the old pond. When I say the old pond, I mean the Atlantic Ocean. Old pond is what I call it in a kind of a joking way.

Well, the wife hadn't never been to Europe, but she was half scared to go on account of seasickness which she even gets it on a bicycle. Personally I am a good sailor. Of course when I say good sailor I don't mean I would be any good sailing a boat, but it's just an expression I got up for a person that don't get sick easy.

Finally the wife agreed to go along provided I would pick out a steady ship so I made inquiries around and got pretty good reports on the Paris. The Paris is a French Line ship and named after Paris, the capital of France. The Paris is a six-day ship, or in other words, it made the run in a little over seven days.

We had to get our pictures taken and send to Washington for what they call a passport and when the passport come back, we had to get it what they call visaed by the consuls from the different countries which we intended to visit. We decided to visit France, Spain, Germany and England. They soaked us ten dollars for each visa, but while I was going around getting the visas, I found out that you can go to Holland for nothing, so we added Holland to the places we would visit if we had the time. The other countries ought to take a tip from the Holland Rotarians or whoever thought up the free gag, as it must draw a lot of customers in the course of a year.

They wasn't much of a passenger list on the Paris, but they was a big crowd down to see us off, if you only counted my children. We left the dock about ten in the morning and was soon out in the middle of North River looking at New York's skyline which I will not describe same here as it has already been mentioned in two or three books and magazines. Suffice it to say that the buildings in downtown New York are very impressive, some of them being several stories high.

We were shown to our cabin by a steward and I made the remark how funny it was that on a train, all the porters and waiters is named George, but on a ship they are all named Stewart. The wife was nervous and did not laugh.

Along about one o'clock a big gong sounded and we went down to lunch, where a steward told us we could not smoke in the dining room, but I soon showed him his mistake.

During the afternoon we unpacked the baggage and also found out the names of some of our fellow passengers. Amongst them was Mr. and Mrs. Reginald Vanderbilt who somebody told me had saved up quite a tidy sum of money and neither one of them has to work.

Another passenger was Gus Wilson, who sets in Georges Carpentier's corner during the Orchid Man's so-called fights and feeds him smelling salts. Mr. Wilson was born in Alsace and took the name Wilson because his own name had so many letters that he couldn't commit it to memory.

Mr. Wilson was chaperoning an American featherweight named Bud Dempsey and a welter named Jack Reed. The two boys was expecting to make some money in France and Germany, especially in Germany where the boxing game is at fever heat and when a bout is over, throngs of fashionable dressed women throw flowers at whoever win.

Messrs. Dempsey and Reed put on a three round exhibition bout previous to the ship's concert, but didn't act like they was very mad at each other. The proceeds of the bout and the proceeds of the concert was as usual donated to the disabled seamen's fund which by this time ought to make the Russian debt look like chicken's food.

At noon of the last day we stopped outside of Plymouth, England, and let off a few passengers that didn't know no better. In the middle of the evening we docked at Havre, but the most of us stayed on the board of the ship all night and got off the next morning and I and the wife took the ferry for Deauville on account of a cousin of mine living near there. It was past the height of the Deauville season, but all you had to do was settle with the hotel to find out why they call it Deauville.

We went to the Casino one night expecting to play roulette, but all as they had was a game called Boule, which has only got nine numbers instead of thirty-six and the ball they roll is rubber. They pay you seven to one on a single number, which don't seem hardly fair, but just the same I cleaned up fifty francs or about two dollars and a half and the croupiers was sure tickled to death when I bid them a fond good-night.

That is about all that happened at Deauville except one afternoon I was setting all alone at a table in the lounge of a hotel and the waiter asked me what would it be and I says dry Martini and pretty soon he came back with three Martinis. He thought I had been talking German. I told this gag to Frazier Hunt a few nights later and he said it was old stuff, but all as I can say is that it happened to me.

We left Deauville one morning at eight o'clock and reached gay Paris at eleven o'clock. I had both wired and written for reservations, but the head clerk hadn't never heard of me. Finally, however, he says to register and he would do what he could in a couple of hours. I forgot to say that when you register at any hotel in Europe you have still got to write your autobiography so the police and military authorities can look you up. This rule went into effect on account of the war and it looks like the hotel people hadn't heard of the armistice.

Well, anyway, while we was waiting, I took the madam over to the Seine which is a big river running right through the town, and also showed her the Eiffel Tower which she said what is it for and I couldn't answer, and I also showed her the Louvre and the Tuileries and finally took her to Maxim's for lunch and it was the first time she ever seen ladies standing up to the bar amongst the boys and several of the ladies smiled at me and she wanted to know where had I met them, so I says they probably recognized me from my pictures.

We got our room after lunch and the man that showed us up to it said that Gloria Swanson and Jackie Coogan was stopping at our hotel though not together, but anyway we stayed in our room all afternoon expecting maybe one of them would call up. The phone didn't ring however, and finally we went down to dinner and then to the Folies-Bergère, which the gals comes out in one scene all dressed up like Eve. In the final scene they have a pool on the stage and the Tiller Girls walk down steps into it clear over their heads. The wife made the remark that it wouldn't hurt none of the costumes in the show if they was submerged a while.

Well, to make a short story out of a long story, why, during this stay in gay Paris we took in all the Montmartre night joints like the Dead Rat and so forth and the only shock I got was when they brought the check around. All the music was American jazz and all the conversation was American and English, though one of the newspaper men told me that they's some old time Parisians that still speaks French.

Next time I run across you I will tell you about Biarritz and Spain and maybe the Riviera, which I know you can't hardly wait.

II

French trains runs like they was on pogo sticks, and when some of your friends sees you getting ready to go on a trip, why, instead of asking where are you bound for they say where are you bounding for.

I and the madam was bounding for Biarritz and left Paris early enough one evening to have dinner on the train. The solid part of the dinner was good; the rest of it spilled itself all over our going-away gowns. However, we was too fascinated watching the French and English eat to care what else happened. Both these nations eat in dead earnest and ambidextrously, and the last course is always an individual toothpick, which is used at great length and with no attempt to deceive, and then replaced in its gold case and put back in the pocket.

When the show was over we went to what is laughingly called the wagon-lit, or sleeping car. The sleeping compartments on a French train was designed by Harry Houdini, and if two people tries to occupy one of them, why, at least one of the people ought to be an experienced traffic policeman.

We arrived in Biarritz in the morning and was escorted to the Palais hotel, which is said to have been one of the residences of the Emperor Napoleon. They's very few places in France that wasn't. As usual, we hit this joint out of season and all the Americans had gone home except the flies.

The concierge informed us that the last bull fight of the year was going to take place at San Sebastian that afternoon. San Sebastian is in Spain. Spain is right near France. So we hired a car and drove over to San Sebastian. We was held up on the border while half a dozen Espagnolas in half a dozen different colored uniforms gathered around and looked at our passport, but they left us go through as soon as they seen I was from Niles, Michigan.

This was my first bull fight, to say nothing about it being my last. They was six bouts on the programme, and we got there in time for the first preliminary. They ain't hardly anybody in the world that ain't described a bull fight, so I will pass it over in a few words.

In the first place, three thirty-year-old horses was rode into the arena by three Spaniards that couldn't make a living no other way. Then come seven or eight guys on foot that they told me was banderilleros, which I don't know what it means but they certainly looked it. They was all carrying different colored coats which they shake in the bull's face and it's supposed to make him mad, but having to be in the same arena as the banderilleros would make him mad enough without no coat shaking.

Well, the picadors parked their three old dobbins at different places against the wall, and then they was a breathless silence and in come the bull.

They tell me that before the bull is sent in they load him up with beer or some other kind of a sedative. He sure looked like he would rather be in bed than where he was at. But, one by one, the bandies managed to get him roused up and attracted his attention to the first horse, and the next thing you know they wasn't no first horse. It was a pretty sight.

Then it was the next horse's turn, and then the last horse's turn, but the bull wasn't satisfied with his job on the last horse and attacked him again after he was down. It was the first time I had ever studied a horse's anatomy from the inside. It was a pretty sight, and no wonder the Spaniards cheered.

A piece of burlap was throwed over each horse, and they was dragged out in turn with a blare of trumpets.

Another breathless silence, and in strode the matador, all dressed up like Escamillo and carrying a sword in one hand and in the other the little old red shawl that Maggie wore. The crowd cheered again, and the banderilleros supplied themselves with banderillas, which is a kind of a barbed dart, which they stuck in the back of the bull's neck to take some of the fight out of him, and finally, when he couldn't even see no more, the bold matador shoved his sword through his bean and the first prelim was over.

I kind of cast a sidelong glance at the madam and she was doing the same thing to me, and without no words passing between us we got up and staggered out of the grand stand, so I can't tell you the results of the last five bouts.

That night we went to a performance of Carmen by a travelling company back in Biarritz, and for some reason another I wished it was the toreador instead of the gal that Don José stabbed.

The next night we had the honor of dining with Mr. Alex Moore, United States ambassador to Spain. The king had gone back to Madrid, but was represented by his secretary, Señor Angel. Señor Angel's name is pronounced as if the "g" was a "h," which is just another sample of what funny people the Spaniards are. Of course we was all in our black suits, and Mr. Moore had on a black tie about a yard long and half as wide which completely hid his collar. He got this habit in his home town of Pittsburgh, where it ain't safe to expose your collar for even a minute.

Mr. Moore treated us grand and took us to the Biarritz Casino, where they left me in as soon as they found out I was a Michigan boy and I was looking forward to roulette, which I have got licked to death, but all they was playing was chemin-de-fer, which I ain't got licked to death, so I watched the others lose theirs.

Well, the next morning I asked the concierge what time could we get a train for Marseilles and how far was it and he says you can get a train at noon and it gets you in there about ten o'clock to-morrow, so I says that sounds pretty bad, but you may as well reserve us a place on the sleeper. Oh, he says, they ain't no sleeper.

Well, to make a short story out of a long story, they was nothing to do but hire a covered wagon, and though it cost a pretty penny we was glad we done it, as it give us a chance at some of the prettiest scenery in la belle France. Most of the way we was in the Pyrenees or alongside of them and I suppose I better explain that the Pyrenees is the mountains that divides la belle France from sunny Spain. France and Spain is right close to each other and would be even closer if it wasn't for the Pyrenees.

I guess all the horses in this part of the country had been used up in the bull fights. Anyway, all along the road we travelled we seen nothing but oxen. On one occasion we come up against a couple of them that seemed to have lost their driver, and no matter how much we honked, they wouldn't get out of the way. The madam begin to get angry, so I says don't get angry; they are just kidding us. Can't you take a yoke of oxen? She didn't laugh and our driver either didn't hear it or else he couldn't understand much English.

We stopped for lunch at a town called Pau, and I pulled a few more gags about the name and got better results. But the prize one was when the wife asked me where was we going to put up for the night and I told her Toulouse. So she says can't we get further than that and I says we could, but the concierge back at the hotel said the trip would take three days at least, so we may as well go easy. We've got nothing Toulouse.

Next time I will tell you about the rest of the drive along the Pyrenees and the arrival on the Riviera and what I done to the boys at Monte Carlo.

Insomnia

IT'S ONLY ten o'clock, but I hardly slept at all last night and I ought to make up for it. I won't read. I'll turn off the light and not think about anything. Just go to sleep and stay asleep till breakfast-time.

Then maybe I'll feel like working.

I've got to get some work done pretty soon.

It's all going out and nothing coming in.

That was a song of Bert Williams'. Let's see; it started:

> Money is de root of evil, no matter where you happen to go.
> But nobody's got any objection to de root, now ain't dat so?
> You know how it is with money, how it makes you feel at ease;
> De world puts on a big broad smile, and your friends is as thick as bees.

Bert sang a song of mine once and I had it published; it was put on phonograph records, too, and I think the total royalties from sheet music and records amounted to $47.50. It's fun writing songs, but I never could make money out of things that were fun, like playing poker or bridge or writing songs or betting on horses.

The only way I can earn money is by writing short stories. Short! By the time I'm half through with one, it's a serial to me.

I wish I were as good as O. Henry and could get by with a thousand or twelve hundred words. I could write a thousand-word short story every day; that is, I could if my head were as full of plots as his must have been. I think of about one plot a year, and then, when I start writing it, I recall that it's somebody else's, maybe two or three other people's.

Just the same, plot or no plot, I'll have to work to-morrow. There's the insurance and notes and interest on mortgages— But I won't get to sleep that way. I mustn't think about anything at all, or at least, I must think about something that doesn't make any difference.

Sheckard, Evers, Schulte, Chance, Steinfeldt, Hofman, Tinker, Kling, Brown.

Twenty years or so ago I was a baseball nut and could recite any club's batting order. Nowadays I hardly know which Waner bats second and which third.

When I was sixteen, I lived in Clayton, Michigan, and sang in the choir. One Christmas day there was a new face in the congregation, a girl's face, the most attractive face I had ever seen. The owner of the face was sitting with a schoolmate of mine, in the fifth or sixth pew from the front.

I saw her at the start of the service and I'm afraid I wasn't of much use to the choir that morning. When the recessional was over, I got out of my cotta and cassock in nothing flat and ran around to the front of the church. My schoolmate generously introduced us. I guess it wasn't generously at that; he didn't lack self-confidence to the extent of considering me a rival.

Her name was Lucy Faulkner. I had always hated the name Lucy, but from then on it was music. We met at several parties and she seemed to like me, in spite of terrific competition. I could say some awfully funny things in those days. I wish I could remember them.

If I had gone to dances, we might have got better acquainted, which probably would have hastened the ruination of my chances, if I had any. You can't be funny all the while, even at sixteen.

Her family, new in town, didn't have much of an opinion of our educational system. They sent her to a boarding school, far away. We started a lopsided correspondence. I wrote her two letters and she didn't answer either of them. But when she came home for spring vacation, she was still quite friendly. As for me, crazy is not the word.

One day our cow got loose and I received the assignment to chase her and bring her home. My pursuit of Cora through the main street of the town afforded the merchants and shoppers a great deal of amusement and me considerable anguish, which developed into suicidal mania when the cow suddenly turned a couple of corners and dashed right into the Faulkners' yard. I realized what a blight to romance would be the spectacle of the perspiring, bedraggled hero chasing a wild, demoniacal cow and losing a length in every two.

My mind was quicker than my feet. I conceded the race, hid behind a tree and prayed that Lucy was not at home, or that if she was, she hadn't seen me and would not recognize Cora.

Luck was with me. The Faulkners were all absent, Cora and I were not observed and Cora, stopping for refreshments on a near-by unmowed lawn was caught and returned to the owner by a friendly hired man.

It was only a postponement of the bitter ending. One night in July, four of us young men about town drank a great many steins of Meusel's singing beer and, at half past two in the morning, decided to go serenading. Our first stop was in front of the Faulkners'. The night was hot and all the windows were open.

Lucy, blessed with youth, slept through the horrible din. Not so her parents. From one of the windows came the sound of a voice that could talk even louder than we could sing and we decided to go somewhere else while a cloud still obscured the moon and kept our features secret.

Well, they never knew who three of us were. But they knew who one of us was. And yet there is said to be a tendency on the part of medium-sized men to envy tall men their height.

Lucy was given some orders at breakfast and obeyed them until she was safely engaged to a decent fella. There was no ban put on the other members of the quartet, though I swear my bass had been barely audible against their deafening whoops.

It must be after midnight. I'll just turn the light on and look at my watch. Eight minutes after ten. Good Lord! Maybe if I read just a little while—— No; that will only make me more wakeful than ever. And if I have to work tomorrow, I must get some sleep.

Ten or eleven high balls or a shot in the arm would be an effective lullaby. The trouble is, the more habits you have, the more you have to snap out of. At that, I guess too much coffee is as bad as too much Scotch. Too much of anything is bad; even too much sleep.

If I had an idea for a story and kind of laid it out in my mind, it would be a lot easier than facing that typewriter tomorrow with no idea at all. I'll try to think of one. No, I mustn't think. You can't go to sleep thinking up an idea for a story.

It is essential, I'm told, that your mind be a perfect blank. Some might say that in my case it wouldn't take much erasing.

It would, though. Perhaps I don't think importantly, but I think just the same.

I wonder if I could make a story out of what Doc Early was telling me the other night. It was about Allan Spears and his wife and his kids. I would have to disguise their names and where they were from or Doc would kill me. I could call the man Leslie Arnold and his wife Amy, and have them live in Janesville, Wisconsin, instead of Rockford, Illinois. I'd have to fake and pad a little, but that's no novelty.

I had heard of Spears, and Mrs. Spears was pointed out to me at the theater, last time I was in Chicago. She is one of the prettiest women I ever saw. A blonde, slight, and with a wonderful complexion. In the story I will make her a brunette and statuesque.

Well, let's see: Spears went to the University of Illinois and won his letter in baseball, football and track three years running. His athletic activities kept him in pretty strict training, but when he got through college, he more than made up for it. He was Rockford's whoopee kid as long as his money held out. It was money (about $6,000) left him by an aunt or something. The money lasted him seven months, and then he had to sober up awhile because everybody knew he was flat and he couldn't even get rat poison on credit.

It was during his involuntary water-wagon ride that Edith Holden fell in love with him. He fell in love with her, too, and I don't suppose he fought very hard against it inasmuch as she was said to have a private fortune of one million dollars. The fortune really amounted to one-fifth of that, but even so——

When Edith broke the news to her parents, their cries could be heard throughout the Middle West. Here was their only child, a young woman so beautiful that when she walked down the street, or up the street for that matter, all of Rockford's male citizens swooned, throwing herself away on a youth who held the world's record for personal consumption of terrible hooch, six thousand dollars' worth in seven months, and who would doubtless try to tie or beat that record as soon as he had the means.

It wouldn't have been so bad if Allan had ever shown an inclination to work. He hadn't.

Mr. Holden made all sorts of threats. He would lock Edith up, he would never speak to her again, he would publicly denounce her, he would shoot young Spears, he would cut her out of his will. (This last item meant something, too, for he was actually a millionaire.) She didn't laugh at him. She cried, and went ahead with plans for an elopement. They ran away to Chicago and were married, and decided to live there. Half of her two hundred thousand dollars was in good bonds, which she put in a safety-deposit box accessible to both her husband and herself. The other hundred thousand in cash was divided evenly and deposited for checking accounts, one his, one her own.

Now you might guess that he was overdrawn within the year, but your guess would be wrong. To his own surprise as well as everybody else's, he stayed on the wagon, went to work for an insurance company, and for the first four years of his married life, earned an average annual income of fifteen thousand.

He and Edith managed to live on this and their coupons without much economizing. And I mustn't forget to mention that he had his own life insured for seventy thousand, with Edith and their twin children, a boy and a girl, named as beneficiaries.

Young Mrs. Spears hoped and prayed that Allan's good behavior and the existence of the twins would soften the hearts of her parents, but not until the beginning of her fifth year away from home did she see an encouraging sign. It came in the form of a letter from her mother, a brief letter to be sure, but still a letter, beginning "Dear Daughter." And Allan chose that otherwise cheering day to fall with a thud.

In two months he had lost his job and thirty thousand dollars, the latter at the race tracks, and had spent five thousand for parties. On the occasions when he came home, unkempt and crazy-looking, the twins ran from him in terror and Edith grew hysterical.

She had no one to call on for help and, besides, she doubted that there was any help for a thing like this. She thought of taking her children to Rockford, but she was not of a temperament that could endure calmly what her mother and father were sure to say.

On the sixty-second day of his bender, Allan was brought to his house in a taxi and carried from the taxi to his bed by the driver and a man Edith had never seen before. Allan was sick, very sick, and she was glad of it. For the moment she didn't care whether he got well or died. However, she did call a doctor.

The doctor said it was a pretty close thing, but that Allan's remarkable constitution would pull him through. That is, it would pull him through this siege. He'd have to stay on the wagon, though, from now on. Another bat would finish him.

When Allan could be talked to, Edith talked to him.

"The doctor says if you ever drink again you'll die. I say if you ever drink again, don't come home. If you do drink again and come home, I'll take the children and go away and never, never come back. I mean it."

Allan was in bed two weeks, up and around the house a week, and then went downtown seeking a job. He was turned down a dozen times a day for a good many days. He was discouraged, blue, despondent.

And then one day he met two alumni of his university, Gilbert White, a classmate, and Harry Myers, an older man credited with having cleaned up in the market and being on the inside of everything that has an inside.

They invited him to luncheon and he accepted. They asked him to have a drink and he declined.

"I'm looking for a job," he said.

"Well," said White, "if you take a drink, Harry will give you something better than a job. He'll give you the tip he's given me and if you play it for all it's worth, you wont need a job."

Allan woke up next morning in a Loop hotel. His head was splitting. He found his coat, which wasn't much trouble since he had not taken it off. He put his hand in a pocket where cigarets might lurk, but the pocket was empty, save for a slip of paper on which Harry Myers' tip was inscribed in his own handwriting.

Allan read the slip with some difficulty and stumbled to the telephone. He called up the brokerage firm of Rogers and King. Sam King, the junior partner, was another alumnus of Illinois.

"What do you think of So-and-so?" asked Allan.

"I think it's the greatest buy there is," said Sam.

"How much margin would I have to put up?"

"Why don't you buy it outright?" said Sam, who had heard, and still thought, that Mrs. Spears had a million in her own name.

"Oh, no," said Allan. "If I did that I'd have to tell my wife and I want to surprise her."

"Well," said Sam, "the amount of margin would depend on the number of shares."

"Make it seven thousand shares," said Allan.

"You're certainly talking big numbers," said Sam, "and your wife *will* be surprised, especially if something happens and the market takes a nose dive."

"What is it selling at this morning?"

"Forty-nine," said Sam.

"Well," said Allan, "you buy me seven thousand shares and I'll be over there inside of an hour with collateral for seventy thousand bucks. And to play it safe, you can sell at forty-four."

Allan hung up the receiver, took it down again and called his home.

"Edith," he said, "I had some drinks last night as you probably guessed. I'm likely to have some more today. I'm going to stay away from home till I'm all through forever. I may see you a month from now, or it may be a year. Yes, I know what the doctor told you, but doctors are always guessing. You won't hear from me again till it's good news. I send the kids a good-by kiss through you. I'm sure that's the way they'd rather have it. And I hope you'll think of me as I am sometimes and not as I am other times."

Allan went to the safety-deposit box, took out seventy thousand dollars' worth of bonds and delivered them to Rogers and King. He returned to the box and deposited the memorandum and receipt.

"It isn't stealing," he told himself. "If the doctor is wrong and Myers is wrong and I lose thirty-five thousand, I'll work till I can pay it back. And no matter whether Myers is wrong, if the doctor is right, the insurance company will pay Edith seventy thousand."

He exchanged what was in his checking account for travelers' checks. Then he got on a train for New York, an Eastern seaport at which you can usually find a ship that will ride you as far as you want to go.

The story I expect to make out of this would be immoral if I allowed Allan himself to profit by what he had done. But the doctor wasn't wrong. And when news of her husband's death, in some remote corner of the earth, reached Edith several months later, she was able to sell Allan's stock at a hundred and fifty-three dollars a share, a profit of $728,000 minus commissions. This chicken feed together with Allan's seventy thousand dollars' worth of life insurance, her hundred thousand in bonds and her fifty thousand dollar bank balance, almost intact, enabled Edith to prove to her parents that she had loved wisely and just about well enough.

Now that's off my mind and I ought to be able to go to sleep. Maybe if I'd exercise every day—— But golf is the only exercise I like and I can't make any money at it. I can't beat anybody. I might if I played three or four times a week.

I'll turn on the light now and see what time it is. Eleven-eighteen. Well, at least it's after eleven. What I should do is get up and make a few notes for my story. And smoke one cigaret, just one. After that, I'll come right back to bed and turn off the light and not think of anything. That's the only way to go to sleep. Not thinking about anything at all.

Eckie

THERE WAS great excitement around the Chicago Inter-Ocean office during the last two or three days of January, 1908. The prophets had declared that if we found the place still open at noon on February second, the paper would exist for six more weeks. Since the beginning of the year it had been common gossip in the town that we were on our last limbs, and the issuance of weekly pay checks was always followed by a foot race downstairs to the bank; the theory being that only the first five or six to reach the paying teller's cage would land in the money.

However, according to the best of my knowledge and belief, all the employes of the I.-O. were paid in full when publication finally ceased. I was not on hand for the funeral, because I received, on February first, an offer from Harry Shroudenbach, sporting editor of the Examiner, to join his staff immediately at the noble salary of twenty-five dollars a week, an increase of $6.50 over what I had been getting. My Inter-Ocean boss, Duke Hutchinson, advised me to grab the offer before it was withdrawn; whether from kindliness or from the fact that he was tired of seeing me around, I shall never know.

With Hugh Fullerton, star baseball writer, hibernating, the Examiner's sporting staff was numerically equal to the Inter-Ocean's. We had Shroudy, the sports editor, Duffy Cornell, his assistant, and Sam Hall and me, domestics. It was important, of course, to get the news into the paper, but more important than that, it seemed, was to write startling, pretty, perfectly fitting headlines of an intricacy which still makes me shiver in retrospect. The sport pages' first and last columns had to be crowned with what were called "Whitney heads," and I don't believe the best copy reader in the world would call them simple. They were triangular in shape, with the base on top and the vertex on the bottom; thus:

GOTCH BREAKS BEALL'S
FOOT WITH TOE HOLD
AS RECORD CROWD

AT COLISEUM
GOES STARK
MAD

Below that was a single cross line, then a double, uneven cross line—both of them common in the heads of today—and finally a symmetrical bank, in small type, that was supposed to tell everything you hadn't told before.

These headlines were undoubtedly a delight to the eye of the reader, but a pain in the neck to the person or persons who wrote them. One in an evening, if you could take your time, was no trouble at all. But when you had to tear off four or six, with a two-minute limit for each, you were ready to spend your off day seeking oblivion.

And that reminds me of three successive off days I took—one of them on the office and the other two on myself—during which so much oblivion was found that it is a wonder the Examiner did not advertise at once for another maid of all work. On Monday, my regular day of recess, I began a preliminary reconnaissance of the South Side. There was so much ground to cover that my explorations were far from complete when someone told me it was Tuesday afternoon and time to report for duty. I reported, and received a note from Shroudy stating that he and Mr. Cornell and Mr. Hall had all left for Milwaukee to handle the big fight. Shroudy was going to write the lead, Mr. Cornell the detail, and Mr. Hall the notes. I can't remember what fight it was, possibly one of the terrific battles between Billy Papke and Stanley Ketchel.

Well, all three of them were good fight writers and any Papke-Ketchel fight was bound to be a good fight; particularly good for a Chicago paper because Papke's home was in Illinois and Ketchel's—whether he ever saw it or not—in Michigan. Just the same, it seemed kind of quaint to leave a hick like me alone in the office to take care of their copy and all the other sport copy that would come in, while the three experienced guys went on a junket to Milwaukee for the simple reason that they were wild-eyed fight fans. Shroudy's instructions said I would have to watch my step, because the stuff would arrive by wire a piece at a time; I would have to figure out whose stuff was whose and keep it all straightened out.

Unseen audience, I wish I had preserved the Examiner's Papke-Ketchel story of that Wednesday morning. Not even a broadcaster could have got things more messed up. Lead, detail and notes were all jumbled together and Round 1 probably read something like this:

> The boys were called to the center of the ring and received instructions from William Hale Thompson, Ernest Byfield, Percy Hammond, Charles Richter, the Spring Valley Thunderbolt tore in as if he had never heard another crowd made the trip as guests of William Lydon on his yacht the Lydonia Steve cut loose with a left uppercut that nearly this makes certain another meeting between the Battling Nelson and Packey McFarland were also introduced. Steve slipped as he was about to. Seven special trains but the majority thought the round was even it was Papke's round.

That and three or four columns more of the same. The stuff had come in just in time to make the first edition; there was no chance for proofreading or rearranging. And when the edition reached the main copy desk it was greeted with such hilarity that even I woke up and took the advice of a reporter friend who told me to get out of the office before the Milwaukee train bearing my boss and his colleagues arrived back in town.

I sought a quiet spot where I knew Walter Eckersall would eventually appear. When a fellow needed a friend, there was none to be found more satisfactory than Eckie. On this occasion he convinced me that it was not my fault and escorted me in a taxi to my lodgings, leaving me, as he thought, to woo forgetfulness in sleep.

But for some reason I was still restless, and ten minutes after he had gone I was in another taxi, on another sight-seeing tour of Chicago. An account of this trip would be extremely dull, even if I were able to recall any of the details. My chauffeur and I probably called on a great many people who have moved since then. Late Wednesday afternoon it occurred to me that the sooner I knew I was fired the sooner I could start looking for a new job. I asked to be taken to the Examiner office. The meter, I was told, read $132 and this was $130.20 more than I had. The chauffeur appeared vexed at my suggestion that we meet later and talk things out, and he was searching his tool box for an instrument with which to express his mortification when who should pour forth from the office door but Shroudy himself!

"What's the matter?" he said, and was soon informed. And within the next ten minutes he saw the cashier, settled with the taxi man, assured me I was still on the staff and that he realized he had overburdened me the night before, and sent me home to sleep till six o'clock Thursday evening, "when," he added, "we'll start all over."

You will realize by this time that my bosses were pretty well supplied with the so-called milk of human kindness. This pleasant surprise, however, was a double play in which Eckie ought to be credited with an assist. I learned long afterward that the latter had pleaded my cause for hours and had even gone to his own boss, Harvey Woodruff, of the Tribune, and persuaded him to make room for me in the event I got the air from the Examiner, though the Trib already employed so many people in the sporting department that half the writers had to buy seats from the agencies or work lying on their stomachs.

Eckie would do almost anything for anybody, but his friendliness toward me was a natural—I was the only person he knew who shared his horror of going to bed. Night after night, until it was almost the next night, we would sit and just talk; nearly always on one subject—football. And I want to testify that never did I hear him brag of his own skill at that sport, skill equaled—in my opinion and that of other experts who have visited or dwelt in the wilderness west of the Hudson River— only by Jim Thorpe, of Carlisle, and George Gipp, of Notre Dame.

Thorpe and Gipp were quadruple-threat men—they could pass, run, point-kick and punt. Eckie was a triple threat; the forward pass was introduced too late for him to work on it. Nevertheless, when you consider his all-around athletic prowess and his ability as a baseball player, you must conclude that he would have been even more valuable in the modern game than in the old.

Study his equipment for a moment. As a track man at Hyde Park High School, he had done the hundred repeatedly in 10 flat. After he entered the University of Chicago, he got down to 09 ⅕ in practice a couple of times and continued to do his 10 consistently in competition. Once, as a stunt, he went the route in 10 ⅕ dressed in his football costume. As a quarterback he was a cool, smart director of play. Perhaps not so hard to bring down as Heston, Mahan or Grange, he was harder to catch because of his terrific speed; he played back on defense, and when an opposing team punted to him it was not punting out of danger but into it. I firmly believe Eckie was the reason for Fielding Yost's insistence that his punters learn to punt out of bounds; when a punter boots a high spiral straight down the field for fifty yards, it disheartens a coach to see the punt brought back forty of those yards in spite of faultless covering by competent ends and tackles. As safety man, he was eluded, so far as I know, just once, and that was by Willie Heston. And when Willie eluded you, you were not disgraced. You were merely grateful that you had not been killed.

Now for his kicking. In the Middle West only Pat O'Dea, of Wisconsin, not a contemporary of Eckie's, was the latter's master in drop-kicking and punting, just as he—Pat—was everybody else's superior in these two specialties. It is unnecessary to take my word for that last clause; the record books will bear me out. But Eckie's punts, well aimed and high, averaged close to forty yards, and if he failed to score on a drop kick from thirty yards out, it was almost as much of a shock to the community as seeing Jimmy Walker in a Mother Hubbard.

Seven or eight years after the close of Eckie's college career —and by this time I was a Tribune man, too—there came into the office one Saturday night a story from Harvard—or wherever Harvard had played that day—saying that Charles Brickley had kicked five goals from field in the game with Yale, breaking the world's record so far as major university competition was concerned. Well, everybody around the office knew that Eckie had done the same thing in a game against Illinois, but to make sure, Harvey Woodruff, the sporting editor, asked him.

"Why, yes," he replied, "but maybe Chicago and Illinois are just prep schools." Then, after a pause, "Listen, Woody; I didn't break a record that time any more than Brickley did this afternoon. Mr. Stagg looked it up and found that I had only tied an old record made by a fella at Purdue."

Now you mustn't ask me who the Purdue fella was. The only prominent athletes from that university whose names I can recall are G. P. Torrence, Elmer Oliphant and George Ade, and I know it was none of these.

I discovered years ago that the best way to judge an athlete's worth was by learning what his opponents, past and to come, really thought of him. It was from the people who had tried to hit, or were about to try to hit, Walter Johnson in his good years that I gleaned the knowledge that no other pitcher of our times was in his class. And the men of Yost's great, but not greatest, Michigan elevens of 1904 and 1905 were unable to hide the fact that the very name of Walter Eckersall gave them a headache.

Eckie's first start against Michigan, however, was a life-sized flop. It was on Thanksgiving Day, 1903, when freshmen were still permitted to play on the varsity. Snow had been predicted, and Marshall Field, in Chicago, was covered with hay until an hour before game time. As soon as the hay was removed, the snowfall began and in an incredibly few minutes there were six inches of it on the ground. The start of the game was delayed until it had ceased falling and the ground keeper and his crew had succeeded in removing it from the field and piling it up a yard out of bounds and behind the goal line.

During the game, which Michigan won, 28 to 0, the regular Chicago quarterback, Lee Maxwell, was hauled from a drift and taken to the locker room by relays of dog teams, to be scraped off and thawed out. Eckie replaced him, and I can still remember his *chef d'œuvre* of the day—a pitiable attempt to punt from a pile of snow in which he was buried a couple of yards behind his own goal. The ball traveled nearly two yards and a half. It was Michigan's ball now and Michigan called Heston's signal, either through sheer venom or because it was the only signal Michigan had. You can guess what happened with half a yard to go.

In 1904, Heston's last year, the Wolverines maintained their

proud record of victories which had begun with the engagement of Fielding Yost as coach three seasons before. They beat
Chicago 22 to 12, I think, but Eckie's beautiful open-field running, which was responsible for his team's twelve points, had my
old home state frightened to such an extent that for months afterward, children hid in the cellar if you said, "Eckersall." In the
same year the late Walter Camp discovered that the United
States was not bounded on the West by Pennsylvania, and hon-
ored both Eckie and Heston with positions on his All-America
team. Eckie was chosen again the following season, and five
years later, when Mr. Camp selected his All-America Team for
All Time, positions were awarded Eckie and two other Middle-
Westerners, Schulz and Heston, of Michigan.

The 145-pound Chicago quarterback really came into his
own in 1905. This was the season in which he kicked five goals
from field against Illinois, and he added to the latter's embar-
rassment by running twenty-five yards for a touchdown. The
battle with Wisconsin was tough, but Eckie won it with a
twenty-five-yard drop kick, after dashes of fifty, forty and thirty
yards had failed to subdue the battling Badgers.

But all games in my memory fade into insignificance compared with the Thanksgiving Day struggle at Marshall Field,
Chicago, when Michigan, thanks to Eckie, suffered its first
defeat in the reign of Yost. This game was so close and so bit-
terly fought, and the hostility it aroused between two formerly
friendly states so marked, that the Chicago ambassador to Ann
Arbor asked for his passports, and vice versa, and athletic relations were severed and stayed severed for years and years and
years.

In common with everybody else from Michigan, I felt mur-
derously inclined toward Eckie that day, and not until I got to
know him would I admit to myself or anyone else that all he
had done was play a great and victorious game of football
against a school that had held a monopoly on football glory in
the hinterlands since 1900. I could write you, from memory,
whole books about that game. Instead, I shall let you off with
a paragraph or two.

Chicago was badly handicapped because one of its star half-
backs, Leo De Tray, was sitting in the stand with a bandage
over one damaged eye. Michigan became equally handicapped

when its star tackle, Joe Curtis, was disqualified for alleged roughing of Eckie on a punt. Michigan made two or three of its familiar marches toward touchdowns, but was always stopped just short. The kicking duel between Eckie and Johnny Garrels was nearly an even thing. The Chicago line was playing over its head and Michigan's defense, led by Tom Hammond, was doing well to keep Bezdek's terrific attack from becoming fatal.

Along in the second half, Chicago had possession of the ball right up against its own goal line. Eckie dropped way back of the goal to punt, but he didn't punt. He ran the ball out nearly to midfield. This is the kind of play that is great if it works, and boneheaded if it doesn't. I have seen Thorpe and Gipp get by with similar plays, which would indicate that Lady Luck is with the stars. Chicago, with Bezdek plunging, was stopped again, and this time Eckie did punt. It was a whale of a punt and came down within inches of Michigan's goal line, where Clark, a substitute back, began to toy with it. He could not make up his mind whether to let it go for a touchback or to run it somewhere. He finally decided on the latter alternative, but it was too late. Just as he gathered the ball into his arms, he was hit, and hit hard, by Catlin and Speik, of Chicago. He was knocked, not for a goal but for a safety, and that's how the game ended, 2 to 0. And it was the first time my girl friend had ever seen me cry.

Ten years elapsed and I was doing a sport column on the Chicago Tribune. My readers had never learned to write, so I was entirely without contributions, and therefore hard up for material. On Thanksgiving morning I printed a dream story of a Michigan-Chicago game that was supposed to take place that afternoon. I wrote an introduction and followed it with a probable line-up, naming players who had been stars ten or twenty years in the past.

Now, there had been no hint of a resumption of athletic relations between Chicago and Michigan. Moreover, Thanksgiving games had been ruled out of the Middle West long, long before, because they interfered with church or turkey or something. Nevertheless, believe it or not, a crowd of more than five hundred people—this is Mr. Stagg's estimate—went to the University of Chicago's football field that day and stood around for hours, waiting for the gates or the ticket windows to open. At length they returned home mad, and many of them telephoned indignant messages to my boss.

This just goes to show that I had Chicago pretty well under my thumb when I sold it to the Sicilians. Also that the type-writer is pretty near as mighty as the rod.

Odd's Bodkins

AUTHOR'S NOTE:

Each morn when the neighbors are through with
    our papers
And stealthily slide them beneath our front door,
I grab the *American*, knowing that there I can
Find O. O. McIntyre's column of lore.
You ask what it's like? I've no copy right here,
But p'rhaps I can give you some sort of idear.

Diary of a Modern New Yorker: Up and out five hours before dawn, and by scooter to the Hermitage Hotel, where the big Seminole Indian Chef, Gwladys, cooked me a flagon of my favorite breakfast dish, beet root and wrestler's knees. Hallooed to Lily Langtry and we fell to arguing over the origin of the word "breakfast," she contending that it was a combination of "break" and "fast," derived from a horse's instructions to a starter in a six-furlong race, and I maintaining that it was five furlongs. We decided to leave it to Percy Hammond, the philatelist, but his nurse told us he was out shoplifting.

Home for a moment to slit my mail and found invitations from Mussolini, Joan Blondell, Joan Crawford, Joan of Arc, President Buchanan, Joe Walcott, and Louisa M. Alcott. Then answered a pleasant long-distance call from Gwladys, the little French chef in the Café des Trois Outfielders in Sydney, her voice as plain as if she were in Melbourne. She had heard I had a cold, she said, and was worried. It was gratifying to hear her whimpers of relief when I assured her the crisis was past.

Breaking bread in the evening at the office of J. P. Morgan & Company and sat between Bernie Shaw, H. J. Wells, Charlie Dickens, Lizzie Barrett, Will Thackeray, Lottie Brontë, Paul Whiteman, and Bill Klem. Chatted for a moment after dinner with *Who's Who* and, finding a heavy rainstorm outside, dismissed my driver, Gwladys, and pirouetted to the lower West Side, where I sat on the New York Central tracks till dawn, watching the operations of a switch engine. I have always been a sucker for a New York Central switch engine in a heavy rainstorm.

Thingumabobs: I once motored around Vienna for two weeks thinking it was Vienna. When I chided the native jehu, Gwladys, he chirped: "Why, Massa, Ah done thought you knowed it was Vienna all de time." . . . If they did not wear identical hats, Jack Dempsey and Connie Bennett could easily pass for sisters. . . . Ellsworth Vines, the golf pro, is a dead ringer for Frank Crowninshield. . . . One-word description of Franklin Delano Roosevelt—President. . . . Otto Kahn always wears a union suit at first nights. . . . There is something about the name Babe Ruth that suggests rare old Dresden filigree work. . . . Mayor O'Brien is the image of Joan Crawford. . . . One of my favorite people—Senator Long. . . . Tallulah Bankhead and Jimmy Durante have profiles exactly alike. . . . Few ladies with as little money can act as grampous as Bernie Baruch. . . . Two of my favorite people—Senator Long.

Thoughts while strolling: Damon Runyon's feet. Kate Smith, a small-town girl who became nationwide in a big city. Rosamond Pinchot and Theodore Dreiser could pass for twins. How did I get to thinking about "The Song of the Shirt"? Oh, yes; it started at tea when Fannie Hurst brought up Arthur Brisbane's quaint method of writing. His syndicated column averages close to 130,000 words a day, yet he writes it all in longhand on his shirt bosom, then forgets it and sends his shirt to the laundry. Damon Runyon's feet.

Mention of the name Rex Cole invariably reminds me of the Mother Goose rhyme, "Old King Cole," etc., and I never can figure out why. The surnames of two successful *Saturday Evening Post* writers, Samuel Blythe and Charles Francis Coe, begin with the second and third letters of the alphabet. Damon Runyon's feet. Personal nomination for the most thrilling of the summer's detective yarns—"Dracula." If you saw only the left side of Theodore Dreiser's face you would swear it was the right side of Ruth Etting's. Rube Goldberg, cover-designer for *Spalding's Base Ball Guide*, never wears a hat to bed. Damon Runyon's feet. One-word description of the Vice-President—Garner.

Insomniacs: While writing a novel "Red" (Socker) Lewis never eats anything but alphabet soup. . . . Irvin S. Cobb cannot eat before, during, or after 5 A.M. . . . Theodore Dreiser always dresses according to the time of day he happens to be writing about. Thus, if an incident in one of his novels takes place in the morning, he puts on a morning coat; if at noon, a noon coat, etc. . . . There is a striking resemblance between Damon Runyon's feet and Ethel Merman. . . . Theodore Dreiser often arises at 2 A.M. and walks for two hours steadily. I once knew a fellow in Gallipolis who often arose at 6 P.M., and at 2 A.M. walked for two hours unsteadily. No dog as cunning as the Cubanola Glide.

PLAYS

The Bull Pen

CAST OF CHARACTERS*

Bill Carney, a pitcher .... AL OCHS
Cy Walters, a pitcher .... WILL ROGERS
Joe Webb, a Busher ....ANDY TOOMBES

SCENE—*"Bull Pen" at the Polo Grounds during a game between the Yankees and Cleveland. Bill and Cy are seated on empty boxes.*

JOE: What innings is it?

CY: Third.

JOE: What's the score?

CY: One and one. And in case you don't know who's playing, it's us and Cleveland. And you're in the American League.

JOE: I know what league I'm in and I know what league I wisht I was in. I wisht I was back in the Central League.

CY: Looks to me like you was going to get your wish.

JOE: They'll keep me longer than they will you.

CY: Well, I've got a good start on you. You only been here part of one season and I was here all last year besides.

JOE: Yes, but how many games did you pitch?

CY: Well, I pitched 154 games last year and about fifty so far this year. And I pitched 'em all right here where we're standing. Some guys gets all swelled up over pitching one no-hit game. Well, the Yankees has played over 200 games since I been with them and nobody's got a hit off me yet.

JOE: I wisht I was where they paid some attention to a man.

CY: That's what I wished the first part of last season. But the last part of the season, I wished they'd ignore me entirely. I used to make ugly faces at Huggins in hopes he'd get mad and quit speaking to me. But just before every game he'd say, "Go down to the Bull Pen and warm up." *WARM UP!*

*As played in the Ziegfeld Follies of 1922.

847

Say, there may be better pitchers than me in this league, but there ain't none that's hotter.

BILL (*commenting on game*): Bob was lucky to get by that inning! Did you see that one Scotty grabbed off Speaker?

JOE: Them guys don't know how to pitch to Speaker.

CY (*gives him a look*): No? How would *you* pitch to him?

JOE: First I'd give him my fast one——

CY: Hold on! Now you're pitching to the next batter. Speaker's on third base.

JOE: How would he get to third base?

CY: He'd slide.

JOE: You ain't seen my fast one when I'm right. It goes zooy! (*Makes motion with hands.*)

CY: Yes, and after it bounced off Speaker's bat, it'd go zeet! (*Makes similar motion.*) Especially this ball they're using these days with a raisin in it.

BILL: The Babe's up. (*Without raising his voice*) Come on, Babe! Bust one!

JOE: He wouldn't bust one if I was pitching!

CY: How would you pitch to *him*?

JOE: High and on the outside.

CY: And that's just where it'd go.

BILL: No, he popped up.

JOE: Just the same, I bet Ruth's glad I ain't with some other club.

CY: He don't know you ain't.

JOE: I bet he don't break no home run record this year.

CY: Look how long he was out!

JOE: Well, it was his own fault. I bet if *I'd* went barnstorming, Landis wouldn't of dast suspend *me* that long!

CY: He wouldn't of suspended you at all. He wouldn't of never heard about it.

BILL: Coveleskie must *have* something in there. He made Baker pop up!

JOE: I wisht I could go in there to the bench.

CY: What for?

JOE (*with a self-conscious smile*): Well, do you remember before the game, when I was up there throwing to Schang? Well, they was a swell dame come in and set down right behind our bench. She looked like a Follies dame. And she give me *some* smile!

CY: She done well to keep from laughing outright.

JOE: She was trying to make me.

CY: She was trying to make you out.

JOE: I bet if Huggins had of left me stay on the bench, I'd be all set by now.

CY: Yes, and that's why Huggins don't let you stay on the bench. He told me the other day, he says, "Cy, old pal, I hope it won't bother you to have this gargoyle down there warming up with you all the time. But it's against the rules to have gals on the bench, and if he was there I simply couldn't keep them off." He says, "I've got a hard enough bunch to manage without adding Peggy Hopkins."

JOE: How do *you* know that's her name?

CY: Oh, I seen her looking at you and I asked one of the ushers.

JOE: Peggy Hopkins! Do you know if she's married?

CY: I can't keep track.

JOE: Do you s'pose her name's in the book?

CY: Well, seems like I've seen it in print *somewheres.*

JOE (*as if to memorize it*): Peggy Hopkins.

BILL: Bob's wild. It's three and nothing on Sewell.

CY (*to Joe*): You better cut loose a little, kid. This may be our day.

JOE: Not both of us.

CY: Sure, providing he picks you first. (*Slight pause.*) But, listen, kid, if I was you I'd leave the dames alone. Wait till you've made good.

JOE: I ain't after no dames. But I can't help the looks they give me.

CY: No more than you can help the looks *God* give you. And he certainly didn't spread himself.

BILL: He's walked Sewell.

JOE: The *gals* seem to think I look O. K.

CY: How do you know?

JOE: The way they act. Do you remember that poor little kid in New Orleans?

CY: What kid?

JOE: The telephone gal in the hotel. She was down to the depot when we went away. But I ducked her. And that dame in Philadelphia.

CY: What do you owe *her*?

JOE: I don't owe her nothin', but she was out to the game every day, tryin' to flirt.

CY: Oh, *that* woman!

JOE: What woman?

CY: That's the woman that goes to the games in Philadelphia. You know those Philadelphia fans? Well, she's their sister.

JOE: I don't know who she is, but she certainly made eyes at me.

CY: She don't mean to make eyes. That's a nervous disease. She's been looking at the Athletics for six years. But you want to quit thinking about the dames and pay attention to your work.

JOE: *I* pay attention to my work!

CY: Well, at that, I can see you've made quite a study of the batters. You know how to pitch to Speaker and Ruth.

JOE: Yes, and some of them other high monkey monks.

CY: Well, how would you go to work on George Sisler?

JOE: Say, that guy won't never get a hit off me.

CY: I guess you're right. He told me one day that when he was through in the big league, he was through.

BILL: There goes Gardner. Another base on balls.

JOE: But there's one guy I *could* fool, is Sisler!

CY: Oh, anybody could *fool* him.

JOE: Well, how would *you* fool him?

CY: I'd say, "Hit this one, George." And then I'd throw him an orange. Then there's another way I bet I could fool him. I could say, "George, come out to the house to dinner to-night. My wife's a great cook. We live at 450 Riverside Drive." When he got there, he'd find out I don't live at that address, and besides, I ain't married.

JOE: Well, I'd like to get a chance at him. And another guy I'd like to pitch against is Cobb.

CY: Irvin?

JOE: That ain't his name is it?

CY: You mean the man that writes the outfield for Detroit. That's Irvin.

JOE: That's right, Irvin.

BILL: He hit O'Neill in the arm. The bases is choked, boys.

CY (*to Joe*): Put something on her, kid! If he can just get Co-veleskie! (*Warming up at top speed*) Listen, kid, if you get in, don't be scared to cut loose! You got nothing to lose.

JOE: Do you think it'll be me?

CY: Well, it's one of us.

BILL (*with feeling*): Damn! Damn! And he had a double play right in front of him. Cy! He's waving to you!

CY (*jumps up and tears off his sweater*): Get out of the way, boy! He wants me in there! (*JOE, dazed, gets out of his way and mournfully goes to the bench and sits down. CY throws one ball.*)

CY: I'm ready. (*He picks up his sweater and goes off-stage, carrying it on his arm.*)

JOE: A fine manager we're workin' for!

(CURTAIN)

I. Gaspiri

(The Upholsterers)

A DRAMA IN THREE ACTS

Adapted from the Bukovinan of Casper Redmonda

CHARACTERS

IAN OBRI, *a Blotter Salesman.*
JOHAN WASPER, *his wife.*
GRETA, *their daughter.*
HERBERT SWOPE, *a nonentity.*
FFENA, *their daughter, later their wife.*
EGSO, *a Pencil Guster.*
TONO, *a Typical Wastebasket.*

ACT I

(*A public street in a bathroom. A man named Tupper has evidently just taken a bath. A man named Brindle is now taking a bath. A man named Newburn comes out of the faucet which has been left running. He exits through the exhaust. Two strangers to each other meet on the bath mat.*)

FIRST STRANGER: Where was you born?
SECOND STRANGER: Out of wedlock.
FIRST STRANGER: That's a mighty pretty country around there.
SECOND STRANGER: Are you married?
FIRST STRANGER: I don't know. There's a woman living with me, but I can't place her.

(*Three outsiders named Klein go across the stage three times. They think they are in a public library. A woman's cough is heard off-stage left.*)

A NEW CHARACTER: Who is that cough?
TWO MOORS: That is my cousin. She died a little while ago in a haphazard way.
A GREEK: And what a woman she was!

(*The curtain is lowered for seven days to denote the lapse of a week.*)

ACT III

(*The Lincoln Highway. Two bearded glue lifters are seated at one side of the road.*)

(TRANSLATOR'S NOTE: *The principal industry in Phlace is hoarding hay. Peasants sit alongside of a road on which hay wagons are likely to pass. When a hay wagon does pass, the hay hoarders leap from their points of vantage and help themselves to a wisp of hay. On an average a hay hoarder accumulates a ton of hay every four years. This is called Mah Jong.*)

FIRST GLUE LIFTER: Well, my man, how goes it?
SECOND GLUE LIFTER: (Sings "My Man," to show how it goes.)

(*Eight realtors cross the stage in a friendly way. They are out of place.*)

CURTAIN

Taxidea Americana

A PLAY IN SIX ACTS

Translated from the Mastoid by
Ring W. Lardner

CHARACTERS

FRED RULLMAN, *an acorn huckster.*
OLD CHLOE, *their colored mammy.*
THOMAS GREGORY, *a poltroon.*
MRS. GREGORY, *his mother, afterward his wife.*
PHOEBE, *engaged to* CHLOE.
PROF. SCHWARTZ, *instructor in Swiss at Wisconsin.*
BUDDY, *their daughter.*
STUDENTS, *policemen, members of the faculty, sailors, etc.*
TIME—*The present.*
PLACE—*Madison, Wisconsin.*

ACT I.

(*In front of the library. Two students in the agricultural college creep across the stage with a seed in their hands. They are silent, as they cannot place one another. Durand and Von Tilzer come down the library steps and stand with their backs to the audience as if in a quandary.*)

DURAND: Any news from home?

(*They go off stage left. Senator LaFollette enters from right and practises sliding to base for a few moments. Ruby Barron comes down the library steps.*)

RUBY: Hello, Senator. What are you practising, sliding to base?

(*The Senator goes out left. Ruby does some tricks with cards and re-enters the library completely baffled. Two students in the pharmacy college, Pat and Mike, crawl on stage from left and fill more than one prescription. On the second refrain Pat takes the obbligato.*)

PAT: I certainly feel sorry for people on the ocean to-night.

MIKE: What makes you think so?

PAT: You can call me whatever you like as long as you don't call me down.

(*They laugh.*)

CURTAIN

(*Note: Acts 2, 3, and 4 are left out through an oversight.*)

ACT 5.

(*Camp Randall. It is just before the annual game between Wisconsin and the Wilmerding School for the Blind. The Wisconsin band has come on the field and the cheer leaders are leading the Wisconsin battle hymn.*)

CHORUS:

Far above Cayuga's waters with its waves of blue,
On Wisconsin, Minnesota and Bully for old Purdue.
Notre Dame, we yield to thee! Ohio State, hurrah!
We'll drink a cup o' kindness yet in praise of auld Nassau!

(*The Wilmerding rooters applaud and then sing their own song.*)

CHORUS:

We are always there on time!
We are the Wilmerding School for the Blind!
Better backfield, better line!
We are the Wilmerding School for the Blind!
Yea!

(*Coach Ryan of Wisconsin appears on the field fully dressed and announces that the game is postponed to permit Referee Birch to take his turn in the barber's chair. The crowd remains seated till the following Tuesday, when there is a general tendency to go home.*)

CURTAIN

ACT 3.

(*Note: The coaches suddenly decide to send in Act 3 in place of Act 6. A livery barn in Stoughton. Slam Anderson, a former Wisconsin end, is making faces at the horses and they are laughing themselves sick. Slam goes home. Enter Dr. Boniface, the landlord of a switch engine on the Soo lines. From the other direction, Farmer Hookle enters on a pogo stick.*)

DR. BONIFACE: Hello, there, Hookle! I hear you are specializing in hogs.

HOOKLE: I don't know where you heard it, but it's the absolute truth.

DR. BONIFACE: Well, do you have much luck with your hogs?

HOOKLE: Oh, we never play for money.

CURTAIN

Clemo Uti—"The Water Lilies"

CHARACTERS

PADRE, *a Priest.*
SETHSO ⎱
GETHSO ⎰ *Both Twins.*
WAYSHATTEN, *a Shepherd's Boy.*
TWO CAPITALISTS.*
WAMA TAMMISCH, *her daughter.*
KLEMA, *a Janitor's third daughter.*
KEVELA, *their mother, afterwards their aunt.*

[TRANSLATOR'S NOTE: *This show was written as if people were there to see it.*]

ACT I

(*The Outskirts of a Parchesi Board. People are wondering what has become of the discs. They quit wondering and sit up and sing the following song.*)

CHORUS:

> What has become of the discs?
> What has become of the discs?
> We took them at our own risks,
> But what has become of the discs?

(*Wama enters from an exclusive waffle parlor. She exits as if she had had waffles.*)

ACTS II & III

(*These two acts were thrown out because nothing seemed to happen.*)

ACT IV

(*A silo. Two rats have got in there by mistake. One of them seems*

---

*NOTE: *The two Capitalists don't appear in this show.*

857

diseased. The other looks at him. They go out. Both rats come in again and wait for a laugh. They don't get it, and go out. Wama enters from an offstage barn. She is made up to represent the Homecoming of Casanova. She has a fainting spell. She goes out.)

KEVELA: Where was you born?
PADRE: In Adrian, Michigan.
KEVELA: Yes, but I thought I was confessing to you.

(*The Padre goes out on an old-fashioned high-wheel bicycle. He acts as if he had never ridden many of them. He falls off and is brought back. He is in pretty bad shape.*)

ACT V

(*A Couple of Salesmen enter. They are trying to sell Portable Houses. The rest of the cast don't want Portable Houses.*)

REST OF THE CAST: We don't want Portable Houses.

(*The Salesmen become hysterical and walk off-stage left.*)

KEVELA: What a man!
WAYSHATTEN (*the Shepherd's Boy*): Why wasn't you out there this morning to help me look after my sheep?
CHORUS OF ASSISTANT SHEPHERDS:

> Why did you lay there asleep
> When you should of looked after his sheep?
> Why did you send telegrams
> When you should of looked after his lambs?
> Why did you sleep there, so old,
> When you should of looked after his fold?

SETHSO: Who is our father?
GETHSO: What of it? We're twins, ain't we?
WAMA: Hush, clemo uti (*the Water Lilies*).

(*Two queels enter, overcome with water lilies. They both make fools of themselves. They don't seem to have any self-control. They quiver. They want to play the show over again, but it looks useless.*)

SHADES

Cora, or Fun at a Spa

AN EXPRESSIONIST DRAMA OF LOVE AND DEATH AND
SEX—IN THREE ACTS

CHARACTERS
(*In the order in which I admire them*)

A FRIEND OF THE PRESIDENT.
PLAGUE BENNETT, *an Embryo Steeplejack.*
ELSA, *their Ward.*
MANAGER OF THE PUMP ROOM.
A MAN WHO LOOKS A GOOD DEAL LIKE HEYWOOD BROUN.
MRS. TYLER.*
CORA.
POULTRY, GAME IN SEASON, ETC.

ACT I

*A Pharmacy at a Spa. The Proprietor is at present out of the city
and Mrs. Tyler is taking his place. She is a woman who seems to
have been obliged to leave school while in the eighth grade. Plague
Bennett enters. His mother named him Plague as tribute to her
husband, who died of it. As Plague enters, Mrs. Tyler is seen replacing a small vial in a case behind the counter.*

PLAGUE: Well, Mrs. T.

MRS. TYLER: "Mrs. T." indeed! I see you're still the same old
    Plague!

PLAGUE: What are you doing?

MRS. TYLER: What do I look like I was doing, spearing eels?
    I'm just putting this bottle of germs back in its place. The
    little fellows were trying to escape. They said they didn't like
    it here. I said, "Don't bacilli!"

(*A Friend of the President enters*)

PLAGUE: Hello, Doctor.

---

*Mrs. Tyler appears only when one of the other characters is out of the city.

859

(*He calls him Doctor*)

FRIEND OF THE PRESIDENT: (*As if to himself*) That old devil sea!

PLAGUE: Well, Doctor, I'm going to Washington to-morrow.

(*He repeatedly calls him Doctor*)

FRIEND OF THE PRESIDENT: What of it?

PLAGUE: Well, they tell me you and the President are pretty close.

FRIEND OF THE PRESIDENT: *He* is.

(END OF FIRST ACT)

ACT II

A poultry yard at a Spa. The chairs and tables are in disarray as if a blotter salesman had been making his rounds. The Manager of the Pump Room is out of the city and the poultry are being fed by Mrs. Tyler. A Dead Ringer for David Belasco enters, crosses stage.

MRS. TYLER: You old master you! (*Aside*) I can never tell whether he's in first speed or reverse.

(*Dead Ringer for David Belasco exits. Manager of the Pump Room returns to the city unexpectedly and Mrs. Tyler goes into pictures. Manager of the Pump Room stands in center stage as if he had been everywhere*)

MANAGER OF THE PUMP ROOM: (*Aside*) I wonder what is keeping Elsa. (*Looks right*) Ah! There she comes now, dancing as usual!

(*Elsa enters left, fooling him completely. She is not even dancing. She looks as if she had taken a bath*)

ELSA: Well——

MANAGER OF THE PUMP ROOM: (*Turns and sees her*) Elsa! I was just thinking about you. I was wondering what was keeping you.

ELSA: I presume you mean who.

(*The curtain is lowered and raised to see if it will work*)

MANAGER OF THE PUMP ROOM: What's the difference between that curtain and Ziegfeld?

ELSA: It works. And that reminds me that I just met a man who looks something like Heywood Broun. Here he comes now, dancing as usual.

(*A Man Who Looks A Good Deal Like Heywood Broun enters*)

MANAGER OF THE PUMP ROOM: (*Aside*) I'll say so!

MAN WHO LOOKS A GOOD DEAL LIKE HEYWOOD BROUN: What's that?

MANAGER OF THE PUMP ROOM: Why, this young lady was just saying she thought you looked something like Heywood Broun.

MAN WHO ETC.: (*Throwing confetti in all directions*) She's conservative.

(END OF SECOND ACT)

ACT III

A Mixed Grill at a Spa. Two Milch Cows sit at a table in one corner, playing draughts. In another corner is seated a gigantic zebu.

FIRST MILCH COW: Don't you feel a draught?

SECOND MILCH COW: No. But we'd better be going. That gigantic zebu is trying to make us.

FIRST MILCH COW: He thinks he is a cow catcher.

SECOND MILCH COW: (*As they rise*) They say there are still a great many buffaloes in Yellowstone Park.

FIRST MILCH COW: So I herd.

(*The Milch Cows go out, followed at a distance by the Zebu. Cora enters. She is dressed in the cat's pajamas. She looks as if she had once gone on an excursion to the Delaware Water Gap*)

CORA: (*Aside*) I wonder if it could be!

(*Plague Bennett and A Friend of the President enter in time to overhear her remark*)

PLAGUE: (*To Friend of the President*) Go on without me,

Doctor. (*He still calls him Doctor. Friend of the President exits and Plague turns to Cora*) You wonder if it could be who?

CORA: Why, I just met a man who looks a little like Heywood Broun. Here he comes now, dancing as usual.

(*A Man Who Looks A Good Deal Like Heywood Broun enters*)

PLAGUE: (*Aside*) He does, at that!

MAN WHO ETC.: At what?

PLAGUE: This little lady was just saying she thought you looked a little like Heywood Broun.

MAN WHO ETC.: A little! She's putting it mildly!

(*Finds he is out of confetti and exits. A poisoned rat dashes into the open air, seeking water*)

PLAGUE: That rat acts like he was poisoned.

CORA: God! You ought to saw me last night!

(END OF THIRD ACT)

Dinner Bridge

CHARACTERS

CROWLEY, *the foreman*
AMOROSI, *an Italian laborer*
TAYLOR, *a Negro laborer*
CHAMALES, *a Greek laborer*
HANSEN, *a Scandinavian laborer*
LLANUZA, *a Mexican laborer*
THE INQUISITIVE WAITER
THE DUMB WAITER

PROGRAM NOTE

This playlet is an adaptation from the Wallachian of Willie Stevens. For a great many years, Long Islanders and Manhattanites have been wondering why the Fifty-ninth Street Bridge was always torn up at one or more points. Mr. Stevens heard the following legend: that Alexander Woollcott, chief engineer in charge of the construction of the bridge, was something of a practical joker; that on the day preceding the completion of the bridge, he was invited to dinner by his wife's brother; that he bought a loaded cigar to give his brother-in-law after the meal, and that the cigar dropped out of his pocket and rolled under the unfinished surface planking. Ever since, gangs of men have been ripping up the surface of the bridge in search of the cigar, but an article the shape of a cigar is apt to roll in any and all directions. This is what has made it so difficult to find the lost article, and the (so far) vain search is the theme of Mr. Stevens' playlet.—*Adapter*.

SCENE: An area under repair on the Fifty-ninth Street Bridge. Part of the surface has been torn up, and, at the curtain's rise, three of the men are tearing up the rest of it with picks. Shovels, axes and other tools are scattered around the scene. Two men are fussing with a concrete mixer. Crowley is bossing the job. Crowley and the laborers are dressed in dirty working clothes. In the foreground is a flat-topped truck or

863

wagon. The two waiters, dressed in waiters' jackets, dickies, etc., enter the scene, one of them carrying a tray with cocktails and the other a tray with caviar, etc. The laborers cease their work and consume these appetizers. The noon whistle blows. The waiters bring in a white table cloth and spread it over the truck or wagon. They also distribute six place cards and six chairs, or camp stools, around the truck, but the "table" is left bare of eating implements.

FIRST WAITER, *to* CROWLEY: Dinner is served.

(CROWLEY *and the laborers move toward the table.*)

TAYLOR, *to* AMOROSI: I believe I am to take you in.

(AMOROSI *gives* TAYLOR *his arm and* TAYLOR *escorts him to the table. The laborers all pick up the place cards to find out where they are to sit.*)

CROWLEY, *to* AMOROSI: Here is your place, Mr. Amorosi. And Taylor is right beside you.

(*Note to producer: Inasmuch as* TAYLOR *and* AMOROSI *do most of the talking, they ought to face the audience. In spite of their nationalities, the laborers are to talk in correct Crownin-shield dinner English, except that occasionally, say every fourth or fifth speech, whoever is talking suddenly bursts into dialect, either his own or Jewish or Chinese or what you will.*

All find their places and sit down. The two waiters now reënter, each carrying one dinner pail. One serves CROWLEY *and the other serves* AMOROSI. *The serving is done by the wait-ers' removing the cover of the pail and holding it in front of the diner. The latter looks into the pail and takes out some viand with his fingers. First he takes out, say, a sandwich. The waiter then replaces the cover on the pail and exits with it. All the labor-ers are served in this manner, two at a time, from their own dinner pails. As soon as one of them has completed the sandwich course, the waiter brings him the pail again and he helps himself to a piece of pie or an apple or orange. But the contents of all the pails should be different, according to the diner's taste. The serv-ing goes on all through the scene, toward the end of which every-one is served with coffee from the cups on top of the pails.*)

CROWLEY, *to* AMOROSI: Well, Mr. Amorosi, welcome to the Fifty-ninth Street Bridge.

AMOROSI: Thank you, I really feel as if this was where I belonged.

HANSON, *politely*: How is that?

AMOROSI: On account of my father. He was among the pioneer Fifty-ninth Street Bridge destroyers. He had the sobriquet of Giacomo "Rip-Up-the-Bridge" Amorosi.

TAYLOR, *sotto voce, aside to* HANSEN: This fellow seems to be quite a card!

LLANUZA: I wonder if you could tell me the approximate date when your father worked here.

AMOROSI: Why, yes. The bridge was completed on the fifth day of August, 1909. So that would make it the sixth day of August, 1909, when father started ripping it up.

TAYLOR, *aside to* HANSEN, *in marked Negro dialect*: I repeats my assertation that this baby is quite a card!

AMOROSI, *in Jewish dialect*: But I guess it must be a lot more fun nowadays, with so much motor traffic to pester.

TAYLOR: And all the funerals. I sure does have fun with the funerals.

CROWLEY, *in Irish brogue*: Taylor has a great time with the funerals.

HANSEN, CHAMALES *and* LLANUZA, *in unison*: Taylor has a great time with the funerals.

AMOROSI, *to* TAYLOR: How do you do it?

TAYLOR, *in dialect*: Well, you see, I'm flagman for this outfit. When I get out and wave my flag, whatever is coming, it's got to stop. When I see a funeral coming, I let the hearse go by and stop the rest of the parade. Then when I see another funeral coming, I stop their hearse and let the rest of *their* procession go on. I keep doing this all morning to different funerals and by the time they get to Forest Hills, the wrong set of mourners is following the wrong hearse. It generally always winds up with the friends and relatives of the late Mr. Cohen attending the final obsequies of Mrs. Levinsky.

CROWLEY, HANSEN, CHAMALES and LLANUZA, *in unison*: Taylor has a great time with the funerals.

AMOROSI: I'm a *trumpet* medium myself.

TAYLOR, *aside to* HANSEN: This boy will turn out to be quite a card!

LLANUZA: Why do you always have to keep repairing it?

CROWLEY: What do you mean, what's the matter?

LLANUZA: Why do they always have to keep repairing it?

AMOROSI: Perhaps Mr. Crowley has the repairian rights.

TAYLOR, *guffawing and slapping* HANSEN *or* CHAMALES *on the back*: What did I tell you?

LLANUZA, *in dialect*: But down in Mexico, where I come from, they don't keep repairing the same bridge.

AMOROSI, *to* LLANUZA: If you'll pardon a newcomer, Mr. ——, I don't believe I got your name.

LLANUZA: Llanuza.

AMOROSI: If you'll pardon a newcomer, Mr. Keeler, I want to say that if the United States isn't good enough for you, I'd be glad to start a subscription to send you back to where you came from.

LLANUZA: I was beginning to like you, Mr. Amorosi.

AMOROSI: You get that right out of your mind, Mr. Barrows. I'm married; been married twice. My first wife died.

HANSEN: How long were you married to her?

AMOROSI: Right up to the time she died.

CHAMALES, *interrupting*: Mr. Amorosi, you said you had been married twice.

AMOROSI: Yes, sir. My second wife is a Swiss girl.

HANSEN: Is she here with you?

AMOROSI: No, she's in Switzerland, in jail. She turned out to be a murderer.

CROWLEY: When it's a woman, you call her a murderess.

TAYLOR: And when it's a Swiss woman, you call her a Swiss-ess.

(*One of the waiters is now engaged in serving* AMOROSI *with his dinner pail.*)

WAITER, *to* AMOROSI: Whom did she murder?

(WAITER *exits hurriedly without seeming to care to hear the answer.*)

AMOROSI, *after looking wonderingly at the disappearing* WAITER: What's the matter with *him*?

TAYLOR: He's been that way for years—a born questioner but he hates answers.

CROWLEY: Just the same, the rest of us would like to know whom your wife murdered.

TAYLOR, HANSEN, CHAMALES and LLANUZA, *to* CROWLEY: Speak for yourself. We don't want to know.

CROWLEY: Remember, boys, I'm foreman of this outfit. (*Aside to* AMOROSI): Who was it?

AMOROSI: (*Whispers name in his ear.*)

CROWLEY: I don't believe I knew him.

AMOROSI: Neither did my wife.

CROWLEY: Why did she kill him?

AMOROSI: Well, you see, over in Italy and Switzerland, it's different from, say, Chicago. When they find a man murdered over in those places, they generally try to learn who it is and put his name in the papers. So my wife was curious about this fellow's identity and she figured that the easiest way to get the information was to pop him.

TAYLOR: I'm a *trumpet* medium myself.

(WAITER *enters and serves one of the laborers from his dinner pail.*)

WAITER: How long is she in for?

(WAITER *exits hurriedly without waiting for the answer.* AMOROSI *again looks after him wonderingly.*)

HANSEN, *to* AMOROSI: Did you quarrel much?

AMOROSI: Only when we were together.

TAYLOR: I was a newspaper man once myself.

LLANUZA, *skeptically*: You! What paper did you work on?

TAYLOR: It was a tabloid—The Porno-graphic.

(WAITER *enters to serve somebody.*)

WAITER, *to* TAYLOR: Newspaper men must have lots of interesting experiences. (*Exits without waiting for a response.*)

AMOROSI: I suppose you've all heard this story——

THE OTHER LABORERS, *in unison*: Is it a golf story?

AMOROSI: No.

THE OTHERS, *resignedly*: Tell it.

AMOROSI, *in dialect*: It seems there was a woman went into a photographer's and asked the photographer if he took pictures of children.

(WAITER *enters to serve somebody.*)

WAITER: How does it end? (WAITER *exits hurriedly.*)

AMOROSI: She asked the photographer if he took pictures of children. "Why, yes, madam," replied the photographer——

TAYLOR: He called her "madam."

AMOROSI: The photographer told her yes, that he did take pictures of children. "And how much do you charge?" inquired the madam, and the photographer replied, "Three dollars a dozen." "Well," said the woman, "I guess I'll have to come back later. I've only got eleven."

(*The other laborers act just as if no story had been told.*)

LLANUZA: Down in Mexico, where I come from, they don't keep repairing the same bridge.

TAYLOR, *to* HANSEN: Can you imitate birds?

HANSEN: No.

TAYLOR, *to* CHAMALES: Can you imitate birds?

CHAMALES: No.

TAYLOR: Can anybody here imitate birds?

THE OTHER LABORERS, *in unison*: No.

TAYLOR: *I* can do it. Long before I got a job on this bridge, while I was helping tear up the crosstown streets, I used to entertain the boys all day, imitating birds.

AMOROSI: What kind of birds can you imitate?

TAYLOR: All kinds.

AMOROSI: Well, what do you say we play some other game?

CROWLEY, *rising*: Gentlemen, we are drawing near to the end of this dinner and I feel we should not leave the table until some one has spoken a few words of welcome to our newcomer, Mr. Amorosi. Myself, I am not much of a talker. (*Pauses for a denial.*)

TAYLOR: You said a full quart.

CROWLEY: Therefore, I will call on the man who is second to me in length of service on the Fifty-ninth Street Bridge, Mr. Harvey Taylor. (*Sits down.*)

TAYLOR, *rising amid a dead silence*: Mr. Foreman, Mr. Amorosi and gentlemen: Welcoming Mr. Amorosi to our little group recalls vividly to my mind an experience of my own on the levee at New Orleans before Prohibition. (*He bursts suddenly into Negro dialect, mingled with Jewish.*) In those days my job was to load and unload those great big bales of cotton and my old mammy used to always be there at the dock to take me in her lap and croon me to sleep.

(WAITER *enters, serves somebody with coffee.*)

WAITER: What was the experience you was going to tell? (*Exits hurriedly.*)

TAYLOR: It was in those days that I studied bird life and learned to imitate the different bird calls. (*Before they can stop him, he gives a bird call.*) The finch. (*The others pay no attention. He gives another call.*) A Dowager. (TAYLOR *is pushed forcibly into his seat.*)

AMOROSI, *rising to respond*: Mr. Foreman and gentlemen: I judge from Mr. Taylor's performance that the practice of imitating birds is quite popular in America. Over where I come from, we often engage in the pastime of mimicking public buildings. For example (*he gives a cry.*) The American Express Company's office at Rome. (*He gives another cry.*) The Vatican. (*He gives another cry.*) Hotel McAlpin. (*A whistle blows, denoting that the dinner hour is over.*)

CROWLEY, *rising*: Shall we join the ladies?

(*All rise and resume the work of tearing up the bridge. The waiters enter to remove the table cloth and chairs.*)

WAITER (*the more talkative one*): How many Mack trucks would you guess had crossed this bridge in the last half hour? (*He exits without waiting for a reply.*)

(CURTAIN)

Abend di Anni Nouveau

A PLAY IN FIVE ACTS

CHARACTERS

ST. JOHN ERVINE, *an immigrant.*
WALTER WINCHELL, *a nun.*
HEYWOOD BROUN, *an usher at Roxy's.*
DOROTHY THOMPSON, *a tackle.*
THEODORE DREISER, *a former Follies girl.*
H. L. MENCKEN, *a kleagle in the Moose.*
MABEL WILLEBRANDT, *secretary of the League of
    American Wheelmen.*
BEN HECHT, *a taxi starter.*
JOHN ROACH STRATON, *a tap dancer.*
CARL LAEMMLE, *toys and games, sporting goods,
    outing flannels.*
ANNE NICHOLS, *a six-day bicyclist.*

ACT I

(*A hired hall. It is twenty-five minutes of nine on New Year's Eve.
A party, to which all the members of the cast were invited, is supposed to have begun at thirty-four minutes after eight. A waiter
enters on a horse and finds all the guests dead, their bodies riddled
with bullets and frightfully garbled. He goes to the telephone.*)

WAITER: (*telephoning*) I want a policeman. I want to report a
    fire. I want an ambulance.

(*He tethers his mount and lies down on the hors d'oeuvres. The
curtain is lowered and partially destroyed to denote the passage of four days. Two policemen enter, neither having had any
idea that the other would come. They find the waiter asleep and
shake him. He wakes and smilingly points at the havoc.*)

WAITER: Look at the havoc.
FIRST POLICEMAN: This is the first time I ever seen a havoc.
SECOND POLICEMAN: It's an inside job, I think.

FIRST POLICEMAN: You WHAT?

WAITER: The trouble now is that we'll have to recast the entire play. Every member of the cast is dead.

FIRST POLICEMAN: Is that unusual?

SECOND POLICEMAN: When did it happen?

WAITER: When did what happen?

SECOND POLICEMAN: I've forgotten.

(END OF ACT 1)

ACT 2

(*The interior of an ambulance. Three men named Louie Breese are playing bridge with an interne. The interne is Louie Breese's partner. Louie leads a club. The interne trumps it.*)

BREESE: Kindly play interne.

INTERNE: I get you men confused.

BREESE: I'm not confused.

THE OTHER TWO BREESES: Neither of us is confused.

(*They throw the interne onto Seventh Avenue. An East Side gangster, who was being used as a card table, gets up and stretches.*)

GANGSTER: Where are we at?

BREESE: Was you the stretcher we was playing on?

GANGSTER: Yes.

BREESE: There's only three of us now. Will you make a fourt'?

GANGSTER: There's no snow.

(END OF ACT 2)

ACTS 3, 4 AND 5

(*A one-way street in Jeopardy. Two snail-gunders enter from the right, riding a tricycle. They shout their wares.*)

FIRST SNAIL-GUNDER: Wares! Wares!

A NEWSBOY: Wares who?

FIRST SNAIL-GUNDER: Anybody. That is, anybody who wants their snails gunded.

(*Three men suddenly begin to giggle. It is a secret, but they give the impression that one of them's mother runs a waffle parlor. They go off the stage still giggling. Two Broadway theatrical producers, riding pelicans, enter almost nude.*)

FIRST PRODUCER: Have you got a dime?
SECOND PRODUCER: What do you think I am, a stage hand?
FIRST PRODUCER: Have you seen my new farce?
SECOND PRODUCER: No. I was out of town that night.

(END OF ACTS 3, 4 AND 5)

Quadroon

A PLAY IN FOUR PELTS WHICH MAY ALL BE
ATTENDED IN ONE DAY OR MISSED IN A GROUP

By Ring Lardner

(AUTHOR'S NOTE: The reason the name of the author is printed so high up in the script is that THE NEW YORKER has a senseless habit of signing your stuff at the bottom or *da capo*, like Alexander Woollcott or Houghton Mifflin, so you are nearly through with it before you wish you had bought a *Graphic* or turned in your trousers to be pressed and try to get that seam out of it where I turned off the radiator.

The characters were all born synonymously; that is, in the "S'uth," they are known as half-castes. The only time the play, or series of plays, was performed with a whole cast, it was stopped by a swarm of little black flies, which don't bite, but are annoying. One time, in Charlotte, Utah, I forget what did happen.

At this point, a word or two concerning the actors may not embarrass you. Thomas Chalmers and Alice Brady are one and the same person. I owned some Alice-Chalmers before the crush in the market and had to give Kimbley & Co. twelve dollars hush money. I asked Mr. Nymeyer one of the partners to get me out of Wall Street and he said he had already moved me as far as Nassau. That is the kind of a friend to have in the stock market. He says one of the men in the firm paid $195,000 for a seat. Imagine, when you can get one for $22.00 to a Ziegfeld opening if you know Goldie or Alice. I can generally most always get one for nothing if he invites me to Boston or Pittsburgh to look at one of his shows and see whether I can improve it. Those kind, as Percy Hammond would say, are usually so good that they can't be improved and after I have heard the second comic's first wow, I wish I had stayed in the hospital, where men are orderlies.

Speaking of hospitals, I turned the last one I visited into a pretty good roadhouse. Harland Dixon came up and tap-danced, Vince Youmans and Paul Lannin dropped in twice and played, and Vic Arden made the piano speak a language with which it was entirely unfamiliar. Phil Ohman would have been there, too, if the doctor had given me a little more nerve tonic and Mrs. Bechlinger, the housekeeper, had had two pianos. Our gracious hostess told me, *con expressione*, that she had never heard of Messrs. Youmans, Lannin, Arden, and Dixon, but had read my stuff ever since she arrived in this country, ten years ago. This gave me a superiority complexion over all musicians and tap-dancers until, at parting, she called me Mr. Gardner. And dropping the subject of roadhouses entirely for the moment, Miss Claudette Colbert came up to call one day and almost instantly, piling in like interferers for Marchmont Schwartz, appeared fifteen internes, to take my temperature. Previously they had treated my room as vacant.

This play, as hinted in the subtitle, is actually four separate plays with four separate titles: "Hic," "Haec," "Hoc," and "Hujus." It can be seen that the original author was a born H lover. He was the first Manny O'Neill and a great friend to William A. Brady. He promised the latter, "If you ever have a daughter, I will provide her with a vehicle." Well, Bill had a daughter, but Manny passed on without leaving her even a roller-coaster. However, he had a great grandson, Eugene (("Greasy")) O'Neill, who acquired a fine sense of after-dinner speaking by playing the outfield for Cincinnati and coaching football at W. and J. He took up the work where the old man had left off, at the top of a blank sheet of fools cap paper, and I kind of monkeyed with it until now it begins at ten in the morning and lasts until Walter Winchell goes to bed.

Remarks have been brandied back and forth concerning the difference in the number of lines given the male and female characters in the piece. The women have a great deal many more lines to speak than the men. There is, of course, a two-fold purpose in this arrangement. The first fold is that it pleases the women. The second fold is that it promotes harmony in the cast. During the intermissions, the ladies, God use his own judgment, have said so much that they are out of lewd words. End of notatum.)

HIC
Part One of "The Quadroon"
CAST
(In Order to Confuse)

CHRISTINE, his sister, played by Alla Nazimova
LAVINIA, her daughter, played by Alice Brady
CASEY JONES, a midwife, played by William A. Brady
Scene: A Park Avenue Push-Wagon, Armistice Day, 1860.

Luncheon Intermission
of Half an Hour

THE ROTH LUNCH
127 West Fifty-second Street
November 22, 1931
SPECIAL LUNCHEON, 65 CENTS.
Chopped Tenderloin Steak
or Calves' Liver and Bacon.
Carrots Shoestring Potatoes String Beans
Choice of Desserts
Rice Pudding   Strawberry Tart
Tea, Coffee or Milk.

HAEC
Part Two of "The Quadroon"
CAST

CHRISTINE, his sister, played by Alice Brady
LAVINIA, her daughter, played by Alla Nazimova
FRANKIE AND JOHNNIE, played by A. H. Woods
Scene: Department of Plant and Structures.
An evening in 1850.

[Christine and Lavinia meet off-stage, dancing.]

LAVINIA: Did you-all evah see me-all in "Hedda Gabler"?

CHRISTINE: Does yo'all mean "Hedda Gabler" by William Anthony McGuire?

LAVINIA: Yo'all done said zac'ly wot Ah'm drivin' at. How did yo'all lak me?

CHRISTINE: Well, Ah seen Mrs. Fiske.

FRANKIE AND JOHNNIE: Let's you and I run up to Elizabeth Arden's and free ourselves from fatigue with an Ardena
Bath.

Dinner Intermission
of One Hour and a Half *

TYPICAL DINNER, $1.50

—

Medaillon of lobster au caviar
Grapefruit
Suprême of fresh fruit, Maraschino
Blue Point oyster cocktail
Fresh shrimp cocktail
or
Cream of lettuce, Parmentier
Clear green turtle, Amontillado

—

(*Choice*)
Filet of sole, Farci Isabella
Broiled Boston scrod, Maître d'Hôtel
Tartelette of Fresh mushrooms,
Lucullus
Country sausages, apple sauce
Breaded spring lamb chop
with Bacon, tomato sauce
Chicken hash au Gratin
Roast sugar cured ham, cider sauce
Omelette Glacé aux Confitures
Cold—Fresh calf's tongue
with chow chow

—

Stewed celery or fresh string beans
Mashed or French fried potatoes

—

(*Choice*)
Pudding Creole   Coffee éclair

*It will doubtless promote good fellowship and good service if, when en-
tering the hotel's dining-room, you say to the man in charge: "Hello, Maître
d'Hôtel."

Assorted cakes
Vanilla, raspberry or chocolate
ice cream and cake

—

Delicious apple   Apple pie
French pastry   Coffee, Tea or Milk

Make the Plaza Central
your New York Home During
the Entire Performance. Ask Arnold.

HOC
Part Three of "The Quadroon"
CAST

LYNN FONTANNE, a Mrs. Lunt, played by Grace George
CASEY JONES, a midwife, played by Bert Lahr
FRANK CASE, proprietor of the Algonquin, played by Alice Brady
Scene: Jimmy Walker's Wardrobe Trunk.
[The Mayor and the Prince of Wales meet outside the stage door, dancing.]
THE MAYOR: New York is the richest market in the world.
THE PRINCE: Not only that, but the New York Theatre Market is an unrivalled concentration of spending power.
THE MAYOR: The New York Magazine Program reaches that market exclusively.
FRANK CASE: Pardon me, Officer, but can either of you boys play a cellophane?

Passengers will Please not Linger in
Washrooms until Other Passengers
Have Completed Their Toilets.

HUJUS
Part Four of "The Quadroon"
CAST

CHRISTINE, her sister, played by Alla Nazimova
LAVINIA, their little one, played by Alice Brady
FRED ASTAIRE, a hoofer, played by Morris Gest

Scene: An ambuscade in the Astor lobby.

[Fred and Lavinia dance.]

LAVINIA: The minute you try Pebeco Tooth Paste you know
by its "bitey" tang that here is a tooth paste that really "gets
somewheres."

FRED: Will you love me always?

LAVINIA: As long as you keep kissable.

[She kills her with an oyster fork.]

*(Leave your ticket check with an usher
and your car will come right
to your seat.)*

The Tridget of Greva

Translated from the Squinch

CHARACTERS

Louis Barhooter, *the Tridget*
Desire Corby, *a Corn Vitter*
Basil Laffler, *a Wham Salesman*

At the rise of the curtain, Barhooter, Corby *and* Laffler *are seated in three small flat-bottomed boats. They are fishing.*

Laffler: Well, boys, any luck?

(*He looks from one to the other. Neither pays any attention.*)

Corby (*After a pause, to* Barhooter): How's your wife, Louis?
Barhooter: She's in pretty bad shape.
Corby (*Who has paid no attention to the reply*): That's fine!
Barhooter: By the way, what was *your* mother's name before she was married?
Corby: I didn't know her then.
Laffler: Do they allow people to fish at the Aquarium?

(Barhooter *and* Corby *ignore him.*)

Barhooter: You sure must know her first name.
Corby: I don't. I always called her Mother.
Barhooter: But your father must have called her something.
Corby: That's a hot one!

(Laffler's *and* Barhooter's *fishlines become entangled.* Barhooter *gets out of his boat, untangles the lines, and resumes his place in the boat.*)

Barhooter (*To* Corby): I wanted to ask you something about your sister, too.
Corby: What about her?
Barhooter: Just anything. For instance, what's the matter with her?

CORBY: Who?

BARHOOTER: Your sister.

CORBY: I'm not married.

(*After a pause,* BARHOOTER *and* CORBY *both laugh.*)

BARHOOTER (*To* LAFFLER): Do you know what we were laughing at?

LAFFLER: I have no idea.

BARHOOTER: I wish I knew who to ask. (*He moistens his finger and holds it up*) The wind's from offstage. (*He draws in his line, discovers the bait is gone*) That fellow got my bait. (*He throws his line "in" again without baiting the hook*)

CORBY: I understand you're an uncle.

BARHOOTER: Yes, my sister is expecting a baby.

CORBY: On what train?

BARHOOTER: Yes, and do you want to hear what happened?

CORBY: No.

BARHOOTER: Well I'll tell you, two days before the baby was born, Big Bertha—that's my *sister*—she and her husband— that's her *husband*—they were driving up a steep man-hole and Harry tried to change into second speed.

CORBY: Who is Harry?

BARHOOTER: The fellow who was driving. He was Big Bertha's husband at the time. He shifted into reverse by mistake and the car went clear to the bottom of the hill.

CORBY: In reverse?

BARHOOTER: Yes. And the baby is very backward.

CORBY: It seems to me there is something wrong with all your sister's children. Look at Julia!

(*Laffler looks in all directions, as if to locate* JULIA.)

LAFFLER: Where?

BARHOOTER (*To* CORBY): Can you imitate birds?

CORBY: I don't know. I never tried.

BARHOOTER: I wish you'd ask somebody—somebody you can rely on. (*To* LAFFLER) Can *you* imitate birds?

LAFFLER: No. Why?

BARHOOTER: I'm always afraid I'll be near somebody that can imitate birds.

CORBY (*To* BARHOOTER): That reminds me, Louis— Do you shave yourself?

BARHOOTER: Who *would* I shave?

CORBY: Well, when you shave, what do you do with your old whiskers?

BARHOOTER: I don't do anything with them.

CORBY: Will you save them for me?

BARHOOTER: What do *you* do with them?

CORBY: I play with them.

BARHOOTER (*With no apparent interest*): You're a scream, Corby. Where were you born?

CORBY: In bed. Where were *you* born?

BARHOOTER: Me? I was born out of wedlock.

CORBY: That's a mighty pretty country around there.

LAFFLER (*To* CORBY): Mr. Corby—

CORBY: Well?

LAFFLER: I often wonder how you spell your name.

CORBY: A great many people have asked me that. The answer is, I don't even try. I just let it go.

LAFFLER: I think that's kind of risky.

BARHOOTER (*To* LAFFLER): If I were you, I'd wait till some one asked me what I thought. You're just making a fool of yourself.

LAFFLER: I'm getting hungry. I wish we could catch some fish.

BARHOOTER: I'm hungry, too, but not for fish.

CORBY: I can't eat fish either. I've got no teeth. (*Opens his mouth and shows his teeth*) About all I can eat is broth.

BARHOOTER: Well, let's go to a brothel.

LAFFLER: Let's—

BLACK OUT

Thompson's Vacation

PLAY IN TWO ACTS

CHARACTERS

THOMPSON, *a plain citizen.*
HAINES, *another.*
DILLON, *another.*

ACT I

August 28. The smoking car of a city-bound suburban train. Thompson is sitting alone. Haines comes in, recognizes him and takes the seat beside him.

HAINES: Hello there, Thompson.
THOMPSON: Hello, Mr. Haines.
HAINES: What's the good word?
THOMPSON: Well——
HAINES: How's business?
THOMPSON: I don't know. I've been on a vacation for two weeks.
HAINES: Where was you?
THOMPSON: Atlantic City.
HAINES: Where did you stop?
THOMPSON: At the Edgar.
HAINES: The Edgar! Who steered you to that joint?
THOMPSON: I liked it all right.
HAINES: Why didn't you go to the Wallace? Same prices and everything up to date. How did you happen to pick out a dirty old joint like the Edgar?
THOMPSON: I thought it was all right.
HAINES: What did you do to kill time down there?
THOMPSON: Oh, I swam and went to a couple of shows and laid around!
HAINES: Didn't you go up in the air?
THOMPSON: No.
HAINES: That's the only thing they is to do in Atlantic City, is go up in the air. If you didn't do that, you didn't do nothing.

882

THOMPSON: I never been up.

HAINES: That's all they is to do down there, especially in August, when it's so hot.

THOMPSON: They was generally always a breeze.

HAINES: Yes, I know what that breeze is in August. It's like a blast out of a furnace. Did you go in any of them cabarets?

THOMPSON: Yes, I was in the Mecca and the Garden.

HAINES: Wasn't you in the La Marne?

THOMPSON: No.

HAINES: If you wasn't in the La Marne, you didn't see nothing.

THOMPSON: I had some real beer in the Mecca.

HAINES: Say, that stuff they give you in the Mecca is dishwater. They's only one place in Atlantic City to get real beer. That's the Wonderland. Didn't you make the Wonderland?

THOMPSON: No.

HAINES: Then you didn't have no real beer. Did you meet many dames?

THOMPSON: Only a couple of them. But they was pips!

HAINES: Pips! You don't see no real pips down there in August. The time to catch the pips down there is—well, June, July, September, May, or any time in the fall or winter or spring. You don't see them there in August. Did you go fishing?

THOMPSON: No.

HAINES: Oh, they's great fishing around there! If you didn't go fishing, you didn't do nothing.

THOMPSON (*rising*): Well, here we are.

HAINES: I think you're a sucker to pick out August for a vacation. May or June or September, that's the time for a vacation.

THOMPSON: Well, see you again.

ACT II

Four minutes later. A downtown subway express. Thompson is hanging on a strap. Dillon enters and hangs on the next strap.

DILLON: Hello there, Thompson.

THOMPSON: Hello.

DILLON: How's everything?

THOMPSON: All right, I guess.
DILLON: Ain't you been on a vacation?
THOMPSON: Yeah.
DILLON: What kind of a time did you have?
THOMPSON: Rotten.
DILLON: Where was you?
THOMPSON: Nowhere.

SONG LYRICS

Gee! It's a Wonderful Game

Who discovered the land of the brave and the free?
I don't know, I don't know.
'Twas Christy Columbus is what they tell me;
Maybe so, I don't know.
There's only one Christy that I know at all,
One Christy that I ever saw,
He's the one who discovered the fade away ball,
And he pitches for Muggsy McGraw.

CHORUS:
Baseball, baseball, ain't it a wonderful game?
Old Christy Colum' found this country, by gum
But the extras don't carry his name.
If old man Columbus had sat in the stand,
Had seen Matty pitching that "fader" so grand,
He'd have said "Boys I'm glad I discovered this land,
Gee! It's a wonderful game."

Who lost out in the battle of old Waterloo?
I don't know, I don't know.
They say 'twas Napoleon, maybe it's true;
Maybe so, I don't know.
The pink sheets don't print Mister Bonaparte's face,
No stories about him today,
'Cause he never could hold down that old second base,
Like his namesake, Big Nap Lay'ooway.

CHORUS:
Baseball, baseball, ain't it a dandy old game?
The Gen'ral of France couldn't lead 'em like Chance,
So no wonder his Waterloo came.
If down in his pocket Napoleon had dug,
Had paid his five francs to see Tyrus Cobb slug,
He'd have said "I give up, I'm a bug, I'm a bug,
Gee! It's a wonderful game."

Prohibition Blues

"What ails you brown man, what makes you frown man"
I ask'd my man so mis'rable
"You look so winnin' when you is grinnin'
With all them gold teeth visible
But now you's always threatnin'
To bust right out and cry
Does yo' dogs fret you?
What has upset you"
Then he made his reply

"I've had news that's bad news about my best pal
His name is Old Man Alcohol but I call him Al
The doctors say he's dyin' as sure as sure can be
And if that's so then oh oh oh
The difference to me

There won't be no sunshine no stars no moon
No laughter no music 'cept this one sad tune
Goodbye forever to my old friend "Booze;
Doggone I've got the Prohibition Blues"

You Can't Get Along Without Me

You're such a wild and reckless child,
I fear for you.
This great, big world is too hard berled,
My dear, for you.
You're so naive, I hate to leave
You all alone.
Your wilful ways upset me; won't you let me
Be your chaperon?

You can't get along without a man like me.
You will get in wrong without a man like me
You're not slick enough to lick the whole universe;
I'll be glad to act as dad and mamma and nurse,
I will be your bodyguard, your governess;
I'll attend you and defend you, free.
Don't be foolish! Don't be mulish! Simply confess
You can't get along without me.

I'll Never Be Young Again

When grandpapa and grandmama were boy and girl,
Their social whirl was tame.
They valued good condition as a priceless pearl;
To survive, stay alive was their game,
But I've got a far diff'rent aim:

I'll never be young again, again, again.
And who would give a damn to live for three score years and
    ten!
Too feeble to misbehave, I'd crave the grave,
So while I'm able, I'll have my fling;
I'll dance and sing and everything,
And when it's over, I'll say "Amen!"
Oh, I'll never be young again!

We're All Just One Big Family

(Duet by a Swell Girl and a Tough Girl)
(For Bowery Scene)

Both: This will merely be a ditty
   Telling you of New York City
   In a plain and not so witty way.
   It's a town where rich and poor folks,
   Mean and bad and clean and pure folks,
      (pointing to different people)
   Hers and his and theirs and your folks stay.

Swell Girl (Pointing to right):
   On my right, if you will please to
   Look, are the Dumont girls, these two
   Go to Hattie Carnegie's to shop.

Tough Girl (Pointing to left):
   On my left you see the Burnses.
   Nellie Burns, she buys at Hearns's
   With the pay her husband earns as cop.

Swell Girl (Pointing to right):
   Missus Higginbotham has a
   Twelve-room hovel at the Plaza;
   She wears pearls and diamonds dazz-a-ling.

Tough Girl (Pointing to left):
   Missus Skolsky, first name Lena,
   Never saw the Park Casina;
   In her life, Pierre's don't mean a thing.

Swell Girl (Pointing to right):
   Missus Latham, when she dances,
   Dolled up by Lucille or Frances,
   At the Lido, just entrances me.

891

Tough Girl (Pointing at herself):
    I, who do not care a dam'll
    Dance at Coney with my Sam'l.

Both: Still we're all just one big family.

        (After the pantomime and musical interlude):

Both: You must not consider this a
    Town where there's no peace or bliss, a
    War zone where all nations disagree.

Tough Girl (to Swell Girl):
    I like you and know my Sam'll.

Swell Girl: Have a Murad. (Handing Tough Girl a cigarette)
Tough Girl: Have a Camel. (Handing Swell Girl a cigarette)

Both: See? We're just one big family.

LETTERS

To Ellis Abbott

What, Rabbits have come home to roost?
Is this what you would tell us?
A full-fledged senior now is she,
But still heart-whole and fancy free,
This girl entitled Ellis?

Why no, she brought her trunk back home,
Its each and every part,
Then what was it she left behind?
Her fertile brain, her brilliant mind?
No, just her Goshen heart.

Far East of here she left her heart;
Is that what you would tell us?
Ah, rather had she left her shoes.
Her powder rag, the gum she chews,
This most forgetful Ellis.

What will she do without her heart?
Why that no one can tell us,
And least of all young Ringlets tall,
Why, no, he cannot tell at all,
So peeved is he and jealous.

We've lived full twenty years and more
And nothing e'er befell us
That stung so much as this same news
That she her Goshen heart did lose;
Is't true? Come, tell us, Ellis.

July 1908

To Ellis Abbott

Dear,—   Sunday.
    No one had enough sleep on the train and almost everyone

went to bed after breakfast this morning. I was going too, but your letter came and changed my schedule. Do you know, before I opened the envelope, I began to feel blue, for I knew, somehow, that there would be "bad news."

I have been thinking about the letter and you for two hours and wondering how to answer. I feel as if I were writing my own death sentence and that's not a pleasant task. I feel as if you were slipping away from me. I don't know how to prevent it and I don't think I ought to try. You ought to know just what I believe and feel about both of us and I'm going to try to tell you. In the first place, there is no doubt at all in my mind about my love for you. You have all of it—to keep and keep forever. I'm simply sick when I'm away from you and I have no real interest in anything but you. You are just everything to me. Please don't think this is an appeal for sympathy—I'm just trying to let you know the truth. When you consider my "circumstances," the fact that I told you I wanted you may seem strange proof of love, but I offer it in evidence anyway. I would be less worthy than I am now if I had told you without meaning it and had asked you to share a lot anything but enviable if I hadn't cared so much that I couldn't help it. I don't believe I made that very clear, but I hope you'll understand it. What I think is the "matter with us" is just this— I don't honestly believe you care as much about me as you sometimes think you do—and you don't know all the time whether you do or not. And in that connection, I have another truth— I think it's a truth—in my mind that it's just impossible to tell you, because you wouldn't understand it, and wouldn't believe it if you did. You can't know how it hurts me to look at these things squarely and to come to the summing up. If I were a "good catch" instead of a bad muff, I could talk differently. As it is, I can say just this—If you don't *know* that you love me, you don't love me enough. I'm not fishing. Ever since that night at Anne's I have felt that it was only a question of time before hell would follow heaven. I believe people get out of life just what they earn. I have not earned such happiness as life with you would be. I don't deserve you. I don't think you want to be bound to me now, and I know you don't want to say so, so I am saying it for you. You are to consider yourself free unless you are *sure* and until you are sure. And if, as I think, you realize it was a mistake and that you never can care, please tell me so. And never reproach yourself for anything, dear. There is no one to blame except me. And you have given me a taste of more happiness than I ever thought of. I'm not trying to pose as a martyr. This all seems, natural, as if it couldn't have happened any other way.

But if I am wrong—I know I ought not to hope I am, but I do—or if you ever do love me truly, so that you feel you can't get along without me—that sounds funny and impossible, I know—don't hesitate about telling me, if it's tomorrow or five years from now, because there'll never be "another girl." I think I do know you as you are, Ellis, but anyway I know I love you as you are.

You can pretend you are keeping that ring for me, if you want to. But please don't hurt my feelings by giving it back to me. That's a favor I'm asking you.

I know this must be tiring you. Write to me—once at least. I still know enough to realize I mustn't ask too much of you. Dear, the very fact that you didn't want to write every other day hurt me and made me see you didn't feel as I did. This has been an awfully hard letter to write and it sounds like a funeral. I know you'll think it is an appeal for sympathy and all I can do is ask you not to think so.

I will try to wind up cheerfully. I don't know whether or not you saw this cartoon. It was a delicate way of telling me I was supposed to "buy." I couldn't see why I should, but I fixed up something for them. The waiter pretended to be taking their orders, which were very elaborate. Then he brought them a ham sandwich, a cup of coffee and a cigar apiece. My guests were very much put out. The paragraph about the feed was written by the boss for their benefit and not for the paper.

Mr. Schulte is with us. Last night, he and I made an agreement to speak to each other only once a week and to try to be "decent" all season.

Ring.

February 27, 1910

To Ellis Abbott

Dearest,—   Monday.
But I'm not enjoying the trip. I'm lonesome and I wish we were training in Goshen.

Last night I told Manager Chance it was my birthday and when he asked me what one and I answered him truthfully, he said: "Do you expect anyone to believe that? You are the oldest looking guy for twenty five that I ever saw." I wish I were about nineteen once more—I mean if you cared for me just the same, for I was very beautiful at that age and I'm not no more. Also, I'm getting to be a worse hand-writer the older I grow.

You know I would go walking with you if I were there and I wouldn't care about wet feet. I'm afraid, Miss Abbott, that you don't take enough precautions about your health. I know I wouldn't make much of a hit lecturing on the subject, but I don't want you to take any chances. If you should be sick, I would be too, so you see you have two people to take care of.

You ought to hear the athletes discuss the relative merits of their babies. There was an argument in my room last night that was the funniest I ever heard. Mr. Hofman's Mary Jane has two teeth and two others just breaking through. She weighs twenty-five pounds. Mr. Reulbach's Edward has four whole teeth and weighs twenty-six. But Mary Jane can pound her fist on the arm of a chair and laugh at the noise. Yes, but Edward is a boy. Whereupon I told them that my four months old nephew—there isn't any such—could dive from a tower ninety feet high into a dishpan full of salt water without making a splash. I wanted to get out of the room so I could go to sleep. One of them left a five o'clock call for my room by way of revenge. Whenever they start their debates in Schulte's presence, he quiets them by saying: "Wait till you hear what *my* dog can do." They don't want to hear so they disperse.

I'm glad you do think of me once in awhile. I think of you all the time and spend my "spare" moments reading your letters. You may tell your grandmother that I don't care whether or not you can keep house. It will be enough to have you there. I know I'll get along all right and I'll be perfectly happy and *contented* as long as I have you. It's awfully hard to wait for the time, though, especially when I don't know just when the time will be. I'm horribly afraid of losing you, dear, and I won't be really "at peace" until I have you all for my own. Did you ever consider the foolishness of quarrels between husbands and wives over practical things and details? There isn't a chance of our quarreling, because I love you too much and because you are too nice.

Isn't it too much to ask you to write every day?

Yours.

Ring

March 7, 1910

To Frank Abbott

Dear Mr. Abbott,—   Chicago, July fifth.

I'm sorry not to have been able to meet you this afternoon, for I know it would have been more satisfactory than writing. I intended leaving here last night, seeing you this morning and returning in time to attend the ball game here. The paper is very much opposed to allowing us to skip a regular game. There is some rule about not taking the signature off a baseball story during the championship season. Tonight we are going east again and, when we come back, about the first of August, I will manage to get over and see you for a few hours anyway.

Of course you have guessed by this time that I care a great deal for Ellis. I can't help it, although I realize that no one is really worthy of such a girl and do not flatter myself that I am. That she cares for me in return is my only excuse for this letter, which is a request for your consent to our marriage. I know the life she has been used to and know I am not "well off." But I do believe I can take care of her. She told me she would like to wait awhile, and, although I want her just as soon as possible, I know it will be better to wait until I have done some more saving.

My present work takes me from home too often to suit me and I intend to have another arrangement after this season ends. I can tell you more about it after this trip. I know how a father must feel about such things and all I can do is to give the assurance that I can take care of her now, and know that I will do better as time goes along.

I realize how much I am asking of you and Mrs. Abbott and Ellis' sisters and brothers. But I care so much for her I can't help asking and hoping that you will give her to me whenever she is ready.

We are going to stop for one day—tomorrow—at Cleveland,

and from there will go to New York to stay from Thursday night until next Tuesday. I would like to hear from you and will be at the Somerset hotel.

Sincerely,
Ring W. Lardner

July 5, 1910

To Jeannette Hascall Abbott

Dear Mrs. Abbott,

I was awfully glad to get your letter, although I never was guilty of imagining that I had been unjustly treated. Ellis told me her father was sick and I was sorry to hear it. But I could not have blamed him for delaying his answer anyway, for I can guess how he must have felt about it—not knowing me at all. I know how a father or a mother must feel about giving up a daughter and especially one like Ellis, who is really so superior. I didn't dream she ever could care for me, and the knowledge that she could and would made me so happy as to cause me to forget for a time some things more important than my own happiness, such as hers, and her separation from her family. But I have thought of them since and can only hope that she will care enough for me to overlook a lot. I know she will not want for love, for she has all of mine.

Of course I want her as soon as I can have her and I know I will be ready to take care of her by the first of the year, but I am *too* grateful over the prospect of having her at all to want to take her from you before you are ready to let her go.

I challenge and defy her ever to discourage me and I don't believe I would care quite so much for her if she were more practical.

I have been trying all summer to get down to Goshen, but I had to wait for rain, and it never came at the right time. However, I'm sure I'll have better luck next month and I will come the first day I can. Thank you for the invitation and also for writing.

Sincerely,
Ring W. Lardner

August Twenty-second.

August 22, 1910

To Ellis Abbott

Dearest Girl,—   Thursday

I'm down at the office and I left your letters at home, but I can remember them I guess. First and foremost, I was awfully glad to get them because I heard from you for a long time.

I've been intending to order the paper for you, but the *country* circulation office manages to close before I get in from the ball game. I'll come down early tomorrow and do it.

I'm afraid, honey, I don't know any more about house-keeping expenses than you do. If this baseball season ever ends, I'll have time to talk things over with Richard and Anne, who ought to know something by this time. Encouraging to me are the thoughts that they got along all right—and he wasn't making any more than I am, although he always had more sense about his money.—and that I spent enough to take care of three people before you and the reform wave came. I know I can be as saving as Tobe because I won't want the things that cost when I have you. Don't worry, dear, you won't have to board. I'm looking forward too gladly to our own home to think of that. I think I'll be making enough by that time so that you can have some one to help you with cooking and other foolish things.

We must have five rooms in our flat. You are not to be shut off from your family and we want room for one or two or three of them whenever they want to come. I know *all* about rents, but that's *none of your business* and I don't think I ought to peddle my knowledge for nothing.

I want to be somewhere near Anne, so I can have an ally when you begin to think of leaving me.

You can't make me believe I ever will be discouraged or cross with you around. I'm afraid of one thing—you'll find out how little brains I possess in those talks of ours, and become disgusted with me. I guess my best play is to keep still.

I must quit.

                         Yours always,
                         Ring

                                        October 6, 1910

To Ellis Abbott

Sweetheart,—   Saturday

I almost missed today, for it rained and we decided all of a sudden to take a five o'clock train for Baltimore. But the train is over an hour late and I have borrowed a hotel across from the station in which to write. If the train goes without me it's your fault.

Dear, I never feel practical and never confidential while I'm on the water wagon. We'll not wait for one of those moods, because you really have a right to know things. So I'll discuss the "delicate subject" briefly. I can't talk by months, for newspapers don't pay that way. The Tribune was giving me $35 a week and I went to St Louis for $50 and came down again to $45 at Boston. It's $45 now and still it isn't, and that's the delicate part. My family used to be "well off," but got over it. My father is kept busy paying for insurance and taxes, and he and my mother and Lena have to have something to live on. Lena makes something and there's no use arguing with her about it. My brother Billy helps when he can. Harry has a crowd for a family of his own, so you see it's up to Rex and me. Each of us ships home $10. Balance for me—$35. If you had been anyone but you, I would have felt obliged to say something before. But I know you. Lena would rather die than ask us (Rex and me) for anything and I guess she thinks I'm going to "stop" when I'm married. But I'm not. R.W. Lardner and Company, which is you, now possess about $800. About $200 of this will go for the Goshen furniture and probably $150 or $200 for the furniture we are still to get. Another $200 for my typewriter (which I must have) and for my trousseau etc., and we'll be lucky to have $200 left when June comes, because I won't be able to save from now on. And I used to swear I'd never get married before I had $1,000 *laid away.* I hadn't known you when I swore that.

There'll be a pay-day on "Little Puff of Smoke" in July and perhaps something from other things some time. These can be used in helping to pay for a piano. I guess you know as much as I do now, and it's awful to leave you with all this. But you brought it on yourself. Perhaps I won't mail this letter, but I guess I will, for you'll have to know about things some time.

I don't want to meet Miss Gibson till you come. If you'll trust me with the flat choosing, there'll be no need of my bothering her. I thought you wanted her approval—of the flat and me.

I am interested in your dresses and you must tell me all about them.

In order that this may not be a business letter exclusively, I'll ask you to tell me you love me. You can pretend it isn't your business to.

I'm in a hurry to get back to Boston, but I suppose the days will drag just the same up there.

I love you and love you and love you and you owe me a long, long letter, with nothing in it but that you love me.

Ring

April 8, 1911

To Ellis Abbott

Sweetheart,—   Friday.

As predicted, I attended supper at the Leaming's last night. Roast beef, mashed potatoes, gravy, *beets*, peas in little round cups cooked with cracker crumb frosting, nut salad with something like maple syrup on it, biscuits, because Mr. Dehman, Mary's father, can't eat plain bread, coffee and strawberry shortcake, which needed sugar, but when it first came on Mary said she hoped, she certainly hoped, she had made it sweet enough this time because Harry was such a sweet tooth, and so, although I wanted sugar, I couldn't use any, and after dinner mints and cigars for me, you know Harry doesn't smoke at all and Mr. D. doesn't either, although he's a fiend for chewing tobacco, and has taken the cure twice and been cured of the habit, but has gone back to it again; he started chewing when he was sixteen and he is pretty old now, and the tobacco must have had the effect of making him nervous, for he talks in his sleep and sometimes even walks; you know he went with the band to Niagara Falls last year and it was the first time he had been on a sleeping car for eight years, and he and the cornet player shared a lower berth, and the rumbling of the car wheels made him dream that the machinery on the floor above the coffee room of the wholesale grocery in which he works was going to fall through the ceiling, and he dreamed that he was trying to escape by jumping out the window, and so he hauled off and smashed his fist through the car window, cutting his hand badly, and was going to throw himself out, when the cornet player awoke and grabbed him. It's hard to sleep on Pullmans when you're not used to it, but of course you're used to it. Don't you get tired of travelling? Mary often sits up in bed and talks and one night last week she dreamed Harry had hit Jack Johnson, the nigger, and that Jack had sworn vengeance, and so Mary thought Jack would kill Harry and she cried in her sleep. Does Ellis ever bother you at night? Gee, I love those Abbott girls. Gee, I love Florence. Gee, I love Ruby. You tell Ellis that I'll break her head for not coming here with you. Is Ruby engaged? When is she going to be married? What kind of fellow is Paull? Will he be good to Florence? Why, says Mary, I thought you knew him. Well, I just met him. Don't you think Wood Spitler is good looking? He's going to marry a little country girl, but she's a peach. He rides his bicycle out to see her. He says he'll trade his bike for my pony if the pony can get over the ground better. Mary sent him a pipe for Christmas and he said he thought at first that it wouldn't be any good because it was too fancy, but after smoking it, he decided that Mary must have pretty good taste in pipes. Mildred certainly likes her beer and she likes to tell how much she can drink. Did you ever meet Aunt —? Well, then you missed the best of the lot. She isn't what you could call pretty, but she's all heart. She gave us this silver and the dining room set. Elizabeth's going to marry a pretty rich fellow, so I suppose Aunt — will spend a lot of money on something small but nice, instead of giving them any furniture. They want a sort of family reunion at Elizabeth's wedding, but it costs too much money to go. Marion and Margaret can travel as much as they please, for Marion gets passes. How can the paper afford to send you all around with the team? says Mary. Why, Lord, don't you know that nine out of every ten people read the sporting page first? Lillian is crazy about baseball, says Mr. D., and I wanted to ask you if it would be all right for a girl to go to the games alone in New York. When do you go to New York? Well, that's very good of you. I got a letter from her yesterday. I'll give it to you, for it has her telephone number and address. Don't you want the letter? says I. Well, yes, I'll tear off the part with the address on it.

I'll bet when you went home last spring you told Ellis all about the tough chicken we gave you. My, but Mary was ashamed of that. We have spoken of it a hundred times since.

Are there any crabs among the ball players? Does Ellis like to take care of the baby, or is it drudgery for her? I've got a picture of Ellis that looks just like a nigger. Why, Harry, it does not. Well, she looks dark.

Lillian finishes her study with Damrosch in June and then she's coming home. Mrs. D. says she thinks she'll make her do all her playing hereafter in the servants' quarters because she's so tired of listening to it.

Perhaps I'll get a letter from you in St. Joe.

R—

Summer 1912

To Franklin P. Adams

Dear. Mr. Adams: Chicago, March 12

I'm glad you liked the Post stuff and also glad that you took the trouble to write to me. It may not sound reasonable, but sometimes I almost prefer appreciation (from real guys) to dough. However, it's dough and the prospect of it that would tempt me to tackle the New York game. I think a gent in this business would be foolish not to go to New York if he had a good chance. From all I can learn, that's where the real money is. I'm not grabbing such a salary from the Trib. that I have any trouble carrying it home. But I do make a little on the side owing to my acquaintance with people hereabouts who want special stunts done—such as vaudeville acts, ads and alleged lyrics for stage songs. (Of course one might expect to get some of that work in New York after a reasonable length of time.) Moreover, I've just finished building a little house in Riverside, the suburb Briggs lived in until he heard I was coming. I suppose I could sell it or rent it, and I mention it merely as a thing I have to consider. I could be torn away from here—and Riverside—for $8,000, and that's probably more than I'm worth. But you see how things are. It's not that I'm swelled on myself as much as some of our well-known diamond heroes, but that I'd have to get something like that to make the change pay. However, I suppose the sooner a person lands in New York, the sooner he feels as if he had a permanent residence. This letter, I'm afraid, is unintelligible in spots. I hope you may be able to make some sense of it. It might have been clearer if Ted Sullivan hadn't come in to see me twice during its composition.

Sincerely,

Ring W. Lardner

Happiest respects, as Jimmy Sheckard says, to Briggs and Rice.

March 12, 1914

To Zelda Fitzgerald

A CHRISTMAS WISH—AND WHAT CAME OF IT.

Of all the girls for whom I care,
And there are quite a number,
None can compare with Zelda Sayre,
Now wedded to a plumber.

I knew her when she was a waif
In southern Alabama.
Her old granddaddy cracked a safe
And found therein her grandma.

A Glee Club man walked up New York
For forty city blocks,
Nor did he meet a girl as sweet
As Mrs. Farmer Fox.

I read the World, I read the Sun,
The Tribune and the Herald,

But of all the papers, there is none
Like Mrs. Scott Fitzgerald.

God rest thee, merry gentlemen!
God shrew thee, greasy maiden!
God love that pure American
Who married Mr. Braden.

If it is dark when home I go
And safety is imperilled,
There's no policeman that I know
Like Zelda Sayre Fitzgerald.

I met her at the football game;
'Twas in the Harvard stadium.
A megaphone announced her name:
"It's Mrs. James S. Braden!"

So here's my Christmas wish for you:
I worship Leon Errol,
But the funniest girl I ever knew
Is Mrs. Scott Fitzgerald.

Christmas 1922

To Maxwell Perkins

Great Neck, New York
Dear Mr. Perkins:— May 9, 1924.
    Sorry you have a cold. We never have them in Great Neck.
    I will be home all day every day next week excepting Monday. My wife says (and we speak as one), can you and Mrs. Perkins come to dinner Tuesday night (or Wednesday, Thursday, Friday or Saturday night)? The telephone is Great Neck 103. If you drive out and can't find the place, call up from the drug store and we'll come and pilot you. Dinner is at seven o'clock and I have outgrown my dinner clothes. If you accept this invitation I will give you my photograph.
    Sincerely,
    R.W.L.

To Scott and Zelda Fitzgerald

Dears Scott and Zelda:—   Thursday, June 5.

Why and the hell don't you state your address, or haven't you any? I'm going to send this registered to plain Hyéres, with a prayer. First the financial news, which I am afraid is bad, but I am enclosing plenty of documentary evidence to support it.

The day after you left, Miss Robinson called up to say that she had rented the house to Mr. and Mrs. Gordon Sarre, née Ruth Shepley, for $1600. "But listen, Miss Robinson," I remonstrated; "Mr. Fitzgerald told me that if you rented it right away, the rent was to be $2000." "But listen, Mr. Lardner," said Miss Robinson: "Mr. Fitzgerald called me up just before he left and said I was to rent it as soon as possible for $1600 as he had given up ideas of making a profit and just wanted it off his mind." Well, she seemed honest so I said all right and I hope it was. Now then, it seems that William and Sally had kind of let things get dirty in out of the way places and Miss Robinson said that both the house and yard needed a thorough renovating, which ought to be at the expense of the last tenants. Not knowing the ethics, I asked Ellis and she said this was according to custom. So I said go ahead and renovate, and all you were soaked for that was $50. Then there was the matter of the oven door, mentioned in one of the enclosures. I said I thought it was up to the owner to repair oven doors, but she said no. I don't think it will amount to more than a very few dollars and will be subtracted from the next rent check.

The Sarres paid $500 down. There was subtracted from that $50 for the cleaning and $80 for Craw's commission, leaving a balance of $370, which I deposited to your account in the Guaranty Trust Company.

Then along came a water bill for $22.08 which I paid because if I hadn't, the company would have shut off the water and Ruth and Gordon would have had to join the Kensington Association in order to use the pool. Sarre is a French name and they ought to get along without baths, but they are kind of Ritzy.

The balance of $1100 in rent is to be paid partly in July and partly in August. Anyway I'll see that it's paid and deposited to your account.

In regards to "How to Write Short Stories": The notices have been what I might call sublime; in fact, readers might think I was having an affair with some of the critics. I'll send the most important ones when I get them all—Mencken, Bunny Wilson and Tom Boyd are yet to be heard from. But listen, if I do send them, will you please send them back? Burton said I was better than Katherine Mansfield, which I really believe is kind of raw, but anyway it got him and Hazel an invitation to come out and spend Sunday with us. Hazel was on the wagon, but her husband was *not*. I enclose his Day Book for June 1 which mentions several of the best writers.

Max Perkins and wife came out to dinner one night. Max brought along twenty-five books for me to autograph (not to sell) and it just happened on this occasion that I could hardly write my name once, let alone twenty-five times. I have promised to be sober next time I see him and her.

John Golden wants me to write a play based on "The Golden Honeymoon," but I don't see how it could be done without introducing a pair of young lovers or something.

Personally I am now reading "The Beautiful and Damned."

We have a parrot which talks, laughs and whistles.

We are going to Cleveland Sunday night for the Republican convention.

Victor Herbert dropped dead a week or so ago. The papers said he spent the forenoon with his daughter, then had lunch with Silvio Hein and died soon after lunch, but Gene says he was with him virtually all day up to the time he died. How he missed being with him when he died or put him in the death business is a mystery to me. Anyway he was the leading pall bearer. I didn't find out whether or not your stunt was going into the Follies because all we could talk about was Victor's death which came like a bolt from the blue.

There's a great murder case in Chicago. Two Jew boys named Loeb and Leopold, aged nineteen apiece, both of whom had graduated from both Michigan and Chicago at the age of eighteen with the best records ever made, were trapped and confessed murdering another Jew boy aged thirteen. It has since been brought out that they had previously murdered two or three other guys and helped themselves to important glands.

Ellis says she will write as soon as she is through with the dentist. Personally I have written a thousand words. Love to one of you.

Mary Esselstyn.

June 5, 1924

To Maxwell Perkins

Great Neck, New York

Dear Max:—   December second.

I am tickled to death with your report on Scott's book. It's his pet and I believe he would take poison if it flopped.

Ellis and I have both read "Three Flights Up" and both liked the two middle stories best. My favorite is "Transatlantic." The last story is way over my head.

I think I am going to be able to sever connections with the daily cartoon early next month. This ought to leave me with plenty of time and it is my intention to write at least ten short stories a year. Whether I can do it or not, I don't know. I started one the other day and got through with about 700 words, which were so bad that I gave up. I seem to be out of the habit and it may take time to get back.

Don Stewart's "Mr. and Mrs. Haddock Abroad" was a blow to me. That is the kind of "novel" I had intended to write, but if I did it now, the boys would yell stop thief.

Five "articles" on the European trip are coming out in Liberty, beginning in January. I don't know whether or not they will be worth putting in a book.

I'm coming to town early next week to call on a dentist. As soon as I know when, I'll telephone you and try to make a date. Not that we don't want you in Great Neck, but I realize that it's no pleasure trip.

Sincerely,
R.W.L.

December 2, 1924

To Scott and Zelda Fitzgerald

Dears Mr. and Mrs. F.—   March 24th.

Max Perkins reports that Mrs. F. is or has been sick, which we hope isn't true, but would like to know for sure.

I read Mr. F's book (in page proofs) at one sitting and liked it enormously, particularly the description of Gatsby's home and his party, and the party in the apartment in New York. It sounds as if Mr. F. must have attended a party or two during his metropolitan career. The plot held my interest, too, and I found no tedious moments. Altogether I think it's the best thing you've done since Paradise.

On the other hand, I acted as volunteer proof reader and gave Max a brief list of what I thought were errata. On Pages 31 and 46 you spoke of the news-stand on the *lower level*, and the cold waiting room on the *lower level* of the Pennsylvania Station. There ain't any lower level at that station and I suggested substitute terms for same. On Page 82, you had the guy driving his car under the elevated at Astoria, which isn't Astoria, but Long Island City. On Page 118 you had a tide in Lake Superior and on Page 209 you had the Chicago, Milwaukee & St. Paul running out of the La Salle Street Station. These things are trivial, but some of the critics pick on trivial errors for lack of anything else to pick on.

Michael Arlen, who is here to watch the staging of The Green Hat, said he thought How To Write Short Stories was a great title for my book and when I told him it was your title, he said he had heard a great deal about you and was sorry to miss you. He also said he had heard that Mrs. Fitzgerald was very attractive, but I told him he must be thinking of somebody else. Mike is being entertained high and low. He was guest of honor at a luncheon given by Ray Long. Irv Cobb and George Doran sat on either side of him and told one dirty story after another. Last Sunday night he was at a party at Condé Nast's, but who wasn't? I was looking forward to a miserable evening, but had the luck to draw Ina Claire for a dinner and evening companion and was perfectly happy, though I regretted being on the wagon. The last previous time I saw her was at the Press Club in Chicago about eight years ago and she says I was much more companionable on that occasion. George Nathan said he heard you were coming home soon. George, they say, is quitting the associate editorship of the Mercury, but will continue to write theaters for it.

So far as I know, Zelda, Mary Hay and Richard are still together; they were when I met them.

Beatrice Kaufman and Peggy Leach have gone abroad.

We had a dinner party at our little nest about two weeks ago; the guests were the Ray Longs, the Grantland Rices, June Walker and Frank Crowninshield. As place cards for Ray, Crownie and Grant, we had, respectively, covers of Cosmopolitan, Vanity Fair and The American Golfer, but this didn't seem to make any impression on June and right after the soup she began knocking Condé Nast in general and his alleged snobbishness in particular. Finally Crownie butted in to defend him and June said, "What do you know about him?" "I live with him," said Crownie. "What for?" said June. "Well," said Crownie, "I happen to be editor of one of his magazines, Vanity Fair." "Oh!" said June. "That's my favorite magazine! And I hate most magazines! For instance, I wouldn't be seen with a Cosmopolitan." After the loud laughter had subsided, I explained to her that Ray was editor of Cosmopolitan. "I'm always making breaks," she said, "and I guess this is one of my unlucky evenings. I suppose that if I said what I think of William R. Hearst, I'd find that even he has a friend here or something."

The annual Dutch Treat show comes off this week. I have a sketch in it which is a born flop.

I met Gene on the train the other day and he said, "Come over and play bridge with us tonight," and I said I couldn't because Arthur Jacks was coming to our house. When I got home, I called up Arthur to inform him of this and he said it was tough luck, but it just happened that he had been invited, several days before, to dine at Gene's that very night.

Write.

Bob Esselstyn.

March 24, 1925

To Scott and Zelda Fitzgerald

Fitzgeralds one and all:—   October 13, 1926.

I have said to myself a hundred times, "Ring, you just must write to those sweet Fitzgeralds," and then I have added (to myself, mind you), "Better wait, perhaps, until there is something to write about." But the days come and the days go and nothing happens—nothing may ever happen. Best not delay any longer.

Very, very glad to hear you are returning soon to God's Country and the Woman. Don't you dare live anywhere but Great Neck, but if I were you, I'd rent awhile before I thought of buying. If you want me to, I will be on the lookout for a suitable furnished house.

Ellis had two babies this summer. They are both girls, giving us two girls and four boys, an ideal combination, we think.

On a party with the Rices, at the Sidney Fishes' in East Hampton, we ran into Esther Murphy and her father and mother. I had an interesting talk with Miss Murphy (Interesting to me, mind you).

The Ziegfeld show (Gene's) didn't do well in New York, but is going better (they say) on the road.

I was in deadly earnest when I said I liked "The Peasants." I knew damn well it would be over your head (Not yours, Zelda).

May Preston reports that she saw you (not you, Zelda) on your way to the hospital, in Paris, and that you were carrying a bouquet of corsets to give your wife.

I enclose a copy (nearly complete) of the story I wrote about the "fight" in Philadelphia. Heywood Broun refused, at the last moment, to cover it and as a favor to Herbert, and to my syndicate, I said I would do it. We had terrible wire trouble on account of the rain and only about half my story got into the World. It broke off (the story) in such a manner that people must have said to themselves that I was very drunk. It made me so mad that I am going to quit newspapers as soon as the last of my present contracts expires, which will be in six months. After that I am going to try to work half as hard and make the same amount of money, a feat which I believe can be done. I bet $500 on Dempsey, giving 2 to 1. The odds ought to have been 7 to 1. Tunney couldn't lick David if David was trying. The thing was a very well done fake, which lots of us would like to say in print, but you know what newspapers are where possible libel suits are concerned. As usual, I did my heavy thinking too late; otherwise I would have bet the other way. The championship wasn't worth a dime to Jack; there was nobody else for him to fight and he had made all there was to be made (by him) out of vaudeville and pictures. The average odds were 3 to 1 and the money he made by losing was money that the income tax collectors will know nothing about.

You ought to meet this guy Tunney. We had lunch with him a few weeks before the fight and among a great many other things, he said he thought the New York State boxing commission was "imbecilic" and that he hoped Dempsey would not think his (Tunney's) experience in pictures had "cosmeticized" him.

I think now (if you care what I think) that the Gibbons–Tunney fight was fixed and that the Dempsey–Gibbons fight was fixed, to let Gibbons stay, and that it was all leading up to this climax—to give the public a popular war hero for champion. Well, he's about as popular as my plays.

We have just had a world's series that neither club had any right to be in, let alone win, and that is all I will say about sports, excepting that Heywood, who has become quite a Negrophile, wrote column after column on the fistic prowess of Harry Wills and the dread that he was held in by Dempsey et al. and how unfair it was not to give Harry a chance, and—Well, last night Wills deliberately fouled Jack Sharkey in the 13th round after Sharkey (who isn't even as good as Tunney) had beaten the life out of him from the very beginning.

I have been on the wagon since early in July, when Ellis' mother died. Before that I had a spree that broke a few records for longevity and dullness.

A couple of months ago, the Metro-Goldwyn people asked me to write a baseball picture for Karl Dane, the man who made such a hit as "Slim," one of the doughboys in "The Big Parade." We talked matters over several times and finally the man asked me how much I would want. I told him I didn't know what authors were getting. He said, "Well, we are giving

Johnnie Weaver $7,500 and Marc Connelly the same," so he asked me again what I wanted and I said $40,000 and he threw up his hands and exclaimed, "Excuse me, Mr. Lardner, for wasting your *valuable* time!" Maybe I told you that before; I have no idea how long ago it was I wrote to you.

It may not be very lively for you, but why not come and stay with us awhile before or after you go to Montgomery.

Keep me posted on your plans and accept the undying love of the madam and

I.

To Jeannette Abbott Kitchell

Hotel Elysée
New York City

Dear Jane:—   Sunday, November ninth.

This is a belated bread and butter (or rather, chicken and jello) note. Thanks for the only meal I had in New England. And please tell Kitch that the three-lettered Cornell man I tried to think of was Kaw.

It would take me years to relate the incredible things that happened after I got back to Boston, and since I have got home. Here is the barest synopsis: I finished the "happy" lyric on the train from Newburyport. It was acceptable (though terrible). Then Flo, on Sunday evening, told me what I and everyone else had been telling him for weeks—that Marilyn's first dance with Fred (to the tune of "Young Man of Manhattan") took her entirely out of her character and, besides, was too hot for her. I must get together with Vince and write a "light" duet that would give the pair a chance to do a dance that she *could* do. Also, I must get Vince to write a tune to which I could set a lyric, a "smart" lyric, with which to open the first act, in place of that remarkable "East River Flows" number where the girls appeared with tail feathers or something. Vince was still in his room, where he had been since Friday, in pajamas. From seven till ten Sunday evening, I struggled to get him at the piano, and the instant I got him there, an explosion in a cleaning and dyeing establishment across LaGrange Street, right outside his window, knocked both of us off our chairs. Before we could get to the window to see what had happened, the dyeing establishment was a mass of flames. We had a beautiful place from which to watch a big fire, and of course there was no hope of getting back to work till it was all over. Vince got statistical and counted over thirty pieces of fire apparatus. It was cold leaning out the window and I had to be his nurse and force a bathrobe and overcoat on him.

After midnight, I succeeded in interesting him in music and was about to accomplish something when several girls and the nutty dance director came in and made it a party. I gave up at two o'clock and went to my room and to bed.

On Monday I made him get up before noon and dress. Then he went to the theater and rearranged the first act finale. Flo told me to forget the duet for Marilyn and Fred and concentrate on the opening. I wrote a lyric that would go to the old "Bambatina" rhythm and tried to make the lyric good enough so that the tune wouldn't matter. Between five and nine I got a tune out of Vince; then I went to the show. Paul Lannin had forgotten the rearrangement of the first act finale. The curtain came down on confusion and I went back stage and found the three stars in hysterics. Flo naturally called Vince up about Paul's mistake and Vince made Paul write a letter of resignation for his own (Paul's) sake, so Vince said. I don't know yet whether Vince was double-crossing Paul. Anyway I felt kind of low about Paul and decided to take some paraldehyde to make me sleep (it works instantly). I asked a boy to get me some orange juice to mix with the paraldehyde, which is terrible tasting stuff. There was a knock at my door and I said, "Come in," thinking it was the boy with the orange juice. Instead, it was the dance director with a confidential, weeping jag. He said: "I'm going to tell you some tragic incidents in my life, and tomorrow I know I'll be sorry I told them to you." I said: "I know I will, too," but that didn't stop him and he went on for an hour. The boy came with the orange juice and I got into bed and drank the paraldehyde and fell asleep with the dance director still telling me tragic incidents.

I wrote another lyric Tuesday and finally got out of town Tuesday midnight. I had been home less than three hours when Flo called up from Boston and said he wanted the Fred–Marilyn duet after all. Fortunately Vince had an old tune in his New York office and I got it. Flo called up again at half past one Thursday morning. I was asleep and Ellis refused to arouse me. He asked her if she would allow me to come back to Boston. She said I wasn't feeling so good, but maybe I would come if it was necessary. He called me up Thursday forenoon and said Marilyn was going to quit the show unless she got a song to sing in place of "Carry On, Keep Smiling." Would I write a lyric? I said, yes, but I must have a tune. Flo said Vince was mailing me a tune. The tune didn't come and Flo asked me to come up to Boston and make Vince write it. I got reservations on the five o'clock Saturday afternoon train, but at noon Saturday, Vince called up (from Boston, of course) and sang me the tune, with some dummy words. I stayed here and did the best I could with it and mailed it to Flo last night. He has mercifully let me alone today, but I have a hunch I'll be back in Boston for a few hours later in the week.

And did I tell you that Fred Astaire pouted over my opening ensemble idea because it required the presence of some Park Avenue women on one side of the stage and he didn't want anybody to appear dressed up before his entrance? And I wrote a lyric for Eddie Foy to sing in place of that dismal thing the girl sings in front of the curtain just ahead of the marvelous bedroom scene. I have written eleven numbers instead of the six I was asked write, and they can't possibly get more than seven of them in, and I have written you the longest letter (about tragic incidents in my life) I ever wrote to any Abbott girl excepting Ellis.

Love to the boys, who seem quite nice.

A Refugee.

November 9, 1930

To Wilma Seavey

East Hampton, Long Island

Dear Miss Seavey:— August 24, 1933

I must apologize for delaying so long in answering your

letter, but my health has prevented me from attending to my correspondence for the last few months.

I don't suppose any author either hates or loves all his characters. I try to write about people as real as possible, and some of them are naturally more likeable than others. In regard to your argument, I think the decision should be awarded to you, because I cannot remember ever having felt any bitterness or hatred toward the characters I have written about. I am grateful to you for your defense of me.

Yours Sincerely,
Ring Lardner

CHRONOLOGY

NOTE ON THE TEXTS

NOTES

Chronology

1885   Born Ringgold Wilmer Lardner on March 6 in Niles, Michigan, ninth and last child of Henry Lardner and Lena Phillips Lardner. Born with a deformed foot, he will wear a metal brace on his leg until he is eleven years old. (Three of Lardner's siblings died in infancy; the others were William; Henry Jr.; Lena; Rex, born 1881; and Anna, later known as Anne, born 1883. Henry Lardner had inherited large landholdings and speculated in real estate. Lena Phillips, a minister's daughter, had taught school before her marriage; she was devoted to music and literature, fond of entertaining on a large scale, and published two books of verse and miscellaneous prose.)

1893   The family visits the Chicago World's Fair during the summer.

1895   Ring, who along with his siblings has been educated at home by his mother, begins to study Latin, mathematics, and geography with a tutor.

1897   With siblings Rex and Anne begins attending Niles Public High School; Ring is admitted as a ninth grader.

1901   Graduates Niles High School. Turns down scholarship at nearby Olivet College. Father's fortune collapses as a result of bad investments. Ring spends summer in Chicago working at a series of short-lived jobs, and staying (as he often will in future years) with family of close childhood friend Arthur Jacks. Returns to Niles and works briefly for Michigan Central Railroad.

1902   With brother Rex, enters Armour Institute in Chicago to study mechanical engineering at their father's urging. Frequents theaters and saloons, and goes repeatedly to the performances of musical comedy star Bert Williams, with whom he later becomes acquainted.

1903   Leaves Armour after spring term, having failed all but one course. Goes back to Niles to live with family. Passes civil service examination and works sporadically at post office. Participates in local theatricals in Niles, writing music and lyrics for musical *Zanzibar*.

1904   Works reading meters and doing other odd jobs for Niles Gas Company.

1905   Hired (partly on the strength of his brother Rex's bur-
        geoning career as a newspaperman) as sports reporter by
        the South Bend *Times*, writing without a byline.

1906   Covers Central League baseball for the *Times*; works as
        scout for the South Bend team. Also covers boxing, bowl-
        ing, horse racing, and college football.

1907   In July, at a picnic in Niles, meets Ellis Abbott of Goshen,
        Indiana, daughter of a prosperous lumber manufacturer,
        and they begin a long courtship. Initiates voluminous cor-
        respondence with Ellis in September when she leaves to
        attend Smith College. On vacation in October in Chicago
        during the World Series, is introduced by a friend to Hugh
        S. Fullerton, baseball writer for the Chicago *Examiner*;
        they establish friendly acquaintance in long drinking ses-
        sion and spend time together during the Series. With
        Fullerton's help, is hired by Chicago *Inter-Ocean* as a sports-
        writer and moves to Chicago in November. Rooms with
        Inter-Ocean colleague Richard Tobin, who becomes a close
        friend; prevails on the paper to hire his brother Rex as a
        writer.

1908   Begins to cover sports for Chicago *Examiner* under
        pseudonym James Clarkson; travels with the Chicago
        White Sox. Accepts job with *Chicago Tribune* writing
        under his own byline. Forms friendship with Doc White of
        the White Sox, with whom he collaborates on writing
        songs.

1909   Goes on the road with the Chicago Cubs in March; con-
        tinues to cover the White Sox as well. Visits Ellis at Smith
        in May; after she graduates in the spring, she visits him in
        Chicago in August, and in October travels to Niles for a
        visit with the Lardner family. Lardner spends Christmas
        with Ellis and her family in Goshen.

1910   Proposes to Ellis in January; she initially accepts, then has
        second thoughts and suggests they wait a year "to learn to
        know each other a little better." Writes to Ellis's father re-
        questing his consent to the marriage, which he delays in
        giving until Lardner visits Goshen in October. Leaves
        Tribune to work as editor of St. Louis *Sporting News*, and
        moves to St. Louis boardinghouse in December.

1911   Contributes "Pullman Pastimes," series of humorous
        sketches of baseball players, to the *Sporting News*. In Feb-
        ruary leaves *Sporting News* after differences with owner
        Charles Spink; accepts job as baseball correspondent for
        Boston *American*. Goes to Augusta, Georgia, for spring

training of Boston Rustlers. Marries Ellis Abbott on June 28 at her parents' home in Goshen; they move into apartment in Brookline, Massachusetts, after the wedding. Promoted to sports editor of Boston *American*, and hires brother Rex for his staff; angered when paper fires Rex while Lardner is away covering World Series. In November returns with Ellis to Chicago, working temporarily as a copy reader for the Chicago *American*.

1912   Resumes position as sportswriter for Chicago *Examiner* in February, covering the White Sox. Publishes article "The Cost of Baseball" in *Collier's* in March. Son John born May 4. Ellis's father dies in September; with money she inherits they buy property in the Chicago suburb of Riverside and begin construction of a house.

1913   Travels with Ellis to California, where he covers White Sox training. In June, takes over daily *Chicago Tribune* column "In the Wake of the News," which he will continue to edit for the next six years; in it he experiments with a variety of forms, including poems, plays, and literary parodies.

1914   Father dies. Son James born May 18. "A Busher's Letters Home," first of the Jack Keefe stories (which will eventually number twenty-six), is published in *Saturday Evening Post* in March, and is followed by others in the same series; the stories make Lardner a popular writer commanding increasingly high rates for his stories. Also publishes "My Roomy" and "Horseshoes" in the *Post*. The Riverside house is completed during the summer.

1915   Son Ringgold Jr. born August 19. Contributes to *Saturday Evening Post*, *Redbook*, *American*, and *McClure's*, including stories "Alibi Ike" and "Harmony"; "Own Your Own Home," first of a series featuring detective Fred Gross and based on Lardner's recent experiences as a suburban property owner, appears in *Redbook*. Publishes *Bib Ballads*, collection of humorous verse about parenthood.

1916   Receives an offer to move to the *Record-Herald*; learning this, the *Tribune* offers him a three-year contract with a raise in salary. Publishes "Gullible's Travels" (*Saturday Evening Post*, August) and "Champion" (*Metropolitan*, October). *You Know Me Al*, collecting the first six Jack Keefe stories, published by George H. Doran. Writes songs and works on scenarios for short baseball movies.

1917   *Gullible's Travels, Etc.* published by Bobbs-Merrill in February. Sells Riverside house. Travels to France in August on an eleven-week assignment as a correspondent for

Collier's, but sees little of activities at the front; eight-part travel account "A Reporter's Diary" appears September 1917–January 1918. Family lives in rented home in Evanston, Illinois.

1918   Mother dies. *Treat 'Em Rough* (a second volume of Jack Keefe stories) and *My Four Weeks in France* (book version of "A Reporter's Diary") published by Bobbs-Merrill. After spending summer at a lake resort in St. Joseph, Michigan, the family moves to a rented apartment in Chicago.

1919   Son David born March 11. Makes deal in New York with John Wheeler to write weekly column for Bell's Syndicate. (When Wheeler offers a written contract to back up their verbal agreement, Lardner writes: "If you knew anything about contracts you would realize we made one in the Waldorf bar before five witnesses, three of whom were sober.") Last installment of "In the Wake of the News" appears in June. Covers Dempsey-Willard prizefight on July 4 in Toledo, Ohio. Loses heavily betting on the White Sox in the year of the Black Sox scandal. Ring and family rent a house in Greenwich, Connecticut. In November begins publishing syndicated feature "Ring Lardner's Weekly Letter." *Own Your Own Home* (collecting the early Fred Gross stories) and *The Real Dope* (stories covering Jack Keefe's exploits in World War I) published by Bobbs-Merrill.

1920   Ring and family move in the spring to East Shore Road in Great Neck, Long Island; his brother Rex and old friend Arthur Jacks are or will soon be neighbors; other Great Neck friends include Franklin P. Adams, Herbert Bayard Swopes, and the sportswriter Grantland Rice, an old acquaintance who becomes one of Lardner's closest friends and a frequent golf partner and traveling companion. In Great Neck enjoys busy social life. Attends Republican Convention in Chicago, where he spends much time with H. L. Mencken. *The Young Immigrunts*, humorous recounting of the move to Connecticut, published by Bobbs-Merrill.

1921   With Rice, plays golf with President Harding in April. "Some Like Them Cold" published in *Saturday Evening Post* in October. Covers disarmament conference in Washington in November. Contributes essay "Sport and Play" to symposium *Civilization in the United States*. *The Big Town* and *Symptoms of Being 35* (reprint of an article from *American*) published by Bobbs-Merrill.

1922   Socializes often with F. Scott and Zelda Fitzgerald, who in October move near him in Great Neck. Drinks heavily and takes sedatives for chronic insomnia. Publishes stories including "A Caddy's Diary" (*Saturday Evening Post*, March) and "The Golden Honeymoon" (*Cosmopolitan*, July). Contributes sketches to the Ziegfeld Follies. Writes continuity for syndicated comic strip based on *You Know Me Al* (series discontinued in 1925).

1923   Contributes regularly to *Cosmopolitan* and *Hearst's International*. At Fitzgerald's urging, Maxwell Perkins of Charles Scribner's Sons writes an admiring letter to Lardner proposing a collection of his short stories; Lardner is open to the idea but acknowledges that he has not kept copies of his stories.

1924   Play "I. Gaspiri" published in *Chicago Literary Times* in February. *How to Write Short Stories*, first major story collection, published in the spring by Scribner's. Sails with Ellis to France in September; they visit the Fitzgeralds (who had relocated to France in April) on the Riviera and go to London briefly before returning at the end of the year.

1925   Publishes stories including "Haircut" (*Liberty*, March), "Mr. and Mrs. Fix-It" (*Liberty*, May), "Zone of Quiet" (*Cosmopolitan*, June), "The Love Nest" (*Cosmopolitan*, August), and "A Day with Conrad Green" (*Liberty*, October). *What of It?*, collection of miscellaneous writing, published by Scribner's.

1926   Publishes stories including "Rhythm" (*Cosmopolitan*, March) and "I Can't Breathe" (*Cosmopolitan*, September). *The Love Nest and Other Stories* published in the spring by Scribner's. After going for a medical checkup during the summer, learns that he has tuberculosis, aggravated by his alcoholism.

1927   Publishes stories including "Sun Cured" (*Cosmopolitan*, January) and "Hurry Kane" (*Cosmopolitan*, May). In March writes final "Weekly Letter." *The Story of a Wonder Man*, humorous autobiography, published by Scribner's. In October covers World Series (between Pittsburgh Pirates and New York Yankees) for the *Chicago Tribune*, the last time he will do so. *The Love Nest*, adapted for the stage by Robert E. Sherwood, opens on Broadway in December for a brief run.

1928   With Grantland Rice, buys tract of land in East Hampton, Long Island, in the spring; builds house he calls Still Pond, where he will lead a social life centered on family and small group of close friends. *Elmer the Great*, stage adaptation of "Hurry Kane" written with George M. Cohan (with Cohan doing most of the writing), opens on Broadway in the fall and runs for 40 performances. Contributes regularly to *Cosmopolitan* and *Collier's*.

1929   Collaborates with George S. Kaufman on play *June Moon*, based on "Some Like Them Cold"; it opens on Broadway in October and enjoys a successful run. Contributes prolifically to *Cosmopolitan* and *Collier's*; "Jersey City Gendarmerie, Je T'Aime" published in *The New Yorker* in November. *Round Up*, collecting new and earlier stories, published by Scribner's. Paramount releases *Fast Company*, film version of *Elmer the Great*, starring Evelyn Brent and Jack Oakie.

1930   Contributes lyrics to Florenz Ziegfeld production *Smiles*, which opens in November. *June Moon* published by Scribner's.

1931   Goes to Desert Sanatorium in Tucson, Arizona, in March; returns to New York in mid-April for stay of several months in Doctors Hospital. Returns to East Hampton for much of summer. After another stay in Doctors Hospital in September, moves in October to a furnished apartment on East End Avenue. Contributes "Cured!" to *Redbook* and "Insomnia" to *Cosmopolitan*; writes series of autobiographical sketches for *Saturday Evening Post* (November 1931–April 1932). Paramount releases film version of *June Moon* starring Jack Oakie and Frances Dee.

1932   Hospitalized again in May and June; visitors include Sherwood Anderson and Claudette Colbert; spends summer in East Hampton. Continues autobiographical series for *Saturday Evening Post* and writes a regular column on radio for *The New Yorker* (June 1932–August 1933) in which he takes songwriters to task for sexually suggestive and grammatically inept lyrics.

1933   On doctors' advice, travels with Ellis to California in February by way of the Panama Canal, spending several months at La Quinta, a resort near Palm Springs, where his visitors include Harold Lloyd and Louella Parsons. Works on a play that remains unfinished. Returns to New York and after a stay in Doctors Hospital goes out to East Hampton in June. *Lose with a Smile* (series of baseball stories) published by Scribner's. Dies of a heart attack in East Hampton on the morning of September 25.

Note on the Texts

This volume presents a selection of Ring Lardner's writing in a range of genres: stories, humorous sketches, reporting, plays, song lyrics, and letters. It contains the full texts of the volumes *You Know Me Al: A Busher's Letters* (1916), *The Real Dope* (1919), *The Young Immigrunts* (1920), and *The Big Town* (1921); selected stories from the collections *Gullible's Travels, Etc.* (1917), *How to Write Short Stories (With Samples)* (1924), *The Love Nest and Other Stories* (1928), and *Round Up* (1929); and four stories that were not collected by Lardner. It also includes seventeen sketches and nonfiction pieces, ten plays, five song lyrics, and seventeen letters. The texts of these works are taken from a variety of sources, detailed below.

You Know Me Al. Lardner's story "A Busher's Letters Home" was first submitted to the Chicago *Tribune*, but was rejected; when published in *The Saturday Evening Post* (March 7, 1914), it was an immediate success, and Lardner continued to produce stories about the fictional Chicago White Sox ballplayer Jack Keefe at a rapid pace. In May the publisher George H. Doran approached Lardner with a proposal for a book collecting the stories. *You Know Me Al* appeared in July 1916. It contained, in addition to "A Busher's Letters Home," the five subsequent Jack Keefe stories: "The Busher Comes Back" (*Saturday Evening Post*, May 23, 1914), "The Busher's Honeymoon" (*Saturday Evening Post*, July 11, 1914), "A New Busher Breaks In" (*Saturday Evening Post*, September 12, 1914), "The Busher's Kid" (*Saturday Evening Post*, October 3, 1914), and "The Busher Beats It Hence" (*Saturday Evening Post*, November 7, 1914). The text of *You Know Me Al* in the present volume has been taken from the first edition.

from Gullible's Travels, Etc. "Carmen" and "Gullible's Travels" both first appeared in *The Saturday Evening Post* (for February 19, 1916, and August 19, 1916, respectively). They were collected in *Gullible's Travels, Etc.* (Indianapolis: Bobbs-Merrill, 1917) along with three other stories ("Three Kings and a Pair," "The Water Cure," and "Three Without, Doubled") about Joe Gullible and his wife. The texts of "Carmen" and "Gullible's Travels" in the present volume are taken from the first edition, published in February 1917.

The Real Dope. *The Real Dope* (Indianapolis: Bobbs-Merrill, 1919)

927

collected six further stories about Jack Keefe. (An earlier Jack Keefe collection, *Treat 'Em Rough*, published in 1918 by Bobbs-Merrill, is not included in this volume.) The stories in *The Real Dope* were originally published in *The Saturday Evening Post*: "And Many a Stormy Wind Shall Blow" (July 6, 1918), "Private Valentine" (August 3, 1918), "Stragety and Tragedy" (August 31, 1918), "Decorated" (October 26, 1918), "Sammy Boy" (December 21, 1918), and "Simple Simon" (January 25, 1919). The text of *The Real Dope* in the present volume has been taken from the first edition, published in February 1919.

The Young Immigrunts. *The Young Immigrunts*, an account of the Lardner family's move from Chicago to Connecticut, was playfully attributed to Lardner's four-year-old son Ring Lardner, Jr., accompanied by "a preface by the father." It was intended as a parody of *The Young Visiters* (1919), written by Daisy Ashford at the age of nine. (Lardner, according to his biographer Jonathan Yardley, doubted the veracity of this well-attested claim.) First printed in *The Saturday Evening Post* on January 31, 1920, *The Young Immigrunts* was published in book form in May. The text in the present volume has been taken from the first edition (Indianapolis: Bobbs-Merrill, 1920).

The Big Town. *The Big Town* was published by Bobbs-Merrill in October 1921. The stories it comprises originally appeared in *The Saturday Evening Post*, sometimes under different titles: "Quick Returns" (March 27, 1920), "Ritchey" (as "Beautiful Katie," July 10, 1920), "Lady Perkins" (as "The Battle of Long Island," November 27, 1920), "Only One" (February 12, 1921), and "Katie Wins a Home" (as "The Comic," May 14, 1921). The text in the present volume is taken from the first edition.

from **How to Write Short Stories (With Samples).** At the urging of F. Scott Fitzgerald, Scribner editor Maxwell Perkins wrote to Lardner in July 1923 asking him to consider putting together a collection of his short stories. Lardner was agreeable to the idea but informed Perkins that he had not retained copies of his stories, which had to be obtained from magazines. *How to Write Short Stories (With Samples)*, a collection of ten stories, was published by Charles Scribner's Sons in May 1924. The present volume includes six of the stories from that collection, along with Lardner's preface. (Lardner's humorous introductory notes on the divisional pages preceding each story are not included in this edition; the stories appear in the order of their first periodical publication rather than of their presentation in the book.) The six stories included here were originally published as follows: "My Roomy" (*Saturday Evening Post*, May 9, 1914), "Alibi Ike" (*Saturday*

Evening Post, July 31, 1915), "Champion" (*Metropolitan*, October 1916), "Some Like Them Cold" (*Saturday Evening Post*, October 1, 1921), "A Caddy's Diary" (*Saturday Evening Post*, March 11, 1922), "The Golden Honeymoon" (*Cosmopolitan*, July 1922). The texts in the present volume are taken from the first edition.

from **The Love Nest and Other Stories.** *The Love Nest and Other Stories*, a collection of nine stories, was published by Charles Scribner's Sons in March 1926. The book was prefaced by a humorous introduction (not included here) attributed to "Sarah E. Spooldripper." The present volume includes eight stories, arranged by order of first periodical publication rather than of appearance in the collection. They were originally published as follows: "Haircut" (*Liberty*, March 28, 1925), "Mr. and Mrs. Fix-It" (*Liberty*, May 9, 1925), "Zone of Quiet" (*Hearst's International-Cosmopolitan*, June 1925), "Women" (*Liberty*, June 20, 1925), "The Love Nest" (*Hearst's International-Cosmopolitan*, August 1925), "A Day with Conrad Green" (*Liberty*, October 3, 1925), "Who Dealt?" (*Hearst's International-Cosmopolitan*, January 1926), "Rhythm" (*Hearst's International-Cosmopolitan*, March 1926). The texts in the present volume are taken from the first edition.

from **Round Up.** *Round Up: The Stories of Ring W. Lardner* (New York: Charles Scribner's Sons) included fourteen previously unpublished stories along with others that had appeared in Lardner's earlier story collections. The present volume includes seven stories from *Round Up*, which had originally been published as follows: "Travelogue" (*Hearst's International-Cosmopolitan*, May 1926), "I Can't Breathe" (*Hearst's International-Cosmopolitan*, September 1926), "Sun Cured" (*Hearst's International-Cosmopolitan*, January 1927), "Liberty Hall" (*Hearst's International-Cosmopolitan*, March 1928), "There Are Smiles" (*Hearst's International-Cosmopolitan*, April 1928), "Ex Parte" (*Hearst's International-Cosmopolitan*, November 1928), "Old Folks' Xmas" (*Hearst's International-Cosmopolitan*, January 1929). They are presented in the order of their first periodical publication rather than their appearance in the collection. The texts in the present volume are taken from the first edition published in April 1929.

Uncollected Stories. The four stories included in this volume that were not collected by Lardner were first published as follows: "Second-Act Curtain" (*Collier's*, April 19, 1930), "Bob's Birthday" (*Red Book*, November 1933), "Poodle" (*Delineator*, January 1934), "Widow" (*Red Book*, October 1935). The texts in the present volume are those of the original periodical publications.

Sketches and Reporting. This volume gathers seventeen of Lardner's short sketches and nonfiction pieces under the rubric "Sketches and Reporting." Texts have been drawn from the following sources: "The Dames," "Bed-Time Stories," "'In Conference,'" "Prohibition," "Tennis by Cable," "Who's Who," and "The Other Side" (parts one and two) from *What of It?* (New York: Charles Scribner's Sons, 1925); "A Literary Diary," "On Conversation," and "Odd's Bodkins" from *First and Last* (ed. Gilbert Seldes; New York: Charles Scribner's Sons, 1934); "Tyrus" from *The American Magazine*, June 1915; a selection from *My Four Weeks in France* (Indianapolis: Bobbs-Merrill, 1918); "Ring Lardner—Himself" from *The Saturday Evening Post*, April 28, 1917; "Insomnia" from *Hearst's International-Cosmopolitan*, May 1931; and "Eckie" from *The Saturday Evening Post*, October 22, 1932.

Plays. The plays by Lardner included in this volume are drawn from the following sources. "The Bull Pen," "Cora, or Fun at a Spa," "Dinner Bridge," "Abend di Anni Nouveau," "Thompson's Vacation": *First and Last* (ed. Gilbert Seldes; New York: Charles Scribner's Sons, 1934). "I. Gaspiri," "Taxidea Americana," "Clemo Uti— 'The Water Lilies'": *What of It?* (New York: Charles Scribner's Sons, 1925). "Quadroon": *The New Yorker*, December 19, 1931. "The Tridget of Griva": *Blackouts: Fourteen Revue Sketches* (ed. Marjorie Rice Levis; New York: Samuel French, 1932).

Song Lyrics. Lardner aspired to success as a songwriter and was a prolific lyricist throughout his writing career. The music for "Gee! It's a Wonderful Game" was written by Chicago White Sox pitcher G. Harris (Doc) White. "Prohibition Blues" was sung by Nora Bayes (who is credited with writing the music) in the musical *Ladies First* (1918); Bayes recorded the song for Columbia. "You Can't Get Along Without Me" and "I'll Never Be Young Again" are among the songs (with music by Paul Lannin) that Lardner wrote for the unproduced musical *All at Sea* (1928–30), book by Lardner, George Abbott, and Joseph Santley. "We're All Just One Big Family" (music by Vincent Youmans) was written for the Florenz Ziegfeld revue *Smiles* (1930). The song lyrics included here are drawn from the following sources. "Gee! It's a Wonderful Game": Sheet music, New York: Jerome H. Remick, 1911. "Prohibition Blues": Sheet music, New York: Jerome H. Remick, 1919. "You Can't Get Along Without Me," "I'll Never Be Young Again," "We're All Just One Big Family": Typescripts, Newberry Library.

Letters. The present volume includes seventeen letters by Lardner, written from 1908 to 1933. Texts have been taken from Clifford M.

Carruthers, ed., *Letters of Ring Lardner* (Washington, D.C.: Orchises, 1995).

This volume presents the texts of the original printings and typescripts chosen for inclusion here, but it does not attempt to reproduce nontextual features of their typographic design. The texts are presented without change, except for the correction of typographical errors. Spelling, punctuation, and capitalization are often expressive features and are not altered, even when inconsistent or irregular. The following is a list of typographical errors corrected, cited by page and line number: 25.28, *Chicago Illinois*; 43.33, to say; 77.21, But is; 108.27, something Maybe; 121.34, no I yes; 165.15, the the horse; 171.31, to-morrow.; 257.34, Wel; 279.8, of him; 349.6, wash-room; 357.28, Delehanty; 379.12, begining; 475.16, going'; 481.39, nothin,"; 485.6, "Me?' said Midge "I; 498.18, goin; 499.17, said,; 528.40, Mr.; 574.28, em; 585.1, York,; 615.32, Jackson,; 617.3, Green."; 625.27, sorry,; 646.10, "It's; 681.27, Landsdowne; 683.29, cream.'; 690.12, dazzingly; 700.3, afternoon.; 705.18, again.; 713.29, Carter's; 717.15, Murdock's; 728.29, damn; 735.1, there so; 748.24, auto" "superintendent-gardener; 770.17, Delehanty; 788.2, Hagan; 789.11, Rubenstein; 843.5, Demspey; 843.17, Runyan's; 843.36, Runyan's; 844.7, Runyan's; 850.5, owe you; 870.11, *Wheelman*.; 873.36, Lanin; 874.6, Lanin.

Notes

In the notes below, the reference numbers denote page and line of this volume (the line count includes titles and headings but not blank lines). No note is made for material included in standard desk-reference books. For the early twentieth-century baseball players frequently referred to by Lardner, a player's name is usually given in the form (often a nickname or shortened version of a first name) used for the player's entry on the website of the Society for American Baseball Research (www.sabr.org), which contains detailed biographies of these players. For further information on Lardner's life and works, and references to other studies, see Matthew J. Bruccoli and Richard Layman, *Ring W. Lardner: A Descriptive Bibliography* (Pittsburgh: University of Pittsburgh Press, 1976); Clifford M. Caruthers, ed., *Letters of Ring Lardner* (Washington, D.C.: Orchises, 1995); *Ring Around Max: The Correspondence of Ring Lardner and Max Perkins* (DeKalb: Northern Illinois University Press, 1973); Donald Elder, *Ring Lardner: A Biography* (New York: Doubleday, 1956); George Hilton, ed., *The Annotated Baseball Stories of Ring W. Lardner, 1914–1919* (Palo Alto, Calif.: Stanford University Press, 1995); and Jonathan Yardley, *Ring: A Biography of Ring Lardner* (New York: Random House, 1977).

YOU KNOW ME AL

1.2   BUSHER'S] Variant of "bush-leaguer," a baseball player in the lower minor leagues; more generally, someone amateurish, inept, and countrified.

3.9   Chicago Americans] I.e., the White Sox, who were in the American League.

3.13–14   show . . . Central League] Keefe had been dealt to the White Sox from the Class B minor league Terre Haute franchise, active from 1903 to 1916 under several team names in the Central League.

3.16   Walsh] Ed Walsh (1881–1959), star White Sox pitcher, whose achievements include winning forty games in 1908 and finishing his career with an earned run average of 1.82, the lowest ever recorded.

3.32   Jack Doyle] "Dirty Jack" Doyle (1869–1958), Irish-born ballplayer, manager, umpire, and scout.

4.2   Comiskey] Charles Comiskey (1859–1931), ballplayer, manager, and owner of the White Sox. With Ban Johnson (1865–1931), the president of the minor league Western League and then the American League, he had overseen the transformation of the American League into a major league association, recognized by the National League as the second major league in 1903.

5.10   president of the league] Ban Johnson (see note 4.2).

5.36   city serious] From 1903 to 1942, the White Sox played the city's National League team, the Cubs, in a "city series" after the regular season ended, unless one of the teams had won their league's pennant.

6.9   *Paso Robles, California*] Site of spring training for the White Sox.

6.29   Kid Gleason . . . Callahan] Kid Gleason (1866–1933), White Sox coach; Nixey Callahan (1874–1934), the team's manager, 1903–4 and 1912–14.

7.29   Scott . . . Russell] White Sox pitchers Jim Scott, nicknamed "Death Valley" (1888–1957), and Reb Russell (1889–1973).

7.34   Lord] White Sox third baseman and captain Harry Lord (1882–1948).

7.38   Walter Johnson's] Walter Johnson (1887–1946), "The Big Train," Washington Senators right-hander who was one of the dominant pitchers of his era, winning 417 games in 21 seasons.

8.19   Collins] White Sox right fielder Shano Collins (1885–1955).

8.31   Bodie . . . Fournier] White Sox center fielder Ping Bodie, born Francesco Pezzolo (1887–1961), and infielder Jack Fournier (1889–1973).

9.9   Chase] White Sox first baseman Hal Chase (1883–1947).

9.15–16   could not get waivers] A player could be sent to the minor leagues only if he was not claimed on waivers by any other team.

9.18   Smith] Louis Smith (1861–1925), owner of the Terre Haute Central League team (see note 3.13–14).

9.32–33   Cotton States League] Class D league based in Mississippi, Alabama, and Florida.

10.24   Weaver] White Sox shortstop Buck Weaver (1890–1956).

11.5   Cobb . . . will steal] Currently fourth on the list of all-time stolen-base leaders, Detroit Tigers outfielder Ty Cobb (1886–1961) was one of baseball's greatest base stealers.

12.4   New England League] A Class B minor league.

12.34   Benz] White Sox pitcher Joe Benz (1886–1957).

13.9   Baker] Philadelphia Athletics third baseman John Franklin "Home Run" Baker (1886–1963), later a player for the New York Yankees.

15.27   Lajoie . . . Jackson] Napoleon Lajoie (1874–1959), second baseman with the Cleveland Naps, a team named for him (later renamed the Cleveland Indians); "Shoeless Joe" Jackson (1887–1951), Cleveland Naps outfielder best known for his later involvement as a White Sox player in throwing the 1919 World Series and his resulting banishment from baseball.

16.26   Bumgardner] St. Louis Browns pitcher George Baumgardner (1891–1970).

16.30   Kuhn] White Sox backup catcher Walt Kuhn (1887–1935).

16.34   Shotten] Browns outfielder Burt Shotton (1884–1962).

16.36   Johnston] Browns outfielder John Johnston (1890–1940).

16.38   Schalk] White Sox starting catcher Ray Schalk (1892–1970).

17.2   Williams] Browns outfielder Gus Williams (1888–1964).

17.7   Pratt] Browns second baseman Del Pratt (1888–1977).

17.14   Easterly] Ted Easterly (1885–1951), primarily a pinch hitter while playing for the White Sox in 1912 and 1913.

17.25   Cicotte] White Sox pitcher Eddie Cicotte (1884–1969), later implicated in throwing the 1919 World Series and banned from baseball.

18.30   Bush and Crawford and Veach] Detroit Tigers shortstop Donie Bush (1887–1972) and outfielders Sam Crawford (1880–1968) and Bobby Veach (1888–1945).

19.18   Moriarty] Tigers third baseman George Moriarty (1884–1964).

19.20   Gainor] Tigers first baseman Del Gainer (1886–1947).

19.21   Stanage] Tigers catcher Oscar Stanage (1883–1964).

20.19   Jennings . . . yelling like an Indian.] Hughie Jennings (1869–1928), manager for the Tigers, 1907–20, was famous for gesticulating theatrically and yelling "Ee-yah" from the third-base coaching box.

23.14   Howard our manager] Del Howard (1877–1956), manager of the San Francisco Seals in the minor league Pacific Coast League, 1912–13.

26.13   Bender] Philadelphia Athletics pitcher Chief Bender (1884–1954), the best pitcher on their staff.

26.15   Collins] Athletics second baseman Eddie Collins (1887–1951), one of the best players of the era.

26.18   Barry] Athletics shortstop Jack Barry (1887–1961).

26.19   Oldring] Athletics outfielder Rube Oldring (1884–1961).

28.9–10   Vitt . . . Osker] Tigers third baseman Oscar "Ossie" Vitt (1890–1963).

28.32   Dubuque, or whatever his name is.] Tigers pitcher Jean Dubuc (1888–1958).

30.14–15   Johnston . . . Turner] Cleveland Naps first baseman Doc Johnston (1887–1961), shortstop Ray Chapman (1891–1920), and third baseman Terry Turner (1881–1960).

30.18   Berger] White Sox infielder Joe Berger (1886–1956).

30.37–38   Wood . . . Smoky Joe] Boston Red Sox pitcher Joe Wood (1889–1985) was nicknamed "Smoky Joe" because of the speed of his fastball.

31.21   the Garden] Madison Square Garden, then located at 26th Street and Madison Avenue.

32.2–3   the Follies] The Ziegfeld Follies, musical revue produced by Florenz Ziegfeld Jr. (1867–1932), which ran in a series of editions from 1907 to 1931.

33.27–29   Bill Sullivan . . . the Monumunt] Washington Senators catcher Gabby Street (1882–1951) caught a ball thrown from the top of the Washington Monument on August 21, 1908; White Sox catcher Billy Sullivan (1875–1965) repeated the stunt on August 24, 1910, catching three of the balls thrown by pitchers Ed Walsh and Doc White (1879–1969).

34.31   Schaefer and Altrock . . . cut up] Senators coaches Germany Schaefer (1876–1919) and Nick Altrock (1876–1965) were crowd favorites for their clownish routines on field before and during ball games.

34.35   Griffith] Senators manager Clark Griffith (1869–1955).

35.9   Milan] Senators center fielder Clyde Milan (pronounced "Millin"; 1887–1953), known for his speed on the basepaths.

35.20   Evans] American League umpire Billy Evans (1884–1956).

35.26   Shanks] Senators left fielder Howie Shanks (1890–1941).

35.39   McBride] Senators shortstop George McBride (1880–1973).

37.23   Zimmerman] Chicago Cubs infielder Heinie Zimmerman (1887–1969).

39.26–27   go to Australia with Mike Donlin's team] Two teams playing as the New York Giants and the Chicago White Sox (with players largely drawn from their ranks) embarked on an international barnstorming tour after the 1913 season, including a stop in Australia. One of the players was the flamboyant outfielder and vaudeville actor Mike Donlin (1878–1933). Lardner was not on the trip but wrote about it in the commemorative pamphlet *March 6th: The Home Coming of Charles A. Comiskey, John J. McGraw and James J. Callahan* (1914), coauthored with Edward G. Heeman.

40.7   Cheney] Cubs pitcher Larry Cheney (1886–1969), at the time the best pitcher on their staff.

40.36   Leach] Cubs outfielder Tommy Leach (1877–1969).

40.38   Schulte the lucky stiff] Cubs power-hitting right fielder Wildfire Schulte (1882–1949), winner in 1911 of the Chalmers Award for the National League, akin to the Most Valuable Player awards instituted in 1931.

41.8   Federal League] Baseball league, 1914–15, established in an attempt to be the third major league; it attracted several major league players and managers in its bid for legitimacy and popularity.

49.14   Texas Oklahoma League] A Class D minor league.

58.35   Tinker] Joe Tinker (1880–1948), longtime Chicago Cubs player who was player-manager of the Chicago Whales in the Federal League, 1914–15.

74.37   Charlie O'Leary] San Francisco Seals shortstop Charley O'Leary (1875–1941), who spent most of his major league career playing for the Detroit Tigers.

76.23–24   Denver . . . Western League] The Denver Bears won the pennant of the Class A Western League's 1913 season.

76.25   Epworth League] Methodist association for adults aged 18 to 35.

78.38   Joe Benz getting married] To his sweetheart Alice Leddy, on March 10, 1914.

81.12   Alcock] White Sox infielder Scotty Alcock (1885–1973).

81.36   Blackburne] White Sox infielder Lena Blackburne (1886–1968).

85.39   left handed stiff Boehling] Washington Senators pitcher Joe Boehling (1891–1941), at the time the best left hander on the Senators' staff.

87.5–6   McInnis] Philadelphia Athletics first baseman Stuffy McInnis (1890–1960).

99.19–20   Mathewson] New York Giants pitcher Christy Mathewson (1880–1925), one of baseball's greatest pitchers.

102.13   O'Day] Chicago Cubs manager Hank O'Day (1862–1935).

102.21   Pierce] Cubs pitcher George Pierce (1888–1935).

102.24   Good . . . Saier that hits a hole lot of home runs] Cubs outfielder Wilbur Good (1885–1963) and first baseman Vic Saier (1891–1967), whose 18 home runs in the 1914 season was second highest in the National League.

106.29   Faber] Red Faber (1888–1976), who had pitched impressively in his rookie season in 1914, the first of a career spent entirely with the White Sox.

112.15–16   N. Y. giants . . . the world.] Based on the 1913 international barnstorming tour (see note 39.27), which would not have been planned for 1914 because of the outbreak of World War I.

115.16   Merkle] New York Giants first baseman Fred Merkle (1888–1956).

115.20   Mcgraw] Giants manager John McGraw (1873–1934).

119.6–7   Steve Evans . . . funny] Outfielder Steve Evans (1885–1943), like Germany Schaefer (see note 34.31), was a popular player because of his clowning. During the 1913–14 world tour Evans played for the White Sox.

120.2   Hern] Giants pitcher Bunny Hearn (1891–1959).

120.3   Wiltse] Giants pitcher Hooks Wiltse (1879–1959).

120.9   Speaker] Tris Speaker (1888–1958), one of baseball's greatest center fielders, who played most of his career for the Boston Red Sox and the Cleveland Indians.

120.24–25   Ted Sullivan . . . trip] Irish-born baseball executive (1851–1929), organizer and director of the 1913–14 barnstorming tour and a close friend of Charles Comiskey.

120.30   Dummy Taylor] Luther Taylor (1875–1958), a deaf-mute pitcher who spent almost his entire major league career with the New York Giants, 1900–1908.

121.17   Doyle and Thorp] New York Giants second baseman Larry Doyle (1886–1974), "Laughing Larry," one of the National League's leading players over several seasons and the winner of the Chalmers Award in 1912; college football star, Olympian, and all-around athlete Jim Thorpe (1888–1953), whose major league baseball career began in 1913 with the New York Giants, the team he played for on the 1913–14 world tour.

131.21   Umpires of Japan] The teams on the 1913–14 tour crossed the Pacific on the steamer *Empress of Japan*.

GULLIBLE'S TRAVELS, ETC.

137.11   Mooratory . . . Farr'r] Lucien Muratore (1876–1954), tenor; Frances Alda (1879–1952), soprano; Geraldine Farrar (1882–1967), soprano who also appeared in silent movies, including Cecil B. De Mille's *Carmen* (1915) and *Joan the Woman* (1917).

140.38   George S. Busy] I.e., Georges Bizet (1838–1875), French composer.

143.27   Sokol Verein] Literally "Falcon Club," a branch of a Czech youth gymnastics and physical-culture organization with a strong nationalist emphasis, founded in 1862 in Prague by Miroslav Tyrš (1832–1884) and Jindřich Fügner (1822–1865). The first American Sokol association was established in 1865.

150.19   *Armour's Do Re Me*] *L'Amore dei Tre Re* (*The Love of the Three Kings*, 1913), opera by Italian composer Italo Montemezzi (1875–1952), with libretto by Italian playwright Sem Benelli (1877–1949).

182.37–38   Bill Sykes . . . Henry Chesterfield] Bill Sikes, brutish character in Charles Dickens's novel *Oliver Twist* (1838); Philip Dormer Stanhope, 4th Earl of Chesterfield (1694–1773), whose letters to his son about polite conduct were published posthumously in 1774.

THE REAL DOPE

188.25   Van Hinburg] German military leader and statesman Paul von Hindenburg (1847–1934), who, with Erich Ludendorff (1865–1937), directed the German army from April 1916 through the end of World War I.

188.36–37   Connie Mack] Born Cornelius McGillicuddy (1862–1956), longtime manager and owner of the Philadelphia Athletics.

189.32   big enough for Nemo Liebold] Nemo Leibold (1892–1977), major league outfielder 5′6″ tall, nicknamed after the comic strip character Little Nemo, a small boy.

191.16–17   Hughey Jennings . . . Oscar Stanage] See notes 20.19 and 19.21.

196.7   Gen. Pershing] General of the Armies John J. Pershing (1860–1948), commander of American Expeditionary Forces during World War I.

200.24   Silk O'Loughlin] American League umpire (1872–1918).

212.7   Terre Haute going after George Sisler] Terre Haute had a Class B minor league team in the Central League (see note 3.13–14); St. Louis Browns first baseman George Sisler (1893–1973) was one of the top players in the major leagues, hitting over .300 for nine consecutive seasons.

215.28   Dummy Taylor] See note 120.30.

219.26   and his eeyah] See note 20.19.

219.34   Manager Rowland] Clarence "Pants" Rowland (1879–1969), manager of the White Sox, 1915–18.

226.21   Rube Oldring] See note 26.19.

226.21   Gandil] White Sox first baseman Chick Gandil (1888–1970).

226.22   Bill Dinneen's] American League umpire Bill Dinneen (1876–1955).

226.25   Robbins one of the Chi paper reporters] *Chicago Daily News* sportswriter George S. Robbins.

228.4   Larry Gardner] Boston Red Sox third baseman (1886–1976).

228.8   Hoblitzel] Red Sox first baseman Dick Hoblitzell (1888–1962).

228.9   Scott] Red Sox shortstop Everett Scott (1892–1960), later a player for the New York Yankees, among other teams.

228.22   Duffy Lewis] Red Sox left fielder (1888–1979).

237.31   Judge] Washington Senators first baseman Joe Judge (1894–1963).

238.8   G.A.R.] Grand Army of the Republic, association of Union veterans from the Civil War.

238.11　Jones] Fielder Jones (1871–1934), manager of the St. Louis Browns, 1916–18.

238.17　Laudermilk] Pitcher Grover Lowdermilk (1885–1968), who played for the Browns from 1917 to 1919.

244.26–28　makeing a Frenchman the gen. . . . Foch] French military leader Ferdinand Foch (1851–1929) was appointed supreme commander of the Allied armies in March 1918.

245.13　Risberg] White Sox shortstop Swede Risberg (1894–1975).

246.28　Wm. Burns] American law enforcement official William J. Burns (1861–1932), founder and head of William J. Burns International Detective Agency, and later the director of the Bureau of Investigation, 1921–24.

247.2–4　Schaefer . . . they called him Germany] See note 34.31.

247.10　first Liberty Loan] The first of five bond issues floated by the U.S. Treasury Department that helped finance World War I.

248.29　W. C. T. U.] Woman's Christian Temperance Union. "Vin Blank" is a misspelling of *vin blanc*, white wine.

250.30　the Elite] The Elite Club, jazz club at 3030 South State Street in Chicago.

250.33　Lincoln Pk.] Chicago's Lincoln Park Zoo.

252.9–13　Field Marshall . . . heim] "Field Marshall Van Hindenburg, c/o The Four Dachshunds, German Army, Flanders. 500,000 U.S. soldiers already in France. In Lauterbach I lost my stocking, and without it I dare not go home." The last sentence is drawn from the well-known German folk song "Zu Lauterbach Hab' Ich Mein Strumpf Verlorn," whose melody was used for American songwriter Septimus Winner's 1864 song "Der Deitcher's Dog" (beginning "Oh where, oh where ish my little dog gone?").

258.10　a Minnie Weffers.] A *Minenwerfer* (literally, "mine-thrower"), German trench mortar.

259.33–34　Schwarz Auge . . . Nase] "Schwarze Auge" is German for "Black Eye"; "Rote Nase" is "Red Nose."

259.34–35　Blumenkohl Ohren] German: cauliflower ears.

275.16　Noir et Blanc] French: black and white.

275.36　Rodeheaver record] Homer Rodeheaver (1880–1955) was a preacher and song leader at evangelist Billy Sunday's revival meetings. Beginning in 1913, he made several recordings of revival hymns and temperance songs.

277.37–38　Young Peoples] Christian youth organization.

279.3–4   Guy Meyer the French ace] French fighter pilot Georges Guyne-
mer (1894–1917), credited with destroying 53 enemy aircraft.

280.31   Ludendorf] Erich Ludendorff; see note 188.25.

282.13   speegle] Mirror, from *Spiegel* in German.

294.26–27   They started . . . 18th of July] In the Second Battle of the
Marne, July 15–August 6, 1918, a German offensive was halted by the Allies in
the vicinity of Reims, July 15–17; the Germans were then driven back by an Allied counteroffensive beginning on July 18. The Allied victory was of decisive
importance for the outcome of the war.

THE YOUNG IMMIGRUNTS

303.9   Rollie Zeider] Infielder (1883–1967) who played in Chicago for both
the White Sox and the Cubs, as well as the Whales in the Federal League.

303.12–13   shirts . . . Artie Hofman] After most of his major league career was over, utility player Artie Hofman (1882–1956), also known as Solly,
opened a haberdashery in Chicago.

303.30–31   Toledo . . . Jessie Willard] Boxer Jack Dempsey (1895–1983)
won the world heavyweight title by defeating his favored opponent and cur-
rent champion, Jess Willard (1881–1968), in Toledo on July 4, 1919. The "big
fellow" (303.32) is Willard, who was much larger than Dempsey.

306.29   Elmer Flick] Outfielder (1876–1971) who played in the major
leagues from 1898 to 1910, mostly for the Philadelphia Phillies and Cleveland
Naps.

308.23–24   Mr. Yost . . . Michigan football team] Fielding Yost (1871–
1946), coach of the University of Michigan Wolverines football team, 1901–23,
1925–26.

330.18–19   Ossining . . . the stripes] Sing Sing prison is located in Ossining,
New York.

330.20–23   Rockfeller . . . Socony] Socony (Standard Oil Company of
New York) was one of the companies established after a 1911 Supreme Court
ruling broke up as an illegal monopoly the Standard Oil Company of New
Jersey (itself formed after the original Standard Oil Trust was dissolved under
the terms of the Sherman Anti-Trust Act in 1892). John D. Rockefeller (1839–
1937) was a founder and president of Standard Oil and its major shareholder.

330.29   Bill Klem . . . Langford] National League umpire Bill Klem
(1874–1951); college football referee W. S. Langford (1875–1950).

THE BIG TOWN

340.37   Oliver Lodge] British physicist and inventor (1851–1940), also
known for his interest in psychic phenomena and the afterlife.

346.25   Sweet and Low] Musical setting by Joseph Barnby (1838–1896) of a poem by Alfred Tennyson.

347.21   Georgie Cohan] George M. Cohan (1878–1942), preeminent musical comedy performer, playwright, and composer.

352.15   Doc Cook] American explorer and physician Frederick Cook (1865–1940), best known for falsely claiming to have reached the North Pole on April 21, 1908.

352.17   Jess Willard's] See note 303.30–31.

357.24   Charley Brickley . . . Eckersall] Brickley (1891–1949), playing for Harvard, kicked five field goals in the 1913 Harvard–Yale game; star University of Chicago quarterback Walter Eckersall (1886–1930) kicked five field goals in games against the University of Wisconsin in 1905 and the University of Nebraska in 1906. Later a sportswriter at the *Chicago Tribune*, Eckersley was a friend of Lardner, who wrote the reminiscence "Eckie" (pp. 833–41 in this volume) about him.

357.26–27   bird named Robertson . . . seven.] Purdue quarterback Edward C. Robertson (1876–1903) kicked seven field goals in a game against Rose Polytechnic, October 27, 1900.

357.28   Bobby Lowe . . . Ed Delahanty] Boston Beaneaters second baseman Bobby Lowe (1865–1951) became the first major league player to hit four home runs in one game on May 30, 1894, in a game against the Cincinnati Reds. Philadelphia Phillies left fielder Ed Delahanty (1867–1903) hit four home runs (two of them inside the park) against the Chicago Colts on July 13, 1896.

357.29   Toledo that time] See note 303.30–31.

362.6   the Follies] See note 32.2–3.

366.30   Eddie Foy's family] Foy (1856–1928), a vaudeville dancer and comedian, performed, 1910–13, with the seven surviving children of his third marriage as Eddie Foy and the Seven Little Foys.

367.26   Rose D. Barry] Rose du Barry, a pink coloring developed as a ceramic glaze in eighteenth-century France.

373.14   Gene Buck] Lyricist (1885–1957), a Great Neck neighbor and sometime collaborator of Lardner.

376.31   Poets and Peasants] Overture to *Dichter und Bauer* (1846), operetta by Austrian composer Franz von Suppé (1819–1895).

393.21   Man o' War] Celebrated thoroughbred racehorse (1917–1947).

396.23   a Perfect Day] Song (1909) by American songwriter Carrie Jacobs-Bond (1862–1946).

404.20   Whispering] Song with lyrics by John Schoenburger and Richard

Coburn, and music by Vincent Rose, an instrumental hit for Paul Whiteman and His Ambassador Orchestra in 1920.

418.35   Bunny Granville] Vaudeville entertainer (1886–1936) associated with the Ziegfeld Follies.

423.39   Hitchcock] Raymond Hitchcock (1865–1929), vaudeville monologist, star of such revues as *Hitchy-Koo* (1917) and *Raymond Hitchcock's Pinwheel* (1922).

424.27   Bert Williams] African American vaudeville comedian and recording star (1874–1922), initially as part of the team of Walker and Williams and subsequently as a solo act.

424.28   Sarah Bernhardt] French actor (1844–1923).

428.37   Lew Fields] Vaudeville comedian (1867–1941), longtime stage partner of Joe Weber (1867–1942).

433.40   Mrs. Fiske] Minnie Maddern Fiske (1865–1932), leading American stage actor.

HOW TO WRITE SHORT STORIES

438.8   Blasco Ibañez] Vicente Blasco Ibáñez (1867–1928), Spanish novelist whose internationally popular works included *Blood and Sand* (1908) and *The Four Horsemen of the Apocalypse* (1916).

441.3–5   Cobb] See note 11.5.

442.18–19   Federals] See note 41.8.

450.5   'Silver Threads Among the Gold.'] Popular ballad, copyrighted in 1873, with lyrics by Eben Rexford and music by Hart Pease Danks.

450.10   Martin Walsh—brother o' Big Ed's] See note 3.16.

462.33   Kid Gleason] See note 6.29.

464.6   Willie Hoppe] American-born billiards champion (1887–1959).

468.9   Big Marquard] Rube Marquard (1886–1980), pitcher for the New York Giants and other teams.

468.33   Doyle] Larry Doyle (see note 121.17).

479.28   Rube Benton and Red Ames] Cincinnati Reds pitchers (in 1915) Rube Benton (1890–1937) and Red Ames (1882–1936).

505.15   Levy's and Goebel's] Leading music publishers.

505.31   Friars club] Private club, established in 1904, whose members include comedians and other show business personalities.

508.16   Robert W. Service] English-born Canadian poet (1874–1958) whose popular verses included "The Shooting of Dan McGrew."

509.22   Berlin or Davis] Irving Berlin (1888–1989), songwriter whose many hits included "White Christmas," "Alexander's Ragtime Band," and "Blue Skies"; Benny Davis (1895–1979), lyricist whose hits included "Baby Face" and "There Goes My Heart."

515.4   Georgie White] Broadway producer (1890–1968) known for his revue *George White's Scandals*, of which there were sixteen editions from 1919 to 1939.

515.24   the Follies] See note 32.2–3.

521.39   Lillian Gish] Film actor (1893–1993) who worked closely with D. W. Griffith starting in 1912, starring in *The Birth of a Nation* (1915), *Intolerance* (1916), and many other films.

547.10–11   Home to Our Mountains and Mother] "Home to Our Mountains," English-language adaptation of "Ai Nostri Monti" from Giuseppe Verdi's opera *Il Trovatore* (1853); "M-O-T-H-E-R," song (1915) with lyrics by Howard Johnson and music by Theodore Morse.

THE LOVE NEST

560.22–24   Gloria Swanson . . . of Virtue] Gloria Swanson (1899–1983), movie star who appeared in *Male and Female* (1919), *Manhandled* (1924), and other films; Thomas Meighan (1879–1936), silent movie star of *Why Change Your Wife?* (1920), *Manslaughter* (1922), and other films; *The Wages of Virtue* (1924), film directed by Allan Dwan and starring Gloria Swanson and Ben Lyon.

567.14   Mrs. Gump] Min, nagging wife of Andy Gump in the comic strip *The Gumps* (1917–59), created by Sidney Smith.

567.24   Robert H. Service] See note 508.16.

569.9–10   Judge Landis] Kenesaw Mountain Landis (1866–1944), federal judge, 1905–22, and first commissioner of Major League Baseball, 1920–44.

572.5–6   "Red" Grange] All-American halfback (1903–1991) for the University of Illinois, and then one of the first stars of professional football, playing mostly for the Chicago Bears.

574.14   the Big Four] Nickname for the Central Pacific Railroad, after its four founders, Leland Stanford, Collis P. Huntington, Mark Hopkins, and Charles Crocker.

574.17   C. & E. I.] Chicago and Eastern Illinois Railroad.

577.9   'What Price Glory?'] Long-running play (1924) by Maxwell Anderson and Laurence Stallings, filmed in 1926.

579.16   'Vanity Fair,'] Novel (1847–48) by William Makepeace Thackeray; magazine noted for its sophisticated literary content, published by Condé Nast, 1913–36, and edited by Frank Crowninshield.

580.18   Peewee Byers] Jazz saxophonist and bandleader.

580.19   Whiteman's] Orchestra led by Paul Whiteman (1890–1967).

581.1–2   Edgar M. Guest] Edgar A. Guest (1881–1959), British-born American poet whose many volumes of popular verse included *A Heap o' Livin'* (1916), *Just Folks* (1917), and *When Day Is Done* (1921).

583.19   Bugs Baer] Arthur "Bugs" Baer (1886–1969), sports journalist and humorist.

584.31   Norma Talmadge] Movie actor (1894–1957) who starred in *Smilin' Through* (1922), *Within the Law* (1923), and other films.

593.15   playin' . . . for McGraw] I.e., for the New York Giants, long managed by John McGraw (see note 115.20).

593.25   Bill Bradley] Bradley (1878–1954) was a third baseman who played most of his career for Cleveland in the American League, a power hitter also possessed of excellent fielding and base-running skills.

606.26–27   'All alone, yes, I'm all alone.'] From Irving Berlin's song "All Alone" (1924).

606.34   Pavlowa] Anna Pavlova (1881–1931), ballerina, principal artist of the Imperial Russian Ballet and Diaghilev's Ballets Russes.

610.1   *Conrad Green*] The character is modeled on Lardner's sometime employer Florenz Ziegfeld Jr. (see note 32.2–3).

611.18   Zuloaga] Ignacio Zuloaga y Zabaleta (1870–1945), Spanish painter.

612.37   Deems Taylor] American composer and music critic (1885–1966).

618.36   Bert Kalmar and Harry Ruby] Kalmar (1884–1947) and Ruby (1895–1974), songwriting team whose many hits included "Who's Sorry Now?" and "Three Little Words."

626.40   "Black Oxen,"] Best-selling novel (1923) by Gertrude Atherton.

629.33   Jack Kearns] Boxing manager (1882–1963), best known as the manager of Jack Dempsey.

629.35   "Humoresque" and "Indian Love Lyrics."] "Humoresque," seventh of Antonín Dvořák's *Humoresques*, op. 101 (1894), of which many popular arrangements were made; "Indian Love Lyrics" (1902), settings by English composer Amy Woodforde-Finden (1860–1919) of four poems by English poet Laurence Hope, pseudonym of Adela Florence Nicolson (1865–1904).

629.36   Ed Wynn] Vaudeville comedian (1886–1966), a star of the Ziegfeld Follies.

629.40   "The Fool" or "Lightnin'."] *The Fool* (1922), play by Channing Pollock (1880–1946); *Lightnin'* (1918), play by Frank Bacon (1864–1922) and Winchell Smith (1871–1933).

631.24–25 Robert Chambers] Robert W. Chambers (1865–1933), prolific popular novelist best remembered for his early volume of supernatural stories, *The King in Yellow* (1895).

631.25 Irving R. Cobb] Irvin S. Cobb (1876–1944), humorist and fiction writer, author of *Cobb's Anatomy* (1912), *Old Judge Priest* (1915), and many other books.

634.5–7 'Gioconda,' . . . Chamounix.'] *La Gioconda* (1876), opera by Amilcare Ponchielli (1834–1886); *Linda di Chamounix* (1842), opera by Gaetano Donizetti (1797–1848).

635.6 Friml] Rudolf Friml (1879–1972), Czech-born American composer of operettas and musicals, including *The Firefly* (1912), *Rose-Marie* (1924), and *The Vagabond King* (1925).

635.18 Gatti-Casazza] Giulio Gatti-Casazza (1869–1940), manager of the Metropolitan Opera, 1908–35.

635.30 Alma Gluck] Soprano (1884–1938), an opera singer and popular recording star.

636.21 Walter Donaldson] Songwriter (1893–1947), composer of many hit songs, including "Yes Sir, That's My Baby," "Love Me or Leave Me," and "My Blue Heaven."

637.8–9 Max Reinhardt . . . Reinald Werrenrath] Reinhardt (1873–1943), internationally renowned Austrian theater producer and director; Werrenrath (1883–1953), American opera and concert singer popular on radio in the 1920s.

637.9–11 Heifetz . . . Tunney] Jascha Heifetz (1901–1987), preeminent violinist; Maria Jeritza (1887–1982), Austrian operatic soprano; Arlen (1895–1956), Armenian writer, born Dikran Kouyoumdjian, author of the popular novel *The Green Hat* (1924); Malone (1882–1950), activist lawyer and politician who ran for governor of New York in 1920; Tunney (1897–1978), boxer who defeated Jack Dempsey for the world heavyweight championship in 1926 and 1927.

637.21 Broun's] Heywood Broun (1888–1939), columnist, sportswriter, and drama critic.

638.15–17 Stephen Jones . . . Gitz-Rice] Stephen O. Jones (1880–1967), songwriter and composer of Broadway shows; Isham Jones (1894–1956), songwriter and bandleader whose compositions included "I'll See You in My Dreams" and "It Had To Be You"; Joe Samuels (d. about 1953), songwriter; Vincent Youmans (1898–1946), Broadway composer whose shows included *No, No, Nanette* (1925) and *Hit the Deck* (1927); Friml, see note 635.6; Dave Stamper, songwriter (1883–1963) associated with the Ziegfeld Follies; Frank Tours (1877–1963), songwriter, composer of "Mother o' Mine"; Irving Berlin, see note 509.22; Harry Tierney (1890–1965), Broadway composer of shows, including *Kid Boots* (1923) and *Rio Rita* (1927); John Raymond Hubbell (1879–1954), songwriter whose songs included "Poor Butterfly"; Silvio Hein (1879–1928), Broadway composer of many shows, including *Moonshine* (1905) and *The Yankee Girl* (1910); Gitz Rice (1891–1947), Canadian songwriter, composer of "Dear Old Pal of Mine."

639.26   Guy Bolton] British-born librettist (1884–1979) of Broadway musicals, including *Very Good Eddie* (1915) and *Leave It to Jane* (1917).

639.33   Ernest Boyd] Critic and journalist (1887–1946).

640.4–5   Stokowski himself] Conductor Leopold Stokowski (1882–1977), longtime leader of the Philadelphia Orchestra.

640.26   Gus Kahn] Lyricist (1886–1941) of popular songs, including "I'll See You in My Dreams," "Ukulele Lady," and "Goofus."

641.35   'Arcady' and 'Marcheta'] "A Song of Arcady" (1914) by English composer Cyril Scott (1879–1970); "Marcheta" (1913) by American composer and songwriter Victor Schertzinger (1888–1941).

ROUND UP

647.1   Eddie Cantor] Comedian, singer, and dancer (1892–1964) who was a star of theater, movies, radio, and early television.

647.34   the House of David] Communal religious society founded by Benjamin Franklin Purnell (1861–1927) and his wife Mary Stallard Purnell (1862–1953); the society was known among other things for the baseball teams it sponsored.

651.18   "Carlyle on Cromwell and Others,"] Book (1925) edited by David Alec Wilson (1864–1933).

651.36   Moran and Mack] Blackface comedy team, also known as the Two Black Crows; the act was founded by Charles Mack (1888–1934) and in its heyday his partner was George Moran (1881–1949).

652.2   Thomas Meighan] See note 560.22–24.

652.2   'Old Home Week.'] Movie (1925) starring Thomas Meighan and Lila Lee.

653.32   Jeanne Eagels in 'Rain'] Eagels (1890–1929) starred as the prostitute Sadie Thompson in *Rain* (1922), play by John Colton (1887–1946) based on a short story by English writer W. Somerset Maugham (1874–1965); it became her most famous role.

657.20–21   "Oh how I miss you tonight"] Song (1925) by Benny Davis, Joe Burke, and Mark Fisher.

658.13   "No Foolin'"] Song (1926) by Gene Buck and James F. Hanley, recorded by The Revelers.

658.20 "Always,"] Song (1925) by Irving Berlin.

660.9 Norma Shearer] Film actor (1902–1983) whose silent vehicles included *He Who Gets Slapped* (1924) and *Lady of the Night* (1925).

660.24 "In a cottage small by a waterfall"] "Just a Cottage Small (By a Waterfall)" (1925), song by Buddy De Sylva and James F. Hanley, popularized by John McCormack.

660.28 Jack Barrymore] John Barrymore (1882–1942), stage and screen actor.

660.28–29 Barney Gallant] Greenwich Village restaurateur (1884–1968) who ran the Village Club, a speakeasy frequented by celebrities.

666.12–13 Norman Kerry . . . Moran] Kerry (1894–1956), silent movie actor who appeared in *Merry-Go-Round* (1923), *The Phantom of the Opera* (1925), and other films; William "Buster" Collier (1902–1987), movie actor whose films included *The Sea Hawk* (1924) and *The College Widow* (1927); Davies (1897–1961), movie actor who starred in *The Patsy* (1928), *Show People* (1928), and other films; Moran (1909–1990), movie actor who appeared in *The Whirlwind of Youth* (1927) and *Behind That Curtain* (1929).

666.36 "Limehouse Blues."] Song (1922) by Douglas Furber and Philip Braham, originally popularized by Gertrude Lawrence.

673.14 American plan] Hotel rate in which meals are included.

679.21 Dillingham] Broadway producer Charles Dillingham (1868–1934).

685.38 "Chevrons."] Novel (1926) by American writer and former soldier Leonard H. Nason (1895–1970), taking place during World War I.

686.17 "Oh! Miss Hannah!" by the Revelers] Released in 1925 by the vocal quintet as the flip side of "Dinah."

689.28 Barney Oldfield] American automobile racer (1878–1946).

693.23 Kaskel's] Kaskel & Kaskel, men's clothing store located (after 1922) at Fifth Avenue and 46th Street.

694.9 Joe Frisco] Vaudeville dancer and comedian (1889–1958).

721.1 "Cradle Snatchers" and "Sex,"] *Cradle Snatchers* (1925) by Russell Medcraft (1897–1962) and Norma Mitchell (1884–1967), and *Sex* (1926) by Mae West (1893–1980) under the pseudonym Jane Mast, both Broadway plays of scandalous reputation; the latter was eventually closed by the New York police.

UNCOLLECTED STORIES

727.5 Heart Throbs] *Heart Throbs in Prose and Verse Dear to the American People* (1905), an anthology of prize entries to a contest sponsored by *The National Magazine*.

727.9   the Insidious Dr. Fu Manchu, by Sax Rohmer] American title of *The Mystery of Dr. Fu-Manchu* (1913), first in Rohmer's series of novels about an archcriminal seeking to rule the world.

727.24   Mr. Payne] John Howard Payne (1791–1852), playwright and actor; "Home, Sweet Home" is a song from his play *Clari; or The Maid of Milan* (1823). The Payne homestead is in East Hampton, Long Island.

727.35–38   "*And she says . . . fordot!*"] From "Mamma's Dirl" by J. M. Lewis.

728.1–8   "*When you see . . . 'Hullo!'*"] From "Hullo!" by Sam Walter Foss (1858–1911).

729.8–9   John Gilbert and Rudy Vallée] Gilbert (1897–1936), leading silent movie actor who appeared in *The Big Parade* (1925), *Flesh and the Devil* (1926), and other films; Vallée (1901–1986), singing star and bandleader whose hits included "My Time Is Your Time" and "I'm Just a Vagabond Lover."

735.7   Kreisler] Fritz Kreisler (1875–1962), renowned Austrian violinist.

741.22   "Tea for Two"] Song from the musical *No, No, Nanette* (1925), with music by Vincent Youmans and lyrics by Irving Caesar.

750.6   Paul Whiteman] See note 580.19.

752.6   "Rhapsody in Blue."] Composition (1924) by George Gershwin for piano and jazz band, premiered by the Paul Whiteman Orchestra.

760.5   "Gates Ajar,"] The phrase can refer to both the widely popular religious novel *The Gates Ajar* (1868) by Elizabeth Stuart Phelps Ward (1844–1911) and the hymn (1870) with words by George Cooper and music by J. R. Thomas.

760.10   "Just As I Am"] Hymn (1835) by English poet and hymn writer Charlotte Elliott (1789–1871), which has been set to a number of different melodies.

760.12–13   "In the Hour of Trial,"] Hymn composed by Spencer Lane (1843–1903) with words by James Montgomery (1771–1854).

SKETCHES AND REPORTING

767.22   Sully] Catcher Billy Sullivan (1875–1965), who spent most of his career with the Chicago White Sox.

767.33   Doc W'ite] Doc White (1879–1969), White Sox pitcher, with whom Lardner sometimes collaborated in writing songs.

768.30   ain't goin' to pull no John Anderson] "Pulling a John Anderson" was baseball slang for attempting to steal an already occupied base (and, by extension, making any base-running blunder), named for St. Louis Browns outfielder John Anderson (1873–1949), who was picked off first base during a game against the New York Highlanders, September 24, 1903. It appears that Anderson was not trying to steal second: with the bases loaded and the count full, he had taken a long lead off first base and had broken toward second with the pitch. The batter struck out and Anderson was thrown out trying to get back to first.

768.37   Doc Cook] Frederick Cook (see note 352.15).

769.2   Connie Mack] See note 188.36–37.

769.14   Bodie] See note 8.31.

770.9   Comiskey] See note 4.2.

770.16–17   Jim Delahanty] Infielder Jim Delahanty (1879–1953), who played with Cobb for the Tigers from 1909 to 1912.

770.19   Harry Davis] First baseman (1873–1947) who played for the Philadelphia Athletics from 1901 to 1911.

770.21–23   Danny Murphy . . . Ira Thomas] Athletics outfielder (1876–1955) and catcher (1881–1958).

770.33   Tannehill] White Sox infielder Lee Tannehill (1880–1938).

771.9   scorin' on kicks . . . Brickley] See note 357.24.

771.16   Ping] Ping Bodie (see note 8.31).

771.17   Weaver] Buck Weaver (see note 10.24).

771.30   Fielder Jones] See note 238.11.

772.23–24   Birmingham] Cleveland Naps center fielder and manager Joe Birmingham (1884–1946).

773.4–5   Big Anderson] John Anderson (see note 768.30).

773.14   Callahan] Nixey Callahan (see note 6.29).

773.33–774.1   Jackson . . . Crawford] Five of Cobb's rivals in hitting: Shoeless Joe Jackson (see note 15.27), Tris Speaker (see note 120.9), Eddie Collins (see note 26.15), Napoleon Lajoie (see note 15.27), and Sam Crawford (see note 18.30).

775.28   Georgia Peach] Cobb's nickname.

775.32   Rossman] Tigers first baseman Claude Rossman (1881–1928).

775.33   Old Nick] Chicago White Sox pitcher Nick Altrock (see also note 34.31).

775.35–36   Hahn . . . Dougherty] White Sox outfielders Ed Hahn (1875–1941) and Patsy Dougherty (1876–1940).

775.39   Smitty] White Sox pitcher Frank Smith (1879–1952).

776.21   Big Ed] Ed Walsh (see note 3.16), also "the Big Moose" at 776.24.

776.27   Davis] White Sox shortstop George Davis (1870–1940).

776.29   Izzy] White Sox second baseman Frank Isbell (1875–1941).

777.7   Jake] White Sox second baseman Jake Atz (1879–1945).

778.12   Donovan] Tigers pitcher Bill Donovan (1876–1923).

779.1   Jennin's] Tigers manager Hughie Jennings (see note 20.19)

779.2   Bush and Mullin and McIntire] Donie Bush (see note 18.30); Tigers pitcher George Mullin (1880–1944) and outfielder Matty McIntire (1880–1920).

781.11   McGraw . . . Eddie Collins] See notes 115.20 and 26.15.

782.4–5   General Sibert . . . General Pershing] Major General William L. Sibert (1860–1935), commander of 1st Infantry Division during World War I; Pershing, see note 196.7.

786.26   Bert A. Williams] See note 424.27.

786.27   Ina Claire] Stage and film actor (1893–1985), who appeared on Broadway in *The Gold Diggers* (1919), *The Last of Mrs. Cheyney* (1925), and *Our Betters* (1928).

787.14   Suzanne Lenglen] French tennis player (1899–1938), leading woman player of the early 1920s.

787.34   Peggy Hopkins] Peggy Hopkins Joyce (1893–1957), socialite notorious for her marriages and affairs with wealthy and titled men.

788.1   Sarazen, Hagen and Barnes] Gene Sarazen (1902–1999), Walter Hagen (1892–1969), and Jim Barnes (1886–1966), champion U.S. golfers.

788.14   "The Prisoner of Zenda,"] Novel (1894) by English novelist and playwright Anthony Hope (1863–1933); it had been filmed in 1914 and 1922.

788.15   Richard Barthelmess] Movie actor (1895–1963), whose silent vehicles included *Broken Blossoms* (1919), *Way Down East* (1920), and *Tol'able David* (1921).

788.23   Stanislaus Zbyszko] Polish strongman and wrestler (1879–1967).

788.35   Maylor Hylan . . . Senator Lodge] John Francis Hylan (1868–1936), mayor of New York, 1918–25; Henry Cabot Lodge (1850–1924), Republican senator from Massachusetts.

789.1–2   Willie Hoppe] See note 464.6.

789.11   Rubenstein] Arthur Rubinstein (1887–1982), classical pianist.

789.17   Gatti-Casazza] See note 635.18.

789.20   Scotti . . . Gerry Farrar] Antonio Scotti (1866–1936), operatic baritone; Farrar, see note 137.11.

790.13   Bill Rogers] Will Rogers (1879–1935), vaudeville performer, humorist, and movie actor.

791.33–34   Gene Buck . . . Dave Stamper] See notes 373.14 and 638.15–17.

792.32   Valentino] Movie idol (1895–1926), star of *The Four Horsemen of the Apocalypse* (1921) and *The Sheik* (1921).

792.34   Tiller gals] The Tiller Girls, troupes of precision dancers under the direction of John Tiller (1854–1925). They performed internationally and appeared in the Ziegfeld Follies.

796.3   Webster Hall] Hall built in 1886 as a venue for meetings, concerts, and public events. During the 1920s it was a center for bohemian culture in New York.

799.23   Luis Firpo] Argentinian boxer (1894–1960), defeated by Jack Dempsey in a celebrated heavyweight championship bout on September 14, 1923.

803.20   Jimmie Montague] James Jackson Montague (1873–1941), journalist and newspaper poet, a friend of Lardner.

803.38   Amy Leslie] Actor and opera singer (1855–1939) who also wrote drama criticism for the *Chicago Daily News*. Lardner is deliberately confusing her with the American *vers libre* poet Amy Lowell (1874–1925).

807.2   Congressman Volstead] Andrew Volstead (1860–1947), U.S. representative from Minnesota, 1903–23, who sponsored the National Prohibition Act of 1919.

807.14   Bernard Shaw on pugilism] An enthusiastic amateur boxer, Shaw wrote often on the subject, as in the novel *Cashel Byron's Profession* (1886).

810.5   Vincent Richards . . . Bill Johnston] Richards (1903–1959) and Johnston (1894–1946) were American tennis champions in the 1920s.

810.28   Tilden . . . Gerald Patterson] Bill Tilden (1893–1953), dominant American tennis player; Patterson (1895–1967), Australian tennis player.

811.25   Hubbard of Michigan] DeHart Hubbard (1903–1976), 1924 Olympic gold medalist in running long jump.

813.14   Casey Stengel] Major league outfielder (1890–1975), best known for his later career as a manager for New York baseball teams.

814.9–11   Walter Johnson . . . Rockne] Walter Johnson, see note 7.38; baseball infielder Rogers Hornsby (1896–1963), hitter with the sport's all-time second highest batting average (.358); heavyweight boxing champion Jack Dempsey (1895–1983); champion American golfers Bobby Jones (1902–1971) and Walter Hagen (1892–1969); Red Grange, see note 572.5–6; star Notre Dame football player and coach Knute Rockne (1888–1931).

819.13–14   Gus Wilson . . . Georges Carpentier's] Alsatian-born trainer and manager Gus Wilson (c. 1887–1951) came to the United States in 1921 while working with the champion French boxer Georges Carpentier (1894–1975), the "Orchid Man," who fought in several weight classes, from welterweight to heavyweight.

820.9–10   Frazier Hunt] Radio announcer and war correspondent (1885–1967); his coverage of World War I appeared in the *Chicago Tribune*.

820.31   Gloria Swanson . . . Jackie Coogan] Swanson, see note 560.22–24; Coogan, child movie actor (1914–1984), featured in *The Kid* (1921) and many other films.

820.37   the Tiller Girls] See note 792.34.

821.27   Harry Houdini] Magician and escape artist (1874–1926).

822.36   Escamillo] Toreador in Georges Bizet's *Carmen* (1875).

822.37   little old red shawl that Maggie wore] A reference to the song "The Little Old Red Shawl My Mother Wore," subsequently parodied as "The Dirty Old Red Drawers That Maggie Wore."

823.11–12   Alex Moore] Alexander Moore (1867–1930), American diplomat who served as ambassador to Spain, 1923–25, and later to Peru.

825.10–15   Money is de root of evil . . . as thick as bees.] From "All Going Out And Nothing Coming In" (1901).

825.16   Bert sang a song of mine] "Home, Sweet Home (That's Where the Real War Is)," performed in the Ziegfeld Follies of 1917.

825.35–36   Sheckard, Evers . . . Brown] Members of the Chicago Cubs in the middle of the first decade of the twentieth century, when the team won three National League pennants and two World Series championships: left fielder Jimmy Sheckard (1878–1947); second baseman Johnny Evers (1881–1947); right fielder Wildfire Schulte, see note 40.38; first baseman and manager Frank Chance (1876–1924); third baseman Harry Steinfeldt (1877–1914); outfielder and utility player Solly Hofman, see note 303.12–13; catcher Johnny Kling (1875–1947); pitcher Mordecai "Three Finger" Brown (1876–1948).

826.2–3   which Waner . . . third.] In the 1920s and 1930s Paul Waner (1903–1965) and his brother Lloyd (1906–1982) played in the outfield for the Pittsburgh Pirates.

833.22   Hugh Fullerton, star baseball writer] Sportswriter and short story writer Hugh Fullerton (1873–1945), who wrote for Chicago newspapers from 1893 through the early 1920s, best known for his involvement in exposing the 1919 World Series "Black Sox" fixing scandal.

833.34   GOTCH . . . BEALL'S] In their third bout within five months, American professional wrestler Frank Gotch (1878–1917) defeated German-born Fred Beell (1876–1933) at the Coliseum in Chicago on April 26, 1907.

834.27   Billy Papke . . . Stanley Ketchel] Middlewight boxers Billy Papke

(1886–1936) and Stanley Ketchel (1886–1910) fought four times in 1908 and 1909, with Ketchel winning three of the bouts. The "Spring Valley Thunderbolt" (835.11–12) refers to Papke, "Steve" (835.13, 16) to Ketchel.

835.9–10   William Hale Thompson . . . Richter] Republican politician William Hale Thompson (1869–1944), twice mayor of Chicago, 1915–23, 1927–31; Chicago restaurateur and hotel owner Ernest Byfield (1890–1950); theater critic Percy Hammond (1873–1936), who wrote for the *Chicago Tribune*, 1908–21; politician Charles Richter, representative in the Illinois General Assembly.

835.12   William Lydon] Chicago businessman (1863–1918), a founder of the Great Lakes Dredge and Dock Company and commodore of the Chicago Yacht Club.

835.14–15   Battling Nelson and Packey McFarland] Lightweight boxers Battling Nelson, born Oscar Nielsen (1882–1954) in Copenhagen, and Chicago-born Packey McFarland (1888–1936); the two fighters never met in the ring.

836.31   Jim Thorpe, of Carlisle, . . . Gipp] Thorpe (see note 121.17) attended the Carlisle Indian School in Carlisle, Pennsylvania; all-American football star George Gipp (1895–1920), known as "The Gipper."

837.8   Heston, Mahan, or Grange] University of Michigan all-American halfback Willie Heston (1878–1963); Harvard all-American halfback Eddie Mahan (1892–1975); Red Grange, see note 572.5–6.

837.12   Fielding Yost] See note 308.23–24.

837.20   Pat O'Dea] Australian-born fullback (1872–1962) for the University of Wisconsin who excelled in drop-kicking and punting.

837.28   Jimmy Walker] James J. Walker (1881–1946), mayor of New York, 1926–32; he resigned in the face of pending corruption charges. A "Mother Hubbard" is a long, loose-fitting woman's dress.

837.32–33   Charles Brickley] See note 357.24.

838.6   G. P. Torrence, Elmer Oliphant and George Ade] George Paull Torrence (1887–1965), who played offensive tackle for Purdue's football team, and went on to a career as a mechanical engineer and executive for the Chicago-based Link-Belt Company; Oliphant (1892–1975), all-American Purdue football player who excelled in several other sports; Ade (1866–1944), humorist and Purdue graduate, who wrote stories on football themes and gave financial support for a stadium at Purdue.

838.11   Walter Johnson] See note 7.38.

839.7–10   Walter Camp . . . All-America team] In 1889 Yale football coach, promoter, writer, and rules reformer Walter Camp (1859–1925) originated the annual All-America Team for college football, a list of players deemed the best at their position in a given year, and for many years selected the team.

839.13　　Schulz] University of Michigan all-American center Germany Schulz (1883–1951).

840.5　　Johnny Garrels] John Garrels (1885–1956), football and track-and-field star at the University of Michigan, who in the 1905 game against the University of Chicago described here started at left end and was the team's punter.

840.6–7　　Tom Hammond . . . Bezdek] Thomas S. Hammond (1883–1950), later a military officer, Republican politician, and business leader, who played several positions for the Michigan Wolverines from 1903 to 1905; Czech-born fullback Hugo Bezdek (1884–1952), later a college and professional football coach and major league baseball manager.

840.17　　Clark] William Dennison Clark (1885–1932), University of Michigan halfback and punt returner.

840.22　　Catlin and Speik] University of Chicago players Mark Catlin (1882–1956) and Fred Speik (1882–1940).

842.7　　O. O. McIntyre] Oscar Odd McIntyre (1884–1938), widely syndicated newspaper writer known for his column "New York Day by Day," of which this piece is a parody.

842.14　　Lily Langtry] British singer and actor (1853–1929).

842.18　　Percy Hammond] See note 835.9–10.

842.21　　Joan Blondell] Movie actor (1906–1979) featured in *Night Nurse* (1931), *Three on a Match* (1932), and other films.

842.22　　Joe Walcott] Jersey Joe Walcott, boxer born Arnold Cream (1914–1994).

842.31　　Bill Klem] See note 330.29.

843.5　　Connie Bennett] Constance Bennett (1904–1965), socialite and movie star whose films included *Born to Love* (1931) and *What Price Hollywood* (1932).

843.6　　Ellsworth Vines] American tennis player (1911–1994), a world champion in the 1930s.

843.6–7　　Frank Crowninshield] Journalist and critic (1872–1947) who edited *Vanity Fair*, 1914–36.

843.8　　Otto Kahn] Investment banker (1867–1934), a prominent philanthropist and patron of the arts.

843.10–11　　Mayor O'Brien] John O'Brien (1873–1951) served as mayor of New York, January–December 1933, following the resignation of Jimmy Walker.

843.12   Senator Long] Huey Long (1893–1935), who served as U.S. senator from Louisiana, 1932–35, following his term as governor, 1928–32.

843.16   Kate Smith] Singer (1907–1986) whose early hits included "Dream a Little Dream of Me" and "River, Stay 'Way from My Door."

843.18–19   Rosamond Pinchot] Stage and screen actor (1904–1938) from a wealthy background.

843.20   "The Song of the Shirt"] Poem (1843) by Thomas Hood.

843.21   Fannie Hurst] Novelist (1889–1968), author of *Back Street* (1931) and *Imitation of Life* (1933).

843.21–22   Arthur Brisbane] Newspaperman (1864–1936), editor at various times of the New York *Sun*, the *New York World*, and the *New York Evening Journal*.

843.26   Rex Cole] Refrigerator designer (1887–1967) whose name was prominently featured in General Electric showrooms and advertisements.

843.29   Samuel Blythe . . . Charles Francis Coe] Blythe (1868–1947), writer and newspaper editor, known for writing on public affairs; Coe (1890–1956), author of novels, stories, and screenplays about boxing and crime.

843.34   Ruth Etting] Popular singer (1897–1978) known for "Ten Cents a Dance," "Love Me or Leave Me," and many other hits.

843.34   Rube Goldberg] Cartoonist (1883–1970) famous for his depiction of elaborate imaginary gadgets.

843.37   Garner] John Nance Garner (1868–1967), Texas politician who served as U.S. vice president, 1933–41.

843.38   "Red" (Socker) Lewis] Novelist Sinclair Lewis (1885–1951) was known by the nickname "Red."

844.1   Irvin S. Cobb] See note 631.25.

PLAYS

847.3–5   AL OCHS . . . TOOMBES] Ochs (1880–1935), Broadway actor of the 1920s and 1930s; Rogers, see note 790.13; Andy Tombes (1885–1976), Broadway actor who played character roles in many films of the 1930s.

847.15   Central League] Class B minor league.

847.29   Huggins] Miller Huggins (1879–1929), manager of the New York Yankees, 1918–29.

848.3–4   Bob . . . Speaker] New York Yankees pitcher Bob Shawkey (1890–1980); Everett Scott (see note 228.9); Tris Speaker (see note 120.9).

848.30 Landis wouldn't of dast suspend me] Commissioner Landis (see note 569.9–10) suspended Babe Ruth for 39 days during the 1922 season because Ruth had joined a barnstorming team after the end of the 1921 season, in violation of the commissioner's rule. Ruth's teammate on the New York Yankees, Bob Meusel, was also suspended, and both players were fined.

848.33 Coveleskie] Cleveland Indians pitcher Stan Coveleski (1889–1984), known for his spitball.

848.34 Baker] Home Run Baker (see note 13.9).

848.38 Schang] Yankees catcher Wally Schang (1889–1965).

849.14 Peggy Hopkins] See note 787.34.

849.23 Sewell] Indians catcher Joe Sewell (1898–1990).

850.21 George Sisler] See note 212.7.

850.25 Gardner] Indians third baseman Larry Gardner (1886–1976).

850.36–37 Cobb . . . Irvin] See notes 11.5 and 844.1.

851.2 O'Neill] Indians catcher Steve O'Neill (1891–1962).

852.9 HERBERT SWOPE] Herbert Bayard Swope (1882–1958), editor of the *New York World* and Lardner's next-door neighbor in Great Neck.

853.13 "My Man,"] "Mon Homme" (1916), French music hall song popularized by Mistinguett; the English-language version was recorded in 1921 by Fanny Brice.

854.23 *Senator LaFollette*] Robert M. LaFollette (1855–1925), U.S. senator from Wisconsin, 1906–25.

855.14–17 Far above Cayuga's waters . . . in praise of auld Nassau!] The passage mixes together phrases from various college anthems and other songs, beginning with the first line of Cornell University's alma mater.

858.4 *Homecoming of Casanova*] Arthur Schnitzler's novel *Casanova's Homecoming* (1918), published in English translation in 1921.

859.10 HEYWOOD BROUN] See note 637.21.

860.2–3 That old devil sea!] A line repeatedly delivered by the seaman Chris Christopherson, father of the title character of Eugene O'Neill's *Anna Christie* (1921).

860.15 *David Belasco*] American theatrical impresario (1853–1931).

863.16 Alexander Woollcott] Critic and humorist (1887–1943).

864.19–20 *Crowninshield*] See note 843.6–7.

870.4–16 ST. JOHN ERVINE . . . NICHOLS] Ervine (1883–1971), Irish playwright; Winchell (1897–1972), gossip columnist and radio commentator;

Broun, see note 637.21; Thompson (1893–1961), journalist and radio commentator; Mencken (1880–1956), journalist and author; Willebrandt (1889–1963), U.S. assistant attorney general, 1921–29, charged with oversight of Volstead Act violations; Hecht (1894–1964), author and screenwriter; Straton (1875–1929), Protestant pastor who led opposition to presidential campaign of Al Smith; Laemmle (1867–1939), motion picture producer; Nichols (1891–1966), playwright, author of long-running comedy *Abie's Irish Rose* (1922).

873.19 Thomas Chalmers . . . Alice Brady] Chalmers (1884–1966), opera singer who subsequently starred as a dramatic actor in Broadway productions of plays by Pirandello, Schnitzler, and O'Neill; Brady (1892–1939), stage and screen actor who costarred with Chalmers in the first production of O'Neill's *Mourning Becomes Electra* (1931).

873.20 Alice-Chalmers] A play on the name of Allis-Chalmers, industrial equipment manufacturer, 1861–1999.

873.21 Kimbley & Co.] New York brokerage house, successor to the firm Sutro & Kimbley, cofounded by Frank R. Kimbley (1874–1938). Dutch-born banker Frederick H. Nymeyer (873.22) was one of its partners.

873.30 Percy Hammond] See note 835.9–10.

873.35 Harland Dixon] Song and dance man (1885–1969); he had a long career in vaudeville and in Broadway revues, sometimes in partnership with James Doyle.

873.36 Vince Youmans] Youmans, see note 638.15–17; Paul Lannin, composer and arranger.

874.1–2 Vic Arden . . . Phil Ohman] Arden and Ohman were a successful duo-piano team.

874.11 Claudette Colbert] Movie actor (1903–1996), star of *The Smiling Lieutenant* (1931), *The Sign of the Cross* (1932), and other films.

874.13 Marchmont Schwartz] Football player (1909–1991) who played for Notre Dame, 1929–31.

874.20 William A. Brady] Actor, theatrical producer, and boxing manager (1863–1950).

875.5 Alla Nazimova] Russian-born actor (1879–1945) who appeared in the original production of Eugene O'Neill's *Mourning Becomes Electra* (1931).

875.9–10 *Luncheon Intermission of Half an Hour*] The Broadway production of *Mourning Becomes Electra* included a one-hour intermission for dinner.

875.26 A. H. Woods] Albert H. Woods, theatrical producer (1870–1951) known for such productions as *Getting Gertie's Garter* (1921), *The Demi-Virgin* (1921), and *The Matrimonial Bed* (1927).

875.31–32 William Anthony McGuire] Actor and theatrical producer (1881–1940).

875.35   Mrs. Fiske] See note 433.40.

877.12   LYNN FONTANNE . . . Grace George] Fontanne (1887–1983), leading stage actor married to Alfred Lunt, with whom she often costarred; George (1879–1961), stage actor, star of *The Two Orphans* (1904), *The New York Idea* (1915), *The New Morality* (1921), and many other productions.

877.13   Bert Lahr] Actor and comedian (1895–1967).

877.14   FRANK CASE] Manager (from 1907) and owner (from 1927) of the Algonquin Hotel until his death in 1946.

877.34   Morris Gest] New York theater producer (1881–1942).

SONGS

887.1   *Gee! It's a Wonderful Game*] The music was written by White Sox pitcher G. Harris "Doc" White (1879–1969).

887.6–8   Christy . . . fade away ball] Christy Matthewson (see note 99.19–20), known as "Matty," was one of the first major league pitchers to throw the "fadeaway," now known as the screwball.

887.9   Muggsy McGraw] New York Giants manager John McGraw (see note 115.20).

887.25   Big Nap Lay'ooway] Napoleon Lajoie; see note 15.27.

888.1   *Prohibition Blues*] The music was written by the singer Nora Bayes (1880–1928), who recorded it in 1919.

889.1   *You Can't Get Along Without Me*] Written for the unproduced musical *All at Sea* (1928–30), with music by Paul Lannin and book by Lardner, George Abbott, and Joseph Santley.

890.1   *I'll Never Be Young Again*] Written for *All at Sea*.

891.1   *We're All Just One Big Family*] Written for the Ziegfeld production *Smiles*, November 18, 1930–January 10, 1931, starring Fred Astaire and Marilyn Miller, with music by Vincent Youmans and lyrics by Clifford Grey and Harold Adamson, with additional lyrics by Lardner.

LETTERS

895.1   *Ellis Abbott*] Abbott (1887–1960) was engaged to Lardner at the time. They married in 1911.

896.32   Anne] Lardner's older sister, born Anna in 1883.

897.29   Mr. Schulte] See note 40.38.

898.1   Manager Chance] See note 825.35–36.

898.17   Mr. Hofman] See note 303.12–13.

898.19   Mr. Reulbach] Chicago Cubs pitcher Ed Reulbach (1882–1961).

901.12   Richard and Anne] Richard G. Tobin, sportswriter who married Lardner's sister Anne.

902.34   "Little Puff of Smoke"] Song (1910) with lyrics by Lardner and music by G. Harris "Doc" White.

904.13   Jack Johnson] Boxer (1878–1946), first African American world heavyweight champion, 1908–15.

905.14   Damrosch] Conductor and composer (1862–1950).

906.1   Briggs] Clare Briggs (1875–1930), comic strip artist, creator of "When a Feller Needs a Friend" and other strips.

906.11   Ted Sullivan] See note 120.24–25.

906.15   Jimmy Sheckard] See note 825.35–36.

906.15   Rice] Grantland Rice (1880–1954), syndicated sportswriter, a close friend of Lardner.

907.6   Mr. Braden] Jim Braden, all-American fullback for Yale in 1919, and later a sportswriter for the *Chicago Daily News*.

907.16   Leon Errol] Vaudeville comedian (1881–1951), later featured in many films.

907.20   *Maxwell Perkins*] Editor (1884–1947); at the suggestion of F. Scott Fitzgerald he approached Lardner and proposed he put together a collection of his magazine stories.

909.7   Bunny Wilson and Tom Boyd] Edmund Wilson (1895–1972), critic who would review *How to Write Short Stories* in *The New Republic*; Thomas Boyd (1898–1935), novelist, author of *Through the Wheat* (1923).

909.8–9   Burton] Burton Rascoe (1892–1957), journalist and critic, literary editor of the *Chicago Tribune*.

909.9   Katherine Mansfield] New Zealand–born author (1888–1923) known for short story collections, including *In a German Pension* (1911) and *The Garden Party and Other Stories* (1922).

909.19   John Golden] Theatrical producer and lyricist (1874–1955).

909.22   "The Beautiful and Damned."] Novel (1922) by F. Scott Fitzgerald.

909.26   Victor Herbert] Composer (1859–1924) of operettas, including *Babes in Toyland* (1903), *The Red Mill* (1906), and *Naughty Marietta* (1910).

909.28   Silvio Hein] See note 638.15–17.

909.28   Gene] Gene Buck; see note 373.14.

909.36   Loeb and Leopold] Nathan Leopold Jr. (1904–1971) and Richard

Loeb (1905–1936) were convicted in September 1924 for the murder of Bobby Franks.

910.13   "Three Flights Up"] Story collection (1924) by Sidney Howard.

910.23   Don Stewart] Donald Ogden Stewart (1894–1980), humorist and screenwriter.

910.26   "articles" on the European trip] The six articles were collected as "The Other Side" in *What of It?* (1925).

911.24–25   Michael Arlen . . . The Green Hat] See note 637.9–11. Arlen's dramatization opened on Broadway in 1925, with Leslie Howard and Katherine Cornell in the leading roles.

911.31–32   Ray Long] Newspaper and magazine editor (1878–1935).

911.32   George Doran] George H. Doran (1869–1956), publisher of Lardner's early books; his publishing house merged with Doubleday, Page & Co. in 1927. He published a memoir, *Chronicles of Barabbas, 1884–1934* (1935).

911.34   Condé Nast] Magazine publisher (1873–1942).

911.35–36   Ina Claire] See note 786.27.

912.3–5   George Nathan . . . Mercury] George Jean Nathan (1882–1958), drama critic. He cofounded *The American Mercury* with H. L. Mencken in 1924.

912.7   Mary Hay and Richard] Star of musical comedies and movies (1901–1957). She married actor Richard Barthelmess (see note 788.15) in 1920; the couple separated in 1925 and were divorced in 1927.

912.9   Beatrice Kaufman and Peggy Leach] Kaufman (1895–1945), fiction writer and editor, wife of playwright George S. Kaufman; Margaret Leech (1893–1974), journalist who later wrote *Reveille in Washington* (1942).

912.11   Grantland Rices] See note 906.15.

912.11–12   June Walker] Stage and film actor (1900–1966), star of the original production of *Gentlemen Prefer Blondes* (1926).

912.29   Dutch Treat] The Dutch Treat Club, an association of writers, illustrators, and performers.

912.33   Arthur Jacks] A lifelong friend with whom Lardner attended high school in Niles, Michigan.

913.16   Sidney Fishes] Fish was an attorney.

913.17   Esther Murphy] Sister of the Fitzgeralds' friend Gerald Murphy; their father was Patrick Murphy, founder of the Mark Cross leather goods company.

913.20   The Ziegfeld show (Gene's)] *No Foolin'* ran for 106 performances in New York, June–September 1926.

913.22   "The Peasants."] Four-volume novel (1904–9) by Wladyslaw Rey-
mont (1867–1925), winner of the Nobel Prize for Literature in 1924; an English translation was published by Knopf in 1925.

913.25   May Preston] Magazine illustrator (1873–1949).

913.29   the "fight" in Philadelphia.] Gene Tunney (see note 637.9–11) defeated Jack Dempsey for the world heavyweight title on September 23, 1926,
at the Sesquicentennial Municipal Stadium in Philadelphia. Lardner's account,
"Ring (Side) Lardner Sees 'Em Through," was published in the *New York
World*.

913.30   Herbert] See note 852.9.

914.18–19   Gibbons–Tunney fight . . . Dempsey–Gibbons fight] Tunney
defeated Tommy Gibbons (1891–1960) at the New York Polo Grounds on
June 5, 1925; Jack Dempsey defeated Gibbons on a decision in Shelby, Mon-
tana, on July 4, 1923.

914.27   Harry Wills] Heavyweight boxer (1889–1958), known as "The
Black Panther," three-time holder of the World Colored Heavyweight Championship.

914.29   Jack Sharkey] Heavyweight boxer (1902–1994).

914.36   Karl Dane] Danish-born silent screen actor (1886–1934).

914.37–38   "The Big Parade."] Film (1925) directed by King Vidor and
starring John Gilbert.

915.1   Johnnie Weaver . . . Marc Connelly] John V. A. Weaver (1893–
1938), novelist and poet who wrote the screenplay for King Vidor's *The Crowd*
(1928) and other films; Connelly (1890–1980), playwright whose plays *Dulcy*
(1921), *Merton of the Movies* (1922), and *Beggars on Horseback* (1924), written
in collaboration with George S. Kaufman, were adapted into films.

915.19–20   things that happened] Lardner was on the road writing additional lyrics for Ziegfeld's *Smiles* (see note 891.1).

915.23   Flo] Florenz Ziegfeld.

915.24   Marilyn] Marilyn Miller (1898–1936), star of Broadway musicals
beginning with *Ziegfeld Follies of 1918*.

915.27   Vince] Vincent Youmans (see note 638.15–17).

917.23   Eddie Foy] See note 366.30.

917.33   *Wilma Seavey*] Seavey had written to Lardner about an argument
with her fiancé about Lardner's attitude toward his characters.

*This book is set in 10 point ITC Galliard Pro, a
face designed for digital composition by Matthew Carter
and based on the sixteenth-century face Granjon. The paper
is acid-free lightweight opaque and meets the requirements
for permanence of the American National Standards Institute.
The binding material is Brillianta, a woven rayon cloth made
by Van Heek–Scholco Textielfabrieken, Holland.
Composition by Dedicated Book Services. Printing and
binding by Edwards Brothers Malloy, Ann Arbor.
Designed by Bruce Campbell.*

THE LIBRARY OF AMERICA SERIES

The Library of America fosters appreciation and pride in America's literary heritage by publishing, and keeping permanently in print, authoritative editions of America's best and most significant writing. An independent nonprofit organization, it was founded in 1979 with seed funding from the National Endowment for the Humanities and the Ford Foundation.

To subscribe to the series or to order individual copies, please visit www.loa.org or call (800) 964.5778.

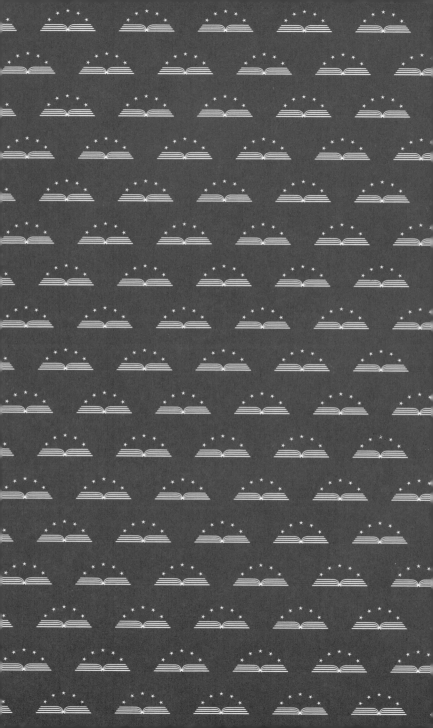